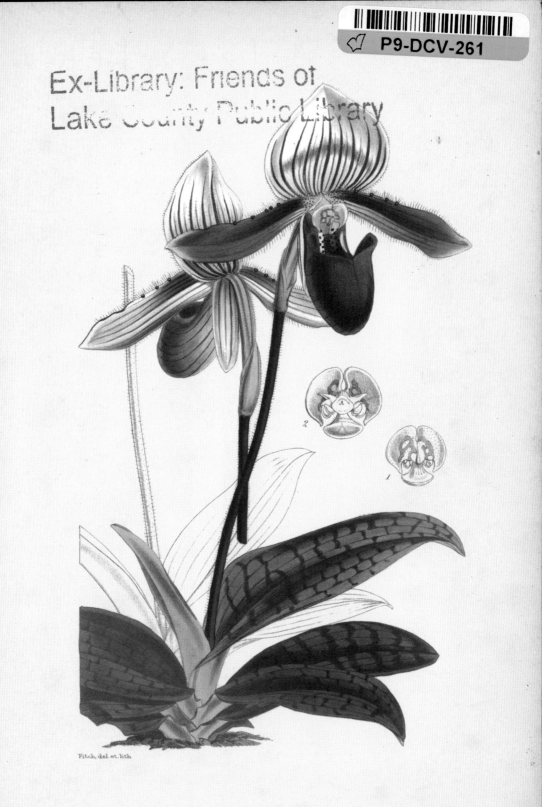

Fitch, del. et. lith.

The
Signature
of All Things

ALSO BY ELIZABETH GILBERT

Pilgrims

Stern Men

The Last American Man

Eat, Pray, Love:
One Woman's Search for Everything
Across Italy, India and Indonesia

Committed: A Love Story

At Home on the Range, by Margaret Yardley Potter

The Signature of All Things

ELIZABETH GILBERT

Viking

VIKING
Published by the Penguin Group
Penguin Group (USA) LLC
375 Hudson Street
New York, New York 10014

USA | Canada | UK | Ireland | Australia | New Zealand | India | South Africa | China
penguin.com
A Penguin Random House Company

LIBRARY OF CONGRESS CATALOGING-IN-PUBLICATION DATA
Gilbert, Elizabeth, date
  The signature of all things : a novel / Elizabeth Gilbert.
    pages cm
  ISBN 978-0-670-02485-8
  ISBN 978-0-670-01585-6 (export edition)
  1. Women botanists—Fiction. 2. Painters—Fiction. 3. Enlightenment—Fiction. 4. Industrial revolution—Fiction. I. Title.
  PS3557.I3415S54 2013
  813'.54—dc23   2013017045

Printed in the United States of America
10 9 8 7 6 5 4 3 2 1

Set in Minion Pro   •   Designed by Elke Sigal

Interior illustrations:
  Page 4: Cinchona calisaya
    48: Dicranaceae
    164: Aerides odoratum
    324: Artocarpus incisa
    436: Juglans laciniosa
The LuEsther T. Mertz Library of The New York Botanical Garden, Bronx, New York.

Endpaper illustrations:
  Front left page: Aerides lindleyanum (rock orchid); Margaret Bushby Lascelles Cockburn; The Natural History Museum / Alamy
  Front right: Cypripedium barbatum (bearded ladies' slipper orchid); Walter Hood Fitch for Sir William Jackson Hooker; Florilegius / Alamy
  Back left: Dendrobium pulchellum; Benjamin Maund; Florilegius / Alamy
  Back right: Ophrys apifera (bee orchid); Pierre Jean-François Turpin; Florilegius / Alamy

For my grandmother

Maude Edna Morcomb Olson

in honor of her hundredth birthday

———————————

What life *is*, we know not. What life *does*, we know well.

—LORD PERCEVAL

Contents

Prologue

Alma Whittaker, born with the century, slid into our world on the fifth of January, 1800.

Swiftly—nearly immediately—opinions began to form around her.

Alma's mother, upon viewing the infant for the first time, felt quite satisfied with the outcome. Beatrix Whittaker had suffered poor luck thus far generating an heir. Her first three attempts at conception had vanished in sad rivulets before they'd ever quickened. Her most recent attempt—a perfectly formed son—had come right to the brink of life, but had then changed his mind about it on the very morning he was meant to be born, and arrived already departed. After such losses, any child who survives is a satisfactory child.

Holding her robust infant, Beatrix murmured a prayer in her native Dutch. She prayed that her daughter would grow up to be healthy and sensible and intelligent, and would never form associations with overly powdered girls, or laugh at vulgar stories, or sit at gaming tables with careless men, or read French novels, or behave in a manner suited only to a savage Indian, or in any way whatsoever become the worst sort of discredit to a good family; namely, that she not grow up to be *een onnozelaar*, a simpleton. Thus concluded her blessing—or what constitutes a blessing, from so austere a woman as Beatrix Whittaker.

The midwife, a German-born local woman, was of the opinion that this had been a decent birth in a decent house, and thus Alma Whittaker was a decent baby. The bedroom had been warm, soup and beer had been freely offered, and the mother had been stalwart—just as one would expect from the Dutch. Moreover, the midwife knew that she would be paid, and paid handsomely. Any baby who brings money is an acceptable baby. Therefore, the midwife offered a blessing to Alma as well, although without excessive passion.

Hanneke de Groot, the head housekeeper of the estate, was less impressed. The baby was neither a boy nor was it pretty. It had a face like a bowl of porridge, and was pale as a painted floor. Like all children, it would bring work. Like all work, it would probably fall on her shoulders. But she blessed the child anyway, because the blessing of a new baby is a responsibility, and Hanneke de Groot always met her responsibilities. Hanneke paid off the midwife and changed the bedsheets. She was helped in her efforts, although not ably, by a young maid—a talkative country girl and recent addition to the household—who was more interested in looking at the baby than in tidying up the bedroom. The maid's name does not bear recording here, because Hanneke de Groot would dismiss the girl as useless the next day, and send her off without references. Nonetheless, for that one night, the useless and doomed maid fussed over the new baby, and longed for a baby herself, and imparted a rather sweet and sincere blessing upon young Alma.

Dick Yancey—a tall, intimidating Yorkshireman, who worked for the gentleman of the house as the iron-handed enforcer of all his international trade concerns (and who happened to be residing at the estate that January, waiting for the Philadelphia ports to thaw so he could proceed on to the Dutch East Indies)—had few words to say about the new infant. To be fair, he was not much given to excessive conversation under any circumstances. When told that Mrs. Whittaker had given birth to a healthy baby girl, Mr. Yancey merely frowned and pronounced, with characteristic economy of speech, "Hard trade, living." Was that a blessing? Difficult to say. Let us give him the benefit of the doubt and take it as one. Surely he did not intend it as a curse.

As for Alma's father—Henry Whittaker, the gentleman of the estate—he was pleased with his child. Most pleased. He did not mind that the infant was not a boy, nor that it was not pretty. He did not bless Alma, but only because he was not the blessing type. ("God's business is none of my business," he frequently said.) Without reservation, though, Henry *admired* his child. Then again, he had made his child, and Henry Whittaker's tendency in life was to admire without reservation everything he made.

To mark the occasion, Henry harvested a pineapple from his largest greenhouse and divided it in equal shares with everyone in the household. Outside it was snowing, a perfect Pennsylvania winter, but this man possessed several coal-fired greenhouses of his own design—structures that made him not only the envy of every plantsman and botanist in the Americas, but also blisteringly rich—and if he wanted a pineapple in January, by God he could have a pineapple in January. Cherries in March, as well.

He then retired to his study and opened up his ledger, where, as he did every night, he recorded all manner of estate transactions, both official and intimate. He began: "A new nobbel and entresting pasennger has joyned us," and continued with the details, the timing, and the expenses of Alma Whittaker's birth. His penmanship was shamefully crabbed. Each sentence was a crowded village of capital letters and small letters, living side by side in tight misery, crawling up on one another as though trying to escape the page. His spelling was several degrees beyond arbitrary, and his punctuation brought reason to sigh with unhappiness.

But Henry wrote up his account, nonetheless. It was important for him to keep track of things. While he knew that these pages would look appalling to any educated man, he also knew that nobody would ever see his writing—except his wife. When Beatrix recovered her strength, she would transcribe his notes into her own ledgers, as she always did, and her elegantly penned translation of Henry's scrawls would become the official household record. The partner of his days, was Beatrix—and a good value, at that. She would do this task for him, and a hundred other tasks besides.

God willing, she would be back at it shortly.

Paperwork was already piling up.

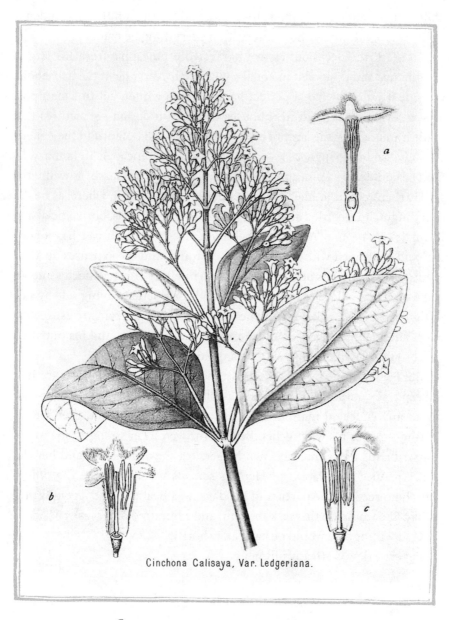

Cinchona Calisaya, Var. Ledgeriana.

Cinchona calisaya, var. ledgeriana

PART ONE

The Tree of Fevers

Chapter One

$\mathbf{F}$or the first five years of her life, Alma Whittaker was indeed a mere passenger in the world—as we all are passengers in such early youth—and so her story was not yet noble, nor was it particularly interesting, beyond the fact that this homely toddler passed her days without illness or incident, surrounded by a degree of wealth nearly unknown in the America of that time, even within elegant Philadelphia. How her father came to be in possession of such great wealth is a story worth telling here, while we wait for the girl to grow up and catch our interest again. For it was no more common in 1800 than it has ever been for a poor-born and nearly illiterate man to become the richest inhabitant of his city, and so the means by which Henry Whittaker prospered are indeed interesting—although perhaps not noble, as he himself would have been the first to confess.

Henry Whittaker was born in 1760 in the village of Richmond, just up the Thames from London. He was the youngest son of poor parents who had a few too many children already. He was raised in two small rooms with a floor of beaten earth, with an almost adequate roof, with a meal on the hearth nearly every day, with a mother who did not drink and a father who did not beat his family—by comparison to many families of the day, in other words, a nearly genteel existence. His mother even had a private spot of dirt behind the house in which to grow larkspurs and lupines, decoratively, like a lady. But Henry was not fooled by larkspurs and lupines. He grew up sleeping one wall away from the pigs, and there was not a moment in his life when poverty did not humiliate him.

Perhaps Henry would have taken less offense at his destiny had he never seen wealth around him against which to compare his own poor circumstances—but the boy grew up witnessing not only wealth, but royalty. There was a palace at Richmond, and there were pleasure gardens there, too, called Kew, cultivated with expertise by Princess Augusta, who had brought with her from Germany a retinue of gardeners eager to make a false and regal landscape out of real and humble English meadows. Her son, the future King George III, spent his childhood summers there. When he became king, George sought to turn Kew into a botanical garden worthy of any Continental rival. The English, on their cold, wet, isolated island, were far behind the rest of Europe on botanizing, and George III was eager to catch up.

Henry's father was an orchardman at Kew—a humble man, respected by his masters, as much as anyone could respect a humble orchardman. Mr. Whittaker had a gift for fruiting trees, and a reverence for them. ("They pay the land for its trouble," he would say, "unlike all the others.") He had once saved the king's favorite apple tree by whip-grafting a scion of the ailing specimen onto sturdier rootstock and claying it secure. The tree had fruited off the new graft that very year, and soon produced bushels. For this miracle, Mr. Whittaker had been nicknamed "the Apple Magus" by the king himself.

The Apple Magus, for all his talents, was a simple man, with a timid wife, but they somehow turned out six rough and violent sons (including one boy called "the Terror of Richmond" and two others who would end up dead in tavern brawls). Henry, the youngest, was in some ways the roughest of them all, and perhaps needed to be, to survive his brothers. He was a stubborn and enduring little whippet, a thin and exploding contrivance, who could be trusted to receive his brothers' beatings stoically, and whose fearlessness was frequently put to the test by others, who liked to dare him into taking risks. Even apart from his brothers, Henry was a dangerous experimentalist, a lighter of illicit fires, a roof-scampering taunter of housewives, a menace to smaller children; a boy who one would not have been surprised to learn had fallen from a church steeple or drowned in the Thames—though by sheer happenstance these scenarios never came to pass.

But unlike his brothers, Henry had a redeeming attribute. Two of them, to be exact: he was intelligent, and he was interested in trees. It would be exaggeration to claim that Henry revered trees, as his father did, but he was interested in trees because they were one of the few things in his impoverished world that could readily be learned, and experience had already instructed Henry that learning things gave a person advantage over other people. If one wanted to continue living (and Henry did) and if one wanted to ultimately prosper (and Henry did), then anything that could be learned, should be learned. Latin, penmanship, archery, riding, dancing—all of these were out of reach to Henry. But he had trees, and he had his father, the Apple Magus, who patiently took the trouble to teach him.

So Henry learned all about the grafter's tools of clay and wax and knives, and about the tricks of budding, booting, clefting, planting, and pruning with a judicious hand. He learned how to transplant trees in the springtime, if the soil was retentive and dense, or how to do it in the autumn, if the soil was loose and dry. He learned how to stake and drape the apricots in order to save them from wind, how to cultivate citruses in the orangery, how to smoke the mildew off the gooseberries, how to amputate diseased limbs from the figs, and when not to bother. He learned how to strip the tattered bark from an old tree and take the thing right down to the ground, without sentimentality or remorse, in order to demand life back out of it for a dozen more seasons to come.

Henry learned much from his father, though he was ashamed of the man, who he felt was weak. If Mr. Whittaker truly was the Apple Magus, Henry reasoned, then why had the king's admiration not been parlayed into wealth? Stupider men were rich—many of them. Why did the Whittakers still live with pigs, when just nearby were the great wide green lawns of the palace, and the pleasant houses on Maid of Honor Row, where the queen's servants slept on French linens? Henry, climbing to the top of an elaborate garden wall one day, had spied a lady, dressed in an ivory gown, practicing manège on her immaculate white horse while a servant played the violin to entertain her. People were living like this, right there in Richmond, while the Whittakers did not even have a floor.

But Henry's father never fought for anything fine. He'd earned the same paltry wage for thirty years, and had never once disputed it, nor had he ever complained about working outdoors in the foulest of weather for so long that his health had been ruined by it. Henry's father had chosen the careful-lest steps through life, particularly when interacting with his betters—and he regarded everyone as his better. Mr. Whittaker made a point never to offend, and never to take advantage, even when advantages may have been ripe for plucking. He told his son, "Henry, do not be bold. You can butcher the sheep only once. But if you are careful, you can shear the sheep every year."

With a father so forceless and complacent, what could Henry expect to receive out of life, aside from whatever he could clutch at with his own hands? A man should profit, Henry started telling himself when he was only thirteen years old. A man should butcher a sheep every day.

But where to find the sheep?

That's when Henry Whittaker started stealing.

By the mid-1770s, the gardens at Kew had become a botanical Noah's Ark, with thousands of specimens already in the collection, and new consign-ments arriving weekly—hydrangeas from the Far East, magnolias from China, ferns from the West Indies. What's more, Kew had a new and ambi-tious superintendent: Sir Joseph Banks, fresh from his triumphant voyage around the world as chief botanist for Captain Cook's HMS *Endeavour.* Banks, who worked without salary (he was interested only in the glory of the British Empire, he said, although others suggested he might be just the slightest bit interested in the glory of Sir Joseph Banks), was now collecting plants with furious passion, committed to creating a truly spectacular national garden.

Oh, Sir Joseph Banks! That beautiful, whoring, ambitious, competitive adventurer! The man was everything Henry's father was not. By the age of twenty-three, a drenching inheritance of six thousand pounds a year had made Banks one of the richest men in England. Arguably, he was also the handsomest. Banks could easily have spent his life in idle luxury, but instead he sought to become the boldest of botanical explorers—a vocation he took up without sacrificing a bit of flash or glamour. Banks had paid for a good deal of Captain Cook's first expedition out of his own pocket, which had afforded him the right to bring along on that cramped ship two black man-servants, two white manservants, a spare botanist, a scientific secretary, two artists, a draftsman, and a pair of Italian greyhounds. During his adventure, Banks had seduced Tahitian queens, danced naked with savages on beaches, and watched young heathen girls having their buttocks tattooed in the moonlight. He had brought home with him to England a Tahitian man named Omai, to be kept as a pet, and he had also brought home nearly four thousand plant specimens—almost half of which the world of science had never before seen. Sir Joseph Banks was the most famous and dashing man in England, and Henry admired him enormously.

But he stole from him anyway.

It was merely that the opportunity was *there*, and that the opportunity was so obvious. Banks was known in scientific circles not merely as a great botanical collector, but also as a great botanical hoarder. Gentlemen of botany, in those polite days, generally shared their discoveries with each other freely, but Banks shared nothing. Professors, dignitaries, and collectors came to Kew from all over the world with the reasonable hope of obtaining seeds and cuttings, as well as samples from Banks's vast herbarium—but Banks turned them all away.

Young Henry admired Banks for a hoarder (he would not have shared his own treasure, either, had he possessed any) but he soon saw opportunity in the angered faces of these thwarted international visitors. He would wait for them just outside the grounds of Kew, catching the men as they were leaving the gardens, sometimes catching them cursing Sir Joseph Banks in French, German, Dutch, or Italian. Henry would approach, ask the men what samples they desired, and promise to procure those samples by week's end. He always carried a paper tablet and a carpenter's pencil with him; if the men did not speak English, Henry had them draw pictures of what they needed. They were all excellent botanical artists, so their needs were easily made clear. Late in the evenings, Henry would sneak into the greenhouses, dart past the workers who kept the giant stoves going through the cold nights, and steal plants for profit.

He was just the boy for the task. He was good at plant identification, expert at keeping cuttings alive, a familiar enough face around the gardens not to arouse suspicion, and adept at covering his tracks. Best of all, he did not seem to require sleep. He worked all day with his father in the orchards, and then stole all night—rare plants, precious plants, lady's slippers, tropical orchids, carnivorous marvels from the New World. He kept all the botanical drawings that the distinguished gentlemen made for him, too, and studied those drawings until he knew every stamen and petal of every plant the world desired.

Like all good thieves, Henry was scrupulous about his own security. He trusted nobody with his secret, and buried his earnings in several caches throughout the gardens at Kew. He never spent a farthing of it. He let his silver rest dormant in the soil, like good rootstock. He wanted that silver to accumulate, until it could burst forth hugely, and buy him the right to become a rich man.

Within a year Henry had several regular clients. One of them, an old orchid cultivator from the Paris Botanical Gardens, gave the boy perhaps the first pleasing compliment of his life: "You're a useful little fingerstink, aren't you?" Within two years, Henry was driving a vigorous trade, selling plants not only to serious men of botany, but also to a circle of wealthy London gentry, who longed for exotic specimens for their own collections. Within three years, he was illicitly shipping plant samples to France and Italy, expertly packing the cuttings in moss and wax to ensure they survived the journey.

At the end, however, after three years of this felonious enterprise, Henry Whittaker was caught—and by his own father.

Mr. Whittaker, normally a deep sleeper, had noticed his son leaving the house one night after midnight and, heartsick with a father's instinctive suspicion, had followed the boy to the greenhouse and seen the selecting, the thieving, the expert packing. He recognized immediately the illicit care of a robber.

Henry's father was not a man who had ever beat his sons, even when they deserved it (and they frequently did deserve it), and he didn't beat Henry that night, either. Nor did he confront the boy directly. Henry didn't even realize he'd been caught. No, Mr. Whittaker did something far worse. First thing the next morning, he asked for a personal audience with Sir Joseph Banks. It was not often that a poor fellow like Whittaker could request a word with a gentleman like Banks, but Henry's father had earned just enough respect around Kew in thirty years of tireless labor to warrant the intrusion, if only just this once. He was an old and poor man, indeed, but he was also the Apple Magus, the savior of the king's favorite tree, and that title bought him entrance.

Mr. Whittaker came at Banks almost upon his knees, head bowed, penitent as a saint. He confessed the shaming story about his son, along with his suspicion that Henry had probably been stealing for years. He offered his resignation from Kew as punishment, if the boy would only be spared arrest or harm. The Apple Magus promised to take his family far away from Richmond, and see to it that Kew, and Banks, would never again be sullied by the Whittaker name.

Banks—impressed by the orchardman's heightened sense of honor—refused the resignation, and sent for young Henry personally. Again, this was an unusual occurrence. If it was rare for Sir Joseph Banks to meet with an illiterate plantsman in his study, it was exceedingly rare for him to meet with an illiterate plantsman's thieving sixteen-year-old son. Probably, he ought to have simply had the boy arrested. But theft was a hanging crime, and children far younger than Henry got the rope—and for far less serious infractions. While the attack on his collection was galling, Banks felt sympathy enough for the father to investigate the problem himself before summoning the bailiff.

The problem, when it walked into Sir Joseph Banks's study, turned out to be a spindly, ginger-haired, tight-lipped, milky-eyed, broad-shouldered, sunken-chested youth, with pale skin already rubbed raw by too much exposure to wind, rain, and sun. The boy was underfed but tall, and his hands were large; Banks saw that he might grow into a big man someday, if he could get a proper meal.

Henry did not know precisely why he had been summoned to Banks's offices but he had sufficient brains to suspect the worst, and he was much alarmed. Only through sheer thick-sided stubbornness could he enter Banks's study without visibly trembling.

God's love, though, what a beautiful study it was! And how splendidly Joseph Banks was dressed, in his glossy wig and gleaming black velvet suit, polished shoe buckles and white stockings. Henry had no sooner passed through the door than he had already priced out the delicate mahogany writing desk, covetously scanned the fine collection boxes stacked on every shelf, and glanced with admiration at the handsome portrait of Captain Cook on the wall. Mother of dead dogs, the mere frame for that portrait must have cost ninety pounds!

Unlike his father, Henry did not bow in Banks's presence, but stood before the great man, looking him straight in the eye. Banks, who was seated, permitted Henry to stand in silence, perhaps waiting for a confession or a plea. But Henry neither confessed nor pleaded, nor hung his head in shame, and if Sir Joseph Banks thought Henry Whittaker was fool enough to speak first under such hot circumstances, then he did not know Henry Whittaker.

Therefore, after a long silence, Banks commanded, "Tell me, then—why should I not see you hang at Tyburn?"

So that's it, Henry thought. I'm snapped.

Nonetheless, the boy grappled for a plan. He needed to find a tactic, and he needed to find it in one quick and slender moment. He had not spent his life being beaten senseless by his older brothers to have learned nothing about fighting. When a bigger and stronger opponent has landed the first blow, you have but one chance to swing back before you will be pummeled into clay, and you'd best come back with something unexpected.

"Because I'm a useful little fingerstink," Henry said.

Banks, who enjoyed unusual incidents, barked with surprised laughter. "I confess that I don't see the use of you, young man. All you have done for me is to rob me of my hard-won treasure."

It wasn't a question, but Henry answered it nonetheless.

"I might've trimmed a bit," he said.

"You don't deny this?"

"All the braying in the world won't change it, do it?"

Again, Banks laughed. He may have thought the boy was putting on a show of false courage, but Henry's courage was real. As was his fear. As was his lack of penitence. For the whole of his life, Henry would always find penitence weak.

Banks changed tack. "I must say, young man, that you are a crowning distress to your father."

"And him to me, sir," Henry fired back.

Once more, the surprised bark of laughter from Banks. "Is he, then? What harm has that good man ever done to you?"

"Made me poor, sir," Henry said. Then, suddenly realizing everything, Henry added, "It were him, weren't it? Who peached me over to you?"

"Indeed it was. He's an honorable soul, your father."

Henry shrugged. "Not to me, eh?"

Banks took this in and nodded, generously conceding the point. Then he asked, "To whom have you been selling my plants?"

Henry ticked off the names on his fingers: "Mancini, Flood, Willink, LeFavour, Miles, Sather, Evashevski, Feuerle, Lord Lessig, Lord Garner—"

Banks cut him off with a wave. He stared at the boy with open astonishment. Oddly, if the list had been more modest, Banks might have been angrier. But these were the most esteemed botanical names of the day. A few of them Banks called friends. How had the boy found them? Some of these men hadn't been to England in years. The child must be *exporting*. What kind of campaign had this creature been running under his nose?

"How do you even know how to handle plants?" Banks asked.

"I always knowed plants, sir, for my whole life. It's like I knowed it all beforehand."

"And these men, do they pay you?"

"Or they don't get their plants, do they?" Henry said.

"You must be earning well. Indeed, you must have accumulated quite a pile of money in the past years."

Henry was too cunning to answer this.

"What have you done with the money you've earned, young man?" Banks pushed on. "I can't say you've invested it in your wardrobe. Without a doubt, your earnings belong to Kew. So where is it all?"

"Gone, sir."

"Gone where?"

"Dice, sir. I have a weakness of the gambling, see."

That may or may not have been true, Banks thought. But the boy certainly had as much nerve as any two-footed beast he had ever encountered. Banks was intrigued. He was a man, after all, who kept a heathen for a pet, and who—to be honest—enjoyed the reputation of being half heathen himself. His station in life required that he at least purport to admire gentility, but secretly he preferred a bit of wildness. And what a little wild cockerel was Henry Whittaker! Banks was growing less inclined by the moment to hand over this curious item of humanity to the constables.

Henry, who saw everything, saw something happening in Banks's face— a softening of countenance, a blooming curiosity, a sliver of a chance for his life to be saved. Intoxicated with a compulsion for self-preservation, the boy vaulted into that sliver of hope, one last time.

"Don't put me to hang, sir," Henry said. "You'll regret it that you did."

"What do you propose I do with you, instead?"

"Put me to use."

"Why should I?" asked Banks.

"Because I'm better than anyone."

Chapter Two

So Henry did not dangle on the gallows at Tyburn, in the end, nor did his father lose his position at Kew. The Whittakers were miraculously reprieved, and Henry was merely exiled, sent away to sea, dispatched by Sir Joseph Banks, to discover what the world would make of him.

It was 1776, and Captain Cook was about to embark on his third voyage around the world. Banks was not joining this expedition. Simply put, he had not been invited. He had not been invited on the second voyage, either, which had rankled him. Banks's extravagance and attention-seeking had soured Captain Cook to him, and, shamefully, he had been replaced. Cook would be traveling now with a humbler botanist, somebody more easily controlled—a man named Mr. David Nelson, who was a timid, competent gardener from Kew. But Banks wanted a hand in this journey somehow, and he very badly wanted to keep an eye on Nelson's botanical collecting. He didn't like the idea of any important scientific work being done behind his back. So he arranged to send Henry on the expedition as one of Nelson's hands, with instructions that the boy watch everything, learn everything, remember everything, and later report everything back to Banks. What better use of Henry Whittaker than to implant him as an informer?

Moreover, exiling Henry to sea was a good strategy for keeping the boy away from Kew Gardens for a few years, while allowing a safe distance in which one could determine exactly what sort of person this Henry might become. Three years on a ship would offer ample opportunity for the boy's true temperament to emerge. If they ended up hanging Henry on the yard-arm as a thief, murderer, or mutineer . . . well, that would be Cook's problem, wouldn't it, not Banks's. Alternatively, the boy might prove himself at something, and then Banks could have him for the future, after the expedition had kicked some of the wildness out of him.

Banks introduced Henry to Mr. Nelson as such: "Nelson, I would like you to meet your new right hand, Mr. Henry Whittaker, of the Richmond Whittakers. He is a useful little fingerstink, and I trust you will find—when it comes to plants—that he knowed it all beforehand."

Later, privately, Banks gave Henry some last advice before he dispatched the boy to sea: "Every day that you are aboard, son, defend your health with vigorous exercise. Listen to Mr. Nelson—he is dull, but he knows more about plants than you ever will. You shall be at the mercy of the older sailors, but you must never complain about them, or things will go badly for you. Stay away from whores, if you don't want to acquire the French disease. There will be two ships sailing, but you'll be on the *Resolution*, with Cook himself. Never put yourself in his way. Never speak to him. And if you do speak to him, which you must never do, certainly do not speak to him in the manner in which you have sometimes spoken to me. He will not find it as diverting as do I. We are not similar, Cook and I. The man is a perfect dragon for protocol. Be invisible to him, and you will be happier for it. Lastly, I should tell you that aboard the *Resolution*, as with all His Majesty's ships, you shall find yourself living amongst an odd cabal of both rogues and gentlemen. Be clever, Henry. Model yourself upon the gentlemen."

Henry's deliberately expressionless face made it impossible for anyone to read him, so Banks could not have realized how strikingly this final admonition was received. To Henry's ear, Banks had just suggested something quite extraordinary—the possibility of Henry's someday becoming a gentleman. More than a possibility, even, it may have sounded like a command, and a most welcome command at that: *Go forth in the world, Henry, and learn how to become a gentleman.* And in the hard, lonely years that Henry was about to spend at sea, perhaps this casual utterance of Banks's would grow only greater in his mind. Perhaps it would be all he ever thought about. Perhaps over time Henry Whittaker—that ambitious and striving boy, so fraught with the instinct for advancement—would come to remember it as having been a *promise.*

Henry sailed from England in July of 1776. The stated objectives of Cook's third expedition were twofold. The first was to sail to Tahiti, to return Sir Joseph Banks's pet—the man named Omai—to his homeland. Omai had grown tired of court life and now longed to return home. He had become sulky and fat and difficult, and Banks had grown tired of his pet. The second task was to then sail north, all the way up the Pacific coast of the Americas, in search of a Northwest Passage.

Henry's hardships began instantly. He was housed belowdecks, with the hen coops and the barrels. Poultry and goats complained all around him, but he did not complain. He was bullied, scorned, harmed by grown men with salt-scaled hands and anvils for wrists. The older sailors derided him as a freshwater eel, who knew nothing of the severities of ocean travel. On every expedition there were men who died, they said, and Henry would be the first to die.

They underestimated him.

Henry was the youngest, but not, as it soon emerged, the weakest. It was not much less comfortable a life than the one he had always known. He learned whatever he was required to learn. He learned how to dry and prepare Mr. Nelson's plants for scientific record, and how to paint botanicals in the open air—beating away the flies who landed in his pigments even as he mixed them—but he also learned how to be useful on the ship. He was made to scrub every crevice of the *Resolution* with vinegar, and forced to pick vermin from the bedding of the older sailors. He helped the ship's butcher to salt and barrel hogs, and learned how to operate the water distillation machine. He learned how to swallow his vomit, rather than displaying his seasickness for anyone's satisfaction. He rode out tempests without showing fear to the heavens or to any man. He ate sharks, and he ate the half-decomposed fish that were in the bellies of sharks. He never faltered.

He landed at Madeira, at Tenerife, at Table Bay. Down in the Cape, he encountered for the first time representatives of the Dutch East India

Company, who impressed him with their sobriety, competence, and wealth. He watched the sailors lose all their earnings at gaming tables. He watched people borrow money from the Dutch, who seemed not to gamble themselves. Henry did not gamble, either. He watched a fellow sailor, a would-be counterfeiter, get caught cheating and be whipped senseless for his crime—at Captain Cook's command. He committed no crimes himself. Rounding the Cape in ice and wind, he shivered at night under one thin blanket, his jaws clattering so hard he broke a tooth, but he did not complain. He kept Christmas on a bitterly cold island of sea lions and penguins.

He landed in Tasmania and met naked natives—or, as the British called them (and all copper-colored people), "Indians." He watched Captain Cook give the Indians souvenir medals, stamped with an image of George III and the date of the expedition, to mark this historic encounter. He watched the Indians immediately hammer the medals into fishhooks and spear tips. He lost another tooth. He watched the English sailors not believe that the life of any savage Indian had any account at all, while Cook tried futilely to teach them otherwise. He saw sailors force themselves on women they could not persuade, persuade women they could not afford, and simply buy for themselves girls from their fathers, if the sailors had any iron to trade for flesh. He avoided all girls.

He spent long days on board the ship, helping Mr. Nelson draw, describe, mount, and classify his botanical collections. He had no particular feelings of affection for Mr. Nelson, though he wished to learn everything that Mr. Nelson already knew.

He landed in New Zealand, which looked to him precisely like England, except with tattooed girls whom you could buy for a few handfuls of penny nails. He bought no girls. He watched his fellow sailors, in New Zealand, purchase two eager and energetic brothers—aged ten and fifteen—from their father. The native boys joined the excursion as hands. They had wanted to come, they indicated. But Henry knew the boys had no idea what it would mean to leave their people. They were called Tibura and Gowah. They tried to befriend Henry, because he was closest to their age, but he ignored them. They were slaves and they were doomed. He did not wish to associate with the doomed. He watched the New Zealand boys eat raw dog meat and pine for home. He knew they would eventually die.

He sailed to the verdant, tufted, perfumed land of Tahiti. He watched

Captain Cook be welcomed back to Tahiti as a great king, as a great friend. The *Resolution* was met by a swarm of Indians, swimming out to the ship and calling Cook's name. Henry watched as Omai—the Tahitian native who had met King George III—was received at home first as a hero and then, increasingly, as a resented outsider. He could see that now Omai belonged nowhere. He watched the Tahitians dance to English hornpipes and bagpipes, while Mr. Nelson, his staid botanical master, got drunk one night and stripped down to the waist, dancing to Tahitian drums. Henry did not dance. He watched Captain Cook order that a native man have both his ears shorn off at the temples by the ship's barber, for twice having stolen iron from the *Resolution*'s forge. He watched one of the Tahitian chiefs try to steal a cat from the Englishmen, and receive a lash of a whip across the face for his troubles.

He watched Captain Cook light fireworks over Matavai Bay, to impress the natives, but it only frightened them. On a quieter night, he saw the million lamps of heaven in the skies over Tahiti. He drank from coconuts. He ate dogs and rats. He saw stone temples littered with human skulls. He climbed up the treacherous avenues of rock cliffs, beside waterfalls, gathering fern samples for Mr. Nelson, who did not climb. He saw Captain Cook struggle to keep order and discipline among his charges, while licentiousness reigned. All the sailors and officers had fallen in love with Tahitian girls, and each girl was reputed to know a special secret act of love. The men never wanted to leave the island. Henry withheld from the women. They were beautiful, their breasts were beautiful, their hair was beautiful, they smelled extraordinary and they inhabited his dreams—but most of them already had the French disease. He held out against one hundred fragrant temptations. He was ridiculed for this. He held out nonetheless. He was planning something bigger for himself. He concentrated on botany. He collected gardenias, orchids, jasmine, breadfruit.

They sailed on. He watched a native in the Friendly Islands have his arm cut off at the elbow, on Captain Cook's orders, for having stolen a hatchet from the *Resolution*. He and Mr. Nelson were botanizing on those same islands when they were ambushed by natives, who stripped them of their clothes, and—far more injuriously—stripped them of their botanical samples and notebooks, as well. Sunburned, nude, and shaken, they returned to the ship, but still Henry did not complain.

With care, he observed the gentlemen on board, appraising their behaviors. He imitated their speech. He practiced their diction. He improved his manners. He overheard one officer tell another, "As much of a contrivance as the aristocracy has always been, it still constitutes the best check against mobs of the uneducated and the unreflecting." He watched how the officers repeatedly bestowed honor upon any native who resembled a nobleman (or, at least, who resembled some English idea of a nobleman). On every island they visited, the *Resolution*'s officers would single out any brown-skinned man who had a finer headpiece than the others, or who wore more tattoos, or who carried a bigger spear, or who had more wives, or who was borne upon a litter by other men, or who—in the absence of any of these luxuries— was simply *taller* than the other men. The Englishmen would treat that person with respect. This would be the man with whom they would negotiate, and upon whom they would bestow gifts, and who, sometimes, they would pronounce "the king." He concluded that wherever English gentlemen went in the world, they were always looking for a king.

Henry went turtling, and ate dolphins. He was eaten by black ants. He sailed on. He saw tiny Indians with giant shells in their ears. He saw a storm in the tropics turn the skies a sickly green color—the only thing that had ever visibly frightened the older sailors. He saw the burning mountains called volcanoes. They sailed farther north. It got cold again. He ate rats again. They landed on the west coast of the continent of North America. He ate reindeer. He saw people who dressed in furs and who traded in beaver pelts. He saw a sailor tangle his leg in the anchor chain and be pulled overboard to die.

They sailed farther north still. He saw houses made of whale's ribs. He bought the hide of a wolf. He collected primroses, violets, currants, and juniper with Mr. Nelson. He saw Indians who lived in holes in the ground, and who hid their women from the English. He ate salted pork studded with maggots. He lost another tooth. He arrived at the Bering Strait and heard beasts howling in the Arctic night. Every dry item he owned became soaked, and then iced. He watched his beard grow in. Sparse as it was, it still collected icicles. His dinner froze to his plate before he could eat it. He did not complain. He did not want it reported back to Sir Joseph Banks that he had ever complained. He traded his wolf hide for a pair of snowshoes. He watched Mr. Anderson, the ship's surgeon, die and be buried at sea in the dreariest prospect a man could ever imagine—a frozen world of constant night. He watched sailors volley rounds of cannon fire at sea lions on shore, for sport, until there was not a creature left alive on that beach.

He saw the land the Russians called Elaskah. He helped make beer out of spruce pine, which the sailors hated, but it was all they had to drink. He saw Indians who lived in dens not one degree more comfortable than the dwellings of the animals they hunted and ate, and he met Russians, stranded at a whaling station. He overheard Captain Cook remark of the leading Russian officer (a tall, handsome blond man), "He is clearly a gentleman of good family." Everywhere, it seemed, even in this dismal tundra, it was important to be a gentleman of good family. In August, Captain Cook gave up. He could find no Northwest Passage, and the *Resolution* was already blocked in by cathedrals of icebergs. They reversed course and headed south.

They barely stopped until they reached Hawaii. They ought never to have gone to Hawaii. They would have been safer starving in the ice. The kings of Hawaii were angry, and the natives were thieving and aggressive. The Hawaiians were not Tahitians—not gentle friends—and moreover, there were thousands of them. But Captain Cook needed fresh water, and had to remain in port until the holds were once more filled. There was much looting by the natives and much punishment by the English. Guns were fired, Indians were wounded, chiefs were appalled, threats were exchanged. Some of the men said that Captain Cook was unraveling, becoming more brutal, exhibiting more theatrical temper tantrums, and more enraged indignation, at every theft. Still, the Indians kept stealing. It could not be permitted. They pried the nails right out of the ship. Boats were stolen, and weapons, too. More guns were fired and more Indians were killed. Henry did not sleep for days in vigilance. Nobody slept.

Captain Cook struck out on land, wishing for an audience with the chiefs, to appease them, but he was met instead by hundreds of furious Hawaiians. Inside of a moment, the crowd became a mob. Henry watched as Captain Cook was killed, pierced through the breast by a native spear and clubbed over the head, his blood mixing with the waves. In one instant, the great navigator was no more. His body was dragged away by natives. Later that night, as a final insult, an Indian in a canoe threw a chunk of Captain Cook's thigh on board the *Resolution*.

Henry watched the English sailors burn the entire settlement in retribution. The English sailors could scarcely be held back from murdering every Indian man, woman, and child on the island. The heads of two Indians were severed and put on pikes—and there would be more of this, the sailors promised, until Captain Cook's body was returned for decent burial. The next day, the rest of Cook's corpse arrived on the *Resolution*, missing his vertebrae and feet, which were never recovered. Henry watched as the remains of his commander were buried at sea. Captain Cook had never spoken a word to Henry, and Henry—who had followed Banks's advice—had never let himself be seen by Cook. But now Henry Whittaker was alive, and Captain Cook was not.

He thought they might return to England after this disaster, but they did not. A man named Mr. Clerke became captain. They still had their mission—to try again at the Northwest Passage. When summer returned, they sailed back north once more, into that awful cold. Henry was pelted with ash and pumice from a volcano. Every fresh vegetable had long ago been consumed, and they drank brackish water. Sharks followed the ship, to dine off the slop from the latrines. He and Mr. Nelson recorded eleven new species of polar duck, and ate nine of them. He saw a giant white bear swim past the ship, paddling with lazy menace. He watched Indians tie themselves into small canoes covered with fur, and navigate the waters as if they and their boats were one animal. He watched the Indians run on the ice, pulled by their dogs. He watched Captain Cook's replacement—Captain Clerke—die at age thirty-eight, and be buried at sea.

Now Henry had outlived two English sea captains.

They gave up once more on the Northwest Passage. They sailed to Macao. He saw fleets of Chinese junks, and again encountered representatives of the Dutch East India Company, who seemed to be everywhere in their simple black clothes and humble clogs. It appeared to him that everywhere in the world, somebody owed money to a Dutchman. In China, Henry found out about a war with France, and a revolution in America. It was the first he had heard of it. In Manila, he saw a Spanish galleon, loaded, it was said, with two million pounds' worth of silver treasure. He traded his snowshoes for a Spanish naval jacket. He fell ill from the flux—they all did—but he survived it. He arrived in Sumatra, and then in Java, where, once more, he saw the Dutch making money. He took note of it.

They rounded the Cape one last time and headed back to England. By October 6, 1780, they were safely returned to Deptford. Henry had been gone four years, three months, and two days. He was now a young man of twenty years. During the entirety of the journey, he had acquitted himself in a gentlemanly manner. He hoped and expected that this would be reported of him. He'd also been a zealous observer and botanical collector, as instructed, and was now prepared to divulge his account to Sir Joseph Banks.

He departed the ship, received his wages, found a ride to London. The city was a filthy horror. The year 1780 had been a dreadful one for Britain— mobs, violence, antipapist bigotry, Lord Mansfield's home burned to the ground, the Archbishop of York's sleeves torn from his clothing and thrown in his face right on the street, prisons broken open, martial law—but Henry knew none of this, and cared about none of it. He walked all the way to 32 Soho Square, straight to Banks's private home. Henry knocked on the door, announced his name, and stood ready to receive his reward.

Banks sent him to Peru.

That would be Henry's reward.

Banks had been rather dumbfounded to discover Henry Whittaker standing at his door. Over the past few years, he had nearly forgotten about the boy, though he was too clever and too polite to reveal this. Banks carried a staggering amount of information in his head, and a good deal of responsibility. He was not only overseeing the expansion of Kew Gardens, but also supervising and funding numberless botanical expeditions all over the world. Hardly a ship arrived in London during the 1780s that did not carry a plant, a seed, a bulb, or a cutting on its way to Sir Joseph Banks. In addition, he held a place in polite society, and kept his hand in every new scientific advancement in Europe, from chemistry to astronomy to the breeding of sheep. Put simply, Sir Joseph Banks was an overoccupied gentleman, who had not been thinking about Henry Whittaker during the past four years quite as much as Henry Whittaker had been thinking about him.

Nonetheless, as he began to recall the orchardman's son, he permitted Henry entry into his personal study and offered him a glass of port, which

Henry refused. He bade the boy to tell him all about the journey. Of course Banks already knew that the *Resolution* had safely arrived in England, and he had been receiving letters from Mr. Nelson along the way, but Henry was the first live person Banks had encountered straight off the ship, and so Banks welcomed him—once he'd remembered who the boy was—with penetrating curiosity. Henry spoke for nearly two hours, in full botanical and personal detail. He spoke with more liberty than delicacy, it must be said, which made his account a treasure. By the end of the narrative, Banks found himself most deliciously informed. There was nothing Banks loved more than knowing things that other people did not realize he knew, and here— long before the official and politically polished logs of the *Resolution* would be made available to him—he already knew all that had occurred on Cook's third expedition.

As Henry spoke, Banks grew impressed. Banks could see that Henry had spent the past few years not so much studying as conquering botany, and that he now had the potential to become a first-rate plantsman. Banks would need to keep this boy, he realized, before someone else filched him away. Banks was a serial filcher himself. He often used his money and éclat to pinch young men of promise away from other institutions and expeditions, and to bring them into the service of Kew. Naturally, he had lost some young men over the years, as well—lured away to safe and lucrative posts as gardeners at wealthy estates. Banks would not lose this one, he decided.

Henry may have been ill-bred, but Banks did not mind an ill-bred man, if he was competent. Great Britain produced naturalists like flaxseed, but most of them were blockheads and dilettantes. Meanwhile, Banks was desperate for new plants. He would gladly have embarked on expeditions himself, but he was nearing fifty years old and suffering awfully from gout. He was swollen and pained, trapped most hours of the day in his desk chair. So he needed to dispatch collectors in his stead. It was not as simple a task as one might think, to find them. There were not as many able-bodied young men as one might hope—young men who wanted to earn wretched salaries in order to die of the ague in Madagascar, or be shipwrecked off the Azores, or assaulted by bandits in India, or taken prisoner in Grenada, or simply to vanish forever in Ceylon.

The trick was to make Henry feel as though he were *already* destined to work for Banks forever, and not to give the boy any time to ponder things, or to have someone warn him off, or to fall in love with some saucily dressed girl, or to make his own plans for his future. Banks needed to convince Henry that the future was prearranged, and that Henry's future already belonged to Kew. Henry was a confident young fellow, but Banks knew that his own position of wealth, power, and fame gave him the advantage here—indeed, gave him the appearance, at times, of being the hand of divine providence itself. The trick was to use the hand unblinkingly and swiftly.

"Fine work," Banks said, after Henry had relayed his stories. "You've done well. Next week I shall send you to the Andes."

Henry had to think for a moment: What were the Andes? Islands? Mountains? A country? Like the Netherlands?

But Banks was talking forward, as though all were decided. "I'm funding a Peruvian botanical expedition, and it departs Wednesday next. You'll be led by Mr. Ross Niven. He's a tough old Scot—perhaps too old, if I may be candid—but he's as hardy as anyone you'll ever meet. He knows his trees and, I daresay, he knows his South America. I prefer a Scotsman to an Englishman for this sort of work, you know. They are more cold-minded and constant, more fit to pursue their object with relentless ardor, which is what you want in your man abroad. Your salary, Henry, is forty pounds a year, and although it is not the sort of salary upon which a young man can fatten his life, the position is an honorable one, which carries along with it the gratitude of the British Empire. As you are still a bachelor, I am certain you can make do. The more frugally you live now, Henry, the richer a man you will someday become."

Henry looked as though he were about to ask a question, so Banks bowled him over. "You don't speak Spanish, I suppose?" he asked, disapprovingly.

Henry shook his head.

Banks sighed in exaggerated disappointment. "Well, you'll learn it, I expect. I'll permit you to go on the expedition regardless. Niven speaks it, although with a comic burr. You'll carry on somehow with the Spanish government there. They are protective of Peru, you know, and they are an annoyance—but it is theirs, I suppose. Though heaven knows I'd like to ransack every jungle in the place, given the chance. I do detest Spaniards,

Henry. I hate the dead hand of Spanish law, impeding and corrupting all it encounters. And their church is ghastly. Can you imagine it—the Jesuits still believe that the four rivers of the Andes are the same four rivers of paradise, as mentioned in the book of Genesis? Think of it, Henry! Mistaking the Orinoco for the Tigris!"

Henry had no idea what the man was talking about, but he stayed silent. He had learned in the past four years to speak only when he knew that which he was speaking about. Moreover, he had learned that silence can sometimes relax a listener into thinking that one might be intelligent. Lastly, he was distracted, still hearing the echo of these words: *The richer a man you will someday become . . .*

Banks rang a bell, and a pale, expressionless servant entered the room, sat down at the secretary, and took out some writing paper. Banks, without another word to the boy, dictated:

"Sir Joseph Banks, having been pleased to recommend you to the Lord Commissioners of His Majesty's Botanic Gardens at Kew, et cetera, et cetera . . . I am commanded by their Lordships to acquaint you that they have been pleased to appoint you, Henry Whittaker, as a collector of plants for His Majesty's garden, et cetera, et cetera . . . for your reward and remuneration and for your board, wages and tracking expenses, you will be allowed a salary of forty pounds a year, et cetera, et cetera, et cetera . . ."

Later, Henry would think that this had been an awful lot of *et cetera*s for forty pounds a year, but what other future did he have? There was a florid scratching of pens, and then Banks was lazily waving the letter in the air to dry, saying, "Your task, Henry, is the cinchona tree. You may know of it as the fever tree. It is the source of Jesuit's bark. Learn all you can about it. It's a fascinating tree and I'd like to see it more deeply studied. Make no enemies, Henry. Protect yourself from thieves, idiots, and miscreants. Take plentiful notes, and be sure to inform me in what sort of soil you find your specimens—sandy, loamy, boggy—so we can try to cultivate them here at Kew. Be tight with your money. Think like a Scot, boy! The less you indulge yourself now, the more you can indulge yourself in the future, when you have made your fortune. Resist drunkenness, idleness, women, and melancholy; you can enjoy all those pleasures later in life, when you are a useless old man like me. Be attentive. Better if you don't let anyone know that you are a man of botany. Protect your plants from goats, dogs, cats, pigeons, poultry, insects, mold, sailors, saltwater . . ."

Henry was listening with half an ear.

He was going to Peru.

On Wednesday next.

He was a man of botany, on assignment from the King of England.

Chapter Three

Henry arrived in Lima after nearly four months at sea. He found himself in a town of fifty thousand souls—a struggling colonial outpost, where Spanish families of rank often had less to eat than the mules that pulled their carriages.

He arrived there alone. Ross Niven, the leader of the expedition (an expedition, by the way, that had consisted entirely of Henry Whittaker and Ross Niven), had died along the way, just off the coast of Cuba. The old Scot should never have been allowed to leave England in the first place. He was consumptive and pale and raising up blood with every cough, but he had been stubborn, and had hidden his illness from Banks. Niven had not lasted a month at sea. In Cuba, Henry had penned a nearly illegible letter to Banks, offering news of Niven's death, and expressing his determination to continue on with the mission alone. He did not wait for a reply. He did not wish to be called home.

Before Niven died, though, the man had usefully bothered to teach Henry a thing or two about the cinchona tree. Around 1630, according to Niven, Jesuit missionaries in the Peruvian Andes had first noticed the Quechua Indians drinking a hot tea made of powdered bark, to cure fevers and chills brought on by the extreme cold of high altitude. An observant monk had wondered whether this bitter powdered bark might also treat the fevers and chills associated with malaria—a disease that did not even exist in Peru but which, in Europe, had forever been the murderer of popes and paupers alike. The monk shipped some cinchona bark to Rome (that sickeningly malarial swamp of a city) along with instructions for testing the powder. Miraculously, it turned out that cinchona did indeed interrupt the path of malaria's ravages, for reasons nobody could understand. Whatever the cause, the bark appeared to cure malaria entirely, with no side effects except lingering deafness—a small price to pay to live.

By the early eighteenth century, Peruvian bark, or Jesuit's bark, was the most valuable export from the New World to the Old. A gram of pure Jesuit's bark was now equal in value to a gram of silver. It was a rich man's cure, but there were plenty of rich men in Europe, and none of them wanted to die of malaria. Then Louis XIV was cured by Jesuit's bark, which only drove up prices steeper. Just as Venice grew rich on pepper and China grew rich on tea, the Jesuits were growing rich on the bark of Peruvian trees.

Only the British were slow to recognize the value of the cinchona— mostly owing to their anti-Spanish, anti-Papist prejudice, but also because of a lingering preference for bleeding their patients, rather than treating them with queer powders. In addition, the extraction of medicine from the cinchona was a complicated science. There were some seventy varieties of the tree, and nobody knew exactly which barks were the most potent. One had to rely on the honor of the bark collector himself, who was usually an Indian six thousand miles away. The powders one often encountered as "Jesuit's bark" in London pharmacies, smuggled into the country through secret Belgian channels, were largely fraudulent and ineffective. Nonetheless, the bark had at last come to the attention of Sir Joseph Banks, who wanted to learn more about it. And now—with the merest hint of potential riches—so did Henry, who had just become the leader of his own expedition.

Soon Henry was moving through Peru like a man goaded by the tip of a bayonet, and that bayonet was his own furious ambition. Ross Niven, before dying, had given Henry three sound pieces of advice about traveling through South America, and the young man wisely followed them all. One: Never wear boots. Toughen up your feet until they look like the feet of an Indian, forsaking forever the rotting embrace of wet animal hide. Two: Abandon your heavy clothing. Dress lightly, and learn to be cold, as the Indians do. You'll be healthier that way. And three: Bathe in a river every day, as the Indians do.

That constituted everything Henry knew, aside from the fact that cinchona was lucrative, and that it could be found only in the high Andes, in a remote area of Peru called Loxa. He had no man, map, or book to further instruct him, so he solved it on his own. To get to Loxa, he had to endure rivers, thorns, snakes, illness, heat, cold, rain, Spanish authorities, and—most dangerous of all—his own team of sullen mules, ex-slaves, and embittered Negroes, whose languages, resentments, and secret designs he could only begin to guess at.

Barefoot and hungry, he pushed on. He chewed coca leaves, like an Indian, to keep up his strength. He learned Spanish, which is to say that he stubbornly decided that he could already speak Spanish, and that people could already understand him. If they could not understand him, he shouted at them with increasing force until they did. He eventually reached the region called Loxa. He found, and bribed, the *cascarilleros*, the "bark cutters," the local Indians who knew where the good trees grew. He kept searching, and found even more hidden groves of cinchona.

Ever the orchardman's son, Henry quickly realized that most of the cinchona trees were in poor condition, sick and overharvested. There were a few trees with trunks as thick as his own midsection, but none any bigger. He began to pack the trees with moss, wherever the bark had been removed, to allow them to heal. He trained the *cascarilleros* to cut the bark in vertical strips, rather than killing the tree by horizontally banding it. He severely coppiced other sick trees, to allow for new growth. When he became sick himself, he kept on working. When he could not walk from illness or infection, he had his Indians tie him to his mule, like a captive, so he could visit his trees every day. He ate guinea pigs. He shot a jaguar.

He stayed up in Loxa for four miserable years, barefoot and cold, sleeping in a hut with barefoot and cold Indians, who burned manure for heat. He continued to nurse the cinchona groves, which legally belonged to the Spanish Royal Pharmacy, but which Henry had silently claimed for his own. He was far enough back in the mountains that no Spaniard ever interfered with him, and after a time the Indians weren't bothered by him, either. He gleaned that the cinchona trees with the darkest bark seemed to produce a more potent medicine than the other varieties, and that the newest growth produced the most powerful bark. Heavy pruning, therefore, was advisable. He identified and named seven new species of cinchona, but most of them he considered useless. He focused his attention on what he called cinchona *roja*—the red tree, the richest. He grafted the *roja* onto the root stock of more sturdy and disease-resistant varieties of cinchona in order to produce a higher yield.

Also, he thought a great deal. A young man alone in a high and distant forest has plenty of time to think, and Henry formulated grand theories. He knew from the late Ross Niven that the trade in Jesuit's bark was bringing in ten million *reales* a year to Spain. Why did Sir Joseph Banks want him to merely study this product, when they could be selling it? And why must production of Jesuit's bark be limited to this inaccessible region of the world? Henry remembered his father's teaching him that every plant of value in human history had been hunted before it was cultivated, and that hunting a tree (like climbing into the Andes to find the blasted thing) was far less efficient than cultivating it (like learning how to grow it elsewhere, in a controlled environment). He knew that the French had tried transplanting the cinchona to Europe in 1730, and that they had failed, and he believed he knew why: because they didn't understand altitude. One cannot grow this tree in the Loire Valley. Cinchona needed high, thin air and a humid forest—and France didn't have such a place. Nor did England. Nor Spain, for that matter. This was a pity. One cannot export climate.

During four years of thinking, though, this is what Henry came up with: India. Henry was willing to bet that the cinchona tree would thrive in the cold, damp Himalayan foothills—a place Henry had never been, but which he had heard about from British officers when he was traveling in Macao. Moreover, why not grow this useful medicinal tree closer to malarial locations themselves, closer to where it was actually needed? Jesuit's bark was in desperate demand in India, to combat debilitating fevers in British troops and native laborers. For now, the drug was far too costly to give to common soldiers and workers, but it needn't remain so. By the 1780s, Jesuit's bark was being marked up some two hundred percent between its source in Peru and its European markets, but most of that expense was due to the costs of shipping. It was time to stop hunting this tree and start cultivating it for profit, closer to where it was needed. Henry Whittaker, now twenty-four years old, believed he was the man to do it.

He left Peru in early 1785, carrying not only notes, an extensive herbarium, and samples of bark packed in linen, but also bare root cuttings and some ten thousand cinchona *roja* seeds. He brought home some capsicum varieties, too, as well as some nasturtiums and a few rare fuchsias. But the real prize was the cache of seeds. Henry had waited two years for those seeds to emerge, waiting for his best trees to put out blossoms untouched by frost. He'd dried the seeds in the sun for a month, turning them every two hours to keep them from growing mold, and had wrapped them in linen at night to protect them from dew. He knew that seeds rarely survived ocean voyages (even Banks had failed at carrying seeds home successfully from his travels with Captain Cook), so Henry decided to experiment with three different packing techniques. He packed some of the seeds in sand, embedded others in wax, and kept the rest loose in dried moss. All were stuffed in ox bladders to keep them dry, and then wrapped in alpaca wool to hide them.

The Spanish still held the monopoly on cinchona, so Henry was now officially a smuggler. As such, he avoided the busy Pacific coast and traveled east, overland across South America, carrying a passport that identified him as a French textile merchant. He and his mules and his ex-slaves and his unhappy Indians took the thieves' route—from Loxa to the river Zamora, to the Amazon, to the Atlantic coast. From there he sailed to Havana, then to Cadiz, then home to England. The return voyage took a year and a half in total. He encountered no pirates, no noteworthy storms, no debilitating illness. He lost no specimens. It wasn't that difficult.

Sir Joseph Banks, he thought, would be pleased.

But Sir Joseph Banks was not pleased, when Henry met up with him again, back in the comforts of 32 Soho Square. Banks was merely older and sicker and more distracted than ever. His gout was tormenting him terribly, and he was struggling with scientific questions of his own design, which he considered important to the future of the British Empire.

Banks was trying to find a way to end England's dependence on foreign cotton, and had thereby dispatched plantsmen to the British West Indies, who were working—unsuccessfully, thus far—on growing cotton there. He was also trying, also unsuccessfully, to break the Dutch monopoly on the spice trade by growing nutmeg and cloves at Kew. He had a proposal before the king to turn Australia into a penal colony (this was a mere hobby idea of his), but nobody as yet was listening. He was working to build a forty-foot-tall telescope for the astronomer William Herschel, who was desirous of discovering new comets and planets. But most of all, Banks wanted balloons. The French had balloons. The French had been experimenting with lighter-than-air gases, and were sending up manned flights in Paris. The English were falling behind! For the sake of science and national security, by God, *the British Empire needed balloons.*

So Banks, that day, was not in a mood to listen to Henry Whittaker's assertion that what the British Empire really needed were cinchona plantations in the midrange altitudes of the Indian Himalayas—an idea that did not further in any manner the causes of cotton, spices, comet hunting, or ballooning. Banks's mind was cluttered and his foot ached like the devil and he was irritated enough by Henry's aggressive presence to disregard the entire conversation. Here, Sir Joseph Banks made a rare tactical error—an error that would ultimately cost England dearly.

But it should be said that Henry, too, made tactical errors that day with Banks. Several of them in a row, in fact. Showing up unannounced was the first error. Yes, he had done it before, but Henry was no longer a cheeky lad, in whom such a lapse in decorum could be excused. He was by now a grown man (and a large man, at that) whose insistent hammering at the front door carried a suggestion of both social impudence and physical threat.

What's more, Henry arrived at Banks's doorstep empty-handed, which a botanical collector must never do. Henry's Peruvian collection was still on board the ship from Cadiz, safely docked in harbor. It was an impressive collection, but how could Banks have known that, when all the specimens were out of sight, hidden away on a distant merchant ship, concealed in ox bladders, barrels, gunnysacks, and Wardian cases? Henry should have brought something to personally place in Banks's hands—if not a cutting of cinchona *roja* itself, then at least a nicely flowering fuchsia. Anything to get the old man's attention, to soften him into believing that the forty pounds a year he'd been pouring into Henry Whittaker and Peru had not been squandered.

But Henry was not a softener. Instead, he verbally hurled himself at Banks with this blunt accusation: "You are wrong, sir, to merely study the cinchona when you should be selling it!" This staggeringly ill-considered statement accused Banks of being a fool, while simultaneously befouling

32 Soho Square with the unpleasant taint of *trade*—as though Sir Joseph Banks, the wealthiest gentleman in Britain, would ever personally need to resort to commerce.

To be fair to Henry, his head was not entirely lucid. He had been alone for many years in a remote forest, and a young man in the forest can become a dangerously unfettered thinker. Henry had discussed this topic with Banks so many times already *in his mind* that he was impatient now with the actual conversation. In Henry's imagination, everything was already arranged and already successful. In Henry's mind, there was only one possible outcome: Banks would now welcome the idea as brilliant, introduce Henry to the proper administrators at the East India Company, clear all permissions, secure all funding, and proceed—ideally by tomorrow afternoon—with this ambitious project. In Henry's dreams, the cinchona plantation was already growing in the Himalayas, he was already the glitteringly wealthy man whom Joseph Banks had once promised he might become, and he had already been welcomed as a gentleman into the embrace of London society. Most of all, Henry had allowed himself to believe that he and Joseph Banks already regarded each other as dear and intimate friends.

Now, it is quite possibly the case that Henry Whittaker and Sir Joseph Banks could have become dear and intimate friends, except for one small problem, which was that Sir Joseph Banks never regarded Henry Whittaker as anything more than an ill-bred and thieving little toiler, whose only purpose in life was to be wrung dry of usefulness in the service of his betters.

"Also," said Henry, while Banks was still recovering from the assault upon his senses, his honor, and his drawing room, "I believe we should discuss my nomination to the Royal Society of Fellows."

"Pardon me," Banks said. "Who on earth has nominated you to the Royal Society of Fellows?"

"I am trusting that you will," said Henry. "As reward for my work and my ingenuity."

Banks was speechless for a long moment. His eyebrows, on their own accord, fled to the top of his brow. He drew a sharp breath. And then—most unfortunately for the future of the British Empire—he laughed. He laughed so heartily that he had to dab his eyes with a handkerchief of Belgian lace, which may very well have cost more than the house in which Henry Whittaker had been raised. It was good to laugh, after such a tiresome day, and he gave in to the hilarity with all his being. He laughed so hard that his manservant, standing outside the door, poked his head into the room, curious about this sudden explosion of merriment. He laughed so hard that he could not speak. Which was probably for the best, because even without the laughter, Banks would have encountered difficulty finding words to express the absurdity of this notion—that Henry Whittaker, who by all rights should have swung from the gallows at Tyburn nine years earlier, who had the ferrety face of a natural-born pickpocket, whose appallingly penned letters had been a real source of entertainment to Banks over the years, whose father (poor man!) had kept company with pigs—that this young *bilker* expected to be invited into the most esteemed and gentlemanly scientific consortium in all of Britain? What a good whacking bit of comedy was this!

Of course, Sir Joseph Banks was the much-loved president of the Royal Society of Fellows—as Henry well knew—and had Banks nominated a crippled badger to the Society, the Society would have welcomed the creature and minted it a medal of honor, besides. But to welcome in Henry Whittaker? To allow this impudent picaroon, this mackerel-backed shaver, this jack-weighted *hob*, to add the initials RSF to his indecipherable signature?

No.

When Banks began to laugh, Henry's stomach collapsed upon itself and folded into a small, hard cube. His throat narrowed as though he were, at last, noosed. He shut his eyes and saw murder. He was capable of murder. He envisioned murder and carefully considered the consequences of murder. He had a long while to ponder murder, while Banks laughed and laughed.

No, Henry decided. Not murder.

When he opened his eyes, Banks was still laughing, and Henry was a transformed human being. Whatever youth had remained in him as of that morning, it was now kicked out dead. From that point forward, his life would be not about who he could become, but about what he could acquire. He would never be a gentleman. So be it. Sod gentlemen. Sod them all. Henry would become richer than any gentleman who had ever lived, and someday he would own the lot of them, from the floor up. Henry waited for Banks to stop laughing, and then he escorted himself from the room without a word.

He immediately went out into the streets and found himself a prostitute. He held her up against an alley wall and battered the virginity out of himself, injuring both the girl and himself in the process, until she cursed him for a brute. He found a public house, drank two jars of rum, pummeled a stranger in the gut, was thrown out in the street and kicked in the kidneys. There, now—it was done. Everything from which he had been abstaining over the last nine years, in the interest of becoming a respectable gentleman, it was all done. See how easy it is? No pleasure in it, to be sure, but it was done.

He hired a boatman to take him up the river to Richmond. It was nighttime now. He walked past his parents' dreadful house without stopping. He would never see his family again—nor did he wish to. He sneaked into Kew, found a shovel, and dug up all the money he had left buried there at age sixteen. There was a fair bit of silver waiting for him in the ground, far more than he remembered.

"Good lad," he told his younger, thieving, hoarding self.

He slept by the river, with a damp sack of coins as his pillow. The next day, he returned to London and bought himself a good-enough suit of clothes. He supervised the removal of his entire Peruvian botanical collection—seeds and bladders and bark samples all—from the ship that had come from Cadiz, and transferred it over to a ship heading to Amsterdam. Legally, the entire collection belonged to Kew. Bugger Kew. Bugger Kew until it bled. Let Kew come and find him.

Three days later, he sailed to Holland, and sold his collection, his ideas, and his services to the Dutch East India Company—whose severe and cunning administrators received him, it must be said, without a trace of laughter.

Chapter Four

Six years later, Henry Whittaker was a rich man on his way to becoming richer still. His cinchona plantation was thriving in the Dutch colonial outpost of Java, growing as happily as weeds in a cool, humid, terraced mountain estate called Pengalengan—an environment nearly identical, as Henry knew it would be, to both the Peruvian Andes and the lower Himalayas. Henry lived on the plantation himself and kept a careful eye on this botanical treasure trove. His partners in Amsterdam were now setting the global prices for Jesuit's bark, and reaping sixty florins for every hundred pounds of cinchona they processed. They couldn't process it fast enough. There was a fortune to be made here, and the fortune was made in specifics. Henry had continued to refine his orchard, which was protected now from crosspollination with lesser stock, and was producing a bark both more potent and more consistent than anything coming out of Peru itself. Furthermore, it shipped well, and—without the corrupting interference of Spanish or Indian hands—was judged by the world as a reliable product.

The colonial Dutch were now the world's biggest producers and consumers of Jesuit's bark, using the powder to keep their soldiers, administrators, and workers free from malarial fever all over the East Indies. The advantage that this gave them over their rivals—particularly over the English—was quite literally beyond calculation. With determined vengefulness, Henry made an effort to keep his product out of British markets entirely, or at least to drive up the price whenever Jesuit's bark found its way to England or her outposts.

Back at Kew, and far behind the game now, Sir Joseph Banks did eventually attempt to cultivate cinchona in the Himalayas, but without Henry's expertise the project lagged. The British were expending wealth, energy, and anxiety growing the wrong species of cinchona at the wrong altitude, and Henry, with cold satisfaction, knew it. By the 1790s, numberless British citizens and subjects were dying every week of malaria in India, lacking access to good Jesuit's bark, while the Dutch pushed forward in rude health.

Henry admired the Dutch and worked well with them. He effortlessly comprehended these people—these industrious, tireless, ditch-digging, beer-drinking, straight-speaking, coin-counting Calvinists, who had been making order out of trade since the sixteenth century, and who slept peacefully every night of their lives with the certain knowledge that God wished for them to be rich. A country of bankers, merchants, and gardeners, the Dutch liked their promises the same way Henry liked his (that is to say, gilded with profit), and thus they held the world captive at steep interest rates. They did not judge him for his rude manners or his aggressive ways. Very soon Henry Whittaker and the Dutch were making each other quite stupendously wealthy. In Holland, there were people who called Henry "the Prince of Peru."

By now, Henry was a rich man of thirty-one years, and it was time for him to orchestrate the remainder of his life. To begin with, he had the opportunity now to start his own business concerns, wholly separate from his Dutch partners, and he combed through his options with care. He had no fascination with minerals or gemstones, because he had no expertise in minerals or gemstones. Likewise with shipbuilding, publishing, or textiles. It would be botany, then. But which sort of botany? Henry had no desire to enter the spice trade, although there were famously large profits to be made in it. Too many nations were already involved in spices, and the costs of defending one's product from pirates and competing navies defeated the gains, as far as Henry could see. He also had no respect for either the sugar or the cotton trades, which he found to be insidious and costly, as well as intrinsically bound to slavery. Henry wanted nothing to do with slavery— not because he found it morally abhorrent, but because he regarded it as financially inefficient, untidy, and expensive, and controlled by some of the most unsavory middlemen on earth. What really interested him were medicinal plants—a market upon which nobody had yet fully capitalized.

So, medicinal plants and pharmacy it would be.

Next, he had to decide where he should live. He owned a fine estate in Java with a hundred servants, but the climate there had sickened him over the years, bestowing upon him tropical diseases that would periodically throw his health into havoc for the rest of his life. He needed a more temperate home. He would cut off his arm before he ever again lived in England. The Continent did not appeal: France was filled with irritating people; Spain was corrupt and unstable; Russia, impossible; Italy, absurd; Germany, rigid; Portugal, in decline. Holland, though favorably disposed toward him, was dull.

The United States of America, he decided, was a possibility. Henry had never been there, but he had heard promising things. He had heard especially promising things about Philadelphia—the lively capital of that young nation. It was said to be a city with a good-enough shipping port, central to the eastern coast of the country, filled with pragmatic Quakers, pharmacists, and hardworking farmers. It was rumored to be a place without haughty aristocrats (unlike Boston), and without pleasure-fearing puritans (unlike Connecticut), and without troublesome self-minted feudal princes (unlike Virginia). The city had been founded on the sound principles of religious tolerance, a free press, and good landscaping, by William Penn—a man who grew tree saplings in bathtubs, and who had imagined his metropolis as a great nursery of both plants and ideas. Everyone was welcome in Philadelphia, absolutely everyone—except, of course, the Jews. Hearing all this, Henry suspected Philadelphia to be a vast landscape of unrealized profits, and he aimed to turn the place to his advantage.

Before he settled anywhere, however, he wanted to be fitted up with a wife, and—because he was not a fool—he wanted a Dutch wife. He wanted a clever and decent woman with the least possible frivolousness, and Holland was the place to find her. Henry had indulged himself at times with prostitutes over the years, and had even kept a young Javanese girl on his estate in Pengalengan, but now it was time to take on a proper wife, and he recalled the advice of a sage Portuguese sailor who had told him, years before, "To be prosperous and happy in life, Henry, it is simple. Pick one woman, pick it well, and surrender."

So he sailed back to Holland to pick one. He chose quickly and calculatingly, plucking a wife from a respectable old family, the van Devenders, who had been custodians of the Hortus botanical gardens in Amsterdam for many generations. The Hortus was one of the foremost research gardens in Europe—one of the oldest links in history between botany, scholarship, and trade—and the van Devenders had always managed it with honor. They were not aristocrats by any means, and certainly not rich, but Henry did not need a rich woman. The van Devenders were, however, a premier European family of learning and science—and that he did admire.

Unfortunately, the admiration was not mutual. Jacob van Devender, the current patriarch of the family and of the Hortus (and a masterful hand at growing ornamental aloes), knew of Henry Whittaker and did not like what he had heard. He knew that this young man had a history of thieving, and also that he had betrayed his own country for profit. This was not the sort of conduct of which Jacob van Devender approved. Jacob was Dutch, yes, and he liked his money, but he was not a banker, not a speculator. He did not measure people's worth by their piles of gold.

However, Jacob van Devender had an excellent prospect of a daughter— or so Henry thought. Her name was Beatrix, and she was neither plain nor pretty, which seemed just about right for a wife. She was stout and bosomless, a perfect little barrel of a woman, and she was already rolling toward spinsterhood when Henry met her. To most suitors' tastes, Beatrix van Devender would have appeared dauntingly overeducated. She was conversant in five living languages and two dead ones, with an expertise in botany equal to any man's. Decidedly, this woman was not a coquette. She was no ornament of the drawing room. She dressed in the full spectrum of colors that one associates with common house sparrows. She nursed a hard suspicion of passion, exaggeration, and beauty, putting her confidence only in that which was solid and credible, and always trusting acquired wisdom over impulsive instinct. Henry perceived her as a living slab of ballast, which was precisely what he desired.

As for what Beatrix saw in Henry? Here, we encounter a slight mystery. Henry was not handsome. He was certainly not refined. In all truth, there was something of the village blacksmith about his ruddy face, his large hands, and his rough manners. To most eyes, he appeared neither solid nor credible. Henry Whittaker was an impulsive, loud, and bellicose man, who had enemies all over the world. He had also become, in the past years, a bit of a drinker. What respectable young woman would willingly choose such a character for a husband?

"The man has no principles," Jacob van Devender objected to his daughter.

"Oh, Father, you are most grievously mistaken," Beatrix corrected him dryly. "Mr. Whittaker has many principles. Just not the best variety of them."

True, Henry was rich, and thus some observers speculated that perhaps Beatrix appreciated his wealth more than she let on. Also, Henry aimed to take his new bride to America, and perhaps—the local wags gossiped—she had some shameful secret reason to leave Holland forever.

The truth, however, was simpler: Beatrix van Devender married Henry Whittaker because she liked what she saw in him. She liked his strength, his cunning, his ascendency, his promise. He was rough, yes, but she was no dainty blossom herself. She respected his bluntness, as he respected hers. She understood what he wanted of her, and felt certain that she could work with him—and perhaps even manage him a bit. Thus, Henry and Beatrix quickly and straightforwardly formed their alliance. The only accurate word for their union was a Dutch word, a business word: *partenrederij*—a partnership based on honest trade and plain dealing, where tomorrow's profits are a result of today's promises, and where the cooperation of both parties equally contributes to prosperity.

Her parents disowned her. Or it may be more precise to say that Beatrix disowned them. They were a rigid family, the whole lot of them. They disagreed over her alliance, and disagreements among van Devenders tended to be eternal. After choosing Henry and leaving for the United States, Beatrix never again communicated with Amsterdam. Her last glimpse of her family was of her young brother, Dees, ten years old, weeping at her departure, pulling at her skirts, crying, "They are taking her away from me! They are taking her away from me!" She uncurled her brother's fingers from her hem, told him to never again shame himself with public tears, and walked away.

Beatrix brought with her to America her personal maidservant—an immensely competent young washbasin of a woman named Hanneke de Groot. She also procured from her father's library a 1665 edition of Robert Hooke's *Micrographia*, and a most valuable compendium of Leonhart

Fuchs's botanical illustrations. She sewed dozens of pockets into her traveling dress, and filled each pocket with the Hortus's rarest tulip bulbs, all swaddled protectively in moss. She brought along, as well, several dozen blank accounting ledgers.

She was already planning her library, her garden, and—it would appear—her fortune.

Beatrix and Henry Whittaker arrived in Philadelphia in early 1793. The city, unprotected by walls or other fortifications, consisted at that time of a busy port, a few blocks of commercial and political interests, a conglomerate of farming homesteads, and some fine new estates. It was a place of expansive, generative possibility—a veritable alluvial bed of potential growth. The First Bank of the United States had opened there just the year before. The entire Commonwealth of Pennsylvania was at war with its forests—and its denizens, armed with axes, oxen, and ambition, were winning. Henry bought 350 acres of sloping pastures and unmolested woodland along the west bank of the Schuylkill River, with the intention to add more land as soon as he could acquire it.

Henry had originally planned to be rich by the age of forty, but he had driven his horses so hard, as the expression went, that he had arrived at his destination early. He was only thirty-two years old, and already had money banked up in pounds, florins, guineas, and even Russian kopecks. He aimed to become even wealthier still. But for now, upon his arrival in Philadelphia, it was time to put on a display.

Henry Whittaker named his property White Acre, a play on his own name, and immediately set to work building a Palladian mansion of lordly dimensions, far more beautiful than any private structure the city had yet seen. The house would be stone, vast, and well balanced—graced with fine east and west pavilions, a columned portico to the south, and a broad terrace to the north. He also built a grand carriage house, a large forge, and a whimsical gatehouse, as well as several botanical structures—including the first of what would eventually be many freestanding hothouses, an orangery modeled after the famous structure at Kew, and the beginnings of a glasshouse of staggering scope. Along the muddy bank of the Schuylkill—where only fifty years earlier Indians had gathered wild onions—he built his own private barge dock, just like the ones at the fine old estates along the Thames.

The city of Philadelphia was, for the most part, still living frugally in those days, but Henry designed White Acre as a brazen affront to the very notion of thrift. He wanted the place to pulse with extravagance. He was not afraid to be envied. Indeed, he found it bloody good sport to be envied, and good business, too, for envy drew people near. His home was designed not only to appear grand from a distance—easily seen from the river, sitting lofty and high upon its promontory, coolly overlooking the city on the other side—but also to express richness with every minute detail. Each doorknob would be brass, and all the brass would gleam. The furniture came straight from Seddon's of London, the walls were hung with Belgian paper, the china plate was Cantonese, the cellar was stocked with Jamaican rum and French claret, the lamps were hand-blown in Venice, and the lilacs around the property had first bloomed in the Ottoman Empire.

He allowed rumors of his wealth to spread unchecked. As rich as he was, it did not hurt for people to imagine him even richer. When neighbors started whispering that Henry Whittaker's horses had their hooves shod in silver, he permitted them to continue believing it. In fact, his horses' hooves were not shod in silver; they were shod in iron, just like everyone else's horses, and what's more, Henry had shod them himself (a skill he had learned in Peru—on poor mules, using poor tools). But why should anyone know that, when the rumor was so much more pleasing and formidable?

Henry understood not only the allure of money, but also the more mysterious allure of power. He knew that his estate must not merely dazzle, but also intimidate. Louis XIV used to take visitors on walks through his pleasure gardens not as an amusing diversion, but as a demonstration of force: every exotic flowering tree and every sparkling fountain and all the priceless Greek statuary were all just a means to communicate a single unambiguous message to the world: *You would not be advised to declare war against me!* Henry wished White Acre to express that same sentiment.

Henry also built a large warehouse and factory down by the Philadelphia harbor, for the receiving of medicinal plants from all over the world: ipecac, simarouba, rhubarb, guaiacum bark, china root, and sarsaparilla. He entered into partnership with a stalwart Quaker pharmacist named James Garrick, and the two men immediately began processing pills, powders, ointments, and tonics.

He started his business with Garrick not one moment too soon. By the summer of 1793, a yellow fever epidemic was battering Philadelphia. The streets were choked with corpses, and orphans clung to their dead mothers in the gutters. People died in pairs, in families, in clusters of dozens—heaving out sickening rivers of black sludge from their gullets and bowels on their way to death. Local physicians had decided that the only possible cure was to violently purge their patients even further, through repeated bouts of vomiting and diarrhea, and the best-known purgative in the world was a plant called jalap, which Henry was already importing in bales from Mexico.

Henry himself suspected that the jalap cure was bogus, and he refused to let anyone in his household take it. He knew that Creole doctors down in the Caribbean—far more familiar with yellow fever than their northern counterparts—treated patients with a less barbarous prescription of restorative liquids and rest. There was no money to be made, however, in restorative liquids and rest, while there was a great deal of money to be made in jalap. This is how it came to pass that, by the end of 1793, one-third of the population of Philadelphia had died of yellow fever, and Henry Whittaker had doubled his wealth.

Henry took his earnings and built two more glasshouses. At Beatrix's suggestion, he started cultivating native American flowers, trees, and bushes for export to Europe. It was a worthy idea; America's meadows and forests were filled with botanical species that looked exotic to a European eye, and could easily be sold overseas. Henry had grown weary of sending his ships out of the Philadelphia harbor with empty holds; now he could make money on both ends. He was still earning a fortune out of Java, processing Jesuit's bark with his Dutch partners, but there was a fortune to be made locally, too. By 1796, Henry was dispatching collectors into the Pennsylvania mountains to gather ginseng root for export to China. For many years to come, in fact, he would be the only man in America who ever figured out how to sell something to the Chinese.

By the end of 1798, Henry was filling his American greenhouses with imported tropical exotics, as well, to sell to new American aristocrats. The United States economy was in steep and abrupt ascent. George Washington and Thomas Jefferson both had opulent country estates, so everyone wanted an opulent country estate. The young nation was suddenly testing the limits of profligacy. Some citizens were getting rich; others were falling into destitution. Henry's trajectory soared only upward. The basis of every one of

Henry Whittaker's calculations was "I shall win," and invariably he did win—at importing, at exporting, at manufacturing, at opportunism of all kinds. Money seemed to love Henry. Money followed him around like a small, excited dog. By 1800, he was easily the richest man in Philadelphia, and one of the three richest men in the Western Hemisphere.

So when Henry's daughter Alma was born that year—just three weeks after the death of George Washington—it was as though she were born to a new kind of creature entirely, such as the world had never before seen: a mighty and newly minted American sultan.

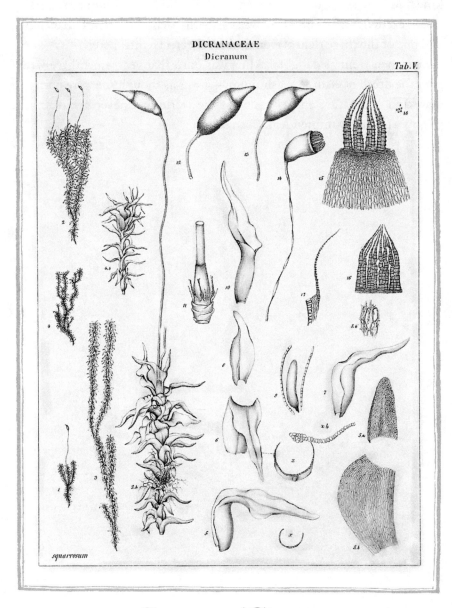

squarrosum

Dicranaceae / Dicranum

PART TWO

The Plum of White Acre

Chapter Five

She was her father's daughter. It was said of her from the beginning. For one thing, Alma Whittaker looked precisely like Henry: ginger of hair, florid of skin, small of mouth, wide of brow, abundant of nose. This was a rather unfortunate circumstance for Alma, although it would take her some years to realize it. Henry's face was far better suited to a grown man than to a little girl. Not that Henry himself objected to this state of affairs; Henry Whittaker enjoyed looking at his image wherever he might encounter it (in a mirror, in a portrait, in a child's face), so he always took satisfaction in Alma's appearance.

"No question who spawned that one!" he would boast.

What's more, Alma was clever like him. Sturdy, too. A right little dromedary, she was—tireless and uncomplaining. Never took ill. Stubborn. From the moment the girl learned to speak, she could not put an argument to rest. If her millstone of a mother had not steadfastly ground the impudence out of her, she might have turned out to be frankly rude. As it was, she was merely forceful. She wanted to understand the world, and she made a habit of chasing down information to its last hiding place, as though the fate of nations were at stake in every instance. She demanded to know why a pony was not a baby horse. She demanded to know why sparks were born when she drew her hand across her sheets on a hot summer's night. She not only demanded to know whether mushrooms were plants or animals, but also—when given the answer—demanded to know *why this was certain.*

Alma had been born to the correct parents for these sorts of restless inquiries; as long as her questions were respectfully expressed, they would be answered. Both Henry and Beatrix Whittaker, equally intolerant of dullness, encouraged a spirit of investigation in their daughter. Even Alma's mushroom question was granted a serious answer (from Beatrix in this case, who quoted the esteemed Swedish botanical taxonomist Carl Linnaeus on how to distinguish minerals from plants, and plants from animals: "Stones grow. Plants grow and live. Animals grow, live, and feel"). Beatrix did not believe a four-year-old child was too young to be discussing Linnaeus. Indeed, Beatrix had commenced Alma's formal education nearly as soon as the child could hold herself upright. If other people's toddlers could be taught to lisp prayers and catechisms as soon as they could speak, then, Beatrix believed, her child could certainly be taught *anything*.

As a result, Alma knew her numbers before the age of four—in English, Dutch, French, and Latin. The study of Latin was particularly stressed, because Beatrix believed that no one who was ignorant of Latin could ever write a proper sentence in either English or French. There was an early dabbling in Greek, as well, although with somewhat less urgency. (Not even Beatrix believed a child should pursue Greek before the age of five.) Beatrix tutored her intelligent daughter herself, and with satisfaction. A parent is inexcusable who does not personally teach her child to think. Beatrix also happened to believe that mankind's intellectual faculties had been steadily deteriorating since the second century anno Domini, so she enjoyed the sensation of running a private Athenian lyceum in Philadelphia, solely for her daughter's benefit.

Hanneke de Groot, the head housekeeper, felt that Alma's young female brain was perhaps overly taxed by so much study, but Beatrix would hear none of it, for this is how Beatrix herself had been educated, as had every van Devender child—male and female—since time immemorial. "Don't be simple, Hanneke," Beatrix scolded. "At no moment in history has a bright young girl with plenty of food and a good constitution perished from *too much learning.*"

Beatrix admired the useful over the vapid, the edifying over the entertaining. She was suspicious of anything one might call "an innocent amusement," and quite detested anything foolish or vile. Foolish and vile things included: public houses; rouged women; election days (one could always expect mobs); the eating of ice cream; the visiting of ice cream houses; Anglicans (whom she felt to be Catholics in disguise, and whose religion, she submitted, stood at odds with both morality and common sense); tea (good Dutch women drank only coffee); people who drove their sleighs in wintertime without bells upon their horses (you couldn't hear them coming up behind you!); inexpensive household help (a troublesome bargain); people who paid their servants in rum instead of money (thus contributing to public drunkenness); people who came to you with their troubles but then refused to listen to sound advice; New Year's Eve celebrations (the new year will arrive one way or another, regardless of all that bell-ringing); the aristocracy (nobility should be based upon conduct, not upon inheritance); and overpraised children (good behavior should be expected, not rewarded).

She embraced the motto *Labor ipse Voluptas*—work is its own reward. She believed there was an inherent dignity in remaining aloof and indifferent to sensation; indeed, she believed that indifference to sensation was the very definition of dignity. Most of all, Beatrix Whittaker believed in respectability and morality—but if pushed to choose between the two, she would probably have chosen respectability.

All of this, she strove to teach her daughter.

As for Henry Whittaker, obviously he could not help with the teaching of the classics, but he was appreciative of Beatrix's educational efforts with Alma. As a clever but unschooled man of botany, he had always felt that Greek and Latin were like two great iron struts, blocking the doorway of knowledge from him; he would not have his child similarly barred. Indeed, he would not have his child barred from anything.

As for what Henry taught Alma? Well, he taught her nothing. That is to say, he taught her nothing directly. He did not have the patience for administering formal instruction, and he did not like to be set round by children. But what Alma learned from her father indirectly constituted a long list. First and foremost, she learned not to irritate him. The moment she irritated her father, she would be banished from the room, so she learned from earliest milky consciousness never to nettle or provoke Henry. This was a challenge for Alma, for it required a stern thrashing down of all her natural instincts (which were, precisely, to nettle and provoke). She learned, however, that her father did not entirely mind a serious, interesting, or articulate question from his daughter—just so long as she never interrupted his speech or (this was trickier) his thoughts. Sometimes her questions even amused him, although she did not always understand why—such as when she asked why the hog took so long at it, climbing up on the lady pig's back, while the bull was always so quick with the cows. That question had made Henry laugh. Alma did not like to be laughed at. She learned never to ask such a question twice.

Alma learned that her father was impatient with his workers, with his houseguests, with his wife, with herself, and even with his horses—but with plants, he never lost his head. He was always charitable and forgiving with plants. This made Alma sometimes long to be a plant. She never spoke of this longing, though, for it would have made her look like a fool, and she had learned from Henry that one must never look like a fool. "The world is a fool who longs to be tricked," he often said, and he had borne it down upon his daughter that there is a mighty gap between the idiots and the clever, and one must come down on the side of cleverness. To show a longing for anything that one cannot have, for instance, is not a clever position.

Alma learned from Henry that there were far distant places in the world, where some men go and never return, but that her father had gone to those places *and had returned from them.* (She liked to imagine that he had returned home for her, in order to be her papa, although he had never insinuated such a thing.) She learned that Henry had endured the world because he was brave. She learned that her father wished for her to be brave, too, even in the most alarming instances—thunder, being chased by geese, a flood on the Schuylkill River, the ape with the chain on its neck that traveled in the wagon with the tinker. Henry would not allow Alma to fear any of those things. Before she even properly understood what death was, he was forbidding her to fear that, as well.

"People die every day," he told her. "But there are eight thousand chances against its being you."

She learned that there were weeks—rainy weeks in particular—when her father's body ailed him more than any man in Christendom should be obliged to bear. He had permanent agony in one leg from a poorly set broken bone, and he suffered from the recurrent fevers that he had acquired in those distant and dangerous places across the world. There were times when Henry could not leave his bed for half a month. He must never be bothered under such circumstances. Even to bring him letters, one must proceed quietly. These ailments were the reason Henry could not travel anymore, and why, instead, he summoned the world to him. This was why there were always so many visitors at White Acre, and why so much business was conducted in the drawing room and at the dining room table. This is also why Henry had the man called Dick Yancey—the terrifying, silent, bald-pated Yorkshireman with gelid eyes, who traveled on Henry's behalf, and who disciplined the world in the name of the Whittaker Company. Alma learned never to speak to Dick Yancey.

Alma learned that her father did not keep the Sabbath, although he did keep, in his name, the finest private pew in the Swedish Lutheran church where Alma and her mother spent their Sundays. Alma's mother did not particularly care for the Swedes, but since there was no Dutch Reformed church nearby, the Swedes were better than nothing. The Swedes, at least, understood and shared the central beliefs of Calvinist teachings: You are responsible for your own situation in life, you are most likely doomed, and the future is terribly grim. That was all comfortingly familiar to Beatrix. Better than any of the other religions, with their false, soft reassurances.

Alma wished she did not have to go to church, and that she could stay home on Sundays as her father did, to work with plants. Church was dull and uncomfortable and smelled of tobacco juice. In the summertime, turkey fowl and dogs sometimes wandered inside the open front door, seeking shade from the insufferable heat. In the wintertime, the old stone building became impossibly cold. Whenever a beam of light shone through one of the tall, wavy-glassed windows, Alma would turn her face up toward it, like a tropical vine in one of her father's botanical forcing houses, wishing to climb her way out.

Alma's father did not like churches or religions, but he did frequently call upon God to curse his enemies. As for what else Henry did not like, the list was long, and Alma came to know it well. She knew that her father detested large men who kept small dogs. Also, he detested people who bought fast horses that they were unskilled to ride. Furthermore, he detested: recreational sailing vessels; surveyors; cheaply made shoes; French (the language, the food, the populace); nervous clerks; tiny porcelain plates which broke in a man's damned hand; poetry (but not songs!); the stooped backs of cowards; thieving sons of whores; a lying tongue; the sound of a violin; the army (any army); tulips ("onions with airs!"); blue jays; the drinking of coffee ("a damned, dirty Dutch habit!"); and—although Alma did not yet understand what either of these words meant—both slavery and abolitionists.

Henry could be incendiary. He could insult and diminish Alma as quickly as another man could button up a waistcoat ("Nobody likes a stupid and selfish little piglet!"), but there were moments, too, when he seemed verifiably fond of her, and even proud of her. A stranger came out to White Acre one day to sell Henry a pony, for Alma to learn to ride. The pony's name was Soames, and he was the color of sugar icing, and Alma loved him immediately. A price was negotiated. The two men settled on three dollars. Alma, who was only six years old, asked, "Excuse me, sir, but does that price also include the bridle and saddle which the pony is currently wearing?"

The stranger balked at the question, but Henry roared with laughter. "She's got you there, man!" he bellowed, and for the rest of that day, he ruffled Alma's hair whenever she came near, saying, "What a good little auctioneer I've got as a daughter!"

Alma learned that her father drank out of bottles in the evening, and that those bottles sometimes contained danger (raised voices; banishment), but could also contain miracles—such as permission to sit on her father's lap, where she might be told fantastical stories, and might be called by her rarest nickname: "Plum." On such nights, Henry told her things like, "Plum, you must always carry enough gold on you to buy back your life in case of a kidnapping. Sew it into your hems, if you must, but never be without money!" Henry told her that the Bedouins in the desert sometimes sewed gemstones under their skin, in case of emergency. He told her that he himself had an emerald from South America sewn under the loose skin of his belly, and that it looked to the unknowing eye like a scar from a gunshot wound, and that he would never, ever show it to her—but the emerald was there.

"You must always have one final bribe, Plum," he said.

On her father's lap, Alma learned that Henry had sailed the world with a great man named Captain Cook. These were the best stories of all. One day a giant whale had come to the surface of the ocean with its mouth open, and Captain Cook had sailed the ship right inside the whale, taken a look around the whale's belly, and had then sailed out again—backward! Once Henry had heard a crying noise at sea, and had seen a mermaid floating on the ocean's surface. The mermaid had been injured by a shark. Henry had pulled the mermaid out of the water with a rope, and she had died in his arms—but not before she had, by God, blessed Henry Whittaker, telling him that he would be a rich man someday. And that was how he acquired this big house—on account of that mermaid's blessing!

"What language did the mermaid speak?" Alma wanted to know, imagining that it would almost have to be Greek.

"English!" Henry said. "By God, Plum, why would I rescue a deuced foreign mermaid?"

Alma was awed and sometimes daunted by her mother, but she adored her father. She loved him more than anything. She loved him more than Soames the pony. Her father was a colossus, and she peered at the world from between his mammoth legs. By comparison to Henry, the Lord of the Bible was dull and distant. Like the Lord of the Bible, Henry sometimes tested Alma's love—particularly after the bottles were opened. "Plum," he would say, "why don't you run as fast as your spindle-shanked legs can carry you, all the way down to the wharf, and see if your papa has any ships arriving from China?"

The wharf was seven miles away, and across the river. It could be nine o'clock on a Sunday night during a bitterly cold March storm, and Alma would leap off her father's lap and start running. A servant would have to catch her at the door and carry her back into the drawing room, or else—at the age of six, without a cloak or bonnet upon her, without a penny in her pocket or the tiniest bit of gold sewn into her hems—by God, she would have done it.

What a childhood this girl passed!

Not only did Alma have these potent and clever parents, but she also had the entire estate of White Acre to explore at her will. It was truly an Arcadia. There was so much to be taken in. The house alone was an ever-unfolding marvel. There was the lumpy stuffed giraffe in the east pavilion, with his alarmed and comical face. There was the threesome of enormous mastodon ribs in the front atrium, dug up in a nearby field by a local farmer, who traded it to Henry for a new rifle. There was the ballroom, gleaming and empty, where once—in the chill of late autumn—Alma had encountered a trapped hummingbird, which had shot past her ear in the most remarkable trajectory (a jeweled missile, it seemed, fired from a tiny cannon). There was the caged mynah bird in her father's study, who came all the way from China, and who could speak with impassioned eloquence (or so Henry claimed) but only in its native tongue. There were the rare snakeskins, preserved with a filling of straw and sawdust. There were shelves stocked with South Sea coral, Javanese idols, ancient Egyptian jewelry of lapis lazuli, and dusty Turkish almanacs.

And there were so many places in which one could eat! The dining room, the drawing room, the kitchen, the parlor, the study, the sunroom, and the verandahs with their shaded arbors. There were luncheons of tea and gingerbread, chestnuts and peaches. (And such peaches—pink on one side, gold on the other.) In the winter, one could drink soup in the upstairs nursery while watching the river below, which glittered under the barren sky like a polished mirror.

But outdoors, the delights were even more plentiful and ripe with mystery. There were the noble greenhouses, filled with cycads, palms, and ferns, all packed in deep, black, stinking tanner's bark to keep them warm. There was the loud and frightening water engine, which kept the greenhouses wet. There were the mysterious forcing houses—always faintingly hot—where the delicate imported plants were brought to heal after long sea voyages, and where orchids were bribed into blooming. There were the lemon trees in the orangery, which were wheeled outside every summer like consumptive patients, to enjoy the natural sun. There was the small Grecian temple, hidden at the end of an avenue of oaks, where one could imagine Olympus.

There was the dairy and, hard beside it, the buttery—with its alluring whiff of alchemy, superstition, and witchcraft. The German dairymaids drew hexes in chalk on the buttery's door, and muttered incantations before entering the building. The cheese would not set, they told Alma, if it was cursed by the devil. When Alma asked her mother about this, she was scolded as a credulous innocent, and given a long lecture in how cheese actually sets—as it turns out, through a perfectly rational chemical trans-mutation of fresh milk treated with rennet, which is then set to age in wax rinds at controlled temperatures. Lesson completed, Beatrix then wiped the hexes from the buttery's door, reprimanding the dairymaids as supersti-tious fools. The next day, Alma noticed, the chalk hexes were drawn back in. One way or another, the cheese continued to set properly.

Then there were the endless sylvan acres of woodland—left purposely uncultivated—filled with rabbits, foxes, and park deer who would eat out of one's hand. Alma was allowed—nay, encouraged!—by her parents to wan-der that woodland at will, in order to learn the natural world. She gathered beetles, spiders, and moths. She watched a large striped snake be eaten alive one day by a much larger black snake—a process that took several hours and was a horrible and spectacular display. She watched tiger spiders dig deep tubes into the duff, and robins gather moss and mud from the river's edge for their nests. She adopted a handsome little caterpillar (handsome by caterpillar standards), and rolled him into a leaf to take home as a friend, though she later accidentally murdered him by sitting on him. That was a severe blow, but one carried on. That is what her mother said: "Stop your weeping and carry on." Animals die, it was explained. Some animals, like sheep and cows, are born for no other purpose *except* to die. One could not mourn every death. By the age of eight Alma had already dissected, with Beatrix's assistance, the head of a lamb.

Alma always went to the woods fitted out in the most sensible dress, armed with her own personal collecting kit of glass vials, tiny storage boxes, cotton wool, and writing tablets. She went out in all weather, because delights could be found in all weather. A late-April snowstorm one year brought the odd sound of songbirds and sleighbells mingled together, and this alone was worth leaving the house for. She learned that walking care-fully in the mud to save one's boots or the hems of one's skirts never rewarded one's search. She was never scolded for returning home with muddied boots and hems, so long as she came home with good specimens for her private herbarium.

Soames the pony was Alma's constant companion on these forays—sometimes carrying her through the forest, sometimes following along behind her like a large, well-mannered dog. In the summer, he wore splen-did silk tassels in his ears, to keep out the flies. In the winter, he wore fur beneath his saddle. Soames was the best botanical collecting partner one could ever imagine, and Alma talked to him all day long. He would do absolutely anything for the girl, except move quickly. Only occasionally did he eat the specimens.

In her ninth summer, completely on her own, Alma learned to tell time by the opening and closing of flowers. At five o'clock in the morning, she noticed, the goatsbeard petals always unfolded. At six o'clock, the daisies and globeflowers opened. When the clock struck seven, the dandelions would bloom. At eight o'clock, it was the scarlet pimpernel's turn. Nine o'clock: chickweed. Ten o'clock: meadow saffron. By eleven o'clock, the process begins to reverse. At noon, the goatsbeard closed. At one o'clock, the chickweed closed. By three o'clock, the dandelions had folded. If Alma was not back to the house with her hands washed by five o'clock—when the globeflower closed and the evening primrose began to open—she would find herself in trouble.

What Alma wanted to know most of all was how the world was regulated. What was the master clockwork behind everything? She picked flowers apart, and explored their innermost architecture. She did the same with insects, and with any carcass she ever found. One late September morning, Alma became fascinated by the sudden appearance of a crocus, a flower that she'd previously believed bloomed only in the spring. What a discovery! She could not get a satisfactory answer from anyone about what in heaven's name these flowers thought they were doing, showing up here at the cold beginning of autumn, leafless and unprotected, just when all else was dying. "They are autumn crocuses," Beatrix told her. Yes, clearly and obviously they were—but to what end? Why bloom now? Were they stupid flowers? Had they lost track of time? To what important office did this crocus need to attend, that it would suffer to put forth bloom during the first bitter nights of frost? Nobody could elucidate. "That is simply how the variety behaves," Beatrix said, which Alma found to be an uncharacteristically unsatisfying answer. When Alma pushed further, Beatrix replied, "Not everything has an answer."

Alma found this to be such a staggering piece of intelligence that she was struck dumb by it for several hours. All she could do was sit and ponder the notion in an amazed stupor. When she recovered herself, she drew the mysterious autumn crocus in her writing tablet, and dated her entry, along with her questions and protestations. She was quite diligent in this way. Things must be kept track of—even things one could not comprehend. Beatrix had instructed her that she must always record her findings in drawings as accurate as she could make them, categorized, whenever possible, by the correct taxonomy.

Alma enjoyed the act of sketching, but her finished drawings often disappointed her. She could not draw faces or animals (even her butterflies looked truculent), though eventually she found that she was not *awful* at drawing plants. Her first successes were some quite good renderings of umbels—those hollow-stemmed, flat-flowered members of the carrot family. Her umbels were accurate, though she wished they were more than accurate; she wished they were beautiful. She said as much to her mother, who corrected her: "Beauty is not required. Beauty is accuracy's distraction."

Sometimes, in her forays through the woodlands, Alma encountered other children. This always alarmed her. She knew who these intruders were, though she never spoke to them. They were the children of her parents' employees. The White Acre estate was like a giant living beast, with half its enormous body needed for servants—the German and Scottish-born gardeners whom her father preferred to hire over the lazier native-born Americans, and the Dutch-born maids upon whom her mother insisted and relied. The household servants lived in the attic, and the outdoor laborers and their families lived in cottages and cabins all across the property. They were quite nice cottages, too—not because Henry cared about his workers' comfort, but because Henry could not abide the sight of squalor.

Whenever Alma encountered the workers' children in the woods, she was struck by fear and horror. She had a method for surviving these encounters, though: she would pretend they were not occurring at all. She rode both past and *above* the children on her stalwart pony (who moved, as always, at the slow and unconcerned pace of cold molasses). Alma held her breath as she passed the children, looking neither to her left nor to her right, until she had cleared the intruders safely. If she did not look at them, she did not have to believe in them.

The workers' children never interfered with Alma. It was likely they had been warned to leave her alone. Everyone feared Henry Whittaker, so the daughter was automatically to be feared, too. Sometimes, though, Alma spied on the children from a safe distance. Their games were rough and incomprehensible. They dressed differently than Alma did. None of these children carried botanical collecting kits slung over their shoulders, and none of them rode ponies with gaily colored silk ear tassels. They shoved and shouted at each other, using coarse language. Alma was more afraid of these children than anything else in the world. She often had nightmares about them.

But here is what one did for nightmares: one went to find Hanneke de Groot, down in the basement of the house. This could be helpful and soothing. Hanneke de Groot, head housekeeper, held authority over the entire cosmos of the White Acre estate, and her authority vested her with a most calming gravitas. Hanneke slept in her own quarters, next to the underground kitchen, down where the fires never went out. She existed within a warm bath of cellar air, perfumed by the salted hams that hung from every beam. Hanneke lived in a cage—or so it appeared to Alma—for her personal rooms had bars over the windows and doors, as it was Hanneke alone who controlled access to the household's silver and plate, and who managed the payroll for the entire staff.

"I do not live in a cage," Hanneke once corrected Alma. "I live in a bank vault."

When Alma could not sleep for nightmares, she would brave the terrifying journey down three flights of darkened stairs, all the way to the farthest corner of the basement, where she clung to the bars of Hanneke's quarters and cried to be let in. Such expeditions were always a gamble. Hanneke would sometimes rise, sleepy and complaining, unlock her jailer's door, and permit Alma to join her in the bed. Sometimes, though, she would not. Sometimes she would scold Alma for a baby, asking her why she must harass a tired Dutch woman, and she would send Alma back up the harrowing dark staircases to her own room.

But for the rare instances when one actually was allowed in Hanneke's bed, it was well worth the ten other times one was repulsed, for Hanneke would tell stories, and Hanneke knew so many things! Hanneke had known Alma's mother forever, since earliest childhood. Hanneke told stories of Amsterdam, which Beatrix never did. Hanneke always spoke Dutch to Alma, and Dutch, to Alma's ears, would forever be the language of comfort and bank vaults and salted ham and safety.

It would never have occurred to Alma to run to her mother, whose bedroom was right next to her own, for assurances during the night. Alma's mother was a woman of many gifts, but the gift of comfort was not among them. As Beatrix Whittaker frequently said, any child who was old enough to walk, speak, and reason ought to be able—without any assistance whatsoever—to comfort herself.

And then there were the houseguests—an unbroken parade of visitors arriving at White Acre nearly every day, in carriages, on horseback, by boat, or on foot. Alma's father lived in terror of being bored, so he liked to summon people to his dinner table, to entertain him, to bring him news of the world, or to give him ideas for new ventures. Whenever Henry Whittaker summoned people, they came—and came gratefully.

"The more money one has," Henry explained to Alma, "the better people's manners become. It is a notable fact."

Henry had a quite robust pile of money by this point. In May of 1803, he had secured a contract with a man named Israel Whelen, a government official who was purveying medical supplies for Lewis and Clark's expedition across western America. Henry had amassed for the expedition potent supplies of mercury, laudanum, rhubarb, opium, columbo root, calomel, ipecac, lead, zinc, sulfate—some of which were actually medically helpful, but all of which were lucrative. In 1804, the drug morphine was first isolated from poppies by German pharmacists, and Henry was an early investor in the manufacture of that useful commodity. The next year, he was granted the contract to supply medical products to the entire U.S. Army. This gave him a certain political power, as well as fiduciary power, and so yes, people came to his dinners.

These were not society dinners, by any means. The Whittakers were never exactly welcomed into Philadelphia's small, rarefied circle of high society. Upon first arriving in the city, the Whittakers had been invited only once to dine with Anne and William Bingham, on Third Street and Spruce, but it had not gone well. Over dessert, Mrs. Bingham—who comported herself as though she were in the Court of St. James's—had asked Henry, "What sort of name is Whittaker? I find it so uncommon."

"Midland England," Henry had replied. "Comes from the word War-wickshire."

"Is Warwickshire your family seat?"

"There, and other places, besides. We Whittakers tend to sit wherever we can find a chair."

"But does your father still own property in Warwickshire, sir?"

"My father, madam, if he is still living, owns two pigs and the privy pot under his bed. I doubt very much he owns the bed."

The Whittakers were not invited back to dine with the Binghams again. The Whittakers did not much care. Beatrix disapproved of the conversation and dress of fashionable ladies, anyway, and Henry disliked the tedious manners of fine drawing rooms. Instead, Henry created his own society, across the river from the city, high upon his hill. Dinners at White Acre were not playing fields of gossip, but exercises in intellectual and commercial stimulation. If there was a bold young man out there in the world somewhere accomplishing interesting feats, Henry wanted that young man summoned to his dinner table. If there was a venerable philosopher passing through Philadelphia, or a well-regarded man of science, or a promising new inventor, those men would be invited, also. Women sometimes came to the dinners, too, if they were the wives of respected thinkers, or the translators of important books, or if they were interesting actresses on tour in America.

Henry's table was a bit much for some people. The meals themselves were opulent—oysters, beefsteak, pheasant—but it was not altogether relaxing to dine at White Acre. Guests could expect to be interrogated, challenged, provoked. Known adversaries were placed side by side. Precious beliefs were pummeled in conversation that was more athletic than polite. Certain notables left White Acre feeling they had suffered the most impressive indignations. Other guests—more clever, perhaps, or thicker of skin, or more desperate for patronage—left White Acre with lucrative agreements, or beneficial partnerships, or just the right letter of introduction to an important man in Brazil. The dining room at White Acre was a perilous playing field, but a victory there could establish a fellow's career for life.

Alma had been welcomed at this combative table from the time she was four years old, and was often seated next to her father. She was allowed to ask questions, so long as her questions were not imbecilic. Some guests were even charmed by the child. An expert in chemical symmetry once proclaimed, "Why, you're as clever as a little book to talk to!"—a compliment Alma never forgot. Other great men of science, as it turned out, were not accustomed to being questioned by a little girl. But some great men of science, as Henry pointed out, were unable to defend their theories to a little girl, and if that was the case, they deserved to be exposed as humbugs.

Henry believed, and Beatrix strongly concurred, that there was no subject too somber, too knotty, or too perturbing to be discussed in front of their child. If Alma did not understand what was being said, Beatrix reasoned, it would merely give her more motive to improve her intellect, so as not to be left behind next time. If Alma had nothing of intelligence to contribute to the conversation, Beatrix taught her to smile at whomsoever had spoken last and murmur politely, "Do go on." If Alma should find herself bored at the table, well, that was certainly no one's concern. Dinner gatherings at White Acre were not ordered around a child's entertainment (indeed, Beatrix submitted that precious few things in life should be ordered around a child's entertainment), and the sooner Alma learned to sit still in a hardbacked chair for many hours on end, listening attentively to ideas far beyond her grasp, the better she would be for it.

Thus Alma spent the tender years of her childhood listening to the most extraordinary conversations—with men who studied the decomposition of human remains; with men who had ideas for importing fine new Belgian fire hoses to America; with men who drew pictures of monstrous medical deformities; with men who believed any medicine that could be swallowed could just as effectively be rubbed over the skin and absorbed into the body; with men who examined the organic matter of sulfuric springs; and with one man who was an expert on the pulmonary function of aquatic birds (a subject which he claimed was more fraught with thrilling interest than any other in the natural world—although, from his droning presentation at the dinner table, this statement did not prove true).

Some of these evenings were entertaining to Alma. She liked it best when the actors and explorers came, and told stirring tales. Other nights were tense with argument. Other nights still were torturously dull eternities. She would sometimes fall asleep at the table with her eyes open, held upright in her chair by nothing more than absolute terror of her mother's censure, and the bracing stays on her formal dress. But the night Alma would remember forever—the night that would later seem to have been the very apogee of her childhood—was the night of the visit from the Italian astronomer.

It was late summer of 1808, and Henry Whittaker had acquired a new telescope. He had been admiring the night skies through his fine German lenses, but he was beginning to feel like a celestial illiterate. His knowledge of the stars was a sailor's knowledge—which is not trifling—but he was not up-to-date on the latest findings. Tremendous advances were being made now in the field of astronomy, and Henry increasingly felt that the night sky was becoming yet another library that he could barely read. So when Maestro Luca Pontesilli, the brilliant Italian astronomer, came to Philadelphia to speak at the American Philosophical Society, Henry lured him up to White Acre by hosting a ball in his honor. Pontesilli, he had heard, was a zealot for dancing, and Henry suspected the man could not resist a ball.

This was to be the most elaborate affair the Whittakers had ever attempted. The finest of Philadelphia's caterers—Negro men in crisp white uniforms—arrived in the early afternoon and set to assembling the elegant meringues and mixing the colorful punches. Tropical flowers that had never before been taken out of the balmy forcing houses were arranged in tableaux all over the mansion. Suddenly an orchestra of moody strangers was milling about the ballroom, tuning their instruments and muttering complaints about the heat. Alma was scrubbed and packed into white crinolines, her cockscomb of unruly red hair forced into a satin bow nearly as big as her head. Then the guests arrived, in billows of silk and powder.

It was hot. It had been hot all month, but this was the hottest day yet. Anticipating the uncomfortable weather, the Whittakers did not commence their ball until nine o'clock, long after the sun had set, but the day's punishing heat still lingered. The ballroom quickly became a greenhouse itself, steaming and damp, which the tropical plants enjoyed, but which the ladies did not. The musicians suffered and perspired. The guests spilled out of doors in search of relief, lounging on the verandahs, leaning against marble statues, trying in vain to draw coolness from the stone.

In an effort to slake their thirst, people drank a good deal more punch than they had perhaps intended to drink. As a natural result, inhibitions melted away, and a general air of lightheaded giddiness took hold of everyone. The orchestra abandoned the formality of the ballroom and set up a lively racket outdoors on the wide lawn. Lamps and torches were brought outside, casting all the guests into turbulent shadows. The charming Italian astronomer attempted to teach the gentlemen of Philadelphia some wild Neapolitan dance steps, and he made his rounds with every lady, too—all of whom found him comical, daring, thrilling. He even tried to dance with the Negro caterers, to general hilarity.

Pontesilli was supposed to have delivered a lecture that night, with elaborate illustrations and calculations, explaining the elliptical paths and velocities of the planets. At some point in the course of the evening, though, this idea was discarded. What gathering, in such an unruly spirit, could fairly be expected to sit still for a serious scientific lecture?

Alma would never know whose idea it had been—Pontesilli's or her father's—but shortly after midnight, it was decided that the famous Italian cosmological maestro would re-create a model of the universe on the great lawn of White Acre, using the guests themselves as heavenly bodies. It would not be an exact scale model, the Italian drunkenly declaimed, but it would at least give the ladies a slight sense about the lives of the planets and their relationships to one another.

With a marvelous air of both authority and comedy, Pontesilli placed Henry Whittaker—the Sun—at the center of the lawn. Then he gathered up a number of other gentlemen to serve as planets, each of whom would radiate outward from their host. To the entertainment of everyone gathered, Pontesilli attempted to choose men for these roles who most closely resembled the planets they were meant to represent. Thus, tiny Mercury was portrayed by a diminutive but dignified grain merchant from Germantown. Since Venus and Earth were bigger than Mercury, but nearly the same size as each other, Pontesilli chose for those planets a pair of brothers from Delaware—two men who were almost perfectly identical in height, girth, and complexion. Mars needed to be bigger than the grain merchant but not quite as big as the brothers from Delaware; a prominent banker with a trim figure fit the bill. For Jupiter, Pontesilli commandeered a retired sea captain, a man of truly hilarious fatness, whose corpulent appearance in the solar system reduced the entire party to hysterical laughter. As for Saturn, a slightly less fat but still amusingly portly newspaperman did the job.

On it went, until all the planets were arranged across the lawn at the proper distance from the sun, and from each other. Then Pontesilli set them into orbit around Henry, desperately trying to keep each intoxicated gentleman in his correct celestial path. Soon the ladies were clamoring to join the amusement, and so Pontesilli arranged them around the men, to serve as moons, with each moon in her own narrow orbit. (Alma's mother played the role of the Earth's moon with cool lunar perfection.) The maestro then created stellar constellations in the outskirts of the lawn, concocted from the prettiest groups of belles.

The orchestra struck up again, and this landscape of heavenly bodies took on the appearance of the most strange and beautiful waltz the good people of Philadelphia had ever seen. Henry, the Sun King, stood beaming at the center of it all, his hair the color of flame, while men large and small revolved around him, and women circled around the men. Clusters of unmarried girls sparkled in the outermost corners of the universe, distant as unknown galaxies. Pontesilli climbed atop a high garden wall and swayed precariously there, conducting and commanding the entire tableau, crying across the night, "Stay at your velocity, men! Do not abandon your trajectory, ladies!"

Alma wanted to be in it. She had never before seen anything so thrilling. She had never before been awake this late—except after nightmares—but she had somehow been forgotten in all the merriment. She was the only child in attendance, as she had been for all her life the only child in attendance. She ran over to the garden wall and cried up to the dangerously unstable Maestro Pontesilli, "Put me in it, sir!" The Italian peered down at her from his perch, troubling himself to try to focus his eyes—who was this child? He might have dismissed her entirely, but then Henry bellowed from the center of the solar system, "Give the girl a *place!*"

Pontesilli shrugged. "You are a comet!" he called down to Alma, while still making a pretense of conducting the universe with one waving arm.

"What does a comet do, sir?"

"You fly about in all directions!" the Italian commanded.

And so she did. She propelled herself into the midst of the planets, ducking and swiveling through everyone's orbits, scuttling and twirling, the ribbon unfurling from her hair. Whenever she neared her father, he would cry, "Not so close to me, Plum, or you will burn to cinders!" and he would push her away from his fiery, combustible self, impelling her to run in another direction.

Astonishingly, at some point, a sputtering torch was thrust into her hands. Alma did not see who gave it to her. She had never before been entrusted with fire. The torch spit sparks and sent chunks of flaming tar spinning into the air behind her as she bolted across the cosmos—the only body in the heavens who was not held to a strict elliptical path.

Nobody stopped her.

She was a comet.

She did not know that she was not flying.

Chapter Six

Alma's youth—or rather, the simplest and most innocent part of it—came to an abrupt end in November of 1809, in the small hours of the night, on an otherwise ordinary Tuesday.

Alma awoke from a deep sleep to raised voices and the sound of carriage wheels dragging through gravel. In places where the house should have been silent at such an hour (the hallway outside her bedroom door, for instance, and the servants' quarters upstairs) there was a skittering of footsteps from all directions. She arose in the cold air, lit a candle, found her leather boots, and reached for a shawl. Her instinct was that some sort of trouble had come to White Acre, and that her assistance might be needed. Later in life, she would recall the absurdity of this notion (how could she have honestly believed she could help with anything?), but at that time, in her mind, she was a young lady of nearly ten years, and she still had a certain confidence in her own importance.

When Alma arrived at the top of the wide staircase she saw below her, in the grand entryway to the home, a gathering of men holding lanterns. Her father, wearing a greatcoat over his night clothes, stood at the center of them all, his face tense with irritation. Hanneke de Groot was there as well, her hair in a cap. Alma's mother was there, too. This must be serious, then; Alma had never seen her mother awake at this hour.

But there was something else, and Alma's eyes went straight to it—a girl, 70 slightly smaller than Alma, with a white-blond plait of hair down her back, stood between Beatrix and Hanneke. The women had one hand each upon the girl's slender shoulders. Alma thought the child looked somehow familiar. The daughter of one of the workers, possibly? Alma could not be sure. The girl, whoever she was, had the most beautiful face—though that face seemed shocked and fearful in the lamplight.

What brought disquiet to Alma, however, was not the girl's fear, but rather the proprietary firmness of Beatrix's and Hanneke's grips on the child's shoulders. As a man approached as though to reach for the girl, the two women closed in tighter, clutching the child harder. The man retreated—and he was wise to, Alma thought, for she had just gotten a glimpse of the expression on her mother's face: unyielding fierceness. The same expression was on Hanneke's face. It was that shared expression of fierceness on the faces of the two most important women in Alma's life that shot her through with unaccountable dread. Something alarming was happening here.

At that point, Beatrix and Hanneke both turned their heads simultaneously, and looked to the top of the staircase, where Alma stood, staring dumbly, holding her candle and her sturdy boots. They turned toward her as though Alma had called out their names, and as though they did not welcome the interruption.

"Go to *bed*," they both barked—Beatrix in English, Hanneke in Dutch.

Alma might have protested, but she was helpless against the power of their united force. Their tight, hardened faces frightened her. She had never seen anything quite like it. She was neither needed nor wanted here, it was clear.

Alma took one more anxious look at the beautiful child in the center of the crowded hall of strangers, then fled to her room. For a long hour, she sat on the edge of her bed, listening until her ears ached, hoping somebody would come to her with explanation or comfort. But the voices diminished, there was the sound of horses galloping away, and still nobody came. Finally Alma collapsed asleep on top of the covers, wrapped in her shawl and cradling her boots. In the morning when she awoke, she found that the entire crowd of strangers had cleared off from White Acre.

But the girl was still there.

***

Her name was Prudence.

Or, rather, it was Polly.

Or, to be specific, her name was Polly-Who-Became-Prudence.

Her story was an ugly one. There was an effort at White Acre to suppress it, but stories like this do not like to be suppressed, and within a few days, Alma would come to learn it. The girl was the daughter of the head vegetable gardener at White Acre, a quiet German man who had revolutionized the design of the melon houses, to lucrative effect. The gardener's wife was a local Philadelphia woman of low birth but famous beauty, and she was a known harlot. Her husband, the gardener, adored her but could never control her. This, too, was widely known. The woman had cuckolded him relentlessly for years, making little effort to conceal her indiscretions. He had quietly tolerated it—either not noticing, or pretending not to notice— until, quite out of nowhere, he stopped tolerating it.

On that Tuesday night in November of 1809, the gardener had awoken his wife from a peaceful sleep beside him, dragged her outside by her hair, and cut her neck from ear to ear. Immediately after, he hanged himself from a nearby elm. The commotion had raised the other workers of White Acre, who came running out of their houses to investigate. Left behind in the wake of all this sudden death was the little girl named Polly.

Polly was the same age as Alma, but daintier and startlingly beautiful. She looked like a perfect figurine carved out of fine French soap, into which someone had inlaid a pair of glittering peacock-blue eyes. But it was the tiny pink pillow of her mouth that made this girl more than simply pretty; it made her an unsettling little voluptuary, a Bathsheba wrought in miniature.

When Polly had been brought to White Acre manor that tragic night, surrounded by constables and big working men—all of them with their hands upon her—Beatrix and Hanneke had immediately foreseen nothing but danger for the child. Some of the men were suggesting the girl be taken to an almshouse, but others were already proclaiming that they would happily assume responsibility for this orphan themselves. Half the men in that room had copulated with that girl's mother at some point or another—as Beatrix and Hanneke well knew—and the women did not like to imagine what might be in store for this pretty thing, for this spawn of the whore.

The two women, acting as one, clutched Polly away from the mob, and kept her away from the mob. This was not a considered decision. Nor was it a gesture of charity, draped in a warm mantle of maternal kindness. No, this was an act of intuition, sprung from a deep and unspoken feminine knowledge of how the world functions. One does not leave so small and beautiful a female creature alone with ten heated men in the middle of the night.

But once Beatrix and Hanneke had safeguarded Polly—once the men had cleared off—what was to be done with her? Then they did make a considered decision. Or rather, Beatrix made the decision, as she alone had the authority to decide. She made, in fact, a rather shocking decision. She decided to keep Polly forever, to adopt her immediately as a Whittaker.

Alma later learned that her father protested the idea (Henry was not happy about having been awoken in the middle of the night, much less about acquiring a sudden daughter), but Beatrix cut short his complaint with a single hard look, and Henry had the good sense not to protest twice. So be it. Their family was too small, anyway, and Beatrix had never been able to enlarge it. Hadn't two more babies been born after Alma? Hadn't those babies never drawn a breath? And weren't those dead infants now buried in the Lutheran churchyard, doing nobody any good? Beatrix had always wanted another child, and now, by dint of providence, a child had arrived. With the addition of Polly to the household, the Whittaker brood could be efficiently doubled overnight. It all made tidy sense. Beatrix's decision was swift and unhesitating. Without another word of protest, Henry conceded. Also, he had no choice.

Anyway, the girl was a pretty thing, and she did not seem to be a complete simpleton. Indeed, once things quieted down, Polly demonstrated an actual decorum—an almost aristocratic composure—that was all the more notable in a child who had just witnessed both of her parents' deaths.

Beatrix saw distinct promise in Polly, as well as no other possible respectable future for the child. In the proper home, Beatrix believed, and with the right moral influence, this girl could be shunted toward a different path of life than the pleasure-seeking gaiety and wickedness for which her mother had paid the ultimate price. The first task was to clean her up. The poor wretch had blood all over her shoes and hands. The second task was to change her name. Polly was a name suitable only to a pet bird or a street girl for hire. From this point forward, the child would be called Prudence—a name that would serve as a signpost, Beatrix hoped and expected, of more righteous direction.

So all was resolved—and resolved within an hour. Which is how it came to pass that Alma Whittaker awoke the next morning to the flabbergasting information that she now had a sister, and that her sister's name was Prudence.

Prudence's arrival changed everything at White Acre. Later in life, when Alma was a woman of science, she would better understand how the introduction of any new element into a controlled environment will alter that environment in manifold and unpredictable ways, but as a child, all she sensed was a hostile invasion and a premonition of doom. Alma did not embrace her interloper with a warm heart. Then again, why should she have? Who among us has ever warmheartedly embraced an interloper?

At first, Alma did not remotely understand why this girl was here. What she would find out eventually about Prudence's history (mined from the dairymaids, and in German, no less!) elucidated much—but on the first day after Prudence's arrival, nobody explained anything. Even Hanneke de Groot, who usually had more information on mysteries than anyone, would say only, "It is God's design, child, and for the best." When Alma pushed the housekeeper for further information, Hanneke whispered sharply, "Find your mercy and ask me no more questions!"

The girls were formally introduced to each other at the breakfast table. No mention was made of the encounter the night before. Alma could not stop staring at Prudence, and Prudence could not stop staring at her plate. Beatrix spoke to the children as though nothing were amiss. She explained that someone named Mrs. Spanner would be coming in from the city later that afternoon, to cut new dresses for Prudence out of more suitable material than her current clothing. There would be a new pony coming, too, and Prudence would need to be taught to ride—the sooner the better. Also, there would thenceforth be a tutor at White Acre. Beatrix had decided that it would tax her energies too extremely to teach two girls at the same time, and since Prudence had received no formal education thus far in life, a young tutor might be a useful addition to the household. The nursery would now be turned into a dedicated schoolroom. Alma would be expected, needless to say, to help teach her sister in penmanship, sums, and figures. Alma was quite far ahead in the training of the mind, of course, but if Prudence toiled sincerely—and if her sister helped—she should be able to excel. A child's intellect, Beatrix said, is an object of impressive elasticity, and Prudence was still young enough to catch up. The human mind, if dutifully trained, should be able to perform anything we ask of it. It is all just a matter of working hard.

While Beatrix spoke, Alma stared. How could anything be as pretty and disturbing as Prudence's face? If beauty were truly accuracy's distraction, as her mother had always said, what did that make Prudence? Quite possibly the least accurate and most distracting object in the known world! Alma's sense of disquiet multiplied by the moment. She was beginning to realize something dreadful about herself, something that she had never before been given reason to contemplate: *she herself was not a pretty thing.* It was only by awful comparison that she suddenly came to perceive this. Where Prudence was dainty, Alma was large. Where Prudence had hair spun from golden-white silk, Alma's hair was the color and texture of rust—and it grew, most unflatteringly, in every direction except downward. Prudence's nose was a little blossom; Alma's was a growing yam. On it went, from head to toe: a most miserable accounting.

After breakfast was completed, Beatrix said, "Now come, girls, and embrace each other as sisters." Alma did embrace Prudence, obediently, but without warmth. Side by side, the contrast was even more notable. More than anything, it felt to Alma, the two of them resembled a perfect little robin's egg and a big homely pinecone, suddenly and inexplicably sharing the same nest.

The realization of all this made Alma want to weep, or fight. She could feel her face settling into a dark sulk. Her mother must have seen it, for she said, "Prudence, please excuse us while I speak to your sister for a moment." Beatrix took Alma by the upper arm, pinching her so firmly that it burned, and escorted her into the hall. Alma felt tears coming, but forced her tears to halt, and then to halt again, and then to halt once more.

Beatrix looked down at her one natural-born child, and spoke in a voice of cool granite: "I do not intend ever again to see such a face upon my daughter as the face I have just seen. Do you understand me?"

Alma managed to say only one wavering word ("*But—*") before she was cut off.

"No outbreak of jealousy or malice has ever been welcomed in God's eyes," Beatrix continued, "nor shall such an outbreak ever be welcomed in the eyes of your family. If you have sentiments within you that are unpleasant or uncharitable, let them fall stillborn to the ground. Become the master of yourself, Alma Whittaker. Am I understood?"

This time, Alma only thought the word (*"But—"*); however, she must have thought it too loudly, because somehow her mother heard it. Now Beatrix had been pushed entirely too far.

"I am sorry on your own account, Alma Whittaker, that you are so selfish in your regard for others," Beatrix said, her face clenched now with true anger. As for her final two words, she spat them out like two sharp chips of ice:

"Improve yourself."

But Prudence also needed improvement, and a good deal of it, too!

To begin with, she was quite far behind Alma in matters of schooling. To be fair, though, what child would not have been behind Alma? By the age of nine, Alma could comfortably read Caesar's *Commentaries* in its original, and Cornelius Nepos. She could already defend Theophrastus over Pliny. (One was the true scholar of natural science, she would argue, while the other was a mere copyist.) Her Greek, which she loved and recognized as a sort of delirious form of mathematics, was growing stronger by the day.

Prudence, by contrast, knew her letters and her numbers. She had a sweet and musical voice, but her speech itself—the very blazing emblem of her unfortunate background—needed much correction. During the beginning of Prudence's stay at White Acre, Beatrix picked at bits of the girl's language constantly, as though with the sharpened tip of a knitting needle, digging away at usage that sounded common or base. Alma was encouraged to make corrections, as well. Beatrix instructed Prudence that she must never say "back and forth," when "backwards and forwards" was so much more refined. The word *fancy* in any context sounded crude, as did the word *folks*. When one wrote a letter at White Acre, it went in the *post*, not the *mail*. A person did not fall *sick*; a person fell *ill*. One would not be leaving for church *soon*; one would be leaving for church *directly*. One was not *partly* there; one was *nearly* there. One did not *stove* along; one *hurried* along. And one did not *talk* in this family; one *conversed*.

A weaker child might have given up on speaking altogether. A more combative child might have demanded to know why Henry Whittaker was allowed to *talk* like a blasted stevedore—why he could sit at the dinner table and call another man "a prick-fed donkey" straight to his face, without ever once being corrected by Beatrix—while the rest of the family must *converse* like barristers. But Prudence was neither weak nor combative. Instead, she turned out to be a creature of steadfast and unblinking vigilance, who perfected herself daily as though honing the blade of her soul, taking care never to make the same error twice. After five months at White Acre, Prudence's speech never again needed refinement. Not even Alma could find an error, though she never stopped looking for one. Other aspects of Prudence's form—her posture, her manners, her daily toilet—also came into quick calibration.

Prudence took all corrections without complaint. Indeed, she actually sought corrections—particularly from Beatrix! Whenever Prudence neglected to perform a task properly, or indulged in an ungenerous thought, or made an ill-considered remark, she would personally report herself to Beatrix, admit her wrongs, and willingly submit to a lecture. In this manner, Prudence made Beatrix not merely her mother, but also her mother-confessor. Alma, who had been hiding her own faults and lying about her own shortcomings since toddlerhood, found this behavior monstrously incomprehensible.

As a result, Alma regarded Prudence with ever-increasing suspicion. There was a diamond-hard quality about Prudence, which Alma believed masked something wicked and perhaps even evil. The girl struck her as cagey and canny. Prudence had a way of sidling out of rooms, never seeming to turn her back on anyone, never making a noise when a door closed behind her. Also, Prudence was altogether too attentive to other people, never forgetting dates that were important to others, always taking care to wish the maids a happy birthday or a pleasant Sabbath at the appropriate time, and all that sort of business. This diligent pursuit of goodness felt altogether too unremitting to Alma, as did the stoicism.

What Alma did know without question was that it advantaged her little to be held by comparison against such a perfectly lacquered person as Prudence. Henry even called Prudence "Our Little Exquisite," which made Alma's old nickname "Plum" feel humble and plain. Everything about Prudence made Alma feel humble and plain.

But there were consolations. In the classroom, at least, Alma always held place of primacy. Prudence could never catch up with her sister there. It was not for lack of effort, either, for the girl was certainly a hard worker. Poor thing, she labored over her books like a Basque stonemason. Each book for Prudence was like a slab of granite, to be hauled uphill in the sun with panting effort. It was nearly painful to watch, but Prudence insisted on persevering, and never once broke into tears. As a result, she did advance—and impressively, one must admit, considering her background. Mathematics would always be a struggle for her, but she did cudgel into her brains the fundamentals of Latin, and after a time she could speak quite passable French, with a nice accent. As for penmanship, Prudence did not cease practicing until it was every bit as fine as a duchess's.

But all the discipline in the world is not enough to close a real gap in the realm of scholarship, and Alma had gifts of the mind that extended far beyond what Prudence would ever be able to reach. Alma had a capital memory for words and an innate brilliance for sums. She loved drills, tests, formulas, theorems. For Alma, to read something once was to have ownership of it forever. She could take apart an argument the way a good soldier can dismantle his rifle—half asleep in the dark, and the thing still comes to pieces beautifully. Calculus put her into fits of ecstasies. Grammar was an old friend—perhaps from having grown up speaking so many languages simultaneously. She also loved her microscope, which felt like a magical extension of her own right eye, enabling her to peer straight down the throat of the Creator Himself.

For all these reasons, one might have supposed that the tutor whom Beatrix eventually hired for the girls would have preferred Alma to Prudence, but in fact he did not. In fact, he was careful not to make known any preference between the two children—both of whom he seemed to regard as a flat and equal duty. The tutor was a rather dull young man, British by birth, with a poxy, waxen complexion and an ever-worried countenance. He sighed a great deal. His name was Arthur Dixon, and he was a recent graduate of the University of Edinburgh. Beatrix had selected him after a rigorous examination process involving dozens of other candidates, all of whom had been rejected for—among other faults—being too stupid, too talkative, too religious, not religious enough, too radical, too handsome, too fat, or too stuttering.

For the first year of Arthur Dixon's tenure, Beatrix often sat in the classroom, too, working at her mending in the corner, watching to ensure that Arthur did not make factual errors, or treat the girls in any sort of unbefitting manner. Eventually she was satisfied: young Dixon was a perfectly boring wizard of academics, who did not appear to be in possession of a single callow or jocular bone. He could be utterly trusted, then, to teach the Whittaker girls, four days a week, a rotating coursework of natural philosophy, Latin, French, Greek, chemistry, astronomy, mineralogy, botany, and history. Alma was also given special extra work in optics, algebra, and spherical geometry, from which Prudence—in a rare gesture of mercy on Beatrix's part—was spared.

On Fridays, there was a departure from this schedule, when a drawing master, a dancing master, and a music master paid visits, to round out the girls' educational curriculum. Mornings, the girls were expected to work alongside their mother in her own private Grecian garden—a triumph of functional mathematics that Beatrix was attempting to arrange, with pathways and topiary, according to strict Euclidean principles of symmetry (all balls and cones and complex triangles, clipped and rigid and exact). The girls were also required to devote several hours a week to improving their needlework skills. During the evenings, Alma and Prudence were called upon to sit at the formal dining table and engage intelligently with dinner guests from all over the world. If there were no guests at White Acre, Alma and Prudence passed their evenings in the drawing room, staying up late into the night, assisting their father and mother with official White Acre correspondence. Sundays were for church. Bedtime brought a long round of nightly prayers.

Apart from that, their time was their own.

But it was not such a trying schedule, really—not for Alma. She was an energetic and engaging young lady, who needed little rest. She enjoyed the work of the mind, enjoyed the labor of gardening, and enjoyed the conversations at the dinner gatherings. She was always happy to spend time helping her father with his correspondence late at night (as this was sometimes her only chance to engage intimately with the man anymore). Somehow she even managed to find hours for herself, and in those hours she created inventive little botanical projects. She toyed with cuttings of willow trees, pondering how it was that they sometimes cast out roots from their buds, and sometimes from their leaves. She dissected and memorized, preserved and categorized, every plant in reach. She built a beautiful *hortus siccus*—a splendid little dried herbarium.

Alma loved botany, more by the day. It was not so much the beauty of plants that compelled her as their magical orderliness. Alma was a girl possessed by a soaring enthusiasm for systems, sequence, pigeonholing, and indexes; botany provided ample opportunity to indulge in all these pleasures. She appreciated how, once you had put a plant into the correct taxonomical order, it stayed in order. There were serious mathematical rules inherent in the symmetry of plants, too, and Alma found serenity and reverence in these rules. In every species, for instance, there is a fixed ratio between the teeth of the calyx and the divisions of the corolla, and that ratio never changes. One could set one's clock to it. It was an abiding, comforting, unfaltering law.

If anything, Alma wished she had even more time to devote to the study of plants. She had bizarre fantasies. She wished that she lived in an army barracks of natural sciences, where she would be woken at dawn by a bugle call and marched off in formation with other young naturalists, in uniforms, to labor all day in woods, streams, and laboratories. She wished that she lived in a botanical monastery or a botanical convent of sorts, surrounded by other devoted taxonomists, where no one interfered with one another's studies, yet all shared their most exciting findings with each other. Even a botanical prison would be nice! (It did not occur to Alma that such places of intellectual asylum and walled isolation did exist in the world, to a point, and that they were called "universities." But little girls in 1810 did not dream of universities. Not even Beatrix Whittaker's little girls.)

So Alma did not mind working hard. But she actively disliked Fridays. Art classes, dancing classes, music classes—all these exertions irritated her, and pulled her from her true interests. She was not graceful. She could not entirely tell one famous painting from another, nor did she ever learn to draw faces without making her subjects look either fear-stricken or deceased. Music was not a gift, either, and around the time Alma turned eleven, her father officially requested that she stop torturing the pianoforte. In all these pursuits, Prudence excelled. Prudence could also sew beautifully, and operate a tea service with masterful delicacy, and had many other small and galling talents besides. On Fridays, Alma was likely to have the blackest and most envious thoughts about her sister. These were the times when she honestly thought, for instance, that she would happily trade in one of her extra languages (any of them, except Greek!) for the simple ability to fold an envelope *just once* as prettily as Prudence could do it.

Despite all this—or perhaps because of it—Alma took real satisfaction in the realms where she excelled over her sister, and the one place where her superiority was most notable was at the Whittakers' famous dining room table, particularly when the room was thick with challenging ideas. As Alma grew older, her conversation became bolder, more certain, more reaching. But Prudence never developed such confidence at the table. She tended to sit mute but lovely, a sort of useless adornment to each gathering, merely filling a chair between guests, contributing nothing but her beauty. In a way, this made Prudence useful. One could seat Prudence next to anyone, and she would not complain. Many a night, the poor girl was deliberately placed beside the most tedious and deaf old professors—perfect mausoleums of men—who picked at their teeth with their forks, or fell asleep over their meals, lightly snoring while debates raged alongside them. Prudence never objected, nor asked for more sparkling dinner companions. It did not seem to make a difference who sat near Prudence, really: her posture and carefully arranged countenance never altered.

Meanwhile, Alma lunged into engagement with every possible topic— from soil management, to the molecules of gases, to the physiology of tears. One night, for instance, a guest came to White Acre who had just returned from Persia, where he had discovered, right outside the ancient city of Esfahan, samples of a plant that he believed produced ammoniacum gum—an ancient and lucrative medicinal ingredient, whose source had thus far been a mystery to the Western world, as its trade was controlled by bandits. The young man had been working for the British Crown, but had grown disillusioned with his superiors and wanted to speak to Henry Whittaker about funding a continued research project. Henry and Alma—working and thinking as one, as they often did at the dining room table—came at the man with questions from both sides, like two sheepdogs cornering a ram.

"What is the climate in that area of Persia?" Henry asked.

"And the altitude?" Alma added.

"Well, sir, the plant grows on the open plains," the visitor replied. "And the gum is so abundant within it, I tell you, that it squeezes out great volumes—"

"Yes, yes, yes," Henry interrupted. "Or so you keep saying, and we must have your word on that, I suppose, for I notice you've brought me nothing but the merest thimbleful of gum as evidence. Tell me, though, how much do you have to pay the officials in Persia? In tributes, I mean, for the privilege of wandering around their country, collecting up gum samples at will?"

"Well, they do demand some tribute, sir, but it seems a small price to pay—"

"The Whittaker Company never pays tribute," Henry said. "I dislike the sound of this. Why have you even let anyone over there know what you're doing?"

"Well, sir, one can hardly play the smuggler!"

"Really?" Henry raised an eyebrow. "Can't one?"

"But could the plant be cultivated elsewhere?" Alma leapt in. "You see, sir, it would do us little good to send you to Esfahan every year on expensive collecting expeditions."

"I have not yet had the chance to explore—"

"Could it be cultivated in Kattywar?" Henry asked. "Do you have associates in Kattywar?"

"Well, I don't know, sir, I merely—"

"Or could it be cultivated in the American South?" Alma put in. "How much water does it require?"

"I'm not interested in any venture that might involve cultivation in the American South, Alma, as you well know," Henry said.

"But, Father, people are saying that the Missouri Territory—"

"Honestly, Alma, can you foresee this pale little English mite thriving in the Missouri Territory?"

The pale little English mite in question blinked, and seemed to have lost his capacity for speech. But Alma pushed on, asking the guest with mounting eagerness, "Do you think the plant you're discussing might be the same one that Dioscorides mentions, sir, in *Materia medica*? That would be a thrill, wouldn't it? We have a splendid early volume of Dioscorides in our library. If you'd like, I could show it to you after dinner!"

Here, Beatrix finally chimed in, admonishing her fourteen-year-old daughter, "I do wonder, Alma, whether it is absolutely necessary for you to put the entire world in possession of your every thought. Why not let your poor guest attempt to answer one question before you assault him with another? Please, young man, try again. What was it you were attempting to say?"

But now Henry was speaking again. "You didn't even bring me cuttings, did you?" he asked the overwhelmed fellow—who by this point did not know which Whittaker he should answer first, and therefore made the grave mistake of answering nobody. In the long silence that ensued, everyone stared at him. Still, the young man could not manage to emit a single word.

Disgusted, Henry broke the silence, turning to Alma and saying, "Ah, put it to rest, Alma. I'm not interested in this one. He hasn't thought things through. And yet look at him! Still he sits there, eating my dinner, drinking my claret, and hoping to get my money!"

So Alma did indeed put it to rest, pursuing no further questions on the subject of ammoniacum gum, or Dioscorides, or the tribal customs of Persia. Instead, she turned brightly to another gentleman at the table—not noticing that this second young fellow had himself turned rather pale—and asked, "So, I see by your marvelous paper that you have found some quite extraordinary fossils! Have you been able yet to compare the bone to modern samples? Do you really think those are hyena teeth? And do you still believe that the cave was flooded? Have you read Mr. Winston's recent article on primeval flooding?"

Meanwhile, Prudence—without anyone's noticing—turned coolly to the stricken young Englishman beside her, the one who had just been so firmly shut down, and murmured, "Do go on."

———————

That night, before bedtime, and after evening accounting and prayers, Beatrix corrected the girls, as per daily custom.

"Alma," she began, "polite discourse should not be a race to the finish line. You may find it both beneficial and civilized, on rare occasions, to permit your victim to actually finish a thought. Your worth as a hostess consists in displaying the talents of your guests, not crowing about your own."

Alma began to protest, "But—"

Beatrix cut her off, and continued, "Moreover, it is not necessary to over-laugh at jests, once they have done their duty and caused amusement. I find lately that you are carrying on with laughter altogether too long. I never met a truly honorable woman who honked like a goose."

Then Beatrix turned to Prudence.

"As for you, Prudence, while I admire that you do not engage in idle and irritating chatter, it is another thing altogether to retreat from conversation entirely. Visitors will think you are a dunce, which you are not. It would be an unfortunate stamp of discredit upon this family if people believed that only one of my daughters had the capacity to speak. Shyness, as I have told you many times, is simply another species of vanity. Banish it."

"My apologies, Mother," Prudence said. "I felt unwell this evening."

"I believe that you *think* you felt unwell this evening. But I saw you with a book of light verse in your hands just before dinner, idling away quite happily as you read. Anyone who can read a book of light verse just before dinner cannot be that unwell a mere hour later."

"My apologies, Mother," Prudence repeated.

"I also wish to speak to you, Prudence, about Mr. Edward Porter's behavior this evening at the dinner table. You should not have let that man stare at you for quite so long as you did. Engrossment of this sort is demeaning to all. You must learn how to abort this sort of behavior in men by speaking to them with intelligence and firmness about serious topics. Perhaps Mr. Porter might have awoken from his infatuated stupor sooner, had you discussed with him the Russian Campaign, for instance. It is not sufficient to be merely good, Prudence; you must also become clever. As a woman, of course, you will always have a heightened moral awareness over men, but if you do not sharpen your wits in defense of yourself, your morality will serve you little good."

"I understand, Mother," Prudence said.

"Nothing is so essential as dignity, girls. Time will reveal who has it, and who has it not."

Life might have been pleasanter for the Whittaker girls if—like the blind and the lame—they had learned how to aid each other, filling in each other's weaknesses. But instead they limped along side by side in silence, each girl left alone to grope through her own deficiencies and troubles.

To their credit, and to the credit of the mother who kept them polite, the girls were never unpleasant to each other. Unkind words were never once exchanged. They respectfully shared an umbrella with each other, arm in arm, whenever they walked in the rain. They stepped aside for each other at doorways, each willing to let the other pass first. They offered each other the last tart, or the best seat, nearest to the warmth of the stove. They gave each other modest and thoughtful gifts at Christmas Eve. One year, Alma bought Prudence—who liked to draw flowers (beautifully, though not *accurately*)—a lovely book on botanical illustration called *Every Lady Her Own Drawing Master: A New Treatise on Flower Painting*. That same year, Prudence made for Alma an exquisite satin pincushion, rendered in Alma's favorite color, aubergine. So they did try to be thoughtful.

"Thank you for the pincushion," Alma wrote to Prudence, in a short note of considered politeness. "I shall be certain to use it whenever I find myself in need of a pin."

Year after year, the Whittaker girls conducted themselves toward each other with the most exacting correctness, although perhaps from different motives. For Prudence, exacting correctness was an expression of her natural state. For Alma, exacting correctness was a crowning effort—a constant and almost physical subduing of all her meaner instincts, stamped into submission by sheer moral discipline and fear of her mother's disapproval. Thus, manners were held, and all appeared peaceful at White Acre. But in truth, there was a mighty seawall between Alma and Prudence, and it did not ever budge. What's more, nobody helped them to budge it.

One winter's day, when the girls were about fifteen years old, an old friend of Henry's from the Calcutta Botanical Gardens came to visit White Acre after many years away. Standing in the entryway, still shaking the snow off his cloak, the guest shouted, "Henry Whittaker, you weasel! Show me that famous daughter of yours I've been hearing so much about!"

The girls were just nearby, transcribing botanical notes in the drawing room. They could hear every word.

Henry, in his great crashing voice, said, "Alma! Come instantly! You are requested to be seen!"

Alma rushed into the atrium, bright with expectation. The stranger looked at her for a moment, then burst out laughing. He said, "No, you bloody fool—that's not what I meant! I want to see the pretty one!"

Without a trace of rebuke, Henry replied, "Oh, so you're interested in

Our Little Exquisite, then? Prudence, come in here! You are requested to be seen!"

Prudence slipped through the entryway and stood beside Alma, whose feet were now sinking into the floor, as into a thick and terrible swamp.

"There we are!" said the guest, looking over Prudence as though pricing her out. "Oh, she *is* splendid, isn't she? I had wondered. I had suspected everyone might have been exaggerating."

Henry waved his hand dismissively. "Ah, you all make too much of Prudence," he said. "To my mind, the homely one is worth ten of the pretty one."

So, you see, it is quite possible that both girls suffered equally.

Chapter Seven

The year 1816 would later be remembered as The Year Without a Summer—not only at White Acre, but across much of the world. Volcanic eruptions in Indonesia filled Earth's atmosphere with ash and darkness, bringing drought to North America and freezing famine to most of Europe and Asia. The corn crop failed in New England, the rice crop withered in China, oat and wheat crops collapsed all across northern Europe. More than a hundred thousand Irish starved to death. Horses and cattle, suffering without grain, were annihilated en masse. There were food riots in France, England, and Switzerland. In Quebec City, it snowed twelve inches in June. In Italy, the snow came down brown and red, terrifying the populace into fears of apocalypse.

In Pennsylvania, for the entirety of June, July, and August of that benighted year, the countryside was enveloped in a deep, frigid, dark fog. Little grew. Thousands of families lost everything. For Henry Whittaker, though, it was not a bad year. The stoves in his greenhouses had managed to keep most of his tropical exotics alive even in the semidarkness, and he'd never made a living off the risks of outdoor farming, anyway. The bulk of his medicinal plants were imported from South America, where the climate was unaffected. What's more, the weather was making people sick, and sick people bought more pharmaceuticals. Both botanically and financially, then, Henry was mostly unaffected.

No, that year, Henry found his prosperity in real estate speculation and his pleasure in rare books. Farmers were fleeing Pennsylvania in droves, heading west in the hopes of finding brighter sun, healthier soil, and a more hospitable environment. Henry bought up a good deal of the property these destroyed people left behind, thus coming into possession of excellent mills, forests, and pastures along the way. Quite a few Philadelphia families of rank and note fell into ruin that year, brought down by the foul weather's spiral of economic decline. This was wonderful news for Henry. Whenever another wealthy family collapsed, he was able to purchase, at steep discount, their land, their furniture, their horses, their fine French saddles and Persian textiles, and—most satisfyingly—their libraries.

Over the years, the acquisition of magnificent books had become something of a mania for Henry. It was a peculiar mania, given that the man could scarcely read English, and most assuredly could not read, say, Catullus. But Henry did not want to read these books; he merely wanted to own them, as prizes for his growing library at White Acre. Medical, philosophical, and exquisitely rendered botanical books he longed for most of all. He was aware that these volumes were every bit as dazzling to visitors as the tropical treasures in his greenhouses. He had even launched a custom before dinner parties of choosing (or, rather, having Beatrix choose) one precious book to show to the gathered guests. He especially enjoyed performing this ritual when famous scholars were visiting, in order to see them catch their breath and go light-headed with desire; most men of letters never really expected to hold in their own hands an early-sixteenth-century Erasmus, with the Greek printed on one side and the Latin on the other.

Henry acquired books voluptuously—not volume by volume, but trunkful by trunkful. Obviously, all these books needed sorting, and, just as obviously, Henry was not the man to sort them. This physically and intellectually taxing job had fallen for years to Beatrix, who would steadily weed through the lots, keeping the gems and unloading much of the dross over to the Philadelphia Free Library. But Beatrix, by late autumn of 1816, had fallen behind in the task. Books were coming in faster than she could sort them. The spare rooms of the carriage house now contained many trunks that had yet to be opened, each filled with more volumes. With new windfalls of entire private libraries coming to White Acre by the week (as one fine family after another met financial ruin), the collection was on the brink of becoming an unmanageable bother.

So Beatrix chose Alma to help her sift and catalogue the books. Alma was the clear choice for the job. Prudence was not much help in such matters, as she was useless in Greek, practically useless in Latin, and could never really be made to understand how to divide botanical volumes accurately between pre- and post-1753 editions (which is to say, before and after the advent of Linnaean taxonomy). But Alma, now aged sixteen, proved to be both efficient and enthusiastic at the task of setting the White Acre library into order. She had a sound historical comprehension of what she was handling, and she was a fevered, diligent indexer. She was also physically strong enough to carry about the heavy crates and boxes. Too, the weather was so poor in 1816 that there was little pleasure to be found outdoors, and not much benefit to be gained by working in the garden. Happily, Alma came to consider her library work as a kind of indoor gardening, with all the attendant satisfactions of muscular labor and beautiful unfoldings.

Alma even found that she had a talent for repairing books. Her experience in mounting plant specimens made her well adept at managing the materials in the binding closet—a tiny dark room with a hidden door just off the library, where Beatrix stored all the paper, fabrics, leather, wax, and glues needed to maintain and restore the fragile old editions. After a few months, in fact, Alma was doing so well at all these tasks that Beatrix put her daughter completely in charge of the White Acre library, both the catalogued and uncatalogued collections. Beatrix had grown too stout and too tired to climb up the library ladders anymore, and was tired of the job.

Now, some people might have questioned whether a respectable and unmarried sixteen-year-old girl really ought to have been left without any supervision in the midst of an uncensored deluge of books, trusted to negotiate her way alone through such a vast flood of unconstrained ideas. Perhaps Beatrix thought she'd already completed her work with Alma, having successfully produced a young woman who appeared pragmatic and decent, and who would surely know how to resist corrupting ideas. Or perhaps Beatrix did not think through what sorts of books Alma might stumble upon when she opened those trunks. Or perhaps Beatrix believed that Alma's homeliness and awkwardness rendered the girl immune to the dangers of, for heaven's sake, *sensuality*. Or perhaps Beatrix (who was nearing fifty years old, and suffering from episodes of dizziness and distraction) was simply getting careless.

One way or another, Alma Whittaker was left alone, and that is how she found the book.

She would never know from whose library it had originated. Alma found the thing in an unmarked trunk, with an otherwise unremarkable collection, mostly medical in nature—some standard Galen, some recent translations of Hippocrates, nothing new or exciting. But in the midst of it all was a thick, sturdy, calfskin-bound volume called *Cum Grano Salis*, written by an anonymous author. Such a funny title: *With a Grain of Salt*. At first, Alma thought it was a treatise on cooking, something like the fifteenth-century Venetian reprint of the fourth-century *De Re Coquinaria*, that the White Acre library already contained. But a swift fanning of its pages revealed that this book was written in English, and contained no illustrations or lists meant for a cook. Alma opened to the first page, and what she read there made her mind jolt wildly.

"It puzzles me," wrote Anonymous, in his introduction, "that we are all bequeathed at birth with the most marvelous bodily pricks and holes, which the youngest child knows are objects of pure delight, but which we must pretend in the name of civilization are abominations—never to be touched, never to be shared, never to be enjoyed! Yet why should we not explore these gifts of the body, both in ourselves and in our fellows? It is only our minds that prevent us from such enchantments, only our artificial sense of 'civilization' that forbids such simple entertainments. My own mind, once locked within a prison of hard civility, has been stroked open for years by the most exquisite of physical pleasures. Indeed, I have found that carnal expression can be pursued as a fine art, if practiced with the same dedication as one might show to music, painting or literature.

"What follows in these pages, respected reader, is an honest accounting of my lifetime of erotic adventure, which some may call *foul*, but which I have pursued happily—and I believe harmlessly—since my youth. If I were a religious man, trapped within the bondage of shame, I might call this book a *confession*. But I do not subscribe to sensual shame, and my investigations have shown that *many human groupings across the world also do not subscribe to shame in regard to the sensual act*. I have come to believe that an absence of such shame may be, indeed, our natural state as a human species—a state that our civilization has sadly warped. For that reason, I do not *confess* my unusual history, but merely *disclose* it. I hope and trust that my disclosures will be read as a guide and a diversion, not only for gentlemen but also for venturous and educated ladies."

Alma closed the book. She knew this voice. She didn't know the author personally, of course, but she recognized him as a type: an educated man of letters, of the sort who frequently dined at White Acre. This was the type of man who could easily write four hundred pages on the natural philosophy of grasshoppers, but who, in this case, had instead decided to write four hundred pages on his sensual adventures. This sense of recognition and familiarity both confused Alma and enticed her. If such a treatise was written by a respectable gentleman, with a respectable voice, did that make it respectable?

What would Beatrix say? Alma knew immediately. Beatrix would say that this book was illicit and dangerous and abhorrent—a mare's nest of wrongness. Beatrix would want this book destroyed. What would Prudence have done, if she ever found such a book? Well, Prudence wouldn't touch it with a barge pole. Or, if Prudence somehow did end up with this book in her hands, she would dutifully present it to Beatrix to be destroyed, and would likely receive a strict punishment in the process for having even touched the thing in the first place. But Alma was not Prudence.

What, then, would Alma do?

Alma would destroy the book, she decided, and say nothing of it to anyone. In fact, she would destroy it right now. This very afternoon. Without reading another word of it.

She opened the book again, to a random page. Again she encountered that familiar, respectable voice, speaking on the most unbelievable topic.

"I wished to discover," the author wrote, "at what age a woman loses her ability to receive sensual pleasure. My friend the brothel owner, who had assisted me in the past in so many experiments, told me of a certain courtesan who had enjoyed her occupation actively from the age of fourteen until the age of sixty-four, and who now, at the age of seventy, lived in a city not far from my own. I wrote to the woman in question, and she responded with a letter of charming candor and warmth. In the space of a month, I had come to visit her, where she allowed me to examine her genitalia, which were not easily distinguished from the genitalia of a much younger woman.

She demonstrated that she was still most capable of pleasure, indeed. Using her fingers and a light coating of nut oil upon her hood of passion, she stroked herself toward a crisis of rapture—"

Alma shut the book. This book must not be kept. She would burn it in the kitchen fire. Not this afternoon, when someone would see her, but later tonight.

She opened it up again, once more at random.

"I have come to believe," the calm narrator continued, "that there are some people who benefit both in body and mind by regular beatings to the naked posterior. Many times, I have seen this practice lift the spirits of both men and women, and I suspect it may be the most salubrious treatment we have at our disposal for melancholia and other diseases of the mind. For two years, I kept company with the most delightful maid, a milliner's girl, whose innocent and even angelic orbs became firm and strong with repeated flagellation, and whose sorrows were routinely erased by the taste of the whip. As I have described earlier in these pages, I once kept in my offices an elaborate couch, made for me by a fine London upholsterer, specially fitted with winches and ropes. This maid liked nothing more than to be tied securely upon that couch, where she would hold my member in her mouth, sucking me as a child enjoys a stick of sugar, whilst a companion—"

Alma shut the book again. Anyone with a mind even remotely above the vulgar would stop reading this thing immediately. But what about the cankerworm of curiosity that lived within Alma's belly? What about its desire to feed daily upon the novel, the extraordinary, the *true*?

Alma opened the book again, and read for another hour, overcome by stimulus, doubt, and havoc. Her conscience tugged at her skirt hems, pleading with her to stop, but she could not make herself stop. What she discovered in these pages made her feel vexed, frothy, and breathless. When she thought she might actually faint from the tangled stalks of imagination that were now waving throughout her head, she slammed shut the book at last, and locked it back into the innocuous trunk from which it had come.

Hurriedly, she left the carriage house, smoothing her apron with her damp hands. Outside it was cool and overcast, as it had been all year, with an unsatisfying mizzle of fog. The air was so thick one nearly could have dissected it with a scalpel. There were important tasks to be completed this day. Alma had promised Hanneke de Groot that she would help supervise the lowering of cider caskets into the basement for winter. Somebody had littered papers beneath the lilacs along the South Wood fence; that would need to be tidied. The shrubbery behind her mother's Grecian garden had been invaded by ivy, and a boy should be dispatched to clear it. She would attend to these responsibilities immediately, with her customary efficiency.

Pricks and holes.

All she could think about were *pricks and holes.*

Evening arrived. The dining room was lit and china laid. Guests were expected presently. Alma was freshly dressed for dinner, bundled in an expensive gown of jaconet muslin. She should have been waiting in the drawing room for the guests, but instead she excused herself for a moment to the library. She locked herself in the binding closet, behind the hidden door, just off the library entrance. It was the nearest door with a solid lock on it. She did not have the book with her. She did not need the book; the images it conjured had been following her about the estate all afternoon, feral and stubborn and searching.

She was full of thoughts, and these thoughts were making wild demands upon her body. Her quim hurt. It felt deprived. This hurt had been accumulating all afternoon. If anything, the painful sense of deprivation between her legs felt like a kind of witchcraft, a devilish haunting. Her quim wanted rubbing in the fiercest way. Her skirts were a hindrance. She was itching and dying in this gown. She lifted her skirts. Sitting there on the small stool in the tiny, dark, locked binding closet, with its smells of glue and leather, she opened her legs and began petting herself, poking at herself, moving her fingers in and around herself, frantically exploring her spongy petals, trying to find the devil who hid in there, eager to erase that devil with her hand.

She found it. She rubbed at it, harder and harder. She felt an unraveling. The hurt in her quim turned to something else—an up-fire, a vortex of pleasure, a chimney-effect of heat. She followed the pleasure where it led. She had no weight, no name, no thoughts, no history. Then came a burst of phosphorescence, as though a firework had discharged behind her eyes, and it was over. She felt quiet and warm. For the first conscious moment of her life, her mind was free from wonder, free from worry, free from work or puzzlement. Then, from the middle of that marvelous furred stillness, a thought took shape, took hold, took over:

I shall have to do this again.

Not a half hour later, Alma was standing in the atrium of White Acre, flustered and embarrassed, receiving dinner guests. That night, the visitors included serious young George Hawkes, a Philadelphia publisher of fine botanical prints, books, periodicals, and journals, and a distinguished older gentleman by the name of James K. Peck, who taught at the College of New Jersey up in Princeton, and who had just published a book about the physiology of Negroes. Arthur Dixon, the girls' pale tutor, dined with the family as usual, although he rarely added much to the conversation, and tended to spend dinner hours looking worriedly at his fingernails.

George Hawkes, the botanical publisher, had been a guest at White Acre many times before, and Alma was fond of him. He was shy but kind, and terribly intelligent, with the posture of a great, awkward, shuffling bear. His clothes were too big, his hat sat wrong on his head, and he never seemed to know precisely where to stand. To coax George Hawkes into speech was a challenge, but once he began speaking, he was a pleasant treasure. He knew more about botanical lithography than anyone else in Philadelphia, and his publications were exquisite. He spoke lovingly of plants and artists and the craft of bookbinding, and Alma enjoyed his company enormously.

As for the other guest, Professor Peck, he was a new addition to the dinner table, and Alma disliked him straight away. He had every mark of a bore, and a determined bore at that. Immediately upon his arrival, he occupied twenty minutes in the atrium of White Acre, relaying in Homeric detail the trials of his coach ride from Princeton to Philadelphia. Once he had exhausted that fascinating topic, he shared his surprise that Alma, Prudence, and Beatrix would be joining the gentlemen at the dinner table, insofar as the conversation would surely be over their heads.

"Oh, no," Henry corrected his guest. "I think you'll soon enough find that my wife and daughters are passably capable of conversation."

"Are they?" the gentleman asked, plainly unconvinced. "In what topics?"

"Well," Henry said, rubbing at his chin as he considered his family,

"Beatrix here knows everything, Prudence has artistic and musical knowledge, and Alma—the big tall one—is a right beast for botany."

"Botany," Professor Peck repeated, with practiced condescension. "A most improving recreation for girls. The only scientific work that is suited to the female sex, I have always surmised, on account of its absence of cruelty, or mathematical rigor. My own daughter does fine drawings of wildflowers."

"How engrossing for her," Beatrix murmured.

"Yes, quite," said Professor Peck, and turned to Alma. "A lady's fingers are more pliant, you see. Softer than a man's. Better suited than a man's hands, some say, for the more delicate operations of plant collection."

Alma, who was not one to blush, blushed to her very bones. Why was this man talking about her fingers, about pliancy, about delicacy, about softness? Now everybody looked at Alma's hands, which, only a short while earlier, had been buried straight up inside her quim. It was dreadful. From the corner of her eye, she saw her old friend George Hawkes smile at her in nervous sympathy. George blushed all the time. He blushed whenever anyone looked at him, and whenever he was forced to speak. Perhaps he was commiserating with her discomfort. With George's eyes upon her, Alma felt herself blushing redder still. For the first time in her life, she could not find speech, and she wished that nobody would look at her at all. She would have done anything to escape dinner that night.

Fortunately for Alma, Professor Peck did not seem particularly interested in anyone but himself, and once dinner was served, he commenced on a long and detailed disquisition, as though he had mistaken White Acre for a lecture hall, and his hosts for students.

"There are those," he began, after an elaborate folding of his napkin, "who have recently submitted that Negroidism is merely a disease of the skin, which could perhaps, using the correct chemical combinations, be *washed off*, as it were, thus transforming the Negro into a healthy white man. This is incorrect. As my research has proven, a Negro is not a diseased white man, but a species of his own, as I shall demonstrate . . ."

Alma found it challenging to pay attention. Her thoughts were on *Cum Grano Salis* and the binding closet. Now, this day did not mark the first occasion upon which Alma had heard of genitalia, or even of human sexual function. Unlike other girls—who were told by their families that Indians brought babies, or that impregnation occurred through the insertion of seeds into small cuts in the side of a woman's body—Alma knew the rudiments of human anatomy, both male and female. There were far too many medical treatises and scientific books around White Acre for her to have remained wholly ignorant on this topic, and the entire language of botany, with which Alma was so intimately familiar, was highly sexualized. (Linnaeus himself had referred to pollination as "marriage," had called flower petals "noble bed curtains," and had once daringly described a flower that contained nine stamens and one pistil as "nine men in the same bride's chamber, with one woman.")

What's more, Beatrix would not have her daughters be raised as self-endangering innocents, particularly given Prudence's natural mother's unfortunate history, so it was Beatrix herself who—with much stuttering and suffering, and a good deal of fanning about the neck—had imparted to Alma and Prudence the essential proceedings of human propagation. This conversation nobody had enjoyed, and everyone had worked together to end it as swiftly as possible—but the information had been transmitted. Beatrix had even once warned Alma that certain parts of the body were never to be touched except in the interest of cleanliness, and that one must never linger at the privy, for instance, due to the dangers of solitary unchaste passions. Alma had paid no mind to the warning at the time because it made no sense: Who would ever want to linger at the privy?

But with her discovery of *Cum Grano Salis*, Alma had suddenly been made aware that the most unimaginable sensual events were transpiring all over the world. Men and women were doing simply astonishing things with each other, and they were doing them not only for procreation but for recreation—as were men and men, and women and women, and children and servants, and farmers and travelers, and sailors and seamstresses, and sometimes even husbands and wives! One could even do the most astonishing things to *oneself*, as Alma had just learned in the binding closet. With or without a light coating of nut oil.

Did other people do this? Not only the gymnastic acts of penetration, but this private rubbing? Anonymous wrote that many people did it—even ladies of gentle birth, by his account and experience. What about Prudence? Did she do this thing? Had she ever experienced the spongy petals, the vortex of up-fire, the bursting of phosphorescence? This was impossible to imagine; Prudence did not even perspire. It was difficult enough to read Prudence's facial expressions, much less surmise at what was hiding beneath her clothes, or buried in her mind.

What about Arthur Dixon, their tutor? Was anything lurking in his mind besides academic tedium? Was anything buried in his body, beyond his twitches and his perpetual dry cough? She stared at Arthur, seeking some sign of sensual life, but his figure, his face, revealed nothing. She could not imagine him in a shudder of ecstasy such as the one she had just experienced in the binding closet. She could scarcely imagine him reclining, and could certainly not imagine him unclothed. He gave every indication of being a man who had been born sitting up, wearing a tight-fitting waistcoat and wool breeches, holding a dense book, and sighing unhappily. If he had urges, where and when did he release them?

Alma felt a cool hand on her arm. It was her mother's.

"What is your opinion, Alma, of Professor Peck's treatise?"

Beatrix knew Alma had not been listening. How did she know that? What else did she know? Alma gathered herself quickly, cast her mind back over the beginning of the dinner, tried to retrieve the few ideas she'd actually heard. Uncharacteristically, she came up with nothing. She cleared her throat and said, "I would prefer to read the entirety of Professor Peck's book before rendering any judgment."

Beatrix cast her daughter a sharp look: surprised, critical, and unimpressed.

Professor Peck, however, took Alma's comment as an invitation to speak more—in fact, to *recite* a good majority of the first chapter of his book, from memory, for the benefit of the ladies at the table. Henry Whittaker would not normally have permitted such an act of perfect tedium in his dining room, but Alma could see by his face that her father was weary and depleted, most likely on the brink of another one of his attacks. Impending illness was the only thing that ever quieted her father like this. If Alma knew Henry, and she did know him, he would be in bed all day tomorrow, and probably for the entirety of the week to come. For the time being, though, Henry endured Professor Peck's droning recitation by pouring himself one liberal dose of claret after another, and by closing his eyes for long periods.

Meanwhile, Alma studied George Hawkes, the botanical publisher. Did he do this thing? Did he ever rub himself to a crisis of pleasure? Anonymous wrote that men practiced onanism even more frequently than women. A young man of health and vigor could reportedly coax himself to ejaculation several times a day. Nobody would describe George Hawkes as being exactly full of vigor, but he was a young man with a large, heavy, perspiring body—a body that did seem to be full of *something*. Had George done this act recently, perhaps even on this day? What was George Hawkes's member doing right now? Resting in languor? Or tending toward desire?

Suddenly, the most astonishing imaginable event occurred.

Prudence Whittaker *spoke*.

"Pardon me, sir," Prudence said, directing her words and her placid gaze precisely at Professor Peck, "if I understand you correctly, it seems you have identified the different textures of human hair as evidence that Negroes, Indians, Orientals, and the white man are all members of different species. But I cannot help but wonder at your supposition. On this very estate, sir, we raise several varieties of sheep. Perhaps you noticed them as you came up the drive earlier this evening? Some of our sheep have silken hair, some have coarse hair, and some have dense woolen curls. Surely, sir, you would not doubt that—despite their differences in coats—they are all sheep. And if you'll excuse me, I believe that all these varieties of sheep can also be inter-bred successfully with one another. Is it not the same with man? Could one not, then, make the argument that Negroes, Indians, Orientals, and the white man are also all one species?"

All eyes turned to Prudence. Alma felt as though she had been jolted awake by a dousing of icy water. Henry's eyes opened. He set down his glass and sat straight up, his attention fully piqued. It would have taken a subtle eye to see it, but Beatrix sat up a bit straighter in her chair, too, as though putting herself on alert. Arthur Dixon, the tutor, widened his eyes at Prudence in alarm, and then immediately looked about anxiously, as though he might be blamed for this outburst. There was much to marvel at here, indeed. This was the longest speech Prudence had ever given at the dinner table—or indeed *anywhere*.

Unfortunately, Alma had not been following the discussion up to this point, so she wasn't entirely certain if Prudence's statement was accurate or relevant, but, by God, the girl had spoken! Everyone was startled, it seemed, except Prudence herself, who gazed upon Professor Peck with her custom-ary cool beauty, unperturbed, blue eyes wide and clear, awaiting a response.

It was as though she had been challenging eminent Princetonians every day of her life.

"We cannot compare humans to sheep, young lady," Professor Peck corrected. "Simply because two creatures can breed . . . well, if your father will excuse my mentioning this topic in front of the ladies?" Henry, quite attentive now, gave a sovereign wave of approval. "Simply because two creatures can breed, does not mean they are members of the same species. Horses can breed with donkeys, as you may know. Also, canaries with finches, roosters with partridge, and the he-goat with the ewe. This does not make them biologically equivalent. Moreover, it is well known that Negroes attract different types of head lice and intestinal worms than whites, thus incontrovertibly proving species differentiation."

Prudence nodded her head politely at the guest. "My error, sir," she said. "Pray, continue."

Alma remained speechless and baffled. Why all this talk of breeding? Tonight of all nights?

"While *differentiation* between races is visibly obvious even to a child," Professor Peck continued, "the *superiority* of the white man should be clear to anyone with the faintest education in human history and origin. As Teutons and Christians, we honor virtue, vigorous health, thrift and morality. We govern our passions. Therefore, we lead. The other races, backward moving from civilization, could never have invented such advances as currency, the alphabet, and manufacturing. But none are so helpless as the Negro. The Negro shows an overexpression of emotional senses, which accounts for his infamous absence of self-control. We see this demonstrated in his facial structure. There is altogether too much eye, lip, nose, and ear— which is to say that the Negro cannot help but become overstimulated by his senses. Thus, he is capable of the warmest affection, but also the darkest violence. What is more, the Negro cannot blush, and is therefore not capable of shame."

At the mere mention of blushing and shame, Alma blushed in shame. She was entirely out of control of her own senses this night. George Hawkes smiled at her again, once more with warm sympathy, causing her to blush only deeper. Beatrix shot Alma a glance of such withering derision that Alma feared for a moment she was about to be slapped. Alma almost wished she *would* be slapped, if only to clear her head.

Prudence—astonishingly—spoke up again.

"I wonder," she posed, in a voice calm and tempered, "whether the wisest Negro is superior in intelligence to the most foolish white man? I ask, Professor Peck, only because last year our tutor, Mr. Dixon, told us of a carnival he'd once attended, where he encountered a former slave named Mr. Fuller, of Maryland, who was famous for his quickness of reckoning. According to Mr. Dixon, if you were to tell this Negro at precisely what date and time you had been born, he could instantly calculate how many *seconds* you had been alive, sir, even accounting for leap years. It was evidently a most impressive display."

Arthur Dixon looked as though he might faint.

The professor, now openly irritated, replied, "Young lady, I have seen carnival mules that can be taught to count."

"As have I," Prudence replied, again in that same pale, unruffled tone. "But I have never yet encountered a carnival mule, sir, that could be taught to calculate leap years."

Professor Peck started a bit at this bold comment, but then nodded curtly and carried on. "Very well, then. To answer your question, there are idiot individuals, and even savant individuals, to be found within every species. Such is not the norm, however, in either direction. I have been collecting and measuring the skulls of white men and Negroes for years, and my research thus far concludes without question that the white man's skull, when filled with water, holds on average four more ounces than the skull of the Negro—thus proving greater intellectual capacity."

"I wonder," Prudence said mildly, "what might have happened if you'd attempted to pour knowledge into the skull of a living Negro, rather than water into the skull of a dead one?"

The table fell into rigid silence. George Hawkes had not yet spoken this evening and clearly he was not about to begin now. Arthur Dixon was doing an excellent imitation of a corpse. Professor Peck's face had taken on a distinctly purplish hue. Prudence, who, as ever, looked porcelain and unimpeachable, waited for a response. Henry stared at his adopted daughter with the beginnings of astonishment, yet for some reason elected not to speak— perhaps feeling too sickly to engage directly, or perhaps simply curious to see where this most unexpected conversation would lead next. Alma, likewise, contributed nothing. Frankly, Alma had nothing *to* add. Never had she found herself with so little to say, and never had Prudence been so loquacious. So the duty fell to Beatrix to put words back upon the dinner table, and she did so with her typical stalwart sense of Dutch responsibility.

"I would be fascinated, Professor Peck," Beatrix said, "to see the research you mentioned earlier, about the varietal difference in head lice and intestinal parasites, between the Negro and the white man. Perhaps you have the documentation with you? I would enjoy looking it over. Biology at the parasitic level is most compelling to me."

"I do not carry the documentation with me, madam," the professor said, pulling himself back slowly toward dignity. "Nor do I need it. Documentation in this case is not necessary. The differentiation in head lice and intestinal parasites between Negroes and the white man is a well-known fact."

It was almost not to be believed, but Prudence spoke *again*.

"What a pity," she murmured, cool as marble. "Forgive us, sir, but in this household we are never permitted to rest upon the assumption that any fact is well known enough to evade the necessity of accurate documentation."

Henry—sick and weary as he was—exploded into laughter.

"And *that*, sir," he boomed at the professor, "is a well-known fact!"

Beatrix, as though none of this was occurring, turned her attention to the butler and said, "It seems we are now ready for the pudding."

———————————————

Their guests were meant to have stayed the night at White Acre, but Professor Peck, flummoxed and irritated, elected instead to take his carriage back to the city, announcing that he would prefer to stay in a downtown hotel and start his arduous journey back to Princeton the next day at dawn. Nobody was sorry to see him go. George Hawkes requested if he might share the carriage back to the center of Philadelphia with Professor Peck, and the scholar gruffly agreed. But before George departed, he asked if he might have a brief moment alone with Alma and Prudence. He had scarcely spoken a word this evening, but now he wanted to say something—and he wanted, apparently, to say it to both girls. So the three of them—Alma, Prudence, and George—all stepped into the drawing room together, while the others milled about in the atrium, gathering up cloaks and parcels.

George directed his comments to Alma, after receiving an almost imperceptible nod from Prudence.

"Miss Whittaker," he said, "your sister tells me that you have written, merely to satisfy your own curiosity, a most interesting paper on the *Monotropa* plant. If you're not too weary, I wonder if you might share with me your central findings?"

Alma was puzzled. This was an odd request, and at such an odd time of day. "Surely you are too weary to speak of my botanical hobbies at this late hour?" she offered.

"Not at all, Miss Whittaker," George said. "I would welcome it. If anything, it would relax me."

At these words, Alma found herself relaxing, too. At last, a simple theme! At last, botany!

"Well, Mr. Hawkes," she said, "as you surely know, *Monotropa hypopitys* grows only in the shade, and is a sickly white color—almost ghostly in tone. Previous naturalists had always assumed that *Monotropa* lacks pigment because of the absence of sunlight in its environment, but this theory makes little sense to me, as some of our most vivid shades of green can also be found in the shade, in such plants as ferns and mosses. My investigations further show that *Monotropa* is just as likely to tilt *away* from the sun as *toward* it, leading me to wonder if it does not gain nourishment from the sun's rays at all, but rather from some other source. I have come to believe *Monotropa* gains its nutrition from the plants in which it grows. In other words, I believe it to be a parasite."

"Which brings us back to an earlier topic of this evening," George said, with a small smile.

Goodness, George Hawkes was making a jest! Alma had not known George was capable of jesting, but upon realizing his joke, she laughed with delight. Prudence did not laugh, but merely sat watching the two of them, pretty and remote as a picture.

"Yes, quite!" Alma said, gaining more momentum. "But unlike Professor Peck and his head lice, I can offer up documentation. I've noticed under the microscope that the stem of *Monotropa* is destitute of those cuticular pores through which air and water are generally admitted in other plants, nor does it seem to have a mechanism to draw moisture from the soil. I believe *Monotropa* takes nourishment and moisture from its foster parent. I believe its corpselike absence of color derives from the fact that it dines upon food that has already been digested, as it were, by the host."

"A most extraordinary speculation," said George Hawkes.

"Well, it is mere speculation at this point. Perhaps someday chemistry will be able to prove what my microscope, for now, only suggests."

"If you wouldn't mind sharing the paper with me this week," said George, "I would like to consider publishing it."

Alma was so enchanted by this unexpected invitation (and so addled by the queer events of the day, and so stirred to be speaking directly to a grown man about whom she had just been nursing sensual thoughts) that she never stopped to consider the strangest element of this entire exchange—namely, the role of her sister Prudence. Why was Prudence even present for this conversation? Why had Prudence given George Hawkes the nod to begin speaking in the first place? And when—at what earlier unknown moment—had Prudence ever had the chance to speak with George Hawkes about Alma's private botanical research projects? When had Prudence even *noticed* Alma's private botanical research projects?

On any other evening, these questions might have inhabited Alma's mind and tugged at her curiosity, but on this evening she dismissed them. On this evening—at the close of what had been the strangest and most distracted day of her life—Alma's mind was spinning and dipping with so many other thoughts that she missed all this. Bemused, tired, and a bit dizzy, she bade good night to George Hawkes, and then sat alone in the drawing room with her sister, waiting for Beatrix to come and contend with them.

With the thought of Beatrix, Alma's euphoria diminished. Beatrix's nightly accounting of her daughters' shortcomings was never to be relished, but tonight Alma dreaded the lecture more than usual. Alma's behavior that day (the discovery of the book, the arousing thoughts, the solitary passion in the binding closet) made her feel as though she visibly emanated guilt. She feared Beatrix would somehow sense it. Moreover, the dinner-table conversation had been catastrophic tonight: Alma had appeared blatantly stupid, while Prudence, unprecedentedly, had been something close to rude. Beatrix would not be pleased with either of them.

Alma and Prudence waited in the drawing room for their mother, quiet as nuns. The two girls were always quiet when they were alone together. Never had they found comfortable conversation. Never had they prattled. Never would they. Prudence sat with her hands folded quietly, while Alma fidgeted with the hem of a handkerchief. Alma glanced at Prudence, seeking something she could not name. Fellowship, maybe. Warmth. Some kind of affinity. Perhaps a reference to any of the evening's proceedings. But Prudence—glittering as hard as ever—invited no intimacy. Despite this fact, Alma decided to attempt it.

"Those ideas of yours which you expressed tonight, Prudence?" Alma asked. "Where did you come by them?"

"From Mr. Dixon, largely. The condition and plight of the African race is a preferred topic of our good tutor."

"Is it? I have never heard him make mention of any such thing."

"Nonetheless, he has strong feelings on the subject," Prudence said, without any change of expression.

"Is he an abolitionist, then?"

"He is."

"Heavens," Alma said, marveling at the idea of Arthur Dixon with strong feelings on *anything*. "Mother and Father had best not hear of that!"

"Mother knows," Prudence replied.

"Does she? And what about Father?"

Prudence did not reply. Alma had more questions—a good many more of them—but Prudence did not seem eager for discussion. Again, the room fell silent. Then suddenly Alma leapt into that silence, allowing a wild and uncontrolled question to burst from her lips.

"Prudence," she asked, "what do you think of Mr. George Hawkes?"

"I think him to be a decent gentleman."

"And I think I am most desperately in love with him!" Alma exclaimed, shocking even herself with this absurd, unanticipated admission.

Before Prudence could respond—indeed, if she ever would have responded at all—Beatrix entered the drawing room and looked at her two daughters sitting on the divan. For a long while, Beatrix said nothing. She held her daughters in a stern, unyielding gaze, studying first one girl, then the other. This was more terrifying to Alma than any lecture, for the silence contained infinite, omniscient, horrifying possibilities. Beatrix could be aware of anything, could know of *everything*. Alma picked at a corner of her handkerchief, tearing it to threads. Prudence's countenance and posture did not alter.

"I am weary this evening," Beatrix said, finally breaking the awful hush.

She looked at Alma and said, "I do not have the will tonight, Alma, to speak of your shortcomings. It will only further injure my temper. Let it only be said that if I ever see such gape-mouthed distraction from you at the dinner table again, I will ask you to take your meals elsewhere."

"But, Mother—" Alma began.

"Do not explain yourself, daughter. It is weak."

Beatrix turned as though to exit the room, but then turned back and leveled her gaze at Prudence, as though she were only just remembering something.

"Prudence," she said. "Fine performance tonight."

This was entirely out of the ordinary. Beatrix never gave praise. But was there anything about this day that was *not* out of the ordinary? Alma, amazed, turned to Prudence, again looking for something. Recognition? Commiseration? A shared sense of astonishment? But Prudence revealed nothing and did not return Alma's gaze, so Alma gave up. She stood from the divan and headed toward the stairs, and bed. At the foot of the stairs, though, she turned to Prudence and surprised herself once more.

"Good night, sister," Alma said. She had never once used that term before.

"And to you," was Prudence's only reply.

Chapter Eight

Between the winter of 1816 and the autumn of 1820, Alma Whittaker wrote more than three dozen papers for George Hawkes, all of which he published in his monthly journal *Botanica Americana*. Her papers were not pioneering, but her ideas were bright, her illustrations free of error, and her scholarship stringent and sound. If Alma's work did not exactly ignite the world, it most certainly ignited Alma, and her efforts were more than good enough for the pages of *Botanica Americana*.

Alma wrote in depth about laurel, mimosa, and verbena. She wrote about grapes and camellias, about the myrtle orange, about the cosseting of figs. She published under the name "A. Whittaker." Neither she nor George Hawkes believed that it would much benefit Alma to announce herself in print as female. In the scientific world of the day, there was still a strict division between "botany" (the study of plants by men) and "polite botany" (the study of plants by women). Now, "polite botany" was often indistinguishable from "botany"—except that one field was regarded with respect and the other was not—but still, Alma did not wish to be shrugged off as a mere polite botanist.

Of course, the Whittaker name was famous in the world of plants and science, so a good number of botanists already knew precisely who "A. Whittaker" was. Not all of them, however. In response to her articles, then, Alma sometimes received letters from botanists around the world, sent to her in care of George Hawkes's print shop. Some of these letters began, "My dear Sir." Other letters were written to "Mr. A. Whittaker." One quite memorable missive even came addressed to "Dr. A. Whittaker." (Alma kept that letter for a long time, tickled by the unexpected honorific.)

As George and Alma found themselves sharing research with each other and editing papers together, he became an even more regular visitor to White Acre. Happily, his shyness relaxed. He could frequently be found speaking at the dinner table now, and sometimes even attempting a witticism.

As for Prudence, she did not speak at the dinner table again. Her outburst about Negroes on the night of Professor Peck's visit must have been some passing act of fever, for she never again repeated the performance, nor did she ever again challenge a guest. Henry had teased Prudence about her views rather relentlessly since that night, calling her "our dusky-loving warrior," but she refused to speak again on the subject. Instead, she retreated back into her cool, distant, mysterious ways, treating everyone and everything with the same indifferent, indecipherable politeness as ever.

The girls grew older. When they turned eighteen, Beatrix discontinued their tutoring sessions at last, announcing their educations complete, and sending away poor, boring Arthur Dixon, who took a position as a tutor of classical languages at the University of Pennsylvania. Thus it seemed the girls were considered children no longer. Any mother other than Beatrix Whittaker might have regarded this period as a time of dedicated husband-seeking. Any other mother might have now ambitiously presented Alma and Prudence into society, encouraging the girls to flirt, to dance, and to court. This might have been a wise moment to order new gowns, adopt new hairstyles, commission new portraits. These activities, however, seem not to have occurred to Beatrix at all.

In truth, Beatrix had never done Prudence or Alma any favors regarding their suitability for marriage. There were those in Philadelphia who whispered that the Whittakers had rendered their girls completely unmarriageable, what with all that education and isolation from the better families. Neither girl had friends. They had only ever dined with grown men of science and trade, so their minds were distinctly unformed. They had not the slightest training in how to speak properly to a young suitor. Alma was the type of girl who, when a visiting young fellow admired the water lilies in one of White Acre's beautiful ponds, would say, "No, sir, you are incorrect. These are not water lilies. These are lotuses. Water lilies float on the surface of water, you see, while lotuses rise just above it. Once you learn the difference, you'll never make the mistake again."

Alma had grown tall as a man by now, with broad shoulders. She looked as though she could swing an ax. (In point of fact, she *could* swing an ax, and often had to, in her botanical fieldwork.) This need not have necessarily precluded her from marriage. Some men liked a larger woman, who promised a stronger disposition, and Alma, it could be argued, had a handsome profile—at least from her left side. She certainly had a fine, friendly nature. Yet she was missing some invisible, essential ingredient, and so, despite all the frank eroticism that lay hidden within her body, her presence in a room did not kindle ideas of ardor in any man.

It did not help that Alma herself believed she was unlovely. She believed this only because she had been told it so many times, and in so many different ways. Most recently, the news of her homeliness had come straight from her father, who—after drinking quite a bit too much rum one evening—had said to her, quite out of nowhere, "Think nothing of it, my girl!"

"Think nothing of what, Father?" Alma asked, looking up from the letter she had been writing for him.

"Don't dismay of it, Alma. It's not everything to have a pleasing face. Plenty of women are loved who are not beauties. Think of your mother. She's never been pretty a day of her life, yet she found a husband, didn't she? Think of Mrs. Cavendesh, down near the bridge! The woman looks a fright, yet her husband finds her adequate enough to have made seven children out of her. So there will be somebody for you, Plum, and I think he will be a fortunate man to have you."

To think that all this was offered by way of *consolation*!

As for Prudence, she was a widely acknowledged beauty—arguably the greatest beauty in Philadelphia—but the entire city agreed that she was cold and unwinnable. Prudence excited envy in women, but it was not clear that she excited passion in men. Prudence had a way of making men feel that they ought not to bother at all, and so, wisely, they didn't. They stared, for one could not help staring at Prudence Whittaker, but they did not approach.

One might have expected the Whittaker girls to attract fortune hunters.

True, there were many young men who coveted the family's money, but the prospect of being Henry Whittaker's son-in-law seemed more like a threat than a windfall, and nobody really believed that Henry would ever part with his fortune, anyway. One way or another, not even dreams of riches brought suitors near White Acre.

Of course, there were always men around the estate—but they came seeking Henry, not his daughters. At any hour of the day, one could find men standing in the atrium of White Acre, hoping for an audience with Henry Whittaker. These were men of all sorts: desperate men, dreaming men, angry men, liars. These were men who arrived at the estate carrying display cases, inventions, drawings, schemes, or lawsuits. They came offering shares of stock, or pleas for loans, or the prototype of a new vacuum pump, or the certainty of a cure for jaundice, if only Henry would invest in their research. But they did not come to White Acre for the pleasures of courtship.

George Hawkes, however, was different. He never sought anything material from Henry, but came up to White Acre merely to converse with him and to enjoy the spoils of the greenhouses. Henry enjoyed George's company, for George published the latest scientific findings in his journals, and knew all that was transpiring in the botanical world. George most certainly did not comport himself as a suitor—he was neither flirtatious nor playful—but he was *aware* of the Whittaker girls, and kind to them. He was always solicitous to Prudence. As for Alma, he engaged with her as though she were a respected botanical colleague. Alma appreciated George's kind regard, but she wished for more. Academic discourse, she felt, is not how a young man speaks to the girl he loves. This was most unfortunate, for Alma indeed loved George Hawkes with all her heart.

He was an odd choice to love. Nobody would ever have accused George of being a handsome man, but in Alma's eyes, he was exemplary. She felt somehow that they made a nice pair, perhaps even an obvious pair. There was no question that George was overly large, pale, awkward, and clumsy—but so was Alma. He always made a hash of dressing, but Alma was not fashionable, either. George's waistcoats were always too tight and his trousers too loose, but if Alma had been a man, this is probably how she would have dressed, as well, for she'd always encountered a similar sort of trouble puzzling out how to arrange her clothing. George had entirely too much forehead and not quite enough chin, but he possessed a thick, damp shock of dark hair, which Alma dearly wanted to touch.

Alma did not know how to play the coquette. She had not the first idea of how to woo George, other than to write him paper after paper on ever more obscure botanical subjects. There had only ever been one moment between George and Alma that might reasonably have been interpreted as tender. In April of 1818, Alma had presented George Hawkes with a beautiful view in her microscope of *Carchesium polypinum* (perfectly lit and living, happily dancing in a tiny pool of pond water, with its spinning cups, waving cilia, and fringed, flowering branches). George had grasped her left hand, pressed it spontaneously between his two large, damp palms, and said, "My stars, Miss Whittaker! What a brilliant microscopist you've become!"

That touch, that pressing of the hand, that praise, had set Alma's heart beating nineteen strokes to the dozen. It had also sent her running to the binding closet, to slake herself once more with her own hands.

Oh, yes—to the binding closet again!

The binding closet had become, ever since the autumn of 1816, a place that Alma visited every day—indeed, sometimes several times a day, with pauses only during her menses. One might have wondered when she found time for such activity, with all her studies and responsibilities, but simply put, there was no question of *not* doing it. Alma's body—tall and mannish, flinty and freckled, large of bone, thick of knuckle, square of hip, and hard of chest—had become, over the years, a most unlikely organ of sexual desire, and she was constantly overcongested with need.

She had now read *Cum Grano Salis* so many times that it was emblazoned in her memory, and she had moved on to other daring reading material. Whenever her father bought up other people's libraries, Alma paid most careful attention while sorting through the books, always on the lookout for something dangerous, something with a trick cover, something illicit hidden among the more innocuous volumes. This is how she had found Sappho and Diderot, and also some quite unsettling translations of Japanese pleasure manuals. She had found a French book of twelve sexual adventures, divided by month, called *L'Année galante*, that told of perverse concubines and lecherous priests, of fallen ballet girls and seduced governesses. (Oh, those long-suffering seduced governesses! Reduced and ruined by the score, they were! They showed up in so many naughty books! Why would anyone be a governess, Alma wondered, if it only led to rape and enslavement?) Alma even read the manual of a secret "Ladies' Whipping Club" in London, as well as numberless tales of Roman orgies and obscene Hindu religious initiations. All of these books, she separated out from the others, and hid in trunks in the old hayloft of the carriage house.

But there was more, too. She also perused medical journals, where she could sometimes find the queerest and most outlandish reports of the human body. She read soberly recounted theories of Adam and Eve's possible hermaphroditism. She read scientific accounts of genital hair that grew in such freakish abundance that it could be harvested and sold as wigs. She read statistics on the health of prostitutes in the Boston area. She read reports of sailors who claimed they had mated with seals. She read comparisons of penis sizes across different races and cultures, and across different mammalian varieties.

She knew she should not be reading any of this material, but she could not stop herself. She wanted to know all she could learn. All this reading filled her mind with a veritable circus parade of bodies—stripped and whipped, degraded and debased, yearning and disassembled (only to be put back together again later, for more debasement). She had also developed a fixation with the idea of putting things into her mouth—things, to be specific, that a lady should never desire to put into her mouth. Parts of other people's bodies, and the like. Most of all, the male member. She desired the male member in her mouth even more than she desired it in her quim, because she wanted the closest possible engagement with the thing. She liked to study things intimately, even microscopically, so it made sense that she longed to see and even taste the most hidden aspect of a man—his most secret nest of being. The thought of all this, coupled with a heightened awareness of her own lips and tongue, became a problematic obsession, which would accumulate within her until she was quite overcome by it. She could solve this problem only with her fingertips, and she could solve it only in the binding closet—in that safe and insulating darkness, with all the familiar smells of leather and glue around her, and the good reliable lock on the door. She could solve it only with one hand between her legs and the other inside her mouth.

Alma knew that her self-violation was the very pinnacle of wrongness, and that it might even bring harm to her health. Again, unable to stop herself from finding things out, she had researched the subject, and what she had learned was not encouraging. In one British medical journal, she read that children brought up with healthy food and fresh air should never feel the faintest sexual impression whatsoever within their bodies, nor should they seek sensual information. The simple amusements of rural life, the author claimed, should entertain young people sufficiently that they should not be overcome with a desire to explore their genitalia at all. In another medical journal, she learned that sexual precocity can be brought on by bedwetting, by too many beatings in childhood, by irritation of the rectal area due to worms, or (and here Alma's breath had tightened) by "premature intellectual growth." That must have been what had happened to her, she thought. For if the mind is overly fostered at a young age, then perversions will inevitably arise, and the victim will seek self-indulgent substitutes for intercourse. This was primarily a problem in the development of boys, she read, but it was, in rare cases, expressed in girls. Young people who self-indulged in their own bodies would someday grow into married people who tormented their spouses with the urge for intercourse every night of the week, until the family would fall into sickness, decay, and bankruptcy. Self-indulgence also destroyed the health of the body, creating a rounded back and a limping gait.

The habit, in other words, did not advertise itself well. But Alma had not originally intended to make such a habit of self-pleasure. She made the most earnest and sincere vows to stop. Or she did so *initially*. She promised herself that she would stop reading salacious material. She promised herself she would stop indulging in sensual reveries about George Hawkes and his damp shock of dark hair. She would never imagine putting his hidden member in her mouth again. She swore never again to visit the binding closet, not even if a book needed repair!

Inevitably, her resolve would wither. She promised herself that she would visit the binding closet just one more time. Just one more time, she would allow her head to fill with these stirring and abhorrent thoughts. Just one more time, she would swirl her fingers about her quim and lips, feeling her legs clench and her face grow heated, and her body yank loose once more into a stew of marvelous havoc. Just one more time.

And then, perhaps, once more again.

Soon it became obvious there was no defeating this, and eventually Alma had no choice but to silently sanction her own behavior and continue on with it. How else could she have dispatched the desire that amassed itself in her, every hour of the day? Moreover, the effects of this self-befoulment upon her health and spirit appeared so markedly different from the warnings in the journals that for a while she wondered if she was doing it incorrectly, such that it was accidentally beneficial, rather than harmful? What else could explain the fact that her secret activity did not bring on any of the dire effects about which the medical journals warned? The act brought Alma relief, not sickness. It flushed her cheeks with healthy color, rather than draining her countenance of all vitality. Yes, the compulsion brought her a sense of shame, but always—once the act was complete—she felt herself swept up into a vivid and precise state of mental clarity. Straight from the binding closet she would run back to her research, where she would labor with a renewed sense of priority, catapulted back into study by energetic lucidity, by a bodily pulse of useful, thrilling animation. It was always afterward that she was at her brightest, her most awake. It was always afterward that her work truly thrived.

What's more, Alma now had a place to work. She had a study of her own—or at least she had something that she called a study. After she had cleared all her father's superfluous books from the carriage house, she had taken over one of the larger, disused ground-floor tack rooms for herself, and had turned it into a place of scholarly refuge. It was a lovely situation. The White Acre carriage house was a beautiful brick building, regal and serene, with tall, vaulted ceilings and wide, generous windows. Alma's study was the finest space within that structure, blessed with steady northern light, a clean tile floor, and a view of her mother's immaculate Grecian garden. The room smelled of hay and dust and horses, and was filled with an agreeable clutter of books, sieves, plates, pans, specimens, correspondence, jars, and old sweets tins. For Alma's nineteenth birthday, her mother had given her a *camera lucida*, which allowed her to magnify and trace botanical specimens for more accurate scientific drawing. She now owned a fine set of Italian prisms, too, which made her feel a bit like Newton. She had a good solid desk, and a wide, simple laboratory bench, for performing experiments. She used old barrels for seats, rather than formal chairs, as she found them easier to get around with her skirts. She had a pair of marvelous

German microscopes, which she had learned to operate—as George Hawkes had noticed!—with the deft touch of a master embroiderer. Initially the winters in the study had been unpleasant (cold enough that her ink wouldn't flow), but Alma soon set herself up with a small Franklin stove, and she personally chinked up the cracks in the walls with dried moss, such that eventually her study became as cozy and lovely a refuge as anyone could hope for, all the year round.

There in the carriage house Alma built up her herbarium, mastered her comprehension of taxonomy, and took on ever more detailed experiments. She read her copy of Philip Miller's *Gardener's Dictionary* so many times that the book itself took on the appearance of old, worn foliage. She studied the latest medical papers about the beneficial effects of digitalis on patients suffering from dropsy, and the use of copaiba for the treatment of venereal diseases. She worked on improving her botanical drawings—which were never exactly beautiful, but always beautifully exact. She worked with untiring diligence, her fingers speeding happily across her tablets and her lips moving as though in prayer.

While the rest of White Acre flowed along in its customary activity and combat, these two locations—the binding closet and the carriage house study—became for Alma twin points of privacy and revelation. One room was for the body; one was for the mind. One room was small and window-less; the other airy and cheerfully lit. One room smelled of old glue; the other of fresh hay. One room brought forth secret thoughts; the other brought forth ideas that could be published and shared. The two rooms existed in separate buildings, divided by lawns and gardens, bisected by a wide gravel drive. Nobody would ever have seen their correlation.

But both rooms belonged to Alma Whittaker alone, and in both rooms, she came into being.

Chapter Nine

Alma was sitting at her desk in the carriage house one day in the autumn of 1819, reading the fourth volume of Jean-Baptiste Lamarck's natural history of invertebrates, when she saw a figure crossing her mother's Grecian garden.

Alma was accustomed to White Acre workers passing by in their duties, and usually there was a partridge or a peacock picking about the grounds as well, but this creature was neither worker nor bird. It was a small, trim, dark-haired girl of about eighteen years, dressed in a most becoming rose-colored walking costume. As she strolled the garden, the girl carelessly swung a green-trimmed, tasseled parasol. It was difficult to be certain, but the girl seemed to be talking to herself. Alma put down Mr. Lamarck and watched. The stranger was not in any hurry, and, indeed, she eventually found a bench to sit upon, and then—more curious still—*to lie upon*, flat on her back. Alma watched, waiting for the girl to move, but it appeared she had fallen asleep.

This was all quite strange. There were visitors at White Acre that week (an expert in carnivorous plants from Yale and a tedious scholar who had written a major treatise on greenhouse ventilation), but none of them had brought daughters. This girl was clearly not related to any of the workers around the estate, either. No gardener could afford to purchase his daughter such a fine parasol as that, and no laborer's daughter would ever walk with such insouciance across Beatrix Whittaker's prized Grecian garden.

Intrigued, Alma left her work behind and walked outside. She approached the girl carefully, not wanting to startle her awake, but upon closer examination saw that the girl was not napping at all—just staring up at the sky, her head pillowed in a pile of glossy black curls.

"Hello," Alma said, peering down at her.

"Oh, hello!" replied the girl, entirely unalarmed by Alma's appearance. "I was just thanking goodness for this bench!"

The girl popped up into a seated position, smiling brightly, and patted the spot beside her, inviting Alma to sit. Alma obediently sat down, studying her seatmate as she settled in. The girl was certainly a queer-looking thing. She had seemed prettier from a distance. True, she had a lovely figure, a magnificent head of hair, and an appealingly matched set of dimples, but from nearby one could see that her face was a bit flat and round—something like a saucer—and her green eyes were altogether too large and demonstrative. She blinked constantly. All of this added up to make her look overly young, not very bright, and just the tiniest bit frantic.

The girl turned her dotty little face up toward Alma and asked, "Now tell me something, did you hear bells ringing last night?"

Alma pondered this question. In fact, she *had* heard bells ringing last night. There had been a fire on Fairmont Hill, and the bells had sounded alarm across the entire city.

"I did hear them," Alma said.

The girl nodded with satisfaction, clapped her hands, and said, "I *knew* it!"

"You knew that I heard bells last night?"

"I knew those bells were *real*!"

"I'm not sure we've met," Alma said cautiously.

"Oh, but we haven't! My name is Retta Snow. I walked all the way here!"

"Did you? May I ask from where?"

One might have almost expected the girl to say, "From the pages of a fairy book!" but instead she said, "From that way," and pointed south. Alma, in a snap, figured it all out. There was a new estate going up just two miles down the river from White Acre. The owner was a wealthy textile merchant from Maryland. This girl must be the merchant's daughter.

"I was hoping there would be a girl my age living around here," said Retta. "How old are you, if I may be so plainspoken?"

"I'm nineteen," said Alma, though she felt much older, especially by comparison to this mite.

"Exceptional!" Retta clapped again. "I am eighteen, which is not such a big difference at all, is it? Now you must tell me something, and I beg your honesty. What is your opinion of my dress?"

"Well . . ." Alma knew nothing about dresses.

"I agree!" Retta said. "It's really not my best dress, is it? If you knew the others, you would agree even more strongly, for I have some dresses that are all the crack! But you don't entirely detest it, either, do you?"

"Well . . ." Alma struggled again for a response.

Retta spared her an answer. "You are far too sweet to me! You don't want to hurt my feelings! I already consider you my friend! Also, you have such a beautiful and reassuring chin. It makes a person want to trust you."

Retta slipped an arm around Alma's waist, and leaned her head against her shoulder, nuzzling in warmly. There was no reason in the world that Alma should have welcomed this gesture. Whosoever Retta Snow may have been, it was obvious she was an absurd person, a perfect little basin of foolishness and distraction. Alma had work to do, and the girl was an interruption.

But nobody had ever called Alma a friend.

Nobody had ever asked Alma what she thought of a dress.

Nobody had ever admired her chin.

They sat on the bench for a while in this warm and surprising embrace. Then Retta pulled away, looked up at Alma, and smiled—childish, credulous, winsome.

"What shall we do next?" she asked. "And what is your name?"

Alma laughed, and introduced herself, and confessed that she did not quite know what to do next.

"Are there other girls?" Retta asked.

"There is my sister."

"You have a sister! You are fortunate! Let us go find her."

So off they went together, wandering about the grounds until they found Prudence working at her easel in one of the rose gardens.

"You must be the sister!" Retta exclaimed, dashing over to Prudence as though she had won a prize, and Prudence was it.

Prudence—poised and correct as ever—set down her brush, and politely offered over her hand for Retta to shake. After pumping Prudence's arm with rather too much enthusiasm, Retta openly took her in for a moment, head cocked to one side. Alma tensed, waiting for Retta to comment on Prudence's beauty, or to demand to know how it could be humanly possible that Alma and Prudence were sisters. Certainly this is what every other person asked, upon seeing Alma and Prudence together for the first time. *How could one sister be so porcelain and the other so ruddy? How could one sister be so dainty and the other so strapping?* Prudence tensed, as well, awaiting these same unwelcome questions. But Retta did not seem captivated or daunted by Prudence's beauty in any manner, nor did she balk at the notion that the sisters were, in fact, sisters. She merely took her time examining Prudence from head to toe, and then clapped her hands in pleasure.

"So now there are three of us!" she said. "What luck! If we were boys, do you realize what we would have to do now? We would have to fall into a terrific scrape with one another, wrestling and fighting and bloodying each other's noses. Then, at the end of our battle, after suffering ghastly injuries, we would come up as fast friends. It's true! I've seen it done! Now, on one hand that seems like a great lot of fun, but I would be sorry to spoil my new dress—although it is not my best dress, as Alma has pointed out—and so I thank heaven today that we are *not* boys. And since we are not boys, this means we can be fast friends right away, without any fighting at all. Don't you agree?"

Nobody had time to agree, as Retta barreled on: "Then it is decided! We are the Three Fast Friends. Somebody should write a song about us. Can either one of you write songs?"

Prudence and Alma looked at each other, dumbstruck.

"Then I'll do it, if I must!" Retta plowed forth. "Give me a moment."

Retta closed her eyes, moved her lips, and tapped her fingers against her waist, as though counting out syllables.

Prudence gave Alma a questioning glance, and Alma shrugged.

After a silence so long it would have felt awkward to anyone in the world except Retta Snow, Retta opened her eyes again.

"I think I've got it," she announced. "Somebody else will have to write the music, for I'm dreadful with music, but I've written the first verse. I think it captures our friendship perfectly. What do you think?" She cleared her throat and recited:

"We are fiddle, fork, and spoon,
We are dancing with the moon,
If you'd like to steal a kiss from us,
You'd better steal one soon!"

Before Alma had a chance to try to decipher this singular little rhyme (to try to work out who was fiddle, who was fork, and who was spoon), Prudence burst into laughter. This was remarkable, for Prudence never laughed. Her laugh was magnificent, brash, and loud—not at all what one would expect from such a doll-like individual.

"Who *are* you?" Prudence asked, when she finally stopped laughing.

"I am Retta Snow, madam, and I am your newest and most undeviating friend."

"Well, Retta Snow," said Prudence, "I believe you might be undeviatingly mad."

"So says everyone!" replied Retta, bowing with a flourish. "But nonetheless—I am here!"

Indeed, she was.

Retta Snow soon became a fixture around the White Acre estate. As a child, Alma had once owned a little cat who'd wandered onto the property and conquered the place in much the same manner. That cat—a pretty little item, with bright yellow stripes—had simply strolled into the White Acre kitchen one sunny day, rubbed herself against everyone's legs, and then settled down beside the hearth with her tail curled around her body, purring lightly, eyes half-closed in contentment. The cat was so comfortable and confident that no one had the heart to inform the creature that it didn't belong—and thus, soon enough, it *did*.

Retta's gambit was similar. She showed up at White Acre that day, put herself at ease, and suddenly it seemed she had always been there. Nobody ever invited Retta, exactly, but Retta did not seem to be the sort of young lady who required invitations for anything. She arrived when she wanted to arrive, stayed for as long as she pleased, helped herself to anything she desired, and departed when she was ready.

Retta Snow lived the most shockingly—even enviably—ungoverned life.

Her mother was a society fixture whose mornings were occupied by long hours spent arranging her toilet, whose afternoons were consumed by visits to other society fixtures, and whose evenings were kept terribly busy with dances. Her father, a man both indulgent and absent, eventually purchased for his daughter a reliable carriage horse and a two-wheeled chaise, in which the girl bounced around Philadelphia quite at her own discretion. She spent her days speeding through the world on her chaise like a happy, roistering bee. If she wished to attend the theater, she attended the theater. If she wished to watch a parade, she found a parade. And if she wished to spend the entire day at White Acre, she did so at her own leisure.

Over the next year, Alma would find Retta in the most surprising places at White Acre: standing atop a vat in the buttery, making the dairymaids laugh as she acted out a scene from *The School for Scandal*; or dangling her feet off the barge dock into the oily waters of the Schuylkill River, pretending to catch fish with her toes; or cutting one of her beautiful shawls in half, in order to share it with a maid who had just complimented it. ("Look, now we each have a bit of the shawl, and so now we are twins!") Nobody knew what to make of her, but nobody ever chased her away. It was not so much that Retta charmed people; it was merely that fending her off was an impossibility. One had no choice but to submit.

Retta even managed to win over Beatrix Whittaker, which was a truly remarkable accomplishment. By all reasonable expectations, Beatrix should have detested Retta, who was the very personification of all Beatrix's deepest fears about girls. Retta was everything Beatrix had raised Alma and Prudence *not* to be—a powdered, hollow-headed, and vain little confection, who ruined expensive dancing slippers in the mud, who was quick to tears and laughter, who pointed crassly at things in public, who was never seen with a book, and who hadn't even the sense enough to keep her head covered in the rain. How could Beatrix ever embrace such a creature as that?

Anticipating this as a problem, Alma had even tried to hide Retta Snow from Beatrix at the beginning of their friendship, fearing the worst should the two ever encounter each other. But Retta was not easily hidden, and Beatrix was not easily deceived. It had taken less than a week, in fact, before Beatrix demanded of Alma one morning at breakfast, "Who is that *child*, with that *parasol*, who is always darting about my property of late? And why do I always see her with *you*?"

Reluctantly, Alma was forced to introduce Retta to her mother.

"How do you do, Mrs. Whittaker," Retta had begun, properly enough, even remembering to curtsey, if perhaps a bit too theatrically.

"How do you do, child?" Beatrix had replied.

Beatrix was not seeking an honest answer to this question, but Retta took the query seriously, pondering it a bit before answering. "Well, I shall tell you, Mrs. Whittaker. I am not at all well. There has been a dreadful tragedy in my household this morning."

Alma looked on in alarm, helpless to intervene. Alma could not imagine where Retta was tending with this line of conversation. Retta had been at White Acre all day, cheerful as can be, and this was the first Alma had heard of a dreadful tragedy in the Snow household. She prayed that Retta would stop speaking, but the girl pushed on, as though Beatrix had urged her to continue.

"Only this morning, Mrs. Whittaker, I suffered the most flurried attack of nerves. One of our servants—my little English maid, to be precise—was in utter tears at breakfast, and so I followed her into her room after the meal was over, to investigate the origins of her sorrow. You shall never guess what I learned! It seems her grandmother had died, exactly three years ago, *to this very day*! Upon learning of this tragedy, I was put into a fit of weeping myself, as I'm certain you can well imagine! I must have wept for an hour on that poor girl's bed. Thank goodness she was there to comfort me. Doesn't it make you want to weep, too, Mrs. Whittaker? To think of losing a grandmother, just three years ago?"

With the mere memory of this incident, Retta's large green eyes filled with tears, and then spilled over.

"What a great heap of nonsense," Beatrix rebuked, emphasizing each word, while Alma flinched at every syllable. "At my age, can you begin to imagine how many people's grandmothers I have seen die? What if I had wept over each one of them? A grandmother's death does not constitute a tragedy, child—and somebody else's grandmother's death from three years past most certainly should not bring on a fit of weeping. Grandmothers *die*, child. It is the proper way of things. One could nearly argue that it is the role of a grandmother to die, after having imparted, one hopes, some lessons of decency and sense to a younger generation. Furthermore, I suspect you were of little comfort to your maid, who would have been better served had you demonstrated for her an example of stoicism and reserve, rather than collapsing in tears across her bed."

Retta took in this admonishment with an open face, while Alma wilted in distress. Well, there's the end of Retta Snow, Alma thought. But then, unexpectedly, Retta laughed. "What a marvelous correction, Mrs. Whittaker! What a fresh way you have of regarding things! You are absolutely in the right! I shall never again think of a grandmother's death as tragedy!"

One could almost see the tears crawling back up Retta's cheeks, reversing themselves and then vanishing completely.

"And now I must take my leave," said Retta, fresh as the dawn. "I intend to go for a walk this evening, so I must go home and select the choicest of my walking bonnets. I do so love walking, Mrs. Whittaker, but not in the wrong bonnet, as I'm sure you can understand." Retta extended her hand to Beatrix, who could not refuse to take it. "Mrs. Whittaker, what a useful encounter this has been! I can scarcely find a way to thank you enough for your wisdom. You are a Solomon among women, and it is little wonder that your children admire you so. Imagine if you were my mother, Mrs. Whittaker—only imagine how stupid I would not be! My mother, you will be sorry to hear, has never had a sensible thought in her life. Worse still, she cakes her face so thickly with wax, paste, and powder that she has every appearance of being a dressmaker's dummy. Imagine my misfortune, then—to have been raised by an unschooled dressmaker's dummy, and not by the likes of you. Well, off I go, then!"

Off she skipped, while Beatrix gaped.

"What a ridiculous conformation of a person," Beatrix murmured, once Retta had taken her leave, and the house had returned to silence.

Daring a defense of her only friend, Alma replied, "Without a doubt she is ridiculous, Mother. But I believe she has a charitable heart."

"Her heart may or may not be charitable, Alma. None but God can judge such a thing. But her face, without a doubt, is absurd. She seems able to shape it into any expression whatsoever, except intelligence."

Retta returned to White Acre the very next day, greeting Beatrix Whittaker with sunny goodwill, as though the initial admonishment had never taken place. She even brought Beatrix a small posy of flowers—plucked from White Acre's own gardens, which was a rather daring play. Miraculously, Beatrix accepted the posy without a word. From that day forward, Retta Snow was permitted to remain a presence on the estate.

As far as Alma was concerned, the disarming of Beatrix Whittaker was Retta's most sterling accomplishment. It almost had the trace of wizardry about it. That it happened so quickly was even more remarkable. Somehow, in only one brief and daring encounter, Retta had managed to inveigle herself into the matriarch's good graces (or good *enough* graces) such that now she had an open warrant to visit whenever she pleased. How had she done it? Alma couldn't be certain, but she had theories. For one thing, Retta was difficult to stifle. What's more, Beatrix was getting older and frailer, and was less inclined these days to battle her objections to the death. Perhaps Alma's mother was not a match for the Retta Snows of the world anymore. But most of all, there was this: Alma's mother may have disliked nonsense, and she was decidedly a difficult woman to flatter, but Retta Snow could scarcely have done better than to have called Beatrix Whittaker "a Solomon among women."

Perhaps the girl was not so foolish as she appeared.

Thus, Retta remained. In fact, as the autumn of 1819 progressed, Alma frequently arrived at her study in the early mornings, ready to work on a botanical project, only to discover that Retta was already there—curled up in the old divan in the corner, looking at fashion illustrations from the latest copy of *Joy's Lady's Book*.

"Oh, hello dearest!" Retta would chirp, looking up brightly, as though they had a prearranged appointment.

As time went on, Alma was no longer startled by this. Retta did not make herself a bother. She never touched the scientific instruments (except the prisms, which she could not resist), and when Alma told her, "For heaven's sake, darling, you must hush now and let me calculate," Retta would hush and let Alma calculate. If anything, it became rather pleasant for Alma to have the silly, friendly company. It was like having a pretty bird in a cage in the corner, making occasional cooing noises, while Alma worked.

There were times when George Hawkes stopped by Alma's study, to discuss the final corrections to some scientific paper or another, and he always seemed taken aback to find Retta there. George never knew quite what to do with Retta Snow. George was such an intelligent and serious man, and Retta's silliness thoroughly unnerved him.

"And what are Alma and Mr. George Hawkes discussing today?" Retta asked one November day, when she was bored of her picture magazines.

"Hornworts," Alma responded.

"Oh, they sound horrid. Are they animals, Alma?"

"No, they are not animals, darling," she replied. "They are plants."

"Can one eat them?"

"Not unless one is a deer," Alma said, laughing. "And a hungry deer at that."

"How lovely to be a deer," Retta mused. "Unless one were a deer in the rain, which would be unfortunate and uncomfortable. Tell me about these hornworts, Mr. George Hawkes. But tell it in such a way that an empty-headed little person such as myself might be made to understand."

This was unfair, for George Hawkes only had one manner of speaking, which was academic and erudite, and not at all tailored for empty-headed little persons.

"Well, Miss Snow," he began awkwardly. "They are among our least sophisticated plants—"

"But that is an unkind thing to say, sir!"

"—and they are autotrophic."

"How proud their parents must be of them!"

"Well . . . er," George stuttered. By now, he was out of words.

Here, Alma stepped in, out of mercy for George. "Autotrophic, Retta, means that they can make their own food."

"So I could never be a hornwort, I suppose," Retta said, with a sad sigh.

"Not likely!" Alma said. "But you might like hornworts, if you came to know them better. They are quite pretty under the microscope."

Retta waved her hand dismissively. "Oh, I never know where to *look*, in the microscope!"

"Where to look?" Alma laughed in disbelief. "Retta—you look through the eyepiece!"

"But the eyepiece is so *confining*, and the view of tiny things is so *alarming*. It makes one feel seasick. Do you ever feel seasick, Mr. George Hawkes, when you look through the microscope?"

Pained by this question, George stared at the floor.

"Hush now, Retta," Alma said. "Mr. Hawkes and I need to concentrate."

"If you continue to hush me, Alma, I shall have to go find Prudence and bother her while she paints flowers on teacups and tries to convince me to be a more noble person."

"Go, then!" Alma said with good cheer.

"Honestly, you two," said Retta, "I simply do not understand why you must always work so much. But if it keeps you out of the arcades and the gin palaces, I suppose it does you no permanent harm . . ."

"Go!" Alma said, giving Retta a fond little push. Off Retta trotted on her hiddy-giddy way, leaving Alma smiling, and George Hawkes entirely baffled.

"I must confess I do not understand a word she speaks," George said, after Retta had vanished.

"Take comfort, Mr. Hawkes. She does not understand you, either."

"But why does she always hover about you, I wonder?" George mused. "Is she trying to improve herself by your company?"

Alma's face warmed in pleasure at this compliment—happy that George might believe her company to be an improving force—but she said merely, "We can never be entirely certain of Miss Snow's motives, Mr. Hawkes. Who knows? Perhaps she is trying to improve *me*."

———————————

By Christmas, Retta Snow had managed to become such good friends with Alma and Prudence that she would invite the Whittaker girls over to her family's estate for luncheons—thus taking Alma away from her botanical research, and taking Prudence away from whatever it was that Prudence did with her time.

Luncheons at Retta's home were ridiculous affairs, as befitted Retta's ridiculous nature. There would be a gallimaufry of ices and trifles and toasts, supervised (if one could call it supervision) by Retta's adorable yet incompetent English maid. Never once was a conversation of value or substance to be heard in this house, but Retta was always prepared for anything foolish, fun, or sportive. She even managed to get Alma and Prudence to play nonsense parlor games with her—games designed for much younger children, such as Post Office, Hunt the Keyhole, or, best of all, Dumb Orator. It was all terribly silly, but also terribly fun. The fact was, Alma and Prudence had never before *played*—not with each other, not alone, not with any other children. Till now, Alma had never particularly understood what play even was.

But play was the only thing Retta Snow ever did. Her favorite pastime was to read aloud the accident reports in the local newspapers for the entertainment of Alma and Prudence. It was indefensible, but amusing. Retta would put on scarves, hats, and foreign accents, and she would act out the most appalling scenes from these accidents: babies falling into fireplaces, workers decapitated by falling tree limbs, mothers of five thrown from carriages into ditches full of water (drowning upside-down, boots in the air, while their children looked on helplessly, screaming in horror).

"This should not be entertaining!" Prudence would protest, but Retta would not cease until they were all gasping with hilarity. There were occasions when Retta was so overtaken by her own laughter, in fact, that she could not stop herself. She would fall quite out of control of her own spirits, overly possessed by a riotous panic of revelry. Sometimes, alarmingly, she would even roll about on the floor. It would appear at these times as though Retta were being driven by, or *ridden* by, some external demonic agency. She would laugh until she started gasping in great, riotous heaves, and her face would darken with something that closely resembled fear. Just when Alma and Prudence were about to become quite worried for her, Retta would regain mastery of her senses. She would jump back up to her feet, wipe her damp forehead, and cry out, "Thank heavens we have an earth! Otherwise, where would we sit?"

Retta Snow was the oddest little miss in Philadelphia, but she played a special role in Alma's life, and in Prudence's too, it appeared. When the three of them were together, Alma very nearly felt like a normal girl, and she had never felt that way before. Laughing with her friend and her sister, she could pretend that she was any regular Philadelphia lass, and not Alma Whittaker of the White Acre estate—not a wealthy, preoccupied, tall, and unlovely young woman full of scholarship and languages, with several dozen academic publications to her name, and a Roman orgy of shocking erotic images floating through her mind. All that faded in Retta's presence, and Alma could be merely a girl, a conventional girl, eating a frosted tart and giggling at a buffoonish song.

Moreover, Retta was the only person in the world who ever made Prudence laugh, and this was a supernatural marvel, indeed. The transformation this laughter brought upon Prudence was extraordinary: it turned her from icy jewel to sweet schoolgirl. At such times, Alma nearly felt as though Prudence could be a regular Philadelphia lass, as well, and she would spontaneously embrace her sister, delighting in her company.

Unfortunately, though, this intimacy between Alma and Prudence existed only when Retta was present. The moment that Alma and Prudence left the Snow estate to walk back to White Acre together, the two sisters would return to silence once more. Alma always hoped they could learn how to sustain their warm rapport after leaving Retta's presence, but it was useless. Any attempt to refer, on the long walk home, to one of the jokes or jests of the afternoon would bring on nothing but woodenness, awkwardness, embarrassment.

During one such walk home in February of 1820, Alma—buoyed and heartened by the day's capers—took a risk. She dared to mention her affection for George Hawkes one more time. Specifically, Alma revealed to Prudence that George had once called her a brilliant microscopist, and that this had pleased her immensely. Alma confessed, "I would like to have a husband like George Hawkes someday—a good man, who encourages my efforts, and whom I admire."

Prudence said nothing. After a long silence, Alma pushed on. "My thoughts of Mr. Hawkes are nearly constant, Prudence. I sometimes even imagine . . . embracing him."

It was a bold assertion, but wasn't this what normal sisters did? All over Philadelphia, weren't regular girls talking to their sisters about the suitors they wished for? Weren't they disclosing the hopes of their hearts? Weren't they sketching dreams of their future husbands?

But Alma's attempt at intimacy did not work.

Prudence replied merely, "I see," and added nothing more to the discussion. They walked the rest of the way home to White Acre in their customary wordlessness. Alma returned to her study, to finish off the work that Retta had interrupted that morning, and Prudence simply vanished, as was her tendency, to tasks unknown.

Alma never again attempted such a confession with her sister. Whatever mysterious aperture Retta pried open between Alma and Prudence, that aperture closed itself up tightly again—as always—as soon as the sisters were once more alone. It was hopeless to remedy. Sometimes, though, Alma could not help but imagine what life might have been like if Retta had been their sister—the littlest girl, the third girl, indulged and foolish, who could disarm everyone, and whisk them all into a state of warmth and affection. If only Retta had been a Whittaker, Alma thought, instead of a Snow! Maybe everything would have been different. Maybe Alma and Prudence, under that familial arrangement, might have learned to be confidantes, intimates, friends . . . sisters!

It was a thought that filled Alma with terrible sadness, but there was nothing to be done for it. Things could only be what they were, as her mother had taught her many times.

As for things that could not be changed, they must stoically be endured.

Chapter Ten

Now it was late July of 1820.

The United States of America was in economic recession, the first period of decline in its short history, and Henry Whittaker, for once, was not enjoying a glittering year of commerce. It was not that he had fallen upon hard times—not by any means—but he was feeling an unaccustomed sense of pressure. The market in exotic tropical plants was saturated in Philadelphia, and Europeans had grown bored of American botanical exports. Worse, it seemed that every Quaker in town these days was opening his own medical dispensary and manufacturing his own pills, ointments, and unguents. No rival had yet surpassed the popularity of Garrick & Whittaker products, but soon enough they might.

Henry longed to have his wife's advice on all this, but Beatrix had not been well all year. She suffered spells of dizziness, and with the summer so hot and uncomfortable, her condition worsened. Her capacity was lagging, and her breath was always short. She never complained, and she tried to keep up with her work, but she was not healthy, and she refused to see a doctor. She did not believe in doctors, pharmacists, or medicines—an irony, given the family trade.

Henry's health was not so capital, either. He was sixty years old now. His bouts of the old tropical maladies lasted longer these days. Dinner gatherings had become difficult to plan, as one could never be certain if Henry and Beatrix would be in the proper condition to receive guests. This made Henry angry and bored, and his anger made everything more difficult at White Acre. His temperamental outbursts were increasingly vitriolic. *Somebody must pay! That bastard's son is finished! I will see him destroyed!* The maids ducked around corners and hid whenever they saw him coming.

There was bad news from Europe, too. Henry's international agent and emissary, Dick Yancey—the tall Yorkshireman who frightened Alma so much as a child—had recently arrived at White Acre with a most disturbing piece of intelligence: a pair of chemists in Paris had recently managed to isolate a substance they were calling "quinine," found in the bark of the cinchona tree. They were claiming that this compound was the mysterious ingredient in Jesuit's bark that was so effective at treating malaria. With this knowledge in hand, French chemists might soon be able to manufacture a better product from the bark—a more lightly powdered, more potent, more efficient product. They could easily undermine Henry's dominance of the fever trade forever.

Henry was berating himself (and berating Dick Yancey a bit, too) that they had not seen this coming. "We should have discovered this ourselves!" Henry said. But chemistry was not Henry's field. He was an unrivaled arborist, a ruthless merchant, and a brilliant innovator, but try as he might, he could not stay abreast of every new bit of scientific progress in the world. Knowledge was advancing too quickly for him. Another Frenchman had recently patented a mathematical calculating machine called an *arithometer*, which could perform long division on its own. A Danish physicist had just announced that a relationship existed between electricity and magnetism, and Henry didn't even understand what the man was talking about.

In short, there were too many new inventions these days, and too many new ideas, all so complex and far-flung. One could no longer be an expert in generalities, making a handsome pudding of profit in all sorts of fields. It was enough to make Henry Whittaker feel old.

But things were not all bad, either. Dick Yancey brought Henry one stunning piece of good news during this visit: Sir Joseph Banks was dead.

That daunting figure, who had once been the handsomest man in Europe, who had been the darling of kings, who had circled the globe, who had slept with heathen queens on open beaches, who had introduced thousands of new botanical species to England, and who had sent young Henry out into the world to become *Henry Whittaker*—that very man was dead.

Dead and rotting in a crypt somewhere in Heston.

Alma, who was sitting in her father's study copying letters when Dick Yancey arrived and delivered this news, gasped in shock, and said, "May God rest him."

"May God curse him," Henry corrected. "He tried to ruin me, but I beat him."

Without a doubt, Henry did seem to have beaten Sir Joseph Banks. At the least, he had matched him. Despite Banks's wounding humiliations so many years earlier, Henry had prospered beyond all imagination. He had not merely been victorious in the cinchona trade, he maintained business interests in every corner of the world. He had become a name. Nearly all his neighbors owed him money. Senators, ship owners, and merchants of every sort sought his blessing, and longed for his patronage.

Over the past three decades, Henry had created greenhouses in West Philadelphia that rivaled anything to be seen at Kew. He'd coaxed orchid varieties to bloom at White Acre that Banks had never found success with along the Thames. When Henry first heard that Banks had acquired a four-hundred-pound tortoise for the menagerie at Kew, he promptly ordered a *pair* of them for White Acre, secured in the Galapagos and personally delivered by the tireless Dick Yancey. Henry had even managed to bring the great water lilies of the Amazon to White Acre—water lilies so big and strong they could support a standing child—while Banks, at the time of his death, had never even *seen* the great water lilies.

What's more, Henry managed to live his life as richly as Banks ever did. He had conjured for himself a far larger and grander estate in America than anything Banks ever inhabited in England. His mansion shone on the hill like a colossal signal fire, casting its impressive light over the entire city of Philadelphia.

Henry had even dressed like Sir Joseph Banks for many years now. He had never forgotten how dazzling that clothing had appeared to him as a boy, and he had made a point—over the course of his life as a rich man—to both imitate and surpass Banks's wardrobe. As a result, by 1820, Henry was still wearing a style of clothing that was much out of date. When every other man in America had long ago turned to simple trousers, Henry still wore silk stockings and breeches, elaborate white wigs with long queues, gleaming silver shoe buckles, deep-cuffed coats, blouses with broad ruffles, and brocaded vests in vivid shades of lavender and emerald.

Dressed in this lordly yet antique manner, Henry looked positively quaint as he strode about Philadelphia in his colorful Georgian finery. He had been accused of looking like a waxwork exhibit from Peale's Arcade, but he did not mind. This was precisely how he wanted to look—exactly as Sir Joseph Banks had first appeared to *him* in the offices of Kew, in 1776, when Henry the thief (thin, hungry, and ambitious) had been summoned before Banks the explorer (handsome, elegant, and sumptuous).

But now Banks was dead. He was a dead baronet, to be sure, but he was still dead. Whereas Henry Whittaker—the poor-born, well-dressed emperor of American botany—was alive and prosperous. Yes, his leg ached, and his wife was ill, and the French were catching up to him in the malaria business, and the American banks were failing all around him, and he had a closetful of aging wigs, and he had never borne a son—but, by God, Henry Whittaker had defeated Sir Joseph Banks at last.

He instructed Alma to go down to the wine cellar, to procure him the finest available bottle of rum, for celebratory purposes.

"Make it two bottles," he said, in afterthought.

"Perhaps you ought not drink overly much this evening," Alma warned, carefully. He had only recently recovered from a fever, and she did not like the look on her father's face. It was a look of frightful emotional distortion.

"We shall drink as much as we wish tonight, my old friend," said Henry to Dick Yancey, as though Alma had not spoken at all.

"*More* than we wish," said Yancey, giving Alma a warning look that chilled her. Lord, she did not like this man, though her father much admired him. Dick Yancey, Alma's father had told her once in a tone of real pride, was a useful fellow to have around in the settling of arguments, as he settled them not with words, but with knives. The two men had met on the docks of Sulawesi in 1788, when Henry had watched Yancey beat a pair of British naval officers into politeness without speaking a single word. Henry had immediately hired him as his agent and enforcer, and the two men had been plundering the world together ever since.

Alma had always been terrified of Dick Yancey. Everybody was. Even

Henry called Dick "a trained crocodile," and had once said, "It's difficult to say which is more dangerous—a trained crocodile or a wild one. One way or another, I would not leave my hand resting in his mouth for long, God bless him."

Even as a child, Alma innately comprehended that there were two types of silent men in the world: one type was meek and deferential; the other type was Dick Yancey. His eyes were a pair of slowly circling sharks, and as he stared at Alma now, those eyes were clearly saying: "Bring the rum."

So Alma went down to the cellar and obediently brought up the rum—two full bottles of it, one for each man. Then she went out to her carriage house, to disappear into her work and escape the drunkenness in store. Long after midnight, she fell asleep on her divan, uncomfortable as it was, rather than return to the house. She awoke at dawn and walked across the Grecian garden to take her breakfast in the big house. As she approached the house, though, she could hear that her father and Dick Yancey were still awake. They were singing sailors' songs at top volume. Henry may not have been to sea in three decades, but he still knew all the songs.

Alma stopped at the entrance, leaned against the door, and listened. Her father's voice, echoing through the mansion in the gray morning light, sounded miserable and lurid and exhausted. It sounded like a haunting from a distant ocean.

Not two weeks later, on the morning of August 10, 1820, Beatrix Whittaker fell down the great staircase at White Acre.

She had woken early that morning, and must have been feeling well enough that she thought she could do some work in the gardens. She had put on her old leather gardening slippers, gathered her hair into her stiff Dutch cap, and headed down the stairs to go to work. But the steps of the staircase had been waxed the day before, and the soles of Beatrix's leather slippers were too slick. She toppled forward.

Alma was in her study in the carriage house already, hard at work editing a paper for *Botanica Americana* on the carnivorous vestibules of the bladderwort, when she saw Hanneke de Groot running across the Grecian garden toward her. Alma's first thought was how comic it was to see the old housekeeper running—skirts flapping and arms pumping, her face red and strained. It was like watching a giant barrel of ale, dressed in a gown, bounce and roll across the yard. She nearly laughed aloud. In the very next moment, however, Alma sobered. Hanneke was obviously alarmed, and this was not a woman who was generally subject to alarm. Something dreadful must have occurred.

Alma thought: *My father is dead.*

She put her hand to her heart. *Please, no. Please, not my father.*

Now Hanneke was at her door, wide-eyed and wild, panting for breath. The housekeeper choked, swallowed, and blurted it out: "*Je moeder is dood.*"

Your mother is dead.

The servants had carried Beatrix back to her bedroom and laid her across the bed. Alma was almost afraid to enter; she had rarely been allowed in her mother's bedroom. She could see that her mother's face had turned gray. There was a contusion rising on her forehead, and her lips were split and bloodied. The skin was cold. Servants surrounded the bed. One of the maids was holding a mirror under Beatrix's nose, looking for any signs of breath.

"Where is my father?" Alma asked.

"Still sleeping," said a maid.

"Don't wake him," Alma commanded. "Hanneke, loosen her stays."

Beatrix had always worn her clothing tight across the bodice—respectably, firmly, suffocatingly tight. They turned the body to its side, and Hanneke released the lacing. Still, Beatrix did not breathe.

Alma turned to one of the younger servants—a boy who looked as though he could run quickly.

"Bring me *sal volatile*," she said.

He stared at her blankly.

Alma realized that, in her haste and agitation, she had just used Latin with this child. She corrected herself. "Bring me ammonium carbonate."

Again, the blank look. Alma spun and glanced at everyone else in the room. All she saw were confused faces. Nobody knew what she was talking about. She wasn't using the right words. She searched her mind. She tried again.

"Bring me spirit of hartshorn," she said.

But, no, that wasn't the familiar term, either—or would not be for these people. Hartshorn was an archaic usage, something only a scholar would know. She clenched shut her eyes and searched for the most recognizable possible name of what she wanted. What did ordinary people call it? Pliny the Elder had called it *hammoniacus sal.* Thirteenth-century alchemists used it all the time. But references to Pliny would be of no help in this situation, nor was thirteenth-century alchemy of much service to anyone in this room. Alma cursed her mind as a dustbin of dead languages and useless particulars. She was losing precious time here.

Finally, she remembered. She opened her eyes and barked out a command that actually worked: "Smelling salts!" she cried. "Go! Find them! Bring them to me!"

Quickly, the salts were produced. It took nearly less time to find them than it had taken Alma to *name* them.

Alma wafted the crystals under her mother's nose. With a wet, rattling gasp, Beatrix took a breath. The circle of maids and servants emitted various bleats and gasps of shock, and one woman shouted, "Praise God!"

So Beatrix was not dead, but she remained senseless for the next week. Alma and Prudence took turns sitting with their mother, watching her throughout the days and the long nights. On the first night, Beatrix vomited in her sleep, and Alma cleaned her. She also wiped away the urine and the foul waste.

Alma had never before seen her mother's body—not beyond the face, the neck, the hands—but when she bathed the inanimate form on the bed, she could see that her mother's breasts were misshapen with several hard lumps in each. Tumors. Large ones. One of the tumors had ulcerated through the skin, and was leaking a dark fluid. The sight of this made Alma feel as though she herself might topple over. The word for it came to her mind in Greek: *Karkinos.* The crab. Cancer. Beatrix must have been diseased for quite a long while. She must have been living in torment for months, if not years. She had never complained. She had merely excused herself from the table, on the days when the suffering became unbearable, and dismissed it as common vertigo.

Hanneke de Groot barely slept at all that week, but brought compresses and broths at all hours. Hanneke wrapped fresh damp linens around Beatrix's head, tended to the ulcerated breast, carried in buttered bread for the girls, tried to get liquids past Beatrix's cracked lips. To her shame, Alma sometimes felt a sense of restlessness at her mother's side, but Hanneke patiently attended to all the duties of care. Beatrix and Hanneke had been together their whole lives. They had grown up side by side at the botanical gardens of Amsterdam. They had come together on the ship from Holland. They had both left their families behind to sail to Philadelphia, never again to see parents or siblings. At times, Hanneke wept over her mistress, and prayed in Dutch. Alma did not weep or pray. Nor did Prudence—not that anyone saw.

Henry stormed in and out of the bedroom at all hours, undone and disquieted. He was of no assistance. It was much easier when he was gone. He would sit with his wife for only a few moments before crying out, "Oh, I cannot bear it!" and leaving in a storm of curses. He grew disheveled, but Alma had little time for him. She was watching her mother wither away beneath the fine Flemish bedlinens. This was no longer the formidable Beatrix van Devender Whittaker; this was a most miserable and insentient object, ripe with stink and sad with decline. After five days, Beatrix was seized with a total suppression of urine. Her abdomen grew swollen, hard, and hot. She could not live long now.

A doctor arrived, sent by the pharmacist James Garrick, but Alma sent him away. It would do her mother no good to be bled and cupped now. Instead, Alma sent a message back to Mr. Garrick, requesting that he prepare for her a tincture of liquid opium that she could release into her mother's mouth by small drops every hour.

On the seventh night, Alma was asleep in her own bed when Prudence—who had been sitting with Beatrix—came and woke her with a touch to the shoulder.

"She's speaking," Prudence said.

Alma shook her head, trying to establish where she was. She blinked at Prudence's candle. Who was speaking? She had been dreaming of horses' hooves and winged animals. She shook her head again, placed herself, remembered.

"What is she saying?" Alma asked.

"She asked me to leave the room," Prudence said without emotion. "She asked for you."

Alma drew a shawl around her shoulders.

"You sleep now," she told Prudence, and took the candle into her mother's room.

Beatrix's eyes were open. One of the eyes was shot red with blood. That eye did not move. The other eye moved across Alma's face, hunting, tracking carefully.

"Mother," Alma said, and looked around for something to give Beatrix to drink. There was a cup of cold tea on the bedside table, a remnant of Prudence's recent vigil. Beatrix would not want blasted English tea, not even on her deathbed. Still, it was all there was to drink. Alma held the cup to her mother's dry lips. Beatrix sipped and then, sure enough, frowned.

"I'll bring you coffee," Alma apologized.

Beatrix shook her head, only very slightly.

"What can I bring you?" Alma asked.

There was no response.

"Do you want Hanneke?"

Beatrix did not seem to hear, so Alma repeated the question, this time in Dutch.

"*Zal ik Hanneke roepen?*"

Beatrix shut her eyes.

"*Zal ik Henry roepen?*"

There was no response.

Alma took her mother's hand, which was cold and small. They had never before held hands. She waited. Beatrix did not open her eyes. Alma had nearly dozed off when her mother spoke, and in English.

"Alma."

"Yes, Mother."

"Never leave."

"I won't leave you."

But Beatrix shook her head. This is not what she had meant. Once more, she closed her eyes. Again, Alma waited, overcome with exhaustion in this dark room ripe with death. It was a long while before Beatrix found the strength to make her full statement.

"Never leave your father," she said.

What could Alma say? What does one promise a woman on her deathbed? Especially if that woman is one's mother? One promises anything.

"I will never leave him," Alma said.

Beatrix searched Alma's face again with her one good eye, as though weighing the sincerity of this vow. Evidently satisfied, she closed her eyes once more.

Alma gave her mother another drop of opium. Beatrix's breathing was quite shallow now and her skin was cold. Alma was certain her mother had already spoken her last words, but nearly two hours later, when Alma had fallen asleep in the chair, she heard a gurgling cough, and woke with a start. She thought Beatrix was choking, but she was only trying to speak again. Once again, Alma wet Beatrix's lips with the hated tea.

Beatrix said, "My head spins."

Alma said, "Let me fetch Hanneke for you."

Astonishingly, Beatrix smiled. "No," she said. "*Het is fijn.*"

It is pleasant.

Then Beatrix Whittaker closed her eyes, and—as though by her own decision—she died.

The next morning, Alma, Prudence, and Hanneke worked together to clean and dress the body, wrap it in the shroud, and prepare it for burial. It was silent, sad work.

They did not lay out the body in the parlor for viewing, despite local custom. Beatrix would not have wished to be viewed, and Henry did not want to see his wife's corpse. He could not bear it, he said. Moreover, in weather this hot a swift burial was the wisest and most hygienic course of action. Beatrix's body had been moldering even before she'd died, and now they all feared a violent putrefaction. Hanneke dispatched one of White Acre's carpenters to build a quick and simple coffin. The three women tucked sachets of lavender all throughout the winding-sheets in order to retard the smell, and as soon as the coffin was built, Beatrix's body was loaded into a wagon and taken to the church, to be stored in the cool basement until the funeral. Alma, Prudence, and Hanneke wound black crepe mourning bands around their upper arms. They were to wear these bands for the next six months. The tightness of the material around her arm made Alma feel like a girded tree.

On the afternoon of the funeral, they walked behind the wagon, following the coffin to the Swedish Lutheran graveyard. The burial was brief, simple, efficient, and respectable. Fewer than a dozen people attended. James Garrick, the pharmacist, was there. He coughed terribly during the entire ceremony. His lungs were ruined, Alma knew, from years of working with the powdered jalap that had made him rich. Dick Yancey was there, his bald pate gleaming in the sun like a weapon. George Hawkes was there, and Alma wished she could have folded herself into his arms. To Alma's surprise, her waxen erstwhile tutor Arthur Dixon was there, too. She could not imagine how Mr. Dixon had even heard about Beatrix's death, nor did she realize he had ever been fond of his old employer, but she was touched that he had come, and she told him so. Retta Snow came, too. Retta stood between Alma and Prudence, holding a hand of each, and she remained uncharacteristically silent. In fact, Retta was nearly as stoic as a Whittaker that day, to her credit.

There were no tears from anyone, nor would Beatrix have wanted any. From birth to death, Beatrix had always taught that one must exude credibility, forbearance, and restraint. It would have been a pity now, after this woman's lifetime of respectability, for things to have gone mawkish at the last moment. Nor, after the funeral, would there be any gathering at White Acre, to drink lemonade and share in remembrances and comfort. Beatrix would not have wished for any of that. Alma knew that her mother had always admired the instructions that Linnaeus—the father of botanical taxonomy—had issued to his own family about his funeral arrangements: "Entertain nobody, and accept no condolences."

The coffin was lowered into the fresh clay grave. The Lutheran minister spoke. Liturgy, litany, the Apostles' Creed—it went swiftly by. There was no eulogy, for that was not the Lutheran way, but there was a sermon, familiar and grim. Alma tried to listen, but the minister droned on until she felt stupefied, and only bits of the sermon rose to her ears. Sin is innate, she heard. Grace is a mystery of God's bequeathing. Grace can be neither earned nor squandered, nor added to, nor diminished. Grace is rare. None shall know who has it. We are baptized unto death. We praise you.

The hot summer sun, setting low, burned cruelly in Alma's face. Everyone squinted in discomfort. Henry Whittaker was benumbed and bewildered. His only request had been this: once the coffin was in the hole, he'd asked that they cover the lid with straw. He wanted to make sure that, when the first shovelfuls of dirt hit his wife's casket, the awful sound would be muffled.

Chapter Eleven

Alma Whittaker, aged twenty, was now the mistress of the White Acre estate.

She slipped into her mother's old role as though she had trained a lifetime for it—which, in a sense, she had done.

The day after Beatrix's funeral, Alma entered her father's study and started sifting through piles of accumulated paperwork and letters, resolved to immediately attend to all the tasks that Beatrix had traditionally executed. To her growing distress, Alma realized that a great deal of important work at White Acre—accounting, invoicing, correspondence—had been left untended in the past few months, even the past year, as Beatrix's health had deteriorated. Alma cursed herself for not having noticed this earlier. Henry's desk had always been a shamble of vital papers all mixed in with the jumble of uselessness, but Alma had not grasped how serious the disorder had grown until she investigated the study more deeply.

Here is what she found: stacks of important papers had been spilling off Henry's desk over the past few months and cumulating on the floor into something like geological strata. Horrifyingly, there were more boxes of unsorted papers hidden in deep closets. In her initial excavations, Alma found bills that had not been paid since the previous May, payrolls that had never been reckoned, and letters—such a thick sludge of letters!—from builders awaiting orders, from business partners with urgent questions, from collectors overseas, from lawyers, from the Patent Office, from botanical gardens across the world, and from various and sundry museum directors. If Alma had known earlier that so much correspondence was being neglected, she would have tended to it months ago. Now it was nearly at the level of crisis. At this very moment, a ship full of Whittaker botanicals was moored in the Philadelphia harbor, collecting steep docking fees, unable to unload its cargo because the captain had not been recompensed.

What was worse, mixed in with all the urgent work were absurd little details, time-wasters, mounds of absolute twaddle. There was a nearly illegible note from a woman in West Philadelphia, saying that her baby had just swallowed a pin and the mother was afraid the child might die—could somebody at White Acre tell her what to do? The widow of a naturalist who had worked for Henry fifteen years earlier in Antigua was claiming destitution and requesting a pension. There was an outdated note from White Acre's head landscaper about a gardener who needed to be fired immediately, for having entertained several young women in his room after hours with a party of watermelon and rum.

Was this the sort of thing her mother had always taken care of, in addition to everything else? Swallowed pins? Disconsolate widows? Watermelon and rum?

Alma saw no choice but to clean out this Augean stable, one piece of paper at a time. She cajoled her father to sit beside her and help her to understand what various items might mean, and whether this or that suit of law needed to be taken seriously, or why the price of sarsaparilla had climbed so steeply since last year. Neither of them could completely translate Beatrix's coded, vaguely Italian, triple-accountancy system, but Alma was the better mathematician, so she puzzled out the ledgers as best she could, while simultaneously creating a simpler method for future use. Alma deputized Prudence to pen page after page of polite correspondence, as Henry—with much loud complaining—dictated the essence of the most vital information.

Did Alma mourn her mother? It was difficult to know. She did not exactly have time for it. She was buried in a swampland of work and frustration, and this sensation was not entirely distinguishable from sorrow itself. She was weary and overwhelmed. There were times when she looked up from her labors to ask her mother a question—looking over to the chair where Beatrix had always sat—and was startled by the nothingness to be found there. It was like looking at a spot on a wall where a clock had hung for years, and seeing only an empty space. She could not train herself not to look; the emptiness surprised her every time.

But Alma was also angry with her mother. As she paged through months' worth of confusing documents, she wondered why Beatrix—knowing herself to be so ill—had not enlisted somebody to help over a year ago. Why had she put documents into boxes and stored them in closets, rather than seeking assistance? Why had Beatrix never taught anyone else her complicated accounting system, or, if nothing else, told someone where to find filed documentation from previous years?

She remembered her mother's having warned her, years ago, "Never put away your labors while the sun is high, Alma, with the hopes of finding more hours to work tomorrow—for you shall never have any more extra time tomorrow than you had today, and once you have fallen behindhand in your responsibilities, you will never catch up."

So why had Beatrix allowed things to fall so behindhand?

Perhaps she had not believed she was dying.

Perhaps her mind had been so addled with pain that she had lost track of the world.

Or perhaps—Alma thought darkly—Beatrix had wanted to punish the living with all this work, long after she was dead.

As for Hanneke de Groot, Alma quickly came to understand that the woman was a saint. Alma had never before realized how much work Hanneke did around the estate. Hanneke recruited, trained, maintained, and reprimanded a staff of dozens. She managed the food cellars and harvested the estate's vegetables as though leading a cavalry charge through fields and gardens. She commandeered her troops to polish the silver, and stir the gravy, and beat the carpets, and whitewash the walls, and put up the pork, and gravel the driveway, and render the lard, and cook the puddings. With her even temper and firm handle on discipline, Hanneke somehow managed the jealousies, laziness, and stupidity of so very many people, and she was clearly the only reason the estate had carried on at all once Beatrix had fallen ill.

One morning, shortly after her mother's death, Alma had caught Hanneke disciplining three scullery maids, whom she had backed up against the wall as though she intended to shoot them.

"One good worker could replace all three of you," Hanneke barked, "and trust me—when I *find* one good worker, all three of you will be dismissed! In the meanwhile, get back to your tasks, and stop shaming yourselves with such carelessness."

"I cannot thank you enough for your service," Alma told Hanneke, once the girls were gone. "I hope to someday be able to assist you more with the management of the household, but for now I will still need you to do everything, as I try to make sense of my father's business affairs."

"I have always done everything," Hanneke replied, uncomplainingly.

"Indeed, it seems you have, Hanneke. It seems you do the work of ten men."

"Your mother did the work of twenty men, Alma—and had to look after your father, too."

As Hanneke turned to leave, Alma reached for the housekeeper's arm.

"Hanneke," she asked, exhausted and frowning, "what does one do for a baby who has just swallowed a pin?"

Without hesitating, or asking why such a question should suddenly arise, Hanneke replied, "Prescribe raw egg white to the child and patience to the mother. Give the mother assurance that the pin will probably slide out the child's sewer hole in a few days, with no ill effects. If it's an older child, you can make it jump a rope, to encourage the process along."

"Does the child ever die from it?" Alma asked.

Hanneke shrugged. "Sometimes. But if you prescribe these steps and speak in a tone of certainty, the mother will not feel so helpless."

"Thank you," Alma said.

As for Retta Snow, the girl came over to White Acre several times during the first weeks after Beatrix's death, but Alma and Prudence—absorbed in catching up with the work of the family business—could find no time for her.

"I can help you!" Retta said, but everyone knew that she could not.

"Then I shall wait for you every day in your study in the carriage house," Retta finally promised Alma, when she had been turned away too many times in a row. "When you are finished with your labors, you will come and see me. I will talk to you while you study impossible things. I will tell you extraordinary stories, and you will laugh and marvel. For I have news of the most shocking variety!"

Alma could not imagine ever again finding the time to laugh or marvel with Retta, much less to continue her own projects. For quite some time after her mother's death, she forgot that she had ever had her own work at all. She was a mere quill-driver now, a scrivener, a slave to her father's desk, and the administrator of a dauntingly large household—wading through a jungle of neglected tasks. For two months, she barely stepped outside her father's study at all. As best she was able, she refused to let her father leave, either.

"I need your help on all these matters," Alma pleaded with Henry, "or we shall never catch up again."

Then, late one October afternoon, right in the middle of all the sorting, calculating, and solving, Henry simply stood up and walked out of his own study, leaving Alma and Prudence with their hands full of papers.

"Where are you going?" Alma asked.

"To get drunk," he said, in a voice fierce and dark. "And by God, how I dread it."

"Father—" she protested.

"Finish it yourself," he commanded.

And so she did.

With Prudence's help, with Hanneke's help, but mostly on her own accord, Alma polished that study to a state of trim perfection. She put each one of her father's affairs in order—solving one onerous problem at a time—until every edict, injunction, mandate, and dictate had been addressed, until every letter was answered, every chit was paid, every investor was assured, every vendor cajoled, and every vendetta settled.

It was the middle of January before she finished, and when she did, she understood the workings of the Whittaker Company from top to bottom. She had been in mourning for five months. She had entirely missed the autumn—seeing it neither arrive nor leave. She stood up from her father's desk and unwound her black crepe armband. She laid the thing across in the last bin of refuse and discards, to be burned with the rest of it. That was enough.

Alma walked to the binding closet just off the library, locked herself in, and pleasured herself quickly. She had not touched her quim in months, and the unfettering of this welcome old release made her want to weep. She had not wept in months, either. No, that was incorrect: she had not wept in years. She also realized that her twenty-first birthday had come and gone the previous week without notice—not even from Prudence, who could usually be counted upon for a small, thoughtful gift.

Well, what did she expect? She was older now. She was the mistress of the grandest estate in Philadelphia, and the head clerk, it now appeared, of one of the largest botanical importing concerns on the planet. The time for childish things had passed.

After Alma left the binding closet, she stripped down and took a bath—though it was not a Saturday—and went to sleep at five o'clock in the afternoon. She slept for thirteen hours. When she awoke, the house was silent. For the first moment in months, the house needed nothing from her. The silence sounded like music. She dressed slowly and enjoyed her tea and toast. Then she walked across her mother's old Grecian garden, glassed over now with ice, until she reached the carriage house. It was time for her to return, if only for a few hours, to her own work, which she had left in mid-sentence the day her mother had fallen down the stairs.

To her surprise, Alma saw a thin tendril of smoke uncurling from the chimney of the carriage house as she approached. When she reached her study, there—as promised—was Retta Snow, curled up on the divan under a thick wool blanket, sound asleep and waiting for her.

"Retta—" Alma touched her friend's arm. "What in the world are you doing here?"

Retta's large green eyes flew open. Clearly, in the first moment in which she awoke, the girl had no idea where she was, and she did not seem to recognize Alma. Something awful came over Retta's face in that instant. She looked feral, even dangerous, and Alma found herself jerking back in fear, as though recoiling from a cornered dog. Then Retta smiled and the effect passed. She was all sweetness again, and she resembled herself once more.

"My loyal friend," said Retta in a sleepy voice, reaching for Alma's hand. "Who loves you most? Who loves you best? Who thinks of you when others rest?"

Alma looked about the room and saw a small cache of empty biscuit tins and a puddle of clothing piled carelessly on the floor. "Why are you sleeping in my study, Retta?"

"Because things have grown impossibly dull at my own house. Things are rather dull here, too, of course, but at least there is the chance at times to see a bright face, if one is patient. Did you know that you have mice in your herbarium? Why do you not keep a pussycat in this room, to manage them? Have you ever seen a witch? I confess, I believe there was a witch in the carriage house last week. I could hear her laughing. Do you think we should tell your father? I can't imagine it's safe to keep a witch about the place. Or perhaps he would merely think I am mad. Though he seems to think so, anyway. Have you got any more tea? Aren't these cold mornings unutterably cruel? Do you not long terribly for summer? Where has your black armband gone?"

Alma sat down and pressed her friend's hand to her lips. It was good to hear utter nonsense again, after all the seriousness of the last months. "I never know which one of your questions to answer first, Retta."

"Start in the middle," Retta suggested, "and then work in both directions."

"What did the witch look like?" Alma asked.

"Ha! Now *you* are the one asking too many questions!" Retta leapt up from the divan and shook herself awake. "Are we working today?"

Alma smiled. "Yes, I believe we are working today—at last."

"And what are we studying, my dear best Alma?"

"We are studying *Utricularia clandestina*, my dear best Retta."

"A plant?"

"Most certainly."

"Oh, it sounds beautiful!"

"Do be assured that it isn't," Alma said. "But it is interesting. And what is Retta studying today?" Alma picked up the ladies' magazine lying on the floor by the divan and thumbed through its incomprehensible pages.

"I am studying the sorts of gowns in which a fashionable girl should wed," Retta said lightly.

"And are you choosing such a gown?" Alma replied, just as lightly.

"Most absolutely!"

"And what will you do with such a gown, my little bird?"

"Oh, I had a plan to wear it on my wedding day."

"An ingenious plan!" Alma said, and turned toward her laboratory bench to see if she could begin putting together her notes from five months earlier.

"But the sleeves are quite short in all these drawings, you see," Retta prattled on, "and I fear I shall be cold. I could wear a shawl, suggests my little maid, but then nobody would be able to enjoy the necklace Mother said I could wear. Also, I wish for a spray of roses, though they are out of season and some say it is inelegant to carry a spray of flowers, in any case."

Alma turned around to face her friend once more. "Retta," she said, this time in a more serious tone. "You aren't truly getting married, are you?"

"I do hope so!" Retta laughed. "I have been told that the only way one *should* get married is truly!"

"And whom do you intend to marry?"

"Mr. George Hawkes," said Retta. "That funny, serious man. It makes me so glad, Alma, that my husband-to-be is somebody you adore so much, which means that we can all be friends. He does admire you so, and you admire him, which must mean he is a good man. It is your affection for George, really, that makes me trust him. He asked for my hand shortly after your mother's death, but I didn't want to speak of it sooner, as you were suffering so much, you poor dear. I had no idea he was even fond of me, but Mother tells me that everyone is fond of me, bless their hearts, because they cannot help themselves."

Alma sat down on the floor. She had no other choice *but* to sit down.

Retta ran over to her friend, and sat down beside her. "Look at you! You are overcome on my behalf! You care about me so!" Retta put her arm around Alma's waist, just as she had done on the day they met, and embraced her closely. "I must confess that I am still a bit overcome myself. What would such a clever man want with such a silly bit of lint like me? My father was most surprised! He said, 'Loretta Marie Snow, I always figured you to be the sort of girl who would marry a handsome, stupid fellow who wore tall boots and hunted foxes for pleasure!' But look at me—instead I shall marry a scholar. Imagine if it eventually makes me clever, Alma, to be married to a man with such a premium mind. Though I must say that George is not nearly as patient as you are, about answering my questions. He says that the subject of botanical publishing is far too complex to explain, and it is true that I still cannot tell the difference between a lithograph and an engraving. Is that what it's called—a lithograph? So I may end up as stupid as ever! Nonetheless, we shall live right across the river, which will be most fun! Father has promised to build us a charming new house, right next to George's print shop. You must come see me every day! And we shall all three of us go to see plays at Old Drury together!"

Alma, still sitting on the floor, had no capacity for speech. She was only grateful that Retta's head was tucked against her chest as she chattered away, so the girl could not see her face.

George Hawkes was to marry Retta Snow?

But George was supposed to be Alma's husband. She had seen it in her mind so vividly for nearly five years now. She had conjured fantasies of him—his body!—when she was in the binding closet. But she had cherished more chaste thoughts of him, as well. She had imagined them working together, in close study. She always pictured herself leaving White Acre, when it came time to marry George. Together, they would live in a small room over his print shop, with its warm smells of ink and paper. She had envisaged them traveling to Boston together, or perhaps even beyond—as far away as the Alps, climbing over boulders to hunt for pasqueflowers and rock-jasmine. He would say to her, "What do you make of this specimen?" and she would say, "It is fine and rare."

He had always been so kind to her. He had once pressed her hand between his hands. They had looked through the same microscope eyepiece *so many times*—one after the other, then back again—trading on and off with the marvel of it.

What could George Hawkes possibly see in Retta Snow? By Alma's recollection, George had barely ever been able to *look* at Retta Snow without baffled embarrassment. Alma remembered how George had always glanced over to her in confusion whenever Retta spoke, as though seeking help, relief, or interpretation. If anything, these little glances between George and Alma *about* Retta had been one of their sweetest intimacies—or at least Alma had dreamed that they were.

But apparently Alma had dreamed many things.

Some part of her still hoped this was just one of Retta's strange games, or perhaps a deluded flight of the girl's imagination. Only a moment earlier, after all, Retta had claimed there were witches living in the carriage house, so anything could be possible. But, no. Alma knew Retta too well.

This was not Retta at play. This was Retta in earnest. This was Retta chattering on about the problem with sleeves and shawls in a February wedding. This was Retta quite seriously worrying over the necklace her mother planned to lend her, which was quite valuable, but not entirely to Retta's liking: *What if the chain is too long? What if it becomes tangled in the bodice?*

Alma stood suddenly and pulled Retta up from the floor. She could not bear it anymore. She could not sit still and listen to another word of this. Without a further plan of action, she embraced Retta. It was so much easier to embrace her than to look at her. It also made Retta stop talking. She held Retta in such a firm press that she heard the girl's breath intake sharply, with a surprised squeak. Just when she thought Retta might begin speaking again, Alma commanded, "Hush," and grasped her friend more securely.

Alma's arms were extraordinarily strong (she had a blacksmith's arms, just as her father did) and Retta was so tiny, with the rib cage of a baby rabbit. There were snakes that could kill this way, with an embrace that only grew tighter and tighter until the breath stopped completely. Alma squeezed tighter. Retta made another small squeaking noise. Alma grasped harder still—so hard that she lifted Retta right from the floor.

She remembered the day they all had met: Alma, Prudence, and Retta. *Fiddle, fork, and spoon.* Retta had said, "If we were boys, we would have to fight now." Well, Retta was no fighter. She would have lost such a battle. She would have lost badly. Alma compressed her arms even tighter around this tiny, useless, precious person. She clenched her eyes shut as hard as she could, but tears bled from the corners nonetheless. She could feel Retta going limp in her grip. It would be so easy to stop her from breathing. Stupid Retta. Cherished Retta, who—even now!—successfully resisted all efforts not to be loved.

Alma dropped her friend to the floor.

Retta landed with a gasp and very nearly bounced.

Alma forced herself to speak. "I congratulate you on your happiness," she said.

Retta sobbed once, and clutched at her bodice with trembling hands. She smiled, so foolish and trusting. "What a good little Alma you are!" Retta said. "And how much you love me!"

In a queer touch of almost masculine formality, Alma extended her hand for Retta to shake, managing to choke forth just one more sentence: "You are most deserving."

———————————————

"Did you *know*?" Alma demanded of Prudence not an hour later, finding her sister at her needlework in the drawing room.

Prudence set her work on her lap, folded her hands, and said nothing. Prudence had a habit of never committing to any conversation before she completely understood the circumstances. But Alma waited nonetheless, wanting to force her sister to speak, wanting to catch her at something. At what, though? Prudence's face had nothing to reveal, and if Alma thought Prudence Whittaker was fool enough to speak first under such hot circumstances, then she did not know Prudence Whittaker.

In the silence that followed, Alma felt her anger turn from blazing indignation to something more tragic and petulant, something spoiled and sad. "Did you know," Alma was finally forced to ask, "that Retta Snow is to marry George Hawkes?"

Prudence's expression did not change, but Alma saw a tiny white line appear for just a moment around her sister's lips, as though the mouth had compressed only the slightest bit. Then the line vanished, quickly as it had arrived. Alma might even have imagined it.

"No," Prudence replied.

"How could this have happened?" Alma asked. Prudence said nothing, so Alma kept speaking. "Retta tells me they have been betrothed since the week of our mother's death."

"I see," said Prudence, after a long pause.

"Did Retta ever know that I . . ." Here Alma hesitated and nearly started weeping. "Did Retta ever know that I had feelings for him?"

"How could I possibly answer that?" Prudence replied.

"Did she learn it from *you*?" Alma's voice was insistent and ragged. "Had you ever told her? You were the only one who could have told her that I loved George."

Now the white line around her sister's lips reappeared, for a slightly longer time. There was no mistaking it. This was anger.

"I would hope, Alma," said Prudence, "that you would better know my character after so many years. Would anybody who came to me for gossip

ever go home satisfied?"

"Did Retta ever come to you for gossip?"

"It matters little whether she did or did not, Alma. Have you ever known me to disclose someone's secrets?"

"*Stop answering me in riddles!*" Alma shouted. Then she lowered her voice: "Did you or did you not ever tell Retta Snow that I loved George Hawkes?"

Alma saw a shadow pass across the door, waver, and then vanish. All she caught was the glimpse of an apron. Somebody—a maid—was about to enter the drawing room, but had evidently changed her mind and ducked out instead. Why was there never any privacy in this house? Prudence had seen the shadow, too, and she did not like it. She stood up now and stepped forward to face Alma directly—indeed, almost threateningly. The sisters could not regard one another eye-to-eye, for their heights were so different, but Prudence somehow managed to stare down Alma, nonetheless, even from one foot below her.

"No," Prudence said. "I have told nothing to anyone, and never shall. What's more, your insinuations insult me, and are unfair to both Retta Snow and Mr. Hawkes, whose business—I should dearly hope—is their own. Worst of all, your inquiry degrades you. I am sorry for your disappointment, but we owe our friends our joy and best wishes at their good fortune."

Alma started to speak again, but Prudence cut her off. "You'd best regain mastery of yourself before you continue speaking, Alma," she warned, "or you shall regret whatever it is you are about to reveal."

Well, that was beyond debate. Alma already *did* regret what she had revealed. She wished that she had never begun this conversation. But it was too late for that. The next best thing would have been to end it right now. This would have been a marvelous opportunity for Alma to stop her mouth. Horribly, though, she could not control herself.

"I only wanted to know if Retta had betrayed me," Alma blurted forth.

"Did you?" Prudence asked evenly. "So is it your supposition that your friend and mine, Miss Retta Snow—the most guileless creature I have ever encountered—willfully stole George Hawkes from you? To what purpose, Alma? For her own sporting satisfaction? And while you are on this line of questioning, do you also believe that I betrayed you? Do you believe that I told Retta your secret, in order to make a mockery of you? Do you believe that I encouraged Retta to pursue Mr. Hawkes, as some sort of wicked game? Do you believe I have some wish to see you punished?"

Sweet mercy, but Prudence could be relentless. Had she been a man, she would have made a formidable lawyer. Alma had never felt so dreadful or appeared so petty. She sat down on the nearest chair and stared at the floor. But Prudence followed Alma to the chair, stood over her, and kept speaking. "In the meanwhile, Alma, I have news of my own to report, which I shall tell you now, for it pertains to a similar concern. I had intended to wait until our family was out of mourning to address this subject, but I see that you have decided that our family is out of mourning already."

Here, Prudence touched Alma's upper right arm—bare of its black crepe band—and Alma nearly flinched.

"I, too, am to wed," Prudence announced, without a trace of triumph or delight. "Mr. Arthur Dixon has asked for my hand, and I have accepted."

Alma's head, for just one moment, emptied: Who in the name of God was Arthur Dixon? Mercifully, she did not speak this question aloud, for in the very next instant, of course, she remembered who he was, and felt absurd for having ever wondered. Arthur Dixon: their tutor. That unhappy and stooped man, who had somehow drummed French into Prudence's head, and who had joylessly helped Alma to master her Greek. That sad creature of damp sighs and sorrowful coughs. That little tedium of a figure, whose face Alma had not thought about since quite literally the last time she had seen it, which had been—when? Four years ago? When he'd finally left White Acre to become Professor of Ancient Languages at the University of Pennsylvania? No, Alma realized with a start, this was incorrect. She had seen Arthur Dixon only recently, at her mother's funeral. She had even spoken to him. He had offered up his kind condolences, and she had wondered what he was doing there.

Well, now she knew. He was there to court his former student, apparently, who also happened to be the most beautiful young woman in Philadelphia, and, it must be said, potentially one of the richest.

"When did this engagement occur?" Alma asked.

"Just before our mother died."

"*How?*"

"In the customary fashion," Prudence replied coolly.

"Did all this occur *at the same time*?" Alma demanded. The idea sickened her. "Did you become engaged to Mr. Dixon at the same time as Retta Snow became engaged to George Hawkes?"

"I have no knowledge of other people's affairs," Prudence said. But then she softened just a trace, and conceded, "But it would appear so—or, close to so. My engagement seems to have occurred a few days earlier. Though it matters not at all."

"Does Father know?"

"He will know soon enough. Arthur was waiting until our mourning had passed, to make his suit."

"But what on earth is Arthur Dixon going to say to Father, Prudence? The man is terrified of Father. I cannot conceive of it. How will Arthur manage to get through the conversation, without fainting dead away? And what will you do for the rest of your life—married to a *scholar*?"

Prudence drew herself up taller and smoothed her skirts. "I wonder if you realize, Alma, that the more traditional response to the announcement of an engagement is to wish the bride-to-be many years of health and happiness—particularly if the bride-to-be is your sister."

"Oh, Prudence, I apologize—" Alma began, ashamed of herself for the dozenth time that day.

"Think nothing of it," Prudence said, and turned toward the door. "I had not expected anything different."

———————————————

In all of our lives, there are days that we wish we could see expunged from the record of our very existence. Perhaps we long for that erasure because a particular day brought us such splintering sorrow that we can scarcely bear to think of it ever again. Or we might wish to blot out an episode forever because we behaved so poorly on that day—we were mortifyingly selfish, or foolish to an extraordinary degree. Or perhaps we injured another person and wish to disremember our guilt. Tragically, there are some days in a lifetime when all three of those things happen at once—when we are heartbroken and foolish and unforgivably injurious to others, all at the same time. For Alma, that day was January 10, 1821. She would have done anything in her power to strike that entire day from the chronicle of her life.

She could never forgive herself that her initial response to the happy news from both her dear friend and her poor sister had been a mean show of jealousy, thoughtlessness, and (in the case of Retta, at least) physical violence. What had Beatrix always taught them? *Nothing is so essential as dignity, girls, and time will reveal who has it.* As far as Alma was concerned, on January 10, 1821, she had revealed herself as a young woman devoid of dignity.

This would trouble her for many years to come. Alma tormented herself by imagining—again and again—all the different ways she might have behaved on that day, had she been in better control of her passions. In Alma's revised conversations with Retta, she embraced her friend with perfect tenderness at the mere mention of George Hawkes's name, and said in a steady voice, "How lucky a man he is to have won you!" In her revised conversations with Prudence, she never accused her sister of having betrayed her to Retta, and certainly never accused Retta of having stolen George Hawkes, and, when Prudence announced her own engagement to Arthur Dixon, Alma smiled warmly, took her sister's hand in fondness, and said, "I cannot imagine a more suitable gentleman for you!"

Unfortunately, though, one does not get second chances at such blundered episodes.

To be fair, by January 11, 1821—merely one day later!—Alma was a much better person. She pulled herself back into order as quickly as she could. She firmly committed herself to a spirit of graciousness about both engagements. She willed herself to play the role of a composed young woman who was genuinely pleased about other people's happiness. And when the two weddings arrived in the following month, separated from each other by only one week, she managed to be a pleasant and cheerful guest at both events. She was helpful to the brides and polite to their grooms. Nobody saw a fissure in her.

That said, Alma suffered.

She had lost George Hawkes. She had been left behind by her sister and by her only friend. Both Prudence and Retta, directly after their weddings, moved across the river into the center of Philadelphia. Fiddle, fork, and spoon were now finished. The only one who would remain at White Acre was Alma (who had long ago decided that she was *fork*).

Alma took some solace in the fact that nobody, aside from Prudence, knew about her past love for George Hawkes. There was nothing she could do to obliterate the passionate confessions she had so carelessly shared with Prudence over the years (and heavens, how she regretted them!), but at least Prudence was a sealed tomb, from whom no secrets would ever leak. George himself did not appear to realize that Alma had ever cared for him, nor that she might ever have suspected him of caring for *her*. He treated Alma no differently after his marriage than he had treated her before it. He had been friendly and professional in the past, and he was friendly and professional now. This was both consoling to Alma and also horribly disheartening. It was consoling because there would be no lingering discomfiture between them, no public sign of humiliation. It was disheartening because apparently there had never been anything at all between them—apart from whatever Alma had allowed herself to dream.

It was all terribly shameful, when one looked back on it. Sadly, one could not often help looking back on it.

Moreover, it now appeared that Alma would be staying at White Acre forever. Her father needed her. This was more abundantly clear every day. Henry had let Prudence go without a fight (indeed, he had blessed his adopted daughter with a quite generous dowry, and he had not been unkind toward Arthur Dixon, despite the fact that the man was a bore and a Presbyterian), but Henry would never let Alma go. Prudence had no value to Henry, but Alma was essential to him, especially now that Beatrix was gone.

Thus, Alma entirely replaced her mother. She was forced to assume the role, because nobody else could manage Henry. Alma wrote her father's letters, settled his accounts, listened to his grievances, minded his rum consumption, offered commentary on his plans, and soothed his indignations. Called into his study at all hours of day and night, Alma never knew exactly what her father might need from her, or how long the task would take. She might find him sitting at his desk, scratching away at a pile of gold coins with a sewing needle, trying to determine if the gold was counterfeit, and wanting Alma's opinion. He might simply be bored, wishing for Alma to bring him a cup of tea, or to play cribbage with him, or to remind him of the lyrics of an old song. On days when his body ached, or if he'd just had a tooth drawn or a blistering plaster applied to his chest, he summoned Alma to his study merely to tell her how much pain he was in. Or, for no reason at all, he might simply wish to inventory his complaints. ("Why must lamb taste like *ram* in this household?" he might demand. Or, "Why must the maids constantly move the carpets about, such that a man never knows where to put his *footing*? How many spills do they want me to suffer?")

On busier, healthier days, Henry might have genuine work for Alma. He might need Alma to write a threatening letter to a borrower who had fallen into arrears. ("Tell him that he must commence paying me back within the fortnight, or I will see to it that his children spend the remainder of their lives in a workhouse," Henry would dictate, while Alma would write, "Dear Sir: With greatest respect, I ask that you bestir yourself to attend this debt...") Or Henry might have received a collection of dried botanical specimens from overseas, which he would need Alma to reconstitute in water and diagram for him swiftly, before they all rotted away. Or he might need her to write a letter to some underling in Tasmania working himself halfway to death at the far reaches of the planet in order to gather exotic plants on behalf of the Whittaker Company.

"Tell that lazy noodle," Henry would say, tossing a writing tablet across the desk at his daughter, "that it does me no good when he informs me that such-and-such a specimen was found on the banks of some creek whose name he has probably invented himself, for all I know, because I cannot find it marked on any map in existence. Tell him that I need *useful* details. Tell him I don't care a row of pins for news of his failing health. My health is failing, too, but do I trouble him to listen to my sorrows? Tell him that I will warrant ten dollars per hundred of every specimen, but that I need him to be *exact* and I need the specimens to be *identifiable.* Tell him that he must stop *pasting* his dried samples to paper, for it destroys them, which he should bloody well know by now. Tell him that he must use *two* thermometers in every Wardian case—one tied to the glass itself and one embedded in the soil. Tell him that, before he ships off any further specimens, he must convince the sailors on board the ship that they must move the cases off the decks at night if frost is expected, because I will not pay him a *wooden tooth* for another shipment of black mold in a box, purporting to be a plant. And tell him that, no, I will not advance his salary again. Tell him that he is fortunate to still have his employment at all, given the fact he is doing his level best to bankrupt me. Tell him I will pay him again when he has earned it." ("Dear Sir," Alma would begin writing, "We here at the Whittaker Company offer our most sincere gratitude for all your recent labors, and our apologies for any discomforts you may have suffered...")

Nobody else could do this work. It had to be Alma. It was all just as Beatrix had instructed on her deathbed: Alma could not leave her father.

Had Beatrix suspected that Alma would never marry? Probably, Alma realized. Who would have her? Who would take this giant female creature, who stood above six feet tall, who was overly stuffed with learning, and who had hair in the color and shape of a rooster's comb? George Hawkes had been the best candidate—the only candidate, really—and now he was gone. Alma knew it would be hopeless ever to find a suitable husband, and she said as much one day to Hanneke de Groot, as the two women clipped boxwoods together in Beatrix's old Grecian garden.

"It will never be my turn, Hanneke," Alma said, out of the blue. She said it not pitifully, but with simple candor. There was something about speaking in Dutch (and Alma spoke only Dutch with Hanneke) that always elicited simple candor.

"Give the situation time," Hanneke said, knowing precisely what Alma was talking about. "A husband may still come looking for you."

"Loyal Hanneke," Alma said fondly, "let us be honest with ourselves. Who will ever put a ring on these fishwife's hands of mine? Who will ever kiss this encyclopedia of a head?"

"I will kiss it," said Hanneke, and pulled Alma down for a kiss on the brow. "There now, it is done. Stop complaining. You always behave as though you know everything, but you do not know all things. Your mother had this same fault. I have seen more of life than you have seen, by a long measure, and I tell you that you are not too old to marry—and you may still raise a family yet. There's no hurry for it, either. Look at Mrs. Kingston, on Locust Street. Fifty years old, she must be, and she just presented her husband with twins! A regular Abraham's wife, she is. Somebody should study her womb."

"I confess, Hanneke, that I do not believe Mrs. Kingston is quite fifty years old. Nor do I believe she wishes us to study her womb."

"I am merely saying that you do not know the future, child, quite as much as you believe you do. And there is something more I need to tell you, besides." Hanneke stopped working now, and her voice became serious. "Everyone has disappointments, child."

Alma loved the sound of the word *child* in Dutch. *Kindje*. This was the nickname that Hanneke had always called Alma when she was young and afraid and would climb into the housekeeper's bed in the middle of the night. *Kindje*. It sounded like warmth itself.

"I am aware that everyone has disappointments, Hanneke."

"I'm not certain you are. You are still young, so you think only of your own self. You do not notice the tribulations that occur all around you, to other people. Do not protest; it is true. I am not condemning you. I was as selfish as you, when I was your age. It is the custom of the young to be selfish. Now I am wiser. It's a pity we cannot put an old head on young shoulders, or you could be wise, too. But someday you will understand that nobody passes through this world without suffering—no matter what you may think of them and their supposed good fortune."

"What are we to do, then, with our suffering?" Alma asked.

This was not a question Alma would ever have posed to a minister, or a philosopher, or a poet, but she was curious—desperate, even—to hear an answer from Hanneke de Groot.

"Well, child, you may do whatever you like with *your* suffering," Hanneke said mildly. "It belongs to you. But I shall tell you what I do with mine. I grasp it by the small hairs, I cast it to the ground, and I grind it under the heel of my boot. I suggest you learn to do the same."

And so Alma did. She learned how to grind her disappointments under the heel of her boot. She had sturdy boots in her possession, too, and thus she was well outfitted for the task. She made an effort to turn her sorrows into a gritty powder that could be kicked into the ditch. She did this every day, sometimes even several times a day, and that is how she proceeded.

The months passed. Alma helped her father, she helped Hanneke, she worked in the greenhouses, and sometimes she arranged formal dinners at White Acre for Henry's diversion. Rarely did she see her old friend Retta. It was rarer still to see Prudence, but it did occur sometimes. From habit alone, Alma attended church services on Sundays, although she often, rather disgracefully, followed up her visits to church with visits to the binding closet, in order to evacuate her mind by touching her body. It was no longer joyful, the habit in the binding closet, but it made her feel somewhat unleashed.

She kept herself occupied, but she was not occupied *enough*. Within a year, she sensed an encroaching lethargy that frightened her severely. She longed for some sort of employment or enterprise that would provide vent for her considerable intellectual energies. At first, her father's commercial matters were helpful in this regard, as the work filled her days with daunting piles of responsibilities, but soon enough Alma's efficiency became her enemy. She carried out her tasks for the Whittaker Company too well and too quickly. Soon, having learned everything she needed to know about botanical importing and exporting, she was able to complete Henry's work for him in the matter of four or five hours a day. This was simply not enough hours. This left far too many remaining hours free, and free hours were dangerous. Free hours created too much opportunity for examining the disappointments she was meant to be grinding under her boot heel.

It was also around this time—the year after everyone married—that Alma came to a significant and even shocking realization: contrary to her childhood belief, she discovered that White Acre was not, in fact, a very large place. Quite the opposite, actually: it was a *tiny* place. Yes, the estate had grown to more than a thousand acres, with a mile of riverfront, with a sizable patch of virgin forest, with an immense house, with a spectacular library, with a vast network of stables, gardens, glasshouses, ponds, and creeks—but if this constituted the boundaries of one's entire world (as it did now for Alma), then it was not large at all. Any place that one could not leave was not large—particularly if one was a naturalist!

The problem was that Alma had already spent her life studying the nature of White Acre, and she knew the place too well. She knew every tree and rock and bird and lady's slipper. She knew every spider, every beetle, every ant. There was nothing new here for her to explore. Yes, she could have studied the novel tropical plants that arrived at her father's impressive greenhouses every week—but that is not discovery! Somebody else had already discovered those plants! And the task of a naturalist, as Alma understood it, was to discover. But there would be no such chance for Alma, for she had reached the limits of her botanical borders already. This realization frightened her and made her unable to sleep at night, which, in turn, frightened her more. She feared the restlessness that was creeping upon her. She could almost hear her mind pacing within her skull, caged and bothered, and she felt the weight of all the years she had yet to live, bearing down upon her with heavy menace.

A born taxonomist with nothing new to classify, Alma kept her uneasiness at bay by setting other things into order. She tidied and alphabetized her father's papers. She smartened up the library, discarding books of lesser value. She arranged the collection jars on her own shelves by height, and she created ever more refined systems of superfluous filing, which is how it came to pass that—early one morning in June of 1822—Alma Whittaker sat alone in her carriage house, poring over all the research articles she had ever written for George Hawkes. She was trying to decide whether to organize these old issues of *Botanica Americana* by subject or by chronology. It was an unnecessary task, but it would fill an hour.

At the bottom of this pile, though, Alma found her earliest article—the one she had written when she was only sixteen years old, about *Monotropa hypopitys*. She read it again. The writing was juvenile, but the science was sound, and her explanation of this shade-loving plant as a clever, bloodless parasite still felt valid. When she looked closely at her old illustrations of *Monotropa*, though, she almost had to laugh at their rudimentary crudeness. Her diagrams looked as though they had been sketched by a child, which, essentially, they had been. Not that she had become a glittering artist over the past years, but these early pictures were quite rough indeed. George had been kind to publish them at all. Her *Monotropa* was meant to be depicted growing out of a bed of moss, but in Alma's depiction, the plant looked to be growing out of a lumpy old mattress. Nobody would have been able to identify those dismal clumps at the bottom of the drawing as moss at all. She ought to have shown much more detail. As a good naturalist, she ought to have made an illustration that depicted quite precisely in which variety of moss *Monotropa hypopitys* grew.

On further consideration, though, Alma realized that she herself did not know in which variety of moss *Monotropa hypopitys* grew. On still further consideration, she realized that she was not entirely certain she could distinguish between different varieties of moss at all. How many were there, anyway? A few? A dozen? Several hundred? Shockingly, she did not know.

Then again, where would she have learned it? Who had ever written about moss? Or even about Bryophyta in general? There was no single authoritative book on the subject that she knew of. Nobody had made a career out of it. Who would have wanted to? Mosses were not orchids, not cedars of Lebanon. They were not big or beautiful or showy. Nor was moss something medicinal and lucrative, upon which a man like Henry Whittaker could make a fortune. (Although Alma did remember her father telling her that he had packed his precious cinchona seeds in dried moss, to preserve them during transport to Java.) Perhaps Gronovius had written something about mosses? Maybe. But the old Dutchman's work was nearly seventy years old by now—very much out of date and terribly incomplete. What was clear was that nobody paid much attention to the stuff. Alma had even chinked up the drafty old walls of her carriage house with wads of moss, as though it were common cotton batting.

She had overlooked it.

Alma stood up quickly, wrapped herself in a shawl, tucked a large magnifying glass into her pocket, and ran outside. It was a fresh morning, cool and somewhat overcast. The light was perfect. She did not have to go far. At a high spot along the riverbank, she knew there to be a large outcropping of damp limestone boulders, shaded by a screen of nearby trees. There, she remembered, she would find mosses, for that's where she had harvested the insulation for her study.

She had remembered correctly. Just at that border of rock and wood, Alma came to the first boulder in the outcropping. The stone was larger than a sleeping ox. As she had suspected and hoped, it was blanketed in moss. Alma knelt in the tall grass and brought her face as near as she could to the stone. And there, rising no more than an inch above the surface of the boulder, she saw a great and tiny forest. Nothing moved within this mossy world. She peered at it so closely that she could smell it—dank and rich and old. Gently, Alma pressed her hand into this tight little timberland. It compacted itself under her palm and then sprang back to form without complaint. There was something stirring about its response to her. The moss felt warm and spongy, several degrees warmer than the air around it, and far more damp than she had expected. It appeared to have its own weather.

Alma put the magnifying lens to her eye and looked again. Now the miniature forest below her gaze sprang into majestic detail. She felt her breath catch. This was a stupefying kingdom. This was the Amazon jungle as seen from the back of a harpy eagle. She rode her eye above the surprising landscape, following its paths in every direction. Here were rich, abundant valleys filled with tiny trees of braided mermaid hair and minuscule, tangled vines. Here were barely visible tributaries running through that jungle, and here was a miniature ocean in a depression in the center of the boulder, where all the water pooled.

Just across this ocean—which was half the size of Alma's shawl—she found another continent of moss altogether. On this new continent, everything was different. This corner of the boulder must receive more sunlight than the other, she surmised. Or slightly less rain? In any case, this was a new climate entirely. Here, the moss grew in mountain ranges the length of Alma's arms, in elegant, pine tree–shaped clusters of darker, more somber green. On another quadrant of the same boulder still, she found patches of infinitesimally small deserts, inhabited by some kind of sturdy, dry, flaking moss that had the appearance of cactus. Elsewhere, she found deep, diminutive fjords—so deep that, incredibly, even now in the month of June—the mosses within were still chilled by lingering traces of winter ice. But she also found warm estuaries, miniature cathedrals, and limestone caves the size of her thumb.

Then Alma lifted her face and saw what was before her—dozens more such boulders, more than she could count, each one similarly carpeted, each one subtly different. She felt herself growing breathless. *This was the entire world.* This was bigger than a world. This was the firmament of the universe, as seen through one of William Herschel's mighty telescopes. This was planetary and vast. These were ancient, unexplored galaxies, rolling forth in front of her—and it was all right here! She could still see her house from here. She could see the familiar old boats on the Schuylkill River. She could hear the distant voices of her father's orchardmen working in the peach grove. If Hanneke had rung the bell for mealtime at that very instant, she would have heard it.

Alma's world and the moss world had been knitted together this whole time, lying on top of each other, crawling over each other. But one of these worlds was loud and large and fast, where the other was quiet and tiny and slow—and only one of these worlds seemed immeasurable.

Alma sank her fingers into the shallow green fur and felt a surge of joyful anticipation. This could belong to her! No botanist before her had ever committed himself uniquely to the study of this undervalued phylum, but Alma could do it. She had the time for it, as well as the patience. She had the competence. She most certainly had the microscopes for it. She even had the publisher for it—because whatever else had occurred between them (or had not occurred between them), George Hawkes would always be happy to publish the findings of A. Whittaker, whatever she might turn up.

Recognizing all this, Alma's existence at once felt bigger and much,

much smaller—but a pleasant sort of smaller. The world had scaled itself down into endless inches of possibility. Her life could be lived in generous miniature. Best of all, Alma realized, she would never learn *everything* about mosses—for she could tell already that there was simply too much of the stuff in the world; they were everywhere, and they were profoundly varied. She would probably die of old age before she understood even half of what was occurring in this one single boulder field. *Well, huzzah to that!* It meant that Alma had work stretched ahead of her for the rest of her life. She need not be idle. She need not be unhappy. Perhaps she need not even be lonely.

She had a task.

She would learn mosses.

If Alma had been a Roman Catholic, she might have crossed herself in gratitude to God at this discovery—for the encounter did have the weightless, wonderful sensation of religious conversion. But Alma was not a woman of excessive religious passion. Even so, her heart rose in hope. Even so, the words she now spoke aloud sounded every bit like prayer:

"Praise be the labors that lie before me," she said. "Let us begin."

Ann. Roy. Bot. Garden, Calcutta, Vol. 8, PLATE 282.

Drawn by R. Pantling.

ÆRIDES ODORATUM, Lour.

Lith by K. D. Chandra.

Aerides odoratum, Lour

PART THREE

The Disturbance of Messages

Chapter Twelve

By 1848, Alma Whittaker was just beginning work on her new book, *The Complete Mosses of North America*. In the previous twenty-six years, she had published two others—*The Complete Mosses of Pennsylvania* and *The Complete Mosses of the Northeastern United States*—both of which were long, exhaustive, and handsomely produced by her old friend George Hawkes.

Alma's first two books had been warmly received within the botanical community. She had been flatteringly reviewed in a few of the more respectable journals, and was generally acknowledged as a wizard of bryophytic taxonomy. She had mastered the subject not only by studying the mosses of White Acre and its surroundings, but also by purchasing, trading, and cajoling samples from other botanical collectors all over the country and the world. These transactions had been easily enough executed. Alma already knew how to import botanicals, and moss was effortless to transport. All one had to do was dry it, box it up, and put it on a ship, and it would survive its journey without the slightest trouble. It took up little space and weighed virtually nothing, so ships' captains did not mind having it as extra cargo. It never rotted. Dried moss was so perfectly designed for transport, in fact, that people had already been using it as packing material for centuries. Indeed, early in her explorations, Alma had discovered that her father's dockside warehouses were already filled with several hundred varieties of mosses from across the planet, all tucked into neglected corners and crates, all ignored and unexamined—until Alma had gotten them under her microscope.

Through such explorations and imports, Alma had been able, over the past twenty-six years, to collect nearly eight thousand species of mosses, which she had preserved in a special herbarium, stored in the driest hayloft of the carriage house. Her body of knowledge in the field of global bryology, then, was almost excruciatingly dense, despite the fact that she herself had never traveled outside Pennsylvania. She kept up correspondence with botanists from Tierra del Fuego to Switzerland, and carefully watched the complex taxonomical debates that raged in the more obscure scientific journals as to whether this or that sprig of *Neckera* or *Pogonatum* constituted a new species, or was merely a modified variation of an already documented species. Sometimes she chimed in with her own opinions, with her own meticulously argued papers.

What's more, she now published under her own full name. She was no longer "A. Whittaker," but simply "Alma Whittaker." No initials were appended to the name—no evidence of degrees, no membership in distinguished gentlemanly scientific organizations. Nor was she even a "Mrs.," with the dignity that such a title affords a lady. By now, quite obviously, everyone knew she was a woman. It mattered little. Moss was not a competitive domain, and that is the reason, perhaps, that she had been allowed to enter the field with so little resistance. That, and her own dogged perseverance.

As Alma came to know the world of moss over the years, she better understood why nobody had properly studied it before: to the innocent eye, there appeared to be so little *to* study. Mosses were typically defined by what they lacked, not by what they were, and, indeed, they lacked much. Mosses bore no fruit. Mosses had no roots. Mosses could grow no more than a few inches tall, for they contained no internal cellular skeleton with which to support themselves. Mosses could not transport water within their bodies. Mosses did not even engage in sex. (Or at least they did not engage in sex in any obvious manner, unlike lilies or apple blossoms—or any other flower, in fact—with their overt displays of male and female organs.) Mosses kept their propagation a mystery to the naked human eye. For that reason, they were also known by the evocative name Cryptogamae—"hidden marriage."

In every way mosses could seem plain, dull, modest, even primitive. The simplest weed sprouting from the humblest city sidewalk appeared infinitely more sophisticated by comparison. But here is what few people understood, and what Alma came to learn: Moss is inconceivably strong. Moss eats stone; scarcely anything, in return, eats moss. Moss dines upon boulders, slowly but devastatingly, in a meal that lasts for centuries. Given enough time, a colony of moss can turn a cliff into gravel, and turn that gravel into topsoil. Under shelves of exposed limestone, moss colonies create dripping, living sponges that hold on tight and drink calciferous water straight from the stone. Over time, this mix of moss and mineral will itself turn into travertine marble. Within that hard, creamy-white marble surface, one will forever see veins of blue, green, and gray—the traces of the antediluvian moss settlements. St. Peter's Basilica itself was built from the stuff, both created by and stained with the bodies of ancient moss colonies.

Moss grows where nothing else can grow. It grows on bricks. It grows on tree bark and roofing slate. It grows in the Arctic Circle and in the balmiest tropics; it also grows on the fur of sloths, on the backs of snails, on decaying human bones. Moss, Alma learned, is the first sign of botanic life to reappear on land that has been burned or otherwise stripped down to barrenness. Moss has the temerity to begin luring the forest back to life. It is a resurrection engine. A single clump of mosses can lie dormant and dry for forty years at a stretch, and then vault back again into life with a mere soaking of water.

The only thing mosses need is time, and it was beginning to appear to Alma that the world had plenty of time to offer. Other scholars, she noticed, were starting to suggest the same notion. By the 1830s, Alma had already read Charles Lyell's *Principles of Geology*, which proposed that the planet was far older than anyone had yet realized—perhaps even millions of years old. She admired the more recent work of John Phillips, who by 1841 had presented a geological timeline even older than Lyell's estimates. Phillips believed that Earth had been through three epochs of natural history already (the Paleozoic, the Mesozoic, and the Cenozoic), and he had identified fossilized flora and fauna from each period—including fossilized mosses.

This notion of an unthinkably ancient world did not shock Alma, though it did shock a good many other people, as it directly contradicted the Bible's teachings. But Alma had her own peculiar theories about time, which were only bolstered by the fossil records in primordial ocean shale to which Lyell and Phillips had referred in their studies. Alma had come to believe, in fact, that there were several different sorts of time that operated simultaneously throughout the cosmos; as a diligent taxonomist, she had even gone so far as to differentiate and name them. Firstly, Alma had determined, there was such a thing as Human Time, which was a narrative of limited, mortal memory, based upon the flawed recollections of recorded history. Human Time was a short and horizontal mechanism. It stretched out straight and narrow, from the fairly recent past to the barely imaginable future. The most striking characteristic of Human Time, however, was that it moved with such amazing quickness. It was a snap of the finger across the universe. Most unfortunately for Alma, her mortal days—like everyone else's mortal days—fell within the purview of Human Time. Thus, she would not be here long, as she was most painfully aware. She was a mere blink of existence, as was everyone else.

At the other end of the spectrum, Alma postulated, there was Divine Time—an incomprehensible eternity in which galaxies grew, and where God dwelled. She knew nothing about Divine Time. Nobody did. In fact, she became easily irritated at people who claimed to have any comprehension whatsoever of Divine Time. She had no interest in studying Divine Time, because she believed there was no way for a human mind to comprehend it. It was time outside of time. So she left it alone. Nonetheless, she sensed that it existed, and she suspected that it hovered in some kind of massive, infinite stasis.

Closer to home, returning to earth, Alma also believed in something she called Geological Time—about which Charles Lyell and John Phillips had recently written so convincingly. Natural history fell into this category. Geological Time moved at a pace that felt *nearly* eternal, nearly divine. It moved at the pace of stone and mountains. Geological Time was in no hurry, and had been ticking along, some scholars were now suggesting, far longer than anyone had yet surmised.

But somewhere between Geological Time and Human Time, Alma posited, there was something else—Moss Time. By comparison to Geological Time, Moss Time was blindingly fast, for mosses could make progress in a thousand years that a stone could not dream of accomplishing in a million.

But relative to Human Time, Moss Time was achingly slow. To the unschooled human eye, moss did not even seem to move at all. But moss did move, and with extraordinary results. Nothing seemed to happen, but then, a decade or so later, all would be changed. It was merely that moss moved so slowly that most of humanity could not track it.

Alma could track it, though. She *was* tracking it. Long before 1848, she had already trained herself to observe her world, as much as possible, through the protracted clockwork of Moss Time. Alma had drilled tiny painted flags into the stones at the edges of her limestone outcropping to mark the progress of each individual moss colony, and she had now been watching this prolonged drama for twenty-six years. Which varieties of mosses would advance across the boulder, and which varieties would retreat? How long would it take? She observed these great, inaudible, slow-moving dominions of green as they expanded and contracted. She measured their progress in fingernail lengths and by half decades.

As Alma studied Moss Time, she tried not to worry about her own mortal life. She herself was trapped within the limits of Human Time, but there was nothing to be done for it. She would simply have to make the best of the short, mayfly-like existence she had been granted. She was already forty-eight years old. Forty-eight years was nothing to a moss colony, but it was a considerable accretion of years for a woman. Her cycles of menstruation had recently finished. Her hair was turning white. If she was fortunate, she thought, she might be permitted another twenty or thirty years in which to live and to study—forty more years at the most. That was the best she could wish for, and she wished for it every day. She had so much to learn, and not enough time in which to learn it.

If the mosses had known how soon Alma Whittaker would be gone, she often thought, they might pity her.

Meanwhile, life at White Acre carried on as ever. The Whittakers' botanical business had not expanded for years, but neither had it contracted; it had stabilized, one could say, into a steady machine of profitable returns. The greenhouses were still the best in America, and there were, just now, more than six thousand different varieties of plants on the property. There was a craze at the moment in America for ferns and palms ("pteridomania," the cheeky journalists called it) and Henry was reaping the benefit of that fad, growing and selling all manner of exotic fronds. There was much money to be made, too, on the mills and farms that Henry owned, and a good bit of his land had been profitably sold to the railroad companies in the past few years. He was interested in the burgeoning rubber trade, and had recently used his contacts in Brazil and Bolivia to begin investing in that uncertain new business.

So Henry Whittaker was still very much alive—perhaps miraculously so. His health, at the age of eighty-eight, had not much declined, which was rather impressive, considering how strenuously he had always lived and how vigorously he had always complained. His eyes gave him trouble, but with a magnifying lens and a good lamp, he could keep track of his paperwork. With a sturdy cane and a dry afternoon, he could still walk his property, dressed—as ever—like an eighteenth-century lord of the manor.

Dick Yancey—the trained crocodile—continued to manage the Whittaker Company's international interests ably, importing new and lucrative medicinal plants like simarouba, chondrodendron, and many others. James Garrick, Henry's old Quaker business partner, was now deceased, but James's son John had taken over the pharmacy, and Garrick & Whittaker medicinal brands still sold briskly across Philadelphia and beyond. Henry's dominance of the international quinine trade had been dealt a blow by French competition, but he was doing well closer to home. He had recently launched a new product, Garrick & Whittaker's Vigorous Pills—a concoction of Jesuit's bark, gum myrrh, sassafras oil, and distilled water, which professed to cure every human malady from tertian fevers and blistering rashes to feminine malaise. The product was a tremendous success. The pills were inexpensive to manufacture and brought in a steady profit, particularly in the summertime, when illness and fever broke out across the city, and every family, rich or poor, lived in fear of pestilence. Mothers would try the pills for anything afflicting their children.

The city had risen up around White Acre. Neighborhoods bustled now where once there had been only quiet farms. There were omnibuses, canals, railroad lines, paved highways, turnpikes, and steam packets. The population of the United States had doubled since the Whittakers had arrived in 1792, and its flag now boasted thirty stars. Trains running in every direction spit hot ash and cinders. Ministers and moralists feared that the vibrations and jostling of such fast travel would throw weak-minded women into sexual frenzies. Poets wrote odes to nature, even as nature vanished before their eyes. There were a dozen millionaires in Philadelphia, where once there had been only Henry Whittaker. All this was new. But there was still cholera and yellow fever and diphtheria and pneumonia and death. All that was old. Thus, the pharmaceutical business remained strong.

After Beatrix's death, Henry had not married again, nor shown any interest in marriage. He had no need for a wife; he had Alma. Alma was good to Henry, and sometimes, once a year or so, he even praised her for it. By now, she had learned how to best organize her own existence around her father's whims and demands. For the most part she enjoyed his company (she could never help her fondness for him) although she was keenly aware that every hour she spent in her father's presence was an hour lost for the study of mosses. She gave Henry her afternoons and evenings, but kept the mornings for her own work. He was ever more slow to rise as he got older, so this schedule functioned well. He sometimes wished for dinner guests, but far less frequently now. They might have company four times a year these days, instead of four times a week.

Henry remained capricious and difficult. Alma might find herself woken during the night by the apparently ageless Hanneke de Groot, telling her, "Your father wants you, child." At which point Alma would rise, wrap herself in a warm robe, and go to her father's study—where she would find Henry sleepless and irritated, shuffling through a lake of papers, demanding a dram of gin and a friendly round of backgammon at three o'clock in the morning. Alma would oblige him without complaint, knowing that Henry would only be more tired the next day, and thus afford her more hours for her own work.

"Have I ever told you about Ceylon?" he would ask, and she would let him talk himself to sleep. Sometimes she would fall asleep, too, to the sound of his old stories. Dawn would break on the old man and his white-haired daughter, both collapsed across their chairs, an unfinished game of backgammon between them. Alma would rise and tidy up the room. She would call for Hanneke and the butler to take her father back to his bed. Then she would bolt down her breakfast and walk either to her study in the carriage house or to her outpost of moss boulders, where she could turn her attention once more to her own labors.

This is how things had been for more than two and a half decades now. This is how she thought things would always be. It was a quiet but not unhappy life for Alma Whittaker.

Not unhappy in the least.

Others, however, had not been so fortunate.

Alma's old friend George Hawkes, for instance, had not found happiness in his marriage to Retta Snow. Nor was Retta in the least bit happy. Knowing this did not bring Alma any consolation or joy. Another woman might have rejoiced at this information, as a sort of dark revenge to her own broken heart, but Alma was not the sort of character who took satisfaction from somebody else's suffering. What's more, however much the marriage had once hurt her, Alma no longer loved George Hawkes. That fire had dimmed years ago. To have continued loving him under the reality of the circumstances would have been immeasurably foolish, and she had already played the fool too far. However, Alma did pity George. He was a good soul, and he had always been a good friend to her, but never had a man chosen a wife more poorly.

The staid botanical publisher had been at first merely baffled by his flighty and mercurial bride, but as time passed he had grown more openly irritated. George and Retta had occasionally dined at White Acre during the first years of their marriage, but Alma soon noticed that George would darken and grow tense whenever Retta spoke, as though he dreaded in advance whatever she was about to say. Eventually he stopped speaking at the dinner table altogether—almost in the hope, it seemed, that his wife would stop speaking, too. If that had been his wish, it hadn't worked. Retta, for her part, became increasingly nervous around her quiet husband, which made her speak only more frantically, which, in turn, only made her husband more determinedly silent.

After a few years of this, Retta had developed a most peculiar habit, which Alma found painful to watch. Retta would flutter her fingers helplessly in front of her mouth as she spoke, as though trying to catch the words as they came out of her—as though trying to *stop* the words, or even thrust them back in. Sometimes Retta was actually able to abort a sentence in the middle of some crazed thought or another, and then she would press her fingers against her lips to prevent more speech from spilling out. But this triumph was even more difficult to witness, for that last, strange, unfinished sentence would hang uncomfortably in the air, while Retta, stricken, stared at her soundless husband, her eyes wild with apology.

After enough of these upsetting performances, Mr. and Mrs. Hawkes stopped coming to dinner at all. Alma saw them only in their own home, when she came down to Arch Street to discuss publishing details with George.

Wifehood, as it turned out, did not suit Mrs. Retta Snow Hawkes. She simply was not crafted for it. Indeed, adulthood itself did not suit her. There were too many restrictions involved in the custom, and far too much seriousness expected. Retta was no longer a silly girl who could go driving about the city so freely in her small two-wheeled chaise. She was now the wife and helpmeet of one of Philadelphia's most respected publishers, and expected to comport herself as such. It was no longer dignified for Retta to be seen at the theater alone. Well, it never had been dignified, but in the past nobody had forbidden it. George forbade it. He did not enjoy the theater. George also required his wife to attend church services—several times a week, in fact—where Retta squirmed, childlike, in tedium. She could not dress so gaily after her marriage, either, nor break into song at the slightest whim. Or, rather, she could break into song, and sometimes did, but it did not look correct, and only infuriated her husband.

As for motherhood, Retta had not been able to manage that responsibility either. Within a year of marriage there had been a pregnancy in the Hawkes household, but that pregnancy had ended in a miscarriage. The next year, there had been another unsuccessful pregnancy, and the year after that, another. After losing her fifth child, Retta had taken to her room in a most violent mania of despair. Neighbors could hear her sobbing, it was reported, from several houses away. Poor George Hawkes had no idea what to do with this desperate woman, and he was quite unable to work for several days in a row on account of his wife's derangement. He had finally sent a message up to White Acre, begging for Alma to please come down to Arch Street and sit with her old friend, who was beyond all consolation.

But by the time Alma had arrived, Retta was already sleeping, with a thumb in her mouth and her beautiful hair splayed across the pillow like bare black branches against a pale winter sky. George explained that the pharmacy had sent over a bit of laudanum, and this had seemed to work.

"Pray, George, try not to make a habit of that," Alma had warned. "Retta has an unusually sensitive constitution, and too much laudanum may do her harm. I know she can be a bit nonsensical at times, and even tragic. But my understanding of Retta is that she requires only patience and love in order to find her own way back to happiness. Perhaps if you give her more time . . ."

"I apologize for having disturbed you," George said.

"Not at all," Alma said. "I am always at your disposal, and Retta's, too."

Alma wanted to say more—but what? She felt she may have spoken too freely already, or perhaps even criticized him as a husband. Poor man. He was exhausted.

"Friendship is here, George," she said, and laid her hand on his arm. "Use it. You may call upon me at any time."

Well, he did. He called upon Alma in 1826, when Retta cut off all her hair. He called upon Alma in 1835, when Retta vanished for three days, and was ultimately found in Fishtown, sleeping amid a pile of street children. He called upon her in 1842, when Retta came after a servant with a pair of sewing scissors, claiming that the woman was a ghost. The servant had not suffered serious injury, but now nobody would take Retta her breakfast. He called upon her in 1846, when Retta had started writing long, incomprehensible letters, composed more of tears than ink.

George did not know how to manage these scenes and muddles. It was all a dreadful distraction to his business and to his mind. He was publishing more than fifty books a year now, along with an array of scientific journals and a new, expensive, subscription-only *Octavo of Exotic Flora* (to be released quarterly, and illustrated with impressively large hand-tinted lithographs of the finest quality). All these endeavors required his absolute attention. He had no time for a collapsing wife.

Alma had no time for it either, but still she came. Sometimes—during particularly bad episodes—she would even spend the night with Retta, sleeping in the Hawkeses' own conjugal bed, with her arms around her trembling friend, while George slept on a pallet in the print shop next door. She got the impression that he usually slept there nowadays, anyway.

"Will you still love me and will you still be kind to me," Retta would ask Alma in the middle of the night, "if I become the very devil himself?"

"I will always love you," Alma reassured the only friend she had ever had. "And you could never be the devil, Retta. You simply must rest, and not trouble yourself or the others anymore . . ."

In the mornings after such episodes, the three of them would breakfast together in the Hawkeses' dining room. This was never comfortable. George was no light conversationalist under the best of circumstances, and Retta—depending on how much laudanum she had been given the night before—would be either frenzied or stupefied. Intervals of lucidity became ever more rare. Sometimes Retta chewed on a rag, and would not let it be taken from her. Alma would search for some topic of conversation that would suit all three of them, but no such topic existed. No such topic had ever existed. She could speak with Retta about nonsense, or she could speak with George about botany, but she could never puzzle out a way to speak to them both.

Then, in April of 1848, George Hawkes called upon Alma again. She was working at her desk—attacking with zeal the puzzle of a poorly preserved *Dicranum consorbrinum* recently sent to her by an amateur collector in Minnesota—when a thin young boy arrived on horseback, carrying an urgent message: Miss Whittaker's immediate presence was please requested at the Hawkes home on Arch Street. There had been an accident.

"What sort of accident?" Alma asked, rising from her work in alarm.

"A fire!" the boy said. It was difficult for him to restrain his glee. Boys always loved fires.

"Dear heavens! Has anyone been injured?"

"No, ma'am," said the boy, visibly disappointed.

Retta, Alma soon learned, had set a fire in her bedroom. For some reason, she had decided that she needed to burn her bedclothes and curtains. Mercifully, the weather was damp, and the fabrics had only smoldered, not ignited. A good deal more smoke than flame had been produced, but the damage to the bedroom was considerable nonetheless. The damage to the morale of the household was even more severe. Two more maids had resigned. No one could be expected to live in this home. No one could bear this demented mistress.

When Alma arrived, George was pale and overwhelmed. Retta had been sedated, and lay heavily asleep across a couch. The house smelled of a brush fire after rain.

"Alma!" George said, rushing to her. He took her hand in his. He had done that only once before, more than three decades earlier. It was different this time. Alma felt ashamed of even remembering the last time. His eyes were wide with panic. "She cannot stay here any longer."

"She is your wife, George."

"I know what she is! I know what she is. But she cannot stay here, Alma. She is not safe, and nobody is safe around her. She could have killed us all, and ignited the print shop, as well. You must find a place for her to stay."

"A hospital?" Alma asked. But Retta had been to the hospital so many times, where, it always seemed, nobody could do much for her. She always returned home from the hospital even more agitated than when she had been admitted.

"No, Alma. She needs a permanent place. A different sort of home. You know of what I speak! I cannot have her here for another night. She must live elsewhere. You must forgive me for this. You know more than anyone, and yet not even you know fully what she has become. I have not slept a night in this past week. Nobody in this household sleeps, for fear of what she will do. She requires two people with her at all times, to ensure that she does not harm herself or another. Do not force me to say more! I know that you understand what I am asking. You must attend to this for me."

Without questioning for a moment why it must be *she* who must attend to this, Alma attended to it. With a few well-placed letters, she was quickly able to secure admission for her friend at the Griffon Asylum in Trenton, New Jersey. The building had just been erected the year prior, and Dr. Victor Griffon—a respected Philadelphia figure who had once been a guest at White Acre—had designed the property himself, for optimum serenity to the disturbed mind. He was the foremost American advocate of moral care for the mentally disturbed, and his methods, it was said, were quite humane. His patients were never chained to the walls, for instance, as Retta had once been chained at the Philadelphia hospital. The asylum was said to be a serene and beautiful place, with fine gardens and, naturally, high walls. It was not unpleasant, people said. Nor was it inexpensive, as Alma had learned when she paid, in advance, for the first year of Retta's stay. She had no wish to trouble George with the bill, and Retta's own parents had long ago passed away, leaving only debts behind them.

It was a sad business for Alma, making these arrangements, but everyone agreed it was for the best. Retta would have her own room at Griffon, such that she could not harm another patient, and she would also have a nurse with her at all hours. Knowing this brought Alma comfort. Moreover, the therapies at the asylum were modern and scientific. Retta's madness would be treated with hydropathy, with a centrifugal spinning board, and with kind moral guidance. She would have no access to either fire or scissors. Alma had been assured of this last fact by Dr. Griffon himself, who had already diagnosed Retta with something he called "exhaustion of the nervous fountain."

So Alma made all the arrangements. George was required only to sign the certificate of insanity and accompany his wife, along with Alma, to Trenton. The three of them went by private carriage, because Retta could not be trusted on a train. They brought a strap with them, in case she needed restraining, but Retta bore herself along lightly, humming little songs.

When they arrived at the asylum, George walked briskly ahead across the great lawn toward the front entrance, with Alma and Retta following just behind him, arm in arm, as though they were enjoying a stroll.

"Such a pretty house this is!" Retta said, admiring the elegant brick building.

"I agree," Alma said, with a surge of relief. "I am happy that you like it, Retta, for this is where you will live now." It was not clear how much Retta understood about what was happening, but she did not seem agitated.

"These are lovely gardens," Retta went on.

"I agree," said Alma.

"I cannot bear to see flowers cut down, though."

"But, Retta, you are so silly to say such a thing! Nobody loves a bouquet of freshly cut flowers more than you!"

"I am being punished for the most unspeakable offenses," Retta replied, quite calmly.

"You are not being punished, little bird."

"I am terrified of God, more than all."

"God has no complaint with you, Retta."

"I am plagued by the most mysterious pains in my chest. It feels sometimes as if my heart will be crushed. Not at the moment, you see, but it comes on so quickly."

"You will meet friends here who can help you."

"When I was a young girl," Retta said in this same relaxed tone, "I used to go on compromising walks with men. Did you know that about me, Alma?"

"Hush, Retta."

"There is no need to hush me. George knows. I've told him many times. I permitted those men to handle me however they liked, and I even allowed myself to take money from them—though you know I never needed the money."

"Hush, Retta. You are not speaking sensibly."

"Did you ever wish to go on compromising walks with men? When you were young, I mean?"

"Retta, please . . ."

"The ladies in the buttery at White Acre used to do it, too. They showed me how to do things to men, and taught me how much money to take for my services. I bought myself gloves and ribbons with the money. I once even bought a ribbon for you!"

Alma slowed her pace, hoping George could not hear them speaking. But she knew he had already heard everything. "Retta, you are so weary, you must save your voice . . ."

"But did you never, Alma? Did you *never* wish to commit compromising acts? Did you never feel a wicked hunger, inside the body?" Retta clutched her arm and gazed up at her friend quite piteously, searching Alma's face. Then she slumped again, resigned. "No, of course you didn't. For you are good. You and Prudence are both good. Whereas I am the very devil himself."

Now Alma felt that her own heart would break. She looked at the wide, hunched shoulders of George Hawkes as he walked ahead of them. She felt overcome with shame. Had she never wished to commit compromising acts with men? Oh, if Retta only knew! If anyone knew! Alma was a forty-eight-year-old spinster with a dried-up womb, and yet she *still* found her way to the binding closet several times a month. Many times a month, even! What's more, all the illicit texts of her youth—*Cum Grano Salis*, and the rest of them—still pulsed in her memory. Sometimes she took those books out of their hidden trunk, in the hayloft of the carriage house, and read them again. What did Alma *not* know of wicked hungers?

Alma felt that it would be immoral of her to say nothing of reassurance or allegiance to this broken little creature. How could Alma let Retta believe she was the only wicked girl in the world? But George Hawkes was right there, walking only a few feet in front of them, and surely he could hear all. So Alma did not console, nor did she offer commiseration. All she said was this: "Once you settle into your new home here, my dear little Retta, you will be able to walk in these gardens every day. Then you will be at peace."

On the carriage ride home from Trenton, Alma and George were mostly silent.

"She will be well taken care of," Alma said at last. "Dr. Griffon assured me of it himself."

"We are each of us born into trouble," George said, by means of reply. "It is a sad fate to come into this world at all."

"That may be true," Alma replied carefully, surprised at the vehemence of his words. "Yet we must find the patience and resignation to endure our challenges as they arise to meet us."

"Yes. So we are taught," George said. "Do you know, Alma, there were times when I wished Retta would find relief in death, rather than suffer this continued torment, or bring such torment to myself and to others?"

She could not imagine what to say in response. He stared at her, his face twisted by darkness and agony. After a few moments, she stumbled forth with this statement: "Where there is life, George, there is still hope. Death is so terribly final. It will come soon enough to us all. I would hesitate to wish it hastened upon anyone."

George shut his eyes and did not answer. This did not seem to have been a reassuring response.

"I will make a practice of coming to Trenton to visit Retta once a month," Alma said, in a lighter tone. "If you wish, you may join me. I will take her copies of *Joy's Lady's Book*. She will like that."

For the next two hours, George did not speak. For a while, it appeared that he was falling in and out of sleep. As they neared Philadelphia, though, he opened his eyes. He looked as unhappy as anyone Alma had ever seen. Alma, her heart going out to the man, elected to change the subject. A few weeks earlier, George had lent Alma a new book, just published out of London, on the subject of salamanders. Perhaps a mention of this would lift his spirits. So she thanked him now for the loan, and spoke of the book in some detail as the carriage moved slowly toward the city, concluding at last, "In general, I found it to be a volume of considerable thought and accurate analysis, though it was abominably written and terribly arranged—so I do have to ask you, George, do these people in England not have editors?"

George looked up from his feet and said, quite abruptly, "Your sister's husband has made some trouble for himself of late."

Clearly, he had not heard a word she'd spoken. Furthermore, the change of subject surprised Alma. George was not a gossip, and it struck her as odd that he would refer to Prudence's husband at all. Perhaps, she supposed, he was so distraught by the day's events that he was not quite himself. She did not wish to make him feel uncomfortable, however, so she took up the conversation, as though she and George always discussed such matters.

"What has he done?" she asked.

"Arthur Dixon has published a reckless pamphlet," George explained wearily, "to which he was foolish enough to append his own name, expressing his opinion that the government of the United States of America is a beastly bit of moral fraudulence on account of its ongoing affiliation with human slavery."

There was nothing shocking in this news. Prudence and Arthur Dixon had been committed abolitionists for many years. They were well known across Philadelphia for antislavery views that leaned toward the radical. Prudence, in her spare hours, taught reading to free blacks at a local Quaker school. She also cared for children at the Colored Orphans' Asylum, and often spoke at meetings of women's abolition societies. Arthur Dixon produced pamphlets frequently—even incessantly—and had served on the editorial board of the *Liberator*. To be frank about it, many people in Philadelphia had grown rather weary of the Dixons, with their pamphlets and articles and speeches. ("For a man who fancies himself an agitator," Henry always said of his son-in-law, "Arthur Dixon is an awful bore.")

"But what of it?" Alma asked George Hawkes. "We all know that my sister and her husband are active in such causes."

"Professor Dixon has gone further this time, Alma. He not only wishes for slavery to be abolished immediately, but he is also of the opinion we should neither pay taxes nor respect American law until that unlikely event occurs. He encourages us to take to the streets with flaming torches and the like, demanding the instant liberation of all black men."

"Arthur *Dixon*?" Alma could not help herself from saying the full name of her dull old tutor. "Flaming torches? That doesn't sound like him."

"You may read it yourself and see. Everyone has been speaking of it. They say he is fortunate to still hold his position at the university. Your sister, it seems, has spoken in agreement with him."

Alma contemplated this news. "That is a bit alarming," she agreed at last.

"We are each of us born to trouble," George repeated, rubbing his hand over his face in exhaustion.

"Yet we must find the patience and resignation—" Alma began again lamely, but George cut her off.

"Your poor sister," he said. "And with young children in her house, besides. Please let me know, Alma, if there is anything I can ever do to help your family. You have always been so kind to us."

Chapter Thirteen

*H*er poor sister?

Well, perhaps . . . but Alma wasn't certain.

Prudence Whittaker Dixon was a difficult woman to pity, and she had remained, over the years, a thoroughly impossible woman to comprehend. Alma pondered these facts the next day, as she examined her moss colonies back at White Acre.

Such a riddle was the Dixon household! Here was another marriage that seemed not at all happy. Prudence and her old tutor had been married now for more than twenty-five years, and had produced six children, yet Alma had never witnessed a single sign of affection, pleasure, or rapport pass between the couple. She had never heard either of them laugh. She had scarcely ever seen them smile. Nor had she ever seen a flash of anger directed by one toward the other. She had never seen emotion of any variety pass between them, in fact. What sort of marriage was this, where people march through the years in diligent dullness?

But there had always been questions surrounding her sister's married life—beginning with the burning mystery that had consumed all of Philadelphia's gossips so many years long ago, when Arthur and Prudence had first wed: What happened to the dowry? Henry Whittaker had blessed his adopted daughter with a tremendous sum of money upon the occasion of her marriage, but there was no sign that a penny of it was ever spent. Arthur and Prudence Dixon lived like paupers on his small university salary. They did not even own their home. Why, they barely *heated* their home! Arthur did not approve of luxuries, so he kept his household as cold and bloodless as his own dry self. He governed his family through a model of abstinence, modesty, scholarship, and prayer, and Prudence had fallen into obedience with it. From the very first day of her career as a wife, Prudence had renounced all finery, and had taken to dressing nearly like a Quaker: flannel and wool and dark colors, and with the most homely imaginable poke bonnets. She did not adorn herself with so much as a trinket or a watch chain, nor would she wear even a speck of lace.

Prudence's restrictions were not limited to her wardrobe, either. Her diet became as simple and restricted as her mode of dress—all cornbread and molasses, by the looks of things. She was never seen to take a glass of wine, or even tea or lemonade. As her children came along, Prudence had raised them in the same miserly manner. A pear plucked from a nearby tree constituted a treat for her boys and girls, whom she trained to turn their faces away from more alluring delicacies. Prudence dressed her children in the same manner in which she dressed herself: in humble clothing, neatly patched. It was as though she wanted her children to look poor. Or perhaps they genuinely were poor, though they had no cause to be.

"What in the deuce has she gone and done with all her gowns?" Henry would sputter, whenever Prudence came to visit White Acre adorned in rags. "Has she stuffed her mattresses with them?"

But Alma had seen Prudence's mattresses, and they were stuffed with straw.

The wags of Philadelphia had a great sport speculating about what Prudence and her husband had done with the Whittaker dowry. Was Arthur Dixon a gambler, who had squandered the riches on horse races and dog fights? Did he keep another family in another city, who lived in luxury? Or was the couple sitting on a buried treasure of unspeakable wealth, hiding it behind a facade of poverty?

Over time, the answer emerged: all the money had gone to abolitionist causes. Prudence had quietly turned over most of her dowry to the Philadelphia Abolitionist Society shortly after her marriage. The Dixons had also used the money to purchase slaves out of captivity, which could cost upwards of $1,300 per life. They had paid for the transport of several escaped slaves to safety in Canada. They had paid for the publication of innumerable agitating pamphlets and tracts. They had even funded black debating societies, which helped train Negroes to argue their own cause.

All these details were revealed back in 1838, in a story that the *Inquirer* had published about Prudence Whittaker Dixon's peculiar living habits. Spurred by a lynch mob's burning of a local abolitionist meeting hall, the newspaper had been looking for interesting—even diverting—stories about the antislavery movement. A reporter had been pointed in the direction of Prudence Dixon when a prominent abolitionist made mention of the quiet generosity of the Whittaker heiress. The newspaperman had been immediately intrigued; the Whittaker name, hitherto, had not exactly been associated around Philadelphia with boundless acts of generosity. What's more, of course, Prudence was vividly beautiful—a fact that always draws attention—and the contrast between her exquisite face and her plain mode of living only made her a more fascinating subject. With her elegant white wrists and delicate neck peeking from within those dreary clothes, she had every appearance of being a goddess in captivity—Aphrodite trapped in a convent. The reporter had been unable to resist her.

The story appeared on the front page of the paper, along with a flattering engraving of Mrs. Dixon. Most of the article was familiar abolitionist material, but what captured the imagination of Philadelphians was that Prudence—brought up in the palatial halls of White Acre—was quoted as having declared that for many years she had denied herself and her family any bit of luxury that was produced by a slave's hands.

"It may seem innocent to wear South Carolina cotton," her quote continued, "but it is not innocent, for this is how evil seeps into our home. It may seem a simple pleasure to spoil our children with a treat of sugar, but that pleasure becomes a sin when the sugar was grown by human beings held in unspeakable misery. For that same reason, in our household, we take no coffee or tea. I urge all Philadelphians of good Christian conscience to do the same. If we speak out against slavery, yet continue to enjoy its plunders, we are naught but hypocrites, and how can we believe that the Lord smiles upon our hypocrisy?"

Later in the article, Prudence went further still: "My husband and I live next door to a family of freed Negroes, consisting of a good and decent man named John Harrington, his wife, Sadie, and their three children. They are impoverished, and thus they struggle. We see to it that we live no richer than they. We see to it that our house is no finer than theirs. Often the Harringtons work alongside us in our home, and we work in theirs. I scrub my hearth alongside Sadie Harrington. My husband cuts wood alongside John Harrington. My children learn their letters and numbers alongside the Harringtons' children. They often dine with us at our own table. We eat the same fare they eat, and we wear the same clothing they wear. In the winters, if the Harringtons have no heat, we ourselves go without heat. We are kept warm by our absence of shame, and by our knowledge that Christ would have done the same. On Sundays, we attend the same services as the Harringtons do, at their humble Negro Methodist church. Their church has no comforts—so why should ours? Their children sometimes have no shoes— why should ours?"

Here, Prudence had gone too far.

Over the following days, the newspaper had been flooded with angry responses to Prudence's words. Some of these letters came from appalled mothers ("Henry Whittaker's daughter keeps her children without shoes!"), but most came from enraged men ("If Mrs. Dixon loves Black Africans as much as she claims, let her marry off her prettiest little white daughter to her neighbor's inkiest-skinned son—I stand eager to see it done!").

As for Alma, she could not help but find the article irritating. There was something about Prudence's manner of living that looked, to Alma's eyes, suspiciously like pride, or even vanity. It was not that Prudence possessed the vanity of normal mortals (Alma had never even caught her peeking in a mirror), but Alma felt Prudence was being vain in some other way here—in a more subtle way, through these excessive demonstrations of austerity and sacrifice.

Look how little I need, Prudence seemed to be saying. *Behold my goodness.*

What's more, Alma could not help but wonder if perhaps Prudence's black neighbors, the Harringtons, might wish to eat something more than cornbread and molasses one night—and why couldn't the Dixons simply buy it for them, instead of also going hungry themselves in such an empty gesture of solidarity?

The newspaper exposure brought trouble. Philadelphia may have been a free city, but this did not mean its citizens loved the mingling of poor Negroes and fine white ladies. At first, there were threats and attacks on the

Harringtons, who were so harassed that they were forced to move. Then Arthur Dixon was pelted with horse dung on his way to work at the University of Pennsylvania. Mothers refused to allow their children to play any longer with the Dixon children. Strips of South Carolina cotton kept appearing on the Dixons' front gate, and small piles of sugar on their doorstep—strange and inventive warnings, indeed. And then one day in mid-1838, Henry Whittaker had received an unsigned letter in the post, which read, "You'd best stop up your daughter's mouth, Mr. Whittaker, or you will soon see your warehouses burned to the ground."

Well, Henry could not stand for this. It was insult enough that his daughter had squandered her generous dowry, but now his commercial property was in danger. He'd summoned Prudence up to White Acre, where he intended to drive some sense into her.

"Be gentle with her, Father," Alma had warned, in advance of the encounter. "Prudence is likely shaken and anxious. She has been much plagued by the events of recent weeks, and she is probably more concerned for the safety of her children than you are for the safety of your warehouses."

"I doubt it," Henry had growled.

But Prudence did not seem cowed or dismayed. Rather, she strode into Henry's study like Joan of Arc, and stood before her father undaunted. Alma tried for a pleasant greeting, but Prudence showed no interest in pleasantries. Nor did Henry. He launched into the conversation with an immediate charge. "See what you have done! You have brought disgrace to this family, and now you bring a lynch mob to your father's doorstep? That's the reward you offer me, for all that I have given you?"

"Pardon me, but I see no lynch mob," Prudence said evenly.

"Well, there may be one soon!" Henry thrust the threatening letter to Prudence, who read it without reaction. "I tell you, Prudence, I will not be happy, operating my business from the charred shell of a destroyed building. What do you think you are at, playing these games? Why are you putting yourself in the newspapers like this? There is no dignity in it. Beatrix would have disapproved."

"I am proud that my words were recorded," Prudence said. "I would proudly speak those same words again, in front of every newspaperman in Philadelphia."

Prudence was not helping the situation.

"You come here dressed in rags," Henry said, in a voice of increasing anger. "You come here penniless, despite my generosity. You come here from the confines of your husband's insolvent hell, expressly to be miserable in our presence and to make us all miserable around you. You meddle where you have no business meddling, and you incite agitation in a cause that will pull this city apart—and destroy my trade with it! And there is no reason for it, besides! There is no slavery within the Commonwealth of Pennsylvania, Prudence! So why do you continue to argue the point? Let the South solve her own sins."

"I regret that you do not share in my beliefs, Father," Prudence said.

"I don't give a farrier's fart about your beliefs. But I swear to you, if my warehouses come to any harm—"

"You are a man of influence," Prudence interrupted. "Your voice could benefit this cause, and your money could do much good for this sinful world. I appeal to the witness within your own bosom—"

"Oh, bugger the witness in my bosom! You only stand to make things more wretched for every hardworking tradesman in this city!"

"Then what would you have me do, Father?"

"I would have you stop your mouth, girl, and attend to your family."

"All who suffer are my family."

"Curse the moon and spare me your sermons—*they are not*. The people in this room are your family."

"No more than any other," said Prudence.

That stopped Henry. Indeed, it took the breath out of him. Even Alma felt walloped by it. The comment made her eyes sting unexpectedly, as though she had just been clouted hard across the bridge of her nose.

"You do not regard us as your family?" Henry asked, once he had regained his composure. "Very well, then. I dismiss you from this family."

"Oh, Father, you mustn't—" Alma protested, in real horror.

But Prudence cut her sister off, launching into a response that was so lucid and calm, one might have thought it had been rehearsed for years. Perhaps it had been.

"As you wish," Prudence said. "But know that you are dismissing from your household a daughter who has always been loyal to you, and who has the right to seek tenderness and sympathy from the one man she ever had the memory of calling Father. Not only is this cruel, but I believe it will bring anguish upon your conscience. I shall pray for you, Henry Whittaker. And when I pray, I shall ask the Lord in heaven whatever happened to my father's ethics—or did he never have any?"

Henry leapt to his feet and pounded both fists on his desk in rage.

"You little idiot!" he roared. *"I never had any!"*

That had been ten years earlier, and Henry had not seen his daughter Prudence since, nor had Prudence made any attempt to see Henry. Alma herself had seen her sister only a handful of times, stopping by the Dixon home in sporadic demonstrations of artificial nonchalance and forced goodwill. She pretended she was passing through the neighborhood anyway, to drop in with small gifts for her nieces and nephews, or to deliver a basket of treats around the Christmas holidays. Alma knew that her sister would only pass along these gifts and treats to a more needy family, but she made the gestures nonetheless. At the beginning of the family rift, Alma had even attempted to offer money to her sister, but Prudence, not surprisingly, had refused it.

These visits had never been warm or comfortable, and Alma was always relieved when they were over. Alma felt shamed whenever she saw Prudence. As irritating as she found her sister's rigidity and morality, Alma could not help but feel that her father had behaved poorly in his final encounter with Prudence—or, rather, that Henry and Alma herself had *both* behaved poorly. The incident had cast them in no lovely light: Prudence had stood firmly (though sanctimoniously) on the side of the Good and the Righteous, while Henry had merely defended his commercial property and disowned his adopted daughter. And as for Alma? Well, Alma had come down on the side of Henry Whittaker—or at least it would appear that she had—by not having spoken up more vehemently in her sister's defense, and by staying on at White Acre after Prudence walked out.

But her father needed her! Henry Whittaker might not be a generous man, and he might not be a kind man, but he was an important man, and he needed her. He could not live without her. Nobody else could manage his affairs, and his affairs were vast and significant. This is what she told herself.

What's more, abolitionism was not a cause dear to Alma's heart. She believed slavery to be abhorrent, naturally enough, but she was occupied with so many other concerns that the question did not consume her conscience on a daily basis. Alma was living in Moss Time, after all, and she simply could not focus upon her work—and take care of her father—while also calibrating herself to the shifting vagaries of everyday human political drama. Slavery was a grotesque injustice, yes, and should be abolished. But there were so *many* injustices: poverty was another, and tyranny, and theft, and murder. One could not set one's hand to eliminating every known injustice while at the same time writing definitive books on American mosses and managing the complex affairs of a global family enterprise.

Was that not true?

And why must Prudence go so far out of her way to make everyone around her look so paltry-hearted and piggish, in comparison to her own mighty sacrifices?

"Thank you for your kindness," Prudence would always say, whenever Alma came calling with a gift or a basket, but she always stopped short of expressing true affection or gratitude. Prudence was nothing if not polite, but she was not warm. Alma would return home to the luxuries of White Acre after these visits to Prudence's impoverished home feeling undone and overly examined—as though she had stood before a strict jurist and had been found lacking. So perhaps it should not be surprising that over the years Alma visited Prudence less and less frequently, and that the two sisters were pulled further apart than ever.

But now, in the carriage returning home from Trenton, George Hawkes had given Alma information that the Dixons might be in some kind of trouble over Arthur Dixon's inflammatory pamphlet. As Alma stood near her boulder field in that spring of 1848, taking notes on the progress of her mosses, she wondered if she should perhaps call upon Prudence again. If her brother-in-law's position at the university was indeed threatened, this was serious. But what could Alma say? What could she do? What help could she offer Prudence, that would not be refused out of pride and a willful show of humility?

Moreover, had the Dixons not put themselves in this pickle? Wasn't all this just the natural consequence of living in such extremity and radicalism? What business did Arthur and Prudence have as parents, putting the lives of their six children in jeopardy? Their cause was a dangerous one. Abolitionists were often dragged through the streets and beaten—even in free northern cities! The North did not love slavery, but it did love peace and stability, and abolitionists disturbed that peace. The Colored Orphans' Asylum, where Prudence volunteered her services as a teacher, had been several times already attacked by mobs. And what about the abolitionist Elijah Lovejoy—murdered in Illinois, and his abolitionist-friendly printing presses destroyed and thrown in the river? That could easily happen here in Philadelphia. Prudence and her husband should be more careful.

Alma turned her attention back to her mossy boulders. She had work to do. She had fallen behind in the last week, committing poor Retta to Dr. Griffon's asylum, and she did not intend to fall even further behind now as a result of her sister's foolhardiness. She had measurements to record, and she needed to attend to them.

Three separate colonies of *Dicranum* grew on one of the largest rocks. Alma had been observing these colonies for twenty-six years, and lately it had become incontrovertibly evident that one of these *Dicranum* varietals was advancing, while the other two had retreated. Alma sat near the boulder, comparing more than two decades of notes and drawings. She could make no sense of it.

Dicranum was Alma's obsession-within-an-obsession—the innermost heart of her fascination with mosses. The world was blanketed with hundreds upon hundreds of species of *Dicranum*, and each variety was minutely different. Alma knew more about *Dicranum* than anybody in the world, yet still this genus bothered her and kept her awake at night. Alma—who had puzzled over mechanisms and origins her entire life—had been consumed for years with fervent questions about this complicated genus. How had *Dicranum* come to be? Why was it so markedly diverse? Why had nature bestowed such pains in making each variety so minutely different from the others? Why were some varietals of *Dicranum* so much hardier than their nearby kin? Had there always been such a vast mix of *Dicranum*, or had they transmuted somehow—metamorphosed from one into another—while sharing a common ancestor?

There had been a good deal of talk within the scientific community lately about species transmutation. Alma had been following the debate most eagerly. It was not an entirely new discussion. Jean-Baptiste Lamarck had originated the subject forty years prior, in France, when he'd argued that every species on earth had transformed since its original creation because of an "interior sentiment" within the organism, which longed to perfect itself. More recently, Alma had read *Vestiges of the Natural History of Creation*, by an anonymous British author who also argued that species were capable of progression, of change. The author did not put forth a convincing mechanism as to *how* a species could change—but he did argue for the existence of transmutation.

Such views were most controversial. To put forth the notion that any entity could alter itself was to question God's very dominion. The Christian position was that the Lord had created all the world's species in one day, and that none of His creations had changed since the dawn of time. But it seemed increasingly clear to Alma that things *had* changed. Alma herself had studied samples of fossilized moss that did not quite match the mosses of the current day. And this was only nature on the tiniest scale! What was one to make of the tremendous fossil bones of the lizardlike creatures that Richard Owen had recently named "dinosaurs"? That these gargantuan animals had once walked the earth, and now—quite obviously—they did not, was beyond dispute. The dinosaurs had been replaced by something else, or they had shifted into something else, or they had simply been erased. How did one account for such mass extinctions and transformations?

As the great Linnaeus himself had written: *Natura non facit saltum.*

Nature does not make leaps.

But Alma thought that nature *did* make leaps. Perhaps only tiny leaps—skips, hops, and lurches—but leaps nonetheless. Nature certainly made alterations. One could see it in the breeding of dogs and sheep, and one could see it in the shifting arrangements of power and dominion between various moss colonies on these common limestone boulders at White Acre's forest edge. Alma had ideas, but she could not quite tack and baste them together. She felt certain that some varieties of *Dicranum* must have grown forth out of other, older varieties of *Dicranum*. She felt certain that one entity could have issued from another entity, or rendered another colony extinct. She could not grasp *how* it occurred, but she was convinced *that* it occurred.

She felt the familiar old constriction in her chest—that combination of desire and urgency. Only two more hours of daylight remained in which to work outdoors before she had to return to her father's evening demands. She needed more hours—many more hours—if she was ever to study these questions as they deserved to be studied. She would never have enough hours. She had already lost so much time this week. Every soul in the world seemed to believe that Alma's hours belonged to him. How was she ever meant to devote herself to proper scientific exploration?

Observing the sun as it lowered, Alma decided that she would not visit Prudence. She simply did not have the time for it. She did not want to read Arthur's latest seditious pamphlet on abolition, either. What could Alma do to help the Dixons? Her sister did not want to hear Alma's opinions, nor did she wish to accept Alma's assistance. Alma felt sorry for Prudence, but a visit would only be awkward, as such encounters were always awkward.

Back to her boulders Alma turned. She took out her tape and measured the colonies again. Hastily, she recorded the data in her notebook.

Only two more hours.

She had so much work to do.

Arthur and Prudence Dixon would have to learn how to take more care with their own lives.

Chapter Fourteen

Later that month, Alma received a note from George Hawkes, asking that she please come to Arch Street, in order to visit his printing shop and see something quite extraordinary.

"I shall not spoil the incredibility of it by telling you more at this point," he wrote, "but I believe you would enjoy viewing this in person, and at your leisure."

Well, Alma had no leisure. Neither did George, though—which is why this note was most unprecedented. In the past, George had contacted Alma only for publishing matters, or emergencies regarding Retta. But there had been no emergencies with Retta since they had placed her at Griffon's, and Alma and George were not working on a book together at the moment. What, then, could be so urgent?

Intrigued, she took a carriage to Arch Street.

She found George in a back room, hulking over a long table covered with the most dazzling multiplication of shapes and colors. As Alma approached, she could see that this was an enormous collection of paintings of orchids, stacked in tall piles. Not only paintings, but lithographs, drawings, and etchings.

"This is the most beautiful work I have ever seen," George said, by means of a greeting. "It's just come in yesterday, from Boston. It's such an odd story. Look at this mastery!"

George thrust into Alma's hand a lithograph of a spotted *Catasetum.*

The orchid had been rendered so magnificently that it seemed to grow off the page. Its lips were spotted red against yellow, and appeared moist, like living flesh. Its leaves were lush and thick, and its bulbous roots looked as though one could shake actual soil off them. Before Alma could thoroughly take in the beauty, George handed her another stunning print—a *Peristeria barkeri*, with its tumbling golden blossoms so fresh they nearly trembled. Whoever had tinted this lithograph had been a master of texture as well as color; the petals resembled unshorn velvet, and touches of albumen on their tips gave each blossom a hint of dew.

Then George handed her another print, and Alma could not help but gasp. Whatever this orchid was, Alma had never seen it before. Its tiny pink lobes looked like something a fairy would don for a fancy dress ball. She had never seen such complexity, such delicacy. Alma knew lithographs, and knew them well. She had been born only four years after the technique was invented, and she had collected for the library at White Acre some of the finest lithography the world had yet produced. She believed she well understood the technical limitations of the medium, yet these prints proved her wrong. George Hawkes knew lithography, too. Nobody in Philadelphia had mastered it better than he. Yet his hand shook as he reached to give Alma another sheet, another orchid. He wanted her to see all of this, and he wanted her to see it all at once. Alma was desperate to keep looking, but she needed to better understand the situation first.

"Wait, George, let us pause for a moment. You must tell me—who made these?" Alma asked. She knew all the best botanical illustrators, but she did not know this artist. Not even Walter Hood Fitch could create work like this. If she had ever before seen the likes of it, she most certainly would have remembered.

"The most extraordinary fellow, it seems," George said. "His name is Ambrose Pike."

Alma had never heard the name.

"Who publishes his work?" she asked.

"Nobody!"

"Who has commissioned this work, then?"

"It is not clear that anyone has commissioned it," George said. "Mr. Pike made the lithographs himself, in a friend's print shop in Boston. He found the orchids, executed the sketches, made the prints, and even did the tint work on his own. He sent all this work to me without a good deal more explanation than that. It arrived yesterday in the most innocuous box you have ever seen. I nearly toppled over when I opened it, as you can imagine. Mr. Pike has been in Guatemala and Mexico for these past eighteen years, he says, and only recently returned home to Massachusetts. The orchids he has documented here are the result of his time in the jungle. Nobody knows of him. We must bring him to Philadelphia, Alma. Perhaps you could invite him to White Acre? His letter was most humble. He has put the entirety of his life toward this endeavor. He wonders if I might publish it for him."

"You *will* publish, won't you?" Alma asked, already imagining these lavish prints in a perfectly executed Hawkes volume.

"Naturally, I will publish! But first I must gather my senses around it all. Some of these orchids, Alma, I've never before seen. Such artistry, I most certainly have never before seen."

"Nor have I," Alma said, turning to the table and gently paging through the other examples. She almost didn't want to touch them, they were that spectacular. They should be behind glass—each and every one. Even the smallest sketches were masterpieces. Reflexively, she glanced up at the ceiling to make sure it was sound, that nothing would leak on this work and destroy it. She feared suddenly for fire or theft. George needed to put a lock on this room. She wished she were wearing gloves.

"Have you *ever*—" George began, but he was so overcome, he couldn't finish the sentence. She had never seen his face so undone by emotion.

"I have never," she murmured. "I have never in my life."

That very evening, Alma wrote a letter to Mr. Ambrose Pike, of Massachusetts.

She had written many thousands of letters in her life—and many of them had been letters of praise or invitation—but she did not know how to begin this one. How does one address true genius? In the end, she decided she must be nothing short of direct.

> Dear Mr. Pike,
>   I fear you have done me a great harm. You have ruined me forever, for admiring anybody else's botanical artwork. The

world of drawing, painting, and lithography will seem sadly drab
and dull to me now that I have seen your orchids. I believe you
may soon be visiting Philadelphia in order to work alongside my
dear friend George Hawkes on the publication of a book. I
wonder if, while you are in our city, I may lure you to White
Acre, my family's estate, for an extended visit? We have
greenhouses stocked with an abundance of orchids—some of
which are nearly as beautiful in reality as yours are in depiction.
I daresay you may enjoy them. Perhaps you might even wish to
draw them. (Any of our flowers would consider it an honor to
have their portraits painted by you!) Without a doubt, my father
and I shall delight in making your acquaintance. If you alert me
as to your expected arrival, I shall send a private carriage to
collect you at the train station. Once you are in our care, we shall
see to your every need. Please do not harm me again by refusing!
Most sincerely yours, Alma Whittaker

He arrived in the middle of May 1848.

Alma was in her study working at her microscope when she saw the carriage pull up in front of the house. A tall, slender, sandy-haired young man in a brown corduroy suit stepped out. From this distance, he appeared to be no more than twenty years old—though Alma knew that to be impossible. He was carrying nothing but a small leather valise, which looked not only as though it had traveled the world a few times already, but as though it might fall apart before the end of this day.

Alma watched for a moment before she went out to greet him. She had witnessed so many arrivals at White Acre over the years, and it was her experience that first-time visitors always did exactly the same thing: they stopped in their tracks to gape at the house before them, for White Acre was both magnificent and daunting, especially upon first sight. The place had been expressly designed to intimidate, after all, and few guests could hide their awe, their envy, or their fear—particularly if they did not know they were being watched.

But Mr. Pike did not even look at the house. In fact, he turned his back to the mansion immediately and regarded, instead, Beatrix's old Grecian garden—which Alma and Hanneke had kept pristine over the decades as a tribute to her. He backed up a bit, as though to get a better sense of it, and then he did the oddest thing: he set down his valise, took off his jacket, walked to the northwest corner of the garden, and then strode in long lengths diagonally to the southeast corner. He stood there for a moment, looked about, and then paced out two contiguous borders of the garden—its length and width—in the long strides of a surveyor measuring a property boundary. When he reached the northwest corner, he took off his hat, scratched his head, paused for a moment, and then burst into laughter. Alma could not hear his laughter, but she could distinctly see it.

This was too much for her to resist, and she rushed out of her carriage house to meet him.

"Mr. Pike," she said, extending her hand as she approached him.

"You must be Miss Whittaker!" he said, smiling warmly and taking her hand in greeting. "My eyes cannot believe what I am seeing here! You must tell me, Miss Whittaker—what mad genius took such pains to fabricate this garden according to strict Euclidian geometric ideals?"

"It was my mother's inspiration, sir. Had she not passed away many years ago, she would have thrilled to know that you recognized her objectives."

"Who would not recognize them? It's the golden ratio! We have double squares here, containing recurring nets of squares—and with the pathways bisecting the entire construction, we make several three-four-five triangles, as well. It's so pleasing! I find it extraordinary that somebody would take the trouble to do this, and on such a magnificent scale. The boxwoods are perfect, too. They seem to serve as equation marks to all the conjugates. She must have been a delight, your mother."

"A delight . . ." Alma considered that possibility. "Well, my mother was blessed with a mind that functioned with delightful precision, to be sure."

"How very remarkable," he said.

He had still not appeared to notice the house.

"It is a true pleasure to meet you, Mr. Pike," Alma said.

"And you, Miss Whittaker. Your letter was most generous. I must say that I enjoyed the private carriage ride—a first, in my long life. I am so accustomed to traveling in close quarters with squalling children, unhappy animals, and loud men smoking thick cigars that I scarcely knew what to do with myself for such a long spell of solitude and tranquility."

"What did you do with yourself, then?" Alma asked, smiling at his enthusiasm.

"I befriended a quiet view of the road."

Before Alma could respond to that charming reply, she saw an expression of concern cross Mr. Pike's face. She turned to see what he was looking at: a servant was walking into White Acre's daunting front doors, carrying Mr. Pike's small piece of baggage with him.

"My valise . . ." he said, reaching out a hand.

"We are merely taking it to your rooms for you, Mr. Pike. It will be there, next to your bed and awaiting you, whenever you need it. "

He shook his head, embarrassed. "Of course you are," he said. "How foolish of me. My apologies. I am not accustomed to servants, and that sort of thing."

"Would you prefer to keep your valise with you?"

"No, not at all. Forgive my reaction, Miss Whittaker. But if one has only a single asset in life, as do I, it is a bit worrisome to watch a stranger walk off with it!"

"You have far more than one asset in life, Mr. Pike. You have your exceptional artistic talent—the likes of which neither Mr. Hawkes nor I has ever before seen."

He laughed. "Ah! You are kind to say so, Miss Whittaker. But everything else that I own is in the valise, and perhaps I value those prized little belongings more!"

Now Alma was laughing, too. The reserve that normally exists between two strangers was thoroughly absent. Perhaps it had never been there at all.

"Now tell me, Miss Whittaker," he said, brightly. "What other marvels do you have at White Acre? And what is this I hear, that you study mosses?"

This is how it came to pass that, by the end of the hour, they were standing together amid Alma's boulders, discussing *Dicranum*. She had intended to show him the orchids first. Or rather, she had never intended to show him the moss beds at all—for nobody else had ever shown an interest in them—but once she had started speaking of her work, he insisted that she take him to see it.

"I should warn you, Mr. Pike," she said, as they walked across the field together, "that most people find mosses to be quite dull."

"That doesn't frighten me," he said. "I've always found fascination in subjects that other people find dull."

"This, we share," said Alma.

"Tell me, though, Miss Whittaker, what is it that you admire in mosses?"

"Their dignity," Alma replied without hesitation. "Also, their silence and intelligence. I like that—as a point of study—they are *fresh*. They are not like other bigger or more important plants, which have all been pondered and poked at by hordes of botanists already. I suppose I admire their modesty, as well. Mosses hold their beauty in elegant reserve. By comparison to mosses, everything else in the botanical world can seem so blunt and obvious. Do you understand what I am saying? Do you know how the bigger, showier flowers can look at times like dumb, drooling fools—the way they bob about with their mouths agape, appearing so stunned and helpless?"

"I congratulate you, Miss Whittaker. You have just described the orchid family to perfection."

She gasped and put her hands to her mouth. "I've offended you!"

But Mr. Pike was smiling. "Not in the least. I am teasing you. I have never defended the intelligence of an orchid, and I never shall. I do love them, but I confess that they do not seem particularly bright—not by your standards of description. But I am much enjoying listening to somebody defend the intelligence of moss! It feels as though you are writing a character reference in their defense."

"Somebody must defend them, Mr. Pike! For they have been so overlooked, and they have such a noble character! In fact, I find the miniature world to be a gift of disguised greatness, and therefore an honor to study."

Ambrose Pike didn't seem to find any of this dull. When they arrived at the boulders, he had dozens of questions for Alma, and he put his face so close to the moss colonies that it appeared as though his beard was growing out of the stones. He listened with care as she explained each variety, and discussed her burgeoning theories of transmutation. Perhaps she spoke overly long. Her mother would have said so. Even as she spoke, Alma feared that she was about to throw this poor man into pure tedium. But he was so welcoming! She felt herself set loose as she spilled forth ideas from her long-overbrimming vaults of private thoughts. There is only so long that a person can keep her enthusiasms locked away within her heart before she longs to share it with a fellow soul, and Alma had many decades of thoughts much overdue for sharing.

Very soon Mr. Pike had thrown himself on the ground so that he could peer under the lip of a larger boulder and examine the moss beds that were hidden in those secret shelves. His long legs flopped out from beneath the rock as he enthused. Alma thought she had never been so pleased in her life. She had always wanted to show this to somebody.

"So here is my question to you, Miss Whittaker," he called from under the rock ledge. "What is the true nature of your moss colonies? They have mastered the trick, as you say, of appearing modest and mild. Yet from what you tell me, they possess considerable faculties. Are they friendly pioneers, your mosses? Or are they hostile marauders?"

"Farmers or pirates, do you mean?" Alma asked.

"Exactly."

"I cannot say for certain," Alma said. "Perhaps a bit of both. I wonder that to myself all the time. It may take me another twenty-five years or so to learn."

"I admire your patience," he said, at last rolling out from under the rock and stretching casually across the grass. As she would come to know Ambrose Pike better over time, she would learn that he was a great one for throwing himself down wherever and whenever he wanted to rest. He would even collapse happily on a carpet in a formal drawing room if the mood struck—particularly if he was enjoying his thoughts and the conversation. The world was his divan. There was such a freedom in it. Alma could not imagine ever feeling so free. On this day, while he sprawled, she sat carefully on a nearby rock.

Mr. Pike was considerably older, Alma could see now, than he had initially appeared. Well, naturally he was—there was no way he could have created such a vast body of work had he been so young as he first seemed. It was only his enthusiastic posture and his brisk walking pace that made him resemble a university student from a distance. That, and his humble brown attire—the very uniform of an impecunious young scholar. Up close, though, one could see his age—especially as he lay in the sun, flopped across the grass without his hat on. His face was faintly lined, tanned and freckled by years of weather, and the sandy hair at his temples was turning gray. Alma would have put him at thirty-five years old, or maybe thirty-six. More than ten years younger than she, but still, no child.

"What profound reward you must glean from studying the world so closely," Ambrose went on. "Too many people turn away from small wonders, I find. There is so much more potency to be found in detail than in generalities, but most souls cannot train themselves to sit still for it."

"But sometimes I fear that my world has become *too* detailed," Alma said. "My books on mosses take me years to write, and my conclusions are excruciatingly intricate, not unlike those elaborate Persian miniatures one can study only with a magnifying lens. My work brings me no fame. It brings me no income, either—so you can see I am using my time wisely!"

"But Mr. Hawkes said your books are well-reviewed."

"Most certainly they are—by the dozen gentlemen on earth who care deeply about bryology."

"A dozen!" Mr. Pike said. "That many? Remember, madam, you are speaking to a man who has published nothing in his long life, and whose poor parents fear him to be a shameful idler."

"But your work is superb, sir."

He waved away the praise. "Do you find dignity in your labors?" he asked.

"I do," Alma said, after considering the question for the moment. "Though sometimes I wonder why. The majority of the world—especially the suffering poor—would be happy, I think, never to work again. So why do I labor so diligently at a subject about which so few people care? Why am I not content simply to admire mosses, or even draw them, if their designs please me so much? Why must I pick at their secrets, and beg them for answers about the nature of life itself? I am fortunate enough to come from a family of means, as you can see, so there is no necessity for me to work at all in my life. Why am I not happy, then, to idle about, letting my mind grow as loosely as this grass?"

"Because you are interested in creation," Ambrose Pike replied simply, "and all its wonderful arrangements."

Alma flushed. "You make it sound grand."

"It is grand," he said, just as simply as before.

They sat in silence for a while. Somewhere in the trees beside them, a thrush was singing.

"What a fine private recital!" Mr. Pike said, after a long spell of listening. "It makes one want to applaud him!"

"This is the finest time of year for birdsong at White Acre," Alma said. "There are mornings when you can sit under a single cherry tree in this meadow, and you will hear every bird in the orchestra, performing for your benefit."

"I would like to hear that some morning. I dearly missed our American songbirds when I was in the jungle."

"But there must have been exquisite birds where you were!"

"Yes—exquisite and exotic. But it is not the same. One gets so homesick, you know, for the familiar noises of childhood. There were times when I would hear mourning doves calling out in my dreams. It was so lifelike, it would break my heart. It made me wish never to wake up."

"Mr. Hawkes tells me you were in the jungle for many years."

"Eighteen," he said, smiling almost abashedly.

"In Mexico and Guatemala, mostly?"

"In Mexico and Guatemala entirely. I meant to see more of the world, but I couldn't seem to leave that region, as I kept discovering new things. You know how it is—one finds an interesting place and begins looking, and then the secrets reveal themselves, one after the other, until one cannot pull away. Also, there were certain orchids I found in Guatemala—the more shy and reclusive epiphytes, particularly—that simply would not do me the courtesy of blooming. I refused to leave until I saw them in bloom. I became quite stubborn about it. But they were stubborn, too. Some of them made me wait for five or six years before allowing me a glimpse."

"Why did you finally come home, then?"

"Loneliness."

He had the most extraordinary frankness. Alma marveled at it. She could never imagine admitting such a weakness as loneliness.

"Also," he said, "I became too ill to continue rough living. I had recurrent fevers. Though they were not entirely unpleasant, I should say. I saw remarkable visions in my fevers, and I heard voices, too. Sometimes it was tempting to follow them."

"The visions or the voices?"

"Both! But I could not do that to my mother. It would have inflicted too much pain upon her soul, to lose a son in the jungle. She would have wondered forever what became of me. Although she still wonders what became of me, I'll wager! But at least she knows I am alive."

"Your family must have missed you, then, all those years."

"Oh, my poor family. I have disappointed them so, Miss Whittaker. They are so respectable, and I have lived my life in such irregular directions. I feel sympathy for them all, and for my mother in particular. She believes, I suppose rightly, that I have been trodding most egregiously upon the pearls that were cast before me. I left Harvard after only a year, you see. I was said to be promising—whatever that word is meant to convey—but collegiate life did not suit me. By some peculiarity of the nervous system, I simply could not bear to sit in a lecture hall. Also, I never courted the cheerful company of social clubs and gangs of young men. You may not know this, Miss Whittaker, but most of university life is arranged around social clubs and gangs of young men. As my mother has expressed it, all I've ever wanted to do is sit in a corner and draw pictures of plants."

"Thank goodness for that!" Alma said.

"Perhaps. I don't think my mother would agree, and my father went to his grave angry at my choice of career—if one can call it a career. Mercifully for my long-suffering mother, my younger brother Jacob has come up behind me to set an example as a most dutiful son. He attended university in my footsteps, but, unlike me, he managed to remain there for the expected duration. He studied courageously, earning every honor and laurel as he did so, though I sometimes feared he would injure his mind through such exertions, and now he preaches from the same Framingham pulpit where my father and grandfather once stood before their own congregations. He is a good man, my brother, and he has prospered. He is a credit to the Pike name. The community admires him. I am entirely fond of him. But I do not envy his life."

"You come from a family of ministers, then?"

"Indeed—and was meant to be one myself."

"What happened?" Alma asked, rather boldly. "Did you fall away from the Lord?"

"No," he said. "Quite the opposite. I fell too close to the Lord."

Alma wanted to ask what he meant by such a curious statement, but she felt that she had pushed overmuch already, and her guest did not elaborate. They rested in silence for a long while, listening to the thrush sing. After a spell, Alma noticed that Mr. Pike had fallen asleep. How suddenly he was gone! Awake one moment and asleep the next! It occurred to her that he must have been utterly exhausted from his long journey—and here she was peppering him with questions, and bothering him with her theories of bryophytes and transmutation.

Quietly, she stood up and crossed to another area of the boulder field, to ponder once more her moss colonies. She felt so pleased and relaxed. How agreeable was this Mr. Pike! She wondered how long he would stay at White Acre. Perhaps she could convince him to remain for the entirety of the summer. What a joy it would be to have this friendly, inquisitive creature about the place. It would be like having a younger brother. She had never before imagined having a younger brother, but now she desperately wanted one, and she wanted him to be Ambrose Pike. She would have to speak to her father about it. Surely they could make a painting studio for him, in one of the old dairy buildings, if he wished to stay.

It was probably half an hour before she noticed Mr. Pike stirring in the grass. She walked back over to him and smiled.

"You fell asleep," she said.

"No," he corrected her. "Sleep overtook me."

Still sprawled in the grass, he stretched out his limbs like a cat, or an infant. He did not seem the least bit uncomfortable about having dozed off in front of Alma, so she did not feel uncomfortable, either.

"You must be weary, Mr. Pike."

"I have been weary for years." He sat up, yawned, and set his hat back on his head. "What a generous person you are, though, to have allotted me this rest. I thank you."

"Well, you were generous to listen to me speak about mosses."

"That was my pleasure. I hope to hear more. I was just thinking, as I nodded off, what an enviable life you lead, Miss Whittaker. Imagine being able to spend one's entire existence in pursuit of something so detailed and fine as these mosses—and all the while surrounded by a loving family and its comforts."

"I should think that my life would appear dull to a man who had spent eighteen years in the jungles of Central America."

"Not in the least. If anything, I have been longing for a life that is a bit more dull than what I have thus far experienced."

"Be careful what you wish for, Mr. Pike. A dull life is not as interesting as you may think!"

He laughed. Alma came closer and sat beside him, right on the grass, tucking her skirts beneath her legs.

"I shall confess something to you, Mr. Pike," she said. "Sometimes I fear that my labors in these moss beds are of no use or value whatsoever. Sometimes I wish I had something more sparkling to offer the world, something more magnificent—like your orchid paintings, I suppose. I am diligent and disciplined, but I do not possess a distinctive genius."

"So you are industrious, but not original?"

"Yes!" Alma said. "Exactly that! Precisely."

"Bah!" he said. "You do not convince me. I wonder why you would even try to convince yourself of something so foolish."

"You are kind, Mr. Pike. You have made an old lady feel quite attended to this afternoon. But I am aware of the truth of my own life. My work in these moss fields excites nobody but the cows and the crows who watch me at it all day."

"Cows and crows are excellent judges of genius, Miss Whittaker. Take my word for it—I have been painting exclusively for their amusement now for many years on end."

That evening, George Hawkes joined them for dinner at White Acre. This would be the first time George had met Ambrose Pike in person, and he was terribly excited about it—or as excited as a solemn old fellow like George could ever become.

"It is my honor to know you, sir," George said, with a smile. "Your work has brought me the most undeviating pleasure."

Alma was touched by George's sincerity. She knew what her friend could not say to the artist—that this past year had been one of acute suffering within the Hawkes household, and that Ambrose Pike's orchids had freed George, fleetingly, from the snares of darkness.

"I offer you my unfeigned thanks for your encouragement," Mr. Pike replied. "Unfortunately, my thanks are the only compensation I can make at the moment, but they are sincere."

As for Henry Whittaker, he was in a foul mood that night. Alma could see it from ten paces away, and she keenly wished that her father were not joining them for dinner. She had neglected to warn her guest about her father's curt nature, and now she regretted it. Poor Mr. Pike would be thrown at the wolf without any preparation, and the wolf was, quite clearly, both hungry and incensed. She also regretted that neither she nor George Hawkes had thought to bring one of the extraordinary orchid paintings to show her father, which meant that Henry had no sense of who this Ambrose Pike was, other than an orchid-chaser and an artist—neither of which was a category of person he tended to admire.

Not surprisingly, the dinner began poorly.

"Who is this individual again?" her father asked, looking straight at his new guest.

"This is Mr. Ambrose Pike," Alma said. "As I told you earlier, he is a naturalist and a painter, whom George has recently discovered. He makes the most exquisite renditions of orchids I have ever seen, Father."

"You draw orchids?" Henry demanded of Mr. Pike, in the same tone in which another man might say, "You rob widows?"

"Well, I attempt to, sir."

"Everybody attempts to draw orchids," Henry said. "Nothing new about that."

"You raise a fair point, sir."

"What is so special about your orchids?"

Mr. Pike contemplated the question. "I could not say," he admitted. "I don't know whether anything is special about them, sir—other than that painting orchids is all I do. It is all I have done now for nearly twenty years."

"Well, that is an absurd employment."

"I disagree, Mr. Whittaker," the artist said, unperturbed. "But only because I would not call it an employment at all."

"How do you make a living?"

"Again, you raise a fair point. But as you can probably see by my mode of dress, it is arguable whether I make a living at all."

"I would not advertise that fact as an attribute, young man."

"Believe me, sir—I do not."

Henry peered at him, taking in the worn suit and the unkempt beard. "What happened, then?" he demanded. "Why are you so poor? Did you squander a fortune like a rake?"

"Father—" Alma attempted.

"Sadly, no," said Mr. Pike, seemingly unoffended. "There was never any
fortune in my family to be squandered."

"What does your father do for a living?"

"Currently, he resides across the divide of death. But prior to that, he was a minister in Framingham, Massachusetts."

"Why are you not a minister, in that case?"

"My mother wonders the same thing, Mr. Whittaker. I am afraid I have too many questions about religion to be a good minister."

"*Religion?*" Henry frowned. "What the deuce does *religion* have to do with being a good minister? It is a profession like any other profession, young man. You fit yourself to the task, and keep your opinions private. That is what all good ministers do—or should!"

Mr. Pike laughed pleasantly. "If only somebody had told me that twenty years ago, sir!"

"There is no excuse for a young man of health and wit in this country not to prosper. Even a minister's son should be able to find industrious activity somewhere."

"Many would agree with you," said Mr. Pike. "Including my late father. Nonetheless, I have been living beneath my station for years."

"And I have been living *above* my station—forever! I first came here to America when I was a young fellow about your age. I found money lying about everywhere, all over this country. All I had to do was pick it up with the tip of my walking stick. What is your excuse for poverty, then?"

Mr. Pike looked Henry directly in the eye and said, without a trace of malice, "The want of a good walking stick, I suppose."

Alma swallowed hard and stared down at her plate. George Hawkes did the same. Henry, however, seemed not to hear. There were times when Alma thanked the heavens for her father's worsening deafness. He had already turned his attention to the butler.

"I tell you, Becker," Henry said, "if you make me eat mutton one more night this week, I will have someone shot."

"He doesn't really have people shot," Alma reassured Mr. Pike, under her breath.

"I had figured that," her guest whispered back, "or else I would be dead already."

For the rest of the meal, George and Alma and Mr. Pike made pleasant conversation—more or less between themselves—while Henry huffed and coughed and complained about various aspects of his dinner, and even nodded off a few times, chin collapsed on his chest. He was, after all, eighty-eight years old. None of it, happily, appeared to concern Mr. Pike, and as George Hawkes was already used to this sort of behavior, Alma eventually relaxed a bit.

"Please forgive my father," Alma said to Mr. Pike in a low voice, during one of Henry's bouts of sleep. "George knows his moods well, but these outbursts can be disquieting to those who do not have experience with our Henry Whittaker."

"He is quite the bear at the dinner table," Mr. Pike replied, with a tone more admiring than appalled.

"Indeed he is," said Alma. "Thankfully, though, like a bear, he sometimes gives us the respite of hibernating!"

This comment even brought a smile to George Hawkes's lips, but Ambrose was still studying the sleeping figure of Henry, pondering something.

"My own father was so grave, you see," he said. "I always found his silences frightening. I should think it would be delightful to have a father who speaks and acts with such liberty. One always knows where one stands."

"One does, at that," Alma agreed.

"Mr. Pike," George said, changing the subject, "may I ask where you are living at the moment? The address to which I sent my letter was in Boston, but you mentioned just now that your family resides in Framingham, so I wasn't certain."

"At the moment, sir, I am without a home," said Mr. Pike. "The address you refer to in Boston is the residence of my old friend Daniel Tupper, who has been kind to me since the days of my short career at Harvard. His family owns a small printing concern in Boston—nothing as fine as your operation, but well run and solid. They are mostly known for pamphlets and local bills of advertisement, that sort of thing. When I left Harvard, I worked for the Tupper family for several years as a typesetter, and found that I had a hand for it. That was also where I first learned the art of lithography. I had been told it was difficult, but I never found it to be. It is much the same as drawing, really, except that one draws on stone—though of course you both already know that! Forgive me. I am unaccustomed to speaking about my work."

"And what took you to Mexico and Guatemala, Mr. Pike?" George continued gently.

"Again, we can credit my friend Tupper with that. I've always had a fascination for orchids, and somewhere along the way, Tupper hatched a scheme that I should go to the tropics for a few years and make some drawings and such, and together we would produce a beautiful book on tropical orchids. I'm afraid he thought it would make us both quite rich. We were young, you know, and he was full of confidence about me.

"So we pooled our resources, such as they were, and Tupper put me on a boat. He instructed me to go off and make a great noise of myself in the world. Sadly for him, I am not much of a noisemaker. Even more sadly for him, my few years in the jungle turned into eighteen, as I have already explained to Miss Whittaker. Through thrift and perseverance I was able to keep myself alive there for nearly two decades, and I am proud to say I never took money from Tupper or anybody, after his initial investment. Nonetheless, I think poor Tupper feels his faith in me was quite misguided. When I finally came home last year, he was kind enough to let me use his family's printing press to make some of the lithographs you've already seen, but— quite forgivably—he long ago lost his desire to produce a book with me. I move too slowly for him. He has a family now, and cannot dally about with such expensive projects. He has been a heroically good friend to me, all the same. He lets me sleep on the couch in his home, and, since returning to America, I have been helping once more in the print shop."

"And your plans now?" Alma said.

Mr. Pike raised his hands, as though in supplication before heaven. "It has been so long since I made plans, you see."

"But what would you *like* to do?" Alma asked.

"Nobody has ever asked me that question before."

"Yet I ask you, Mr. Pike. And I wish for you to give me an honest answer."

He turned his light brown eyes upon her. He did look awfully weary. "Then I shall tell you, Miss Whittaker," he said. "I would like never to travel again. I would like to spend the rest of my days in a place so silent—and working at a pace so slow—that I would be able to hear myself living."

George and Alma exchanged glances. As though sensing that he was being left behind, Henry woke up with a start, and pulled the attention back to himself.

"Alma!" he said. "That letter from Dick Yancey last week. You read it?"

"I did read it, Father," she replied, briskly changing tone.

"What do you make of it?"

"I think it unfortunate news."

"Obviously it is. It has put me in a ghastly temper. But what do your friends here make of it?" Henry asked, waving his glass at his guests.

"I do not believe they know of the situation," Alma said.

"Then tell them the situation, daughter. I need opinions."

This was most odd. Henry did not generally seek opinions. But he urged her again with a wave of the wineglass, and so she began to speak, addressing herself to George and Mr. Pike both.

"Well, it's about vanilla," she said. "Fifteen years or so ago, my father was convinced by a Frenchman to invest in a vanilla plantation in Tahiti. Now we learn the plantation has failed. And the Frenchman has vanished."

"Along with my investment," Henry added.

"Along with my father's investment," Alma confirmed.

"A considerable investment," Henry clarified.

"A *most* considerable investment," Alma agreed. She knew this well, for she had arranged the transfers of payment herself.

"It should have worked," Henry said. "The climate is perfect for it. And the vines grew! Dick Yancey saw them himself. They grew to sixty-five feet tall. The blasted Frenchman said that vanilla would grow happily there, and he was right about it. The vines produced blossoms as big as your fist. Exactly as he said they would. What was it the little Frenchman told me, Alma? 'Growing vanilla in Tahiti will be easier than farting in your sleep.'"

Alma blanched, glancing at her guests. George politely folded his napkin in his lap, but Mr. Pike smiled in frank amusement.

"So what went wrong, sir?" he asked. "If I may pry?"

Henry glared at him. "The vines did not bear fruit. The blossoms bloomed and withered, and never produced a single blasted pod."

"May I ask where the original vanilla plants came from?"

"Mexico," Henry growled, staring Mr. Pike down in a spirit of full challenge. "So you be the one to tell me, young man—what went wrong?"

Alma was slowly beginning to glean something here. Why did she ever underestimate her father? Was there anything the old man missed? Even in his foul temper, even in his semideafness, even in his *sleep*, he had somehow garnered exactly who was sitting at his table: an orchid expert who had just spent nearly two decades of study in and around Mexico. And vanilla, Alma now remembered, was a member of the orchid family. Their visitor was being put to the test.

"*Vanilla planifolia*," Mr. Pike said.

"Exactly," Henry confirmed, and set down his wineglass on the table. "That is what we planted in Tahiti. Go on."

"I saw it all over Mexico, sir. Mostly around Oaxaca. Your man in Polynesia, your Frenchman, he was correct—it is a vigorous climber, and it would happily take to the climate of the South Pacific, I suspect."

"Then why are the blasted plants not fruiting?" Henry demanded.

"I could not say for certain," Mr. Pike said, "having never laid eyes on the plants in question."

"Then you are nothing but a useless little orchid-sketcher, aren't you?" Henry snapped.

"Father—"

"However, sir," Mr. Pike went on, unconcerned with the insult, "I could posit a theory. When your Frenchman was originally procuring his vanilla plants in Mexico, he may have accidentally purchased a varietal of *Vanilla planifolia* that the natives call *oreja de burro*—donkey's ear—which never bears fruit at all."

"He was an idiot then," Henry said.

"Not necessarily, Mr. Whittaker. It would take a mother's eye to see the distinction between the fruiting and nonfruiting versions of the *planifolia*. It is a common mistake. The natives themselves often confuse the two varieties. Few men of botany can even tell the difference."

"Can *you* tell the difference?" Henry demanded.

Mr. Pike hesitated. It was evident he did not wish to disparage a man he had never met.

"I asked you a question, boy. Can you tell the difference between the two varieties of *planifolia*? Or can you not?"

"Generally, sir? Yes. I can tell the difference."

"Then the Frenchman was an idiot," Henry concluded. "And I was a bigger idiot to have invested in him, for now I have wasted thirty-five acres of fine lowland in Tahiti, growing an infertile variety of vanilla vines for the past fifteen years. Alma, write a letter to Dick Yancey tonight, and tell him to yank up the entire lot of vines and feed it to the pigs. Tell him to replace it with yams. Tell Yancey, too, that if he ever finds that little shit of a Frenchman, he can feed *him* to the pigs!"

Henry stood up and limped out of the room, too angry to finish his meal. George and Mr. Pike stared in silent wonder at the retreating figure—so quaint in his wig and old velvet breeches, yet so fierce.

As for Alma, she felt a strong surge of victory. The Frenchman had lost, and Henry Whittaker had lost, and the vanilla plantation in Tahiti was most certainly lost. But Ambrose Pike, she believed, had won something tonight, during his first appearance at the White Acre dinner table.

It was a small victory, perhaps, but it might count toward something in the end.

That night, Alma awoke to a strange noise.

She had been lost in dreamless sleep and then, as suddenly as though she'd been slapped, she was awake. She peered into the darkness. Was there somebody in her room? Was it Hanneke? No. Nobody was there. She rested back into her pillow. The night was cool and serene. What had broken her slumber? Voices? She was reminded for the first time in years of the night that Prudence had been brought to White Acre as a child, surrounded by men and covered with blood. Poor Prudence. Alma really should go visit her. She must make more of an effort with her sister. But there was simply no time. There was silence all around her. Alma began to settle back into sleep.

She heard the sound again. Once more, Alma's eyes snapped open. What *was* it? Indeed, it seemed to be voices. But who would be awake at this hour?

She rose and wrapped her shawl around her, and expertly lit her lamp. She walked to the top of the stairs and looked over the banister. A light was on in the drawing room; she could see it glowing from under the door. She could hear her father's laughter. Who was he with? Was he talking to himself? Why had nobody woken her, if Henry needed something?

She came down the stairs and found her father sitting next to Ambrose Pike on the divan. They were looking over some drawings. Her father was wearing a long white nightdress and an old-fashioned sleeping cap, and he was flushed with drink. Mr. Pike was still in his brown corduroy suit, with his hair even more disarranged than earlier in the day.

"We've awoken you," Mr. Pike said, looking up. "My apologies."

"Can I assist you with something?" Alma asked.

"Alma!" Henry cried. "Your boy here has come up with a piece of brilliance! Show it to her, son!"

Henry wasn't drunk, Alma realized; he was simply ebullient.

"I had trouble sleeping, Miss Whittaker," Mr. Pike said, "because I was thinking about the vanilla plants in Tahiti. It occurred to me that there might be another possibility as to why the vines have not fruited. I should have waited until morning so as to not disturb anyone, but I did not want to lose the idea. So I rose and came down, looking for paper. I fear I woke your father in the process."

"Look what he's done!" Henry said, thrusting a paper at Alma. It was a lovely sketch, minutely detailed, of a vanilla blossom, with arrows pointing to particular bits of the plant's anatomy. Henry stared at Alma expectantly, while she studied the page, which meant nothing to her.

"I apologize," Alma said. "I was asleep only a moment ago, so my mind is perhaps not clear . . ."

"Pollination, Alma!" Henry cried, clapping his hands once, and then pointing at Mr. Pike, indicating that he should explain.

"What I believe may have occurred, Miss Whittaker—as I was telling your father—is that your Frenchman may have, indeed, collected the correct variety of vanilla from Mexico. But perhaps the reason the vines have not fruited is that they have not been successfully pollinated."

It may have been the middle of the night, and Alma may have been asleep only moments earlier, but still her mind was a fearfully well-trained machine of botanical calculation, which is why she instantly heard the abacus beads in her brain begin clicking toward an understanding.

"What is the pollination mechanism for the vanilla orchid?" she asked.

"I could not say for certain," Mr. Pike said. "Nobody is certain. It could be an ant, it could be a bee, it could be a moth of some sort. It could even be a hummingbird. But whatever it is, your Frenchman did not transport it to Tahiti along with his plants, and the native insects and birds of French Polynesia do not seem capable of pollinating your vanilla blossoms, which do have a difficult shape. Thus—no fruit. No pods."

Henry clapped once again. "No profit!" he added.

"So what are we to do?" Alma asked. "Collect every insect and bird in the Mexican jungle and try to ship them, alive, to the South Pacific, with the hopes of finding your pollinator?"

"I don't believe you will need to," Mr. Pike said. "This is why I couldn't sleep, because I've been considering that same question, and I think I've come up with an answer. I think you could pollinate it yourself, by hand. Look, I've made some drawings here. What makes the vanilla orchid so troublesome to pollinate is the exceptionally long column, you see, which contains both the male and female organs. The rostellum—right here— separates the two, to prevent the plant from pollinating itself. You simply need to lift the rostellum, and then insert a small twig into the pollinia cluster, gather up the pollen on the tip of the twig, and then reinsert the twig into the stamen of a different blossom. You are essentially playing the role of the bee, or the ant, or whoever would be doing this in nature. But you could be far more efficient than any animal, because you could hand-pollinate every single blossom on the vine."

"Who would do this?" Alma asked.

"Your workers could do it," Mr. Pike said. "The plant only puts out blooms once a year, and it would take but a week to finish the task."

"Wouldn't the workers crush the blossoms?"

"Not if they were carefully trained."

"But who would have the delicacy for such an operation?"

Mr. Pike smiled. "All you need is little boys with little fingers and little sticks. If anything, they will enjoy the task. I myself would have enjoyed it, as a child. And surely there is an abundance of little boys and little sticks on Tahiti, no?"

"Aha!" Henry said. "So what do you think, Alma?"

"I think it's brilliant." She was also thinking that first thing tomorrow, she would need to show Ambrose Pike the White Acre library's copy of the sixteenth-century Florentine codex, with those early Spanish Franciscan illustrations of vanilla vines. He would much appreciate it. She couldn't wait to show it to him. She hadn't even shown him the library yet at all. She had barely shown him anything at White Acre. They had so much more explor-ing ahead of them!

"It's merely an idea," Mr. Pike said. "It probably could have waited until daylight."

Alma heard a noise and turned. Here was Hanneke de Groot, standing
at the door in her nightclothes, looking plump and puffy and irritable.

"Now I've woken the entire household," Mr. Pike said. "My sincerest apologies."

"*Is er een probleem?*" Hanneke asked Alma.

"There's no problem, Hanneke," Alma said. "The gentlemen and I were simply having a discussion."

"At two o'clock in the morning?" Hanneke demanded. "*Is dit een bordeel?*"

Is this a bordello?

"What is she saying?" Henry asked. Apart from his failing hearing, he had never mastered Dutch—despite having been married to a Dutch-woman for decades, and having worked alongside Dutch speakers for much of his life.

"She wants to know if anyone would like tea or coffee," Alma said. "Mr. Pike? Father?"

"I will have tea," Henry said.

"You're all kind, but I will take my leave," Mr. Pike said. "I will return to my rooms now, and I promise not to disturb anyone again. Moreover, I've just realized that tomorrow is the Sabbath. Perhaps you will all be rising early, for church?"

"Not I!" Henry said.

"You will find in this household, Mr. Pike," Alma said, "that some of us keep the Sabbath, some of us do not keep it, and some of us keep it only halfway."

"I understand," he replied. "In Guatemala, I often lost track of the days, and I fear I missed many Sabbaths."

"Do they honor the Sabbath in Guatemala, Mr. Pike?"

"Only through the acts of drinking, brawling, and cockfighting, I'm afraid."

"Then off to Guatemala we go!" Henry cried.

Alma had not seen her father in such high spirits in years.

Ambrose Pike laughed. "You may go to Guatemala, Mr. Whittaker. I daresay they would appreciate you there. But I myself am finished with jungles. For tonight, I should simply return to my rooms. When I have the opportunity to sleep in a proper bed, I would be fool to waste it. I bid you both a good night, I thank you again for your hospitality, and I apologize most sincerely to your housekeeper."

After Mr. Pike left the room, Alma and her father sat in silence for a while. Henry stared at Ambrose's sketch of the vanilla orchid. Alma could almost hear him thinking; she knew her father all too well. She waited for him to say it—what she knew was coming—while at the same time trying to figure out how she was going to combat it.

Meanwhile, Hanneke returned with a tray, which held tea for Alma and Henry, and coffee for herself. She set it down with a grumbling sigh, then plopped herself in an armchair across from Henry. The housekeeper poured her own cup first, and put her gouty old ankle up on a finely embroidered French footstool. She left Henry and Alma to serve themselves. Protocol at White Acre had grown relaxed over the years. Perhaps too relaxed.

"We should send him to Tahiti," Henry said at last, after a good five minutes of silence. "We will put him in charge of the vanilla plantation."

So there it was. Exactly what Alma had seen coming.

"An interesting idea," she said.

But she could not let her father dispatch Mr. Pike to the South Seas. She knew this with as much certainty as she had ever known anything in her life. For one thing, she sensed that the artist himself would not welcome the assignment. He had said as much himself—that he was finished with jungles. He did not wish to travel any longer. He was weary and homesick. And yet he had no home. The man needed a home. He needed to rest. He needed a place to work, to make the paintings and prints he was born to make, and to hear himself living.

What's more, though—Alma needed Mr. Pike. She felt overcome with a wild necessity to keep this person at White Acre forever. What a thing to decide, after knowing him less than a day! But she felt ten years younger today than she had felt the day before. This had been the most illuminating Saturday Alma had spent in decades—or perhaps even since childhood—and Ambrose Pike was the source of the illumination.

This situation reminded her of when she was young, and she had found a fox kitten in the woods, orphaned and tiny. She had brought it home and begged her parents to allow her to keep it. This was back in the halcyon days before Prudence had arrived, back when Alma had been given the run of the whole universe. Henry had been tempted, but Beatrix had put a stop to the plan. *Wild creatures belong in wild places.* The kit was taken from Alma's hands, not to be seen again.

Well, she would not lose *this* fox. And Beatrix was not here anymore to

prevent it.

"I think it would be a mistake, Father," Alma said. "It would be a waste of Mr. Pike to send him to Polynesia. Anyone can manage a vanilla plantation. You just heard the man explain it himself. It's simple. He's even made the instruction drawings already. Send the sketches to Dick Yancey, and have him enlist someone to implement the pollination program. I think you could find better use for Mr. Pike right here at White Acre."

"Doing what, exactly?" Henry asked.

"You have not yet seen his work, Father. George Hawkes thinks Ambrose Pike to be the best lithographer of our age."

"And what need do I have for a lithographer?"

"Maybe it's time to publish a book of White Acre's botanical treasures. You have specimens in these greenhouses that the civilized world has never seen. They should be documented."

"Why would I do such an expensive thing, Alma?"

"Let me tell you something that I've heard recently," Alma said, by means of an answer. "Kew is planning to publish a catalog of fine prints and illustrations of its most rare plants. Had you heard that?"

"For what purpose?" Henry asked.

"For the purpose of boasting, Father," Alma said. "I heard it from one of the young lithographers who works for George Hawkes down on Arch Street. The British have offered this boy a small fortune, to lure him over to Kew. He is fairly gifted, though he's no Ambrose Pike. He is considering to accept the invitation. He says the book is intended to be the most beautiful botanical collection ever printed. Queen Victoria herself is investing in it. Five-color lithographs, and the best watercolorists in Europe to finish them off. It will be a large volume, too. Nearly two feet tall, the boy says, and thick as a Bible. Every botanical collector will want a copy of it. It is meant to announce the renaissance of Kew."

"The renaissance of Kew," Henry scoffed. "Kew will never be what it was, now that Banks is gone."

"I hear differently, Father. Since they've built the Palm House, everyone claims the place is becoming magnificent again."

Was this shameless of her? Even sinful? To stir up Henry's old rivalry with Kew Gardens? But it was true, what she said. It was all true. So let Henry brew up some antagonism, she decided. It did not feel wrong to evoke this force. Things had become too torpid and slow at White Acre over these last years. A bit of competition would harm no one. She was merely raising up the blood in Henry Whittaker's old bones—and in herself, too. Let this family have a pulse again!

"No one has yet heard of Ambrose Pike, Father," she pushed on. "But once George Hawkes publishes his orchid collection, everyone will know the name. Once Kew publishes *its* book, every other prominent botanical garden and greenhouse will want to commission a florilegium, as well—and they'll all want Mr. Pike to make the prints. Let us not wait, only to lose him to a rival garden. Let us keep him here, and offer him shelter and patronage. Invest in him, Father. You've seen how clever he is, how useful. Give him the opportunity. Let us produce a folio of White Acre's collection that surpasses anything the world of botanical publishing has ever seen."

Henry said nothing. Now she could hear *his* abacus clicking. She waited. It was taking him a long time to think. Too long. Meanwhile, Hanneke was slurping at her coffee with what appeared to be deliberate insouciance. The noise seemed to be distracting Henry. Alma wanted to knock the cup out of the old woman's hands.

Raising her voice, Alma made one last effort. "It should not be difficult, Father, to persuade Mr. Pike to stay here. The man is in need of a home, but he lives on precious little, and it would require nearly nothing to support him. His worldly belongings fill a valise that would fit on your lap. As you have witnessed tonight, he is agreeable company. I think you may even enjoy having him about. But whatever you do, Father, I lay the most urgent stress upon you *not* to send this man to Tahiti. Any fool can grow a vanilla vine. Get another Frenchman for that job, or a hire a missionary gone bored. Any blockhead's brother can manage a plantation, but no one can make botanical illustrations in the manner of Ambrose Pike. Do not let the chance slip for you to keep him here with us. I seldom give you such strong counsel, Father, but I must plead with you tonight in the plainest terms—do not lose this one. You shall regret it."

There was another long silence. Another slurp from Hanneke.

"He will need a studio," Henry said at last. "Printing presses, that sort of thing."

"He can share the carriage house with me," Alma said. "I have plenty of room for him."

So it was decided.

Henry limped off to bed. Alma and Hanneke were left staring at each other. Hanneke said nothing, but Alma did not like the expression on her face.

"*Wat?*" Alma finally demanded.

"*Wat voor spelletje speel je?*" Hanneke asked.

"I don't know what you're talking about," Alma said. "I am not playing a game."

The old housekeeper shrugged. "As you insist," she said, in deliberately accentuated English. "You are the mistress of this house."

Then Hanneke stood up, quaffed back the last of her coffee, and returned to her rooms in the basement—leaving a mess behind in the drawing room for someone else to clean up.

Chapter Fifteen

They became inseparable, Alma and Ambrose. They soon spent nearly every moment together. Alma instructed Hanneke to move Mr. Pike out of the guest wing and into Prudence's old bedroom, on the second floor of the house, directly across the hall from Alma's own room. Hanneke protested the incursion of a stranger into the family's private living quarters (it was not proper, she said, nor safe, and most especially, *we do not know him*), but Alma overruled her, and the move was made. Alma herself cleared space for Ambrose in the carriage house, in a disused tack room next to her own study. Within a fortnight, his first printing presses had arrived. Soon after that, Alma purchased for him a fine bureau-escritoire, with pigeonholes and stacks of broad, shallow drawers to hold his drawings.

"I've never before had my own desk," Ambrose told her. "It makes me feel uncharacteristically important. It makes me feel like an aide-de-camp."

A single door separated their two studies—and that door was never closed. All day long, Alma and Ambrose walked back and forth into each other's rooms, looking in on the other's progress, and showing each other some item or other of interest in a specimen jar, or on a microscope slide. They ate buttered toast together every morning, had gypsy lunches out in the fields, and stayed up late into the night, helping Henry with his correspondence, or looking over old volumes from the White Acre library. On Sundays, Ambrose joined Alma for church with the dull, droning Swedish Lutherans, dutifully reciting prayers alongside her.

They spoke or they were silent—it did not seem to matter much one way or the other—but they were never apart.

During the hours that Alma worked in the moss beds, Ambrose sprawled out on the grass nearby, reading. While Ambrose sketched in the orchid house, Alma pulled up a chair beside him, working on her own correspondence. She had never before spent much time in the orchid house, but since Ambrose's arrival, it had been transformed into the most stunning location at White Acre. He had spent nearly two weeks cleaning each of the hundreds of glass panes so that sunlight entered in crisp, unfiltered columns. He mopped and waxed the floors until they glittered. What's more—and rather astonishingly—he spent another week burnishing the leaves of every individual orchid plant with banana peels, until they all shone like tea services polished by a loyal butler.

"What's next, Ambrose?" Alma teased. "Shall we now comb out the hair of every fern on the property?"

"I do not think the ferns would object," he said.

In fact, something curious had occurred at White Acre right after Ambrose brought such shine and order to the orchid house: the rest of the estate suddenly seemed drab by comparison. It was as though someone had polished only a single spot on a dingy old mirror, and now, as a result, the rest of the mirror looked truly filthy. One wouldn't have noticed it before, but now it was obvious. It was as though Ambrose had opened an inlet to something previously invisible, and Alma could finally see a truth she would otherwise have been blind to forever: White Acre, elegant as it was, had incrementally fallen into a state of crumbling neglect over the past quarter century.

With this realization, Alma got it in her mind to bring the rest of the estate up to the same sparkling standard as the orchid house. After all, when was the last time every single pane of glass in any of the other greenhouses had been cleaned? She could not recall. There was mildew and dust everywhere she looked now. The fences all needed whitewashing and repair, weeds grew in the gravel drive, and cobwebs filled the library. Every rug needed a stout banging, and every furnace was in need of overhaul. The palms in the great glasshouse were nearly bursting through the roof, they had not been cut back in so many years. There were desiccated animal bones in the corners of the barns from years of marauding cats, the carriage brass had been allowed to tarnish, and the maids' uniforms appeared to be decades out of date—because they were.

Alma hired seamstresses to make new uniforms for everyone on the staff, and she even commissioned two new linen frocks for herself. She offered a new suit to Ambrose, but he asked if he could have four new paint-brushes, instead. (Exactly four. She offered five. He did not need five, he said. Four would be luxury enough.) She enlisted a squadron of fresh young help to assist in bringing the place back up to shine. She realized that, as older White Acre workers had died or been dismissed over the years, they had never been replaced. Only a third as many staff worked at the estate now as there had been twenty-five years ago, and that was simply not enough.

Hanneke resisted the new arrivals at first. "I do not have the strength of body or mind anymore to make good workers out of bad ones," she complained.

"But, Hanneke," Alma protested. "Look how cleverly Mr. Pike has spruced up the orchid house! Don't we want everything at the estate to look so fine?"

"We have far too much cleverness in this world already," Hanneke replied, "and not enough good sense. Your Mr. Pike is only making work for others. Your mother would spin in her grave, to know that people are going about polishing flowers by hand."

"Not the flowers," Alma corrected. "The leaves."

But in time even Hanneke surrendered, and it wasn't long before Alma saw her delegating the new young staff to haul out the old flour barrels from the cellar, to dry them in the sun—a chore that had not been performed, as far as Alma could remember, since Andrew Jackson had been president.

"Don't go too far with the cleaning," Ambrose cautioned. "A little neglect can be of benefit. Have you ever noticed how the most splendid lilacs, for instance, are the ones that grow up alongside derelict barns and abandoned shacks? Sometimes beauty needs a bit of ignoring, to properly come into being."

"So speaks the man who polishes his orchids with banana peels!" Alma said, laughing.

"Ah, but those are *orchids*," Ambrose said. "That's different. Orchids are holy relics, Alma, and need to be treated with reverence."

"But, Ambrose," Alma said, "this entire estate was beginning to look like a holy relic . . . after a holy war!"

They called each other "Alma" and "Ambrose" now.

May passed. June passed. July arrived.

Had she ever been this happy?

She had never been this happy.

Alma's existence, before the arrival of Ambrose Pike, had been a good enough one. Yes, her world may have looked small, and her days repetitive, but none of it had been unbearable to her. She had made the best of her fate. Her work with mosses occupied her mind, and she knew that her research was unimpeachable and honest. She had her journals, her herbarium, her microscopes, her botanical disquisitions, her correspondence with botanists and collectors overseas, her duties toward her father. She had her customs, habits, and responsibilities. She had her dignity. True, she was something like a book that had opened to the same page every single day for nearly thirty straight years—but it had not been such a bad page, at that. She had been sanguine. Contented. By all measures, it had been a good life.

She could never return to that life now.

In mid-July of 1848, Alma went to visit Retta at the Griffon Asylum for the first time since her friend had been interned there. Alma had not kept her word to visit Retta every month, as she had promised George Hawkes she would, but White Acre had been so busy and pleasant since Ambrose's arrival that she had put Retta out of her mind. By July, though, Alma's conscience was beginning to scratch at her, and thus she made arrangements to take her carriage up to Trenton for the day. She wrote a note to George Hawkes, asking if he would like to join her, but he demurred. He gave no explanation as to why, although Alma knew he simply could not bear to see Retta in her current state. Ambrose, however, offered to keep Alma company for the day.

"But you have so much work to do here," Alma said. "Nor is it likely to be a pleasurable visit."

"The work can wait. I would like to meet your friend. I have a curiosity, I must confess, about diseases of the imagination. I would be interested to see the asylum."

After an uneventful ride to Trenton, and a short conversation with the supervising doctor, Alma and Ambrose were escorted to Retta's room. They found her in a small private chamber with a neat bedstead, a table and chair, a strip of carpet, and an empty space on the wall where a mirror had once hung, before it had to be removed—the nurse explained—because it was upsetting the patient.

"We tried to put her in with another lady for a spell," the nurse said, "but she wouldn't have it. Became violent. Fits of disquiet and terror. There is reason to fear for anyone left in a room with her. Better off on her own."

"What do you do for her do when she suffers such fits?" Alma asked.

"Ice baths," said the nurse. "And we block her eyes and ears. It seems to calm her."

It was not an unpleasant room. It had a view of the back gardens, and the light was plentiful, but still, Alma thought, her friend must be lonely. Retta was dressed neatly and her hair was clean and braided, but she looked apparitional. Pale as ashes. She was still a pretty thing, but mostly, by now, she was just a *thing*. She did not appear either pleased or alarmed to see Alma, nor did she show any interest in Ambrose. Alma went and sat beside her friend, and held her hand. Retta allowed it without protest. A few of her fingers, Alma noticed, were bandaged at the tips.

"What has happened there?" Alma asked the nurse.

"She bites herself at night," the nurse explained. "We can't get her to quit off doing it."

Alma had brought her friend a small bag of lemon candies and a paper funnel full of violets, but Retta merely looked at the gifts as though she was not certain which to eat and which to admire. Even the recent edition of *Joy's Lady's Book* that Alma had purchased along the way was met with indifference. Alma suspected that the flowers, the sweets, and the magazine would ultimately go home with the nurse.

"We have come to visit you," Alma said to Retta, rather lamely.

"Then why are you not here?" Retta asked, in a voice blunted by laudanum.

"We are here, darling. We are right here before you."

Retta looked at Alma blankly for a while, then turned to look out the window again.

"I had meant to bring her a prism," Alma said to Ambrose, "but I've gone and forgotten it. She always loved prisms."

"You should sing her a song," Ambrose suggested quietly.

"I am not a singer," Alma said.

"I do not think she would object."

But Alma couldn't even think of a song. Instead she leaned over to Retta's ear and whispered, "Who loves you most? Who loves you best? Who thinks of you when others rest?"

Retta failed to respond.

Alma turned to Ambrose, and asked, almost in a panic, "Do you know a song?"

"I know many, Alma. But I don't know *her* song."

In the carriage ride home, Alma and Ambrose were thoughtful and quiet. At last, Ambrose asked, "Was she always this way?"

"Stupefied? Never. She was always a bit mad, but she was such a delight as a girl. She had wild humor and no small amount of charm. All who knew her loved her. She even brought gaiety and laughter to me and to my sister—and, as I've told you, Prudence and I were never ones for shared gaiety. But her disturbances increased over the years. And now, as you see . . ."

"Yes. As I see. Poor creature. I have such sympathy for the mad. Whenever I am around them, I feel it straight to my soul. I think anyone who claims never to have felt insane is lying."

Alma pondered this. "I honestly do not believe I have ever felt insane," she said. "I wonder if I'm telling a falsehood when I say that to you. I don't think so."

Ambrose smiled. "Of course not. I should have made an exception for you, Alma. You are not like the rest of us. You have a mind of such solidity and substance. Your emotions are durable as a strongbox. This is why people feel so reassured around you."

"Do they?" Alma asked, genuinely surprised to hear it.

"Indeed, they do."

"That's a curious thought. I've never heard it expressed," Alma looked out the window of the carriage, and contemplated further. Then she remembered something. "Or perhaps I have heard it expressed. You know, Retta herself used to say that I possessed a rather reassuring chin."

"The entirety of your being is reassuring, Alma. Even your voice is reassuring. For those of us who sometimes feel as though we are blowing about our lives like chaff on a miller's floor, your presence is a most appreciated consolation."

Alma did not know how to respond to this surprising statement, so she tried to dismiss it. "Come now, Ambrose," she said. "You are such a steady-minded man—surely you have never felt insane?"

He thought for a moment, selecting his words carefully: "One cannot help but feel how closely one lies to the same condition as your friend Retta Snow."

"No, Ambrose, surely not!"

When he did not immediately reply, she felt herself grow anxious.

"Ambrose," she said more gently. "Surely not, yes?"

Again, he was careful, and took a long time to answer. "I refer to the sense of dislocation from this world—coupled with a feeling of alignment to some other world."

"To what other world?" Alma asked.

His hesitation to reply made her feel as though she had overreached, so she attempted a more casual tone. "I apologize, Ambrose. I have a dreadful habit of not resting on questions until I have found a satisfactory answer. It's my nature, I'm afraid. I hope you will not think me rude."

"You are not rude," Ambrose said. "I enjoy your curiosity. It's merely that I'm uncertain how to offer you a satisfactory answer. One does not wish to lose the fondness of people one admires by revealing too much of oneself."

So Alma released the topic, hoping, perhaps, that the subject of madness would never be mentioned again. As though to neutralize the moment, she brought out a book from her purse and attempted to read. The carriage was too jolting for comfortable reading, and her mind was much distracted by what she had just heard, but she pretended to be absorbed in her book regardless.

After a long while, Ambrose said, "I have not yet told you why I left Harvard, those many years ago."

She put the book away and turned to him.

"I suffered an episode, Alma," he said.

"Of madness?" Alma asked. She spoke in her customary direct way, although her stomach fell in fear at how he might reply.

"It may have been. I'm not certain what one would call it. My mother thought it was madness. My friends thought it was madness. The doctors believed it to be madness. I myself felt it was something else."

"Such as?" she asked, again in her normal voice, although her trepidation was mounting by the moment.

"Possession by spirits, perhaps? A gathering of magic? An erasure of material boundaries? Inspiration, winged with fire?" He did not smile. He was quite serious.

This confession gave Alma such severe pause that she could not reply. There was no place in her thinking for the erasure of material boundaries. Nothing brought more goodness and assurance to Alma Whittaker's life than the heartening certainty of material boundaries.

Ambrose regarded her carefully before continuing. He looked at her as though she were a thermometer or a compass—as though he were trying to gauge her, as though he were choosing a direction in which to turn based entirely on the nature of her response. She endeavored to keep alarm from her face. He must have been satisfied with what he saw, for he went on.

"When I was nineteen years old, I discovered a collection of books in the Harvard library written by Jacob Boehme. Do you know of him?"

Naturally she knew of him. She had her own copies of these works in the White Acre library. She had read Boehme, though she never admired him. Jacob Boehme was a sixteenth-century cobbler from Germany who had mystical visions about plants. Many people considered him an early botanist. Alma's mother, on the other hand, had considered him a cesspool of residual medieval superstition. So there was considerable conflict of opinion surrounding Jacob Boehme.

The old cobbler had believed in something he called "the signature of all things"—namely, that God had hidden clues for humanity's betterment inside the design of every flower, leaf, fruit, and tree on earth. All the natural world was a divine code, Boehme claimed, containing proof of our Creator's love. This is why so many medicinal plants resembled the diseases they were meant to cure, or the organs they were able to treat. Basil, with its liver-shaped leaves, is the obvious ministration for ailments of the liver. The celandine herb, which produces a yellow sap, can be used to treat the yellow discoloration brought on by jaundice. Walnuts, shaped like brains, are helpful for headaches. Coltsfoot, which grows near cold streams, can cure the coughs and chills brought on by immersion in ice water. *Polygonum*, with its spattering of blood-red markings on the leaves, cures bleeding wounds of the flesh. And so on, ad infinitum. Beatrix Whittaker had always been scornful of this theory ("Most leaves are shaped like livers—are we meant to eat them all?"), and Alma had inherited her mother's skepticism.

But now was not the time to speak of skepticism, for again Ambrose was reading Alma's face. He was searching her expression most desperately, it seemed, for permission to proceed. Again, Alma kept her countenance impassive, although she felt much disturbed. Again, he proceeded.

"I know that the science of today takes issue with Boehme's ideas," he said. "I understand the objections. Jacob Boehme worked in the opposite direction of proper scientific methodology. He lacked the rigor of orderly thinking. His writings were filled with shattered, splintered, mirror-fragments of insight. He was irrational. He was credulous. He saw only what he wished to see. He overlooked anything that contradicted his certainties. He started with his beliefs, then sought to make the facts fit around them. Nobody could rightly call that science."

Beatrix Whittaker could not have said it better herself, Alma thought—but again, she merely nodded.

"And yet . . ." Ambrose trailed off.

Alma gave her friend time to collect his thoughts. He was quiet for such a long while that she thought perhaps he had decided to end there. But after a long silence, he continued: "And yet Boehme said that God had *pressed* Himself into the world, and had left marks there for us to discover."

The parallel was unmistakable, Alma thought, and she could not help but point it out. "Like a printmaker," she said.

At these words, Ambrose spun to look at her, his face flooded with relief and gratitude. "Yes!" he said. "Precisely that. You understand me. You can see what that idea would have meant to me, as a young man. Boehme said that this divine *imprimatur* is a kind of holy magic, and that this magic is the only theology we will ever need. He believed that we could learn to read God's prints, but that we must first swing ourselves into the fire."

"Swing ourselves into the fire," Alma repeated, keeping her voice neutral.

"Yes. By renouncing the material world. By renouncing the church, with its stone walls and liturgies. By renouncing ambition. By renouncing study. By renouncing the desires of the body. By renouncing possessiveness and selfishness. By renouncing even speech! Only then could one see what God had seen, at the moment of creation. Only then could one read the messages the Lord had left behind for us. So you see, Alma, I could not become a minister after hearing of this. Nor a student. Nor a son. Nor—it seemed—a living man."

"What did you become, instead?" Alma asked.

"I tried to become the fire. I ceased all activities of normal existence. I stopped speaking. I even stopped eating. I believed that I could survive on sunlight and rain alone. For quite a long while—though it seems impossible to imagine—I tell you that I *did* survive on sunlight and rain alone. It did not surprise me. I had faith. I had always been the most devout of my mother's children, you see. Where my brothers possessed logic and reason, I had always felt the Creator's love more innately. As a child, I used to fall so deeply into prayer that my mother would shake me in church and punish me for sleeping during services, but I had not been sleeping. I had been . . . corresponding. Now, after reading Jacob Boehme, I wanted to meet the divine even more intimately. That is why I gave up everything in the world, including sustenance."

"What happened?" Alma asked, once more dreading the answer.

"I met the divine," he said, eyes bright. "Or, I believed I did. I had the most magnificent thoughts. I could read the language hidden inside trees. I saw angels living inside orchids. I saw a new religion, spoken in a new botanical language. I heard its hymns. I cannot remember the music now, but it was exquisite. Also, there was a full fortnight when I could hear people's thoughts. I wished they could hear mine, but they did not appear to. I was kept joyous by exalted feeling, by rapture. I felt that I could never be injured again, never touched. I was no harm to anyone, but I did lose my desire for this world. I was . . . unparticled. Oh, but there was more. Such knowledge came into me! For instance, I renamed all the colors! And I saw new colors, hidden colors. Did you know that there is a color called *swissen*, which is a sort of clear turquoise? Only moths can see it. It is the color of God's purest anger. You would not think God's anger would be pale and blue, but it is."

"I did not know that," Alma admitted, carefully.

"Well, I saw it," Ambrose said. "I saw halos of *swissen*, surrounding certain trees, and certain people. In other places, I saw crowns of benevolent light where there should have been no light at all. This was light that did not have a name, but it had a sound. Everywhere I saw it—or, rather, everywhere I heard it—I followed. Soon after that, however, I nearly died. My friend Daniel Tupper found me in a bank of snow. Sometimes I think that if winter had not come, I might have been able to continue."

"Without food, Ambrose?" Alma asked. "Surely not . . ."

"Sometimes I think so. I do not claim it to be rational, but I think so. I wished to become a plant. Sometimes I think that—just for a very short while, driven by faith—I became a plant. How else could I have endured two months with nothing but rain and sunlight? I recalled Isaiah: 'All flesh is grass . . . surely the people is grass.'"

For the first time in years, Alma remembered how, as a child, she had also longed to be a plant. Of course, she had been a mere child, wishing for more patience and affection from her father. But even so—she had never actually believed that she *was* a plant.

Ambrose went on. "After my friends found me in the snowbank, they took me to a hospital for the insane."

"Similar to where we just were?" Alma asked.

He smiled with infinite sadness. "Oh, no, Alma. Not at all similar to where we just were."

"Oh, Ambrose, I am so sorry," she said, and now she felt thoroughly sickened. She had seen more typical hospitals for the insane in Philadelphia, when she and George used to commit Retta to such houses of despair for short periods of time. She could not imagine her gentle friend Ambrose in such a place of squalor and sorrow and suffering.

"One need not be sorry," Ambrose said. "It has passed. Fortunately for my mind, I have forgotten most of what occurred there. But the experience of the hospital left me, forever after, more frightened than I had been in the past. Too frightened to ever again experience full trust. When I was released, Daniel Tupper and his family took me into their care. They were kind to me. They gave me shelter, and offered work for me to do in their print shop. I hoped that perhaps I might be able to reach the angels once again, but through a more material manner this time. A safer manner, I suppose you could say. I had lost my courage to swing myself into the fire once more. So I taught myself the art of printmaking—in imitation of the Lord, really, though I know it sounds sinful and prideful to confess that. I wanted to press my own perceptions into the world, though I have still never made work as fine as what I wish it to be. But it brings me occupation. And I contemplated orchids. There was comfort in orchids."

Alma hesitated, then asked, not without discomfort, "Were you ever able to reach the angels again?"

"No." Ambrose smiled. "I'm afraid not. But the work brought its own pleasures—or its own distractions. Thanks to Tupper's mother, I began eating again. But I was a changed person. I avoided all the trees and all people whom I had seen tinted by God's angry *swissen* during my episode. I longed for the hymns of the new religion I had witnessed, but I could not remember the words. Soon after that, I went off to the jungle. My family thought it was a mistake—that I would encounter madness there again, and that the solitude would harm my constitution."

"Did it?"

"Perhaps. It is difficult to say. As I told you when first we met, I suffered fevers there. The fevers diminished my strength, but I also welcomed them. There were moments during fever when I believed I could nearly see God's imprimatur again, but only nearly. I could see that edicts and stipulations were written into the leaves and vines. I could see that the tree branches around me were bent into a disturbance of messages. There were signatures everywhere, lines of confluence everywhere, but I could not read them. I heard strains of the old familiar music, but I could not capture it. Nothing was revealed to me. When I was ill I sometimes saw glimpses of the angels hidden inside the orchids again—but only the edges of their raiment. The light had to be pure, and everything quite silent, even for that to occur. Yet it was not enough. It was not what I had seen before. Once one has seen angels, Alma, one is not satisfied with the edges of their raiment. After eighteen years, I knew that I would never again witness what I had seen once— not even in the deepest solitude of the jungle, not even in a state of deluded fever—and so I came home. But I suppose I will always long for something else."

"What do you long for, precisely?" Alma asked.

"Purity," he said, "and communion."

Alma, overcome with sadness—and also overcome by a jarring fear that something beautiful was being taken away from her—took all this in. She did not know how to bring Ambrose comfort, though he did not seem to be asking for it. Was he a madman? He did not seem a madman. In a way, she told herself, she should feel honored he had entrusted her with such secrets. But such alarming secrets! What was one to make of them? She had never seen angels, or witnessed the hidden color of God's true anger, or swung into the fire. She was not even entirely certain what that meant—to "swing into the fire." How would one do it? *Why* would one do it?

"What plans do you have now?" she asked. Even as she spoke these words, she cursed her plodding and corporeal mind, which could think only in terms of mundane strategies: *A man has just spoken of angels, and you ask him his plans.*

But Ambrose smiled. "I wish for a restful life, though I am not convinced I have earned it. I am grateful that you have provided me with a place to live. I enjoy White Acre enormously. It is a sort of heaven for me— or as close as one can reach to heaven, I suppose, while still living. I am sated by the world, and wish for peace. I am fond of your father, who does not seem to condemn me, and who permits me to stay. I am grateful to have work to produce, which brings me occupation and satisfaction. I am most grateful for your companionship. I have felt lonely, I must confess, since 1828—since my friends first brought me out of the snowbank and back into the world. After what I have seen, and because of what I can no longer see, I am always somewhat lonely. But I find that I am less lonely in your company than I am at other times."

Alma nearly felt she would cry when she heard this. She considered how to respond. Ambrose had always given so freely of his confidences, and yet she had never shared her own. He was brave with his admissions. Although his admissions frightened her, she should return his bravery in kind.

"You bring me respite from my loneliness, as well," Alma said. This was difficult for her to confess. She could not bear to look at him as she said it, but at least her voice did not waver.

"I would not have known that, dear Alma," Ambrose said kindly. "You always appear so stalwart."

"None of us is stalwart," Alma replied.

They returned to White Acre, back to their normal and pleasant routine, but Alma remained distracted by what she had been told. Sometimes when Ambrose was busy working—drawing an orchid or preparing a stone for lithographic printing—she would watch him, looking for signs of a sickly or sinister mind. But she could see no evidence of it. If he was suffering from, or longing for, spectral illusions or uncanny hallucinations, he did not reveal this, either. There appeared no evidence of a distempered reason.

Whenever Ambrose glanced up and caught her looking at him, he would merely smile. He was so guileless, so gentle and unsuspecting. He did not seem wary of being watched. He did not appear anxious to hide anything. He did not seem to regret what he had shared with Alma. If anything, his deportment toward her was only warmer. He was only more appreciative, more encouraging, and more helpful than before. His good temperament was ever so fixed. He was patient with Henry, with Hanneke, with everyone. At times he appeared fatigued, but that was to be expected, for he worked hard. He worked as hard as Alma did. Naturally he would be fatigued at times. But otherwise he was much the same as before: her dear, unguarded friend. Nor was he seized by excessive religiosity, not so far as Alma could tell. Aside from his dutiful appearances with Alma at church every Sunday, she never even saw him in prayer. In every way, he appeared a good man at peace.

Alma's imagination, on the other hand, had been raked up and kindled by their discussion during the journey home from Trenton. She could not put any of it into sense, and she longed for a cogent answer to this puzzle: Was Ambrose Pike mad? And if Ambrose Pike was not mad, then what was he? She had trouble swallowing marvels and miracles, but she had equal trouble regarding her dear friend as a bedlamite. So what had he seen, during his episode? She herself had never met the divine, nor had she ever longed to meet it. She had lived her life committed to a comprehension of the real, the material. Once, while having a tooth pulled under the influence of ether, Alma had seen dancing stars inside her mind—but this, she had known even at the time, was the normal effect of the drug upon one's wits, and it did not cause her to ascend into the gearworks of heaven. But Ambrose had not been under the influence of ether or any other substance during his visions. His madness had been . . . clearheaded madness.

In the weeks following her conversation with Ambrose, Alma often woke in the night and crept down to the library to read the volumes of Jacob Boehme. She had not studied the old German cobbler since her youth, and she tried now to approach the texts with respect and an open mind. She knew that Milton had read Boehme, and that Newton had admired him. If such luminaries had found wisdom in these words—and if someone as extraordinary as Ambrose had been so stirred by them—then why not Alma?

But she found nothing in the texts that aroused her to a state of mystery or wonder. To Alma, Boehme's writings were full of extinct principles, both opaque and occultist. He was of the old mind, the medieval mind, distracted by alchemy and bezoars. He believed that precious stones and metals were imbued with power and divine virtue. He saw the cross of God hidden in a slice of cabbage. Everything in the world, he believed, was an embodied revelation of eternal potency and divine love. Each piece of nature was a *verbum fiat*—a spoken word of God, a created utterance, a marvel made flesh. He believed that roses did not symbolize love, but in fact *were* love: love made literal. He was both apocalyptic and utopian. This world must soon end, he said, and humanity must reach an Edenic state, where all men would become male virgins, and life would be joy and play. Yet God's wisdom, he insisted, was female.

Boehme wrote, "The wisdom of God is an eternal virgin—not a wife, but rather chastity and purity without flaw, who stands as an image of God. . . . She is the wisdom of miracles without number. In her, the Holy Spirit beholds the image of the angels. . . . Although she give the body to all the fruits, she is not the corporeality of the fruits, but rather the gracefulness and beauty within them."

None of this made sense to Alma. A good deal of it irritated her. It certainly did not make her long to stop eating, or studying, or speaking, or to give up the pleasures of the body and live upon sunlight and rain. On the contrary, Boehme's writing made her long for her microscope, for her mosses, for the comforts of the palpable and the concrete. Why was the material world not sufficient for people such as Jacob Boehme? Was it not wonderful enough, what one could see and touch and know to be real?

"True life stands in the fire," Boehme wrote, "and then one mystery takes hold of the other."

Alma had been taken hold of, to be sure, but her mind did not ignite. Nor, however, did it settle. Her reading of Boehme led her to other works in the White Acre library—other dusty treatises on the intersection of botany and divinity. She felt both skeptical and provoked. She paged through all the old theologians and the quaint, extinct thaumaturges. She examined

Albertus Magnus. She dutifully studied what monks had written four hundred years earlier about mandrakes and unicorn horns. The science was all so flawed. There were holes in their logic so gaping that one could feel gusts of wind blowing through the arguments. They had believed such outlandish notions in the past—that bats were birds, that storks hibernated under water, that gnats sprang from the dew, that geese hatched from barnacles, and that barnacles grew on trees. As a purely historical matter it was interesting enough—but why honor it? she wondered. Why would Ambrose have been seduced by medieval scholarship? It was a fascinating trail, yes, but it was a trail of errors.

In the middle of one hot night at the end of July, Alma was in the library with a lamp before her and her spectacles upon the tip of her nose, looking at a seventeenth-century copy of the *Arboretum sacrum*—whose author, like Boehme, had tried to read sacred messages into all the plants mentioned in the Bible—when Ambrose entered the room. She was startled when she saw him, but he seemed undisturbed. If anything, he appeared concerned about her. He sat beside her at the long table in the center of the great room. He was wearing his daytime clothes. Either he had changed out of his nightclothes, out of deference to Alma, or he had never gone to bed that evening at all.

"You cannot pass so many nights in a row without sleep, my dear Alma," he said.

"I am using the quiet hours to conduct research," she replied. "I hope I have not disturbed you."

He looked at the titles of the great old books lying open before them. "But you are not reading about mosses," he said quietly. "What is your interest in all this?"

She found it difficult to lie to Ambrose. In general, she was not adept at untruths, and he, in particular, was not a person she wished to deceive. "I cannot make sense of your story," she confessed. "I am looking for answers in these books."

He nodded, but said nothing in reply.

"I started with Boehme," Alma went on, "whom I find simply incomprehensible, and now I've moved on to . . . all the others."

"I've troubled you by what I've told you about myself. I was afraid that might occur. I ought to have said nothing."

"No, Ambrose. We are the dearest of friends. You may always confide in me. You may even trouble me at times. I was honored by your confidences. But in my desire to better understand you, I am afraid I am falling quite out of my depth."

"And what do these books tell you about me?"

"Nothing," Alma replied. She could not help but laugh, and Ambrose laughed with her. She was quite exhausted. He looked weary as well.

"Then why do you not ask me yourself?"

"Because I do not wish to gall you."

"You could never gall me."

"But it needles me, Ambrose—the errors in these books. I wonder why the errors do not needle you. Boehme makes such leaps, such contradictions, such confusions of thought. It is as though he wishes to vault directly into heaven upon the strength of his logic, but his logic is deeply impaired." She reached across the table for a book and flung it open. "In this chapter here, for instance, he is trying to find keys to God's secrets hidden inside the plants of the Bible—but what are we to make of it, when his information is simply incorrect? He spends a full chapter interpreting 'the lilies of the field' as mentioned in the book of Matthew, dissecting every letter of the word 'lilies,' looking for revelation within the syllables . . . but Ambrose, 'the lilies of the field' itself is a mistranslation. It would not have *been* lilies that Christ discussed in his Sermon on the Mount. There are only two varieties of lily native to Palestine, and both are exceedingly rare. They would not have flowered in such abundance as to have ever filled a meadow. They would not have been familiar enough to the common man. Christ, tailoring his lesson to the widest possible audience, would more likely have referred to a ubiquitous flower, in order that his listeners would comprehend his metaphor. For that reason, it is exceedingly probable that Christ was talking about the anemones of the field—probably *Anemone coronaria*—though we cannot be certain . . ."

Alma trailed off. She sounded didactic, ridiculous.

Ambrose laughed again. "What a poet you would have made, dear Alma! I would enjoy to see your translation of the Holy Scripture: '*Consider the lilies of the field; they neither toil nor spin—though most probably they were not lilies, in any case, but rather* Anemone coronaria, *though we cannot be certain, but regardless, we can all agree that they neither toil nor spin.*'

What a hymn that would make, to fill the rafters of any church! One would love to hear a congregation sing it. But tell me, Alma, while we are on the subject, what do you make of the willows of Babylon, upon which the Israelites hung their harps and wept?"

"Now you are baiting me," said Alma, her pride both stung and stirred. "But I suspect, given the region, that they were probably poplars."

"And Adam and Eve's apple?" he probed.

She felt like a fool, but she could not stop herself. "It was either an apricot or a quince," she said. "More likely an apricot, because quince is not so sweet as to have attracted a young woman's desire. One way or another, it could not have been an apple. There were no apples in the Holy Land, Ambrose, and the tree in Eden is often described as having been shady and inviting, with silvery leaves, which could describe most varietals of apricot . . . so when Jacob Boehme speaks of apples and God and Eden . . ."

Now Ambrose was laughing so hard that he had to wipe his eyes. "My dear Miss Whittaker," he said, with utmost tenderness. "What a marvel is your mind. This sort of dangerous reasoning, by the way, is precisely what God feared would happen, if a woman were allowed to eat from the tree of knowledge. You are a cautionary example to all womankind! You must cease at once all this intelligence and immediately take up the mandolin, or mending, or some other useless activity!"

"You think me absurd," she said.

"No, Alma, I do not. I think you remarkable. I am touched that you are trying to comprehend me. A friend could not be more loving. I am more touched, still, that you are trying to understand—through rational thought—that which cannot be understood at all. There is no exact principle to be found here. The divine, as Boehme said, is *unground*—unfathomable, something outside the world as we experience it. But this is a difference of our minds, dearest one. I wish to arrive at revelation on wings, while you advance steadily on foot, magnifying glass in hand. I am a smattering wanderer, seeking God within the outer contours, searching for a new way of knowing. You stand upon the ground, and consider the evidence inch by inch. Your way is more rational and more methodical, but I cannot change my way."

"I do have a dreadful love for understanding," Alma admitted.

"Indeed you do love it, though it is not dreadful," Ambrose replied. "It is the natural result of having been born with a mind so exquisitely calibrated. But for me, to experience life through mere reason is to feel about in the dark for God's face while wearing heavy gloves. It is not enough only to study and depict and describe. One must sometimes . . . *leap*."

"Yet I simply do not comprehend the Lord toward whom you are leaping," Alma said.

"Why must you, though?"

"Because I would wish to better know you."

"Then question me directly, Alma. Do not look for me within these books. I sit here before you, and I shall tell you anything you like about myself."

Alma shut the dense volume before her. She might have shut it a touch too firmly, for it closed with a thud. She turned her chair to face Ambrose, folded her hands in her lap and said, "I do not understand your interpretation of nature, and this, in turn, fills me with a sense of alarm about the condition of your mind. I do not understand how you can overlook the points of contradiction and the sheer foolishness in these discredited old theories. You presume that our Lord is a benevolent botanist, hiding clues for our betterment within every variety of plant, yet I see no consistent evidence for that. There are just as many plants in our world that poison us as heal us. Why does your botanist deity give us the fetterbush and the privet, for instance, to kill off our horses and cows? Where is the hidden revelation there?"

"But why should our Lord not be a botanist?" Ambrose asked. "What occupation would you prefer your deity to have?"

Alma considered the question seriously. "Perhaps a mathematician," she decided. "Scratching and erasing at things, you know. Adding and subtracting. Multiplying and dividing. Toying with theories and new calculations. Discarding earlier mistakes. It appears a more sensible idea to me."

"But the mathematicians I have met, Alma, are not particularly compassionate souls, nor do they nourish life."

"Precisely," said Alma. "This would go a long way toward explaining the suffering of mankind and the random nature of our fates—as God adds and subtracts us, divides and erases us."

"What a grim view! I wish you did not consider our lives so bleakly. On the whole of things, Alma, I still see more wonder in the world than suffering."

"I know you do," said Alma, "and that is why I worry for you. You are an idealist, which means that you are destined to be disappointed, and perhaps even wounded. You seek a gospel of benevolence and miracle, which leaves no room for the sorrows of existence. You are like William Paley, arguing that the perfection of every design in the universe is proof of God's love for us. Do you recall Paley's claim that the mechanism of the human wrist—so exquisitely suited to gathering food and creating works of artistic beauty—is the very imprint of the Lord's affection toward man? But the human wrist is also perfectly suited to swinging a murderous ax at one's neighbor. What proof of love, therein? Moreover, you make me feel like a horrid little marplot, because I sit here making such dull arguments and because I cannot live in the same shining city upon the hill that you inhabit."

They sat quietly for a spell, then Ambrose asked, "Are we arguing, Alma?"

Alma considered the question. "Perhaps."

"But why must we quarrel?"

"Forgive me, Ambrose. I am weary."

"You are weary because you have been sitting in this library every night, asking questions of men who have been dead for hundreds of years."

"I have spent most of my life conversing with such men, Ambrose. Older ones, as well."

"Yet because they do not answer questions to your liking, you now assail me. How can I offer you satisfactory answers, Alma, if far superior minds than my own have already disappointed you?"

Alma put her head in her hands. She felt strained.

Ambrose continued, but now in a more tender voice. "Only imagine what we could learn, Alma, if we could unshackle ourselves from argument."

She looked up at him again. "I cannot unshackle myself from argument, Ambrose. Recall that I am Henry Whittaker's daughter. I was born into argument. Argument was my first nursemaid. Argument is my lifelong bedfellow. What's more, I believe in argument and I even love it. Argument is our most steadfast pathway toward truth, for it is the only proven arbalest against superstitious thinking, or lackadaisical axioms."

"But if the end result is only to drown in words, and never to *hear* . . ." Ambrose trailed off.

"To hear *what*?"

"Each other, perhaps. Not each other's words, but each other's thoughts.

Each other's spirit. If you ask me what I believe, I shall tell you this: the whole sphere of air that surrounds us, Alma, is alive with invisible attractions—electric, magnetic, fiery and thoughtful. There is a universal sympathy all around us. There is a hidden means of knowing. I am certain of this, for I have witnessed it myself. When I swung myself into the fire as a young man, I saw that the storehouses of the human mind are rarely ever fully opened. When we open them, nothing remains unrevealed. When we cease all argument and debate—both internal and external—our true questions can be heard and answered. That is the powerful mover. That is the book of nature, written neither in Greek nor in Latin. That is the gathering of magic, and it is a gathering that, I have always believed and wished, can be shared."

"You speak in riddles," Alma said.

"*And you speak too much,*" Ambrose replied.

She could find no reply to this. Not without speaking more. Offended, confused, she felt her eyes sting with tears.

"Take me someplace where we can be silent together, Alma," Ambrose said, leaning in to her. "I trust you so thoroughly, and I believe that you trust me. I do not wish to quarrel with you any longer. I wish to speak to you without words. Allow me to try to show you what I mean."

This was a most startling request.

"We can be silent together right here, Ambrose."

He looked around the vast, elegant library. "No," he said. "We cannot. It is too large and too loud in here, with all these dead old men arguing around us. Take me somewhere hidden and quiet, and let us listen to each other. I know it sounds mad, but it is not mad. I know this one thing to be true—that all we need for communion is our consent. I have come to believe that I cannot reach communion on my own because I am too weak. Since I have met you, Alma, I feel stronger. Do not make me regret what I have told you already of myself. I ask so little of you, Alma, but I must beg of you this request, for I have no other way to explain myself, and if I cannot show you what I believe to be true, then you will always think me deranged or idiotic."

She protested, "No, Ambrose, I could never think such things of you—"

"*But you do already,*" he interrupted, with desperate urgency. "Or you will eventually. Then you will come to pity me, or detest me, and I shall lose the companion whom I hold most dear in the world, and this would bring me tribulation and sorrow. Before that sad event occurs—if it has not already occurred—permit me to try to show you what I mean, when I say that nature, in her limitlessness, has no concern for the boundaries of our mortal imaginations. Allow me to try to show you that we can speak to each other without words and without argument. I believe that enough love and affection passes between us, my dearest friend, that we can achieve this. I have always hoped to find somebody with whom I can communicate silently. Since meeting you, I have hoped it even more—for we share, it seems, such a natural and sympathetic understanding of each other, which extends far beyond the crass or the common affections . . . do we not? Do you not also feel as though you are more powerful when I am near?"

This could not be denied. Nor, however, out of dignity, could it be admitted.

"What is it that you wish from me?" Alma asked.

"I wish for you to listen to my mind and my spirit. And I wish to listen to yours."

"You are speaking of mind reading, Ambrose. This is a parlor game."

"You may call it whatever you wish. But I believe that without the impediment of language, all will be revealed."

"But I do not believe in such a thing," Alma said.

"Yet you are a woman of science, Alma—so why not try? There is nothing to be lost, and perhaps much to be learned. But for this to succeed, we shall need deepest stillness. We shall need freedom from interference. Please, Alma, I will ask this of you only once. Take me to the most quiet and secret place that you know, and let us attempt communion. Let me show you what I cannot tell you."

What choice did she have?

She took him to the binding closet.

Now, this was not the first that Alma had heard of mind reading. If anything, it was a bit of a local fashion. Sometimes it felt to Alma that every other lady in Philadelphia was a divine medium these days. There were "spirit ambassadors" everywhere one looked, ready to be hired by the hour. Sometimes their experiments leaked into the more respectable medical and scientific journals, which appalled Alma. She had recently seen an article on the subject of pathetism—the idea that chance could be induced by suggestion—which seemed to her like mere carnival games. Some people called these explorations science, but Alma, irritated, diagnosed them as entertainment—and a rather dangerous variety of entertainment, at that.

In a way, Ambrose reminded her of all these spiritualists—yearning and susceptible—yet at the same time, he was not like them in the least. For one thing, he had never heard of them. He lived in far too much isolation to have noticed the mystical manias of the moment. He did not subscribe to the phrenology journals, with their discussions of the thirty-seven different faculties, propensities, and sentiments represented by the bumps and valleys of the human skull. Nor did he visit mediums. He did not read *The Dial*. He had never mentioned to Alma the names of Bronson Alcott or Ralph Waldo Emerson—because he had never encountered the names of Bronson Alcott or Ralph Waldo Emerson. For solace and fellowship, he looked to medieval writers, not contemporary ones.

Moreover, he actively sought the God of the Bible, as well as the spirits of nature. When he attended the Swedish Lutheran church every Sunday with Alma, he knelt and prayed in humble accord. He sat upright in the unyielding oak pew, and took in the sermons without discomfort. When he was not in prayer, he worked in silence over his printing presses, or industriously made portraits of orchids, or helped Alma with her mosses, or played long games of backgammon with Henry. Truly, Ambrose had no idea what was occurring in the rest of the world. If anything, he was trying to escape the world—which meant that he had arrived at his curious bundle of ideas all by himself. He did not know that half of America and most of Europe were attempting to read each other's minds. He merely wanted to read Alma's mind, and to have her read his.

She could not refuse him.

So when this young man asked her to take him someplace quiet and secret, she took him into the binding closet. She could think of nowhere else to go. She did not want to wake anyone by marching through the house to a more distant location. She did not wish to be caught in a bedroom with him. What's more, she knew of no quieter or more private place than this. She told herself that these were the reasons she took him there. They may even have been true.

He had not known that the door was there. Nobody knew it was there—so cleverly were its seams hidden behind the elaborate old plaster molding of the wall. Since Beatrix's death, Alma was the only person who ever entered the binding closet. Perhaps Hanneke knew of its existence, but the old housekeeper seldom came to this wing of the house, to the far distant library. Henry probably knew of it—he had designed it, after all—but he, too, seldom frequented the library anymore. He had probably forgotten the place years earlier.

Alma did not bring a lamp with them. She was all too familiar with the tiny room's contours. There was a stool, where she had sat when she came to be so shamefully and pleasurably alone, and there was a small work table on which Ambrose could now sit, directly facing her. She showed him where to sit. Once she shut and locked the door, they were in absolute darkness together, in this tiny, hidden, stifling place. He did not seem alarmed by darkness, or the cramped quarters. For this was what he had requested.

"May I take your hands?" he asked.

She reached out cautiously across the darkness until her fingertips touched his arms. Together, they found each other's hands. His hands were slender and light. Hers felt heavy and damp. Ambrose laid his hands across his knees, palms facing upward, and she allowed her palms to settle atop his. She did not expect what she encountered in that first touch: the fierce, staggering onrush of love. It went through her like a sob.

But what had she expected? Why should it have felt anything less than elevated, exaggerated, exalted? Alma had never before been touched by a man. Or, rather, just twice—once, in the spring of 1818, when George Hawkes had pressed Alma's hand between both of his and had called her a brilliant microscopist; and once again by George, more recently, when he was in distress about Retta—but in both cases that had been only *one* of her hands, coming in contact nearly accidentally with a man's flesh. Never had she been touched with anything that might fairly be called intimacy. Numberless times over the decades, she had sat on this very stool with her legs open and her skirts up about her waist, with this very door locked behind her, leaning back against the embrace of this very wall behind her, sating her hunger as best she could with the grappling of her own fingers. If there were molecules in this room that differed from the other molecules of White Acre—or indeed, from the other molecules of the world—then these molecules were permeated by dozens and hundreds and thousands of impressions of Alma's carnal exertions. Yet now she was here in this closet, in the same familiar darkness, surrounded by those molecules, alone with a man ten years her junior.

But what was she to do about this sob of love?

"Listen for my question," Ambrose said, holding Alma's hands lightly. "And then ask me your own. There will be no further need to speak. We shall know when we have heard each other."

Ambrose closed his grip gently around her hands. The sensation that this provoked up her arms was beautiful.

How could she extend this?

She considered pretending that she was reading his mind, if only to draw out the experience. She considered whether there might be a way to repeat this event in the future. But what if they were ever discovered in here? What if Hanneke found them alone in a closet? What would people say? What would people think of Ambrose, whose intentions, as ever, had seemed so unmingled with anything foul? He would appear a rake. He would be banished. She would be shamed.

No, Alma understood, they would never do this again after tonight. This was to be the one moment in her life when a man's hands would be clasped around hers.

She closed her eyes and leaned back a bit, putting her full weight against the wall. He did not let go of her. Her knees nearly brushed against his knees. A good deal of time passed. Ten minutes? A half hour? She drank in the pleasure of his touch. She wished to never forget this.

The pleasant sensation that had begun in her palms and traveled up her arms now advanced into her torso, and eventually pooled between her legs. What had she supposed might happen? Her body had been tuned to this room, trained to this room—and now this new stimulus had arrived. For a while, she contended against the sensation. She was grateful that her face could not be seen, for a most contorted and flushed countenance would have been revealed, had there been a trace of light. Though she had forced this moment, she still could not quite believe this moment: There was a man sitting across from her, right here in the dark of the binding closet, inside the deepest penetralia of her world.

Alma attempted to keep her breath even. She resisted what she was feeling, yet her resistance only increased the sensation of pleasure growing between her legs. There is a Dutch word, *uitwaaien*, "to walk against the wind for pleasure." That is what this felt like. Without moving her body at all, Alma leaned against the rising wind with all her power, but the wind only pushed back, with equal force, and so did her pleasure increase.

More time passed. Another ten minutes? Another half hour? Ambrose did not move. Alma did not move, either. His hands did not so much as tremble or pulse. Yet Alma felt consumed by him. She felt him everywhere within her and around her. She felt him counting the hairs at the base of her neck, and examining the clusters of nerves at the bottom of her spine.

"Imagination is gentle," Jacob Boehme had written, "and it resembles water. But desire is rough and dry as a hunger."

Yet Alma felt both. She felt both the water and the hunger. She felt both the imagination and the desire. Then, with a sort of horror and a fair amount of mad joy, she knew that she was about to reach her old familiar vortex of pleasure. Sensation was rising quickly through her quim, and there was no question of stopping it. Without Ambrose touching her (aside from her hands), without her touching herself, without either of them moving so much as an inch, without her skirts lifted above her waist or her hands at work within her own body, without even a change of breath—Alma tumbled into climax. For a moment, she saw a flash of white, like sheet lightning across a starless summer sky. The world turned milky behind her closed eyes. She felt blinded, rapturous—and then, immediately, shamed.

Dreadfully shamed.

What had she done? What had he felt? What had he heard? Dear God, what had he *smelled*? But before she could react or pull away, she felt something else. Though Ambrose still did not move or stir or react, she suddenly felt as though he were brushing against the soles of her feet with a persistent stroke. As the moments passed, she perceived that this stroking sensation was, in fact, a question—an *utterance* coming into being, right out of the floor. She felt the question enter through the bottoms of her feet and rise through the bones of her legs. Then she felt the question creep up into her womb, swimming through the wet path of her quim. It was nearly a spoken voice that was gliding up into her, nearly an articulation. Ambrose was asking something of her, but he was asking it from inside her. She heard it now. Then there it was, his question, perfectly formed:

Will you accept this of me?

She pulsed silently with her reply: *YES.*

Then she felt something else. The question that Ambrose had placed within her body was twisting into something else. It was now turning into *her* question. She had not known that she had a question for Ambrose, but now she did have one—most urgently. She let her question rise through her torso and out through her arms. Then she placed her question upon his awaiting palms:

Is this what you want of me?

She heard him draw in his breath sharply. He clutched her hands so tightly that he nearly hurt her. Then he shattered the silence with one spoken word:

"Yes."

Chapter Sixteen

Only one month later, they were married.

In the years to come, Alma would puzzle over the mechanism by which this decision had been reached—this most inconceivable and unexpected leap into wedlock—but in the days after the experience within the binding closet, matrimony felt like an inevitability. As for what had actually transpired in that tiny room, all of it (from Alma's chaste climax, to the silent transmission of thought) seemed a miracle, or at least a phenomenon. Alma could find no logical explanation for what had transpired. People cannot hear each other's thoughts. Alma knew this to be true. People cannot convey that sort of electricity, that sort of longing and frank erotic disruption with the mere touch of hands. Yet—it had happened. Without question, it had happened.

When they had walked out of the closet that night, he had turned to her, his face flushed and ecstatic, and he said, "I would like to sleep beside you every night for the rest of my life, and listen to your thoughts forever."

That is what he had said! Not telepathically, but *aloud*. Overwhelmed, she'd had no words for a reply. She'd merely nodded her assent, or her agreement, or her wonder. Then they had both gone off to their respective bedrooms, across the hall from each other—although, of course, she had not slept. How could she have?

The following day, as they walked toward the moss beds together,

Ambrose began speaking casually, as though they were in the middle of an ongoing conversation. Quite out of nowhere, he said, "Perhaps the difference in our stations in life is so vast that it is of no consequence. I possess nothing in this world that anyone would desire, and you possess everything. Perhaps we inhabit such extremes that there is balance to be found within our differences?"

Alma had not an inkling where he was tending with this line of conversation, but she allowed him to keep speaking.

"I have also wondered," he reflected mildly, "if two such diverse individuals as we could find harmony in matrimony."

Both her heart and stomach lunged at the word: *matrimony*. Was he speaking philosophically, or literally? She waited.

He continued, though he was still far from direct: "There will be people, I suppose, who might accuse me of reaching for your wealth. Nothing could be further from the truth. I live my life in strictest economy, Alma, not only out of habit, but also out of preference. I have no riches to offer you, but I would also take no riches from you. You will not become wealthier by marrying me, but nor will you grow poorer. That truth may not satisfy your father, but I hope it will satisfy you. In any case, our love is not a typical love, as is typically felt between men and women. We share something else between us—something more immediate, more cherishing. That has been evident to me from the beginning, and I pray it has been evident to you. My wish is that we two could live together as one, both contented and elevated, and ever-seeking."

It was only later that afternoon, when Ambrose asked her, "Will you speak to your father, or shall I?" that Alma definitively pieced it together: this had indeed been a marriage proposal. Or, rather, it had been a marriage *assumption*. Ambrose did not precisely ask for Alma's hand—for in his mind, apparently, she had already given it to him. She could not deny that this was true. She would have given him anything. She loved him so deeply that it pained her. She was only just confessing this to herself. To lose him now would be an amputation. True, there was no sense to be made of this love. She was nearly fifty years old, and he was still a fairly young man. She was homely and he was beautiful. They had known each other for only a few weeks. They believed in different universes (Ambrose in the divine; Alma in the actual). Yet, undeniably—Alma told herself—this was love. Undeniably,

Alma Whittaker was about to become a wife.

"I shall speak to Father myself," Alma said, cautiously overjoyed.

She found her father in his study that evening before dinner, deep in papers.

"Listen to this letter," he said by way of greeting. "This man here says he can no longer operate his mill. His son—his stupid gambling dicer of a son—has ruined the family. He says he has resolved to pay off his debts, and wishes to die unencumbered. This from a man who, in twenty years, has not taken one step of common sense. Well, a fine chance he has for *that*!"

Alma did not know who the man in question was, or who the son was, or which mill was at stake. Everyone today was speaking to her as though from the midst of a preexisting conversation.

"Father," she said. "I wish to discuss something with you. Ambrose Pike has asked for my hand in marriage."

"Very well," said Henry. "But listen, Alma—this fool here wishes to sell me a parcel of his cornfields, too, and he's trying to convince me to purchase that old granary he's got on the wharf, the one that is falling into the river already. You know the one, Alma. What he thinks that wreck of a building is worth, or why I would wish to be saddled with it, I cannot imagine."

"You are not listening to me, Father."

Henry did not so much as glance up from his desk. "I am listening to you," he said, turning over the paper in his hand and peering at it. "I am listening to you with captive fascination."

"Ambrose and I wish to marry soon," Alma said. "There need be no spectacle or festivity, but we would like it to be prompt. Ideally, we would like to be married before the end of the month. Please be assured that we will remain at White Acre. You will not lose either of us."

At this, Henry looked up at Alma for the first time since she'd walked into the room.

"Naturally I will not lose either of you," said Henry. "Why would either of you leave? It is not as though the fellow can support you in your accustomed manner on the salary of—what is his profession?—orchidist?"

Henry settled back into his chair, crossed his arms over his chest, and gazed at his daughter over the rims of his old-fashioned brass eyeglasses. Alma was not certain what to say next.

"Ambrose is a good man," she finally uttered. "He has no longing for fortune."

"I suspect you may be correct in that," Henry replied. "Though it does not speak highly of his character that he prefers poverty to riches. Nonetheless, I thought the situation out years ago—long before you or I ever heard of Ambrose Pike."

Henry rose somewhat unsteadily and peered at the bookcase behind him. He pulled out a volume on English sailing vessels—a book that Alma had seen on the shelves her whole life, but had never opened, as she held no interest in English sailing vessels. He paged through the book until he found a folded sheet of paper tucked inside, stamped with a wax seal. Above the seal was written "Alma." He handed it to her.

"I drew up two of these documents, with the assistance of your mother, around 1817. The other, I gave your sister Prudence when she married that crop-eared spaniel of hers. It is a decree for your husband to sign, asserting that he will never own White Acre."

Henry was nonchalant about this. Alma took the document, wordlessly. She recognized her mother's hand in the straight-backed capital *A* of her own name.

"Ambrose has no need of White Acre, nor any desire for it," Alma said, defensively.

"Excellent. Then he will not mind signing it. Naturally, there will be a dowry, but my fortune, my estate—it will never be his. I trust we are understood?"

"Very well," she said.

"Very well, indeed. Now, as to the suitability of Mr. Pike as a husband, that is your business. You are a grown woman. If you believe such a man can render you satisfied in wedlock, you have my blessing."

"Satisfied in wedlock?" Alma bristled. "Have I ever been a difficult figure to satisfy, Father? What have I ever asked for? What have I ever demanded? How much trouble could I possibly present to anybody as a wife?"

Henry shrugged. "I could not say. That is for you to learn."

"Ambrose and I share a natural sympathy with each other, Father. I know that it may seem an unconventional pairing, but I feel—"

Henry cut her off. "Never explain yourself, Alma. It makes you appear weak. In any case, I do not dislike the fellow." He returned his attention to the papers on his desk.

Did that constitute a blessing? Alma could not be certain. She waited for him to say more. He did not. It did seem, however, that permission to marry had been granted. At the very least, permission had not been declined.

"Thank you, Father." She turned toward the door.

"One further matter," Henry said, looking up again. "Before her wedding night, it is customary that a bride be advised on certain matters of the conjugal chamber—presuming that you are still innocent of such things, which I suspect you are. As a man and as your father, I cannot advise you. Your mother is dead, or she'd have done it. Do not trouble yourself asking Hanneke any questions on the matter, for she is an old spinster who knows nothing, and she would die of shock if she ever knew what transpired between men and women in their beds. My advice is that you pay a visit to your sister Prudence. She is a long-married wife and the mother of half a dozen children. She may be able to edify you on some points of matrimonial conduct. Do not blush, Alma—you are too old to blush and it makes you look ridiculous. If you are to have a go at marriage, then by God, go at it properly. Arrive prepared to the bed, as you do with everything else in life. It may be worth your effort. And post these letters for me tomorrow, if you are going into town anyway."

Alma had not even had time to properly contemplate the notion of marriage, yet now it all seemed arranged and decided. Even her father had proceeded immediately to the topics of inheritance and the marital bed. Events moved even more swiftly after that. The next day, Alma and Ambrose walked to Sixteenth Street to have a daguerreotype made of themselves: their wedding portrait. Alma had never before been photographed, and neither had Ambrose. It was such a dreadful likeness of them both that she hesitated even to pay for the picture. She looked at the image only once, and never wanted to see it again. She appeared so much older than Ambrose! A stranger, looking at this picture, might have thought her the younger man's large-boned, heavy-jawed, rueful mother. As for Ambrose, he looked like a starved, mad-eyed prisoner of the chair that held him. One of his hands was a blur. His tousled hair made it appear as though he had been roughly awoken from a tormented sleep. Alma's hair was crooked and tragic. The whole experience made Alma feel terribly sad. But Ambrose only laughed when he saw the image.

"Why, this is *slander!*" he exclaimed. "How unkind a fate, to see oneself so honestly! Nonetheless, I will send the picture to my family in Boston. One hopes they will recognize their own son."

Did events generally move this hastily for other people who were engaged to marry? Alma did not know. She had not seen much of courtships, engagements, the rituals of matrimony. She had never studied the ladies' magazines, or enjoyed the light novels about love, written for dewy, innocent girls. (She had certainly read salacious books about coupling, but they did not clarify the larger situation.) In short, she was far from an expert belle. If Alma's experiences in the realm of love had not been so markedly scarce, she might have found her courtship, such as it was, both abrupt and unlikely. In the three months that she and Ambrose had known each other, they had never exchanged a love letter, a poem, an embrace. The affection between them was clear and constant, but passion was absent. Another woman might have regarded this situation with suspicion. Instead Alma felt only drunken, and befuddled by questions. They were not necessarily unpleasant questions, but they swarmed within her to the point of distraction. Was Ambrose now her lover? Could she fairly call him that? Did she belong to him? Could she hold his hand at any time now? How did he regard her? What would his body look like, beneath his clothing? Would her body bring him satisfaction? What did he expect from her? She could not conjecture answers to any of it.

She was also hopelessly in love.

Alma had always adored Ambrose, of course, from the moment she had met him, but—until his marriage proposal—she had never considered allowing herself to fall backward into the full expression of that adoration; it would have felt audacious to do so, if not dangerous. It had always been enough simply to have him near. Alma would have been willing to regard Ambrose as merely a dear companion, if it would have kept him at White Acre forever. To share buttered toast with him every morning, to observe his ever-illuminated face as he spoke of orchids, to witness the mastery of his printmaking, to watch him throw himself down upon her divan to listen to theories of species transmutation and extinction—truly, all that would have been plenty. She would never have presumed to wish for more. Ambrose as friend—as brother—more than sufficed.

Even after the events of the binding closet, Alma would not have asked for more. Whatever had transpired between them in the dark, she was easily prepared to regard as a unique moment, perhaps even a mutual hallucination. She could have talked herself into believing that she had imagined the current of communication that had moved between them across the silence, and imagined the riotous effect that his hands against hers had wrought throughout her entire body. Given enough time, she might have even learned to forget that it ever occurred. Even after that encounter, she would not have allowed herself to love him so desperately, so thoroughly, so helplessly—not without his permission.

But now they were to be married, and that permission had been granted. There was no chance anymore for Alma to restrain her love—and no reason to. She allowed herself to plummet directly into it. She felt inflamed by amazement, rampant with inspiration, enthralled. Where she had once seen light in Ambrose's face, she now saw celestial light. Where his limbs had before looked only pleasing, they now looked like Roman statuary. His voice was an evensong. His slightest glance bruised her heart with fearful joy.

Cast loose for the first time in her life into the realm of love, imbued with impossible energy, Alma barely recognized herself. Her capacities seemed limitless. She barely had need for sleep. She felt she could row a boat up a mountainside. She moved through the world as though in a corona of fire. She was *zoetic*. It was not merely Ambrose whom she regarded with such vivid purity and thrill—but everything and everybody. All was suddenly miraculous. She saw lines of convergence and grace everywhere she looked. Even the smallest matters became revelatory. She was doused by a sudden surfeit of the most astonishing self-confidence. Quite out of the blue, she found herself solving botanical problems that had vexed her for years. She wrote furiously paced letters to distinguished men of botany (men whose reputations had always cowed her), laying challenge to their conclusions as she had never before permitted herself to do.

"You have presented your *Zygodon* with sixteen cilia and no outer peristome!" she scolded.

Or, "Why are you so certain this is a *Polytrichum* colony?"

Or, "I do not agree with Professor Marshall's conclusion. It can be discouraging, I know, to achieve consensus in the field of cryptogamia, but I caution you against your haste in declaring a new species before you have thoroughly studied the accumulated evidence. These days, one may see as many names for a given specimen as there are bryologists studying it; that does not mean the specimen is either new or rare. I have four such specimens in my own herbarium."

She had never before possessed the courage for such remonstrance, but love had emboldened her, and her mind felt like an immaculate engine. A week before the wedding, Alma woke in the night with an electrified start, abruptly realizing that there was a link between algae and mosses. She had been looking at mosses and algae for decades, but she had never before seen the truth of it: the two were cousins. She had no trace of a doubt about it. In essence, she apprehended, mosses did not merely *resemble* algae that had crawled up on dry land; mosses *were* algae that had crawled up on dry land. How mosses had made this elaborate transformation from aquatic to terrestrial, Alma did not know. But these two species shared an entwined history. They must do. The algae had *decided* something, long before Alma or anyone else was watching them, and in that point of decision, had moved up into the dry air and transformed. She did not know the mechanism behind this transformation, but she knew that it had occurred.

Realizing all this, Alma wished to run across the hall and leap into bed with Ambrose—with he who had ignited such wildness within her body and mind. She wished to tell him everything, to show him everything, to prove the workings of the universe to him. She could not wait for daylight, when they could speak again at breakfast. She could not wait to look upon his face. She could not wait for the time when they would never need to be separated—not even at night, not even in sleep. She lay in her own bed, trembling with anticipation and sentiment.

What a long distance it felt, between their two rooms!

As for Ambrose himself, as the wedding approached, he became only more serene, only more attentive. He could not have been kinder to Alma. She sometimes feared he might change his mind, but there was no sign of it. She had felt a shudder of apprehension when she handed him Henry Whittaker's decree, but Ambrose had signed it without hesitation or complaint—indeed, without even reading it. Each night, before they went to their separate rooms, he kissed her freckled hand, right below the knuckles. He called her "my other soul, my better soul."

He said, "I am such a strange man, Alma. Are you certain you can endure my unusual ways?"

"I can endure you!" she promised.

She felt that she was in danger of igniting.

She feared she might die of gladness.

Three days before the wedding—which was to be a simple ceremony held in the drawing room at White Acre—Alma finally visited her sister Prudence. It had been many months since they had last seen each other. But it would be utterly rude of her not to invite her sister to the wedding, so Alma had written Prudence a note of explanation—that she was to be wed to a friend of Mr. George Hawkes—and then made plans for a brief visit. Furthermore, Alma had decided to follow her father's advice, and speak to Prudence on the matter of the conjugal bed. It was not a conversation she was eagerly anticipating, but she did not wish to come into Ambrose's arms unprepared, and she did not know whom else to ask.

It was an early evening in mid-August when Alma arrived at the Dixon home. She found her sister in the kitchen, making a mustard poultice for her youngest boy, Walter, who was sick in bed, ill in the stomach from having eaten too much green watermelon rind. The other children were milling about the kitchen, working at various chores. The room was suffocatingly hot. There were two small black girls whom Alma had never before seen, sitting in the corner with Prudence's thirteen-year-old daughter, Sarah; together, the three of them were carding wool. All the girls, black and white, were dressed in the humblest imaginable frocks. The children, even the black ones, approached Alma and kissed her politely, called her "auntie," and returned to their tasks.

Alma asked Prudence if she could help with the poultice, but Prudence refused assistance. One of the boys brought Alma a tin cup of water from the pump in the garden. The water was warm, and tasted murky and unpleasant. Alma did not want it. She sat on a long bench, and did not know where to put the cup. Nor did she know what to say. Prudence—who had received Alma's note earlier in the week—congratulated her sister on her upcoming nuptials, but that perfunctory exchange took only a moment, and then the subject was closed. Alma admired the children, admired the cleanliness of the kitchen, admired the mustard poultice, until there was nothing left to admire. Prudence looked thin and weary, but she did not complain, nor did she share any news of her life. Alma did not ask any news. She dreaded to know details of the circumstances the family might be facing.

After a long while, Alma roused the courage to ask, "Prudence, I wonder if I might have a private word with you."

If the request surprised Prudence, she did not show it. But then, Prudence's smooth countenance had always been incapable of expressing such a base emotion as surprise.

"Sarah," Prudence said to the eldest girl. "Take the others outdoors."

The children filed out of the kitchen solemnly and obediently, like soldiers on the way to battle. Prudence did not sit, but stood with her back braced against the large wooden slab that called itself a kitchen table, her hands folded prettily against her clean apron.

"Yes?" she asked.

Alma searched her mind for where to begin. She could not find a sentence that did not seem vulgar or rude. Suddenly she deeply regretted having taken her father's advice on the matter. She wished to run from this house—back to the comforts of White Acre, back to Ambrose, back to a place where the water from the pump was fresh and cold. But Prudence gazed at her, expectant and silent. Something would need to be said.

Alma began, "As I approach the shores of matrimony . . ."

Alma trailed off and stared at her sister, helpless, wishing against all reason that Prudence would glean from this senseless fragment of a statement precisely what Alma was attempting to ask.

"Yes?" Prudence said.

"I find myself without experience," Alma completed the statement.

Prudence gazed on, in unperturbed silence. *Help me, woman!* Alma wanted to cry out. If only Retta Snow had been here! Not the new, mad Retta—but the old, joyful, unrestrained Retta. If only Retta had been there, too, and if only they were all nineteen years old again. The three of them, as girls, might have been able to approach this subject in safety, somehow. Retta would have made it amusing and candid. Retta would have released Prudence from her reserve, and taken away Alma's shame. But nobody was there now to help the two sisters to behave as sisters. What's more, Prudence did not appear interested in making this discussion any easier, as she did not speak up at all.

"I find myself without experience of conjugality," Alma clarified, in a burst of desperate courage. "Father suggested that I speak with you for guidance on the subject of delighting a husband."

One of Prudence's eyebrows lifted, minutely. "I am sorry to hear that he thinks me an authority," she said.

This had been a misguided idea indeed, Alma realized. But there was no backing out of it now.

"You take me wrongly," Alma protested. "It is only that you have been married so long, you see, and you have so many children . . ."

"There is more to marriage, Alma, than that to which you allude. Further, I am prevented by certain scruples from discussing that to which you allude."

"Of course, Prudence. I do not wish to offend your sensibilities or intrude in your privacy. But that of which I speak remains cryptic to me. I beg you not to misunderstand me. I do not need to consult with a doctor; I am familiar with the essential workings of anatomy. But I do need to consult with a married woman, so as to comprehend what might be welcome to my husband, or unwelcome to him. How to present myself, I mean, in regards to the art of pleasing . . ."

"There should be no art to it," Prudence replied, "unless one is a woman for hire."

"*Prudence!*" Alma cried with a force that surprised even herself. "Look at me! Do you not see how ill-prepared I am? Do I look like a young woman to you? Do I appear an item of desire?"

Until this moment, Alma had not realized how afraid she was of her wedding night. Naturally she loved Ambrose, and she was consumed with anticipatory thrill, but she was also terror-stricken. That terror gave partial explanation to her sleepless bouts of nighttime shuddering these past few weeks: she did not know how to comport herself as a man's wife. True, Alma had been consumed for decades by a rich, indecent, carnal imagination—but she was also an innocent. An imagination is one thing; two bodies together is something else entirely. How would Ambrose regard her? How could she enchant him? He was a younger man, and a lovely man, whereas a true assessment of Alma's appearance at the age of forty-eight would have called for this truth to be revealed: she was far more bramble than rose.

Something in Prudence softened, marginally.

"You need only be willing," Prudence said. "A healthy man presented with a willing and acquiescent wife will need no particular coaxing."

This information brought Alma nothing. Prudence must have suspected as much, for she added, "I assure you that the duties of conjugality are not overly discomforting. If he is tender to you, your husband will not much injure you."

Alma wanted to crumple to the floor and weep. Honestly, did Prudence think that Alma feared *injury*? Who or what could ever injure Alma Whittaker? With hands as callused as these? With arms that could have picked up the oaken slab against which Prudence so delicately rested, and thrown it across the room with ease? With this sunburned neck and this thistle-patch of hair? It was not injury that Alma feared on her wedding night, but *humiliation*. What Alma desperately wanted to know was how she could possibly present herself to Ambrose in the form of an orchid, like her sister, and not a mossy boulder, like herself. But such a thing cannot be taught. This was a useless exchange—a mere preamble to humiliation, if anything.

"I have taken up enough of your evening," Alma said, standing up. "You have a sick child to attend. Forgive me."

For a moment, Prudence hesitated, as though she might reach forward, or ask her sister to stay. The moment passed quickly, though, if it had ever existed at all. She merely said, "I am pleased that you visited."

Why do we differ so? Alma wanted to beg. *Why can we not be close?*

Instead she asked, "Will you join us at the wedding on Saturday?" although she already suspected the answer would be a demurral.

"I fear not," Prudence replied. She did not supply a reason. Both of them knew why: because Prudence would never again set foot at White Acre. Henry would not accept it, and nor would Prudence herself.

"All good wishes to you, then," concluded Alma.

"And to you," Prudence replied.

It was only when Alma was halfway up the street that she realized what she had just done: she had not only asked a weary forty-eight-year-old mother—with a sick child in the house!—for advice on the art of copulation, but she had asked *the daughter of a whore* for advice on the art of copulation. How could Alma have forgotten Prudence's shameful origins? Prudence could never have forgotten it herself, and was likely living an existence of perfect rigor and righteousness in order to counter the infamous depravities of her natural mother. Yet Alma had barreled into that humble, decent, and constrained household nonetheless, with questions on the tricks and trade of seduction.

Alma sat down on an abandoned barrel in a posture of dejection. She wished to go back to the Dixon house and apologize, but how could she? What could she say, that would not make the situation even more distressing?

How could she be such a blundering clod?

Where on earth had all her good sense gone?

The afternoon before her wedding, two items of interest arrived in the post for Alma.

The first item was an envelope postmarked Framingham, Massachusetts, with the name "Pike" written in the corner. Alma immediately assumed this must be a letter for Ambrose, as it was obviously from his family, but the envelope was unmistakably addressed to her, so she opened it.

> *Dear Miss Whittaker—*
>
> *I apologize that I shall be unable to attend your wedding to my son, Ambrose, but I am much the invalid, and such a long journey is far outside my capabilities. I was pleased, however, to receive the information that Ambrose is soon to enter into the state of holy matrimony. My son has lived for so many years in seclusion from family and society that I had long ago abandoned the hope of his ever taking a bride. What's more, his young heart was so deeply injured long ago by the death of a girl whom he had much admired and adored—a girl from a fine Christian family in our own community, whom we had all assumed he would wed—that I feared his sensibilities had been irreparably harmed, such that he could never again know the rewards of natural affection. Perhaps I am speaking too freely, though*

certainly he has told you all. The news of his engagement, then, was welcome, for it showed evidence of a healed heart.

I have received your wedding portrait. You appear a capable woman. I see no sign of foolery or frivolity in your countenance. I do not hesitate to say that my son needs just such a woman. He is a clever boy—quite my cleverest—and as a child he was my chiefest joy, yet he has spent far too many years idly gazing at clouds and stars and flowers. I fear, too, that he believes he has outwitted Christianity. You may be the woman to correct him of that misconception. One prays that a decent marriage shall cure him of playing the moral truant. In conclusion, I regret that I cannot see my son wed, but I hold high hopes for your union. It would warm this mother's heart to know that her child was elevating his mind with contemplation of God through the discipline of scriptural study and regular prayer. Please see to it that he does.

His brothers and I welcome you to the family. I suppose that is understood. Notwithstanding, it bears saying.

Yours, Constance Pike.

The only thing Alma gleaned from this letter was: *a girl whom he had much admired and adored.* Despite his mother's certainty that he had told all, Ambrose had told nothing. Who had the girl been? When had she died? Ambrose had left Framingham for Harvard when he was but seventeen years old, and had never lived in the town since. The love affair must have been before that early age, then, if it had even been a love affair. They must have been children, or nearly children. She must have been beautiful, this girl. Alma could see her now: a sweet thing, a pretty little collie, a chestnut-haired and blue-eyed paragon who sang hymns in a honeyed voice, and who had walked with young Ambrose through spring orchards in full bloom. Had the death of the girl contributed to his mental collapse? What had been the girl's name?

Why had Ambrose not spoken of this? On the other hand, why ought he have? Was he not entitled to the privacy of his own former stories? Had Alma ever told Ambrose, for instance, of her dog-eared, useless, misdirected love for George Hawkes? Should she have told him? But there had been nothing to tell. George Hawkes had not even known that he was an actor in a love story, which meant that there had never been a love story in the first place.

What was Alma to do with this information? More immediately, what was she to do with this letter? She read it again, memorized its contents, and hid it. She would reply to Mrs. Pike later, in some cursory and innocuous manner. She wished she had never received such a missive. She must teach herself to forget what she had just learned.

What had been the girl's name?

Fortunately, there was another piece of mail to distract her—a parcel wrapped in brown waxed paper, secured with twine. Most surprisingly, it came from Prudence Dixon. When Alma opened the parcel, she discovered that it was a nightdress of soft white linen, trimmed with lace. It looked to be the right size for Alma. It was a lovely and simple gown, modest but feminine, with voluminous folds, a high neck, ivory buttons, and billowing sleeves. The bodice shone quietly with delicate embroidered flowers rendered in threads of pale yellow silk. The nightdress had been folded neatly, scented with lavender, and tied with a white ribbon, under which was tucked a note in Prudence's immaculate handwriting: "With all best wishes."

Where had Prudence come by such a luxurious item as this? She would not have had time to sew it herself; she must have purchased it from a skilled seamstress. How much it must have cost her! Where had she found the money? These were exactly the sorts of materials the Dixon family had long ago renounced: silk, lace, imported buttons, finery of any kind. Prudence had worn nothing this smart in nearly three decades. All of which is to say, it must have cost Prudence *a great deal*—both financially and morally—to procure this gift. Alma felt her throat pinch with emotion. What had she ever done for her sister, to deserve such a kindness? Especially considering their most recent encounter, how could Prudence have made such an offering?

For a moment, Alma thought she must refuse it. She must package this nightdress up and send it right back to Prudence, who could cut it into pieces and make pretty frocks out of it for her own daughters, or—more likely—sell it for the abolitionist cause. But no, that would appear rude and ungrateful. Gifts must not be returned. Even Beatrix had always taught that.

Gifts must never be returned. This had been an act of grace. It must be received with grace. Alma must be humble and thankful.

It was only later, when Alma went to her bedroom and closed the door, stood before her long mirror, and put the nightdress on, that she understood more fully what her sister was telling her to do, and why the garment could never be returned: Alma needed to wear this lovely item on her wedding night.

She actually looked pretty in it.

Chapter Seventeen

The wedding took place on Tuesday, August 29, 1848, in the drawing room at White Acre. Alma wore a brown silk dress made specially for the occasion. Henry Whittaker and Hanneke de Groot stood as witnesses. Henry was cheerful; Hanneke was not. A judge from West Philadelphia, who had done business in the past with Henry, conducted the vows as a favor to the master of the house.

"Let friendship instruct you," he concluded, after promises had been exchanged. "Let you be anxious of each other's misfortunes, and encouraging of each other's joys."

"Partners in science, trade, and life!" Henry bellowed, quite unexpectedly, and then blew his nose with considerable force.

There were no other friends or family in attendance. George Hawkes had sent a crate of pears as congratulations, but he was ill with fever, he wrote, and could not join them. Also, a large bouquet had arrived the day before, care of the Garrick Pharmacy. As for Ambrose, no one attended as his guest. His friend Daniel Tupper, in Boston, had sent a telegraph that morning reading simply, "WELL DONE PIKE," but Tupper did not travel down for the wedding. It would have been only half a day from Boston by train, but still—nobody came down to stand for Ambrose.

Alma, looking around her, realized how small a household they had become. This was far too small a gathering. This was simply not enough people. It was barely enough for a legal wedding. How had they become so isolated? She remembered the ball that her parents had held in 1808, exactly forty years earlier: how the verandah and the great lawn had swirled with dancers and musicians, and how she had run among them with her torch. It was impossible to imagine now that White Acre had ever been the site of such a spectacle, such laughter, such wild doings. It had become a constellation of silence since then.

As a wedding gift, Alma gave Ambrose an exceedingly fine antiquarian edition of Thomas Burnet's *Sacred Theory of the Earth*, originally published in 1684. Burnet was a theologian who surmised that the planet—before Noah's flood—had been a smooth sphere of absolute perfection, which had "the beauty of youth and blooming nature, fresh and fruitful, not a wrinkle, scar or fracture in all its body; no rocks nor mountains, no hollow caves, nor gaping channels, but even and uniform all over." He, Burnet, had called this "The First Earth." Alma thought her husband would like it, and indeed he did. Notions of perfection, dreams of unsullied exquisiteness—all of this was Ambrose, through and through.

As for Ambrose, he presented Alma with a beautiful square of Italian paper, which he had folded into a tiny, complex sort of envelope, and had covered with seals in four different colors of wax. Every seam was sealed, and every seal was different. It was a pretty object—small enough to sit on the palm of her hand—but it was strange and nearly cabalistic. Alma turned the curious little item over and over.

"How is one meant to open such a gift?" she asked.

"It is not to be opened," Ambrose said. "I ask you never to open it."

"What does it contain?"

"A message of love."

"Really?" said Alma, delighted. "A message of love! I should like to see such a thing!"

"I would prefer that you imagine it."

"My imagination is not as rich as yours, Ambrose."

"But for you who loves knowledge so much, Alma, it will do your imagination good to keep something unrevealed. We will come to know each other so well, you and I. Let us leave something unopened."

She put the gift in her pocket. It sat there all day—a strange, light, mysterious presence.

They dined that evening with Henry and his friend the judge. Henry and the judge drank too much port. Alma took no spirits, nor did Ambrose. Her husband smiled at her whenever she glanced his way—but then he always had done that, even before he was her husband. It felt like any other evening, except that she was now Mrs. Ambrose Pike. The sun went down slowly that night, like an old man taking his time to hobble downstairs.

At last, after dinner, Alma and Ambrose retired to Alma's bedroom for the first time. Alma sat on the edge of the bed, and Ambrose joined her. He reached for her hand. After a long silence, she said, "If you'll excuse me . . ."

She wished to put on her new nightdress, but did not want to disrobe in front of him. She took the nightdress into the small water closet off the corner of her bedroom—the one that had been installed, with a bathtub and cold-water taps, in the 1830s. She undressed and put on the gown. She did not know if she should keep her hair up, or let it down. It did not always look nice when she let it down, but it was uncomfortable to sleep in pins and fasteners. She hesitated, then decided to leave it up.

When she reentered the bedroom, she found that Ambrose had also changed into his nightshirt—a simple linen affair, which hung to his shins. He had folded his clothes neatly and set them on a chair. He stood on the far side of the bed from her. Nervousness ran over her like a cavalry charge. Ambrose did not seem nervous. He did not say anything about her nightdress. He beckoned her to the bed, and she climbed in. He came into the bed from the other side, and met her in the middle. Immediately she had the awful thought that this bed was far too small for the both of them. She and Ambrose were both so tall. Where were their legs supposed to go? What about their arms? What if she kicked him in her sleep? What if she put an elbow into his eye, without knowing?

She turned sideways, he turned sideways, and they faced each other.

"Treasure of my soul," he said. He took one of her hands, brought it to his lips, and kissed it, just above the knuckles, as he had been doing every night for the last month, since their engagement. "You have brought me such peace."

"Ambrose," she replied, amazed by his name, amazed by his face.

"It is in our sleep that we most closely glimpse the power of spirit," he said. "Our minds will speak across this narrow distance. It will be here, together in nocturnal stillness, that we shall finally become unbound by time, by space, by natural law and physical law. We shall roam the world however we like, in our dreams. We shall speak with the dead, transform into animals and objects, fly across time. Our intellects shall be nowhere to be found, and our minds will be unfettered."

"Thank you," she said, senselessly. She could not think of what else to say, in response to such an unexpected speech. Was this some sort of wooing? Was this how they proceeded with things, up in Boston? She worried that her breath did not smell sweet. His breath smelled sweet. She wished that he would extinguish the lamp. Immediately, as though hearing her thoughts, he reached over and extinguished the lamp. The dark was better, more comfortable. She wanted to swim toward him. She felt him take up her hand again and press it to his lips.

"Good night, my wife," he said.

He did not let go of her hand. Within a matter of moments—she could tell it by his breathing—he was asleep.

Of everything Alma had imagined, hoped for, or feared as to what might transpire on her wedding night, this course of events had never occurred to her.

Ambrose dozed on, steady and peaceful beside her, his hand clasped lightly and trustingly around hers, while Alma, eyes wide in the dark, lay still in the spreading silence. Bewilderment overcame her like something oily and dank. She sought possible explanations for this strange occurrence, paging through her mind for one interpretation after another, as one would do in science, with any experiment gone wildly wrong.

Perhaps he would awaken, and they would recommence—or rather *commence*—with their marital pleasures? Perhaps he had not liked her nightdress? Perhaps she had appeared too modest? Or too eager? Was it the dead girl that he wanted? Was he thinking of his lost love from Framingham, all those years ago? Or perhaps he had been overcome by a fit of nerves? Was he unequal to love's duties? But none of these explanations made sense, particularly not the last one. Alma knew enough of such matters to understand that the inability to conduct intercourse brought men the severest imaginable shame—but Ambrose did not seem ashamed at all. Nor had he even *attempted* intercourse. On the contrary, he slept as easefully as a man could possibly sleep. He slept like a rich burgher in a fine hotel. He slept like a king after a long day of boar hunting and jousting. He slept like a princely Mohammedan, sated by a dozen comely concubines. He slept like a child under a tree.

Alma did not sleep. The night was hot, and she was uncomfortable lying on her side for so long, afraid to move, afraid to withdraw her hand from his. The pins and fasteners in her hair pressed into her scalp. Her shoulder was growing numb below her. After a long while, she finally released herself from his clasp and turned over onto her back, but it was useless: rest would not find her this night. She lay there in stiffness and alarm, her eyes wide open, her armpits damp, her mind searching without success for a comforting conclusion to this most surprising and unfavorable turn of affairs.

At dawn, every bird on earth, merrily oblivious to her dread, began to sing. With the first rays of sunlight, Alma allowed herself to throw forward a spark of hope that her husband would awaken in the dawn and embrace her now. Perhaps they would begin it in the daylight—all the expected intimacies of matrimony.

Ambrose did awaken, but he did not embrace her. He woke in a lively instant, fresh and contented. "What dreams!" he said, and reached his arms above him in a languorous stretch. "I have not had such dreams in years. What an honor it is, to share the electricity of your being. Thank you, Alma! What a day we shall have! Did you have such dreams, too?"

Alma had dreamed nothing, of course. Alma had passed the night boxed up within a waking horror. Nonetheless, she nodded. She did not know what else to do.

"You must promise me," Ambrose said, "that when we die—whichever of us shall die first—that we will send vibrations to each other across the divide of mortality."

Again, senselessly, she nodded. It was easier than trying to speak.

Stale and silent, Alma watched her husband rise and splash his face in the basin. He took his clothing from the chair and politely excused himself to the water closet, returning fully dressed and saturated with good cheer. What lurked behind that warm smile? Alma could see nothing behind it but more warmth. He looked to her exactly as he had looked the first day she had glimpsed him—like a lovely, bright, and enthusiastic man of twenty years.

She was a fool.

"I shall leave you to your privacy," he said. "And I shall be waiting for you at the breakfast table. What a day we shall have!"

Alma's entire body ached. In a terrible cloud of stiffness and despair, she moved out of bed slowly, like a cripple, and dressed herself. She looked in the mirror. She should not have looked. She had aged a decade in one night.

Henry was at the breakfast table when Alma finally descended. He and Ambrose were engaged in a light tinsel of conversation. Hanneke brought Alma a fresh pot of tea and threw her a sharp look—the sort of look that all women get on the morning after their wedding—but Alma avoided her eyes. She tried to keep her face from appearing moony or grim, but her imagination was fatigued and she knew that her eyes were red. She felt over-grown by mildew. The men did not seem to notice. Henry was telling a story Alma had heard a dozen times already—of the night he had shared a bed in a filthy Peruvian tavern with a pompous little Frenchman, who had the thickest imaginable French accent, but who tirelessly insisted he was not French.

Henry said, "The dunderhead kept saying to me, '*Hi emm en Heenglish-man!*' and I kept telling him, 'You are not an Englishman, you idiot, you are a Frenchman! Just listen to your cussed accent!' But no, the bloody dunder-head kept saying it: '*Hi emm en Heenglishman!*' Finally I said to him, 'Tell me, then—how is it possible that you are an Englishman?' And he crowed, '*Hi emm en Heenglishman because Hi 'ave en Heenglish wife!*'"

Ambrose laughed and laughed. Alma stared at him as if he were a specimen.

"By that logic," Henry concluded, "I am a bloody Dutchman!"

"And I am a Whittaker!" Ambrose added, still laughing.

"More tea?" Hanneke asked Alma, again with that same penetrating look.

Alma clamped shut her mouth, which she realized had been hanging a bit too far open. "I have had enough, Hanneke, thank you."

"The men will be carting in the last of the hay today," Henry said. "See to it, Alma, that it is done properly."

"Yes, Father."

Henry turned to Ambrose again. "She is good value, that wife of yours, especially when there is work to be done. A regular Farmer John in skirts, she is."

The second night was the same as the first—and the third night, and the fourth and fifth. All the nights to follow, all the same. Ambrose and Alma would undress in privacy, come to the bed and face each other. He would kiss her hand and praise her goodness, and extinguish the lamp. Ambrose would then fall into the sleep of an enchanted figure in a fairy tale, while Alma lay in silent torment beside him. The only thing that changed over time was that Alma finally managed to receive a few fitful hours of sleep a night, merely because her body would collapse with exhaustion. But her sleep was interrupted by clawing dreams and awful spells of restless, roaming, wakeful thought.

By day, Alma and Ambrose were companions as ever in study and contemplation. He had never seemed more fond of her. She woodenly went about her own work, and helped him with his. He always wanted to be near her—as near to her as possible. He did not seem aware of her discomfort. She tried not to reveal it. She kept hoping for a change. More weeks passed. October arrived. The nights turned cool. There was no change.

Ambrose appeared so at ease with the terms of their marriage that Alma—for the first time in her life—feared herself to be going mad. Here she wanted to ravish him to a pulp, but he was happy to merely kiss the one square inch of skin below the middle knuckle of her left hand. Had she been misinformed as to the nature of conjugality? Was it a trick? She was enough of a Whittaker to seethe at the thought of having been played as a fool. But then she would look at Ambrose's face, which was the furthest imaginable thing from the face of a scoundrel, and her rage, once more, would render down back into unhappy bewilderment.

By early October, Philadelphia was enjoying the last days of Indian summer. The mornings were crowning glories of cool air and blue skies, and the afternoons balmy and lazy. Ambrose behaved as though he was more inspired than ever, springing out of bed every morning as though shot forth by a cannon. He had managed to get a rare *Aerides odorata* to bloom in the orchid house. Henry had imported the plant years ago from the foothills of the Himalayas, but it had never put forth a single bud until Ambrose took the orchid out of its pot on the ground and hung it high from the rafters, in a bright spot of sun, in a basket made of bark and dampened moss. Now the thing had ignited into sudden flower. Henry was elated. Ambrose was elated. Ambrose was making drawings of it from every angle. It would be the pride of the White Acre florilegium.

"If you love anything enough, it will eventually show you its secrets," Ambrose told Alma.

She might have begged to differ, had her opinion been asked. She could not possibly have loved Ambrose more, but no secrets were forthcoming from him. She found herself unpleasantly jealous of his victory with the *Aerides odorata*. She envied the plant itself, and the care he had shown it. She could not focus on her own work, yet here he was thriving in his. She began to resent his presence in the carriage house. Why was he always interrupting her? His printing presses were loud, and smelled of hot ink. Alma could no longer bear it. She felt as though she were rotting. Her temper grew short. She was walking through the White Acre vegetable gardens one day when she came upon a young worker, sitting on his shovel, lazily picking at a splinter in his thumb. She had seen this one before—this little splinter-picker. He was far more often to be found sitting on his shovel than working with it.

"Your name is Robert, isn't it?" she asked, approaching him with a warm smile.

"I'm Robert," he confirmed, looking up at her with mild unconcern.

"What is your task this afternoon, Robert?"

"To turn over this rotty old pea patch, ma'am."

"And do you plan to get at it one of these days, Robert?" she probed, her voice dangerously low.

"Well, I've got this splinter here, see . . ."

Alma leaned over him, casting his whole tiny body in shadow. She picked him up by his collar, a full foot off the ground, and—shaking him like a sack of feed—she bellowed, "Get back at your work, you useless little lobcock, before I take off your balls with that shovel of yours!"

She tossed him back to the ground. He landed hard. He scrambled out from under her shadow like a rabbit, and began digging furiously, haphazardly, fearfully. Alma walked away, shaking loose the muscles of her arms, and immediately recommenced her thoughts of her husband. Was it possible that Ambrose simply didn't *know*? Could anyone be such an innocent as to have entered matrimony unaware of its duties, or oblivious to the sexual mechanisms between man and wife? She remembered a book she had read years ago, back when she had begun collecting those licentious texts in the loft of the carriage house. She had not thought of this book for at least two decades. It had been rather tedious, compared to the others, but it came back to her mind now. It bore the title *The Fruits of Marriage: A Gentleman's Guide to Sexual Continence; A Manual for Married Couples*, by Dr. Horscht.

This Dr. Horscht had written the book, he claimed, after counseling a modest young Christian couple who did not possess any knowledge—either theoretical or practical—of the sexual relation, and who had baffled themselves and each other with such peculiar feelings and sensations upon entering the conjugal bed that they felt they were under a spell. Finally, a few weeks after their wedding, the poor young groom had quizzed a friend, who had given him the shocking information that the newlywed husband needed to place his organ directly inside his bride's "watering hole" for the proper relations to occur. This thought had brought such fear and shame upon the poor young fellow that he ran to Dr. Horscht with questions as to whether this outlandish-sounding act could possibly be either performable or virtuous. Dr. Horscht, in pity for the baffled young soul, had written his guidebook on the engine of sexuality, to assist other newly married men.

Alma had scorned the book when she'd read it years earlier. To be a young fellow and to hold such complete ignorance of the genito-urinary function seemed beyond absurd to her. Surely such people could not exist?

Yet now she wondered.

Did she need to *show* him?

That Saturday afternoon, Ambrose retired to their bedroom early and excused himself to bathe before dinner. She followed him to the room. She sat on the bed, and listened to the water running into the large porcelain tub on the other side of the door. She heard him humming. He was happy. She, on the other hand, was inflamed with misery and doubt. He must be undressing now. She heard muted splashes as he entered the bath, and then a sigh of pleasure. Then silence.

She stood up and undressed, too. She removed everything—drawers and chemise, even the pins from her hair. If she'd had anything more to take off, she would have done so. Her nude form was not beautiful, and she knew it, but it was all she had. She went and leaned against the door of the water closet, listening with her ear pressed against it. She did not have to do this. There were alternatives. She could learn to endure things as they were. She could patiently submit to her suffering, to this strange and impossible marriage-that-was-not-a-marriage. She could learn how to conquer everything that Ambrose brought forth within her—her appetite for him, her disappointment in him, her sense of tormenting absence whenever she was near him. If she could learn how to defeat her own desire, then she could keep her husband—such as he was.

No. No, she could not learn that.

She turned the knob, pushed against the door, and entered as silently as she could. His head turned toward her, and his eyes grew wide with alarm. She said nothing, and he said nothing. She looked away from his eyes and allowed herself to examine his entire body, just submerged under the cool bath water. There he was, in all his naked loveliness. His skin was milky white—so much whiter in his chest and legs than on his arms. There was only a trace of hair on his torso. He could not have been more perfectly beautiful.

Had she worried that he might not have genitalia at all? Had she imagined that this might have been the problem? Well, this was not the problem. He had genitalia—perfectly adequate, and even impressive, genitalia. She allowed herself to observe with care this lovely appendage of his—this pale, waving sea creature, which floated between his legs in its thatch of wet and private fur. Ambrose did not move. Nor did his penis stir at all. It did not like being looked at. She realized this immediately. Alma had spent enough time in the woods gazing upon shy animals to know when a creature did not want to be seen, and this creature between Ambrose's legs did not wish to be seen. Still, she gazed at it because she could not look away. Ambrose allowed her to do this—not so much because he was permissive, but because he was paralyzed.

At last, she looked up to his face, desperate to find some opening, some conduit, into him. He appeared frozen in fear. Why *fear*? She dropped to the floor beside the bathtub. It almost looked as though she were kneeling before him in supplication. No—she *was* kneeling before him in supplication. His right hand, with its long and tapered fingers, was resting on the edge of the tub, clutching at the porcelain rim. She loosened this hand, one finger at a time. He allowed her to loosen it. She took his hand and brought it toward her mouth. She put three of his fingers in her mouth. She could not help herself. She needed something of him inside her. She wanted to bite down on him, just enough to keep his fingers from slipping out of her mouth. She did not wish to frighten him, but she did not wish to let him go, either. Instead of biting down, she began to suck. She was perfectly concentrated in her yearning. Her lips made a noise—a rude sort of wet noise.

At that, Ambrose came alive. He gasped, and yanked his fingers from her mouth. He sat up quickly, making a loud splash, and covered his genitals with both his hands. He looked as though he were going to die of terror.

"Please—" she said.

They stared at each other, like a woman and a bedchamber intruder—but she was the intruder, and he was the terrified quarry. He stared at her as though she were a stranger who had put a knife to his throat, as though she intended to use him for the most evil pleasures, then sever his head, carve out his bowels, and eat his heart with a long, sharpened fork.

Alma relented. What other choice did she have? She stood and walked slowly from the water closet, gently pulling the door closed behind her. She dressed again. She walked downstairs. Her heart was so broken that she did not know how it was possible she could still be alive.

She found Hanneke de Groot sweeping the corners of the dining room. With a clenched voice, she requested that the housekeeper please make up the guest bedroom in the east wing for Mr. Pike, who would be sleeping there from now on, until other arrangements could be made.

"*Waarom*?" Hanneke asked.

But Alma could not tell her why. She was tempted to fall into Hanneke's arms and weep, but resisted it.

"Is there any harm in an old woman's question?" Hanneke asked.

"You will please inform Mr. Pike yourself of this new arrangement," Alma said, and walked away. "I find myself unable to tell him."

———————————

Alma slept on her divan in the carriage house that night, and did not take dinner. She thought of Hippocrates, who believed that the ventricles of the heart were not pumps for blood, but for air. He believed the heart was an extension of the lungs—a sort of great, muscular bellows, which fed the furnace of the body. Tonight, Alma felt as if it were true. She could feel a huge gushing and sucking of wind inside her chest. It felt as though her heart was gasping for air. As for her lungs, they seemed full of blood. She was drowning with every breath. She could not shake this sense of drowning. She felt mad. She felt like crazed little Retta Snow, who also used to sleep on this couch, when the world became too frightening.

In the morning, Ambrose came to find her. He was pale and his face was contorted with pain. He sat beside her, and reached for her hands. She pulled them away. He stared at her for a long while without speaking.

"If you are trying to communicate something to me silently, Ambrose," she said at last, in a voice tight with anger, "I will be unable to hear it. I ask that you speak to me directly. Do me that courtesy, please."

"Forgive me," he said.

"You must tell me what I am to forgive you *for*."

He struggled. "This marriage . . ." he began, and then lost his words.

She laughed a hollow laugh. "What is a marriage, Ambrose, when it is cheated of the honest pleasures any husband and wife could rightly expect?"

He nodded. He looked hopeless.

"You have misled me," she said.

"Yet I believed we understood each other."

"Did you? What did you believe was understood? Tell me in words: What did you think our marriage would be?"

He searched for an answer. "An exchange," he finally said.

"Of what, exactly?"

"Of love. Of ideas and comfort."

"As did I, Ambrose. But I thought there might be other exchanges as well. If you wished to live like a Shaker, why did you not run off and join them?"

He looked at her, baffled. He had no idea what a Shaker was. Lord, there was so much this boy did not know!

"Let us not dispute each other, Alma, or stand in conflict," he begged.

"Is it the dead girl whom you long for? Is that the problem?"

Again, the baffled expression.

"The dead girl, Ambrose," she repeated. "The one your mother told me of. The one who died in Framingham years ago. The one you loved."

He could not have been more perplexed. "You spoke to my mother?"

"She wrote me a letter. She told me of the girl—of your true love."

"My mother wrote you a letter? About Julia?" Ambrose's face was swimming in bewilderment. "But I never loved Julia, Alma. She was a dear child and the friend of my youth, but I never loved her. My mother may have wished me to love her, for she was the daughter of an upstanding family, but Julia was nothing more than my innocent neighbor. We drew flowers together. She had a small genius for it. She was dead at the age of fourteen. I have scarcely thought of her these many years. Why on earth are we speaking of Julia?"

"Why can you not love me?" Alma asked, hating the desperation in her voice.

"I could not love you *more*," Ambrose said, with desperation to match her own.

"I am ugly, Ambrose. I have never been unaware of that fact. Also, I am old. Yet I am in possession of several things that you wanted—comforts, companionship. You could have had all those things without humiliating me through marriage. I had already given you those things, and would have given them to you forever. I was content to love you like a sister, perhaps even like a mother. But *you* were the one who wished to wed. You were the one who introduced to me the idea of matrimony. You were the one who said that you wanted to sleep next to me every night. You were the one who allowed me to long for things that I long ago overcame desiring."

She had to stop speaking. Her voice was rising and cracking. This was shame upon shame.

"I have no need of wealth," Ambrose said, his eyes wet with sorrow. "You know this of me."

"Yet you are reaping its benefits."

"You do not understand me, Alma."

"I do not understand you at all, Mr. Pike. Edify me."

"I asked you," he said. "I asked you if you wanted a marriage of the soul—a *mariage blanc*." When she did not immediately answer, he said, "It means a chaste marriage, without exchange of flesh."

"I know what a *mariage blanc* is, Ambrose," she snapped. "I was speaking French before you were born. What I fail to understand is why you would imagine that I wanted one."

"Because I asked you. I asked if you would accept this of me, and you agreed."

"*When?*" Alma felt that she would tear his hair straight out of his scalp if he did not speak more directly, more truthfully.

"In your book-repair closet that night, after I found you in the library. When we sat in silence together. I asked you, silently, 'Will you accept this of me?' and you said, 'yes.' I *heard* you say yes. I felt you say it! Do not deny it, Alma—you heard my question across the divide, and you answered me in the affirmative! Is that not true?"

He was staring at her with panicked eyes. Now she was struck dumb.

"And you asked me a question, too," Ambrose went on. "You asked me silently if this is what I wanted of you. I said yes, Alma! I believe I even said it aloud! I could not have answered more clearly! You heard me say it!"

She cast her mind back to that night in the binding closet, to her silent detonation of sexual pleasure, to the sensation of his question running through her, and of her question running through him. *What had she heard?* She had heard him ask, clear as a ringing church bell, "Will you accept this of me?" Of course she had said yes. She thought he had meant, "Will you accept sensual pleasures such as this from me?" When she had asked in reply, "Is this what you want of me?" she had meant, "Do you want these sensual pleasures with me?"

Dear Lord in heaven, they had misunderstood each other's questions! They had *supernaturally* misunderstood each other's questions. It had been the one and only categorical miracle of Alma Whittaker's life, and she had misunderstood it. This was the worst jest she had ever heard.

"I was only asking you," she said wearily, "if you wanted *me*. Which is to say—if you wanted me *fully*, in the way that lovers typically want each other. I thought you were asking me the same."

"But I would never ask for anyone's corporeal body in the manner of which you speak," Ambrose said.

"Why ever not?"

"Because I do not believe in it."

Alma could not comprehend what she was hearing. She was unable to speak for a long while. Then she asked, "Is it your opinion that the conjugal act—even between a man and his wife—is something vile and depraved? Surely you know, Ambrose, what other people share with each other, in the privacy of marriage? Do you think me debased, for wanting my husband to be a husband? Surely you have heard tales of such enjoyments between men

278 and women?"

"I am not like other men, Alma. Can that honestly surprise you to learn, at this late date?"

"What do you imagine you are, then, if not like other men?"

"It is not what I imagine I am, Alma—it is what I wish to be. Or rather, what I once was, and wish to be again."

"Which is what, Ambrose?"

"An angel of God," Ambrose said, in a voice of unspeakable sadness. "I had hoped we could be angels of God together. Such a thing would not be possible unless we were freed of the flesh, bound in celestial grace."

"Oh, for the godforsaken mercy of the twice-buggered mother of *Christ!*" Alma cursed. She wanted to pick him up and shake him, as she'd shaken Robert the garden boy the other day. She wanted to argue scripture with him. The women of Sodom, she wanted to tell him, had been punished by Jehovah for having sexual communion with angels—*but at least they had gotten their chance!* Just her luck, to have been sent an angel so beautiful, yet so uncomplying.

"Come, Ambrose!" she said. "Awaken yourself! We do not live in the celestial realm—not you, and most certainly not I. How can you be so dim? Put your eyes upon me, child! Your real eyes—your mortal eyes. Do I look like an angel to you, Ambrose Pike?"

"Yes," he said, with sad simplicity.

The rage passed out of Alma, and was replaced by leaden, bottomless sorrow.

"Then you have been much mistaken," Alma said, "and now we find ourselves in a deuce of a mess."

He could not stay on at White Acre.

This became evident after only a week had passed—a week during which Ambrose slept in the guest chambers in the east wing, and Alma slept on the divan in the carriage house, both of them enduring the grins and titters of the young maids. To be wed only a few weeks and already sleeping not only in different rooms, but in different *buildings* . . . well, this was far too glorious a scandal for the busybodies about the estate to resist.

Hanneke tried to keep the staff silent, but the rumors dipped and flew like bats at twilight. They said that Alma was too old and ugly for Ambrose to endure, regardless of the fortune that came tucked inside her dried-up cunny. They said that Ambrose had been caught stealing. They said that Ambrose liked the pretty young girls, and that he had been found with his hand on the arse of a dairymaid. They said whatever they wanted to say; Hanneke could not dismiss everyone. Alma overheard some of it herself, and what she did not overhear, she could easily imagine. The looks they gave her were despicable enough.

Her father called her into his study on a Monday afternoon in late October.

"What is this, then?" he said. "Bored of your new toy already?"

"Do not ridicule me, Father—I swear to you, I cannot bear it."

"Then make an explanation to me."

"It is too shameful to explain."

"I cannot imagine that to be true. Do you fancy that I have not heard the bulk of rumors already? Nothing you could tell me would be more shameful than what people are already saying."

"There is much that I cannot tell you, Father."

"Has he been untrue to you? *Already?*"

"You know him, Father. He would not do that."

"None of us much know him, Alma. So what is it? Stolen from you— from *me*? Is he rutting you half to death? Beating you with a leather strop? No, somehow I cannot see any of that. Put a name to it, girl. What is his crime?"

"He cannot stay here any longer, and I cannot tell you why."

"Do you take me for a specimen of man who would faint at the truth? I am old, Alma, but not yet entombed. And don't think I will not guess it, either, if I go at the question long enough. Are you frigid? Is that the trouble? Or does he hang limp?"

She did not reply.

"Ah," he said. "Something like that, then. So there has been no settlement of the marital duties?"

Again, she did not reply.

Henry clapped his hands. "Well, what of it? You enjoy each other's companionship, regardless. That's more than most people are allotted in their marriages. You are too old to bear children, anyway, and many marriages are not happy in the bedchamber. Most of them, really. Poorly matched pairings are thick as flies in this world. Your marriage may have soured faster than others, but you will bear up and endure it, Alma, like the rest of us do—or did. Haven't you been raised to bear up and endure things? You will not have your life felled by one setback. Make the best of it. Think of him as a brother, if he does not tickle you under the coverlets to your satisfaction. He would make a good enough brother. He is pleasant company to us all."

"I am not in need of a brother. I am telling you, Father, *he cannot stay here*. You must make him leave."

"And I am telling you, daughter, that not three months ago we two stood in this very room and I listened to you insist that you must marry this man—a man about whom I knew nothing, and about whom you knew only a penny's worth more. Now you wish me to chase him away? What am I to be, your bull terrier? I confess, I do not approve of it, no, I do not. There is no dignity in it. Is it the gossip you don't like? Face it down like a Whittaker. Go and be seen by those who mock you. Knock somebody's head about, if you don't like the way they look at you. They'll learn. They'll find something else to gossip about soon enough. But to cast this young man out forever, for the crime of—what? Not entertaining you? Take up with one of the gardeners, if you must have a young buck in your bed. There are men you can pay for such diversions, same as men pay for women. People desirous of money will do anything, and you have ample money. Use your dowry to establish a harem of young men for your pleasure, if you wish it."

"Father, please—" she begged.

"But meanwhile, what do you propose I *do* with our Mr. Pike?" he went on. "Drag him behind a carriage through the streets of Philadelphia, painted with tar? Sink him in the Schuylkill, tied to a barrel full of rocks? Put a blindfold on him, and shoot him against a wall?"

She could only stand there in shame and sorrow, unable to speak. What had she thought her father would say? Well—foolish as it seemed now—she had thought Henry might defend her. She thought Henry would be outraged on her behalf. She had half expected him to stomp around the house in one of his famous old theatrical rants, arms waving like a player in a farce: *How could you do this to my daughter?* That sort of thing. Something to match the pitch and depth of her own loss and fury. But why would she think that? Whom had she ever seen Henry Whittaker defend? And if he was defending anyone in this case, it appeared he was defending Ambrose.

Instead of coming to her rescue, her father was belittling her. What's more, Alma now remembered the conversation she and Henry had had about her marriage to Ambrose, not three months earlier. Henry had warned her—or at least, he'd raised the question—about whether "this sort of man" could bring her satisfaction in matrimony. What had he known then, that he hadn't expressed? What did he know now?

"Why did you not stop me marrying him?" Alma asked at last. "You suspected something. Why did you not speak?"

Henry shrugged. "It was not my domain three months ago to make up your mind for you. Nor is it now. If something is to be done with the young man, you must do it yourself."

The thought of this staggered Alma: Henry had been making up Alma's mind for her forever, since she was the smallest mite of a girl—or that was how she had always perceived things.

She could not stop herself from asking, "But what do you think I should do with him?"

"Do what you damned well like, Alma! This decision is yours. Mr. Pike is not mine to dispose of. You brought this thing into our household, you get rid of it—if that is what you wish. Be swift about it, too. It is always better to cut than to tear. One way or another, I want this matter resolved. A certain amount of common sense has exited this family in the last few months, and I would like to see it restored. We have too much work on hand for this sort of foolery."

In years to come, Alma would try to convince herself that she and Ambrose had made the decision together—about where he was to go next in his life—but nothing could have been further from the truth. Ambrose Pike was not a man who made decisions for himself. He was an untethered balloon, fabulously susceptible to the influence of those more powerful than he—and everyone was more powerful than he. Always, he had done just as he was told. His mother had told him to go to Harvard, and so he had gone to Harvard. His friends had pulled him out of a snowbank and sent him to a ward for the mentally insane, and he had obediently allowed himself to be locked away. Daniel Tupper up in Boston had told him to go to the jungles of Mexico and paint orchids, and he had gone to the jungle and painted orchids.

George Hawkes had invited him to Philadelphia, and he had come to Philadelphia. Alma had established him at White Acre and instructed him to make a grand florilegium of her father's plant collection, and he had set to it without question. He would go wherever he was led.

He wanted to be an angel of God, but Lord protect him, he was just a lamb.

Did she honestly try to think of a plan that would be best for him? She told herself later that she did. She would not divorce him; there was no reason to put either of them through such scandal. She would provide him with ample funds—not that he had ever asked for any, but because it was the proper thing to do. She would not send him back to Massachusetts, not only because she detested his mother (just from that one letter, she detested his mother!) but also because the thought of Ambrose sleeping forever on his friend Tupper's couch brought her anguish. She could not send him back to Mexico, either, that was certain. He had almost died of fever there already.

Yet she could not keep him in Philadelphia, because his presence brought her too much suffering. Mercy, how he had diminished her! Yet she still loved his face—pale and troubled though he had become. Just to see that face brought forth such a gaping, vulgar need within her that she could scarcely bear it. He would have to go elsewhere—somewhere far away. She could not risk encountering him in the years to come.

She wrote a letter to Dick Yancey—to her father's iron-fisted business manager—who was at the moment in Washington, D.C., arranging some business with the nascent botanical gardens there. Alma knew that Yancey would soon be embarking for the South Pacific on a whaling ship. He was going to Tahiti to investigate the Whittaker Company's struggling vanilla plantation, and to attempt to put into place the artificial-pollination tactic that Ambrose himself had suggested to Alma's father, on the first night of his visit to White Acre.

Yancey planned to leave for Tahiti soon, within the fortnight. It was best to sail before the late-autumn storms, and before the harbor froze.

Alma knew all this. Why should Ambrose not go to Tahiti with Dick Yancey, then? It was a respectable, even ideal, solution. Ambrose could take over management of the vanilla plantation himself. He would excel at it, would he not? Vanillas were orchids, weren't they? Henry Whittaker would be pleased with the plan; sending Ambrose to Tahiti was exactly what he'd wanted in the first place, before Alma talked him out of it, to her own severe detriment.

Was this a banishment? Alma attempted not to think so. Tahiti was said to be a paradise, Alma told herself. It was hardly a penal colony. Yes, Ambrose was delicate, but Dick Yancey would see that no harm befell him. The work would be interesting. The climate was fine and healthy there. Who would not envy this opportunity to see the fabled shores of Polynesia? It was an opportunity that any man of botany or commerce would welcome—and it was all paid for, besides.

She pushed aside the voices within her who protested that, yes, this was most certainly a banishment—and a cruel one. She ignored what she knew all too well—that Ambrose was neither a man of botany nor a man of commerce, but rather a being of unique sensitivities and talents, whose mind was a delicate thing, and who was perhaps not at all suited to a long journey on a whaling vessel, or life on an agricultural plantation in the distant South Seas. Ambrose was more child than man, and he had said to Alma many times that he wanted nothing more in life than a secure home and a gentle companion.

Well, there are many things in life that we want, she told herself, and we do not always get them.

Besides, there was nowhere else for him to go.

Having decided everything, Alma then established her husband at the United States Hotel for two weeks—right across the street from the large bank where her father's money was stored in great secret vaults—while she waited for Dick Yancey to return from Washington.

It was in the lobby of United States Hotel, a fortnight later, that Alma at last introduced her husband to Dick Yancey—to towering, silent Dick Yancey, with the fearsome eyes and the jaw carved out of rock, who did not ask questions, and who did only as he was ordered. Well, Ambrose did only as he was ordered, too. Stooped and pale, Ambrose asked no questions. He did not even ask how long he would be expected to remain in Polynesia. She would not have known how to answer that question, in any case. It was not a banishment, she continued to tell herself. Yet even she did not know how long it would last.

"Mr. Yancey will take care of you from here," she said to Ambrose. "Your comforts will be attended to, as much as possible."

She felt as though she were leaving a baby in the care of a trained crocodile. At that moment, she loved Ambrose every bit as much as she ever had loved him—which was *entirely*. Already, she felt a wide-open absence at the thought of him sailing to the other side of the world. Then again, she had felt nothing but wide-open absence since her wedding night. She wanted to embrace him, but she had *always* wanted to embrace him, and she could not do that. He would not permit it. She wanted to cling to him, to beg him to stay, to beg him to love her. None of it was permitted. There was no use in it.

They shook hands, as they had done in her mother's Grecian garden on the day they had met. The same small worn leather valise sat beside Ambrose's feet, filled with all his belongings. He wore the same brown corduroy suit. He had taken nothing with him from White Acre.

The last thing she said to him was, "I pray of you, Ambrose, do me the service of not speaking to anyone you may meet about our marriage. Nobody need know what has transpired between us. You will travel not as the son-in-law of Henry Whittaker, but as his employee. Anything further than that would only lead to questions, and I do not long for the world's questions."

He agreed by nodding. He said nothing more. He looked sick and exhausted.

Alma did not need to ask Dick Yancey to keep secret her history with Mr. Pike. Dick Yancey did nothing but keep secrets; that was why the Whittakers had kept him around for such a very long time.

Dick Yancey was useful that way.

Chapter Eighteen

Alma heard nothing whatsoever from Ambrose over the next three years; in fact, she scarcely even heard anything *about* him. In the early summer of 1849, Dick Yancey sent word that they had safely arrived in Tahiti after an uneventful sail. (Alma knew that this did not mean it had been an *easy* sail; to Dick Yancey, any journey that did not end in shipwreck or capture by pirates was uneventful.) Yancey reported that Mr. Pike had been left at Matavai Bay, in the care of a botanizing missionary named the Reverend Francis Welles, and that Mr. Pike had been introduced to the duties of the vanilla plantation. Soon after, Dick Yancey had left Tahiti to attend to Whittaker business in Hong Kong. After that, no more news arrived.

This was a time of much despair for Alma. Despair is a tedious business and quickly becomes repetitive, which is how it came to pass that each day for Alma became a replica of the day that had preceded it: sad, lonely, and indistinct. The first winter was the worst. The months seemed colder and darker than any winter Alma had known, and she felt invisible birds of prey hovering over her whenever she walked between the carriage house and the mansion. The bare trees stared at her starkly, begging to be warmed or clothed. The Schuylkill froze so fast and thick that men made bonfires on its surface at night and roasted oxen on spits. Whenever Alma stepped outside, the wind hit her, captured her, and wrapped around her like a stiff and frozen cloak.

She stopped sleeping in her bedroom. She quite nearly stopped sleeping at all. She had been more or less living in the carriage house since her confrontation with Ambrose; she could not imagine ever sleeping in her matrimonial chamber again. She ceased taking meals with the household, and ate the same fare at dinner as she had taken at breakfast: broth and bread, milk and molasses. She felt listless, tragic, and slightly murderous. She was irritable and prickly with exactly those people who were kindest to her—Hanneke de Groot, for instance—and she left off all care and concern for the likes of her sister Prudence, or her poor old friend Retta. She avoided her father. She barely kept up with the official work of White Acre. She complained to Henry that he had treated her unfairly—that he had always treated her as a servant.

"I never claimed fairness!" he shouted, and banished her back to the carriage house until she could become master of herself again.

She felt as though the world mocked her, and thus the world was difficult to face.

Alma had always been of sturdy constitution and had never known the desolations of a sickbed, but during that first winter after Ambrose left, she found it difficult to rise at all in the mornings. She lost her nerve for study. She could not imagine why she had ever been interested in mosses—or in anything. All her old enthusiasms were grown over with weeds. She invited no guests to White Acre. She had no will for it. Conversation was unbearably tiresome; silence worse. Her thoughts were a cloud of contagion that did her no good. If a maid or gardener dared to cross her path, she was likely to cry out, "Why am I not allowed a moment's privacy?" and storm off in the other direction.

Casting about for answers about Ambrose, she searched his study, which he had left intact. She found a notebook filled with his writings in the top drawer of his desk. It was not her place to read such a private relic, and she knew it, yet she told herself that if Ambrose had intended to keep his innermost thoughts secret, he would not have stored the record of them in such an obvious place as the unlocked top drawer of his desk. The notebook, however, brought forth no answers. If anything, it confused and alarmed her more. The pages were not filled with confessions or longings, nor was this a simple log of daily transactions, such as the journals her father kept. None of the entries were even dated. Many of the sentences were barely sentences at all—just fragments of thought, trailed by long dashes and ellipses:

What is thy will—? . . . An eternal forgetting of all strife . . . to yearn only for that which is robust and pure, hewing to the divine standard of self-rule alone . . . Find everywhere contained that which is attached. . . . Do angels twist so painfully against themselves and rank flesh? All that is spoiled within me to be ceaseless and regained in un-self-mangled reform! . . . . To be thoroughly—regenerated!—in benevolent firmness! . . . Only by stolen fire or by stolen knowledge does wisdom advance! . . . No strength in science, but in the compilation of the two—the axis where fire gives birth to water . . . Christ, be my merit, set inside me the example! . . . TORRID hunger, when fed, gives birth to only more hunger!

There were pages and pages of this. It was a confetti of thinking. It began nowhere, led to nothing, and concluded nothing. In the world of botany, such confusing language would have been called *nomina dubia* or *nomina ambigua*—which is to say, misleading and obscure names of plants that render the specimens impossible to classify.

One afternoon Alma finally broke down and cracked open the seals on the elaborately folded piece of paper Ambrose had given her on their wedding day—the curious object, the "message of love" he had specifically asked her never to open. She unfolded its many pleats and smoothed it out. In the center of the page was one word, written in his elegant, unmistakable hand: ALMA.

Useless.

Who was this person? Or rather—who had he been? And who was Alma, now that he was departed? *What* was she, she further wondered? She was a married virgin who had shared a chaste bed with her exquisite young husband for scarcely more than a month. Could she even call herself a wife? She did not believe so. She could not bring herself to be referred to any longer as "Mrs. Pike." The name was a cruel joke, and she barked at anyone who dared use it. She was still Alma Whittaker, and always had been Alma Whittaker.

She could not help but think that if only she had been a more beautiful woman or a younger woman, she might have convinced her husband to love her as a husband should. Why had Ambrose even marked her as a candidate for a *mariage blanc*? Surely because she looked the part: a homely figure of no appeal. She also tormented herself over the question of whether she ought to have taught herself to endure the humiliation of their marriage, as her father had advised. Perhaps she should have accepted Ambrose's terms. Had she been able to swallow her pride or quash her desires, she would still have him beside her now—the companion of her days. A stronger individual might have been able to bear it.

Only a year previous, she had been a contented, useful, and industrious woman, who had never even heard of Ambrose Pike, and now her existence had been blighted by him. This person had arrived, he had illuminated her, he had ensorcelled her with notions of miracle and beauty, he had both understood and misunderstood her, he had married her, he had broken her heart, he had looked upon her with those sad and hopeless eyes, he had accepted his banishment, and now he was gone. What a stark and stunning thing was life—that such a cataclysm can enter and depart so quickly, and leave such wreckage behind!

Seasons passed, but grudgingly. It was now 1850. Alma woke one night in early April from a violent, faceless nightmare. She was clutching at her own throat, choking dryly on the last crumbs of terror. Panicked, she did the oddest thing. She leapt from her divan in the carriage house and ran, barefoot, across the gravel drive, across the frosted yard, across her mother's Grecian garden and toward the house. She dashed around the corner to the kitchen door at the back and pushed in, heart pounding and lungs gasping for breath. She ran downstairs—her feet knowing every worn wooden step in the dark—and did not stop running until she had reached the bars that surrounded Hanneke de Groot's bedroom, in the warmest corner of the basement. She grasped the bars and shook them like a crazed inmate.

"Hanneke!" Alma cried. "Hanneke, I am frightened!"

If she had paused for even an instant between waking and running, she might have stopped herself. She was a fifty-year-old woman running into the arms of her old nursemaid. It was absurd. But she did not stop herself.

"*Wie is daar?*" Hanneke shouted, startled.

"*Ik ben het. Alma!*" Alma said, falling into the warm, familiar Dutch. "You must help me! I have had bad dreams."

Hanneke rose, grumbling and baffled, and unlocked the gate. Alma ran into her arms—into those great salty hams of arms—and wept like an infant. Surprised but adapting, Hanneke guided Alma to the bed and sat her down, embracing her and allowing her to sob.

"There, there," said Hanneke. "It will not kill you."

But Alma thought it *would* kill her, this profundity of sorrow. She could not sound out the bottom of it. She had been sinking into it for a year and a half, and feared she would sink forevermore. She cried herself out on Hanneke's neck, sobbing forth the harvest of her long-darkened spirits. She must have poured a tankard of tears down Hanneke's bosom, but Hanneke did not move or speak, except to repeat, "There, there, child. It will not kill you."

When Alma finally recovered herself somewhat, Hanneke reached for a clean cloth and wiped them both down with cursory efficiency, just as she might have wiped tables in the kitchen.

"One must bear what cannot be escaped," she told Alma, as she rubbed clean her face. "You will not die of your grief—no more than the rest of us ever have."

"But how does one bear it?" Alma begged.

"Through the dignified performance of one's duties," Hanneke said. "Be not afraid to work, child. There you will find consolation. If you are healthy enough to weep, you are healthy enough to work."

"But I loved him," Alma said.

Hanneke sighed. "Then you made an expensive error. You loved a man who thought the world was made of butter. You loved a man who wished to see stars by daylight. He was nonsense."

"He was not nonsense."

"He was *nonsense*," Hanneke repeated.

"He was singular," Alma said. "He did not wish to live in the body of a mortal man. He wished to be a celestial figure—and he wished me to be one, too."

"Well, Alma, you make me say it again: he was nonsense. Yet you treated him like he was a heavenly visitant. Indeed, all of you did!"

"Do you think he was a scoundrel? Do you think he had a wicked soul?"

"No. But he was no heavenly visitant, either. He was just a bit of nonsense, I tell you. He ought to have been harmless nonsense, but you fell prey. Well, we all fall prey to nonsense at times, child, and sometimes we are fool
enough to even love it."

"No man will ever have me," Alma said.

"Probably not," Hanneke decided firmly. "But now you must endure it—and you won't be the first. You have been indulging yourself in a slough of sadness for a long time now, and your mother would be ashamed of you. You are growing soft, and it is disgraceful. Do you think you are the only one to suffer? Read your Bible, child; this world is not a paradise but a vale of tears. Do you think God made an exception for you? Look around you, what do you see? All is anguish. Everywhere you turn there is sorrow. If you do not see sorrow at first glance, look more carefully. You will soon enough see it."

Hanneke spoke sternly, but the mere sound of her voice was reassuring. Dutch was not a mellifluous language like French, or a powerful language like Greek, or a noble language like Latin, but it was as comforting as porridge to Alma. She wanted to put her head in Hanneke's lap and be scolded forever.

"Blow the dust off yourself!" Hanneke went on. "Your mother will haunt me from her grave if I allow you to continue simpering around this place, sucking on the rump-end of sorrow, as you have been doing now for months. Your bones are not broken, so stand up on your own two shanks. Do you wish us to mourn for you forever? Has somebody stuck a twig in your eye? No, they have not—so stop moping about, then! Stop sleeping like a dog on that couch in the carriage house. Take care of your duties. Take care of your father—can you not see he is sick and elderly and soon to die? And leave me alone. I am too old a woman for this foolishness, and so are you. At this point in your life, after everything you have been taught, it would be a pity if you could not better control yourself. Go back to your room, Alma—to your *proper* room, in this house. You will take your breakfast tomorrow morning at the table with the rest of us, just as ever, and furthermore, I expect to see you properly dressed for the day when you sit down to eat it. You will eat every bite of it, too, and you will thank the cook. You are a Whittaker, child. Recover yourself. This is enough."

So Alma did as she was told. She returned, albeit cowed and worn, to her bedroom. She returned to the breakfast table, to her responsibilities toward her father, to the management of White Acre. As best as possible, she returned to her life as it had been before the advent of Ambrose. There was no cure for the gossip of the maids and gardeners, but—as Henry had predicted—eventually they moved on to other scandals and dramas, and for the most part stopped chatting about Alma's woes.

She herself did not forget her woes, but she sewed up the rents in the fabric of her life quite as well as she could, and carried on. She noticed for the first time that her father's health was indeed deteriorating, and rapidly, as Hanneke de Groot had pointed out. This should have come as no surprise (the man was ninety years old!), but she had always seen him as such a colossus, such a piece of human invincibility, that his new frailty amazed and alarmed her. Henry took to his bedroom for longer periods of time, frankly uninterested in matters of important business. His eyesight was dim; his hearing was almost gone. He required an ear trumpet to hear much of anything anymore. He needed Alma both more and less than he had ever needed her before: more as a nurse, less as a clerk. He never mentioned Ambrose. Nobody did. Reports came through Dick Yancey that the vanilla vines in Tahiti were fruiting at last. This was the closest Alma came to hearing news of her lost husband.

Yet Alma never stopped thinking about him. The silence from the printing studio next door to her study in the carriage house was a constant reminder of his absence, as was the dusty neglect of the orchid house, and the tedium at the dinner table. There were conversations to be had with George Hawkes, about the upcoming publication of Ambrose's orchid book—which Alma was now overseeing. That, too, was a reminder, and a painful one. But there was nothing to be done for any of this. One cannot erase every reminder. In fact, one cannot erase *any* reminders. Her sadness was ceaseless, but she kept it quarantined in a governable little quarter of her heart. It was the best she could do.

Once more, as she had done during other lonely moments of her life, she turned to her own work for solace and distraction. She returned to her labors on *The Mosses of North America*. She returned to her boulder fields and inspected her tiny flags and markings. She observed once more the slow advance or decline of one variety against another. She revisited the inspiration she'd had two years before—in those heady, joyful weeks before her wedding—about the similarities between algae and mosses. She could not regain her original wild confidence about the idea, but it still seemed to her entirely possible that the aquatic plant might have transformed into the land plant. There was something to it, some sort of confluence or connection, but she could not solve the riddle.

Looking for answers, seeking intellectual occupation, she returned her attention to the ongoing debates about species mutation. She read Lamarck once more, and carefully. Lamarck had surmised that biological transmutation occurred because of overuse or disuse of a particular body part. For instance, he claimed, giraffes had such long necks because certain individual giraffes across history had stretched themselves up so high, in order to eat from treetops, that they had *caused* their necks to actually grow, within their own lifetimes. Then they had passed on that trait—neck elongation—to their young. Conversely, penguins had such ineffective wings because they had stopped using them. The wings had withered through neglect, and this trait—a pair of stumped and flightless appendages—had been passed along to penguin young, thus shaping the species.

It was a provocative theory, but it did not entirely make sense to Alma. By Lamarck's reasoning, she reckoned, there should be far more transmutation occurring on earth than there actually was. By this logic, Alma surmised, the Jewish people, after centuries of practicing circumcision, should long ago have started producing boys who were born without foreskins. Men who shaved their faces for their entire lives should produce sons who never grew beards. Women who curled their hair daily should produce daughters born with curls. Clearly none of this had occurred.

Yet things *changed*—Alma was certain of it. It was not only Alma who believed this, either. Nearly everyone in the scientific world was discussing the possibility that species could shift from one thing into another—not before one's eyes, perhaps, but over long periods of time. It was extraordinary, the theories and battles that had begun to rage over the subject. Only recently, the word *scientist* had been coined, by the polymath William Whewell. Many scholars had objected to this blunt new term, as it sounded so sinisterly similar to that awful word *atheist*; why not simply continue to call themselves *natural philosophers*? Was that designation not more godly, more pure? But divisions were being drawn now between the realm of nature and the realm of philosophy. Ministers who doubled as botanists or geologists were becoming increasingly rare, as far too many challenges to biblical truths were stirred up through investigation of the natural world. It used to be that God was revealed in the wonders of nature; now God was being challenged by those same wonders. Scholars were now required to choose one side or the other.

As old certainties quaked and trembled upon ever-eroding ground, Alma Whittaker—alone at White Acre—indulged in her own dangerous thoughts. She pondered Thomas Malthus, with his theories about population growth, disease, cataclysm, famine, and extinction. She pondered John William Draper's brilliant new photographs of the moon. She pondered Louis Agassiz's theory that the world had once seen an Ice Age. She took a long walk one day to the museum at Sansom Street to see the fully reconstructed bones of a giant mastodon, which caused her to think once again about the ancientness of this planet—and, indeed, of all the planets. She reconsidered algae and mosses, and how one might have turned into the other. She focused again on *Dicranum*, wondering anew how this particular moss genus could exist in so many minutely diverse forms; what had shaped it into all these hundreds upon hundreds of silhouettes and configurations?

In late 1850, George Hawkes brought forth Ambrose's orchid book into the world—a lavish and expensive publication called *The Orchids of Guatemala and Mexico*. All who encountered the book declared Ambrose Pike to be the finest botanical artist of the age. All the most prominent gardens wanted to commission Mr. Pike to document their own collections, but Ambrose Pike was gone—lost on the other side of the world, growing vanilla, far out of reach. Alma felt guilt and shame over this, but she did not know what to do about it. She spent time with the book every day. The beauty of Ambrose's work brought her pain, but she could not stay away from it, either. She arranged for George Hawkes to send a copy of the book to Ambrose in Tahiti, but she never heard whether the volume had arrived. She arranged that Ambrose's mother—the formidable Mrs. Constance Pike—should receive all the earnings from the book. This led to some polite exchanges of letters between Alma and her mother-in-law. Mrs. Pike, most unfortunately, believed that her son had run away from his new wife in order to pursue his reckless dreams—and Alma, even more unfortunately, did not disabuse her of that misconception.

Once a month, Alma went to see her old friend Retta at the Griffon Asylum. Retta no longer knew who Alma was—nor, it seemed, did Retta know who she herself was.

Alma did not see her sister Prudence, but heard news every now and again:

poverty and abolition, abolition and poverty, always the same grim tale.

Alma thought about all these things, but did not know what to make of any of it. Why had their lives turned this way, and not another way? She thought again about the four distinct and concurrent varieties of time, as she had once named them: Divine Time, Geological Time, Human Time, Moss Time. It occurred to her that she had spent most of her life wishing she could live within the slow, microscopic realm of Moss Time. That had been an odd enough desire, but then she'd met Ambrose Pike, whose yearnings were even more extreme than hers: he had wanted to live within the eternal emptiness of Divine Time—which is to say, he had wanted to live outside of time altogether. He had wanted her to live there with him.

One thing was certain: Human Time was the saddest, maddest, most devastating variety of time that had ever existed. She tried her best to ignore it.

Nevertheless, the days passed by.

———

In early May of 1851, on a cool, rainy morning, a letter came to White Acre addressed to Henry Whittaker. There was no return address, but the edges of the envelope had been inked with a black border, signifying mourning. Alma read all of Henry's mail, so she opened this envelope, too, as she dutifully caught up with correspondence in her father's study.

> *Dear Mr. Whittaker—*
>
> *I write today both to introduce myself and to share unfortunate news. My name is the Reverend Francis Welles, and I have been the missionary at Matavai Bay, Tahiti, for thirty-seven years. At times in the past, I have conducted business with your good representative, Mr. Yancey, who knows me to be an enthusiastic amateur in the field of botany. I have collected samples for Mr. Yancey and shown him places of botanical interest, &c., &c. Also, I have sold him marine specimens, coral and seashells—a special interest of mine.*
>
> *Of late, Mr. Yancey had enlisted my aid in the attempt to preserve your vanilla plantation here—an endeavor that was much assisted by the arrival, in 1849, of a young employee of yours, by the name of Mr. Ambrose Pike. It is my sad duty to inform you that Mr. Pike has passed away, owing to the sort of*

infection that—all too easily in this torrid climate—can lead the
sufferer to a fast and early death.

You may wish to alert his family that Ambrose Pike was
called to our Lord on November 30, 1850. You may also wish to
inform his loved ones that Mr. Pike was given a proper Christian
burial, and that I have arranged for a small stone to mark his
grave. I much regret his passing. He was a gentleman of the
highest morality and purest character. Such are not easily found
in these parts. I doubt I shall ever meet another like him.

I can offer no consolation, aside from the certainty that he
lives now in a better place, and that he will never suffer the
indignities of old age.

Yours most sincerely, The Reverend F. P. Welles.

The news hit Alma with all the force of an ax head striking granite: it clanged in her ears, shuddered her bones, and struck sparks before her eyes. It knocked a wedge of something out of her—a wedge of something terribly important—and that wedge was sent spinning into the air, never to be found again. If she had not been sitting, she would have fallen down. As it was, she collapsed forward onto her father's desk, pressed her face against the Reverend F. P. Welles's most kind and thoughtful letter, and wept like to pull down every cloud from the vaults of heaven.

———————————

How could she possibly grieve Ambrose more than she had already grieved him? Yet she did. There is grief below grief, she soon learned, just as there are strata below strata in the ocean floor—and even more strata below that, if one keeps digging. Ambrose had been gone from her for so long, and she must have known he would be gone forever, but she had never considered that he might die before she did. The simple magic of arithmetic should have precluded that: he was so much younger than she. How could he die first? He was the picture of youth. He was the compilation of all the innocence that youth had ever known. Yet he was dead, and she was alive. She had sent him away to die.

There is a level of grief so deep that it stops resembling grief at all. The pain becomes so severe that the body can no longer feel it. The grief cauterizes itself, scars over, prevents inflated feelings. Such numbness is a kind of mercy. This is the level of grief that Alma reached, once she lifted her face from her father's desk, once she stopped sobbing.

She moved forward as though manipulated by some blunt, relentless external force. The first thing she did was tell her father the sorry news. She found him lying in bed, eyes closed, gray and weary, looking like a death mask unto himself. Ingloriously, she had to shout the news of Ambrose's death into Henry's ear trumpet before he was made to understand what had transpired.

"Well, there goes that," he said, and shut his eyes again.

She told Hanneke de Groot, who pursed her lips, pressed her hands to her chest, and said only, "God!"—a word that is the same in Dutch as in English.

Alma wrote a letter to George Hawkes explaining what had happened and thanking him for the kindness he had shown Ambrose, and for honoring Mr. Pike's memory through the exquisite orchid book. George responded immediately with a note of perfect tenderness and polite sorrow.

Shortly thereafter, Alma received a letter from her sister Prudence, expressing condolence for the loss of her husband. She did not know who had told Prudence. She did not ask. She wrote Prudence a note of gratitude in reply.

She wrote a letter to the Reverend Francis Welles, which she signed in her father's name, thanking him for conveying the sad news about the death of this most respected employee, and asking if there was anything the Whittakers could do for him in return.

She wrote a note to Ambrose's mother, into which she transcribed every word of the Reverend Francis Welles's letter. She dreaded to send it. Alma knew that Ambrose had been his mother's favorite son, despite what Mrs. Pike referred to as "his ungovernable ways." Why would he not have been her favorite? Ambrose was everyone's favorite. This news would destroy her. What's worse, Alma could not help but feel that she had murdered this woman's favorite son—the best one, the jewel, the angel of Framingham. Mailing the dreadful letter, Alma could only hope that Mrs. Pike's Christian faith would shield her at least somewhat from this blow.

As for Alma, she did not have the comfort of that sort of faith. She believed in the Creator, but she had never turned to Him in moments of despair—and she would not do so now, either. Hers was not that sort of belief. Alma accepted and admired the Lord as the designer and prime mover of the universe, but to her mind He was a daunting, distant, and even pitiless figure. Any being who could create a world of such acute suffering was not the being to approach for solace from the tribulations of that world. For such solace, one could only turn to the likes of Hanneke de Groot.

After Alma's sad duties had been carried out—after all those letters about Ambrose's death were written and posted—there was naught else for her to do but settle into her widowhood, her shame, and her sadness. More from habit than desire, she returned to her studies of mosses. Without that task, she felt she might have died herself. Her father grew sicker. Her responsibilities grew larger. The world became smaller.

And that is what the rest of Alma's life might have looked like, had it not been for the arrival—only five months later—of Dick Yancey, who came striding up the steps of White Acre on a fine October morning, carrying in his hand the small, worn, leather valise that had once belonged to Ambrose Pike, and asking for a private word with Alma Whittaker.

Chapter Nineteen

Alma led Dick Yancey into her father's study and closed the door behind them. She had never before been in a room alone with him. He had been a presence in her life since earliest memory, but he had always made her feel chilled and uneasy. His towering height, his corpse-white skin, his gleaming bald head, his icy gaze, the hatchet of his profile—all of it combined to create a figure of real menace. Even now, after nearly fifty years of acquaintance, Alma could not determine how old he was. He was eternal. This only added to his fearsomeness. The entire world was afraid of Dick Yancey, which was exactly how Henry Whittaker wanted it. Alma had never understood Yancey's loyalty to Henry, or how Henry managed to control him, but one thing was clear: the Whittaker Company could not function without this terrifying man.

"Mr. Yancey," Alma said, and gestured toward a chair. "I beg of you, make yourself at ease."

He did not sit. He stood in the middle of the room and held Ambrose's valise loosely in one hand. Alma tried not to stare at it—the only possession of her late husband. She did not sit, either. Evidently, they would not be making themselves at ease.

"Is there something you wished to speak with me about, Mr. Yancey? Or would you prefer to see my father? He has been unwell lately, as I know you are aware, but today is one of his better days and his head is clear. He can receive you in his bedchamber, if that would suit you."

Still, Dick Yancey did not speak. This was a famous tactic of his: silence as a weapon. When Dick Yancey did not speak, those around him, nervous, filled the air with words. People said more than they meant to say. Dick Yancey would watch from behind his silent fortification as secrets flew. Then he would bring those secrets home to White Acre. This was a function of his power.

Alma resolved not to fall into his trap and speak without thinking. Thus, they stood in silence together for what must have been another two minutes. Then Alma couldn't bear it. She spoke again: "I see you are carrying my late husband's valise. I assume you have been to Tahiti, and have retrieved it there? Have you come to return it to me?"

He neither moved nor said a word.

Alma went on. "If you are wondering whether I would like to have that valise back, Mr. Yancey, the answer is yes—I would like it very much. My late husband was a man of few belongings, and it would mean a good deal to me to keep as a remembrance the one item that I know he himself valued enormously."

Still, he did not speak. Was he going to make her beg for it? Was she meant to pay him? Did he want something in exchange? Or—the thought crossed her mind in an errant, illogical flash—was he hesitating for some reason? Could he be feeling uncertain? There was no telling with Dick Yancey. He could never be read. Alma began to feel both impatient and alarmed.

"I really must insist, Mr. Yancey," she said, "that you explain yourself."

Dick Yancey was not a man who ever explained himself. Alma knew this as well as anybody alive. He did not squander words on such petty uses as explanation. He did not squander words at all. From earliest childhood, in fact, Alma had rarely heard him speak more than three words in a row. As for this day, however, Dick Yancey was able to make his point clear in a mere two words, which he now growled from the corner of his mouth as he strode past Alma and out the door, thrusting the valise into her arms as he brushed by her.

"Burn it," he said.

Alma sat alone with the valise in her father's study for an hour, staring at the object as though trying to determine—through its worn and salt-stained leather exterior—what lurked within. Why on earth would Yancey have said such a thing? Why would he take the trouble to bring her this valise from the other side of the planet, only to instruct her now to burn it? Why had he not burned it himself, if it needed burning? And did he mean that she should burn it *after* opening it and reviewing its contents, or *before*? Why had he hesitated so long before handing it over?

Asking him any of these questions, of course, was quite outside the realm of possibility: he was long gone. Dick Yancey moved with improbable speed; he could be halfway to Argentina by now, for all she knew. Even if he had remained at White Acre, though, he would not have answered any further queries. She knew that. That sort of conversation would never be part of Dick Yancey's service. All she knew was that Ambrose's precious valise was in her possession now—and so was a dilemma.

She decided to take the thing out to her own study, in the carriage house, that she might contemplate it in privacy. She set it down upon the divan in the corner—where Retta used to chat with her so many years ago, where Ambrose used to sprawl out comfortably with his long legs dangling, and where Alma had slept in the dark months after Ambrose left. She studied the valise. It was about two feet long, a foot and a half wide, and six inches deep—a simple rectangle of cheap, honey-colored cowhide. It was scuffed and stained and humble. The handle had been repaired with wire and leather lacing several times. The hinges were corroded from sea air and age. One could barely make out, above the handle, the faintly embossed initials "A.P." Two leather belts circled the valise, buckling it closed, like cinch straps around a horse's belly.

There was no lock, which was entirely characteristic of Ambrose. His was such a trusting nature—or rather, it had been. Perhaps, had there been a lock on the valise, she would not have opened it. Perhaps all it would have taken was one faint sign of secretiveness, and she would have backed away. Or perhaps not. Alma was the sort of person who was born to investigate things regardless of the consequences, even if it meant breaking a lock.

She opened the valise with no difficulty. Folded inside was a brown corduroy jacket, instantly recognizable, which made her throat clench with feeling. She lifted it out and pressed it to her face, hoping to smell something of Ambrose in its fibers, but all she could detect was a trace of mildew. Underneath the jacket she found a thick stack of paper: sketches and drawings on wide, toothy paper the color of eggshell. The topmost drawing was a depiction of a tropical *Pandanus* tree, immediately recognizable by its helices of leaves and thick roots. Here was Ambrose's virtuosic botanical hand at work, in typically perfect detail. It was a mere pencil sketch, but it was quite magnificent. Alma studied it, then set it aside. Underneath this drawing was another—a detail of a vanilla bloom, drawn in ink and delicately tinted, which seemed almost to flutter across the page.

Alma felt hope rising within her. The valise, then, contained Ambrose's botanical impressions from the South Pacific. This was comforting on multiple counts. For one thing, it meant that Ambrose had taken solace in his craftsmanship while he was in Tahiti, and had not merely withered away in idle despair. For another, by taking possession of these pictures, Alma would have *more* of Ambrose now—something exquisite and tangible to remember him by. Not least, these drawings would be a window into his final years: she would be able to see what he had seen, as though looking straight through his eyes.

The third drawing was a coconut palm, simply and quickly sketched, unfinished. The fourth drawing, however, stopped her short. It was a face. This was a surprise, for Ambrose—to Alma's knowledge—had never shown any interest in depicting the human form. Ambrose was no portraitist, and had never claimed to be. Yet here was a portrait, drawn in pen and ink in Ambrose's exacting hand. It was the head of a young man in right profile. His features pointed to Polynesian ancestry. Broad cheekbones, flat nose, wide lips. Attractive and strong. Hair cut short, like a European's.

Alma turned to the next sketch: another portrait of the same youth, in left profile. The next picture depicted a man's arm. It was not Ambrose's arm. The shoulder was wider than his, the forearm sturdier. Next came an intimate detail of a human eye. It was not Ambrose's eye (Alma would have known Ambrose's eye anywhere). It was someone else's eye, distinctive for its feathery lashes.

Then came a full-length study of a young man, nude, from behind, seemingly walking away from the artist. His back was broad and muscled. Every vertebral knob had been meticulously rendered. Yet another nude showed the young man resting against a coconut palm. His face was already familiar to Alma—the same proud brow, the same wide lips, the same almond-shaped eyes. Here, he looked somewhat younger than in the other drawings—not much more than a boy. Perhaps seventeen or eighteen years old.

There were no more botanical studies. All of the remaining drawings, sketches, and watercolors in the valise were nudes. There must have been more than a hundred of them—all of the same young native with the short European hair. In some, he appeared to be sleeping. In others, he was running, or carrying a spear, or lifting a stone, or hauling a fishing net—not unlike the athletes or demi-gods on ancient Greek pottery. In none of the images did he wear a scrap of clothing—not so much as a shoe. In most of the studies, his penis was flaccid and relaxed. In others it was decidedly not. In these, the youth's face turned toward the portraitist with frank, and perhaps even amused, candor.

"My God," Alma heard herself say aloud. Then she realized she had been saying this all along, with every new and shocking picture.

My God, my God, my God.

Alma Whittaker was a woman of quick calculation, and far from a sensual innocent. The sole possible conclusion to be reached regarding the valise's contents was this: Ambrose Pike—paragon of purity, the angel of Framingham—was a sodomite.

Her mind flew back to his first night at White Acre. Over dinner, he had dazzled them, Henry and Alma both, with his ideas about the hand-pollination of vanilla orchids in Tahiti. What was it he had said? It would be so easy, he'd promised: *All you need is little boys with little fingers and little sticks.* It had sounded so playful. Now, in echoing retrospect, it sounded perverse. But it also answered for much. Ambrose had been unable to consummate their marriage not because Alma was old, not because Alma was ugly, and not because he wanted to emulate the angels—but because he wanted little boys with little fingers and little sticks. Or big boys, by the looks of these drawings.

Dear God, what he had put her through! What lies he had told! What manipulations! What self-disgust he had made her feel for her own entirely natural longings. The way he had looked at her from the bathtub that afternoon when she had taken his fingers into her mouth—as though she were some sort of succubus, come to devour his flesh. She remembered a line from Montaigne, something she had read years ago, which had always

303

stayed with her, and which now felt horribly pertinent: "These are two things that I have always observed to be in singular accord: supercelestial thoughts and subterranean conduct."

She had been made a fool by Ambrose and his supercelestial thoughts, by his grand dreams, his false innocence, his pretense at godliness, his noble talk of communion with the divine—and look where he had ended up! In a louche paradise, with a willing catamite, and a fine upstanding cock!

"You duplicitous son of a whore," she said aloud.

Another woman might have taken Dick Yancey's counsel to burn the valise and everything inside it. Alma, however, was far too much the scientist to burn evidence of any kind. She put the valise under the divan in her study. Nobody would find it there. Nobody ever came into that room, in any case. Loath to have her work disturbed, she had never permitted anyone but herself to even clean her study. Nobody cared what an old spinster like Alma did inside her room full of silly microscopes and tedious books and vials of dried moss. She was a fool. Her life was a comedy—a terrible, sad comedy.

She went to dinner and paid no attention to her food.

Who else had known?

She had heard the worst gossip about Ambrose in the months after their marriage—or thought she had—but she didn't recall anyone ever having accused him of being a Miss Molly. Had he buggered the stable boys, then? Or the young gardeners? Was that what he had been up to? But when would he have done it? Someone would have said something. They were always together, Alma and Ambrose, and secrets that salacious do not stay secrets long. Rumors are a precious currency that burn holes in the pocket and are always, eventually, spent. Yet no one had spoken a word.

Had Hanneke known? Alma wondered, looking at the old housekeeper. Was that why she had been opposed to Ambrose? *We do not know him*, she had said, so many times . . .

What about Daniel Tupper in Boston—Ambrose's dearest friend? Had he been more than a friend? The telegram he had sent on the day of their wedding, WELL DONE PIKE—had it been some sort of cheeky code? But Daniel Tupper was a married man with a houseful of children, Alma remembered. Or so Ambrose had said. Not that it mattered. People could be many things, apparently, and all at once.

What about his mother? Had Mrs. Constance Pike known? Was this what she meant, when she had written, "Perhaps a decent marriage shall cure him of playing the moral truant"? Why had Alma not read that letter more carefully? Why had she not investigated?

How could she not have seen this?

After dinner, she paced her rooms. She felt bisected and dislocated. She felt awash in curiosity, polished bright by anger. Unable to stop herself, she walked back over to the carriage house. She went into the printing studio she had so carefully (and expensively) outfitted for Ambrose more than three years earlier. All the machinery rested beneath sheets now, and the furniture, too. She found Ambrose's notebook once more in the top drawer of his desk. She opened to a random page, and found a sample of the familiar, mystical drivel:

Nothing exists but the MIND, and it is propelled by FORCE . . . To not darken the day, to not glitter in shift . . . Away with the outwardly, away with the outwardly!

She closed the book and made a rude noise. She could not bear another word of it. Why could the man never be *clear*?

She went back to her study and pulled the valise from under the divan. This time she looked more methodically at the contents. It was not a pleasant task, but she felt she must do it. She dug around the edges of the valise, seeking a hidden compartment, or anything she may have missed on her first examination. She combed through the pockets of Ambrose's timeworn jacket, but found only a pencil stub.

Then she returned to the pictures again—the three adept drawings of plants, and the dozens of obscene drawings of the same beautiful young man. She wondered if, upon closer examination, she could arrive at some alternate conclusion, but no; the portraits were too blunt, too sensual, too intimate. There was no other interpretation for this. Alma turned over one of the nudes, and noticed something written on the back, in Ambrose's lovely, graceful script. It was tucked into a corner, like a faint and modest signature. But it was not a signature. It was two words only, in lowercase letters: *tomorrow morning.*

Alma turned over another nude and saw, in the same lower right-hand corner, the same two words: *tomorrow morning*. One by one, she turned over every drawing. Each one said the same thing, in the same elegant, familiar handwriting: *tomorrow morning, tomorrow morning, tomorrow morning*...

What was this supposed to mean? Was everything a deuced code?

She took up a piece of paper and picked apart the letters of "tomorrow morning," rearranging them into other words and phrases:

NO ROOM, TRIM WRONG

RING MOON, MR. ROOT

O GRIM—NO WORT, MORN!

None of it made sense. Nor did translating the words into French, Dutch, Latin, Greek, or German bring edification. Nor did reading them backward, nor assigning them numbers corresponding to their places in the alphabet. Perhaps, then, it wasn't a code. Perhaps it was a deferral. Perhaps something was always going to happen with this boy *tomorrow morning*, or at least according to Ambrose. Well, that was very much like Ambrose, in any case: mysterious and off-putting. Perhaps he was simply delaying consummation with his handsome native muse: "I shall not bugger you now, young man, but I shall get around to it first thing *tomorrow morning*!" Perhaps this was how he had kept himself pure, in the face of temptation. Perhaps he had never touched the boy. Then why draw him naked in the first place?

Another thought occurred to Alma: Had these drawings been a commission? Had somebody—some other sodomite, perhaps, and a rich one—paid Ambrose to make pictures of this boy? But why would Ambrose have needed money, when Alma had seen to it that he was so well provided for? And why would he have accepted such a commission, when he was a person of such delicate sensibilities—or purported to be? If his morality was merely a pretense, then clearly he had kept up the performance even after leaving White Acre. His reputation in Tahiti had not been that of a degenerate, or else the Reverend Francis Welles would not have taken the trouble to eulogize Ambrose Pike as "a gentleman of highest morality and purest character."

Why, then? Why *this* boy? Why a nude and aroused boy? Why such a handsome young companion with such a distinctive face? Why take so much effort to make so *many* pictures? Why not draw flowers instead? Ambrose had loved flowers, and Tahiti was overrun with flowers! Who was this muse? And why had Ambrose gone to his death constantly planning to do something with this boy—and to do it, forever and endlessly, *tomorrow morning*?

Chapter Twenty

Henry Whittaker was dying. He was a ninety-one-year-old man, so this ought not to have been shocking, but Henry was both shocked and enraged to find himself in such a reduced state. He had not walked in months and could scarcely draw a full breath anymore, but still he could not believe his fate. Trapped in his bed, weak and diminished, his eyes trawled the room wildly, as though seeking a means of escape. He looked as though he were trying to find someone to bully, bribe, or cajole into keeping him alive. He could scarcely believe there was no escape from this. He was appalled.

The more appalled he became, the more Henry turned tyrant to his poor nurses. He wanted his legs rubbed constantly, and—fearing suffocation from his inflamed lungs—demanded that his bedstead be tilted up at a steep angle. He refused all pillows for fear they would drown him in his sleep. He grew more belligerent by the day, even as he declined. "What a beggarly mess you have made of this bed!" he would shout after some pale, frightened girl as she ran from the room. Alma marveled at how he could possibly find the strength to bark like a chained dog, even as he was vanishing away upon the sheets. He was difficult, but there was something admirable in his fight, too, something kingly in his refusal to quietly die.

He weighed nothing. His body had become a loose envelope filled with long, sharp bones, and covered all over with sores. He could take nothing but beef tea, and not much of it. But for all that, Henry's voice was the last part of his body to fail him. This was a pity, in a way. Henry's voice caused the good maids and nurses around him to suffer, for—like a brave English sailor going down with his ship—he took to singing bawdy songs, as though to keep up his courage in the face of doom. Death was trying to pull him down with both hands, but he was singing it away.

"*With a red flag flying, let it pass! Shove it up the maiden's ass!*"

"That will be all, Kate, thank you," Alma would say to the unfortunate young nurse who happened to be on duty, escorting the poor girl to the door, even as Henry sang out, "*Good old Kate in Liverpool! Once she ran a whoring school!*"

Henry had never cared much for civilities, but now he cared for them not a whit. He said whatever he wanted to say—and perhaps, it occurred to Alma, even more than he wanted to say. He was staggeringly indiscreet. He shouted about money, about deals gone sour. He accused and probed, attacked and parried. He even picked fights with the dead. He debated with Sir Joseph Banks, trying again to convince him to grow cinchona in the Himalayas. He ranted to his deceased wife's long-gone father: "I will show you, you skunk-faced old pig-dog of a Dutchman, what a rich man I intend to become!" He accused his own long-dead father of being a fawning boot-lick. He demanded that Beatrix be summoned to take care of him and to bring him cider. Where was his wife? For what purpose did a man have a wife, if not to tend him upon his sickbed?

Then one day he looked Alma straight in the eye and said, "And you think I don't know what that husband of yours was!"

Alma hesitated a moment too long to send the nurse from the room. She ought to have done it right away, but she waited, instead, uncertain of what her father was trying to say.

"You think I have not met such men as that in my travels? You think I was not once such a man as that myself? You think they took me on the *Resolution* for my able navigating? I was a hairless little boy, Plum—a hairless little shaver from the land, with a fine clean arsehole. There's no shame in saying it!"

He was addressing her as "Plum." He had not called her that name in years—in decades. He had not even recognized her at times during the past months. But now, with the use of the beloved old pet name, it was apparent that he knew precisely who she was—which meant that he also knew precisely what he was saying.

"You may leave now, Betsy," Alma directed the nurse, but the nurse did not seem in a hurry to leave.

"Ask yourself what they did to me on that ship, Plum! The youngest shaver there, I was! Oh, by God, but they had their fun with me!"

"Thank you, Betsy," Alma said, moving now to escort the nurse to the door herself. "You may close the door behind you. Thank you. You've been most helpful, then. Thank you. Off you go."

Henry was now singing an awful verse Alma had never heard before: "*They whacked me up and whacked me down, The mate he buggered me round and round!*"

"Father," Alma said, "you must stop." She drew near and placed her hands on his chest. "You *must* stop."

He stopped singing and looked at her with fiery eyes. He grabbed her wrists with his bony hands.

"Ask yourself why he married you, Plum," Henry said, in a voice as clear and strong as youth itself. "Not for the money, I'll wager! Not for your clean little arsehole, either. For something else, it must be. It don't make sense to you, do it? Not to me neither, it don't make sense."

Alma pulled her arms from her father's grip. His breath smelled like rot. Most of him was already dead.

"Cease your talking, Father, and take some beef tea," she said, tilting the cup to his mouth, and avoiding his gaze. She had a feeling the nurse was listening from behind the door.

He sang, "*Oh, we're running away around the Cape! Some for debt and some for rape!*"

She tried to pour the broth into his mouth—to stop him singing, as much as anything—but he spat it out and knocked her hand away. The broth rained across the sheets and the cup spun across the floor. He still had strength in him, the old fighter. He grabbed for her wrists again and caught one of them.

"Don't be simple, Plum," he said. "Don't believe a single thing any cunt or bastard ever tells you in this world. *You go find out!*"

Over the next week, as Henry slid closer toward death, he would say and sing many more things—most of them filthy and all of them unfortunate—but that one phrase of his struck Alma as so cogent and deliberate that she would always think of it as having been her father's final words: *You go find out.*

Henry Whittaker died on October 19, 1851. It was like a storm blowing out to sea. He thrashed till the end, fought to the last breath he drew. The calm at the end of it, once he finally left, was staggering. Nobody could believe they had survived him. Hanneke, wiping away a tear of exhaustion as much as sadness, said, "Oh, to those who already dwell in heaven—good luck for what is coming!"

Alma helped to wash her father's body. She asked to be alone with his corpse. She did not wish to pray. She did not wish to weep. There was something she needed to find. Lifting the sheet off her father's naked corpse, she explored the skin around his abdomen, searching with fingers and eyes for something like a scar, like a lump, something odd, small, and out of place. She was looking for the emerald that Henry had sworn to her, decades ago when she was a child, that he had sewn beneath his own flesh. She did not flinch to look for it. She was a naturalist. If it was there, she would find it.

You must always have one final bribe, Plum.

It wasn't there.

She was astonished. She'd always believed everything her father told her. But then, she thought, perhaps he had offered the emerald up to Death, right near the end. When the songs hadn't worked and the courage hadn't worked and all his cunning had failed to negotiate a way out of this final frightful contract, maybe he had said, "Take my best emerald, too!" And maybe Death had taken it, Alma thought—but then took Henry, as well.

Not even her father could buy his way out of that covenant.

Henry Whittaker was gone, and his last trick gone with him.

She inherited everything. The will—produced only a day after the funeral, by Henry's old solicitor—was the simplest imaginable document, not more than a few sentences long. To his "one natural-born daughter," the will instructed, Henry Whittaker left his entire fortune. All his land, all his business concerns, all his wealth, all his holdings—all of it was to be Alma's exclusively. There were no provisions made for anyone else. There was no mention of his adopted daughter, Prudence Whittaker Dixon, nor his loyal staff. Hanneke would receive nothing; Dick Yancey would receive nothing.

Alma Whittaker was now one of the richest women in the New World. She controlled the largest botanical importing concern in America, the affairs of which she had singlehandedly managed over the last five years, and she was half owner of the prosperous Garrick & Whittaker Pharmaceutical Company. She was the sole inhabitant of one of the grandest private homes in the Commonwealth of Pennsylvania, she held the rights to several lucrative patents, and she owned thousands of acres of productive land. Under her direct command were scores of servants and employees, while numberless people around the world worked for her on a contractual basis. Her greenhouses and glasshouses rivaled any to be found in the finest European botanical gardens.

It did not feel like a blessing.

Alma was weary and saddened by the death of her father, of course, but she also felt burdened, rather than honored, by his mammoth bequest. What interest did she have in a vast botanical importing concern, or a busy pharmaceutical manufacturing operation? What need did she have to own half a dozen mills and mines across Pennsylvania? What use did she have for a thirty-four-room mansion filled with rare treasures and a challenging staff? How many greenhouses did one lady botanist need in order to study mosses? (That answer, at least, was simple: none.) Yet it was all hers.

After the solicitor left, Alma, feeling stunned and self-pitying, went to find Hanneke de Groot. She longed for the comfort of the most familiar person left in the world to her. She found the old housekeeper standing upright inside the large, cold fireplace in the kitchen, poking a broom handle up into the chimney, trying to unloose a swallow's nest, while unleashing upon herself a coating of soot and grime.

"Surely someone else can do that for you, Hanneke," Alma said in Dutch, by means of greeting. "Let me find a girl."

Hanneke backed out of the fireplace, huffing and filthy. "Do you think I haven't asked them to?" she demanded. "But do you think there is another Christian soul in this household who would stick their neck up a fireplace chimney except me?"

Alma brought Hanneke a damp cloth to wipe clean her face, and the two women sat down at the table.

"The solicitor has left already?" Hanneke asked.

"Gone just these five minutes ago," Alma said.

"That was swift."

"It was a simple business."

Hanneke frowned. "So he left it all to you, then, did he?"

"Indeed," said Alma.

"Nothing to Prudence?"

"Nothing," said Alma, noticing that Hanneke had not asked after her own interests.

"Curse him, then," Hanneke said, after a moment's silence.

Alma winced. "Be kind, Hanneke. My father is not a day in his grave."

"Curse him, I say," the housekeeper repeated. "Curse him as a stubborn sinner, to disregard his other daughter."

"She would not have accepted anything from him anyway, Hanneke."

"You do not know that to be true, Alma! She is part of this family, or should be. Your much-lamented mother wanted her to be part of this family. I expect you will look after Prudence yourself, then?"

This took Alma aback. "In what manner? My sister scarcely wishes to see me, and she turns away all gifts. I cannot offer her so much as a teacake without her claiming it to be more than she needs. You cannot honestly believe she would allow me to share our father's wealth with her?"

"She is a proud girl, that one," Hanneke said, with more admiration than concern.

Alma wished to change the subject. "What will White Acre be like now, Hanneke, without my father? I do not look forward to running the estate without his presence. It feels as though a great, living heart has been ripped out of this home."

"I will not permit you to disregard your sister," Hanneke said, as though Alma had not spoken at all. "It is one thing for Henry to be sinful, stupid, and selfish in his grave, but another thing altogether for you to behave the same way in life."

Alma bristled. "I come to you today for warmth and counsel, Hanneke, yet you insult me." She stood up, as if to leave the kitchen.

"Oh, sit down, child. I insult nobody. I only mean to tell you that you owe your sister a significant debt, and you should see to it that debt is paid."

"I owe my sister no debt."

Hanneke threw up her arms, still blackened with soot. "Do you see *nothing*, Alma?"

"If you refer, Hanneke, to the lack of warmth between Prudence and myself, I urge you not to lay the blame for it exclusively upon my shoulders. The fault has been every bit as much hers as mine. We have never been at ease in each other's society, the two of us, and she has warded me off, all these many years."

"I do not speak of sisterly warmth. Many sisters have no warmth with each other. I speak of sacrifice. I know everything that occurs in this house, child. Do you imagine you are the only one who ever came to me in tears? Do you imagine you are the only one who ever knocked on Hanneke's door when sorrow overwhelmed? I know all the secrets."

Bewildered, Alma tried to imagine her aloof sister Prudence ever falling into the housekeeper's arms in tears. No, it could not be pictured. Prudence had never had Alma's closeness with Hanneke. Prudence had not known Hanneke from infancy, and Prudence did not even speak Dutch. How could intimacy exist at all?

Still, Alma had to ask it: "What secrets?"

"Why do you not ask Prudence yourself?" Hanneke replied.

Now the housekeeper was being intentionally coy, Alma felt, and she could not endure it. "I cannot command you to tell me anything, Hanneke," Alma said, switching over to English. She was too irritated now to speak in the old, familiar Dutch. "Your secrets belong to you, if you choose to keep them. But I do command you to cease toying with me. If you have information about this family that you believe I should know, then I wish you would reveal it. But if your sport is merely to sit here and mock my ignorance—my ignorance of *what*, I cannot possibly know—then I regret coming to speak to you today at all. I face important decisions about everyone in this household, and I deeply grieve my father's passing. I carry much responsibility now. I do not have the time or the fortitude to play guessing games with you."

Hanneke looked at Alma carefully, squinting a bit. At the end of Alma's speech she nodded, as though she approved the tone and tenor of Alma's words.

"Very well, then," Hanneke said. "Did you ever ask yourself why Prudence married Arthur Dixon?"

"Stop speaking in puzzles, Hanneke," Alma snapped. "I warn you, I cannot bear it today."

"I am not speaking in puzzles, child. I am trying to tell you something. Ask yourself—did you ever wonder at that marriage?"

"Of course I did. Who would marry Arthur Dixon?"

"Who, indeed? Do you think Prudence ever loved her tutor? You saw them together for years, when he lived here and was teaching both of you. Did you ever observe any sign of love from her to him?"

Alma thought back. "No," she admitted.

"Because she did not love him. She loved another, and always had. Alma, your sister loved George Hawkes."

"George Hawkes?" Alma could only repeat the name. She saw the botanical publisher suddenly in her mind—not as he looked today (a worn-out man of sixty years, with a stooped back and an insane wife) but as he had looked thirty years earlier when she herself had loved him (a large and comforting presence, with a shock of brown hair and a smile of shy kindness). "George *Hawkes*?" she asked again, most foolishly.

"Your sister Prudence loved George Hawkes," Hanneke repeated. "And I tell you something more: George Hawkes loved her in return. I'll wager she loves him still, and I'll wager he still loves her, to this very day."

This made no sense to Alma. It was as if she were being told that her mother and father were not her real parents, or that her name was not Alma Whittaker, or that she did not live in Philadelphia—as though some great and simple truth were being shaken apart.

"Why would Prudence have loved George Hawkes?" Alma asked, too baffled to ask a more intelligent question.

"Because he was *kind* to her. Do you think, Alma, that it is a gift to be as beautiful as your sister? Do you remember what she looked like at sixteen years old? Do you remember how men stared at her? Old men, young men, married men, workers—all of them. There was not a man who set foot on this property who did not look at your sister as if he wished to purchase her for a night's entertainment. It had been like that for her since she was a child. Same with her mother, but her mother was weaker, and she did sell herself away. But Prudence was a modest girl, and a good girl. Why do you think your sister never spoke at the table? Do you think it was because she was too foolish to have an opinion on anything? Why do you think she always arranged her face without any expression at all? Do you think it was because she never felt anything? All Prudence ever wished for, Alma, was not to be seen. You cannot know what it feels like, to be stared at by men your whole life as though you are standing on an auction block."

This Alma could not deny. She most certainly did *not* know what that felt like.

Hanneke went on, "George Hawkes was the only man who ever looked at your sister kindly—not as an item, but as a soul. You well know Mr. Hawkes, Alma. Can you not see how a man like that could make a young woman feel safe?"

By all means she could see that. George Hawkes had always made Alma herself feel safe. Safe and recognized.

"Did you ever wonder why Mr. Hawkes was always here at White Acre, Alma? Do you think he came by so often in order to see your father?" Hanneke, mercifully, did not add, "Do you think he came by so often in order to see *you*?" but the question, unspoken, hung in the air. "He loved your sister, Alma. He was courting her, in his quiet way. What's more, she loved him."

"As you keep saying," Alma interjected. "This is difficult for me to hear, Hanneke. You see, I once loved George Hawkes myself."

"Do you think I don't know that?" Hanneke exclaimed. "Of course you loved him, child, for he was polite to you! You were innocent enough to confess your love to your sister. Do you think a young woman as principled as Prudence would have married George Hawkes, knowing that you had feelings for him? Do you think she would have done that to you?"

"Did they wish to *marry*?" Alma asked, incredulous.

"Naturally, they wished to marry! They were young and in love! But she would not do that to you, Alma. George asked for her hand, shortly before your mother died. She turned him away. He asked again. She turned him away again. He asked several more times. She would not reveal her reasons for refusing him, in order to protect *you*. When he kept asking, she went and threw herself down the throat of Arthur Dixon, because he was the nearest and easiest man to marry. She knew Dixon well enough to know that he would not cause her harm, in any case. He would never beat her or bring debasement upon her. She even had some regard for him. He had introduced her to those abolitionist ideas of hers, back when he was your tutor, and those ideas affected her conscience greatly—as they still do. So she respected Mr. Dixon, but she did not love him, and she does not love him today. She simply needed to marry somebody—*anybody*—in order to remove herself from George's prospects, with the hope, I must tell you, that George would then marry *you*. She knew that George was fond of you as a friend and she hoped he might learn to love you as a wife, and bring you happiness. That is what your sister Prudence did for you, child. And you stand before me claiming that you owe her no debt."

For a long while, Alma could not speak.

Then, stupidly, she said, "But George Hawkes married Retta."

"So it didn't work, then—did it, Alma?" Hanneke asked, in a firm voice. "Do you see that? Your sister gave up the man she loved for nothing. He did not go and marry you, after all. He went and did the same thing Prudence had done: he threw himself down the throat of the next person who passed by, just to be wedded to someone."

He never even considered me, Alma realized. Shamefully, this was her first thought, before she even began to take in the scope of her sister's sacrifice.

He never even considered me.

But George had never seen Alma as anything but a colleague in botany and a good little microscopist. Now it all made sense. Why would he have even noticed Alma? Why would he have even recognized Alma as a woman at all, when exquisite Prudence was so near? George had never known for a moment that Alma loved him, but Prudence knew it. Prudence always knew it. Prudence must also have known, Alma realized in mounting sorrow, that there were not many men in this world who could be an appropriate husband for Alma, and that George was probably the best hope. Prudence, on the other hand, could have had anyone. That must have been how she saw it.

So Prudence had given George up for Alma—or had tried to, in any case. But it was all for nothing. Her sister had forfeited love, only to go live her life in poverty and abnegation with a parsimonious scholar who was incapable of warmth or affection. She had forfeited love, only for brilliant George Hawkes to go live his life with a crazed little pretty wife who had never even read a book and who now resided in an asylum. She had forfeited love, only for Alma to go live her life in absolute loneliness—leaving Alma vulnerable in middle age to enthrallment by a man like Ambrose Pike, who was repelled by her desire, and who wished only to be an angel (or, it now appeared, who wished only to love naked Tahitian boys). What a wasted gesture of kindness, then, had been Prudence's youthful sacrifice! What a long chain of sorrows it had caused for everyone. What a sad mess this was, and what a deep series of mistakes.

Poor Prudence, Alma thought—at last. After a long moment, she added in her mind: Poor George! Then: Poor Retta! And then, for that matter: Poor Arthur Dixon!

Poor all of them.

"If what you say is true, Hanneke," Alma said, "then you tell a melancholy tale."

"What I say *is* true."

"Why have you never told me this before?"

"To what end?" Hanneke shrugged.

"But why would Prudence have done such a thing for me?" Alma asked. "Prudence was never even fond of me."

"It matters little what she thought of you. She is a good person, and she lives her life according to good principles."

"Did she pity me, Hanneke? Was that it?"

"If anything, she admired you. She always tried to emulate you."

"Nonsense! She never did."

"You are the one filled with nonsense, Alma! She always admired you, child. Think of what you must have looked like to her, when first she came here! Think of all you knew, of your capabilities. She always tried to win your admiration. You never offered it, though. Did you ever once praise her? Did you ever once see how hard she worked, to catch up with you in her studies? Did you ever admire her talents, or did you scorn them as less worthy than your own? How is it that you have so stubbornly remained blind to her admirable qualities?"

"I have never understood her admirable qualities."

"No, Alma—you have never believed in them. Concede it. You think her goodness is a posture. You believe her to be a charlatan."

"It is only that she wears such a *mask* . . ." Alma murmured, struggling to find ground upon which to defend herself.

"Indeed she does, for she prefers neither to be seen nor known. But I know her, and I tell you that behind that mask is the best, the most generous, the most admirable of women. How do you not see this? Do you not witness how commendable she is to this very day—how sincere in her good works? What more must she do, Alma, to earn your regard? Yet still you have never praised her, and now you mean to utterly spurn your sister, without a trace of uneasiness, as you inherit a pirate's cave of riches from your dead fool of a father—a man who was just as blind as you have always been to the sufferings and sacrifice of others."

"Be careful, Hanneke," Alma warned, fighting back a tidal surge of grief. "You have given me a great shock, and now you attack me, while I am still in a state of amazement. So I must beg of you—please be careful with me today, Hanneke."

"But everyone has been careful with you already, Alma," the old housekeeper replied, relenting not an inch. "Perhaps they have been careful with you for too long."

Alma, shaken, fled to her study in the carriage house. She sat on the shabby divan in the corner, unable to bear her own weight anymore on her own two feet. Her breath came shallow and fast. She felt like a foreigner to herself. The compass within her—the one that had always oriented her to the simplest truths of her world—spun wildly, searching for a secure point upon which to land, but finding nothing.

Her mother was dead. Her father was dead. Her husband—whatever he had been or not been—was dead. Her sister Prudence had destroyed her own life on Alma's account, with benefit to absolutely nobody. George Hawkes was an utter tragedy. Retta Snow was a ruined and lacerated little disaster. And now it looked as if Hanneke de Groot—the last living person Alma loved and admired—had no respect for her whatsoever. Nor should she.

Sitting in her study, Alma forced herself at last to take an honest accounting of her own life. She was a fifty-one-year-old woman, healthy in mind and body, as strong as a mule, as educated as a Jesuit, as rich as any peer of the realm. She was not beautiful, admittedly, but she still had most of her teeth and she was plagued by not a single physical ailment. What would she ever have to complain about? She had been suffused in luxury since birth. She was without a husband, true, but she also had no child or—now—parent demanding her care. She was competent, intelligent, diligent, and (she had always believed, although now she was not so certain) brave. Her imagination had been exposed to the most daring ideas of science and invention the century had to offer, and she had met, in her very own dining room, some of the finest minds of her day. She owned a library that would have made a Medici weep with longing, and she had read through that library several times over.

With all that learning and all that privilege, what had Alma created of her life? She was the authoress of two obscure books on bryology—books that the world had not by any means cried out for—and she was now at work on a third. She had never given a moment of herself over to the betterment of anyone, with the exception of her selfish father. She was a virgin and a widow and an orphan and an heiress and an old lady and an absolute fool.

She thought she knew much, but she knew nothing.

She knew nothing about her sister.

She knew nothing about sacrifice.

She knew nothing about the man she had married.

She knew nothing about the invisible forces that had dictated her life.

She had always thought herself to be a woman of dignity and worldly knowledge, but really she was a petulant and aging princess—more mutton than lamb, by this point—who had never risked anything of worth, and who had never traveled farther away from Philadelphia than a hospital for the insane in Trenton, New Jersey.

It should have been unbearable to face this sorry inventory, yet for some reason it was not. In strange point of fact, it was a relief. Alma's breath slowed. Her compass spun itself out. She sat quietly with her hands in her lap. She did not move. She let herself imbibe all this new truth, and she did not flinch from any of it.

The next morning Alma rode out alone to the offices of her father's long-time solicitor, and there she spent the next nine hours sitting with that man at his desk, drawing up papers and executing provisions and overriding objections. The solicitor did not approve of anything she was doing. She did not listen to a word he said. He shook his old yellow head until the jowls under his chin wagged, but he did not sway her in the least. The decisions were hers alone to make, as they were both well aware.

With that business concluded, Alma rode her horse to Thirty-ninth Street, to her sister's house. It was evening by now, and the Dixon family were finishing their meal.

"Come take a walk with me," Alma said to Prudence, who—if she was surprised by Alma's sudden visit—did not reveal it.

The two women strolled down Chestnut Street, latched politely together, arm in arm.

"As you know," Alma said, "our father has passed away."

"Yes," said Prudence.

"I thank you for the note of condolence."

"You are most welcome," said Prudence.

Prudence had not attended the funeral. Nobody would have expected her to.

"I've spent the day with our father's solicitor," Alma went on. "We were reviewing the will. I found it full of surprises."

"Before you continue," Prudence interjected, "I must tell you that I cannot in good conscience accept any money from our late father. There was a rift between us that I was unable or unwilling to mend, and it would not be ethical of me to profit by his largesse now that he has gone."

"You need not worry," Alma said, stopping in her path and turning to look at her sister directly. "He left you nothing."

Prudence, controlled as ever, gave no reaction. She merely said, "Then it is simple."

"No, Prudence," Alma said, taking her sister's hand. "It is far from simple. What Father did was rather surprising, in fact, and I beg you to listen carefully. He left the entirety of the White Acre estate, along with the vast majority of his fortune, to the Philadelphia Abolitionist Society."

Still, Prudence did not react or respond. *My stars, but she's strong,* Alma marveled, nearly wanting to bow in admiration of her sister's great reserve. Beatrix would have been proud.

Alma went on. "But there was an additional provision written into the will. He directed that he would leave his estate to the Abolitionist Society only under the condition that the house at White Acre become a school for Negro children, and that you, Prudence, administer it."

Prudence stared at Alma penetratingly, as though looking for evidence of trickery on Alma's face. Alma had no trouble arranging her countenance into an expression of truth, for indeed this was what the documents said—or, at least, this was what the documents said *now*.

"He left a quite long letter of explanation," Alma went on, "which I can summarize for you here. He said that he felt he'd done little good with his life, although he had prospered handsomely. He felt he'd offered the world nothing of value, in return for his own tremendous good fortune. He felt you would be the best person to see to it that White Acre, in the future, would become a seat of human kindness."

"He wrote those words?" Prudence asked, canny as ever. "Those very words, Alma? Our father, Henry Whittaker, referred to 'a seat of human kindness'?"

"Those very words," Alma insisted. "The deeds and instructions have already been drawn up. If you do not accept these provisions—if you do not move back to White Acre along with your family, and take command over running a school there, as our father wished—then all the money and property simply reverts to the two of us, and we shall have to sell it all off or divide it some other way. That being the case, it seems a pity not to honor his wishes."

Prudence searched Alma's face again. "I do not believe you," she said at last.

"You need not believe me," Alma said. "Yet that is how it is. Hanneke will stay on to manage the household and ease you into the role of running White Acre. Father left Hanneke a most generous endowment, but I know she will wish to remain there and to help you. She is an admirer of yours, and she likes to be kept useful. The gardeners and landscapers will stay on, to maintain the property. The library will remain intact, for the betterment of the students. Mr. Dick Yancey will continue to administer our father's overseas interests, and he will take over the Whittaker share of the pharmaceutical company, with all the profits flowing back into the school, into the salaries of the workers, and to abolitionist causes. Do you understand?"

Prudence did not reply.

Alma went on, "Ah, but there is but one more provision. Father has set aside a generous bequest to pay for the expenses of our friend Retta at the Griffon Asylum for the remainder of her days, such that George Hawkes should not suffer the burden of her care."

Now Prudence seemed to be losing control of something in her face. Her eyes grew damp, as did her hand, clasped in Alma's.

"There is nothing you can say," Prudence said, "that will ever convince me that our father wished for any of these things."

Still, Alma did not back down. "Do not let it surprise you so. You know that he was an unpredictable man. And you will see, Prudence—the papers of ownership and the provisions of transfer are all quite clear and legal."

"I well know, Alma, that you yourself have a facility for drawing up clear legal papers."

"But you have known me for such a long while, Prudence. Have you ever known me to do anything in life beyond what our father permitted me to do, or instructed me to do? Think of it, Prudence! Have you ever?"

Prudence looked away. Then her face collapsed upon itself, her reserve fractured at last, and she fell apart into tears. Alma pulled her sister—her extraordinary, brave, little-known sister—into her arms, and the two women stood for a long while, embracing in silence, while Prudence wept.

At last, Prudence pulled away and wiped her eyes. "And what did he leave *you*, Alma?" she asked, her voice shaken. "What did that most generous father of ours leave you, amid this unexpected beneficence?"

"Do not worry yourself with that now, Prudence. I have far more than I will ever need."

"But what did he leave you *exactly*? You must tell me."

"A bit of money," Alma said. "And the carriage house, as well—or, rather, all of my possessions within it."

"Are you meant to live forever in a carriage house?" Prudence asked, overwhelmed and confused, and clutching again at Alma's hand.

"No, dear one. I shall not live anywhere near White Acre, ever again. It is all in your care now. But my books and my belongings will remain at the carriage house, while I go away for a while. Eventually I shall settle someplace, and then I shall send for all that I need."

"But where are you going?"

Alma could not help but laugh. "Oh, Prudence," she said. "If I were to tell you, you would only think I was mad!"

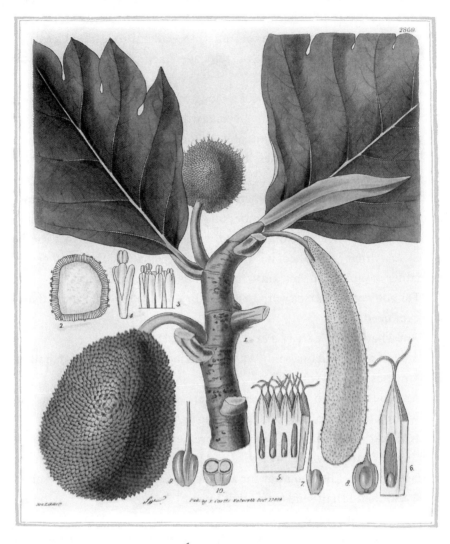

Artocarpus incisa

PART FOUR

The Consequence of Missions

Chapter Twenty-one

Alma sailed for Tahiti on the thirteenth day of November, 1851.

The Crystal Palace had just been erected in London for the Great Exhibition. Foucault's pendulum was newly installed at the Paris Observatory. The first white man had recently glimpsed Yosemite Valley. A submarine telegraph cable was spooling across the Atlantic Ocean. John James Audubon was dead of old age; Richard Owen won the Copley Medal for his work on paleontology; the Female Medical College of Pennsylvania was about to graduate its first class of eight women doctors; and Alma Whittaker—aged fifty-one years—was a paying passenger on a whaling ship headed for the South Seas.

She sailed without a maid, without a friend, without a guide. Hanneke de Groot had wept on Alma's neck at the news she was leaving, but had quickly regained her senses and commissioned for Alma a collection of practical garments, including two specially made travel dresses: humble frocks of linen and wool, with reinforced buttons (not much different from what Hanneke had always worn), which Alma could tend without assistance. So attired, Alma rather resembled a servant herself, but she was exceedingly comfortable and could move about with ease. She wondered why she had not dressed this way her entire life. Once the travel dresses were completed, Alma instructed Hanneke to sew secret compartments into the hems of two of the dresses, which Alma used to conceal the gold and silver coins she would need to pay for her travels. These coins consti-tuted a large portion of Alma's remaining wealth in the world. It was not a fortune by any means, but it was enough—Alma dearly hoped—to sustain a frugal traveler for two or three years.

"You have been always so kind to me," Alma said to Hanneke, when the dresses were presented.

"Well, I shall miss you," Hanneke replied, "and I shall cry again when you go, but let us admit to it, child—we are both of us too old now to fear the great changes of life."

Prudence presented Alma with a commemorative bracelet, braided from strands of Prudence's own hair (still as pale and beautiful as sugar) together with strands of Hanneke's hair (gray as polished steel). Prudence knotted the bracelet herself onto Alma's wrist, and Alma promised never to remove it.

"I could not think of a more precious gift," Alma said, and she meant it.

Immediately upon making her decision to go to Tahiti, Alma had penned a letter to the missionary in Matavai Bay, the Reverend Francis Welles, alerting him that she would be coming for an indefinite period of time. She knew there was a strong chance she would arrive at Papeete before her letter did, but there was nothing to be done for it. She needed to sail before winter set in. She did not want to wait so long that she changed her mind. She could only hope that when she arrived in Tahiti, there would be a place for her to stay.

It took her three weeks to pack. She knew precisely what to take, as she had been instructing botanical collectors for decades on the subject of safe and useful travel. Thus, she packed arsenical soap, cobbler's wax, twine, camphor, forceps, cork, insect boxes, a plant press, several waterproof Indian rubber bags, two dozen durable pencils, three bottles of India ink, a tin of watercolor pigments, brushes, pins, nets, lenses, putty, brass wire, small scalpels, washing flannels, silk thread, a medical kit, and twenty-five reams of paper (blotting, writing, plain brown). She considered bringing a gun, but as she was not an expert shot, she decided that a scalpel would have to do at close range.

She heard her father's voice as she prepared, remembering all the times she had taken dictation for him, or had overheard him instructing young botanists. *Be wakeful and watchful,* she heard Henry say. *Make sure you are not the only member of your party who can write or read a letter. If you need to find water, follow a dog. If you are starving, eat insects before you waste your energy on hunting. Anything that a bird can eat, you can eat. Your biggest dangers are not snakes, lions, or cannibals; your biggest dangers are blistered feet, carelessness, and fatigue. Be certain to write your diaries and maps legibly; if you die, your notes may be of use to a future explorer. In an emergency, you can always write in blood.*

Alma knew to wear light colors in the tropics in order to stay cool. She knew that soapsuds worked into fabric and dried overnight would waterproof clothing perfectly. She knew to wear flannel next to the skin. She knew that it would be appreciated if she took gifts for both the missionaries (recent newspapers, vegetable seeds, quinine, hand axes, and glass bottles) and the natives (calico, buttons, mirrors, and ribbon). She packed one of her beloved microscopes—the lightest one—though she much feared it would be destroyed on the journey. She packed a gleaming new chronometer and a smallish traveling thermometer.

All of this, she loaded into trunks and wooden boxes (cushioned lovingly with dried moss) which she then stacked into a small pyramid just outside the carriage house. Alma felt a quiver of panic when she saw her life's essentials reduced to such a minimal pile. How could she survive with so little? What would she do without her library? Without her herbarium? How would it feel to wait sometimes six months for news of family, or of science? What if the ship should sink, and all these essentials be lost? She felt a sudden sympathy for all the intrepid young men the Whittakers had sent out on collecting expeditions in the past—for the fear and uncertainty they must have felt, even as they purported to be confident. Some of those young men had never been heard from again.

In her preparations and packing, Alma made certain to give herself every appearance of a *botaniste voyageuse*, but the truth was, she was not going to Tahiti to search for plants. Her actual motive could be found in one item, buried at the bottom of one of the larger boxes: Ambrose's leather valise, buckled securely, and filled with the drawings of the nude Tahitian boy. She intended to look for that boy (whom she had come to refer to in her mind as The Boy) and she was certain that she could find him. She intended to search for The Boy across the entire island of Tahiti if necessary, searching for him almost *botanically*, as though he were a rare orchid specimen.

She would recognize him as soon as she saw him, she plainly knew. She would know that face till the end of her days. Ambrose had been a brilliant artist, after all, and the features were so vividly depicted. It was as if Ambrose had left her a map, and now she was following it.

She did not know what she would do with The Boy once she had found him. But she would find him.

Alma took the train to Boston, spent three nights in an inexpensive harbor hotel (redolent of gin, tobacco, and the sweat of former guests) and then embarked from there. Her ship was the *Elliot*—a 120-foot whaler, broad and sturdy as an old mare—heading to the Marquesas Islands for the dozenth time since she had been built. The captain had agreed, for a handsome fee, to sail 850 miles out of his way and deliver Alma to Tahiti.

The captain was a Mr. Terrence, out of Nantucket. He was a sailor much admired by Dick Yancey, who had secured Alma her place on his vessel. Mr. Terrence was as hard as a captain should be, Yancey promised, and he enforced better discipline in his men than most. Terrence was known more for being daring than careful (he was famous for raising his canvases in a storm, rather than subtracting them, in the hopes of gaining speed from the gales), but he was a religious man and a sober one, who strove for a high moral tone at sea. Dick Yancey trusted him and had sailed with him many times. Dick Yancey, who was always in a hurry, preferred captains who sailed fast and fearlessly, and Terrence was just such a type.

Alma had never before been on a ship. Or, rather, she had been on many ships, when she used to go with her father down to the docks of Philadelphia to inspect arriving cargo, but she had never *sailed* on a ship before. When the *Elliot* pulled out of its slip, she stood on the deck with her heart drumming as though to burst from her chest. She watched as the last of the dock's piles were ahead of her, and then—with breathtaking swiftness—were suddenly behind her. Then they were flying across the great Boston harbor, with smaller fishing boats bobbing in their wake. By the close of the afternoon, Alma was on the open ocean for the first time in her life.

"I will pay you every service in my power to make you comfortable on this voyage," Captain Terrence had sworn to Alma when first she boarded. She appreciated his solicitousness, but it soon became clear there was not much that would be comfortable about this journey. Her berth, right next to the captain's stateroom, was small and dark, and reeked of sewage. The drinking water smelled of a pond. The ship was carrying a cargo of mules to New Orleans, and the animals were unrelenting in their complaints. The food was both unpleasant and binding (turnips and salt biscuits for break-fast; dried beef and onions for dinner) and the weather was, at best, an uncertain affair. For the first three weeks of the journey she did not once see the sun. Immediately, the *Elliot* encountered gales that broke crockery and knocked sailors about at a most remarkable rate. She sometimes had to tie herself to the captain's table in order to eat her dried beef and onions in safety. She ate it gallantly, though, and without complaint.

There was not another woman on board, nor an educated man. The sail-ors played cards long into the night, laughing and shouting and keeping her awake. Sometimes the men danced on the deck like spirits possessed, until Captain Terrence threatened to break their fiddles if they did not stop. They were all rough sorts, aboard the *Elliot*. One of the sailors caught a hawk off the coast of North Carolina, cut its wings, and watched it hop across the deck, for sport. Alma found this barbaric, but she said nothing. The next day, the sailors, bored and distracted, staged a wedding between two mules, decorating the animals in festive paper collars for the event. There was a fine ruckus of hooting and yelling. The captain let it happen; he saw no harm in it (perhaps, Alma thought, because it was a *Christian* wedding). Alma had never before in her life seen the likes of such behavior.

There was nobody for Alma to speak to of serious matters, so she decided to stop speaking of serious matters. She resolved to be of good cheer and to make simple conversation with everyone. She vowed to make no enemies. As they would all be at sea together for the next five to seven months, this looked to be a sensible strategy. She even allowed herself to laugh at jests, so long as the men were not too coarse. She did not worry about coming to harm; Captain Terrence would not permit familiarity, and the men dis-played no licentiousness toward Alma. (This did not surprise her. If men had not been interested in Alma at nineteen years, surely none would take notice of her at fifty-one.)

Her closest companion was the small monkey that Captain Terrence kept as a pet. His name was Little Nick, and he would sit with Alma for hours, picking over her gently, always looking for new and odd things. He had a most intelligent and curious disposition. More than anything, the monkey was fascinated by the woven-hair bracelet that Alma wore around her wrist. He could never get over his perplexion that there was not a similar bracelet on her other wrist—although every morning he checked to see if a bracelet had grown there during the night. Then he would sigh and give Alma a resigned look, as though to say, "Why can you not just once be *symmetrical*?" Over time, Alma learned to share her snuff with Little Nick. He would daintily place a crumb of it in one of his nostrils, sneeze cleansingly, and then fall asleep in her lap. She did not know what she would have done without his company.

They rounded the tip of Florida and stopped in New Orleans to deliver the mules. Nobody mourned to see the mules go. In New Orleans, Alma saw the most extraordinary fog over Lake Pontchartrain. She saw bales of cotton and casks of cane sugar piled on the wharfs, awaiting shipment. She saw steamboats lined up in rows, as far as the eye could see, waiting to paddle up the Mississippi. She found good use for her French in New Orleans, though the accent was confusing. She admired the little houses with their gardens of seashells and clipped shrubbery, and she was dazzled by the women with their elaborate fashions. She wished she had more time for exploration, but was all too soon ordered back on board.

Southward they sailed along the coast of Mexico. An outbreak of fever swept the ship. Scarcely anyone escaped it. There was a doctor on board, but he was more than useless, and so Alma soon found herself dispensing treatments from her own precious cache of purgatives and emetics. She did not think of herself as much of a nurse, but she was a fairly capable pharmacist, and her assistance won her a small group of admirers.

Soon Alma herself fell ill, and was forced to keep to her berth. Her fevers gave her distant dreams and vivid fears. She could not keep her hands away from her quim, and woke in paroxysms of both pain and pleasure. She dreamed constantly of Ambrose. She had been making a heroic effort not to think of him, but the fever weakened the fortress of her mind, and his memory forced itself in—but distorted horribly. In her dreams, she saw him in the bathtub—just as she had seen him, nude, that one afternoon—but now his penis grew beautiful and erect, and he grinned at her lecherously while bidding her to suck him until she choked for breath. In other dreams, she watched Ambrose drown in the bathtub, and she woke in a panic, feeling certain she had murdered him. She heard his voice one night whispering, "So now you are the child and I am the mother," and she woke with a scream, arms flailing. But nobody was there. His voice had been in German. Why would it be in German? What did it mean? She lay awake the rest of the night, struggling to comprehend the word *mother—Mutter*, in German—a word that, in alchemy, also meant "crucible." She could make no sense of the dream, but it felt most heavily like a curse.

She had her first thoughts of regret about attempting this journey.

The day after Christmas, one of the sailors died of the fever. He was wrapped in sailcloth, weighted with a cannonball, and slid quietly into the sea. The men took his death without any evident sign of grief, auctioning off his belongings among themselves. By evening, it was as if the man had never existed. Alma imagined her belongings auctioned off among these fellows. *What would they make of Ambrose's drawings?* Who was to say? Perhaps such a trove of sodomitic sensuality would be valuable to some of these men. All types of men went to sea. Alma well knew this to be true.

Alma recovered from her sickness. A fair wind brought them to Rio de Janeiro, where Alma saw Portuguese slave ships bound north for Cuba. She saw beautiful beaches, where fishermen risked their lives on rafts that looked no sturdier than the roofs of henhouses. She saw the great fan palms, bigger than any in White Acre's greenhouses, and wished to the point of agony that she could have shown them to Ambrose. She could not keep him from her thoughts. She wondered if he had seen these palms, too, when he had passed through here.

She kept herself distracted with inexhaustible walks of exploration. She saw women who wore no bonnets, and who smoked cigars as they walked down the street. She saw refugees, commercial men, dirty Creoles and courtly Negroes, demi-savages and elegant quadroons. She saw men selling parrots and lizards for food. Alma feasted on oranges, lemons, and limes. She ate so many mangoes—sharing a few of them with Little Nick—that she broke out in a rash. She saw the horse races and the dancing amusements. She stayed at a hotel run by a mixed-raced couple—the first she had ever seen of such a thing. (The woman was a friendly, competent Negro, who did nothing slowly; the man was white and old, and did nothing at all.) Not a day went by that she did not see men marching slaves through the streets of Rio, offering these manacled beings for sale. Alma could not bear the sight of it. It left her sick with shame, for all the years that she had taken no notice of this abhorrence.

Back at sea, they headed for Cape Horn. As they approached the Cape, the weather became so unseasonably fierce that Alma—already wrapped in several layers of flannel and wool—added a man's greatcoat and a borrowed Russian hat to her wardrobe. So bundled, she was now indistinguishable from any man on board. She saw the mountains of Tierra del Fuego, but the ship could not land, as the weather was too fierce. Fifteen days of misery followed as they rounded the Cape. The captain insisted on carrying all sail, and Alma could not imagine how the masts endured the strain. The ship lay first on one side, then the other. The *Elliot* herself seemed to scream in pain—her poor wooden soul beaten and whipped by the sea.

"If it is God's will, we shall go clear," Terrence said, refusing to lower the sails, trying to run out another twenty knots before darkness.

"But what if someone should be killed?" Alma shouted across the wind.

"Burial at sea," the captain shouted back, and pushed on.

It was forty-five days of bitter cold after this. The waves came in endless, rolling assault. Sometimes the storms were so bad that the older sailors sang psalms for comfort. Others cursed and blustered, and a few remained silent—as though they were already dead. The storms loosened the hencoops from their stays, and sent chickens flying across the decks. One night, the boom was smashed into dainty chips, like kindling. The next day, the sailors tried to raise a new boom, and failed. One of the sailors, knocked over by a wave, fell down the hold and broke his ribs.

Alma hovered the entire time between hope and fear, certain she would die at any moment—but never once did she cry out in panic, or raise her voice in alarm. At the end of it all, when the weather cleared, Captain Terrence said, "You are a right little daughter of Neptune, Miss Whittaker," and Alma felt she had never been so mightily praised.

Finally, in mid-March, they docked at Valparaiso, where the sailors found ample houses of prostitution in which to attend to their amorous wants, while Alma explored this elaborate and welcoming city. The area down by the port was a degenerate mudflat, but the houses along the steep hills were beautiful. She hiked the hills for days, and felt her legs grow strong again. She saw nearly as many Americans in Valparaiso as she'd seen in Boston—all of them en route to San Francisco to hunt for gold. She filled her belly with pears and cherries. She saw a religious procession half a mile long, for a saint who was unfamiliar to her, and she followed it all the way to a formidable cathedral. She read newspapers and sent letters home to Prudence and Hanneke. One clear and cool day, she climbed to the highest point of Valparaiso, and from there—in the far and hazy distance—she could see the snow-covered peaks of the Andes. She felt a deep bruise of absence for her father. This provided her with a strange relief—to miss Henry, and not, for once, Ambrose.

Then they sailed again, out into the broad waters of the Pacific. The days grew warm. The sailors became calm. They cleaned between the decks, and scrubbed away old mold and vomit. They hummed as they worked. In the mornings, in the bustle of activity, the ship felt like a small country village. Alma had become used to the want of privacy, and she was comforted by the presence of the sailors now. They were familiar to her, and she was glad they were there. They taught her knots and chanteys, and she cleaned their wounds and lanced their boils. Alma ate an albatross, shot by a young seaman. They passed the bloated, floating carcass of a whale—its blubber stripped away clean by other whalers—but they did not see any living whales.

The Pacific Ocean was vast and empty. Alma could understand now for the first time why it had taken the Europeans so long to find Terra Australis in this tremendous expanse. The early explorers had assumed there must be a southern continent as large as Europe someplace down here, in order to keep the planet perfectly balanced. But they had been wrong. There was little down here but water. If anything, the Southern Hemisphere was a *reverse* of Europe: it was a huge continent of ocean, dotted with tiny lakes of land spread very far apart, indeed.

Days upon days of blue emptiness followed. On every side, Alma saw prairies of water, as far as her mind could imagine. Still, they saw no whales. They saw no birds, either, but they could see weather coming from one hundred miles away, and it often looked bad. The air was voiceless until the storms came, and then the winds would shriek in distress.

In early April, they encountered a most alarming change of weather, which blackened the sky before their eyes, murdering the day in the middle of the afternoon. The air felt heavy and menacing. This sudden transformation worried Captain Terrence enough that he lowered the sails—all of them—as he watched chains of lightning come at them from all directions. The waves became rolling mountains of black. But then—as quickly as it had come upon them—the storm cleared, and skies grew light again. Instead of relief, though, the men cried out in alarm, for immediately they saw a waterspout drawing near. The captain ordered Alma belowdecks, but she would not move; the waterspout was too magnificent a sight. Then another cry went up, as the men realized there were, in point of fact, *three* waterspouts now surrounding the ship at distances much too close for comfort. Alma felt herself hypnotized. One of the spouts drew near enough that she could see the long strands of water spiraling upward from the ocean all the way into the sky, in one great swirling column. It was the most majestic thing she had ever seen, and the most holy, and the most awesome. The pressure in the air was so thick, Alma's eardrums seemed in danger of bursting, and it was a struggle to pull breath into her lungs. For the next five minutes, she was so overcome that she did not know if she was alive or dead. She did not know what world this was. It struck Alma that her time in this world was over. Curiously, she did not mind. There was no one she longed for. Not a single soul she had ever known crossed her mind—not Ambrose, not anyone. She had no regrets. She stood in rapt amazement, prepared for anything that might occur.

After the waterspouts finally passed and the sea was tranquil once more, Alma felt it had been the happiest experience of her life.

They sailed on.

To the south, distant and impossible, was icy Antarctica. To the north was nothing, apparently—or so said the bored sailors. They kept sailing west. Alma missed the pleasures of walking and the smell of soil. With no other botany around to study, she asked the men to pull up seaweed for her to examine. She did not know her seaweeds well, but she knew how to distinguish things, one from the other, and she soon learned that some seaweeds had conglomerate roots, and some had compressed. Some were textured; some were smooth. She tried to puzzle out how to preserve the seaweeds for study, without turning them into slime or black flakes of nothingness. She never really mastered it, but it gave her something to do. She was also delighted to discover that the sailors packed their harpoon tips in wads of dried moss; this gave her something wonderful and familiar to examine again.

Alma came to admire sailors. She could not imagine how they endured such long periods of time away from the comforts of land. How did they not go mad? The ocean both stunned and disturbed her. Nothing had ever put more of an impression upon her being. It seemed to her the very distillation of matter, the very masterpiece of mysteries. One night they sailed through a diamond field of liquid phosphorescence. The ship churned up strange molecules of green and purple light as it moved, until it appeared that the *Elliot* was dragging a long glowing veil behind herself, wide across the sea. It was so beautiful that Alma wondered how the men did not throw themselves into the water, drawn down to their deaths by this intoxicating magic.

On other nights, when she could not sleep, she paced the deck in her bare feet, trying to toughen up her soles for Tahiti. She saw the long reflections of stars on the calm water, shining like torches. The sky above her was as unfamiliar as the sea around her. She saw a few constellations that reminded her of home—Orion, the Pleiades—but the northern pole star was gone, and the Great Bear, too. These missing treasures from the vault of the sky caused her to feel most desperately and helplessly disoriented. But there were new gifts to be seen in the heavens, as compensation. She could see the Cross of the South now, and the Twins, and the vast, spilling nebulae of the Milky Way.

Amazed by the constellations, Alma said to Captain Terrence one night, "*Nihil astra praeter vidit et undas.*"

"What does that mean?" he asked.

"It's from the Odes of Horace," she said. "It means there is nothing to be seen but stars and waves."

"I'm afraid I don't know Latin, Miss Whittaker," he apologized. "I am not a Catholic."

One of the older sailors, who had lived in the South Seas many years, told Alma that when the Tahitians picked a star to follow for navigation, they called it their *aveia*—their god of guidance. But in general, he said, the more common Tahitian word for a star was *fetia*. Mars was the red star, for instance: the *fetia ura*. The morning star was the *fetia ao*: the star of light. The Tahitians were extraordinary navigators, the sailor told her with undisguised admiration. They could navigate on a starless, moonless night, he said, reckoning themselves merely by the feel of the ocean's current. They knew sixteen different kinds of wind.

"I always wondered if they ever went to visit us in the north, before we visited them in the south," he said. "I wonder if they came up to Liverpool or Nantucket in their canoes. Could've done, you know. Could've sailed right up there and watched us while we slept, then paddled away before we saw them. I wouldn't be a bit surprised to learn of it."

So now Alma knew a few words of Tahitian. She knew *star*, and *red*, and *light*. She asked the sailor to teach her more. He offered what he could, trying to be helpful, but mostly he only knew the nautical terms, he apologized, and all the things you say to a pretty girl.

Still they saw no whales.

The men were disappointed. They were bored and restless. The seas were hunted to depletion. The captain feared bankruptcy. Some of the sailors—the ones that Alma had befriended, anyway—wanted to show off to her their hunting skills.

"It is such a thrill as you will never know," they promised.

Every day they looked for whales. Alma looked, too. But she never did get to see one, for they landed in Tahiti in June of 1852. The sailors went one way and Alma went the other, and that was the last she ever heard of the *Elliot*.

Chapter Twenty-two

$\mathbf{A}$lma's first glimpse of Tahiti, as seen from the deck of the *Elliot*, had been of abrupt mountain peaks rising hard into cloudless cerulean skies. She had just awoken on this fine, clear morning, and had walked onto the deck to survey her world. She was not expecting what she saw. The sight of Tahiti grabbed the breath from Alma's chest: not its beauty, but its strangeness. All her life, she'd heard stories of this island, and she'd seen drawings and paintings, too, but still she had no idea the place would be so *tall*, so extraordinary. These mountains were nothing like the rolling hills of Pennsylvania; these were verdant and wild slopes—shockingly steep, alarmingly jagged, staggeringly high, blindingly green. Indeed, everything about the place was overdressed with green. Even right down to the beaches, it was all excessive and green. Coconut palms gave the impression of growing straight from the water itself.

It unnerved her. Here she was, quite literally in the middle of nowhere—halfway between Australia and Peru—and she could not help but wonder: Why is there an island here at all? Tahiti felt to her like an uncanny interruption of the Pacific's vast, endless flatness—an eerie and arbitrary cathedral, thrusting up from the center of the sea for no reason at all. She had expected to view it as a kind of paradise, for that was how Tahiti had always been described. She had expected to be overcome by its beauty, to feel as though she had landed in Eden. Hadn't Bougainville called the island La

Nouvelle Cythère, after the island of Aphrodite's birth? But Alma's first reaction, to be quite honest, was fear. On this bright morning, in this balmy climate, faced with the sudden appearance of this famous utopia, she was conscious of nothing but a sense of menace. She wondered, What had Ambrose made of this? She did not want to be left alone here.

But where else was she to go?

The old pacer of a ship slid smoothly into the harbor at Papeete, with seabirds of a dozen varieties spinning and wheeling about the masts faster than Alma could count or identify them. Alma and her luggage were dispatched onto the bustling, colorful wharf. Captain Terrence, quite kindly, went to see if he could hire Alma a carriage to take her to the mission settlement at Matavai Bay.

Her legs were shaky, after months at sea, and she was nearly overcome by nerves. She saw people around her of all sorts—sailors and naval officers and men of commerce, and somebody in clogs, who looked as though he might be a Dutch merchant. She saw a pair of Chinese pearl traders, with long queues down their backs. She saw natives and half-natives and who knew what else. She saw a burly Tahitian man wearing a heavy woolen pea jacket, which he had clearly acquired from a British sailor, but he wore no trousers—just a skirt of grass, and a disconcertingly nude chest beneath the jacket. She saw native women dressed in all sorts of ways. Some of the older ones quite brazenly displayed their breasts, while the younger women tended to wear long frocks, with their hair arranged in modest plaits. They were the new converts to Christianity, Alma supposed. She saw a woman wrapped in what appeared to be a tablecloth, wearing men's European leather shoes several sizes too big for her feet, selling unfamiliar fruits. She saw a fantastically dressed fellow, wearing European trousers as a sort of jacket, with his head all aflutter in a crown of leaves. She thought him a most extraordinary sight, but no one else paid him any notice.

The native people here were bigger than the people Alma was used to. Some of the women were quite as large as Alma herself. The men were even larger. Their skin was burnished copper. Some of the men had long hair and looked frightening; others had short hair and looked civilized.

Alma saw a sad knot of prostitutes rush toward the *Elliot*'s sailors with immediate, brazen suggestions, just as soon as the men's feet touched the dock. These women wore their hair down, reaching below their waists in glossy black waves. From the back, they all looked the same. From the front, one could see the differences in age and beauty. Alma watched the negotiations begin. She wondered how much something like that cost. She wondered what the women offered, specifically. She wondered how long these transactions took, and where they occurred. She wondered where the sailors went if they wanted to purchase boys instead of girls. There was no sign of that sort of exchange on the dock. Probably it happened in a more discreet place.

She saw all manner of infants and children—in and out of clothes, in and out of the water, in and out of her way. The children moved like schools of fish, or flocks of birds, with every decision rendered in immediate, collective concurrence: *Now we shall jump! Now we shall run! Now we shall beg! Now we shall mock!* She saw an old man with a leg inflamed to twice its natural size. His eyes were white from blindness. She saw tiny carriages, pulled by the saddest little ponies imaginable. She saw a group of small brindled dogs tangling with each other in the shade. She saw three French sailors, arm in arm, singing lustily, drunk already on this fine morning. She saw signs for a billiards hall, and, remarkably, a printing shop. The solid land swayed beneath her feet. She was hot in the sun.

A handsome black rooster spotted Alma and marched toward her with an officious strut, as though he were an emissary dispatched to welcome her. He was so dignified that she would not have been surprised had he worn a ceremonial sash across his chest. The rooster stopped directly in front of her, magisterial and watchful. Alma nearly expected him to speak, or demand to see her documents. Not knowing what else to do, she reached down and stroked the courtly bird, as if he were a dog. Astonishingly, he allowed it. She stroked him some more, and he clucked at her in rich satisfaction. Eventually the rooster settled at her feet and fluffed out his feathers in handsome repose. He showed every sign of feeling that their interaction had gone precisely according to plan. Alma felt comforted, somehow, by this simple exchange. The rooster's quietude and assurance helped put her at ease.

Then the two of them—bird and woman—waited together silently on the docks, waiting for whatever would happen next.

It was seven miles between Papeete and Matavai Bay. Alma took such pity on the poor pony who had to haul her luggage that she stepped out of the carriage and walked along beside it. It was exquisite to use her legs after so many stagnant months at sea. The road was lovely and shaded overhead by a latticework of palms and breadfruit trees. The landscape felt both familiar and confounding to Alma. Many of the palm varieties she recognized from her father's greenhouses, but others were mysterious concoctions of pleated leaves and slippery, leathery bark. Having known palms only in greenhouses, Alma had never before *heard* palm trees. The sound of the wind through their fronds was like rustling silk. Sometimes, in the stronger gusts, their trunks creaked like old doors. They were all so loud and alive. As for the breadfruit trees, they were grander and more elegant than she would ever have imagined. They looked like the elms of home: glossy and magnanimous.

The carriage driver—an old Tahitian man with a disturbingly tattooed back and a well-oiled chest—was perplexed by Alma's insistence on walking. He seemed to fear this meant he wouldn't be paid. To reassure him, she tried to pay him halfway to their destination. This brought only more confusion. Captain Terrence had negotiated a price beforehand, but that arrangement now looked to be void. Alma offered payment in American coins, but the man attempted to make change for her from a handful of dirty Spanish piastres and Bolivian pesos. Alma could not figure out how he was possibly calculating this currency exchange, until she realized he was trading in his dull old coins for her shiny new ones.

She was deposited in a fringe of shade under a banana grove in the middle of the mission settlement at Matavai Bay. The carriage driver stacked her luggage into a tidy pyramid; it looked just as it had looked seven months earlier, outside the carriage house at White Acre. Left alone, Alma took in her surroundings. It was a pleasant enough situation here, she thought, though more modest than she had imagined. The mission church was a humble little structure, whitewashed and thatched, surrounded by a small cluster of similarly whitewashed and thatched cottages. There couldn't have been more than a few dozen people altogether living there.

The community, such as it was, was built along the banks of a small river that let out straight into the sea. The river bisected the beach, which was long and curved, and formed of dense, black, volcanic sand. Because of the color of the sand, the bay here was not the shining turquoise one normally associates with the South Seas; instead it was a stately, heavy, slow-rolling inlet of ink. A reef about three hundred yards out kept the surf fairly calm. Even from this distance, Alma could hear the waves smashing against that distant reef. She took up a handful of the sand—the color of soot—and let it pour through her fingers. It felt like warm velvet, and it left her fingers clean.

"Matavai Bay," she said aloud.

She could scarcely believe she was here. All the great explorers of the last century had been here. Wallis had been here, and Vancouver, and Bougainville. Captain Bligh had spent six months camped on this very beach. Most impressive of all, to Alma's mind, was that this was the same beach where Captain Cook had first landed in Tahiti, in 1769. To Alma's left, in the near distance, was the high promontory where Cook had observed the transit of Venus—that vital movement of a tiny black planetary disc across the face of the sun, which he had traveled across the world to witness. The gentle little river to Alma's right had once marked the last boundary in history between the Tahitians and the British. Directly after Cook's landfall, the two peoples had stood on the opposite sides of this stream, regarding each other with wary curiosity for several hours. The Tahitians thought the British had sailed out of the sky, and that their huge, impressive ships were islands—*motu*—that had broken loose from the stars. The English tried to determine if these Indians would be aggressive or dangerous. The Tahitian women came right to the edge of the river and teased the English sailors on the other side with playful, provocative dances. There seemed to be no danger here, decided Captain Cook, and he let his men loose upon the girls. The sailors exchanged iron nails with the women for sexual favors. The women took the nails and planted them in the ground, hoping to grow more of this precious iron, as one would grow a tree from a sprig.

Alma's father had not been on that voyage. Henry Whittaker had come to Tahiti eight years later, on Cook's third expedition, in August of 1777. By that point, the English and the Tahitians were well accustomed to each other—and fond of each other, too. Some of the British sailors even had island wives waiting among the women, and island children, as well. The Tahitians had called Captain Cook "Toote" because they could not pronounce his name. Alma knew all this from her father's stories—stories she had not thought of in decades. She remembered them all now. Her father had bathed in this very river as a young man. Since that time, the missionaries had started using it, Alma knew, for baptisms.

Now that she was here at last, Alma was not certain what to do next. There was not a soul in sight, with the exception of a child playing alone in the river. He could not have been more than three years old, was absolutely nude, and acted quite unperturbed about having been left unattended in the water. She did not wish to leave her luggage unguarded, so she simply sat down on the pile and waited for someone to come along. She was terribly thirsty. She had been too excited that morning to eat her ship's breakfast, so she was hungry, too.

After a long spell, a stout Tahitian woman in a long, modest dress and a white bonnet emerged from one of the more distant cottages, carrying a hoe. She stopped when she saw Alma. Alma stood up and straightened her dress. "*Bonjour*," she cried out. Tahiti officially belonged to France now; Alma imagined French was her best option.

The woman smiled beautifully. "We speak English here!" she cried back.

Alma wanted to approach, so they would not have to shout at each other, but—foolishly—she still felt bound to her luggage. "I am looking for the Reverend Francis Welles!" she called.

"He is in the corral today!" the woman called back cheerfully, and went on her way down the road toward Papeete, leaving Alma once more alone with her trunks.

The corral? Did they have cattle here? If so, Alma could neither see nor smell any sign of them. What could the woman have meant?

Over the next hours, a few more Tahitians wandered past Alma and her pile of crates and trunks. All of them were friendly, yet none seemed especially intrigued by her presence, and none talked with her for long. All reiterated the same piece of information: that the Reverend Francis Welles was in the corral for the day. And what time would he be back from the corral? Nobody knew. Before dark, they all dearly hoped.

A few young boys gathered round Alma and played a daring game of tossing pebbles at her luggage, and sometimes at her feet, until a large older woman with a glowering face chased them away, and they dashed off to play in the river. As the day wore on, some men with tiny fishing poles walked past Alma down to the beach and waded into the sea. They stood up to their necks in the gently rolling surf, casting about for fish. Her thirst and hunger had become urgent. Still, she did not dare go wandering and leave her belongings behind.

Dusk comes on fast in the tropics. Alma had already learned this in her months at sea. The shadows grew longer. The children ran out of the river and dashed back inside their cottages. Alma watched the sun lowering swiftly over the steep peaks of the island of Moorea, far across the bay. She began to panic. Where would she sleep tonight? Mosquitoes flitted around her head. She was now invisible to the Tahitians. They went about their business around her, as if she and her luggage were a stone cairn that had stood there on the beach since the dawn of history itself. The evening swallows emerged from the trees to hunt. Light glared off the water in dazzling blazes from the setting sun.

Then Alma saw something in the water, something heading toward the beach. It was a small outrigger canoe, quick and narrow. She shaded her eyes with her hand and squinted against the reflected sunlight, trying to make out the figures inside. No, it was just one figure, she saw, and that figure was paddling most energetically. The canoe shot up onto the beach with remarkable force—a little arrow of perfect momentum—and out sprang an elf. Or such was Alma's first thought: Here is an elf! Further scrutiny, however, revealed the elf to be a man, a white man, with a wild corona of snowy hair and a fluttering beard to match. He was tiny and bowlegged and spry, and he hauled the canoe up the beach with surprising strength for one so small.

"Reverend Welles?" she shouted with hope, waving her arms in a gesture that utterly lacked dignity.

The man approached. It was difficult to say what was more remarkable about him—his diminutive stature or his gaunt frame. He was half the size of Alma, with a child's body, and a quite skeletal body, at that. His cheeks were hollow and his shoulders were sharp and pointed beneath his shirt. His trousers were held around his pinched waist by a doubled-up length of rope. His beard reached far down his chest. He was wearing some sort of strange sandals, also made of rope. He did not wear a hat, and his face was deeply sunburned. His clothes were not entirely in rags, but quite nearly. He looked like a broken parasol. He looked like an elderly, miniature castaway.

"Reverend Welles?" she asked again, hesitant as he drew nearer.

He looked up at her—*far* up at her—with frank and bright blue eyes. "I am the Reverend Welles," he said. "At least, I believe that I still am, you see!"

He spoke with a light, clipped, indeterminate British accent.

"Reverend Welles, my name is Alma Whittaker. I hope you received my letter?"

He tilted his head: birdlike, interested, unperturbed. "Your letter?"

It was just as she had feared. She was not expected here. She took a deep breath and tried to think how best to explain herself. "I have come to visit, Reverend Welles, and to perhaps stay for a while—as you can probably see." She made an apologetic gesture toward her pyramid of luggage. "I have an interest in natural botany and I would like to study your native plants. I know that you are something of a naturalist yourself. I come from Philadelphia, in the United States. I have also come to survey the vanilla plantation my family owns. My father was Henry Whittaker."

He raised his wispy white eyebrows. "Your father *was* Henry Whittaker, do you say?" he asked. "Has that good man passed away?"

"I'm afraid he has, Reverend Welles. Just this last year."

"I regret to hear it. May the Lord take him to His breast. I worked for your father over the years, you see, in my own small way. I sold him many specimens, for which he was kind enough to pay me fairly. I never met your father, you see, but I worked through his emissary, Mr. Yancey. He was always a most generous and upright man, your good father. Many times over the years, the earnings from Mr. Whittaker helped to save this little settlement. We cannot always count on the London Missionary Society to come through for us, can we? But we have always been able to count on Mr. Yancey and Mr. Whittaker, you see. Tell me, do you know Mr. Yancey?"

"I know him well, Reverend Welles. I have known him all my life. He arranged for my travel here."

"Certainly! Certainly you do. Then you know him to be a good man."

Alma could not say that she would ever have accused Dick Yancey of being "a good man," but she nodded nonetheless. Likewise, she had never before heard her father described as generous, upright, or kind. These words would take some getting accustomed to. She remembered a man in Philadelphia who'd once referred to her father as "a biped of prey." Think how surprised that man would be now, to see how well regarded was the biped's name here, in the middle of the South Seas! The thought of it made Alma smile.

"I would be most happy to show you the vanilla plantation," the Reverend Welles continued. "A native man from our mission has taken over management of it, ever since we lost Mr. Pike. Did you know Ambrose Pike?"

Alma's heart pirouetted inside her chest, but she kept her face neutral. "Yes, I knew him a bit. I worked rather closely with my father, Reverend Welles, and it was the two of us, in fact, who made the decision to dispatch Mr. Pike to Tahiti."

Alma had decided months ago, even before leaving Philadelphia, that she would tell nobody in Tahiti of her relationship to Ambrose. During the entirety of her journey, she had traveled as "Miss Whittaker," and had allowed the world to regard her a spinster. In a very real sense, of course, she *was* a spinster. No sane person would have regarded her marriage to Ambrose as any sort of marriage at all. What's more, she certainly looked like a spinster—and felt like one. Generally speaking, she did not like to tell lies, but she had come here to fit together the story of Ambrose Pike, and she much doubted that anyone would be candid with her if they knew that Ambrose had been her husband. Assuming that Ambrose had honored her request and told nobody of their marriage, she did not imagine anyone would suspect a link between them, aside from the fact that Mr. Pike had been her father's employee. As for Alma, she was merely a traveling naturalist, and the daughter of a quite famous botanical importer and pharmaceuticals magnate; it should make every bit of sense to anyone that she might come to Tahiti for her own purposes—to study its mosses, and to look in on the family's vanilla plantation.

"Well, we sorely miss Mr. Pike," the Reverend Welles said, with a sweet smile. "Perhaps I miss him most of all. His death was a loss to our small settlement, you see. We wish that all strangers who came here would set such a good example to the natives as did Mr. Pike, who was a friend to the fatherless and fallen, an enemy of rancor and viciousness, and all that sort of thing, you see. He was a kind man, your Mr. Pike. I admired him, you see, because I felt he was able to show the natives—as so many Christians *cannot* seem to show the natives—what a Christian temperament should truly be. The conduct of so many other visiting Christians, you see, does not always seem calculated to raise the esteem of our religion in the eyes of these simple people. But Mr. Pike was a model of goodness. What's more, he had a gift for befriending the natives such as I have rarely seen in others. He spoke to everyone in such a plain and generous manner, you see. It is not always done that way, I am afraid, with the men who come to this island from far away. Tahiti can be a dangerous paradise, you see. For those who are accustomed to, let us say, the more rigorous moral landscape of European society, this island and its people can present temptations that are difficult to resist. Visitors take advantage, you see. Even some missionaries, I am sorry to say, sometimes exploit these people, who are a childlike and innocent people, you see, though with the help of the Lord we try to teach them to be more self-preserving. Mr. Pike was not such a type—to take advantage, you see."

Alma felt bowled over. She found this to be quite the most remarkable speech of introduction she had ever heard (barring, she supposed, the first time she had met Retta Snow). The Reverend Welles had not probed whatsoever into why Alma Whittaker had come all the way from Philadelphia to sit upon a pile of crates and trunks in the middle of his mission, and yet here he was, already discussing Ambrose Pike! She had not expected this. Nor had she expected that her husband, with his valise filled with secret and lewd drawings, would be praised quite so passionately as a moral example.

"Yes, Reverend Welles," she managed to say.

Astonishingly, the Reverend Welles continued even further on the subject: "What's more, you see, I came to love Mr. Pike as a most cherished friend. You cannot imagine the comfort of an intelligent companion in a place so lonely as this. Verily I would walk many miles to see his face again or to grasp his hand once more in friendship, if only that were possible—but such a miracle will never exist for as long as I breathe, you see, for Mr. Pike has been called home to paradise, Miss Whittaker, and we are left here alone."

"Yes, Reverend Welles," Alma said again. What else could she say?

"You may call me Brother Welles," he said, "if I may call you Sister Whittaker?"

"Certainly, Brother Welles," she said.

"You may now join us for evening prayer, Sister Whittaker. We are in a bit of a rush, you see. We will start later than usual this evening, for I have spent the day out in the coral, you see, and I have lost track of time."

Ah, Alma thought—the *coral*. Of course! He had been out at sea all day in the coral reefs, not looking after cattle.

"Thank you," Alma said. She looked again to her luggage, and hesitated. "I wonder where I might place my belongings in the meanwhile, to keep them safe? In my letter, Brother Welles, I had inquired if I might stay at the settlement for some time. I study mosses, you see, and I had hoped to explore the island . . ." She trailed off, unnerved by the man's candid blue eyes upon her.

"Certainly!" he said. She waited for him to say more, but he did not. How unquestioning he was! He could not have been less discommoded by her presence if they had planned this rendezvous for ten years.

"I have a comfortable amount of money," Alma said uncomfortably, "which I could offer to the mission in exchange for lodging . . ."

"Certainly!" he chirped again.

"I am not yet decided as to how long I might stay . . . I shall make every effort not to be a bother . . . I do not expect comforts . . ." She trailed off again. She was answering questions that he was not asking. Over time, Alma would learn that the Reverend Welles never asked questions of anyone, but for now she found it extraordinary.

"Certainly!" he said, for the third time. "Now join us in evening prayer, Sister Whittaker."

"Certainly," she said, and gave up.

He led her away from her luggage—away from all that she owned and all that was precious to her—and strode toward the church. All she could do was follow.

The chapel was not more than twenty feet long. Inside, it was lined with simple benches, and its walls were whitewashed and clean. Four whale-oil lanterns kept the place dimly lit. Alma counted eighteen worshippers, all of them native Tahitians. Eleven women and seven men. To the degree possible (she did not wish to be rude), Alma examined the faces of all the men. None of them was The Boy from Ambrose's drawings. The men were dressed in simple European-style trousers and shirts and the women wore those long, loose frocks that Alma had been seeing everywhere since she'd arrived. Most of the women wore bonnets, but one—Alma recognized her as the hard-faced lady who had shooed away the young boys—wore a wide-brimmed straw hat, decorated with an elaborate array of fresh flowers.

What followed was the most unusual religious service Alma had ever witnessed, and by far the shortest. First, they sang a hymn in the Tahitian language, though no one had a hymnal. The music was odd to Alma's ears—dissonant and sharp, with voices layered upon voices in patterns she could not follow, accompanied by naught but a single drum, played by a boy of about fourteen. The drum's rhythm did not seem to match the song—not in any way that Alma could identify. The women's voices rose up in piercing cries above the chants of the men. She could find no melody hidden within this strange music. She kept listening for a familiar word (Jesus, Christ, God, Lord, Jehovah) but nothing was recognizable. She felt self-conscious sitting in silence while the women around her sang so loudly. She could add nothing to this event.

After the singing ended, Alma expected the Reverend Welles to deliver a sermon, but he remained sitting with his head bowed in prayer. He did not even look up as the large Tahitian woman with the flowers on her hat stood and approached the simple pulpit. The woman read briefly, in English, from the book of Matthew. Alma marveled that this woman could read, and in English, as well. Though Alma had never been the prayerful sort, there was comfort in the familiar words. Blessed are the poor, the meek, the merciful, the pure in heart, the reviled and persecuted. Blessed, blessed, blessed. So many blessings, so generously expressed.

Then the woman closed the Bible and—still speaking in English—gave a quick, loud, and strange sermon.

"We are *born*!" she shouted. "We *crawl*! We *walk*! We *swim*! We *work*! We give *children*! We grow *old*! We walk with a *stick*! But only in God there is *peace*!"

"*Peace!*" said the congregation.

"If we fly to heaven, God is *there*! If we sail the sea, God is *there*! If we walk the land, God is *there*!"

"*There!*" said the congregation.

The woman stretched out her arms and opened and closed her hands in quick succession, many times in a row. Then she opened and closed her mouth rapidly. She made antics like a puppet on strings. Some of the congregation giggled. The woman did not seem to mind the laughter. Then she stopped moving about and shouted, "Look at us! We are cleverly *made*! We are full of *hinges*!"

"*Hinges!*" said the congregation.

"But the hinges will *rust*! We will *die*! Only God *remains*!"

"*Remains!*" said the congregation.

"The king of bodies has no *body*! But he brings us *peace*!"

"*Peace!*" said the congregation.

"Amen!" said the woman in the flower-covered hat, and returned to her seat.

"*Amen!*" said the congregation.

Then the Reverend Welles moved to the altar and offered communion. Alma stood in line with the rest of them. The Reverend was so tiny, she had to bend nearly double at the waist to receive his offering. There was no wine, but the juice of a coconut served the purpose of Christ's blood. As for the body of Christ, it was a small rolled ball of something sticky and sweet that Alma could not identify. She welcomed it; she was famished.

The Reverend Welles offered an impressively short prayer: "Give us the will, oh Christ, to endure every affliction that is our portion. Amen."

"*Amen,*" said the congregation.

This concluded the service. It could not have lasted fifteen minutes. Yet it was just enough time that—when Alma walked back outside—she found that the sky had grown completely dark, and every last one of her belongings was gone.

"Taken *where*?" Alma demanded. "And by whom?"

"Hmm," said the Reverend Welles, scratching his head and looking at the spot where Alma's luggage had rested only so very recently. "Now, that is not easily answered. Probably the young boys took it all, you see. It is usually the young boys, for this sort of thing. But most certainly it has been taken."

This confirmation was not helpful.

"Brother Welles!" she said, frantic with alarm. "I asked you if we should safeguard it! I need those items most urgently! We could have put it all in a house somewhere, safe behind a locked door, perhaps! Why did you not suggest it?"

He nodded in earnest agreement, but without any trace of consternation. "We could have put your luggage in a house, yes. But, you see, everything would have been taken regardless. They would take it now, you see, or they would take it later."

Alma thought of her microscope, of her reams of paper, her ink, her pencils and medicines and collection vials. What of her clothing? Dear God, what of Ambrose's valise, filled with all those dangerous, unspeakable drawings? She thought she would weep.

"But I brought gifts for the natives, Brother Welles. They did not have to steal from me. I would have given them things. I brought them scissors and ribbons!"

He gave a bright smile. "Well, it appears your gifts have been received, you see!"

"But there are items that I will need to have returned to me—items of unspeakable value and tenderness."

He was not entirely unsympathetic. She had to grant him that. He nodded kindly, and took notice, at least somewhat, of her distress. "That must make you sorrowful, Sister Whittaker. But please be assured—none of it has been eternally stolen. It has simply been taken, perhaps only temporarily. Some of it may be returned, if you are patient. If there is anything of particular value to you, I can ask for it specifically. Sometimes if I ask in the proper manner, items reappear."

She thought over all that she had packed. What did she most desperately need? She could not ask for the valise filled with Ambrose's sodomite drawings, though it was torture to have lost it, for it was her most important belonging.

"My microscope," she said, faintly.

He nodded again. "That may be difficult, you see. A microscope would be an item of considerable novelty around here. Nobody will have ever seen one. I don't believe I have ever seen one myself! Still, I shall start asking immediately. We can only hope, you see! As for tonight, we must find you lodging. Down the beach about a quarter of a mile is the small cottage we helped build for Mr. Pike, when he came to stay. It has been left much as it was when he passed away, may God rest him. I had thought that one of the natives might claim the place as his own home, but it seems nobody will go inside. It is tainted by death, you see—to their minds, I mean. These are a superstitious people, you see. But it is a pleasing cottage with comfortable furniture, and if you are not a superstitious person, you should be at ease there. You are not a superstitious person, are you, Sister Whittaker? You do not strike me as such. Shall we go look at it?"

Alma felt like crumpling to the ground. "Brother Welles," she said, struggling to keep her voice from breaking. "Please forgive me. I have come a long way. I am far from all that is familiar to me. I am much shocked to have lost my belongings, which I managed to safeguard for fifteen thousand miles of travel, only to have it vanish just a moment ago! I have not had a bite to eat, with the exception of your kind communion, since my dinner on the whaling ship yesterday afternoon. All is new, and all is strange. I am much burdened and much distracted. I ask you to forgive me . . ." Alma stopped talking. She had lost track of the purpose of this speech. She did not know what she was asking forgiveness *for*.

He clapped his hands. "To eat! Certainly, you must eat! My apologies, Sister Whittaker! You see, I do not eat myself—or quite rarely. I forget that others must do so! My wife would lace me up and give me the evils, if she knew of my poor manners!"

Without another word, and without any supplemental explanation as to the subject of his wife, the Reverend Welles ran off and knocked on the door of the cottage closest to the church. The large Tahitian woman—the same one who had delivered the sermon earlier that evening—answered the door. They exchanged a few words. The woman glanced at Alma, and nodded. The Reverend Welles rushed back to Alma with his springy, bow-legged step.

Alma wondered, could that be the Reverend's wife?

"Then it is done!" he said. "Sister Manu will provide for you. We eat simply here, but yes, at minimum you should eat! She will bring something to your cottage. I also asked her to bring you an *ahu taoto*—a sleeping shawl, which is all we use around here at night. I shall bring you a lamp, too. Now let us find our way. I cannot think of another thing you will possibly need."

Alma could think of many things she needed, but the promise of food and sleep was enough to sustain her for the time being. She walked behind the Reverend Welles down the black sand beach. He walked at an impressive speed for one with such short, crooked legs. Even with her long strides, Alma had to rush to keep up with him. He swung a lantern beside him, but did not light it, for the moon had risen and was bright in the sky. Alma was startled by large, dark shapes scurrying across the sand in their path. She thought they were rats, but on closer look discovered they were crabs. They unsettled her. They were quite sizable, with one large pincer claw each, which they dragged beside them as they scuttled along, clicking awfully. They came too close to her feet. She might have preferred rats, she thought.

She was grateful to be wearing shoes. The Reverend Welles had somehow lost his sandals between the church service and now, but he was unconcerned with the crabs. He prattled along as he walked.

"I am intrigued to see how you will find Tahiti, Sister Whittaker, from a botanical point of view, you see," he said. "Many are disappointed by it. It is a lush climate, you see, but we are a small island, so you will find that there is more abundance here than variety. Sir Joseph Banks most certainly found Tahiti lacking—botanically, I mean. He felt the people were far more interesting than the plants. Perhaps he had a point! We have only two varieties of orchids—Mr. Pike was so sorry to hear of that, though he avidly searched for more of them—and once you learn the palms, which you will do in a snap, there is not much more to discover. There is a tree called *apage*, you see, which will remind you of a gum tree, and it rises to forty feet—but not very magnificent for a woman raised in the deep forests of Pennsylvania, I wager! Ha-ha-ha!"

Alma did not have the energy to tell the Reverend Welles that she had not been raised in a deep forest.

He went on: "There is a lovely sort of laurel called *tamanu*—useful, good. Your furniture is made of it. Impervious to insects, you see. Then a sort of a magnolia, called the *hutu*, which I sent to your good father in 1838. Hibiscus and mimosa are to be found everywhere by the seashore. You will like the *mape* chestnut—perhaps you saw it by the river? I find it the most beautiful tree on the island. The women make their clothing from the bark of a sort of paper-mulberry tree—they call it *tapa*—but now many of them prefer the cotton and calico that the sailors bring."

"I brought calico," Alma murmured sadly. "For the women."

"Oh, they will appreciate that!" the Reverend Welles said breezily, as though he had already forgotten that Alma's belongings had been stolen. "Did you bring paper? Books?"

"I did," Alma said, feeling more mournful by the moment.

"Well, it is difficult here with paper, you will see. The wind, the sand, the salt, the rain, the insects—never was there a climate less conducive to *books*! I have watched all my papers vanish before my eyes, you see!"

As have I, just now, Alma nearly said. She did not think she had ever been this hungry in her life, or this tired.

"I wish I had a Tahitian's *memory*," the Reverend Welles went on. "Then one would have no need for papers! What we keep in libraries, they keep in their minds. I feel such a half-wit, in comparison. The youngest fisherman here knows the names of two hundred stars! What the old ones here know, you could not imagine. I used to keep documents, but it was too discouraging to watch them be eaten away, even as I laid down the words. The ripening climate here produces fruit and flower in abundance, you see, but also mold and rot. It is not a land for scholars! But what is history to us, I ask? So brief is our stay in the world! Why make such a bother to record our flickering lives? If the mosquitoes trouble you too severely in the evenings, you may ask Sister Manu to show you how to burn dried pig dung by your door; it keeps them down a bit. You will find Sister Manu most useful. I used to preach the sermons here, but she enjoys it more than I do, and the natives prefer her sermons to mine, so now she is the preacher. She has no family, and so she tends to the pigs. She feeds them by hand, you see, to encourage them to stay near the settlement. She is wealthy, in her way. She can trade a single piglet for a month of fish and other treasures. The Tahitians value roasted piglet. They used to believe that the smell of flesh draws near the gods and spirits. Of course, some of them still believe that, despite being Christians, ha-ha-ha! In any case, Sister Manu is good to know. She has a fine singing voice. To a European ear, the music of Tahiti wants in every quality that would render it pleasurable, but you may learn to tolerate it with time."

So Sister Manu was *not* the Reverend Welles's wife, Alma thought. Who was his wife, then? Where was his wife?

He kept talking, tirelessly: "If you see lights out on the bay at night, do not be alarmed. It is only the men, gone fishing with lanterns. It is most picturesque. The flying fish are drawn to the light, and they land in the canoes. Some of the boys are able to catch them by hand. I tell you— whatever natural variety is lacking on the land in Tahiti, it is more than made up for by the abundance of wonders at sea! If you like, I will show you the coral gardens tomorrow, out by the reefs. There, you shall witness the Lord's inventiveness most impressively evidenced. Here we are, then—Mr. Pike's house! Now it shall be your house! Or, I should say, your *fare*! In Tahitian, we call a house a *fare*. It is not too soon to begin learning a few words, you see."

Alma repeated the word in her head: *fah-ray*. She committed it to memory. She was exhausted, but even so, Alma Whittaker would have to be far more exhausted than this not to prick up her ears at a new and unfamiliar language. In the dim glow of moonlight, just up a slight slope from the beach, she could see the tiny *fare* hidden under a fretwork of palms. It was not much bigger than the smallest garden shed at White Acre, but it was pleasant enough to look at. If anything, it resembled an English seaside cottage, but much shrunken in scale. A crazy zigzagged path of crushed seashells led from the beach to the door.

"It is a queer path, I know, but the Tahitians made it," said the Reverend Welles with a laugh. "They see nothing advantageous in making a straight path, for even the shortest distances! You will grow accustomed to such marvels as this! But it is good to be a bit off the beach. You are four yards above highest tide, you see."

Four yards. It did not seem like much.

Alma and the Reverend Welles approached the cottage up the crooked path. Alma could see that the purpose of a door was answered by a simple screen of plaited palm fronds, which he pushed open easily. Clearly, there was no lock here—nor had there ever been one. Once inside, he lit the lamp. They stood together in the one small open room, beneath a simple thatched roof. Alma could just barely stand up without hitting her head on the lowest rafter. A lizard skittered across the wall. The floor was dried grass that rustled under Alma's feet. There was a small rough wooden bench with no cushion, but at least it had a back and arms. There was a table with three chairs—one of which was broken and tipped over. It looked like a child's table, in a poor nursery. Curtainless, glassless windows opened on all sides. The final bit of furniture was a small bed—barely bigger than the bench—with a thin pallet slung on top. The pallet appeared to be made from an old canvas sail, stuffed with something or other. The whole room, such as it was, seemed much more suitable to somebody of the Reverend Welles's size than her own.

"Mr. Pike lived as the natives live," he said, "which is to say—he lived in one room only. But if you want partitions, I suppose we could make partitions for you."

Alma could not imagine where one would put a partition in this tiny place. How do you divide nothing into parts?

"You may wish at some point to move back to Papeete, Sister Whittaker. Most do. There is more civilization to be found there in the capital,

I suppose. More vice, as well, and more evil. But there you could find a Chinaman to do your laundry, and that sort of thing. There are all manner of Portuguese and Russians there—all those sorts who fall off whaling boats and never leave. Not that Portuguese and Russians constitute a civilization, but it is more variety of mankind than you will find in our small settlement out here, you see!"

Alma nodded, but she knew she would not be leaving Matavai Bay. This had been Ambrose's banishment; now it would be hers.

"You will find a spot to cook in the back, by the garden," the Reverend Welles went on. "Do not expect much of your garden, although Mr. Pike tried nobly to cultivate it. Everyone tries, but once the pigs and goats have finished their forays, there are not many pumpkins left for us! We can get you a goat, if you would like fresh milk. You can ask Sister Manu."

As though summoned by the sound of her name, Sister Manu appeared at the doorway. She must have been right on their heels. There was almost not enough room for her to enter, with Alma and the Reverend Welles already in the cottage. Alma wasn't sure Sister Manu would even fit through the door, with that wide, flower-covered hat on her head. Somehow, though, they all squeezed in. Sister Manu opened a bundle of cloth and began to lay food out on the tiny table, using banana leaves as plates. It took all of Alma's reserve not to dive into the meal immediately. Sister Manu handed Alma a length of bamboo with a stopper of cork.

"Water for you to *drink*!" Sister Manu said.

"Thank you," said Alma. "You are kind."

They all stared at each other for quite a while after this: Alma exhaustedly, Sister Manu guardedly, the Reverend Welles cheerfully.

Finally, the Reverend Welles bowed his head and said, "We thank you, Lord Jesus and God our Father, for the safe delivery of your servant Sister Whittaker. We ask that you hold her in your special favor. Amen."

Then he and Sister Manu left at last, and Alma plunged into the food with both hands, swallowing it in such quick gulps that she did not pause even for a moment to determine what, exactly, it was.

She awoke in the middle of the night to the taste of warm iron in her mouth. She smelled blood and fur. There was an animal in her room. A mammal. She identified this fact before she even remembered where she was. Her heart beat rapidly as she sought more information. She was not on the ship. She was not in Philadelphia. She was in Tahiti—there, she had oriented herself! She was in Tahiti in the cottage where Ambrose had stayed and where he had died. What was the word for her cottage? *Fare*. She was in her *fare*, and there was an animal in it with her.

She heard a whining noise, high and eerie. She sat up in the tiny, uncomfortable bed and looked around. Enough moonlight shone through the window that she could see it now—the dog who stood in the middle of her room. It was a small dog, maybe twenty pounds. Its ears were back and it was baring its teeth at her. Their eyes fastened on each other. The dog's whine turned to a growl. Alma did not want to fight a dog. Not even a small dog. This thought came to her simply, even calmly. Next to the bed was the short length of bamboo that Sister Manu had given her, filled with fresh water. It was the only thing in reach that might serve as a weapon. She tried to determine whether she could reach for the bamboo without alarming the dog further. No, she most certainly did not want to have a fight with a dog, but if she must fight, she wanted it to be a fair match. She stretched her arm slowly down toward the floor, not taking her eyes off the creature. The dog barked and came nearer. She pulled back her arm. She tried again. The dog barked again, this time with increased anger. There would be no chance for her to find a weapon.

So be it. She was too tired to be afraid.

"What is your complaint with me?" she asked the dog, in a weary tone.

At the sound of her voice, the dog unleashed a great torrent of complaints, barking with such force that his whole body seemed to lift from the floor with every syllable. She stared at him dispassionately. It was the dead of night. She had no lock on her door. She had no pillow for her head. She had lost all her belongings and was sleeping in her filthy traveling dress, with its hems full of hidden coins—all the money she had left to her, now that her belongings had been stolen. She had nothing but a short length of bamboo with which to defend herself, and she could not even reach that. Her house was surrounded by crabs and infested with lizards. And now this: an angry Tahitian dog in her room. She was so exhausted, she nearly felt bored.

"Go away," she told him.

The dog barked louder. She gave up. She turned her back to him, rolled over, and attempted, once more, to find a comfortable arrangement on the thin pallet. He barked and barked. His indignation had no limits. Attack me, then, she thought. She fell asleep to the sound of his outrage.

A few hours later Alma woke again. The light had changed. It was near dawn. Now there was a boy sitting cross-legged in the center of her floor, staring at her. She blinked, and suspected magic: What sorcerer had come and turned a little dog into a little child? The boy had long hair and a solemn face. He looked to be approximately eight years old. He wore no shirt, but Alma was relieved to see that he possessed trousers—although one leg was ripped to a short length, as though he had pulled himself out of a trap and left the remainder of his clothing behind.

The boy jumped to his feet, as if he had been waiting for her to awaken. He approached the bed. She drew back in alarm, but then saw that he was holding something, and, what's more, offering it to her. The object gleamed in the dim morning light, balanced on his palm. It was something slender and brass. He placed it on the edge of her bed. It was the eyepiece to her microscope.

"Oh!" she exclaimed. At the sound of her voice, the boy ran away. The flimsy object that called itself a door swung closed behind him without a sound.

Alma could not fall asleep again after that, but she did not immediately rise, either. She was every bit as weary now as she had been the night before. Who would come to her room next? What sort of a place was this? She must find a means to block the door somehow—but with what? She could move the little table in front of the door at night, but that could easily be shuffled aside. And with windows that were nothing but holes cut in the walls, what good would it do to block the door at all? She fingered the brass eyepiece in her hand with confusion and longing. Where was the rest of her beloved microscope? Who was that child? She should have chased him, to see where he was hiding everything else she owned.

She closed her eyes and listened to the unfamiliar sounds around her. She felt almost as though she could hear the dawn breaking. Most certainly, she could hear the waves just outside her door breaking. The surf sounded disquietingly close. She would prefer to be a bit farther away from the sea. Everything felt too close, too dangerous. A bird, perched on the roof directly over her head, uttered a strange cry. Its call sounded something like: "*Think! Think! Think!*"

As though she ever did anything else!

Alma rose at last, resigned to wakefulness. She wondered where to find a privy, or a spot that might serve as a privy. Last night she had squatted behind the *fare*, but she hoped for a better arrangement nearby. She stepped out the front door and nearly tripped over something. She looked down and saw—sitting right on her doorstep, if one could call it a doorstep— Ambrose's valise, waiting politely for her, unopened and tightly buckled as ever. She knelt down, undid the buckles, and threw it open, then quickly dug through the contents: all the pictures were still there.

Up and down the beach, as far as she could see in the dim morning light, there was not a sign of anyone—neither woman nor man, neither boy nor dog.

"*Think!*" shrieked the bird over her head. "*Think!*"

Chapter Twenty-three

Because time does not object to passing—not even in the strangest and most unfamiliar situations—time passed for Alma in Matavai Bay. Slowly, haltingly, she began to comprehend her new world.

Just as she had in childhood, when first awaking to cognizance, Alma began by studying her house. This did not take long, for her minuscule Tahitian *fare* was not exactly White Acre. There was nothing but the one room, the halfhearted door, the three empty windows, the sticks of crude furniture, and the thatched roof full of lizards. That first morning, Alma searched the house quite thoroughly for some vestige of Ambrose, but nothing existed. She looked for signs of Ambrose even before she began the (completely fruitless) search for her own lost luggage. What had she hoped to find? A message to her, written on a wall? A cache of drawings? Maybe a packet of letters, or a diary that actually revealed something other than inscrutable mystical longings? But there was nothing of him here.

Resigned, she borrowed a broom from Sister Manu and swept clean the cobwebs from the walls. She replaced the old dried grass on the floor with new dried grass. She plumped her mattress and accepted the *fare* as her own. She also accepted, as instructed by the Reverend Welles, the frustrating reality that her belongings would either show up eventually or they would not, and that there was nothing—absolutely nothing—that could be done about it. Though this news was distressing, something about it felt strangely apt, and even just. To be stripped of all that was precious made for a kind of immediate penance. It made her feel somehow closer to Ambrose; Tahiti was where they had both come to lose everything.

Wearing her one remaining dress, then, she continued to explore her environs.

Behind the house was something called a *himaa*, an open oven, where she learned to boil water and cook a limited assortment of foods. Sister Manu taught her how to manage the local fruits and vegetables. Alma did not think the final product of her cooking was meant to taste quite as much like soot or sand as it did, but she persevered, and felt proud that she could feed herself, which—in her entire long life—she had never before had to do. (She was autotrophic, she thought with a rueful smile; how proud Retta Snow would have been!) There was a sorry patch of garden, but not much to be done about it; Ambrose had built his house upon the burning sand, so it was futile even to try. There was nothing to be done about the lizards, either, who scampered across the rafters all night. If anything, they helped to abate mosquitoes, so Alma tried not to mind them. She knew they meant her no harm, though she did wish they would not crawl over her while she slept. She was happy they were not snakes. Tahiti, mercifully, was not snake country.

It was, however, crab country, but Alma soon taught herself not to be bothered by the crabs of all sizes that scuttled around her feet on the beach. They, too, meant her no harm. As soon as they glimpsed her with their waving, stalked eyes, they skimmed off in the other direction in a quick, clicking panic. She took to walking barefoot as soon as she recognized how much safer it was. Tahiti was too hot, too wet, too sandy, and too slippery for shoes. Fortunately, the environs welcomed bare feet; the island did not have even a single thorned plant, and most of the paths were smooth rock or sand.

Alma learned the shape and character of the beach, and the general habits of the tide. She was not a swimmer, but she encouraged herself to wade into the slow, dark water of Matavai Bay a bit deeper every week. She was grateful for the reef, which kept the bay fairly calm.

She learned to bathe in the river in the mornings with the other settlement women, all of whom were as thickset and strong as Alma herself. They were fiends for personal cleanliness, the Tahitians, washing their hair and bodies every day with the foaming sap of the ginger plants along the banks. Alma, who was not accustomed to bathing every day, soon wondered why she had not been doing this her entire life. She learned to ignore the groups of little boys who stood around the river, laughing at the women in their nakedness. There was no point in trying to hide from them; there was no hour of the day or night when the children would not find you.

The Tahitian women did not object to the children's laughter. They seemed far more worried about Alma's wiry, coarse, faded hair, which they fussed over with both sadness and concern. They all had such beautiful hair, which fell in black, billowing sweeps down their backs, and they felt simply terrible for Alma that she did not share this spectacular feature. She felt simply terrible about it herself. One of the first things Alma learned how to convey in Tahitian was an apology for her hair. She wondered if there was any place she could go in the world, ever, where her hair would not be considered a tragedy. She suspected not.

Alma picked up as much Tahitian as she was able, from anybody who would speak to her. She found the people to be warm and helpful, and they encouraged her efforts as a kind of play. She started with the words for the commonest items around Matavai Bay: the trees, the lizards, the fish, the sky, and the sweet little doves called *uuairo* (a word that sounded exactly like their soft, bubbling cry). She moved on to grammar as quickly as she was able. The inhabitants of the mission settlement spoke English at varying levels of proficiency—some were quite fluent, some simply inventive—but Alma, always the linguist, was determined to keep her interactions in Tahitian whenever possible.

But Tahitian, she found, was not a simple language. It sounded to her ears more like birdsong than speech, and she was not musical enough to master it. Alma determined that Tahitian was not even a reliable language. It did not have the sturdy injunctions of Latin or Greek. The people of Matavai Bay were especially kittenish and rascally with words, changing them by the day. Sometimes they mixed in bits of English or French, inventing imaginative new words. The Tahitians loved abstruse puns that Alma could never have comprehended unless her grandparents' grandparents had been born here. Moreover, the people at Matavai Bay spoke differently from the people in Papeete, a mere seven miles away, and *those* people spoke differently from the people in Taravao or Teahupo. You could not trust a sentence to mean the same thing on one side of the island as across it, or to mean the same thing today as it meant yesterday.

Alma studied the people around her carefully, trying to learn the disposition of this curious place. Sister Manu was the most important, for she not only tended the pigs, but policed the entire settlement. She was a strict mistress of protocol, that one, keenly alert to manners and missteps. While everyone at the settlement loved the Reverend Welles, they feared Sister Manu. Sister Manu—whose name meant "bird"—was as tall as Alma, and as heavily muscled as a man. She could have carried Alma on her back. There were not many women about whom one could say *that*.

Sister Manu always wore her broad straw hat, dressed with different fresh flowers every day, but Alma had seen during bath time in the river that Manu's forehead was covered with a hash of blunt white scars. Two or three of the older women had similar mysterious marks on their foreheads, but Manu was scarred in another way besides: she was missing the last phalanx of each of her pinky fingers. It seemed such a strange injury to Alma, so neat and symmetrical. She could not imagine what a person could have been doing, to have lost both pinky tips so tidily. She dared not ask.

Sister Manu was the one who rang the bell for worship every morning and evening, and the people—all eighteen of the settlement's adults— dutifully came. Even Alma tried never to miss religious services at Matavai Bay, for it would have offended Sister Manu, and Alma could not have survived long without her favor. In any case, Alma found that the services were not difficult to sit through; they seldom lasted more than a quarter of an hour, and Sister Manu's sermons in her stubborn English were always entertaining. (If the Lutheran gatherings in Philadelphia had been as simple and diverting as this, Alma thought, she might have become a better Lutheran.) Alma paid close attention and in due course pulled out words and phrases from the dense Tahitian-language chants.

Te rima atua: the hand of God.

Te mau pure atua: the people of God.

As for the boy who had brought Alma her microscope eyepiece the first night, she learned that he was one of a pack of five small boys who roamed the mission settlement with no apparent occupation other than to play ceaselessly until they collapsed with exhaustion onto the sand, and—like dogs—slept where they fell. It took Alma weeks to tell the boys apart.

The one who had shown up in her room and handed her the microscope eyepiece was, she learned, named Hiro. His hair was the longest and he seemed to hold the highest status within the gang. (She later learned that in Tahitian mythology, Hiro was the king of thieves. It amused her that her first encounter with Matavai Bay's little king of thieves was when he returned something that had been stolen from her.) Hiro was the brother of the boy called Makea, although perhaps they were not actual brothers. They also claimed to be brothers with Papeiha and Tinomana and another Makea, but Alma thought this could not possibly be true, because all five boys appeared to be the same age and two of them had the same name. She could not for the life of her determine who their parents might be. There was not the slightest sign that anyone took care of these children but themselves.

There were other children around Matavai Bay, but they approached life far more seriously than the five boys whom Alma came to think of as "the Hiro contingent." These other children came to the mission school for classes in English and reading every afternoon, even if their parents were not residents of the Reverend Welles's settlement. These were little boys with neat, short hair, and little girls with beautiful braids, long dresses, and bright smiles. They took their classes in the church, where they were taught by the bright-faced young woman who had called out to Alma on her first day, "We speak English here!" That woman's name was Etini—"white flowers strewn along the road"—and she spoke English perfectly, with a crisp British accent. It was said she had been personally taught as a child by the Reverend Welles's wife, and now Etini was considered the best English teacher on the entire island.

Alma was impressed by the tidy and disciplined schoolchildren, but she was far more intrigued by the five wild and uneducated boys of the Hiro contingent. She had never before seen children as free as Hiro, Makea, Papeiha, Tinomana, and the other Makea. Tiny lords of liberty, they were, and mirthful ones at that. Like some mythical blend of fish, bird, and monkey, they seemed equally at home in the water, in the trees, and on land. They hung from vines and swung into the river with fearless cheers. They paddled out to the reef on little wooden boards and then, incredibly, they *stood up* on those boards, and sailed across the foaming, billowing, breaking waves. They called this activity *faheei*, and Alma could not imagine the nimbleness and confidence they must have felt to ride the breaking surf with such ease. Back on the beach, they boxed and wrestled each other tirelessly. Another favorite game was when they would build stilts for themselves, cover their bodies with some kind of white powder, prop open their eyelids with twigs, and chase each other across the sand like tall, queer monsters. They also flew the *uo*—a kite made of dried palm fronds. At quieter moments, they played a game like jacks, using small stones instead of jacks. They kept as pets a rotating menagerie of cats, dogs, parrots, and even eels (the eels were bricked up into watery pens in the river; at the sound of the boys' whistles, they would raise their heads up eerily above the surface of the water, ready to be fed bits of fruit by hand). Sometimes the Hiro contingent ate their pets, skinning them and roasting them on a makeshift spit. Eating dog was common practice here. The Reverend Welles told Alma that Tahitian dog was just as tasty as English lamb—but then again, the man had not tasted English lamb in decades, so she was not sure he could be trusted. Alma hoped nobody would eat Roger.

For Roger, Alma had learned, was the name of the little dog that had visited her that first night in her *fare*. Roger did not seem to belong to anyone, but apparently he had been somewhat fond of Ambrose, who had bestowed upon him his dignified, robust name. Sister Etini explained all this to Alma, along with this unsettling bit of advice: "Roger will never bite you, Sister Whittaker, unless you try to feed him."

For the first few weeks of Alma's stay, Roger came to her small room night after night, to bark at her with all his heart. For a long time, she never saw him during the day. Gradually, and with visible reluctance, his indignation wore away, and his episodes of outrage became briefer. One morning, Alma awoke to find Roger sleeping on the floor right next to her bed, which meant that he had entered her house the previous night without barking at all. That seemed significant. At the sound of Alma stirring, Roger growled and ran away, but he was back the next night, and was silent from then on. Inevitably, she did indeed try to feed him, and he did indeed try to bite her. Other than that, they fared well enough together. It was not that Roger became friendly, exactly, but he no longer appeared desirous of removing her throat from her body, and that was an improvement.

Roger was a dreadful-looking dog. He was not only orange and mottled, with an irregularly shaped jaw and a bad limp, but it appeared that something had worked rather relentlessly to chew off a large section of his tail. Also, he was *tuapu'u*—hunchbacked. Still, Alma came to appreciate the dog's presence. Ambrose must have loved him for some reason, she thought, and that intrigued her. She would gaze at the dog for hours and wonder what he knew about her husband—what he had witnessed. His companionship became a comfort. While she could not claim that Roger was protective or loyal toward *her*, he did seem to feel some sort of connection to the house. This made her feel somewhat less afraid to fall asleep alone at night, knowing that he was coming.

This was good, for Alma had abandoned hope for any other measure of security or privacy. There was no gain to be had in even attempting to define boundaries around her home or her few remaining belongings. Adults, children, fauna, weather—at any hour of the day or night, for any reason at all, everybody and everything in Matavai Bay felt quite free to enter Alma's *fare*. They did not always come empty-handed, to be fair. Pieces of her belongings reappeared over time, in bits and fragments. She never knew who brought these items back to her. She never saw it happen. It was as if the island itself were slowly coughing up portions of her swallowed luggage.

In the first week, she recovered some paper, a petticoat, a vial of medicine, a bolt of cloth, a ball of twine, and a hairbrush. She thought, If I wait long enough, it will all be returned. But that was not true, for items were just as likely to vanish as to appear. She did get back her one other travel dress— its hemful of coins amazingly intact—which was a true blessing, though she never recovered any of her spare bonnets. Some of her writing paper found its way back to her, but not much of it. She never again saw her medicine kit, but several glass vials for botanical collection showed up on her doorstep in a neat row. One morning she discovered that a shoe was gone—just one shoe!—though she could not imagine what somebody wanted with just one shoe, while, at the same time, a quite useful set of watercolors had been returned. Another day, she recovered the base of her prized microscope, only to see that somebody had now taken back the eyepiece in exchange. It was as if there were a tide ebbing and flowing in and out of her house, depositing and withdrawing the flotsam of her old life. She had no alternative but to accept it, and to marvel, day after day, at what she found and lost, and then found and lost once more.

Ambrose's valise, however, was never taken from her again. The very morning it was returned to her doorstep, she placed it on the little table inside her *fare*, and there it remained—absolutely untouched, as though guarded by an invisible Polynesian Minotaur. Furthermore, not a single one of the drawings of The Boy ever disappeared. She did not know why this valise and its contents were treated with such reverence, when nothing else was safe at Matavai Bay. She would not have dared to ask anyone, *Why do you not touch this object, or steal these pictures?* But how could she have explained what the drawings were, or what the valise meant to her? All she could do was keep silent, and understand nothing.

Alma's thoughts were on Ambrose at all times. He had left no trace in Tahiti, other than everyone's residual fondness for him, but she sought signs of him ceaselessly. Everything she did, everything she touched, caused her to wonder: Had he done this also? How had he spent his time here? What had he thought of his tiny house, the curious food, the difficult language, the constant sea, the Hiro contingent? Had he loved Tahiti? Or, like Alma, had he found it too alien and peculiar to love? Had he burned under the sun, as Alma now burned on this black sand beach? Had he missed the cool violets and quiet thrushes of home, as Alma did, even as she admired the lush hibiscus and the loud green parrots? Had he been melancholy and sorrowful, or was he full of joy to have discovered Eden? Had he thought of Alma at all when he was here? Or had he forgotten her rapidly, relieved to be free of her discomfiting desires? Had he forgotten her because he fell in love with The Boy? And as for The Boy, where was he now? He wasn't really a *boy*— Alma had to admit this to herself, especially when she studied the drawings again. The figure in them was more of a boy on the brink of manhood. By this time, some two or three years later, he must be a fully grown man. In Alma's mind, though, he was still The Boy, and she never stopped looking for him.

But Alma could find no trace or mention of The Boy at Matavai Bay. She looked for him in the face of every man who came through the settlement, and in the faces of all the fishermen who used the beach. When the Reverend Welles told Alma that Ambrose had taught a native Tahitian the secret to tending vanilla orchids (*little boys, little fingers, little sticks*),

Alma thought, That must be him. But when she went to the plantation to investigate, it wasn't The Boy at all: it was a stout older fellow, with a cast over one eye. Alma took several outings to the vanilla plantation, pretending an interest in the proceedings there, but never saw anyone who remotely resembled The Boy. Every few days or so, she would announce that she was going botanizing, but she would actually return to the capital of Papeete, borrowing a pony from the plantation for the long ride in. Once there, she would walk the streets all day and well into the evening, looking at every passing face. The pony followed behind her—a skeletal, tropical version of Soames, her old childhood friend. She looked for The Boy at the docks, outside the brothels, in the hotels full of fine French colonists, in the new Catholic cathedral, in the market. Sometimes she would see a tall, well-built native man with short hair walking ahead of her, and she would run to him and tap him on the shoulder, ready to ask him any question, merely to make him turn around. At every encounter she was certain: This will be him.

It was never him.

She knew that soon she would need to expand her search, go look for him beyond the environs of Papeete and Matavai Bay, but she wasn't certain how to begin. The island of Tahiti was thirty-five miles long and twelve miles wide, shaped something like a lopsided figure eight. Great stretches of it were difficult or impossible to traverse. Once one left the shaded, sandy road that wound partly around the coastline, the terrain became dauntingly challenging. Terraced plantations of yams crawled up the hills, along with coconut groves and waves of short scrub grass, but then, quite suddenly, there was nothing but tall cliffs and inaccessible jungle. Few people lived in the highlands, Alma was told, except the cliff dwellers—who were nearly mythical, and who had extraordinary capacity as climbers. These people were hunters, not fishermen. Some had never even touched the sea. The cliff-dwelling Tahitians and the coastal Tahitians had always regarded each other warily, and there were boundaries that neither was meant to cross. Perhaps The Boy had been from among the cliff-dwelling tribes? But Ambrose's drawings depicted him at the seaside, carrying a fisherman's nets. Alma could not puzzle it out.

It was also possible that The Boy was a sailor—a hand on a visiting whaling ship. If that was the case, she would never find him. He could be anywhere in the world by now. He could even be dead. But absence of proof—as Alma well knew—was not proof of absence.

She would have to keep looking.

She certainly gleaned no information from within the mission settlement. There was never any wicked gossip about Ambrose—not even at the bathing river, where all the women gossiped so freely. Nobody had made so much as a sidewise comment about the much-missed and much-lamented Mr. Pike. Alma had even gone so far as to ask the Reverend Welles, "Did Mr. Pike have any particular friend when he was here? Somebody he may have cared for more than the others?"

He had merely fixed her with his frank gaze and said, "Mr. Pike was loved by all."

This was on the day they had gone to visit Ambrose's grave. Alma had asked him to take her there, such that she could pay her respects to her father's deceased employee. On a cool and overcast afternoon, they had hiked together all the way to Tahara Hill, where a small English cemetery had been established near the top of the ridge. The Reverend Welles was a most agreeable walking companion, Alma found, for he moved quickly and ably over any terrain, and called out all manner of fascinating information as they strode along.

"When first I came here," he said that day, as they climbed the steep hill, "I tried to determine which of the plants and vegetables here were indigenous to Tahiti, and which had been brought here by ancient settlers and explorers, but it is most vexingly difficult to determine such things, you see. The Tahitians themselves were not much help in this endeavor, for they say that all the plants—even the agricultural plants—were placed here by the gods."

"The Greeks said the same thing," Alma said, between huffs of breath. "They said the grapevines and olive groves had been planted by the gods."

"Yes," said the Reverend Welles. "It seems that people forget what they themselves created, doesn't it? We know now that all the people of Polynesia carry taro root and coconut palm and breadfruit with them when they settle a new island, but they themselves will tell you that the gods planted these things here. Some of their stories are quite fabulous. They say that the breadfruit tree was crafted by the gods to resemble a human body, as a clue to humans, you see—to tell us that the tree is useful. They say that this is why the leaves of the breadfruit resemble hands—to show humans that they should reach toward this tree and find sustenance there. In fact, the Tahitians say that *all* the useful plants on this island resemble parts of the human body, as a message from the gods, you see. This is why coconut oil, which is helpful for headaches, comes from the coconut, which looks like a head. *Mape* chestnuts are said to be good for kidney ailments, for they resemble kidneys themselves, or so I am told. The bright red sap of the *fei* plant is meant to be useful for blood ailments."

"The signature of all things," Alma murmured.

"Yes, yes," the Reverend Welles said. Alma was not sure if he had heard her. "Plantain branches, like these ones here, Sister Whittaker, are also said to be symbolic of the human body. Because of that shape, plantains are used as gestures of peace—as gestures of *humanity*, you might say. You throw one on the ground at the feet of your enemy, to show your surrender or your willingness to consider compromise. It was most useful for me to discover this fact when first I arrived in Tahiti, I tell you! I was tossing about plantain branches in every direction, you see, hoping not to be killed and eaten!"

"Would you have been killed and eaten, truly?" Alma asked.

"Most likely not, though missionaries are always afraid of such things. Do you know, there is a fine and witty example of missionary humor, which asks, 'If a missionary is eaten by a cannibal, and the missionary is digested, and then the cannibal dies, will the missionary's digested body be resurrected on the Day of Judgment? If not, how does Saint Peter know which bits to send to heaven and which bits to hell?' Ha-ha-ha!"

"Did Mr. Pike ever speak to you about that notion you just mentioned a moment ago?" Alma asked, only half listening to the missionary's jest. "About the gods creating plants in various peculiar shapes, I mean, in order to display their uses for the assistance of man?"

"Mr. Pike and I spoke of so many things, Sister Whittaker!"

Alma did not know how to ask for specifics without revealing too much of herself. Why should she have cared so much about her father's employee? She did not want to arouse suspicions. But he was such an odd arrangement of a man! She found him to be candid and inscrutable, all at the same time. Whenever Ambrose was discussed, Alma studiously examined the Reverend Welles's face for clues, but the man was impossible to read. He always gazed upon the world with the same unperturbed countenance. His spirit was unchanging in any situation. He was as constant as a lighthouse. His sincerity was so complete and so perfect, it was almost a mask.

They reached the cemetery at last, with its small bleached headstones, some carved into crosses. The Reverend Welles took Alma straight to Ambrose's grave, which was tidy and marked by a small stone. It was a lovely spot, looking over the entirety of Matavai Bay, and out to the bright sea beyond. Alma had feared that, when she saw the actual grave, she might be unable to contain her emotions, but instead she felt unruffled—even remote. She could sense nothing of Ambrose here. She could not imagine him buried under this stone. She remembered the way he used to sprawl across the grass with his wonderful long legs, speaking to her of marvels and mysteries while she studied her mosses. She felt that he existed more in Philadelphia, more in her memory, than he did here. She could not imagine his bones moldering beneath her feet. Ambrose did not belong to the soil; he belonged to the air. He was barely of the earth when he was *alive*, she thought. How could he possibly be inside the earth now?

"We did not have lumber to spare for a coffin," the Reverend Welles said, "so we wrapped Mr. Pike in native cloth and buried him in the keel of an old canoe, as is sometimes done here. Planking is such difficult work here without the proper tools, you see, and when the natives do get proper lumber, they prefer not to waste it in a grave, so we make do with old canoes. But the natives showed such tender consideration to Mr. Pike's Christian beliefs, you see. They oriented his grave east to west, you see—so he faces the rising sun, as do all Christian churches. They were fond of him, as I have said. I pray he died happy. He was the best of men."

"Did he seem happy when he was here, Brother Welles?"

"He found much to please him about the island, as we all learn to. I am certain he wished for more orchids, you see! Tahiti can be disappointing, as I have said, for those who come to study natural history."

"Did Mr. Pike ever seem troubled to you?" Alma dared to push.

"People come to this island for many reasons, Sister Whittaker. My wife used to say they wash up upon our shores, these jostled strangers, and most of the time they do not know where they have landed! Some of them seem like perfect gentlemen, yet later we discover they were convicts in their countries of origin. On the other hand, you see, some of them were perfect gentlemen in their European lives, but they come here to behave like convicts! One can never know the state of another man's heart."

He had not answered her question.

What of Ambrose? she wanted to ask. What was the state of his heart? She held her tongue.

Then the Reverend Welles said, in his usual bright voice, "You will see the graves of my daughters here, on the other side of that low wall."

The statement knocked Alma into silence. She had not known that Reverend Welles had daughters, much less that they had died here.

"They are just wee graves, you see," he said, "for the girls did not live long. None of them saw their first year. They are Helen, Eleanor, and Laura on the left. Penelope and Theodosia rest beside them, on the right."

The five gravestones were tiny, smaller than bricks. Alma could find no words to offer as comfort. It was the saddest thing she had ever seen.

The Reverend Welles, regarding her stricken face, smiled kindly. "But there is comfort. Their youngest sister, Christina, lives, you see. The Lord gave us one daughter whom we were able to usher into life, and she lives still. She resides in Cornwall, where she is the mother now of three little sons herself. Mrs. Welles stays with her. My wife resides with our living child, you see, while I reside here, to keep company with the departed."

He glanced over Alma's shoulder. "Ah, look!" he said. "The frangipani is in bloom! We shall pick some, and take it back to Sister Manu. She can dress her hat freshly for tonight's service. Won't she enjoy that?"

The Reverend Welles would always bewilder Alma. Never had she met a man so cheerful, so uncomplaining, who had lost so much, and who lived upon—and with—so little. Over time, she discovered that he did not even have a home. There was no *fare* that belonged to him. The man slept in the mission church, on one of the pews. Often he did not even have an *ahu taoto* to sleep under. Like a cat, he was able to doze off anywhere. He had no belongings aside from his Bible—and even that sometimes vanished for weeks on end before somebody would eventually return it. He kept no livestock of his own, nor did he tend a garden. The small canoe that he liked to take out to the coral reef belonged to a fourteen-year-old boy who was generous enough to lend it. There was not a prisoner or a monk or a beggar in the world, Alma thought, who had less than this man.

But it had not always been this way, Alma learned. Francis Welles had been raised in Cornwall, in Falmouth, right on the sea, in a large family of prosperous fishermen. While he did not vouchsafe to Alma the precise details of his youth ("I would not wish you to think less of me, if you knew the acts I committed!"), he indicated that he had been a rough lad. A knock on the head brought him to the Lord—or at least that was how the Reverend Welles reported his conversion experience: a tavern, a brawl, "a bottle to my loaf," and then . . . revelation!

From there, he turned to learning and a life of piety. Soon he married a girl named Edith, the educated and virtuous daughter of a local Methodist minister. Through Edith, he learned to speak, think, and behave in a more dutiful and honorable way. He became fond of books and had "all sorts of high thoughts," as he put it. He undertook ordination. Young and vulnerable to fanciful ideals, the newly Reverend Francis Welles and his wife Edith applied to the London Missionary Society, pleading to be dispatched to the most distant of heathen lands, to introduce the word of the Redeemer abroad. The London Missionary Society welcomed Francis, for it was unusual to find a man of God who was also a rugged and able sailor. For this line of work, one does not want a soft-handed Cambridge gentleman.

The Reverend Francis and Mrs. Welles arrived in Tahiti in 1797, on the first mission ship ever to reach the island, along with fifteen other English evangelicals. At that time, the god of the Tahitians was embodied by a six-foot length of wood, wrapped in *tapa* cloth and red feathers.

"When first we landed," he told Alma, "the natives showed the greatest wonderment at our clothing. One of them pulled off my shoe, and, taking glimpse of my sock, jumped back in fear. He thought I had no toes, you see! Well, soon enough, I had no shoes, for he took them!"

Francis Welles liked the Tahitians immediately. He liked their wit, he said. They were gifted mimics, who loved to tease. It reminded him of the humor and play of the Falmouth docks. He liked how, whenever he wore a straw hat, the children would follow him around shouting, "Your head is thatched! Your head is thatched!"

He liked the Tahitians, yes, but he had no luck converting them.

As he told Alma, "The Bible instructs us, 'As soon as they hear of me, they shall obey me: the strangers shall submit themselves unto me.' Well, Sister Whittaker, perhaps two thousand years ago it was thus! But it was not thus when first we landed in Tahiti! The mildness of these people notwithstanding, you see, they resisted all our efforts at conversion—and most heartily! We could not even sway the children! Mrs. Welles arranged a school for the young ones, but their parents complained, 'Why do you detain my son? What riches will he gain through your God?' The lovely thing about our Tahitian students, you see, was that they were so good and kind and polite. The troublesome thing was that they were not interested in our Lord! They would only laugh at poor Mrs. Welles, when she tried to teach them the catechism."

Life was arduous for the pioneering missionaries. Misery and perplexity dogged their ambitions. Their gospel was met with indifference or mirth. Two of their members died in the first year. The missionaries were blamed for every calamity that struck Tahiti, and credited for none of the godsends. Their belongings either rotted away, or were eaten by rats, or were looted from beneath their noses. Mrs. Welles had brought along only one family treasure from England: a beautiful cuckoo clock that chimed on the hour. The first time the Tahitians heard the clock strike, they fled in terror. The second time, they brought fruit to the clock and bowed before it in awed supplication. The third time, they stole it.

"It is difficult to convert anyone," he said, "who is less intrigued about your god than he is about your scissors! Ha-ha-ha! But how can you fault a body for wanting scissors, when he has never before seen them? Would not a pair of scissors seem a miracle, by comparison to a blade fashioned of shark's teeth?"

For nearly twenty years, Alma learned, neither the Reverend Welles nor anyone else on this island was able to convince a single Tahitian to embrace Christianity. While so many other Polynesian islands came willingly toward the True God, Tahiti remained stubborn. Friendly, but stubborn. The Sandwich Islands, the Navigators, the Gambier Islands, the Hawaiian Islands—even the fearsome Marquesas!—they all embraced Christ, but Tahiti did not. So lovely and gay were the Tahitians, and yet so obdurate. They smiled and laughed and danced, and simply would not let go their hedonism. "Their souls are cast from brass and iron," complained the English.

Weary and frustrated, some of the original group of missionaries returned home to London, where they soon found themselves able to make a handsome living by relating their South Seas adventures in speeches and books. One missionary was driven off Tahiti at spear-point for having attempted to dismantle one of the island's most sacred temples, in order to build a church from the stones. As for those men of God who remained in Tahiti, some drifted into other, simpler pursuits. One became a trader in muskets and gunpowder. One opened a hotel in Papeete, taking up not one but two young native wives to warm his bed. One fellow—Edith Welles's tender young cousin James—simply lost his faith, fell into despair, set off to sea as a common sailor, and was never heard from again.

Dead, banished, lapsed, or exhausted—so it came to pass that all the original missionaries were weeded out, except Francis and Edith Welles, who remained at Matavai Bay. They learned Tahitian and lived without comforts. In their early years, Edith bore the first of their girls—Eleanor, Helen, and Laura—who each died, one after another, in infancy. Still, the Welleses would not relent. They built their little church, largely by themselves. The Reverend Welles figured out how to make whitewash out of bleached coral, by baking it in a rudimentary kiln until it powdered. This made the church look more inviting. He made bellows out of goatskin and bamboo. He attempted to plant a garden with sad, damp, English seeds. ("After three years of effort, we finally managed to produce one strawberry," he told Alma, "and we divided it between ourselves, Mrs. Welles and I. The taste of it was enough to make my good wife weep. I have never managed to grow another one since. Though I have been fairly lucky, at times, with cabbage!") He acquired, and subsequently lost to theft, a herd of four cows. He attempted to grow coffee and tobacco, and failed. Likewise potatoes, wheat, and grapes. The pigs of the mission did well, but no other livestock took to the climate.

Mrs. Welles taught English to the natives of Matavai Bay, whom she found to be quick and clever with language. She taught dozens of local children to read and write. Some of the children moved in with the Welleses. There was a little boy who progressed—in the space of eighteen months—from absolute illiteracy to the ability to read the New Testament without stumbling over a single word, but the boy did not become a Christian. None of them did.

The Reverend Welles told Alma, "They often asked me, the Tahitians, What is the proof of your god? They wanted me to speak of miracles, Sister Whittaker. They wanted evidence of boons for the deserving, you see, or punishments administered to the guilty. I had a man with a missing leg ask me to please instruct my god to grow him a new leg. I told him, 'Where can I find you a new leg, in this country or any other?' Ha-ha-ha! I could not make miracles, you see, so they were not much impressed. I watched a young Tahitian boy stand at the grave of his infant sister and ask, 'Why did God Jesus plant my sister in the ground?' He wanted me to instruct God Jesus to raise that child up from death—but I could not even raise up my own children from death, you see, so how could I perform such a marvel? I could offer no evidence of my savior, Sister Whittaker, but that which my good wife Mrs. Welles calls my 'internal evidence.' I knew then and I know now only what my heart feels to be true, you see—that without the love of our Lord, I am a wretch. This is the only miracle I can evidence, and sufficient miracle it remains for me. For others, perhaps it is not sufficient. I can scarcely fault them, for they cannot see into my heart. They cannot see the darkness that was once there, nor can they see what has replaced it. But to this day, it is the only miracle I have to offer, you see, and it is a humble one."

Also, Alma learned, there was much confusion amid the natives as to what sort of god this was—the god of the Englishman—and where did that god live? For a long while, the natives at Matavai Bay believed that the Bible Reverend Welles carried was, in fact, his god. "They found it most disturbing that I carried my god so casually tucked under my arm, or that I left my god sitting unattended on the table, or that sometimes I lent my god to others! I tried to explain to them that my god was everywhere, you see. They wanted to know, 'Then why can we not see him?' I said, 'Because my god is invisible,' and they said, 'Then how do you not trip over your god?' and I said, 'Verily, my friends, sometimes I do!'"

The London Missionary Society sent nothing in the way of assistance. For nearly ten years, the Reverend Welles did not hear from London at all—no instructions, no aid, no encouragement. He took his religion into his own hands. For one thing, he commenced with baptizing anyone who wanted to be baptized. This was much at odds with the guidelines of the London Missionary Society, which insisted that nobody receive baptism until it was *quite certain* they had renounced their old idols and embraced the True Redeemer. But the Tahitians *wanted* to be baptized, because it was so entertaining—while at the same time wishing to maintain their old beliefs. The Reverend Welles relented. He baptized hundreds of nonbelievers, and half-believers, too.

"Who am I to stop a man from receiving baptism?" he asked, to Alma's amazement. "Mrs. Welles did not approve, I must say. She believed that potential Christians should be put to the strictest test of sincerity before baptism, you see. But to me, this felt like an Inquisition! She often reminded me that our colleagues in London wished us to enforce a uniformity of faith. But there does not even exist a uniformity of faith between me and Mrs. Welles! As I frequently said to my good wife, 'Dear Edith, did we come all this great distance only to become Spaniards?' If a man wants a dunking in the river, I shall give him a dunking in the river! If a man is ever to come to the Lord, you see, it shall be through the will of the Lord—not through anything that I do or do not do. So what is the harm of a baptism? The man comes out of the river a bit cleaner than he went in, and perhaps a bit closer to heaven, too."

In some cases, the Reverend Welles confessed, he baptized people several times a year, or dozens of times in a row. He simply could not see the harm in it.

Over the next few years, the Welleses had two more daughters: Penelope and Theodosia. They, too, died in infancy, and were laid to rest on the hill, beside their sisters.

New missionaries arrived in Tahiti. They tended to stay away from Matavai Bay, and from the Reverend Welles's dangerously liberal notions. These new missionaries were firmer with the natives. They established codes of law against adultery and polygamy, against trespass, Sabbath-breaking, theft, infanticide, and Roman Catholicism. Meanwhile, Francis Welles drifted even further from orthodox missionary practices. In 1810, he translated his Bible into Tahitian without first securing approval from London. "I did not translate the entire Bible, you see, but only the bits I thought the Tahitians might enjoy. My version is far briefer than the Bible with which you are familiar, Sister Whittaker. I left out any mention of Satan, for instance. I've come to feel it is best not to discuss Satan overtly, you see, for the more the Tahitians hear about the Prince of Darkness, the more respect and intrigue they feel toward him. I have seen a young married woman kneeling in my own church, praying most earnestly for Satan to please send her a boy as her firstborn. When I tried to correct her from this sad direction, she said, 'But I wish to earn the favor of the one god whom all the Christians fear!' So I desist from discussing Satan anymore. One must be adaptive, Miss Whittaker. One must be adaptive!"

The London Missionary Society eventually heard about these adaptations and, much displeased, sent word that the Welleses were to stop preaching and return home to England immediately. But the London Missionary Society was quite on the other side of the world, so how could they enforce anything? Meanwhile, the Reverend Welles already *had* stopped preaching, and was allowing the woman named Sister Manu to deliver sermons, despite the fact that she had not yet *quite* renounced all her other gods. But she liked Jesus Christ, and she spoke of him most eloquently. News of this angered London further.

"But I simply cannot answer to the London Missionary Society," he told Alma, almost apologetically. "Their law is left behind in England, you see. They have no idea how things are. Here, I can answer only to the Author of all our mercies, and I have always believed that the Author of all our mercies is fond of Sister Manu."

Still, not a single Tahitian had embraced Christianity fully until 1815, when the king of Tahiti—King Pōmare—sent all his holy idols to a British missionary in Papeete, along with a letter, in English, saying that he wished for his old gods to be committed to flames: he wanted to become a Christian at last. Pōmare hoped his decision would save his people, as Tahiti was in much distress. With every new ship came new plagues. Whole families were dying—from measles, from smallpox, from the dreadful diseases of prostitution. Where Captain Cook had estimated the Tahitian population at two hundred thousand souls in 1772, it had plunged to some eight thousand by 1815. Nobody was exempt from illness—not the high chiefs or the landowners or the lowborn. The king's own son died of consumption.

The Tahitians, as a result, began to doubt their gods. When death visits so many homes, all certainties are questioned. As maladies spread, so spread the rumors that the God of the Englishmen was punishing the Tahitians for having rejected His son Jesus Christ. This fear readied the Tahitians for the Lord, and King Pōmare was the first to convert. His initial act as a Christian was to prepare a feast and to eat the food in front of everyone without first making an offering to the old gods. Crowds gathered around their king in panic, certain he would be struck dead by the angry deities before their eyes. He was not struck dead.

After that, they all converted. Tahiti, weakened, humiliated, and decimated, became Christian at last.

"Weren't we fortunate?" Reverend Welles said to Alma. "Weren't we fortunate, indeed?"

He said this in the same sunny tone with which he always spoke. This was the puzzling thing about the Reverend Welles. Alma found it impossible to comprehend what, if anything, lay behind that eternal good cheer. Was he a cynic? Was he a heretic? Was he a simpleton? Was his innocence practiced or natural? One could never tell from his face, which was perpetually bathed in the clear light of ingenuousness. He had a face so open it would shame the suspicious, the greedy, the cruel. It was a face that would shame a liar. It was a face that sometimes shamed Alma, for she had never been candid with him about her own history or motives. Sometimes she wanted to reach down and take his small hand in her giant one, and— forgoing their respectable titles of Brother Welles and Sister Whittaker—to say to him simply, "I have not been forthright with you, Francis. Let me tell you my entire story. Let me tell you about my husband and our unnatural marriage. Please help me to understand who Ambrose was. Please tell me what you knew about him, and please tell me what you know about The Boy."

But she did not. He was a minister of the Lord and an honorable, married Christian. How could she speak to him of such things?

The Reverend Welles told Alma his entire story, though, and held little back. He told her that, only a few years after King Pōmare's conversion, he and Mrs. Welles, quite unexpectedly, had another baby girl. This time, the infant lived. Mrs. Welles saw it as a sign of the Lord's approval—that the Welleses had helped to Christianize Tahiti. As such, they named the child Christina. During this time, the family was living in the nicest cottage in the settlement, right next to the church, in the very cottage where Sister Manu now lived, and happy they were indeed. Mrs. Welles and her daughter grew snapdragons and larkspurs, and they made a right little English garden of the place. The girl learned to swim before she could walk, like any other island child.

"Christina was my joy and my reward," said the Reverend Welles. "But

Chapter Twenty-four

October arrived.

The island entered the season the Tahitians call *Hia'ia*—the season of cravings, when breadfruit is difficult to find and the people sometimes go hungry. There was no hunger at Matavai Bay, thankfully. There was no abundance, to be sure, but neither did anyone starve. Fish and taro root took care of that.

Oh, taro root! Tedious, tasteless taro root! Pounded and mashed, boiled and slippery, baked over coals, rolled into damp little balls called *poi*, and used for everything from breakfast to communion to pig food. The monotony of taro root was sometimes interrupted by the addition of tiny bananas to the menu—sweet and wonderful bananas that could nearly be swallowed whole—but even these were now difficult to come by. Alma looked at the pigs longingly, but Sister Manu, it appeared, was saving them for another day, for a hungrier day. So there was no pork to be enjoyed, simply taro root at every meal, and sometimes, if one was lucky, a good-sized fish. Alma would have given anything to have a day without taro root—but a day without taro root meant a day without food. She began to understand why the Reverend Welles had given up on eating altogether.

The days were quiet, hot, and still. Everyone grew listless and lazy. Roger the dog dug a hole in Alma's garden and slept there more or less all day long, tongue hanging out. Bald chickens scratched for food, gave up, and squatted in the shade, discouraged. Even the Hiro contingent—those most active of little lads—dozed all afternoon in the shade, like old dogs. Sometimes they stirred themselves to lackadaisical employments. Hiro had got hold of an ax head, which he hung from a rope and banged on with a rock, as a gong. One of the Makeas beat on an old barrel hoop with a stone. It was a kind of music they were making, Alma supposed, but to her it sounded uninspired and weary. All of Tahiti was bored and tired.

In her father's time, this place had been lit up by the torches of war and lust. The beautiful young Tahitian men and women had danced so obscenely and wildly around fires on this very beach that Henry Whittaker—young and unformed—had needed to turn his head away in alarm. Now it was all dullness. The missionaries, the French, and the whaling ships, with their sermons and bureaucracy and diseases, had driven the devil out of Tahiti. The mighty warriors had all died. Now there were just these lazy children napping in the shade, clanging on ax heads and barrel hoops as a barely sufficient means of diversion. What were the young to do with their wildness anymore?

Alma continued to search for The Boy, taking longer and longer walks, alone, with Roger the dog, or with the unnamed skinny pony. She explored the little villages and settlements around the shoreline of the island in both directions from Matavai Bay. She saw all sorts of men and boys. She saw some handsome youths, yes, with the noble forms that the early European visitors had so admired, but she also saw young men with severe elephantiasis of the legs, and boys with scrofula in their eyes from the venereal diseases of their mothers. She saw children bent and twisted with tuberculosis of the spine. She saw youngsters who ought to have been comely, but were marked by smallpox and measles. She found nearly empty villages, vacated over the years by illness and death. She saw mission settlements considerably more strict than Matavai Bay. She sometimes even attended church services at these other missions, where nobody chanted in the Tahitian language; instead, the people sang anodyne Presbyterian hymns in heavy accents. She did not see The Boy in any of these congregations. She passed tired laborers, lost rovers, quiet fishermen. She saw one quite old man who sat in the baking sun, playing the Tahitian flute in the traditional way, by blowing into it with one nostril—a sound so melancholy that it caused Alma's lungs to ache with nostalgia for her own home. But still, she never saw The Boy.

Her searches were fruitless, her census came up empty every day, but she was always glad to return to Matavai Bay and the routines of the mission. She was always grateful when the Reverend Welles invited her to join him in the coral gardens. Alma realized that his coral gardens were something akin to her own moss beds back at White Acre—something rich and slow-growing that could be studied for years on end, as a means of passing the decades without collapsing into loneliness. She much enjoyed the conversations on their excursions to the reef. He had asked Sister Manu to weave for Alma a pair of reef sandals just like his own, of thickly knotted pandanus fronds, so she could walk along the sharp coral without cutting her feet. He showed Alma the circus show of sponges, anemones, and corals—all the absorbing beauty of the shallow, clear tropical waters. He taught her the names of the colorful fish, and told her stories about Tahiti. He never once asked her questions about her own life. This brought her relief; she did not have to lie to him.

Alma also grew fond of the little church at Matavai Bay. The structure was decidedly absent of riches or glory (Alma saw far finer churches elsewhere across the island), but she always enjoyed Sister Manu's short, emphatic, inventive sermons. She learned from the Reverend Welles that—to the Tahitian mind—there were elements of familiarity about the story of Jesus, and these strands of familiarity had helped the first missionaries introduce Christ to the natives. In Tahiti, the people believed that the world was divided into the *pô* and the *ao*, the darkness and the light. Their great lord Taroa, the creator, was born in the *pô*—born at night, born into darkness. The missionaries, once they learned of this mythology, explained to the Tahitians that Jesus Christ, too, had been born in the *pô*—born into the night, sprung from the darkness and suffering. This had captured the attention of the Tahitians. It was a dangerous and mighty destiny to be born at night. The *pô* was the world of the dead, the incomprehensible and the frightful. The *pô* was fetid and decayed and terrifying. Our Lord, taught the Englishmen, came to lead mankind out of the *pô* and into the light.

This all made a certain amount of sense to the Tahitians. At the very least, it caused them to admire Christ, since the boundary between the *pô* and the *ao* was dangerous territory, and only a notably brave soul would cross from one world to the other. The *pô* and the *ao* were akin to heaven and hell, the Reverend Welles explained to Alma, but there was more intercourse between them, and in the places where they mixed, things became demented. The Tahitians had never stopped fearing the *pô*.

"When they think I am not looking," he said, "they still make offerings to those gods who live in the *pô*. They make these offerings, you see, not because they honor or love those gods of darkness, but to bribe them into staying in the world of ghosts, to keep them far away from the world of the light. The *pô* is a most difficult notion to defeat, you see. The *pô* does not cease to exist in the mind of the Tahitian, simply because daytime has arrived."

"Does Sister Manu believe in the *pô*?" Alma asked.

"Absolutely not," said the Reverend Welles, imperturbable as always. "She is a perfect Christian, as you know. But she respects the *pô*, you see."

"Does she believe in ghosts, then?" Alma pushed on.

"Certainly not," said the Reverend Welles mildly. "That would be unchristian of her. But she does not *like* ghosts, either, and she does not want them coming around the settlement, so sometimes she has no choice but to make them offerings, you see, to keep them away."

"So she *does* believe in ghosts," said Alma.

"Of course she doesn't," corrected the Reverend Welles. "She simply manages them, you see. You will find that there are certain parts of this island, too, that Sister Manu does not approve of anyone in our settlement visiting. In the highest and most inaccessible places of Tahiti, you see, it is said that a person can walk into a bank of fog and dissolve forever, straight back into the *pô*."

"But does Sister Manu truly believe that could happen?" Alma asked. "That a person could dissolve?"

"Not at all," said the Reverend Welles cheerfully. "But she disapproves of it most heartily."

Alma wondered: Had The Boy simply vanished away into the *pô*? Had Ambrose?

———

Alma heard nothing from the outside world. No letters came to her in Tahiti, although she frequently wrote home to Prudence and Hanneke, and sometimes even to George Hawkes. She diligently sent her letters away on whaling ships, knowing that the likelihood of their ever reaching Philadelphia was slim. She had learned that sometimes the Reverend Welles did not hear from his wife and daughter in Cornwall for two years at a time. Sometimes, when letters did arrive, they were waterlogged and unreadable after the long voyage at sea. This felt more tragic to Alma than never hearing from one's family at all, but her friend accepted it as he accepted all vexations: with calm repose.

Alma was lonely, and the heat was insufferable—no cooler at night than during the day. Alma's little house became an airless oven. She awoke one night with a man's voice whispering straight into her ear, *"Listen!"* But when she sat up, no one was in the room—none of the Hiro contingent, and not Roger the dog, either. There was not even a trace of wind. She stepped outside, her heart beating strongly. Nobody was there. She saw that Matavai Bay had become, in the hushed and balmy night, as smooth as a mirror. The entire canopy of stars above her was reflected perfectly in the water, as though there were two heavens now: one above, one below. The silence and purity of this was formidable. The beach felt heavy with presences.

Had Ambrose ever seen such a thing while he was here? Two heavens, in one night? Had he ever felt this dread and wonderment, this sense of both loneliness and presence? Was he the one who had just awoken her, with that voice in her ear? She tried to recall if it had sounded like Ambrose's voice, but she could not say for sure. Would she even know Ambrose's voice anymore, if she heard it?

It would have been precisely like Ambrose, though, to wake her up and encourage her to *listen*. Certainly, yes. If ever a dead man would try to speak to the living, it would be Ambrose Pike—he, with all his lofty fancies of the metaphysical and the miraculous. He had even halfway convinced Alma herself of miracles, and she was not susceptible to such beliefs. Had they not seemed like sorcerers, that night in the binding closet—speaking to each other without words, speaking through the soles of their feet and the palms of their hands? He had wanted to sleep beside her, he'd said, so he could listen to her thoughts. She had wanted to sleep beside him so that she could fornicate at last, put a man's member inside her mouth—but he had merely wanted to listen to her thoughts. Why could she not have allowed him to simply listen? Why could he not have allowed her to reach for him?

Had he ever thought of her, even once, when he was here in Tahiti?

Perhaps he was attempting to send messages to her now, but the breach was too wide. Maybe the words grew soggy and indecipherable across the great gulf between death and earth—just like those sad, ruined letters that the Reverend Welles sometimes received from his wife in England.

"Who *were* you?" Alma asked Ambrose in the leaden night, looking across the silent, reflective bay. Her voice on the empty beach was so loud that it startled her. She listened for an answer until her ears ached, but she heard nothing. There was not so much as a tiny wave lapping the beach. The water might as well have been molten pewter, and the air, too.

"Where are you now, Ambrose?" she asked, more quietly this time.

Not a sound.

"Show me where I can find The Boy," she requested, in a low whisper.

Ambrose did not answer.

Matavai Bay did not answer.

The sky did not answer.

She was blowing on cold embers; nothing was here.

Alma sat down and waited. She thought of the story the Reverend Welles had told her of Taroa, the original god of the Tahitians. Taroa, the creator. Taroa, born in a seashell. Taroa lay silently for countless ages as the only thing living in the universe. The world was so empty that when he called out across the darkness, there was not even an echo. He nearly died of loneliness. Out of that inestimable solitude and emptiness, Taroa brought forth our world.

Alma lay back on the sand and shut her eyes. It was more comfortable out here than on her mattress in her stuffy *fare*. She did not mind the crabs, who tottered and skittered busily around her. They, inside their shells, were the only things moving on the beach, the only things alive in the universe. She waited on that small sliver of earth between the two heavens until the sun rose and all the stars vanished from both the sky and the sea, but still nobody told her anything.

Then Christmas came, and with it the rainy season. The rain brought relief from the infernal heat, but it also brought snails of amazing size, and damp patches of mold that grew in the folds of Alma's increasingly shabby skirts. The black sand beach of Matavai Bay grew sodden as pudding. Drenching rainstorms kept Alma in her house all day, where she could scarcely hear her own thoughts over the thundering water on her roof. Nature increasingly took over her tiny living space. The lizard population in Alma's ceiling tripled overnight—a near-biblical pestilence—and they left thick drops of excrement and of half-digested insects throughout the *fare*. The one shoe that Alma had left in the world sprouted mushrooms within its festering depths. She hung her bunches of bananas from the rafters, to keep wet and insistent rats from absconding with them.

Roger the dog showed up one night, as per his usual evening patrol, and then stayed for days; he simply did not have the heart to face down the rain. Alma wished he would take on the rats, but he did not seem to have the heart for that, either. Roger would still not allow Alma to feed him by hand without snapping at her, but he would now sometimes share her food if she put it on the floor for him and turned her back. Sometimes he permitted her to stroke his head while he dozed.

Storms came in irregularly timed onslaughts. One could hear the storms building from far across the sea—steady roaring gales from the southwest that grew louder and louder, like an oncoming train. If the storm promised to be unusually severe, sea urchins would crawl out of the bay, seeking higher, safer ground. Sometimes they took shelter in Alma's house: another reason to watch where she stepped. Rain came like a spray of arrows. The river at the other end of the beach churned with mud, and the surface of the bay boiled and spat. As the storm grew heavier, Alma would watch as her world closed in on her. Fog and darkness would approach from the sea. First the horizon would disappear, then the island of Moorea in the distance would vanish, then the reef was gone, then the beach, and then she and Roger would be all alone in the mist. The world was now as small as Alma's tiny and not particularly waterproof house. The wind blew sideways, the thunder bellowed frightfully, and the rain attacked with full force.

Then the rain would stop for a spell and the blistering sun would return—sudden, brilliant, stunning—though never long enough that Alma could properly dry out her sleeping pallet. Steam rose off the sand in billowing waves. Currents of humid wind swept down the mountainside. The air across the beach snapped and shimmied, like a bedsheet shaken out—as though the beach itself were shaking off the violence that had just been visited upon it. Then a humid calm would prevail, for a few hours or a few days, until another storm rolled in.

These were days to miss a library and a vast, dry, warm mansion. Alma might have fallen into terrible despair during the rainy season in Tahiti, but for one delightful discovery: the children of Matavai Bay loved the rain. The Hiro contingent loved it most of all—and why wouldn't they? For this was the season of mudslides and puddle-splashing and dangerous rides through the wild torrential currents of the now-swollen river. The five little boys turned into five otters, not merely undaunted by the wet, but delighted by it. All the indolence they had demonstrated during the hot and dry season of cravings was now washed away, replaced by vivid, sudden *life*. The Hiro contingent were like mosses, Alma realized; they might dry out and go limp in the heat, but they could be revived instantly by a good soaking. Resurrection engines themselves, were these extraordinary children! They had such purpose and vigor and ebullience as they sprang back to action in this newly soaked world that it caused Alma to think back to her own childhood. The rain and mud had never stopped her from exploring, either. This recollection raised a sharp and sudden question: So why was she cowering inside her house now? She had never avoided inclement weather as a girl, so why avoid it now, as an adult? If there was no place to shelter on this island where a person could stay dry, then why not simply get wet? This question provoked Alma to another sudden question: Why had she not enlisted the help of the Hiro contingent in her search for The Boy? Who better to find a missing Tahitian youth than other Tahitian youth?

Upon these realizations, Alma ran out of her house and hailed down those five wild boys, who—at that moment—were throwing mud at each other with a tremendous sense of purpose. They came running over to Alma as one slippery, muddy, laughing mass. It amused them to see the white lady standing on their beach in the middle of a rainstorm in her soggy dress, getting drenched before their eyes. It was good entertainment, and it cost them nothing.

Alma drew the boys near and spoke to them in a mixture of Tahitian, English, and passionate hand gestures. Later, she would not remember quite how she managed to present the idea, but her central message had been this: *'Tis the season for adventure, lads!* She asked them if they knew the places in the center of the island where Sister Manu did not like people of the settlement to go. Did they know *all* of the forbidden places, where the cliff people dwelled, and where the most remote heathen villages could be found? Would they like to take Sister Whittaker there, on some grand adventures?

Would they? Why, of course they would! It was such a diverting notion that they started off that very day. In fact, they started off immediately, and Alma followed them without hesitation. Without shoes, without maps, without food, without—heaven forfend—*umbrellas*, the boys led Alma straight up into the hills beyond the mission settlement, far from the safe little coastal villages she had already explored on her own. Straight up they went, into the fog, into the rain clouds, into the jungle peaks that Alma had first seen from the deck of the *Elliot*, and which had appeared so fearsome and alien to her at the time. Up they went—and not only on this day, either, but every single day for the next month. Each day, they explored ever more remote trails and ever more wild destinations, often in the driving rain, and always with Alma Whittaker on their heels.

At first Alma worried she would not be able to keep up with them, but soon enough she realized two things: that her years of botanical collecting had rendered her exceptionally fit, and that these children were rather sweetly considerate of their guest's limitations. They slowed down for Alma at particularly perilous spots, and did not ask her to leap across deep crevasses as they did, or scale wet cliffs by hand, as they could with easy proficiency. Sometimes the Hiro contingent got behind her on a particularly steep climb and pushed her up rather ignobly, with their hands on her broad bottom, but Alma didn't mind: they were merely trying to help. They were generous with her. They cheered when she made ascents, and if night fell while they were still deep in the jungle, they held her hands as they guided her back toward the safety of the mission. On these dark walks, they taught her warrior chants in Tahitian—the songs that men sing, to summon courage in the face of danger.

The Tahitians were known across the South Seas as deft climbers and fearless hikers (Alma had heard of islanders who could march thirty miles a day through this inaccessible terrain without faltering), but Alma was not one to falter, either—not when she was on a hunt, and she felt strongly that this was the hunt of her life. This was her best chance to find The Boy. If he was still anywhere on this island, these tireless children would track him down.

Alma's increasingly long absences from the mission did not go unnoticed.

When sweet Sister Etini asked Alma at last, with a worried face, where she was spending her days, Alma said simply, "I am hunting for mosses, with the help of your five most able-bodied young naturalists!"

Nobody doubted her, for it was the perfect season for moss. Alma, indeed, spotted all manner of intriguing bryophytes on the stones and trees that they passed, but she did not pause to look closely. The mosses would always be there; she was looking for something more ephemeral, more urgent: a man. A man who knew secrets. To find him, she had to move in Human Time.

The boys, for their part, loved this unexpected game of leading the peculiar old lady all over Tahiti, to see all that was forbidden and to meet the most remote of peoples. They took Alma to abandoned temples and to sinister-looking caves, where human bones could still be glimpsed in the corners. There were sometimes living Tahitians haunting these grim locales, too, but The Boy was never among them. They took her to a small settlement on the banks of Lake Maeva, where the women still dressed in grass skirts, and where the men had faces covered with macabre tattoos, but The Boy was not there, either. The Boy was not in the company of the hunters they passed on these slippery trails, either, nor on the slopes of Mount Orohena, nor Mount Aorii, nor in the long volcanic tunnels. The Hiro contingent took her to an emerald ridge on the top of the world, so high that it seemed to bisect the very sky—for it was raining on one side of the ridge, but sunny on the other. Alma stood on this precarious peak with darkness to her left and brightness to her right, but even here—at the highest imaginable vantage point, at the collision of weather itself, at the intersection of the *pô* and the *ao*—The Boy was nowhere to be seen.

Because they were clever, the children eventually gleaned that Alma was looking for something, but it was Hiro—always the cleverest—who realized she was looking for some*body.*

"He not here?" Hiro asked Alma with concern, at the end of each day. Hiro had taken to speaking English, and fancied himself quite supreme at it.

Alma never confirmed she was looking for a person, but she never denied it, either.

"We find he tomorrow!" Hiro would swear every day, but January passed and February passed and still Alma did not find The Boy.

"We find he next sabbath!" Hiro promised—for "sabbath" was the local term for "a week." But four more Sabbaths passed, and never did Alma find The Boy. Now it was April already. Hiro began to grow concerned and morose. He could think of nowhere new to take Alma on their wild jaunts around the island. This was no longer an amusing diversion; this had clearly become a serious campaign, and Hiro knew he was failing at it. The other members of the contingent, sensing Hiro's heavy spirits, lost their joy as well. This was when Alma decided to unshoulder the five boys of their responsibilities. They were too young to be carrying the burden of *her* burden; she would not see them weighted with by worry and responsibility, just to chase down a phantom figure on her behalf.

Alma released the Hiro contingent from the game and never went hiking with them again. As thanks, she gave each of the five boys a piece of her precious microscope—which they themselves had returned to her *nearly* intact over the last several months—and she shook their hands. Speaking in Tahitian, she told them they were the greatest warriors who had ever lived. She thanked them for their courageous tour of the known world. She told them she had found all that she needed to find. Then she sent them off on their way, to recommence their previous career of constant, directionless play.

The rainy season ended. Alma had been in Tahiti for nearly a year. She cleared the moldering grass off the floor of her house, and brought in new grass once more. She restuffed her rotting mattress with dry straw. She watched the lizard population diminish as the days grew brighter and crisper. She made a new broom and swept the walls free of cobwebs. One morning, overcome by a need to refresh her sense of mission, she opened Ambrose's valise to look yet again at the drawings of The Boy, only to find that—over the course of the rainy season—they had been utterly consumed by mold. She tried to separate the pages one from the other, but they dissolved in her hands into pasty green morsels. Some sort of moth had been at the drawings, too, and had made a meal of the crumbs. She could not salvage any of it. She could not see a trace of The Boy's face anymore, nor the beautiful lines made by Ambrose's hand. The island had eaten the only remaining evidence of her inexplicable husband and his incomprehensible, chimeric muse.

The disintegration of the drawings felt like another death to Alma: now, even the phantom was gone. It made her wish to weep, and most certainly made her begin doubting her judgment. She had seen so many faces in Tahiti over the previous ten months, but now she wondered whether she truly could have identified The Boy at all, even if he had been standing in front of her. Perhaps she had seen him, after all? Mightn't he have been one of those young men at the wharf in Papeete, on the first day she'd arrived? Mightn't she have walked past him, any number of times? Mightn't he possibly even live here at the settlement, and she had simply grown immune to his face? She had nothing to check her memory against anymore. The Boy had barely existed, and now he did not exist at all. She closed the valise as though closing the lid of a coffin.

Alma could not remain in Tahiti. She knew this now without a doubt. She ought never to have come at all. What an awful lot of energy and resolve and *expense* it had required to get herself to this island of riddles, and now she was stranded, and for no good reason. Worse, she had become a burden to this small settlement of honest souls, whose food she had eaten, whose resources she had strained, whose children she had deputized for her own irresponsible purposes. What a fine state of affairs, was this! Alma felt she had fully lost the thread of her life's purpose, whatever flimsy thread it had ever been. She had interrupted her dull but honorable study of mosses to advance this feeble search for a ghost—or, rather, *two* ghosts: for Ambrose and The Boy, both. And for what? She knew no more about Ambrose now than she had known before she arrived here. All reports in Tahiti declared her husband to have been precisely the man he'd always seemed: a gentle virtuous soul, incapable of malfeasance, too good for this world.

It was beginning to dawn upon her that, very possibly, The Boy may never have existed at all. Otherwise Alma would have found him by now, or somebody would have spoken of him—even if in the most roundabout manner. Ambrose must have invented him. This idea was sadder than anything else Alma could have imagined. The Boy had been the figment of a lonely man with an unsound mind. Ambrose had so longed for a companion, he'd drawn himself one. Through his conjuring of a friend—a beautiful phantom lover—he had found the spiritual marriage for which he'd always longed. It made a certain sense. Ambrose's mind had never been steady, not even under the best of circumstances! This was a man whose dearest friend had committed him to a hospital for the insane, and who had believed that he could see God's fingerprints pressed into the botanical. Ambrose was a man who saw angels in orchids, and who once believed he was an angel himself—to think of it! She had come halfway around the world, looking for a wraith concocted from a lonely man's fragile and demented imagination.

It was a simple story, yet she had complicated it with her futile investigations. Perhaps she had wished for the tale to be more sinister, if only to render her own story more tragic. Perhaps she had wished Ambrose to be guilty of abominable things, of pederasty and depravity, such that she could despise him, rather than long for him. Perhaps she had wished to find evidence not of one Boy here in Tahiti, but of *many* boys—a throng of catamites, whom Ambrose had violated and ruined, one after the other. But there was no evidence of any such thing. The truth was merely this: Alma had been foolish and libidinous enough to marry an innocent young man possessed of faulty sanity. When that young man disappointed her, she had been cruel and angry enough to exile him here to the South Seas, where he had died lonely and unhinged, adrift in fantasies, lost in a hopeless little settlement governed—if one could even call it governance!—by a guileless, ineffectual old missionary.

As for why Ambrose's valise and his drawings had remained untouched (except by nature) in Alma's unguarded *fare* in Tahiti for nearly a year, when all of her other possessions had been borrowed, pilfered, picked apart, or ransacked . . . well, she simply did not have the imagination to solve that mystery. What's more, she did not have the remaining will to contend with yet another impossible question.

There was nothing more to be learned here.

She could find no inducement to stay. She would need to assemble a plan for the remaining years of her life. She had been impulsive and misguided, but she would leave on the next whaling ship heading north, and find someplace to live. She knew only that she must not go back to Philadelphia. She had relinquished White Acre and could never return there; it would be unfair to Prudence, who had the right to take possession of the estate without Alma hovering about as a nuisance. In any case, it would be a humiliation to return home. She would need to begin anew. She would also need to find a way to support herself. She would send word tomorrow to Papeete that she was looking for a berth on a good ship with a respectable captain who had heard of Dick Yancey.

She was not at peace, but at least she was decided.

Chapter Twenty-five

Four days later Alma awoke at dawn to joyous shouting from the Hiro contingent. She stepped outside her *fare* to discover the source of the commotion. Her five wild little boys were running up and down the beach, turning flips and somersaults in the early morning light, shouting in enthusiastic Tahitian. When Hiro saw her, he ran up the zigzagged pathway to her door with wild speed.

"Tomorrow morning is here!" he shouted. His eyes were blazing with excitement, such as she had never before seen, even in this quite excitable child.

Baffled, Alma took his arm, trying to slow him down and make sense of him.

"What are you saying, Hiro?" she asked him.

"Tomorrow morning is here!" he shouted again, jumping up and down as he spoke, unable to contain himself.

"Tell me in Tahitian," she commanded, in Tahitian.

"*Teie o tomorrow morning!*" he shouted back, which was merely the same nonsense in Tahitian as it was in English: "Tomorrow morning is here."

Alma looked up and saw a crowd gathering on the beach—everyone from the mission, as well as people from the nearby villages. All were as excited as the little boys. She saw the Reverend Welles running toward the shore with his funny, crooked gait. She saw Sister Manu running, and Sister Etini, and the local fishermen, too.

"Look!" said Hiro, directing Alma's eyes to the sea. "Tomorrow morning is arrive!"

Alma looked out to the bay and saw—how could she not have noticed immediately?—a fleet of long canoes slicing across the water toward the beach with incredible speed, powered by dozens of dark-skinned rowers. In all her time in Tahiti, she had never lost her wonder at the power and agility of such canoes. When flotillas such as this came rushing across the bay, she always felt as though she were watching the arrival of Jason and the Argonauts, or Odysseus's fleet. Most of all, she loved the moment when, drawing close to shore, the rowers heaved their muscles in one last push, and the canoes flew out of the sea as though shot forth by great invisible bows, landing on the beach in a dramatic, exuberant arrival.

Alma had questions, but Hiro had already dashed over to greet the canoes, as had the rest of the growing crowd. Alma had never before seen so many people on the beach. Caught up in the excitement, she, too, ran toward the boats. These were exceptionally fine, even majestic, canoes. The grandest must have been sixty feet, and in its bow stood a man of impressive height and build—clearly the leader of this expedition. He was Tahitian, but as she drew nearer, she could see that he was impeccably dressed in the suit of a European man. The villagers gathered around him, chanting songs of welcome, carrying him from the canoe like a king.

The people carried the stranger to the Reverend Welles. Alma pushed through the throng, drawing as near as she could. The man bent down over the Reverend Welles, and the two pressed their noses together in the customary greeting of deepest affection. She heard the Reverend Welles say, in a voice wet with tears, "Welcome back to your home, blessed son of God."

The stranger pulled back from the embrace. He turned to smile at the crowd, and Alma caught her first direct look at his face. If she had not been propped up by the crush of so many people, she might have fallen over with the force of recognition.

The words *tomorrow morning*—which Ambrose had written on the backs of all the drawings of The Boy—had not been a code. "Tomorrow morning" was not some sort of dreamy wish for a utopian future, or an anagram, or any manner of occult concealment whatsoever. For once in his life, Ambrose Pike had been perfectly straightforward: Tomorrow Morning was simply a person's name.

And now, indeed, Tomorrow Morning had arrived.

It enraged her.

That was her initial reaction. She felt—perhaps irrationally—that she had been tricked. Why, in all her months of search and privation, had she never heard mention of him—this regal figure, this adored visitant, this man who brought all of northern Tahiti running and cheering to the shoreline to greet him? How had his name or his existence never been alluded to, not even faintly? Nobody had once used the words *tomorrow morning* with Alma, unless in literal reference to something that was planned for the next day, and certainly nobody had ever mentioned the island's universal adoration of some elusive, handsome native who might someday arrive out of nowhere and be worshipped. There had never even been a rumor of such a figure. How could someone of this much consequence simply *appear*?

While the rest of the crowd moved along toward the mission church in a cheering, chanting mass, Alma stood quietly on the beach, struggling to make sense of all this. New questions replaced old beliefs. Whatever certainties she had felt only last week were now breaking up, like an ice dam at the beginning of spring. The apparition she had come here to seek indeed existed, but he was not a Boy; rather, he appeared to be some sort of king. What business did Ambrose have with an island king? How had they met? Why had Ambrose depicted Tomorrow Morning as a simple fisherman, when clearly he was a man of considerable power?

Alma's stubborn, relentless, internal-speculation engine began to spin once more. This sensation only angered her further. She was so weary of speculation. She could not bear anymore to invent new theories. All her life, she felt, she had lived in a state of speculation. All she had ever wanted was to *know things*, yet still and now—even after all these years of tireless questioning—all she did was ponder and wonder and guess.

No more speculation. No more of it. She would now need to know everything. She would insist on knowing.

Alma could hear the church before she reached it. The singing coming from within that humble building was like nothing she had ever heard. It was a roar of jubilation. There was no room inside the church for her; she stood outside with the jostling, chanting crowd, and listened. The hymns that Alma had heard in this church in the past—the voices of the eighteen congregants of the Reverend Welles's mission—had been thin and reedy tunes compared to what she was hearing now. For the first time, she could understand what Tahitian music was truly meant to be, and why it needed hundreds of voices roaring and bellowing together in order to perform its function: to outsing the ocean. That's what these people were doing now, in a crashing expression of veneration, both beautiful and dangerous.

At last it quieted, and Alma could hear a man speaking—clearly and powerfully—to the congregation. He spoke in Tahitian, in a disquisition that, at times, was almost a chant. She pushed closer to the door and peered in: it was Tomorrow Morning, tall and splendid, standing at the pulpit, arms raised, calling out to the congregation. Alma's command of Tahitian was still too basic for her to follow the entire sermon, but she could comprehend that this man was offering up a passionate testament to the living Christ. But that was not all he was doing; he was also cavorting with this gathering of people, the same way Alma had many times watched the boys of the Hiro contingent cavort with the waves. His mettle and nerve were unwavering. He pulled laughter and tears from the congregation, as well as solemnity and riotous joy. She could feel her own emotions being tugged along by the timbre and intensity of his voice, even as his words themselves remained largely incomprehensible.

Tomorrow Morning's performance went on for well over an hour. He had them singing; he had them praying; he had them prepared, it seemed, to attack at dawn. Alma thought, My mother would have despised this. Beatrix Whittaker had never gone in for evangelical passions; she'd believed that frenzied people were in danger of forgetting their manners and their reason, and then where would we be as a civilization? In any case, Tomorrow Morning's riproarious soliloquy was unlike anything Alma had ever before heard at the Reverend Welles's church—or *anywhere*, for that matter. This was not a Philadelphia minister, dutifully dispensing Lutheran teachings, or Sister Manu and her simple, monosyllabic homilies; this was oration. This was the drums of war. This was Demosthenes defending Ctesiphon. This was Pericles honoring the dead of Athens. This was Cicero rebuking Catiline.

What Tomorrow Morning's speech most certainly did *not* bring to Alma's mind was the humility and gentleness she had come to associate with this modest little mission by the sea. There was nothing humble or gentle about Tomorrow Morning. Indeed, she had never seen such an audacious, self-possessed figure. An adage of Cicero's came to her in its original, mighty Latin (the only language, she felt, that could stand up to the thundering groundswell of native eloquence she was right now witnessing): "Nemo umquam neque poeta neque orator fuit, qui quemquam meliorem quam se arbitraretur."

Never did there exist a poet or an orator who thought there was another better than himself.

The day became only more fervid from there.

Through the terrifically effective native telegraph system of Tahiti (fleet-footed boys with loud voices), word spread quickly that Tomorrow Morning had arrived, and the beach at Matavai Bay grew more crowded and exuberant by the hour. Alma wanted to find the Reverend Welles, to ask him many questions, but his tiny form kept disappearing into the mob, and she could only catch fleeting glimpses of him, his white hair flying in the breeze, beaming with happiness. She could not draw near Sister Manu, either, who was so electrified that she lost her giant flowered hat, and who was weeping like a schoolgirl in a crowd of chattering, euphoric women. The Hiro contingent was nowhere to be seen—or, rather, they were everywhere to be seen, but they moved far too quickly for Alma to catch and question them.

The crowd on the beach—as though by unanimous decision—turned into a revel. Space was cleared for wrestling and boxing matches. Young men flung off their shirts, applied coconut oil, and began to tussle. Children galloped across the shoreline in spontaneous footraces. A ring appeared in the sand, and suddenly a cockfight was under way. As the day went on, musicians arrived, carrying everything from native drums and flutes to European horns and fiddles. On another part of the beach, men were industriously digging a fire pit and lining it with stones. They were planning a tremendous roast. Then Alma saw Sister Manu, quite out of nowhere, catch a pig, pin it down, and kill it—much to the consternation of the pig. Alma could not but feel a bit resentful at the sight of this. (How long had she been waiting for a taste of pork? All it took, apparently, was Tomorrow Morning's arrival, and the deed was done.) With a long knife and a confident hand, Manu cheerfully took the pig apart. She pulled out the viscera, like a woman pulling taffy. She and a few of the stronger women held the pig's carcass over the open flames of the fire pit to burn off the bristles. Then they wrapped it in leaves and lowered it onto the hot stones. More than a few chickens, helpless in this tidal surge of celebration, followed the pig to its death.

Alma saw pretty Sister Etini rushing by, her arms filled with breadfruit. Alma lunged forward, touched Etini on the shoulder, and said, "Sister Etini—please tell me: who is Tomorrow Morning?"

Etini turned with a wide smile. "He is the Reverend Welles's son," she said.

"The Reverend Welles's *son*?" Alma repeated. The Reverend Welles had only daughters—and only one living daughter, at that. If Sister Etini's English were not so nimble and fluent, Alma might have assumed the woman had misspoken.

"His son by *taio*," Etini explained. "Tomorrow Morning is his son by adoption. He is my son, too, and Sister Manu's. He is the son of all in this mission! We are all family by *taio*."

"But where does he come from?" Alma asked.

"He comes from here," Etini said, and she could not disguise her tremendous pride in that fact. "Tomorrow Morning is ours, you see."

"But where did he arrive from just today?"

"He arrived from Raiatea, where he now lives. He has a mission of his own there. He has found great success in Raiatea, on an island that was once most hostile to the true God. The people he has brought along with him today, they are his converts—some of his converts, that is. To be sure, he has many more."

To be sure, Alma had many more questions, but Sister Etini was eager to attend to the feast, so Alma thanked her and sent her off. She went over to a guava bush by the river and sat down in its shade, to think. There was a great deal to think about and piece together. Desperate to make sense out of all this astonishing new information, she harkened back to a conversation she'd had months ago with the Reverend Welles. She dimly remembered the Reverend Welles having told her of his three adopted sons—the three most exemplary products of the mission school at Matavai Bay—who now led respected missions on various outer islands. She pushed herself to recall the details of that single, long-ago conversation, but her recollection was frustratingly indistinct. Raiatea may indeed have been one of the islands he had mentioned, Alma felt, but she was certain he had never brought up the name "Tomorrow Morning." Alma would have taken note of that name, had she ever heard it. Those words would have immediately alerted her attention, brimming as they did with personal associations. No, she had never heard the name spoken before. The Reverend Welles had called him by something else.

Sister Etini rushed past again, arms empty this time, and once more Alma darted forth and detained her. She knew she was being a pest, but could not stop herself.

"Sister Etini," she asked. "What is Tomorrow Morning's name?"

Sister Etini looked puzzled. "His name is Tomorrow Morning," she said simply.

"What does Brother Welles call him, though?"

"Ah!" Sister Etini's eyes lit up. "Brother Welles calls him by his Tahitian name, which is Tamatoa Mare. But Tomorrow Morning is a nickname he invented for himself, when he was just a little boy! He prefers to be called that. He was always so facile with language, Sister Whittaker—quite the best student Mrs. Welles and I ever had, and you will find that he speaks far better English than do I—and he could hear, even from earliest childhood, that his Tahitian name sounded like those English words. He was always so clever. Now the name suits him, we all agree, for he brings such hope, you understand, to everyone he meets. Like a new day."

"Like a new day," Alma repeated.

"Exactly, yes."

"Sister Etini," Alma said. "I am sorry, but I have one last question. When was the last time Tamatoa Mare was here at Matavai Bay?"

Sister Etini answered without hesitation. "November of 1850."

Sister Etini rushed off. Alma sat down in the shade again and watched the mirthful mayhem unfold. She watched it with no joy. She felt an indentation in her heart, as though somebody were pressing a thumbprint through her chest, deep and firm.

Ambrose Pike had died here in November of 1850.

It took Alma some time to come near Tomorrow Morning. That night was a mighty celebration—a feast worthy of a monarch, which was certainly how the man was regarded. Hundreds of Tahitians crowded the beach, eating roasted pigs, fish, and breadfruit, and enjoying arrowroot pudding, yams, and countless coconuts. Bonfires were lit, and the people danced—not the most obscene dances, of course, for which Tahiti was once so infamous, but the least offensive traditional dance, the one they called the *hura*. Even this would not have been permitted in any other mission settlement on the island, but Alma knew that the Reverend Welles sometimes allowed it. ("I simply cannot see the harm in it," he had once told Alma, who had begun to think of this oft-repeated phrase as a perfect motto for the Reverend Welles.)

Alma had never seen the dance performed before, and she was as captivated as anyone else. The young female dancers wore their hair ornamented with triple strands of jasmine and gardenia blossoms, and flowers draped over their necks. The music was slow and undulating. Some of the girls had faces marked by the pox, but in the firelight all were equally beautiful. One could get a sense of the women's limbs and hips in motion, even underneath their long-sleeved, shapeless, missionary-prescribed dresses. It was very much the most provocative dance Alma had ever seen (their hands alone were provocative, she marveled), and she could not begin to imagine what this dance must have looked like to her father back in 1777, when the women performing it wore grass skirts and nothing else. Quite a show it must have been, for a young boy from Richmond attempting to uphold his virtue.

From time to time athletic men jumped into the dance ring to perform comic, buffoonish interruptions to the *hura*. The point of this, Alma thought at first, was to break the sensual mood with mirth, but they, too, soon began testing the limitations of lewdness in their movements. There was a recurrent joke of the men grasping toward the female dancers, while the girls gracefully darted away without missing a step. Even the youngest children appeared to understand the underlying allusion to desire and rebuke playing itself out in the performance, and they howled with a degree of laughter that made them seem far more sophisticated than their years. Even Sister Manu—that shining example of Christian propriety—leapt into the fray at one point and joined the *hura* dancers, swaying her bulk with surprising agility. When one of the young male dancers came after her, she allowed herself to be caught, to the roaring delight of the crowd. The dancer then pressed himself against her hip, in a series of motions whose frank ribaldry could be misconstrued by nobody; Sister Manu merely fixed him with a comically inflated flirtatious gaze, and kept dancing.

Alma kept an eye on the Reverend Welles, who appeared simply charmed by all that he saw. Beside him sat Tomorrow Morning, poised with perfect posture, immaculately dressed like a London gentleman. Throughout the evening, people came to sit by his side, to press their noses against his nose, and to bring him salutations. He received everyone with a spirit of both finesse and largesse. Truly, Alma had to admit, she had never seen a more beautiful human being in all her life. Of course, beauty in the physical form was everywhere to be found in Tahiti, and one grew accustomed to it after a while. Men were beautiful here, women yet more beautiful, and children even more beautiful still. What a pale and spindle-armed group of hunchbacks most Europeans seemed by comparison to the extraordinary Tahitians! It had been said a thousand times, by a thousand awestruck foreigners. So, yes, beauty was in no short supply here, and Alma had seen much of it—but Tomorrow Morning was the most beautiful of all.

His skin was dark and burnished, his smile a slow moonrise. When he gazed upon anyone, it was an act of generosity, of luminescence. It was impossible not to stare at him. Notwithstanding his handsome countenance, his size alone commanded attention. He was truly prodigious in stature, an Achilles in the flesh. Most certainly, one would follow such a man into battle. The Reverend Welles had once told Alma that in the old days in the South Seas, when the islanders went to war against each other, the victors would pick through their opponents' corpses, looking for the tallest and darkest bodies among the dead. Once they had found those slain behemoths, they would carve open their corpses and remove their bones, from which they made fishhooks, chisels, and weapons. The bones of the largest men, it was believed, were charged with tremendous power, and hence the tools and weapons carved from them would endow their holder with invincibility. As for Tomorrow Morning, Alma thought ghoulishly, they could have made an armory's worth of weaponry out of him—if they could've managed to kill him in the first place.

Alma hovered around the outskirts of the firelight, to remain somewhat inconspicuous while she took in the situation. Nobody took notice of her, so consumed were they by their joy. The revelry went on long into the night. The fires burned high and bright, casting shadows so dark and so twisting that one almost feared to trip over them, or to be clutched by them and pulled down into the *pô*. The dancing grew wilder and the children behaved like spirits possessed. Alma might have assumed that a visit from a prominent Christian missionary would not have produced *quite* so much roistering and carousing—but then again, she was still new to Tahiti. None of it disturbed the Reverend Welles, who had never looked happier, never more buoyant.

Long after midnight, the Reverend Welles noticed Alma at last.

"Sister Whittaker!" he called out. "Where are my manners? You must meet my son!"

Alma approached the two men, who were sitting so near the fire that they appeared ablaze themselves. It was an awkward meeting, for Alma was standing and the men—as per local custom—remained seated. She was not about to sit. She was not about to press her nose to anyone else's nose. But Tomorrow Morning reached up with his long arm and offered a polite handshake.

"Sister Whittaker," said the Reverend Welles, "this is my son, of whom you have heard me speak. And my dear son, this is Sister Whittaker, you see, who visits us from the United States of America. She is a naturalist of some renown."

"A naturalist!" said Tomorrow Morning in a fine British accent, nodding with interest. "As a child, I had quite a fondness for natural history. My friends thought me mad, to value that which no one else valued—leaves, insects, coral, and the like. But it was a pleasure and education. What a worthy life, to make so deep a study of the world. How fortunate you are in your vocation."

Alma gazed down at him. To see his face so close at long last—this indelible face, this face that had so troubled and fascinated her for so long, this face that had brought her here from the other side of the globe, this face that had probed so stubbornly at her imagination, this face that had beleaguered her to the point of obsession—was simply staggering. His face had such a powerful effect upon her that it struck her as incredible that he, in turn, was not equally staggered by seeing *her*: How could she know him so intimately, and he know her not at all?

But why in heaven would he?

Placidly, he returned her gaze. His eyelashes were so long, it was an absurdity. They seemed not only excessive, but almost confrontational—this spectacle of eyelashes, this needlessly luxuriant fringe. She felt irritation rising within her—nobody required eyelashes such as these.

"It is a pleasure to meet you," she said.

With statesmanlike grace, Tomorrow Morning insisted that, no, the pleasure was entirely his own. Then he released her hand, Alma excused herself, and Tomorrow Morning returned his attention to the Reverend Welles—to his happy, elfin, little white father.

He stayed at Matavai Bay a fortnight.

She rarely took her eyes off him, keen to learn—by observation and proximity—whatever she could. What she learned, and quite quickly, was that Tomorrow Morning was beloved. It was close to exasperating, in fact, how beloved he was. She wondered if it was ever exasperating for him. He was never given a moment to himself, although Alma kept watching for one, hoping for a private word with him. It seemed there would never be a chance for it; there were meals and meetings and gatherings and ceremonies all around him, at all hours. He slept in Sister Manu's house, which buzzed with constant visitors. Queen 'Aimata Pōmare IV Vahine of Tahiti invited Tomorrow Morning for tea at her palace in Papeete. All wanted to hear—in English or Tahitian, or both—the story of Tomorrow Morning's extraordinary success as a missionary on Raiatea.

Nobody wanted to hear about it more than Alma, and over the duration of Tomorrow Morning's sojourn, she managed to piece together the entire story from various onlookers and admirers of the Great Man. Raiatea, she learned, was the cradle of Polynesian mythology, and thus a most unlikely place ever to have embraced Christianity. The island—large and rugged—was the birthplace and residence of Oro, the god of war, whose temples were honored by human sacrifice and littered with human skulls. Raiatea was a serious place (Sister Etini used the word *weighty*). Mount Temehani, in the center of the island, was considered to be the eternal residence of all the dead of Polynesia. A permanent shroud of fog hung over the tallest pinnacle of this mountain, it was said, for the dead did not like the sunlight. The Raiateans were not a laughing people; they were a firm people—a people of blood and grandeur. They were not the Tahitians. They had resisted the English. They had resisted the French. They had not resisted Tomorrow Morning. He had first arrived there six years earlier in a most spectacular manner: he came alone in a canoe, which he abandoned as he neared the island. He stripped naked and swam to shore, paddling easily over the thunderous breakers, holding his Bible over his head and chanting, "I sing the word of Jehovah, the one true God! I sing the word of Jehovah, the one true God!"

The Raiateans took notice.

Since then Tomorrow Morning had built an evangelizing empire. He had erected a church—just near Raiatea's pagan mother temple—that might easily have been mistaken for a palace, had it not been a house of worship. It was now the largest structure in Polynesia. It was held up by forty-six columns, hewn from the trunks of breadfruit trees, and sanded smooth with sharkskin.

Tomorrow Morning numbered his converts at some three and a half thousand souls. He had watched the people feed their idols to the fire. He had watched the old temples undergo a rapid transformation, from shrines of violent sacrifice to harmless piles of mossy rocks. He had put the Raiateans in modest European clothing: men in trousers, women in long dresses and bonnets. Young boys stood in line to have their hair cut short and respectable by him. He had supervised the construction of a community of tidy white cottages. He taught spelling and reading to a people who, prior to his arrival, had never seen the alphabet. Four hundred children a day attended school now and learned their catechism. Tomorrow Morning saw to it that the people did not merely ape the words of the Gospel, but understood what they meant. As such, he had already trained seven missionaries of his own, whom he had recently sent forth to even more distant islands; they, too, would swim to shore with the Bible held high, chanting the name of Jehovah. The days of disturbance and fallacy and superstition were over. Infanticide was over. Polygamy was over. Some called Tomorrow Morning a prophet; he was rumored to prefer the word *servant*.

Alma learned that Tomorrow Morning had taken a wife on Raiatea, Temanava, whose name meant "the welcoming." He had two young daughters there as well, Frances and Edith, named after the Reverend and Mrs. Welles. He was the most honored man in the Society Islands, Alma learned. She heard it so many times, she was growing weary of hearing it.

"And to think," said Sister Etini, "that he came from our little school at Matavai Bay!"

Alma did not find a moment to speak with Tomorrow Morning until late one night, ten days after his arrival, when she caught him walking alone the short distance between Sister Etini's house, where he had just enjoyed dinner, and Sister Manu's house, where he intended to sleep.

"May I have a word with you?" she asked.

"Certainly, Sister Whittaker," he agreed, remembering her name with ease. He gave the appearance of being completely unsurprised to see her coming out of the shadows toward him.

"Is there someplace more quiet where we might speak?" she asked. "What I need to discuss with you, I would like to address in privacy."

He laughed comfortably. "If ever you have managed to experience such a thing as privacy here at Matavai Bay, Sister Whittaker, I salute you. Anything you wish to say to me, you may say here."

"Very well, then," she said, although she could not help but glance around to see if anyone might overhear. "Tomorrow Morning," she began, "you and I are—I believe—more closely affixed to each other's destinies than one might think. I have been introduced to you as Sister Whittaker, but I need you to understand that for a short period of my life, I was known as Mrs. Pike."

"I will not make you go any further," he said gently, putting up a hand. "I know who you are, Alma."

They looked at each other in silence for what felt like a long time.

"So," she said, at last.

"Quite," he replied.

Again, the long silence.

"I know who you are, too," she finally said.

"Do you?" He did not appear the least bit alarmed. "Who am I, then?"

But now—pushed to answer—she found that she could not easily respond to the question. Needing to say something, though, she said, "You knew my husband well."

"Indeed, I did. What's more, I miss him."

This response shocked Alma, but she preferred this—the shock of his admission—to an argument, or a denial. Anticipating this conversation over the previous days, Alma had thought she might go mad, were Tomorrow Morning to accuse her of nefarious lies, or pretend never to have heard of Ambrose. But he did not seem inclined to resist or repudiate. She looked at him closely, seeking something in his face besides relaxed assuredness, but could see nothing amiss.

"You miss him," she repeated.

"And I always will, for Ambrose Pike was the best of men."

"So says everyone," said Alma, feeling vexed and slightly outplayed.

"For it was true."

"Did you love him, Tamatoa Mare?" she asked, again searching his face for a break in his equanimity. She wanted to catch him by surprise, as he had caught her. But his face displayed not a whit of unease. He did not even blink at the use of his given name.

He replied, "All who met him, loved him."

"But did you love him *particularly*?"

Tomorrow Morning put his hands in his pockets and looked up toward the moon. He was not in a hurry to reply. He looked for all the world like a man waiting leisurely for a train. After a while, he returned his gaze to Alma's face. They were not far from the same height, she noticed. Her shoulders were not so much narrower than his.

"I suppose you wonder about things," he said, by means of an answer.

She felt she was losing ground here. She would need to be even more direct.

"Tomorrow Morning," she said. "May I speak to you with candor?"

"Please do," he encouraged.

"Allow me to tell you something about myself, for it might help you to speak more freely. Implanted in my very disposition—though I do not always consider it either a virtue or a blessing—is a desire to understand the nature of things. As such, I would like to understand who my husband was.

I've come all this distance to understand him better, but it has thus far been fruitless. The little that I have been given to understand about Ambrose has brought me only more confusion. Ours was admittedly neither a customary marriage nor a long one, but this does not negate the love and concern that I felt toward my husband. I am not an innocent, Tomorrow Morning. I do not require protection from the truth. Please understand that my aim is neither to assail you nor to make you my enemy. Neither are your secrets in any peril, should you entrust them to my care. I do have reason, however, to suspect that you possess secrets about my late husband. I have seen the drawings that he made of you. Those drawings, as I am certain you can understand, compel me to ask for the truth of your association with Ambrose. Can you honor a widow's request, and tell me what you know? My feelings do not require sparing."

Tomorrow Morning nodded. "Do you have the day free tomorrow, to spend with me?" he asked. "Perhaps well into the evening?"

She nodded.

"How able is your body?" he asked.

The question and its incongruity rattled her. He noted her discomfort and clarified, "What I mean to ascertain is, are you capable of hiking a long distance? I would suppose that as a naturalist you are fit and hale, but still, I must ask. I would like to show you something, but I do not wish to overtax you. Can you manage climbing uphill in steep terrain, and that sort of thing?"

"I should think so," Alma replied, irritated once more. "I have traversed the entirety of this island over the past year. I have seen everything there is to see in Tahiti."

"Not everything, Alma," Tomorrow Morning corrected her, with a benevolent smile. "Not all of it."

Just after dawn the next day, they departed. Tomorrow Morning had procured a canoe for their journey. Not a risky little gambit of a canoe, such as the one the Reverend Welles used when he visited his coral gardens, but a finer one, solid and well made.

"We shall be going to Tahiti-iti," he explained. "It would take us days to get there overland, but we can reach it in five or six hours by navigating the coastline. You're comfortable on the water?"

She nodded. She found it difficult to tell whether he was being considerate or condescending. She had packed a bamboo tube of fresh water for herself and some *poi* for lunch, wrapped in a square of muslin that she could tie to her belt. She was wearing her most tired dress—the one that had already endured the island's worst abuses. Tomorrow Morning glanced at her bare feet, which, after a year on Tahiti, were as tough and callused as a plantation worker's. He made no mention of it, but she saw him take notice. His feet were also bare. From the ankles up, though, he was the perfect European gentleman. He wore his customary clean suit and white shirt, though he removed his jacket, folded it neatly, and used it as a seat cushion in the canoe.

There was no point in conversation on the journey to Tahiti-iti—the small, roundish, rugged, and remote peninsula on the opposite side of the island. Tomorrow Morning had to concentrate, and Alma did not wish to turn around every time she needed to speak. Thus, they proceeded in silence.

Traveling around the coastline was difficult going in certain areas, and Alma wished that Tomorrow Morning had brought a paddle for her, too, so she could feel as though she were helping along their progress—though, truthfully, he did not seem to need her. He carved the water with elegant efficiency, threading through the reefs and channels without hesitation, as though he had made this trip already hundreds of times—which, she suspected, he probably had. She was grateful for her wide-brimmed hat, as the sun was strong, and the glare off the water made spots dance across her eyes.

Within five hours, the cliffs of Tahiti-iti were on their right. Alarmingly, it appeared as if Tomorrow Morning was aiming straight for them. Were they to dash themselves against the rocks? Was that to be the morbid aim of this journey? But then Alma saw it—an arched opening in the cliff face, a dark aperture, an entrance to a sea-level cave. Tomorrow Morning synchronized the canoe to the rolling of a strong wave and then—thrillingly, fearlessly—shot them straight through that opening. Alma thought for certain they would be sucked back into the daylight by the receding water, but he paddled fiercely, almost standing up in the canoe, such that they were pitched up on the wet gravel of a rocky beach, deep inside the cave. It was nigh a feat of magic. Not even the Hiro contingent, she thought, would have risked such a maneuver.

"Jump out, please," he commanded, and although he did not quite bark at her, she gathered that she had to move quickly, before the next wave came in. She leapt out and scurried to the highest level—which, to be honest, did not feel quite high enough. One big wave, she thought, and they would be washed away forever. Tomorrow Morning did not seem concerned. He pulled the canoe up behind him onto the beach.

"May I ask you to help me?" he said politely. He pointed to a ledge above their heads, and she saw that he meant to put the canoe up there, for safe-keeping. She helped him lift the canoe, and together they pushed it up onto the ledge, far above the reach of the breaking waves.

She sat down, and he sat beside her, breathing heavily with exertion.

"Are you comfortable?" he asked her at last.

"Yes," she said.

"Now we must wait. When the tide goes out fully, you will see that there is a kind of narrow route that we can walk on along the cliff, and then we can climb upward, to a plateau. From there, I can take you to the place I wish to show you. If you feel that you can manage it, that is?"

"I can manage it," she said.

"Good. For now, we will rest for a spell." He lay back against the cushion of his jacket, stretched out his legs, and relaxed. When the waves rolled in, they nearly reached his feet—but not quite. He must know exactly how the tides operated within this cave, she could see. It was quite extraordinary. Looking at Tomorrow Morning stretched out beside her, she had a sudden poignant memory of the way Ambrose used to sprawl so comfortably across any surface—across grass, across a couch, across the floor of the drawing room at White Acre.

She gave Tomorrow Morning about ten minutes to rest, but then could contain herself no longer.

"How did you meet him?" she asked.

The cave was not the quietest place to speak, what with the water rushing back and forth up over the stones, and all the variations of damp echoes. But there was something about the thrumming rush of sound, too, that made this place feel like the safest spot in the world for Alma to demand things, and to have secrets revealed. Who could hear them? Who would ever see them? Nobody but the spirits. Their words would be dragged from this cave by the tide and pulled out to sea, broken up in the churning waves, eaten by fish.

Tomorrow Morning replied without sitting up. "I returned to Tahiti to visit the Reverend Welles in August of 1850, and Ambrose was here—just as you are now here."

"What did you think of him?"

"I thought he was an angel," he said without hesitation, without even opening his eyes.

He was answering her questions almost too quickly, she thought. She did not want glib answers; she wanted the complete story. She did not want only the conclusions; she wanted the in-between. She wanted to see Tomorrow Morning and Ambrose as they met. She wanted to observe their exchanges. She wanted to know what they had been thinking, what they had been feeling. Most certainly, she wanted to know what they had done. She waited, but he was not more forthcoming. After they had been in silence for a long while, Alma touched Tomorrow Morning's arm. He opened his eyes.

"Please," she said. "Continue."

He sat up, and turned to face her. "Did the Reverend Welles ever tell you how I came to the mission?" he asked.

"No," she said.

"I was only seven years old," he said. "Perhaps eight. My father died first, then my mother died, then my two brothers died. One of my father's surviving wives took responsibility for me, but then she died. There was another mother, too—another of my father's wives—but subsequently she died. All the children of my father's other wives died, in short order. There were grandmothers, too, but they also died." He paused, considering something, and then continued, correcting himself: "No, I am mistaking the order of the deaths, Alma, please excuse me. It was the grandmothers who died first, as the weakest members of the family. So, yes, first it was my grandmothers who died, and then my father, and then so forth, as I have said. I, too, was sick for a spell, but I did not die—as you can see. But these are common stories in Tahiti. Surely you have heard them before?"

Alma was not sure what to say, so she said nothing. While she knew of the ruinous death toll across Polynesia over the past fifty years, nobody had told her any stories of their personal losses.

"You've seen the scars on Sister Manu's forehead?" he asked. "Has anyone explained to you their origin?"

She shook her head. She did not know what any of this had to do with Ambrose.

"Those are grief scars," he said. "When the women here in Tahiti mourn, they cut their heads with sharks' teeth. It is gruesome, I know, to a European mind, but it is a means for a woman to both convey and unloose her sorrow. Sister Manu has more scars than most because she lost the entirety of her family, including several children. This is perhaps why she and I have always been so fond of each other."

Alma was struck by his use of the quiet word *fond* as a means of expressing the allegiance between a woman who had lost all her children and a boy who had lost all his mothers. It did not seem a forceful enough word.

Then Alma thought of Sister Manu's other physical anomaly. "What about her fingers?" she asked, holding up her own hands. "The missing tips?"

"That is another legacy of loss. Sometimes people here will cut off their fingertips as an expression of grief. This became easier to do when the Europeans brought us iron and steel." He smiled ruefully. Alma did not smile in return; it was too awful. He continued. "Now, as for my grandfather, whom I have not yet mentioned, he was a *rauti*. Do you know about the *rauti*? The Reverend Welles has tried over the years to enlist my help in translating this word, but it's difficult. My good father uses the word 'haranguer,' but that does not convey the dignity of the position. 'Historian' comes close, but it is not quite accurate, either. The task of the *rauti* is to run alongside men as they charge into battle, and to keep up their courage by reminding them of who they are. The *rauti* sings out the bloodlines and the lineage of each man, reminding the warriors of the glory of their family history. He ensures that they do not forget the heroism of their forefathers. The *rauti* knows the lineage of every man on this island, all the way back to the gods, and he chants out their courage for them. One could say it is a kind of sermon, but a violent one."

"What were the verses like?" Alma asked, reconciling herself to this long, incongruous story. He had brought her here for a reason, she supposed, and he must be telling her this for a reason.

Tomorrow Morning turned his face toward the cave entrance, and thought for a moment. "In English? It does not have the same power, but it would be something along the lines of, '*Give forth all your vigilance until their will is severed! Hang upon them like lightning! You are Arava, the son of Hoani, the grandson of Paruto, who was born of Pariti, who sprang from Tapunui, who claimed the head of the mighty Anapa, the father of eels—you are that man! Break over them like the sea!'"* Tomorrow Morning thundered out these words, and they reverberated across the stones, drowning out the waves. He turned back to Alma—who had gooseflesh up her arms now, and who could not imagine the impact this must have had in Tahitian, if it stirred her so greatly in English—and said in his conversational voice, "Women fought, too, at times."

"Thank you," she said, though she could not have identified why she said it. "What became of your grandfather?"

"He died with the rest of them. After my family died, I was a child alone. In Tahiti, this is not so grave a fate for a child as it might be, I suppose, in London or Philadelphia. Children here are given independence from a young age, and anyone who can climb a tree or cast a line can feed himself. Nobody here will freeze to death in the night. I was similar to the young boys you see on the beach at Matavai Bay, who are also without family, although perhaps I was not as happy as they seem to be, for I did not have a little gang of fellows. The problem for me was not starvation of the body, but starvation of the spirit, do you see?"

"Yes," said Alma.

"So I found my way to Matavai Bay, where there was a settlement of people. For several weeks, I watched the mission. I saw that, as humbly as they lived, they still had better things than elsewhere on the island. They had knives sharp enough to kill a pig in one stroke, and axes that could fell a tree with ease. To my eyes, their cottages were luxurious. I saw the Reverend Welles, who was so white that he looked to me like a ghost, though not a malevolent ghost. He spoke the language of ghosts, yes, but he spoke some of my language, too. I watched his baptisms, which were entertaining to everyone. Sister Etini was operating the school already, along with Mrs. Welles, and I saw the children going in and out. I lay outside the windows and listened to the lessons. I was not uneducated, completely. I could name one hundred and fifty kinds of fish, you see, and I could draw a map of the stars in the sand, but I was not educated in the European manner. Some of these children had small slates, for their lessons. I tried to construct myself a slate, out of a dark flake of lava stone that I polished smooth with sand. I dyed my chalkboard blacker still, using the sap of the mountain plantain, and then I scribbled lines on it with white coral. It was nearly a successful invention—although, unfortunately it did not erase!" He smiled at the memory. "You had quite a library as a child, I understand? And Ambrose told me that you spoke several languages, from the earliest age?"

Alma nodded. So Ambrose had spoken of her! She felt a tremor of pleasure at this revelation (*he had not forgotten her!*) but there was disturbance in it, as well: what else did Tomorrow Morning know about her? Far more, clearly, than she knew about him.

"It has been a dream of mine to someday see a library," he said. "I would also like to see stained glass windows. In any case, one day the Reverend Welles spied me and approached me. He was kind. I am certain you need not stretch your imagination to understand how kind he was, Alma, for you have met the man. He gave me a task. He needed to convey a message, he said, to a missionary in Papeete. He asked me if I could take the message to his friend. Naturally, I agreed. I asked him, 'What is the message?' He simply handed me a slate with lines written upon it, and said, in Tahitian, 'This is the message.' I was dubious, but I took off running. In several hours, I had found the other missionary at his church by the docks. This man did not speak Tahitian at all. I did not understand how it would be possible for me to convey to him the message, when I did not even know what the message was, and we could not communicate! But I handed him the slate. He looked at it, and went into his church. When he came out, he handed me a small stack of writing paper. This was the first time I had ever encountered paper, Alma, and I thought it was the finest and whitest *tapa* cloth I had ever seen—though I did not understand what sort of clothing anyone could make out of such small pieces. I supposed it could be sewn together into some kind of garment.

"I hurried back to Matavai Bay, running the entire seven miles, and handed the paper to the Reverend Welles, who was delighted, for—he told me—this had been his message: he had wished to borrow some writing paper. I was a Tahitian child, Alma, which meant that I knew of magic and miracles—but I did not understand the magic of this trick. Somehow, it appeared to me, the Reverend Welles had convinced the slate to *tell something* to the other missionary. He must have commanded the slate to speak on his behalf, and thus, his wish had been granted! Oh, I wanted to know this magic! I whispered a commandment to my poor imitation of a slate, and I scribbled some lines on it with coral. My commandment was, 'Bring back my brother from the dead.' It puzzles me now why I did not ask for my mother, but I must have missed my brother more at that time. Perhaps because he was protective. I had always admired my brother, who was far more courageous than I was. You will not be surprised, Alma, to learn that my attempt at magic did not work. However, when the Reverend Welles saw what I was doing, he sat to speak with me, and that was the beginning of my new education."

"What did he teach you?" Alma asked.

"The mercy of Christ, firstly. Secondly, English. Lastly, reading." After a long pause, he spoke again. "I was a good student. I understand that you were also a good student?"

"Yes, always," said Alma.

"The ways of the mind were easy for me, as I believe they were easy for you?"

"Yes," said Alma. What else had Ambrose told him?

"The Reverend Welles became my father, and since then I have always been my father's favorite. He loves me more, I daresay, than he loves his own daughter and his own wife. He certainly loves me more than he loves his other adopted sons. I understand from what Ambrose told me that you were your father's favorite, as well—that Henry loved you even more, perhaps, than he loved his own wife?"

Alma started. It was a shocking statement. She felt wholly unable to reply. What loyalty did she feel toward her mother and toward Prudence across all the years and miles—and even across the divide of death—that she could not bring herself to answer this question honestly?

"But one knows when one is the favorite of our father, Alma, don't we?" Tomorrow Morning asked, probing more gently. "It transfers to us a unique power, does it not? If the person of most consequence in the world has chosen to prefer us over all others, then we become accustomed to having what we wish for. Wasn't that the case with you, as well? How can we not feel that we are strong—people like you and me?"

Alma searched herself to determine if this was true.

But of course it was true.

Her father had left her everything—the entirety of his fortune, at the exclusion of everyone else in the world. He had never allowed her to leave White Acre, not only because he had needed her, she suddenly realized, but also because he had loved her. Alma remembered him gathering her onto his lap when she was a small child, and telling her fanciful stories. She remembered her father's saying, "To my mind, the homely one is worth ten of the pretty one." She remembered the night of the ball at White Acre, in 1808, when the Italian astronomer had arranged the guests into a *tableau vivant* of the heavens, and had conducted them into a splendid dance. Her father—the sun, the center of it all—had called out across the universe, "Give the girl a *place!*" and had encouraged Alma to run. For the first time in her life, it occurred to her that it must have been he, Henry, who had thrust the torch into her hands that night, entrusting her with fire, releasing her as a Promethean comet across the lawn, and across the wide open world. Nobody else would have had the authority to entrust a child with fire. Nobody else would have bestowed upon Alma the right to have a *place.*

Tomorrow Morning went on. "My father has always regarded me as a sort of prophet, you know."

"Is that how you regard yourself?" she asked.

"No," he said. "I know what I am. For one thing, I am a *rauti.* I am a haranguer, as my grandfather was before me. I come to the people and chant out encouragement. My people have suffered a great deal, and I push them to be strong again—but in the name of Jehovah, because the new god is more powerful than our old gods. If that were not true, Alma, all my people would still be alive. This is how I minister: with power. I believe that on these islands the news of the Creator and of Jesus Christ must be communicated not through gentleness and persuasion, but through power. That is why I have found success where others have failed."

He was quite casual, revealing this to Alma. He almost shrugged it off as an easy thing.

"But there is something more," he said. "In the old ways of thinking, there were known to be intermediary beings—messengers, as it were, between gods and men."

"Like priests?" Alma asked.

"Like the Reverend Welles, you mean?" Tomorrow Morning smiled, looking again at the mouth of the cave. "No. My father is a good man, but he is not the sort of being to which I refer here. He is not a divine messenger. I am thinking of something other than a priest. I suppose you could say . . . what is the word? An *emissary.* In the old ways of thinking, we believed that each god had his own emissary. In emergencies, the Tahitian people would pray to these emissaries for deliverance. 'Come to the world,' they would pray. 'Come to the light, and help us, for there is war and hunger and fear, and we suffer.' The emissaries were neither of this world nor the next, but they moved between the two."

"Is that how you regard yourself?" Alma asked again.

"No," he said. "That is how I regarded Ambrose Pike."

He turned to her immediately after he said this, and his face—for just a moment—was stricken with pain. Her heart clutched, and she had to catch herself, to hold her composure.

"You saw him the same way, too?" he asked, searching her face for an answer.

"Yes," she said. At last they had come to it. At last they had come to Ambrose.

Tomorrow Morning nodded, and looked relieved. "He could hear my thoughts, you know," he said.

"Yes," Alma said. "That was something he could do."

"He wanted me to listen to his thoughts," Tomorrow Morning said, "but I do not have that capacity."

"Yes," said Alma. "I understand. Nor do I."

"He could see evil—the way that it gathers in clusters. That was how he explained evil to me, as a clustering of sinister color. He could see doom. He could see good, as well. Billows of goodness, surrounding certain people."

"I know," said Alma.

"He heard the voices of the dead. Alma, he heard my brother."

"Yes."

"He told me that one night he could hear starlight—but it was only for that one night. It saddened him that he could never hear it again. He thought that if he and I attempted together to hear it, if we put our minds together, we could receive a message."

"Yes."

"He was lonely on earth, Alma, for nobody was similar to him. He could find no home."

Alma again felt the clutch in her heart—a clenching of shame and guilt and regret. She balled up her hands into fists and pressed them into her eyes. She willed herself not to cry. When she put down her fists and opened her eyes, Tomorrow Morning was watching her as though waiting for a signal, as though waiting to see if he should stop speaking. But all she wanted was for him to continue speaking.

"What did he wish for, with you?" Alma asked.

"He wanted a companion," Tomorrow Morning said. "He wanted a twin. He wanted us to be the same. He was mistaken about me, you understand. He thought I was better than I am."

"He was mistaken about me, too," Alma said.

"So you see how it is."

"What did you wish for, with him?"

"I wanted to couple with him, Alma," Tomorrow Morning said grimly, but without a flinch.

"As did I," she said.

"So we are the same, then," said Tomorrow Morning, though the thought did not appear to bring him comfort. It did not bring her comfort, either.

"*Did* you couple with him?" she asked.

Tomorrow Morning sighed. "I allowed him to believe that I was also an innocent. I think he saw me as The First Man, as a new kind of Adam, and I allowed him to believe that of me. I allowed him to draw those pictures of me—no, I *encouraged* him to draw those pictures of me—for I am vain. I told him to draw me as he would draw an orchid, in blameless nakedness. For what is the difference, in the eyes of God, between a naked man and a flower? This is what I told him. That is how I brought him near."

"But did you couple with him?" she repeated, steeling herself for a more direct answer.

"Alma," he said. "You have given me to understand what sort of a person you are. You have explained that you are compelled by a desire for comprehension. Now let me give you to understand what sort of a person I am: I am a conqueror. I do not boast to say it. It is merely my nature. Perhaps you have never before met a conqueror, so it is difficult for you to understand."

"My father was a conqueror," she said. "I understand more than you might imagine."

Tomorrow Morning nodded, conceding the point. "Henry Whittaker. By all accounts, yes. You may be correct. Perhaps, then, you can understand me. The nature of a conqueror, as you surely know, is to acquire whatever he wishes to acquire."

For a long while after that, they did not speak. Alma had another question, but she could scarcely bear to ask it. But if she did not ask it now, she never would know, and then the question would chew holes through her for the rest of her life. She girded her courage again and asked, "How did Ambrose die, Tomorrow Morning?" When he did not reply at once, she added, "I was informed by the Reverend Welles that he died of infection."

"He did die of infection, I suppose—by the end of it. That is what a doctor would have told you."

"But how did he truly die?"

"It is not pleasant to speak of," said Tomorrow Morning. "He died of grief."

"What do you mean—of grief? But how?" Alma pushed on. "You must tell me. I did not come here for a pleasant exchange, and I assure you that I am capable of withstanding whatever I hear. Tell me—what was the mechanism?"

Tomorrow Morning sighed. "Ambrose cut himself, quite severely, some days prior to his death. You will remember my telling you how the women here—when they have lost a loved one—will take a shark's tooth to their own heads? But they are Tahitians, Alma, and it is a Tahitian custom. The women here know how to do this dreadful thing safely. They know precisely how deeply to cut themselves, such that they can bleed out their sorrows without causing dire harm. Afterward, they tend to the wound immediately. Ambrose, alas, was not practiced in this art of self-wounding. He was much distressed. The world had disappointed him. I had disappointed him. Worst of all, I believe, he had disappointed himself. He did not stay his own hand. When we found him in his *fare*, he was beyond saving."

Alma shut her eyes and saw her love, her Ambrose—his good and beautiful head—drenched in the blood of his self-mortification. She had disappointed Ambrose, as well. All he had wanted was purity, and all she had wanted was pleasure. She had banished him to this lonely place, and he had died here, horribly.

She felt Tomorrow Morning touch her arm, and she opened her eyes.

"Do not suffer," he said calmly. "You could not have stopped this thing from occurring. You did not lead him to his death. If anybody led him to his death, it was I."

Still, she was unable to speak. But then another awful question rose, and she had no choice but to ask it: "Did he cut off his fingertips, too? In the manner of Sister Manu?"

"Not all of them," Tomorrow Morning said, with commendable delicacy.

Alma shut her eyes again. Those artist's hands! She remembered— though she did not wish to remember it—the night she had put his fingers in her mouth, trying to take him into her. Ambrose had flinched in fear, had recoiled. He had been so fragile. How had he managed to commit this awful violence upon himself? She thought she would be sick.

"This is my burden to carry, Alma," Tomorrow Morning said. "I have strength enough for this burden. Allow me to carry it."

When she found her voice again, she said, "Ambrose took his own life. Yet the Reverend Welles gave him a proper Christian burial."

It was not a question, but a statement of amazement.

"Ambrose was an exemplary Christian," Tomorrow Morning said. "As for my father, may God preserve him, he is a man of unusual mercy and generosity."

Alma, slowly piecing together more of the story, asked, "Does your father know who I am?"

"We should assume that he does," said Tomorrow Morning. "My good father knows everything that happens on this island."

"Yet he has been so kind to me. He has never pried, never inquired . . ."

"This should not surprise you, Alma. My father is kindness incarnate."

Another long pause. Then: "But does that mean he knows about you, Tomorrow Morning? Does he know what transpired between you and my late husband?"

"Again, we may reasonably assume so."

"Yet he remains so admiring—"

Alma could not finish her thought, and Tomorrow Morning did not bother replying. Alma sat in astonished silence for a long while after this. Clearly, the Reverend Francis Welles's tremendous capacity for compassion and forgiveness was not something to which one could apply logic, or even words.

Eventually, though, yet another terrible question rose in her mind. This question made her feel bilious and somewhat crazed, but—once more—she needed to know.

"Did you force yourself upon Ambrose?" she asked. "Did you bring injury to him?"

Tomorrow Morning did not take offense at this implicit accusation, but he did suddenly look older. "Oh, Alma," he said sadly. "It appears that you do not quite understand what a conqueror is. It is not necessary for me to force things—once I am decided, the others have no choice. Can you not see this? Did I force the Reverend Welles to adopt me as his son, and to love me more than he loves even his own flesh-and-blood family? Did I force the island of Raiatea to embrace Jehovah? You are an intelligent woman, Alma. Try to comprehend this."

Alma pressed her fists against her eyes again. She would not allow herself to weep, but now she knew a dreadful truth: Ambrose had *permitted* Tomorrow Morning to touch him, whereas he had only recoiled from her in abhorrence. It was possible this information made her feel worse than anything else she had yet learned today. It shamed her that she could concern herself with such a petty and selfish matter after hearing such horrors, but she could not help herself.

"What is it?" Tomorrow Morning asked, seeing her stricken face.

"I longed to couple with him, too," she confessed at last. "But he would not have me."

Tomorrow Morning looked at her with infinite tenderness. "So this is where we are different, you and I," he said. "For you relented."

Now the tide was low at last, and Tomorrow Morning said, "Let us go quickly, while we have our opportunity. If we are to do this at all, we must move now."

They left the canoe behind on its unreachable ledge, and exited the cave. There was, as Tomorrow Morning had promised, a narrow route along the bottom of the cliff, upon which they could safely walk. They walked for a few hundred feet and then began to ascend. From the canoe, the cliff had seemed sheer, vertical, and unscalable, but now, as she followed Tomorrow Morning, putting her feet and hands just where he put his, she could see that there was, indeed, a pathway upward. It was almost as if stairs had been cut, with footholds and handholds placed precisely where they would be needed. She did not look down at the waves below, but trusted—as she had learned to trust the Hiro contingent—in her guide's competence and her own sure-footedness.

About fifty feet up, they came to a ridge. From there, they entered a thick belt of jungle, scrambling up a steep slope of damp roots and vines. After her weeks with the Hiro contingent, Alma was in fine hiking trim, with the heart of a Highland pony, but this was a truly treacherous climb. Wet leaves under her feet made for dangerous slips, and even barefoot it was difficult to find purchase. She was tiring. She could see no sign of a path. She didn't know how Tomorrow Morning could possibly tell where he was going.

"Be careful," he said over his shoulder. "*C'est glissant.*"

He must be weary, too, she realized, for he did not even seem to recognize that he just had spoken to her in French. She hadn't known that he spoke French at all. What else did he have in that mind of his? She marveled at it. He had done well for an orphan boy.

The steepness leveled out a bit, and now they were walking alongside a stream. Soon she could hear a dim rumbling in the distance. For a while, the noise was just a rumor, but then they came around a bend and she could see it—a waterfall about seventy feet tall, a ribbon of white foam that emptied noisily into a churning pool. The force of the falling water created gusts of wind, and the mist gave form to this wind, like ghosts made visible. Alma wanted to pause here, but the waterfall was not Tomorrow Morning's destination. He leaned in to her to make himself heard, pointed toward the sky, and shouted, "Now we go up again."

Hand over hand, they climbed beside the waterfall. Soon Alma's dress was soaked through. She reached for sturdy clumps of mountain plantain and bamboo stalks to steady herself, and prayed they would not come unrooted. Near the top of the waterfall was a comfortable hummock of smooth stone and tall grasses, as well as a tumble of boulders. Alma determined that this must be the plateau of which he had spoken—their destination—though she could not at first determine what was so special about this place. But then Tomorrow Morning stepped behind the largest boulder, and she followed him. There, quite suddenly, was the entrance to a small cave—as tidily cut into the cliff as a room in a house, with walls eight feet up on every side. The cave was cool and silent, and smelled of minerals and soil. And it was covered—thoroughly carpeted—with the most luxuriant mantle of mosses Alma Whittaker had ever seen.

The cave was not merely mossy; it throbbed with moss. It was not merely green; it was frantically green. It was so bright in its verdure that the color nearly spoke, as though—smashing through the world of sight—it wanted to migrate into the world of sound. The moss was a thick, living pelt, transforming every rock surface into a mythical, sleeping beast. Improbably, the deepest corners of the cave glittered the brightest; they were absolutely studded, Alma realized with a gasp, with the jewellike filigree of *Schistotega pennata*.

Goblin's gold, dragon's gold, elfin gold—*Schistotega pennata* was that rarest of cave mosses, that false gem that gleams like a cat's eye from within the permanent twilight of geologic shade, that unearthly sparkling plant that needs but the briefest sliver of light each day to sparkle like glory forever, that brilliant trickster whose shining facets have fooled so many travelers over the centuries into believing that they have stumbled upon hidden treasure. But to Alma, this *was* treasure, more stunning than actual riches, for it bedecked the entire cave in the uncanny, glistering, emerald light that she had only ever before seen in miniature, in glimpses of moss seen through a microscope . . . yet now she was standing fully within it.

Her first reaction upon entering this miraculous place was to shut her eyes against the beauty. It was unendurable. She felt as though this were something she should not be allowed to see without permission, without some sort of religious dispensation. She felt undeserving. With her eyes closed, she relaxed and allowed herself to believe that she had dreamed this vision. When she dared open them again, however, it was all still there. The cave was so beautiful that it made her bones ache with longing. She had never before coveted anything as much as she coveted this glimmering spectacle of mosses. She wanted to be swallowed by it. Already—although she was standing right there—she began to miss this place. She knew she would miss it for the rest of her days.

"Ambrose always thought you would like it here," Tomorrow Morning said.

Only then did she begin to sob. She sobbed so hard that she did not make a sound—she could not make a sound—and her face twisted into a mask of tragedy. Something in the center of her broke apart, splintering her heart and lungs. She fell forward into Tomorrow Morning, the way a soldier, shot, falls into the arms of his comrade. He held her up. She shook like a rattling skeleton. Her sobbing did not subside. She clung to him with such force that it would have broken the ribs of a lesser man. She wanted to press straight through him and come out the other side—or, better still, be blotted out by him, absorbed into his guts, erased, negated.

In her paroxysm of grief, she did not at first sense it, but at length she perceived that he, too, was weeping—not great gusting sobs, but slow tears. She was holding him up as much as he was holding her. And so they stood together in the tabernacle of mosses and wept out his name.

Ambrose, they lamented. *Ambrose.*

He was never coming back.

In the end they dropped to the ground, like trees hacked down. Their clothing was soaked and their teeth chattered with cold and fatigue. Without discussion or discomfort, they removed their wet clothes. It had to be done, or they would die of the chill. Now they were not only exhausted and sodden, they were laid bare. They lay down on the moss and regarded each other. It was not an assessment. It was not a seduction. Tomorrow Morning's form was beautiful—but this was evident, unsurprising, beyond argument, and unimportant. Alma Whittaker's form was not beautiful—but this, too, was evident, unsurprising, beyond argument, and unimportant.

She reached for his hand. She put his fingers in her mouth, like a child. He allowed it. He did not recoil from her. Then she reached for his penis, which had been—like the penis of every Tahitian boy—circumcised during youth with the tooth of a shark. She needed to touch him more intimately; he was the one person who had ever touched Ambrose. She did not ask permission of Tomorrow Morning for this touch; permission issued from the man, unspoken. All was understood. She moved down his large, warm body, and took his member into her mouth.

This act was the one thing in her life she had ever really wanted to do. She had given up so much, and she had never complained—but could she not, at least once, have this? She did not need to be married. She did not need to be beautiful, or desired by men. She did not need to be surrounded by friends and frivolity. She did not need an estate, a library, a fortune. There was so much that she did not need. She did not even need to have the unexplored terrain of her ancient virginity excavated at long last, at the wearisome age of fifty-three—though she knew Tomorrow Morning would oblige her, had she wished.

But—if only for one moment of her life—she did need *this*.

Tomorrow Morning did not hesitate, nor did he rush her along. He allowed her to investigate him, and to fit whatever she could fit of him inside her mouth. He allowed her to suck on him as though drawing breath through him—as though she were underwater and he was her only link to air. Her knees in the moss, her face in his secret nest, she felt him grow heavier in her mouth, and warmer, and even more permissive.

It was just as she had always imagined it would be. No, it was more than she had ever imagined it would be. Then he poured himself into her mouth, and she received it like a dedicatory offering, like an almsgiving.

She was grateful.

After that, they did not weep anymore.

They spent the night together, in that high grotto of mosses. It was far too dangerous now, in the darkness, to return to Matavai Bay. While Tomorrow Morning did not object to canoeing at night (indeed, he claimed to prefer it, as the air was cooler), he did not think it safe for them to climb down the waterfall and the cliff face with no light. Knowing the island as he did, he must have realized all along that they would have to spend the night. She did not mind his assumption.

Bedding down in the outdoors did not promise a comfortable night's sleep, but they made the best of the situation. They built a small fire pit with billiard-sized rocks. They gathered up dry hibiscus, which Tomorrow Morning was able to coax into flame in a matter of minutes. Alma collected breadfruit, which she wrapped in banana leaves and baked until it crumbled open. They made bedding from mountain plantain stalks, which they beat with stones into a soft, clothlike material. They slept together under this crude plantain bedding, pressed against each other for warmth. It was damp, but not insufferable. They denned down like brother foxes. In the morning, Alma awoke to find that the sap of the plantain stalks had left dark blue stains on her skin—although it didn't show up, she noticed, on Tomorrow Morning's skin. His skin had absorbed the stain, while hers, paler, displayed it openly.

It seemed wise not to speak of the previous evening's events. They remained silent on the subject not out of shame, but out of something that more closely resembled regard. Also, they were exhausted. They dressed, ate the remaining breadfruit, descended the waterfall, picked their way down the cliffs, reentered the cave, found the canoe high and dry, and reversed their journey back to Matavai Bay.

Six hours later, as the familiar black beach of the mission settlement came into view, Alma turned to face Tomorrow Morning, and put her hand on his knee. He paused his paddling.

"Forgive me," she said. "May I trouble you with one final question?"

There was one last thing she needed to know, and—as she was not certain they would ever see each other again—she had to ask him now. He nodded his head respectfully, inviting her to continue.

"For nearly a year now, Ambrose's valise—filled with his drawings of you—has been sitting in my *fare* on the beach. Anybody could have taken it. Anybody could have distributed those pictures of you all over the island. Yet not one person on this island has so much as touched the thing. Why is that?"

"Oh, that is simple to answer," Tomorrow Morning said easily. "It is because they are all terrified of me."

Then Tomorrow Morning took up the paddle once again, and pulled them back toward the beach. It was almost time for evening services. They were welcomed home with warmth and joy. He gave a beautiful sermon.

Not a single person dared to ask where they had been.

Chapter Twenty-six

Tomorrow Morning left Tahiti three days later, to return to his mission on Raiatea—and to his wife and children. For the most part, over the course of those days, Alma kept to herself. She spent a good bit of time in her *fare*, alone with Roger the dog, contemplating all she had learned. She felt simultaneously relieved and burdened: relieved of all her old questions; burdened by the answers.

She skipped the morning baths in the river with Sister Manu and the other women, for she did not want them to see the blue dye that still faintly marked her skin. She went to church services, but she stayed near the back of the crowd, and made herself inconspicuous. She and Tomorrow Morning never had a moment alone together again. In fact, from what she could see, he never had a moment to himself, either. It was a miracle she had ever been able to find seclusion with him at all.

The day before Tomorrow Morning's departure, there was another celebration in his honor—a duplicate of the remarkable festivities two weeks prior. Again, there was dancing and feasting. Again, there were musicians, and wrestling matches, and cockfights. Again, there were fire pits and slaughtered pigs. Alma could see more clearly now how venerated Tomorrow Morning was, even more than he was loved. She could also see the position of responsibility he held, and how ably he conducted himself in that position. The people draped numberless strands of flowers around his neck;

the flowers hung heavily upon him, like chains. He was presented with gifts: a pair of green doves in a cage, a drove of protesting young pigs, an ornate eighteenth-century Dutch gun that could no longer shoot, a Bible bound in goatskin, jewelry for his wife, bolts of calico, sacks of sugar and tea, a fine iron bell for his church. The people laid the gifts at his feet, and he received them with grace.

At dusk, a group of women with brooms came down to the shoreline and began to sweep clean the beach for a game of *haru raa puu*. Alma had never before seen a game of *haru raa puu*, but she knew what it was, for the Reverend Welles had told her. The game—whose name translated as something like "seizing the ball"—was traditionally played by two teams of women, who faced off against each other across a stretch of beach approximately one hundred feet in length. At either end of this ad hoc field they drew a line in the sand, to signify a goal. The function of a ball was served by a thick bundle of tightly twisted plantain fronds, about the diameter of a medium-sized pumpkin, though not as heavy. The point of the game, as Alma had learned, was to seize the ball from the opposing team and to scramble down to the opposite end of the field without being tackled by one's opponents. If the ball happened to go into the sea, the game would continue in the waves. A player was permitted to do absolutely anything to stop her opponents from scoring.

Haru raa puu was considered by the English missionaries to be both unladylike and stimulating, and was therefore forbidden at all the other settlements. Indeed, to be fair to the missionaries, the game went quite a bit beyond unladylike. Women were routinely injured in matches of *haru raa puu*—limbs broken, skulls cracked, blood shed. It was, as the Reverend Welles stated admiringly, "a stunning show of savagery." But violence was quite the point of it. In the olden times, as men practiced for war, the women had practiced *haru raa puu*. Thus the ladies, too, would be prepared, should the time come to fight. Why had the Reverend Welles allowed *haru raa puu* to continue, then, when the other missionaries had banned it as an unchristian expression of pure savagery? Why, for the same reason as always: he simply could not see the harm in it.

Once the game began, though, Alma could not help but think that the Reverend Welles had been gravely mistaken on this point: there was potential for tremendous harm in a match of *haru raa puu*. The moment the ball was in play, the women were transformed into creatures both formidable and frightening. These kind and hospitable Tahitian ladies—whose bodies Alma had seen at morning baths, whose food she had shared, whose babies she had dandled upon her knee, whose voices she had heard uplifted in earnest prayer, and whose hair she had seen ornamented so prettily with flowers—rearranged themselves immediately into rival battalions of demonic hellcats. Alma could not determine whether the point of the game was, indeed, to seize the ball or to tear off the limbs of one's opponents—or perhaps a combination of both. She saw sweet Sister Etini (*Sister Etini!*) make a grab for another woman's hair and throw her to the ground—and her opponent had not even been near the ball!

The crowd on the beach loved the spectacle and raised a clamor of cheers. The Reverend Welles cheered, too, and Alma saw for the first time the Cornish dockside ruffian he had once been, before Christ and Mrs. Welles had saved him from his belligerent ways. Watching the women attack the ball and each other, the Reverend Welles no longer looked like a harmless little elf; he more resembled a fearless little rat terrier.

Then quite suddenly, absolutely out of nowhere, Alma was run over by a horse.

Or that was what it felt like. It was not a horse, however, that had knocked her to the ground; it was Sister Manu, who'd come running off the field to charge at Alma sideways with full might. Sister Manu gripped Alma by the arm and dragged her onto the field of play. The crowd loved this. The clamor grew louder. Alma caught a glimpse of the Reverend Welles's face, bright with the thrill of this surprising turn of events, shouting his delight. She glanced at Tomorrow Morning, whose demeanor was polite and reserved. He was far too much the majestic figure to laugh at such an exhibition, but neither was he disapproving.

Alma did not want to play *haru raa puu*, but nobody had conferred with her on this point. She was in the game before she knew it. She felt as though she was being attacked from all sides, but this was most likely because she *was* being attacked from all sides. Somebody thrust the ball into her hands and pushed her. It was Sister Etini.

"RUN!" she shouted.

Alma ran. She did not get far before she was knocked to the ground again. Somebody had struck her with an arm to the throat, and she was flung on her back. She bit her tongue on the way down, and tasted blood. She considered simply staying down on the sand to avoid more severe injury, but she feared a trampling by the pitiless herd. She got to her feet. The crowd cheered again. She did not have time to think. She was pulled into a scrimmage of women and had no choice but to go where they were going. She had not the faintest notion of where the ball was. She could not imagine how anyone could know where the ball was. The next thing she knew, she was in the water. She was knocked down again. She came up gasping, salt water in her eyes and down her throat. Somebody pushed her farther out, deeper.

Now she began to feel truly alarmed. These women, like all Tahitians, had learned to swim before they could walk, but Alma had neither confidence nor proficiency in the water. Her skirts were soaked and heavy, which alarmed her more. The waves were not large, but nevertheless they were waves, and they swelled over her. The ball hit her in the ear; she did not see who had thrown it. Somebody called her a *poreito*—which, strictly translated, meant "shellfish," but vernacularly was a quite rude term for the female genitalia. What had Alma done to deserve this insult of *poreito*?

Then she was underwater again, knocked over by three women who were attempting to run over her. They succeeded: they ran over her. One of them pushed off Alma's chest with her feet—using Alma's body for leverage, as one would use a rock in a pond. Another kicked her in the face, and now she was fairly certain her nose was broken. Alma struggled again to the surface, fighting for breath and spitting out blood. She heard somebody call her a *pua'a*—a hog. She was pushed under again. This time, she felt sure it was intentional; her head had been shoved down from the back by two strong hands. She surfaced once more, and saw the ball fly past her. She dimly heard the cheers of the crowd. Again, she was trampled. Again, she went under. When she tried to surface this time, she could not: somebody was actually sitting on her.

What happened next was an impossible thing: a complete halting of time. Eyes open, mouth open, nose streaming blood into Matavai Bay, immobilized and helpless underwater, Alma realized she was about to die. Shockingly, she relaxed. It was not so bad, she thought. It would be so easy, in fact. Death—so feared and so dodged—was, once you faced it, the simplest thing going. In order to die, one merely had to stop attempting to live.

One merely had to agree to vanish. If Alma simply remained still, pinned beneath the bulk of this unknown opponent, she would be effortlessly erased. With death, all suffering would end. Doubt would end. Shame and guilt would end. All her questions would end. Memory—most mercifully of all—would end. She could quietly excuse herself from life. Ambrose had excused himself, after all. What a relief it must have been to him! Here she had been pitying Ambrose his suicide, but what a welcome deliverance he must have felt! She ought to have been envying him! She could follow him straight there, straight into death. What reason did she have to claw for the air? What point was in the fight?

She relaxed even more.

She saw pale light.

She felt invited toward something lovely. She felt summoned. She remembered her mother's dying words: *Het is fign.*

It is pleasant.

Then—in the seconds that remained before it would have been too late to reverse course at all—Alma suddenly knew something. She knew it with every scrap of her being, and it was not a negotiable bit of information: she knew that she, the daughter of Henry and Beatrix Whittaker, had not been put on this earth to drown in five feet of water. She also knew this: if she had to kill somebody in order to save her own life, she would do so unhesitatingly. Lastly, she knew one other thing, and this was the most important realization of all: she knew that the world was plainly divided into those who fought an unrelenting battle to live, and those who surrendered and died. This was a simple fact. This fact was not merely true about the lives of human beings; it was also true of every living entity on the planet, from the largest creation down to the humblest. It was even true of mosses. This fact was the very mechanism of nature—the driving force behind all existence, behind all transmutation, behind all variation—and it was the explanation for the entire world. It was the explanation Alma had been seeking forever.

She came up out of the water. She flung away the body on top of her as though it were nothing. Nose streaming blood, eyes stinging, wrist sprained, chest bruised, she surfaced and sucked in breath. She looked around for the woman who had been holding her under. It was her dear friend, that fearless giantess Sister Manu, whose head was scarred to pieces from all the various awful battles of her own life. Manu was laughing at the expression on Alma's face. The laughter was affectionate—perhaps even comradely—but still, it was laughter. Alma grabbed Manu by the neck. She gripped her friend as though to crush her throat. At the top of her voice, Alma thundered, just as the Hiro contingent had taught her:

"*OVAU TEIE!*
TOA HAU A'E TAU METUA I TA 'OE!
E 'ORE TAU 'SOMORE E MAE QE IA 'EO!"

THIS IS ME!
MY FATHER WAS A GREATER WARRIOR THAN YOUR FATHER!
YOU CANNOT EVEN LIFT MY SPEAR!

Then Alma let go, releasing her grip on Sister Manu's neck. Without a moment's hesitation, Manu howled back in Alma's face a magnificent roar of approval.

Alma marched toward the beach.

She was oblivious to everyone and everything in her midst. If anyone on the beach was either cheering for her or against her, she could not possibly have noticed.

She came striding out of the sea like she was born from it.

Pl. 37.

Bessa del.

1

2

Gabriel Sc.

Thick Shell bark Hickory.

Juglans laciniosa.

Juglans laciniosa

PART FIVE

The Curator of Mosses

Chapter Twenty-seven

Alma Whittaker arrived in Holland in mid-July of 1854.

She had been at sea for more than a year. It had been an absurd voyage—or, rather, it had been a *series* of absurd voyages. She had departed Tahiti in mid-April the year before, sailing on a French cargo ship heading to New Zealand. She had been forced to wait in Auckland for two months before she found a Dutch merchant ship willing to take her on as a passenger to Madagascar, whence she'd traveled in the company of a large consignment of sheep and cattle. From Madagascar, she'd sailed to Cape Town on an impossibly antique Dutch *fluyt*—a ship that represented the finest of seventeenth-century maritime technology. (This had been the only leg of the voyage where, in fact, she truly feared she might die.) From Cape Town, she had proceeded slowly up the western coast of the African continent, stopping to change vessels in the ports of Accra and Dakar. From Dakar, she'd found another Dutch merchant ship heading first to Madeira, then up to Lisbon, across the Bay of Biscay, through the English Channel, and all the way to Rotterdam. In Rotterdam, she had purchased a ticket on a steam-powered passenger boat (the first steamer she'd ever been on), which carried her up and around the Dutch coast, finally heading down the Zuiderzee to Amsterdam. There, on July 18, 1854, she disembarked at last.

Her journey might have been both swifter and easier if she'd not had Roger the dog along with her. But she did have him, for when the time had come to leave Tahiti at last, she'd found herself morally incapable of leaving him behind. Who would take care of unlovable Roger, in her absence? Who would risk his bites, in order to feed him? She could not be entirely certain that the Hiro contingent would not eat Roger once she was gone. (Roger would not have made for much of a meal; nonetheless, she could not bear to imagine him turning on a spit.) Most significantly of all, he was Alma's last tangible link to her husband. Roger had probably been there in the *fare* when Ambrose had died. Alma imagined the constant little dog standing guard in the center of the room during Ambrose's final hours, barking out protection against ghosts and demons and all the attendant horrors of extraordinary despair. For that reason alone she was honor bound to keep him.

Unfortunately, few sea captains welcome the company of woebegone, hunchbacked, unfriendly little island dogs on their ships. Most had simply refused Roger, and thus sailed on without Alma, delaying her journey considerably. Even when they had not refused, Alma sometimes had been required to pay double fare for the privilege of Roger's company. She paid. She sliced open yet more hidden pockets in the hems of her traveling dresses, and pulled out yet more gold, one coin at a time. One must always have a bribe.

Alma did not mind the onerous length of her journey, not in the least. In fact, she needed every hour of it, and had welcomed those long months of isolation on strange ships and in foreign ports. Since her near-drowning in Matavai Bay during that raucous game of *haru raa puu*, Alma had been balancing on the keenest edge of thought she had ever experienced, and she did not want her thinking disturbed. The idea that had struck her with such force while she was underwater now inhabited her, and it would not be shaken. She could not always identify whether the idea was chasing her, or whether she was chasing it. At times, the idea seemed like a creature in the corner of a dream—drawing closer, then vanishing, and then reappearing. She pursued the idea all day long, in page after page of scrawling, vigorous notes. Even at night, her mind tracked the footsteps of this idea so relentlessly that she would awaken every few hours with the need to sit up in bed and write more.

Alma's greatest strength was not as a writer, it must be said, although she had already authored two—nearly three—books. She had never claimed
 literary talent. Her books on mosses were nothing that anyone would read

for pleasure, nor were they even exactly *readable*, except to a small cadre of bryologists. Her greatest strength was as a taxonomist, with a bottomless memory for species differentiation and a bludgeoningly relentless capacity for minutiae. Decidedly, she was no storyteller. But ever since fighting her way to the surface that afternoon in Matavai Bay, Alma believed that she now had a story to tell—an immense story. It was not a cheerful story, but it explained a good deal about the natural world. In fact, she believed, it explained everything.

Here is the story that Alma wanted to tell: The natural world was a place of punishing brutality, where species large and small competed against each other in order to survive. In this struggle for existence, the strong endured; the weak were eliminated.

This in itself was not an original idea. Scientists had been using the phrase "the struggle for existence" for many decades already. Thomas Malthus used it to describe the forces that shaped population explosions and collapses across history. Owen and Lyell used it as well, in their work on extinction and geology. The struggle for existence was, if anything, an obvious point. But Alma's story had a twist. Alma hypothesized, and had come to believe, that the struggle for existence—when played out over vast periods of time—did not merely *define* life on earth; it had *created* life on earth. It had certainly created the staggering variety of life on earth. Struggle was the mechanism. Struggle was the explanation behind all the most troublesome biological mysteries: species differentiation, species extinction, and species transmutation. Struggle explained everything.

The planet was a place of limited resources. Competition for these resources was heated and constant. Individuals who managed to endure the trials of life generally did so because of some feature or mutation that made them more hardy, more clever, more inventive, or more resilient than others. Once this advantageous differentiation was attained, the surviving individuals were able to pass along their beneficial traits to offspring, who were thus able to enjoy the comforts of dominance—that is, until some other, superior, competitor came along, or a necessary resource vanished. During the course of this never-ending battle for survival, the very design of species inevitably shifted.

Alma was thinking somewhat along the lines of what the astronomer William Herschel had called "continuous creation"—the notion of something both eternal and unfolding. But Herschel had believed that creation could be continuous only at the scale of the cosmos, whereas Alma now believed that creation was continuous *everywhere*, at all levels of life—even at the microscopic level, even at the human level. Challenges were omnipresent, and with every moment, the conditions of the natural world changed. Advantages were gained; advantages were lost. There were periods of abundance, followed by periods of *hia'ia*—the seasons of craving. Under the wrong circumstances, anything was capable of extinction. But under the right circumstances, anything was capable of transmutation. Extinction and transmutation had been occurring since the dawn of life, were still occurring now, and would continue to occur until the end of time—and if that did not constitute "continuous creation," then Alma did not know what did.

The struggle for existence, she was certain, had also shaped human biology and human destiny. There was no better example, Alma thought, than Tomorrow Morning, whose entire family had been annihilated by unfamiliar diseases brought upon them by the Europeans' arrival in Tahiti. His bloodline had *nearly* been rendered extinct, but for some reason Tomorrow Morning had not died. Something in his constitution had enabled him to survive, even while Death had come harvesting with both hands, taking all others around him. Tomorrow Morning had endured, though, and had lived to produce heirs, who may even have inherited his strengths and his extraordinary resistance to illness. This is the sort of event that shapes a species.

What's more, Alma thought, the struggle for existence also defined the *inner* life of a human being. Tomorrow Morning was a pagan who had transmuted into a devout Christian—for he was cunning and self-preserving, and had seen the direction the world was taking. He had chosen the future over the past. As a result of his foresight, Tomorrow Morning's children would thrive in a new world, where their father was revered and powerful. (Or, at least, his children would thrive until another wave of challenge arrived to confront them. Then they would have to make their own way. That would be their battle, and nobody could spare them it.)

On the other hand, there was Ambrose Pike, a man whom God had blessed fourfold with genius, originality, beauty, and grace—but who simply did not have the gift of endurance. Ambrose had misread the world. He had wished for the world to be a paradise, when in fact it was a battlefield. He had spent his life longing for the eternal, the constant, and the pure. He desired an airy covenant of angels, but was bound—as is everyone and everything—by the hard rules of nature. Moreover, as Alma well knew, it was not always the most beautiful, brilliant, original, or graceful who survived the struggle for existence; sometimes it was the most ruthless, or the most lucky, or maybe just the most stubborn.

The trick at every turn was to endure the test of living for as long as possible. The odds of survival were punishingly slim, for the world was naught but a school of calamity and an endless burning furnace of tribulation. But those who survived the world shaped it—even as the world, simultaneously, shaped them.

Alma called her idea "A Theory of Competitive Alteration," and she believed she could prove it. Naturally, she could not prove it using the examples of Tomorrow Morning and Ambrose Pike—although they would live forever in her imagination as outsized, romantic, illustrative figures. Even to make mention of them would be grossly unscientific.

She could, however, prove it with mosses.

Alma wrote quickly and copiously. She did not slow down to revise, but would simply tear up old drafts and begin again from scratch, nearly every day. She could not slow her pace; she was not interested in slowing her pace. Like a besotted drunk—who can run without falling, but who cannot *walk* without falling—Alma could only propel herself through her idea with blind speed. She was afraid to slow down and write more carefully, for she feared she might tumble over, lose her nerve, or—worse!—lose her idea.

To tell this story—the story of species transmutation, as demonstrable through the gradual metastasis of mosses—Alma did not need notes, or access to the old library at White Acre, or her herbarium. She needed none of this, for a vast comprehension of moss taxonomy already existed within her head, filling every corner of her cranium with well-remembered facts and details. She also had at her fingertips (or, rather, at her mind's fingertips) all the ideas that had already been written over the last century on the subject of species metamorphosis and geological evolution. Her mind was like a terrific repository of endless shelves, stacked with untold thousands of books and boxes, organized into infinite, alphabetized particulars.

She did not need a library; she *was* a library.

For the first few months of her journey, she wrote and rewrote the fundamental guiding assumptions for her theory, until she finally felt she had it correctly and irreducibly distilled to these ten:

That the distribution of land and water across the face of the earth has not always been where it is now.

That, based upon the fossil record, mosses appear to have endured all geological epochs since the dawn of life.

That mosses appear to have endured these diverse geological epochs through a process of adaptive change.

That mosses can change their fate either by altering their location (i.e., moving to a more favorable climate), or by altering their internal structure (i.e., transmutation).

That the transmutation of mosses has expressed itself over time in a nearly infinite appropriation and discarding of traits, leading to such adaptations as: increased resistance to drying, a decreased reliance upon direct sunlight, and the ability to revive after years of drought.

That the rate of change within moss colonies, and the extent of that change, is so dramatic as to suggest perpetual change.

That competition and the struggle for existence is the mechanism behind this state of perpetual change.

That moss was almost certainly a different entity (most likely algae) before it was moss.

That moss—as the world continues to transform—may itself eventually become a different entity.

That whatever is true for mosses must be true for all living things.

Alma's theory felt audacious and dangerous, even to herself. She knew she was in treacherous territory—not only from a religious perspective (though this did not much concern her), but also from a scientific perspective. As she marched toward her conclusion like a mountaineer, Alma knew she was at risk of falling into the trap that had consumed so many grandiose French thinkers over the centuries—namely, the trap of *l'esprit de système*, where one dreams up some giant and thrilling universal explanation, and then tries to force all facts and reason to bend to that explanation, regardless of whether it makes any sense. But Alma was certain that her theory *did* make sense. The trick would be to prove it in writing.

A ship was as good a place as anywhere to write—and several ships, one after another, moving ponderously across the empty seas, were better still. Nobody disturbed Alma. Roger the dog lay in the corner of her berth and watched her work, panting and scratching at himself and often looking terribly disappointed in life, but he would have done that wherever in the world he happened to be. At night, he would sometimes jump into her bunk and curl up against the crook of her legs. Sometimes he woke Alma with his little moans.

Sometimes Alma, too, uttered little moans in the night. Just as she had found during her first voyage at sea, she discovered that her dreams were vivid and powerful, and that Ambrose Pike figured prominently in them. But now Tomorrow Morning made frequent appearances in her dreams, as well—sometimes even melding with Ambrose into strange, sensual, chimeric figures: Ambrose's head on Tomorrow Morning's body; Tomorrow Morning's voice emerging from Ambrose's throat; one man, during sexual congress with Alma, suddenly transforming into the other. But it was not only Ambrose and Tomorrow Morning who blended together in these strange dreams—*everything* seemed to be merging. In Alma's most compelling nighttime reveries, the old binding closet at White Acre metamorphosed into a cave of mosses; her carriage house became a tiny but pleasant room at the Griffon Asylum; the sweet-smelling meadows of Philadelphia transformed into fields of warm black sand; Prudence was suddenly dressed in Hanneke's clothing; Sister Manu tended to the boxwoods in Beatrix Whittaker's Euclidean garden; Henry Whittaker paddled up the Schuylkill River in a tiny Polynesian outrigger canoe.

Arresting though these images may have been, the dreams somehow did not disturb Alma. Instead, they filled her with the most astonishing sensation of synthesis—as though all the most disparate elements of her biography were at last knitting together. All the things that she had ever known or loved in the world were stitching themselves up and becoming *one thing*. Realizing this made her feel both unburdened and triumphant. She had that feeling again—that feeling she had experienced only once before, in the weeks leading up to her wedding with Ambrose—of being most spectacularly alive. Not merely alive, but outfitted with a mind that was functioning at the uppermost limits of its capacity—a mind that was seeing everything, and understanding everything, as though watching it all from the highest imaginable ridge.

She would awaken, catch her breath, and immediately begin writing again.

Having established the ten guiding principles of her daring theory, Alma now harnessed her most quivering, electrified energies, and wrote the history of the Moss Wars of White Acre. She wrote the story of the twenty-six years she had spent observing the advance and retreat of competing colonies of moss across one tumble of boulders at the edge of the woods. She focused her attention most specifically upon the genus *Dicranum*, because it demonstrated the most elaborate range of variation within the moss family. Alma knew of *Dicranum* species that were short and plain, and others that were dressed in exotic fringe. There were species that were straight-leafed, others that were twisted, others that lived only on rotting logs beside stones, others that claimed the sunniest crests of tall boulders, some that proliferated in puddled water, and one that grew most aggressively near the droppings of white-tailed deer.

Over her decades of study, Alma had noticed that the most similar *Dicranum* species were the ones that could be found right next to each other. She argued that this was not accidental—that the rigors of competition for sunlight, soil, and water had forced the plants, over the millennia, into evolving minuscule adaptations that would advantage them ever so slightly over their neighbors. This is why three or four variations of *Dicranum* could simultaneously exist on one boulder: they had each found their own niche in this contained, compressed environment, and were now defending their individual territory with slight adaptations. These adaptations did not have to be extraordinary (the mosses did not need to grow flowers, or fruit, or wings); they simply needed to be different *enough* to outcompete rivals—and no rival in the world was more threatening than the rival who was brushing right up against you. The most urgent war is always the one fought at home.

Alma reported in exhaustive detail battles whose victories and defeats were measured in inches, and over decades. She recounted how climate alterations over those decades had given advantages to one variety over another, how birds had transformed the destiny of the mosses, and how—when the old oak beside the pasture fence fell and the pattern of shade shifted overnight—the whole universe of the rock field changed with it.

She wrote, "The greater the crisis, it seems, the swifter the evolution."

She wrote, "All transformation appears to be motivated by desperation and emergency."

She wrote, "The beauty and variety of the natural world are merely the visible legacies of endless war."

She wrote, "The victor shall win—but only until he no longer wins."

She wrote, "This life is a tentative and difficult experiment. Sometimes there will be victory after suffering—but nothing is promised. The most precious or beautiful individual may not be the most resilient. The battle of nature is not marked by evil, but by this one mighty and indifferent natural law: that there are simply too many life forms, and not enough resources for all to survive."

She wrote, "Ongoing battle between and among species is inescapable, as is loss, as is biological modification. Evolution is a brutal mathematics, and the long road of time is littered with the fossilized remnants of incalculable failed experiments."

She wrote, "Those who are ill-prepared to endure the battle for survival should perhaps never have attempted living in the first place. The only unforgivable crime is to cut short the experiment of one's own life before its natural end. To do so is a weakness and a pity—for the experiment of life will cut itself off soon enough, in all our cases, and one may just as well have the courage and the curiosity to stay in the battle until one's eventual and inevitable demise. Anything less than a fight for endurance is cowardly. Anything less than a fight for endurance is a refusal of the great covenant of life."

Sometimes she had to cross out entire pages of work, when she looked up from her writing only to realize that hours had passed, and she had not stopped scribbling for a moment, but was no longer exactly discussing mosses.

Then she would go for a brisk circumambulation of the ship's deck—whatever ship it happened to be—with Roger the dog trailing behind her. Her hands would be trembling and her heart racing with emotion. She would clear her head and her lungs, and reconsider her position. Afterward, she would return to her berth, sit down with a fresh sheet of paper, and begin writing all over again.

She repeated this exercise hundreds of times, for close to fourteen months.

By the time Alma arrived in Rotterdam, her thesis was nearly complete. She did not consider it entirely complete, for something about it was still missing. The creature in the corner of the dream was still gazing at her, unsatisfied and unsettled. This sense of incompletion chewed at her, and she resolved to keep at the idea until she had conquered it. That said, she did feel that most of her theory was irrefutably accurate. If she was correct in her thinking, then she was holding in her hand a rather revolutionary forty-page scientific document. And if, instead, she was incorrect in her thinking? Well, then she had—at the very least—written the most detailed description of life and death in a Philadelphia moss colony that the scientific world would ever see.

In Rotterdam, she rested for a few days at the only hotel she could find that would accept Roger's presence. She and Roger had walked the city for much of an afternoon, in an all but futile search for lodging. Along the way, she'd become increasingly irritated by the bilious looks that hotel clerks kept throwing their way. She could not help but think that if Roger were a more handsome dog, or a more charming dog, she would not have encountered so much trouble finding a room. This struck Alma as terribly unjust, for she had come to regard the little orange mongrel as noble in his own fashion. Had he not just crossed the world? How many supercilious hotel clerks could say the same? But she supposed this was the way of life—prejudice and ignominy and their sorry like.

As for the hotel that did accept them, it was a squalid place, run by a rheumy old woman who peered at Roger over the desk and said, "I once had a cat who looked just like him."

Dear God! Alma thought in horror at the idea of such a sad beast.

"You aren't a whore, are you?" asked the woman, just to be certain.

This time, Alma uttered her "Dear God!" aloud. She simply could not help herself. Her answer seemed to satisfy the proprietress.

The tarnished mirror in the hotel room revealed to Alma that she did not look much more civilized than Roger. She could not arrive in Amsterdam looking like this. Her wardrobe was a ruin and a havoc. Her hair, which had grown increasingly white, was a ruin and a havoc, as well. There was nothing to be done about the hair, but over the next few days she had several new frocks quickly sewn up. They were nothing fine (she modeled them on Hanneke's original, practical pattern) but at least they were new, clean, and intact. She purchased new shoes. She sat in a park and wrote long letters to both Prudence and Hanneke, alerting them that she had reached Holland, and that she intended to remain here indefinitely.

She was nearly out of money. She still had a bit of gold sewn into her tattered hems, but not much. She'd kept precious little of her father's inheritance to begin with, and now—over these last years of travel—the better part of her modest bequest had been spent, one precious coin at a time. She was left with a sum not nearly sufficient to meet the simplest demands of life. Of course, she knew she could always get more money, if true emergency were to arise. She supposed she could walk into any countinghouse at the Rotterdam docks and—using Dick Yancey's name and her father's legacy—easily draw a loan against the Whittaker fortune. But she did not wish to do this. She did not feel that the fortune was rightfully hers. It struck her as a matter of utmost personal consequence that she—from this point forth—make her own way in the world.

Letters posted and a fresh wardrobe procured, Alma and Roger left Rotterdam on a steamboat—by far the easiest part of their journey—and headed to the Port of Amsterdam. Upon their arrival, Alma left her luggage at a modest hotel near the docks and hired a coachman (who, for an additional fee of twenty stivers, was finally persuaded to accept Roger as a passenger). The coach took them all the way to the quiet neighborhood of Plantage, straight to the gates of the Hortus Botanicus.

Alma stepped out into the slanting early-evening sun outside the botanical garden's tall brick walls. Roger was by her side; under her arm was a parcel wrapped in plain brown paper. A young man in a tidy guard's uniform stood at the gate, and Alma approached, asking in her easy Dutch whether the director was on the premises today. The young man confirmed that the director was indeed on the premises, because the director came to work every day of the year.

Alma smiled. Naturally he does, she thought.

"Would it be possible to have a word with him?" she asked.

"Might I ask who you are, and what your business is?" asked the young man, aiming condemnatory looks at both her and Roger. She did not object to his questions, but she certainly objected to his tone.

"My name is Alma Whittaker, and my business is the study of mosses and the transmutation of species," she said.

"And why should the director want to see you?" the guard asked.

She drew herself up to her most formidable height and, like a *rauti*, launched into an imposing recitation of her bloodline. "My father was Henry Whittaker, whom some in your country once called 'The Prince of Peru.' My paternal grandfather was the Apple Magus to His Majesty King George III of England. My maternal grandfather was Jacob van Devender, a master of ornamental aloes, and the director of these gardens for thirty-some years—a position that he inherited from his father, who, in turn, had inherited it from *his* father, and so forth, all the way back to the original founding of this institution in 1638. Your current director is, I believe, a man named Dr. Dees van Devender. He is my uncle. His older sister was named Beatrix van Devender. She was my mother, and a virtuoso of Euclidean botany. My mother was born, if I am not mistaken, just around the corner from where we are now standing, in a private home outside the walls of the Hortus—where all van Devenders since the middle of the seventeenth century have been born."

The guard gaped at her.

She concluded, "If this is too much information for you to retain, young man, you may simply tell my uncle Dees that his niece from America would very much like to meet him."

Chapter Twenty-eight

Dees van Devender stared at Alma from across a cluttered table in his office.

Alma allowed him to stare. Her uncle had not spoken to her since she had been ushered into his chambers a few minutes earlier, nor had he invited her to have a chair. He was not being impolite; he was simply Dutch, and therefore cautious. He was taking her in. Roger sat at Alma's side, looking like a crooked little hyena. Uncle Dees took in the dog, as well. Generally speaking, Roger did not like to be looked at. Normally, when strangers stared at Roger, he would turn his back on them, hang his head, and sigh in misery. But suddenly Roger did the strangest thing. He left Alma's side, walked under the table, and lay down with his chin upon Dr. van Devender's feet. Alma had never seen the likes of it. She was about to comment upon it, but her uncle—completely unconcerned about the cur on his shoes—spoke first.

"*Je lijkt niet op je moeder,*" he said.

You do not look like your mother.

"I know," Alma replied in Dutch.

He went on: "You look precisely like that father of yours."

Alma nodded. She could tell by his tone that this was not a point in her favor, her resemblance to Henry Whittaker. Then again, it never had been.

He stared some more. She stared back. She was as riveted by his face as he was by hers. If Alma did not look like Beatrix Whittaker, then this man most certainly *did*. It was a most marked similarity—her mother's face all over again, but elderly, male, bearded, and, at the moment, suspicious. (Well, to be honest, the suspicion only heightened his resemblance to Beatrix.)

"Whatever became of my sister?" he asked. "We heard of the rise of your father—everyone in European botany did—but we never heard from Beatrix again."

Nor did she hear from you, Alma thought, but she did not say it. She did not really blame anyone in Amsterdam for never having attempted to communicate with Beatrix since—when was it?—1792. She knew how the van Devenders were: stubborn. It would never have worked. Her mother would never have yielded.

"My mother lived a prosperous life," Alma replied. "She was content. She made a most remarkable classical garden, much admired throughout Philadelphia. She worked alongside my father in the botanicals trade, straight up to her death."

"Which was when?" he asked, in a tone that would have befitted an officer of the police.

"In August of 1820," she replied.

Hearing the date caused a grimace to cross her uncle's face. "So long ago," he said. "Too young."

"She had a sudden death," Alma lied. "She did not suffer."

He looked at her for a while longer, then took a leisurely sip of coffee and helped himself to a bite of *wentelteefje* from the small plate before him. Clearly, she had interrupted an evening snack. She would have given almost anything for a taste of that *wentelteefje*. It looked and smelled wonderful. When was the last time she'd had cinnamon toast? Probably the last time Hanneke had made it for her. The aroma made her weak with nostalgia. But Uncle Dees did not offer her any coffee, and he certainly did not offer her a share of his beautiful, golden, buttery *wentelteefjes*.

"Would you like me to tell you anything about your sister?" Alma asked at length. "I believe your memories of her would be a child's memories. I could tell you stories, if you like."

He did not respond. She tried to imagine him as Hanneke had always depicted him—as a sweet-natured ten-year-old boy, weeping at his older sister's elopement to America. Hanneke had told Alma many times of how

Dees had clung to Beatrix's skirts, until he'd had to be pried off. She'd also described how Beatrix had scolded her little brother to never again let the world see his tears. Alma found it difficult to picture. He looked dreadfully old now, and dreadfully grave.

She said, "I grew up with Dutch tulips all around me—descendants of the bulbs that my mother took with her to Philadelphia from right here at the Hortus."

Still, he did not speak. Roger sighed, shifted, and curled up even closer to Dees's legs.

After a spell, Alma changed tack. "I should also let you know that Hanneke de Groot still lives. I believe you may have known her long ago."

Now a new expression crossed the old man's face: wonderment.

"Hanneke de Groot," he marveled. "I have not thought of her in years. Hanneke de Groot? Imagine it . . ."

"Hanneke is strong and healthy, you'll be happy to hear," Alma said. There was a bit of wishful thinking in this statement, as Alma had not seen Hanneke in nearly three years. "She remains the head housekeeper of my late father's estate."

"Hanneke was my sister's maid," Dees said. "She was so young when she came to us. She was a sort of nursemaid to me, for a while."

"Yes," said Alma, "she was a sort of nursemaid to me, too."

"Then we were both fortunate," he said.

"I agree. I consider it one of the finest blessings of my life, to have passed my youth in Hanneke's care. She formed me, nearly as much as my own parents formed me."

The staring recommenced. This time, Alma allowed the silence to stand. She watched as her uncle took a forkful of *wentelteefje* and dipped it in his coffee. He enjoyed his bite unhurriedly, without making so much as a drip or a crumb. She needed to learn where she could procure such fine *wentelteefjes* as this.

At last, Dees wiped his mouth on a plain napkin and said, "Your Dutch is not awful."

"Thank you," she said. "I spoke much of it, as a child."

"How are your teeth?"

"Quite well, thank you," said Alma. She had nothing to hide from this man.

He nodded. "The van Devenders all have good teeth."

"A lucky inheritance."

"Did my sister have any other children, apart from you?"

"She had one other daughter—adopted. That is my sister Prudence, who now operates a school from within my father's old estate."

"Adopted," he said neutrally.

"My mother was not blessed with fecundity," Alma elaborated.

"What of you?" he asked. "Do you have children?"

"I, like my mother, was also not blessed with fecundity," Alma said. This understated the situation considerably, but at least it answered the question.

"A husband?" he asked.

"Deceased, I'm afraid."

Uncle Dees nodded, but did not offer condolence. This amused Alma; her mother would have responded the same way. Facts are facts. Death is death.

"And you, sir?" she ventured. "Is there a Mrs. van Devender?"

"Dead, you know."

She nodded, exactly as he had nodded. It was a bit perverse, but she was enjoying everything about this frank, blunt, desultory conversation. With no sense of when or where it all might end, or whether her destiny was or was not meant to intertwine with the destiny of this old man, she felt she was on familiar territory here—Dutch territory, van Devender territory. She had not felt so at home in ages.

"How long do you intend to stay in Amsterdam?" Dees asked.

"Indefinitely," Alma said.

This took him aback. "If you've come seeking charity," he said, "we have nothing to offer."

She smiled. Oh, Beatrix, she thought, how I have missed you these many years.

"I am not in need of charity," she said. "My father left me well provided for."

"Then what are your intentions for your stay in Amsterdam?" he asked, with undisguised wariness.

"I would like to work here, at the Hortus Botanicus."

Now he looked genuinely alarmed. "Dear heavens!" he said. "In what possible capacity?"

"As a botanist. Specifically, as a bryologist."

"A *bryologist*? But what on earth do you know about mosses?"

Here Alma could not help but laugh. It was a marvelous thing, to laugh. She could not think of the last time she had laughed. She laughed so hard, she had to put her face in her hands for a spell, in order to hide her hilarity. This spectacle only seemed to unnerve her poor old uncle more. She was not helping her own cause.

Why had she thought her modest reputation might have preceded her? Oh, foolish pride!

Once Alma had contained herself, she wiped her eyes and smiled at him. "I know I have taken you by surprise, Uncle Dees," she said, falling naturally into a warmer and more familiar tone. "Please forgive me. I wish you to understand that I am a woman of independent means, who does not come here to disrupt your life in any manner. However, it is also the case that I am possessed of certain abilities—both as a scholar and as a taxonomist—which might be of use to an institution such as yours. I can say without reservation that it would bring me the greatest pleasure and contentment to spend the rest of my working life here, giving my time and energies to an institution that has figured so prominently both in the history of botany, and in the history of my own family."

With this, she took the brown-wrapped parcel from under her arm and set it on the edge of his table.

"I will not ask you to take my word for my abilities, Uncle," she said. "This package contains a theory I have recently brought forth, based upon research I have conducted over the past thirty years of my life. Some of the ideas may strike you as rather bold, but I ask only that you read it with an open mind—and, needless to say, that you keep its findings to yourself. Even if you don't agree with my conclusions, I think you will get a sense of my scientific aptitude. I ask you to treat this document with respect, for it is all that I have and all that I am."

He made no commitment.

"You do read English, I assume?" she asked.

He raised one white eyebrow, as though to say, *Honestly, woman—show some respect.*

Before Alma passed the small package to her uncle, she reached for a pencil on his desk and asked, "May I?"

He nodded, and she wrote something on the outside of the parcel.

"This is the name and address of the hotel where I am currently staying, near the port. Take your time in reading this document, and let me know if you would like to speak to me again. If I have heard no word from you within a week, I shall return here, collect my thesis, bid you farewell, and go on about my way. After that, I promise, I shan't bother you or anyone in the family again."

As Alma was saying this, she watched her uncle spear another small triangle of *wentelteefje* on his fork. Rather than carry the fork to his mouth, though, he tilted sideways in his chair, slowly sliding one shoulder down, in order to offer the food to Roger the dog—even as he kept his eye on Alma, pretending to listen to her with complete absorption.

"Oh, do be careful . . ." Alma leaned over the table in concern. She was about to warn her uncle that this dog had a terrible habit of biting anyone who tried to feed him, but before she could speak, Roger had raised up his misshapen little head and—as delicately as a fine-mannered lady—removed the cinnamon toast from the tines of the fork.

"Well, I'll be," Alma marveled, backing off.

Her uncle had still made no overt mention of the dog, though, so Alma said nothing more on the matter.

She brushed off her skirts and collected herself. "It has been a most sincere pleasure to meet you," she said. "This encounter has meant more to me, sir, than you could possibly suspect. I have never before had the pleasure of knowing an uncle, you see. I do hope you will enjoy my paper, and that it will not overly shock you. Good day, then."

He responded with nothing more than a nod.

Alma started for the door. "Come, Roger," she said, without turning to look behind her.

She waited, holding the door open, but the dog did not move.

"Roger," she said more firmly, turning to look at him. "Come now."

Still, the dog did not move from Uncle Dees's feet.

"Go on, dog," said Dees, not very convincingly, and without moving so much as an inch.

"Roger!" Alma demanded, bending down to see him more clearly under the table. "Come now, don't be silly!"

She had never before needed to call for him; he had always simply followed her. But Roger put back his ears and held his ground. He was not going to leave.

"He's never behaved like this before," she apologized. "I'll carry him out."

But her uncle put up a hand. "Perhaps the little fellow can stay here with me for a night or two," he suggested casually, as though it meant nothing to him whatsoever, one way or the other. He did not even meet Alma's eye as he said it. He looked—for just a moment—like a young boy, trying to persuade his mother to permit him to keep a stray.

Ah, Uncle Dees, she thought. Now I can see you.

"Of course," Alma said. "If you're quite certain it's not a bother?"

Dees shrugged, nonchalant as could be, and stabbed another piece of *wentelteefje*.

"We will manage," he said, and fed the dog again, straight from the fork.

Alma walked briskly away from the Hortus Botanicus, in the general direction of the port. She did not wish to take a hackney cab; she felt far too animated to sit in a coach. She felt empty-handed and lighthearted and somewhat shaken and very much alive. And hungry. She kept turning her head and looking for Roger, out of force of habit, but he was not trailing behind her. Dear heavens, she had just left both her dog and her life's work in that man's office, after a mere fifteen-minute interview!

What an encounter! What a risk!

But it was a risk she had had to take, for this is where Alma wanted to be—if not at the Hortus, then here in Amsterdam, or at least in Europe. She had dearly missed the northern world during her time in the South Seas. She had missed the change of seasons, and the hard, bright, bracing sunlight of winter. She had missed the rigors of a cold climate, and the rigors of the mind, as well. She was simply not made for the tropics—neither in complexion nor in disposition. There were those who loved Tahiti because it felt to them like Eden—like the beginning of history—but Alma did not wish to live at the beginning of history; she wished to live within humanity's most recent moment, at the cusp of invention and progress. She did not wish to inhabit a land of spirits and ghosts; she desired a world of telegraphs, trains, improvements, theories, and science, where things changed by the day. She longed to work again in a productive and serious environment, surrounded by productive and serious people. She desired the comforts of crowded bookshelves, collection jars, papers that would not be lost to mold, and microscopes that would not go missing in the night. She longed for access to the latest scientific journals. She longed for peers.

More than anything, she longed for family—and the sort of family with whom she'd been raised: sharp, inquiring, challenging, and intelligent. She wanted to feel like a Whittaker again, surrounded by Whittakers. But since there were no more Whittakers left in the world (aside from Prudence Whittaker Dixon, who was busy with her school; and aside from whatever members of her father's appalling and unknown clan had not yet died in English prisons) then she wanted to be around the van Devenders.

If they would have her.

But what if they would not have her? Well, that was the gamble. The van Devenders—whatever remained of *them*—might not long for her company quite as profoundly as she longed for theirs. They might not welcome her offered contributions to the Hortus. They might see her as nothing but an interloper, an amateur. It had been a precarious play for Alma to have left her treatise with her uncle Dees. His reaction to her work might be anything— from boredom (*the mosses of Philadelphia?*), to religious offense (*continuous creation?*), to scientific alarm (*a theory for the* entire *natural world?*). Alma knew that her paper ran the risk of making her look reckless, arrogant, naive, anarchistic, degenerate, and even a tiny bit French. Yet her paper was also—more than anything else—a portrait of her capacities, and she wished for her family to know her capacities, if they were to know her at all.

Should the van Devenders and the Hortus Botanicus turn Alma away, however, she resolved to square her shoulders and carry on. Perhaps she would take up residence in Amsterdam regardless, or perhaps she would return to Rotterdam, or perhaps she would move to Leiden and live near the university there. If not Holland, there was always France, always Germany. She could find a position elsewhere, perhaps even at another botanical garden. It was difficult for a woman, but not impossible—especially with her father's name and Dick Yancey's influence to lend her credibility. She knew of all the prominent professors of bryology in Europe; many had been her correspondents over the years. She could seek them out, and ask to become somebody's assistant. Alternatively, she could always teach—not at the university level, but one could always find a position as a governess within an affluent family somewhere. If not botany, she could teach languages. Heaven knows, she had enough of them in her head.

She walked the city for hours. She was not ready to return to the hotel. She could not imagine sleeping. She both missed Roger and felt liberated without him trailing along behind her. She did not yet have a grasp of Amsterdam's geography, so she wandered, losing and finding herself, through the city's curious shape—meandering all around its great half-drawn bow, with its five giant, curving canals. She crossed over waterways again and again, on dozens of bridges whose names she did not know. She strolled along Herengracht, admiring the handsome homes with their forked chimneys and jutting gables. She passed the Palace. She found the central post office. She found a café, where she was at last able to order a plate of her own *wentelteefjes*, which she ate with more pleasure than any meal she could remember—while at the same time reading an oldish copy of *Lloyd's Weekly Newspaper*, which some kind British tourist had probably left behind.

Night fell, and she kept walking. She passed ancient churches and new theaters. She saw taverns and gin shops and arcades and worse. She saw old Puritans in short cloaks and neck ruffs, looking as if they had stepped out of the time of Charles I. She saw young women with their arms bared, beckoning men into darkened doorways. She saw—and smelled—the herring-packing concerns. She saw the houseboats along the canals, with their thrifty potted gardens and prowling cats. She walked through the Jewish quarter, and saw the workshops of the diamond cutters. She saw foundling hospitals and orphanages; she saw printing houses and banks and countinghouses; she saw the tremendous central flower market, shuttered for the night. All around her—even at this late hour—she sensed the hum of commerce.

Amsterdam—built on silt and stilts, protected and maintained by pumps, sluices, valves, dredging machines, and dikes—struck Alma not so much as a city, but as an *engine*, a triumph of human industriousness. It was the most contrived place one could ever imagine. It was the sum of human intelligence. It was perfect. She never wanted to leave.

It was long after midnight when she finally returned to her hotel. Her feet were blistering in their new shoes. The proprietress did not respond kindly to her late-night knock on the door.

"Where is your dog?" demanded the woman.

"I've left him with a friend."

"Humph," said the woman. She could not have looked more disapproving if Alma had said, "I've sold him to a gypsy."

She handed Alma her key. "No men in your room tonight, remember."

Not tonight, nor any other night, my dear, thought Alma. But thank you for even imagining it.

The next morning, Alma was awakened by a pounding on her door. It was her old friend, the peevish hotel proprietress.

"There's a coach waiting for you, lady!" the woman yelled, in a voice as pure as tar.

Alma stumbled to the door. "I am not expecting a coach," she said.

"Well, it's expecting you," yelled the woman. "Get dressed. The man says he ain't leaving without you. Take your bags, he says. He paid your room already. I don't know where these people get the idea that I am a messenger service."

Alma, muzzy-headed, dressed and packed her two small bags. She took a little extra time to make her bed—perhaps conscientiously, or perhaps because she was stalling. What coach? Was she being arrested? Expatriated? Was this some sort of a flimflam, a trick played on tourists? But she wasn't a tourist.

She came downstairs and found a liveried driver, waiting for her beside a modest private carriage.

"Good morning, Miss Whittaker," he said, tipping his hat. He tossed her bags up by his seat in the front. She had the worst feeling she was about to be put on a train.

"I'm sorry," she said. "I don't believe I requested a coach."

"Dr. van Devender sent me," he said, opening the carriage door. "Up you go, now—he's waiting, and anxious to see you."

It took nearly an hour to wind through the city back to the botanical gardens. Alma thought it would have been far faster to walk. More soothing, too. She would have been less agitated, could she have walked. The driver delivered her at last, next to a fine brick house just behind the Hortus, on Plantage Parklaan.

"Go on," he said over his shoulder, fussing with her bags. "Let yourself in—door's open. He's waiting for you, I say."

It was somewhat unsettling for Alma to let herself in to a private home unannounced, but she did as directed. Then again, this home was not entirely foreign, either. If she was not mistaken, her mother had been born here.

She saw an open door just off the receiving hallway, and peeked inside. It was the parlor. She saw her uncle sitting on a divan, waiting for her.

The first thing she noticed was that Roger the dog—incredibly—was curled up on his lap.

The second thing she noticed was that Uncle Dees was holding her treatise in his right hand, resting it lightly on Roger's back, as though the dog were a portable writing desk.

The third thing she noticed was that her uncle's face was wet with tears. His shirt collar was also soaked. His beard appeared to be soaked, as well. His chin was trembling, and his eyes were alarmingly red. It looked as if he had been weeping for hours.

"Uncle Dees!" She rushed to his side. "Whatever is the matter?"

The old man swallowed and took her hand in his. His hand was hot and damp. For some time he could not speak at all. He clutched her fingers tightly. He would not let go of her.

At last, with his other hand, he held up her treatise.

"Oh, Alma," he said, and he did not bother to brush away his tears. "May God bless you, child. You have your mother's mind."

Chapter Twenty-nine

Four years passed.

They were happy years for Alma Whittaker, and why would they not have been? She had a home (her uncle had moved her straight into the van Devender household); she had a family (her uncle's four sons, their lovely wives, and their broods of growing children); she was able to communicate regularly by mail with Prudence and Hanneke back in Philadelphia; and she held a position of considerable responsibility at the Hortus Botanicus. Her official title was Curator van Mossen—the Curator of Mosses. She was given her own office, on the second floor of a pleasant building only two doors down the street from the van Devender residence.

She sent for all her old books and notes from the carriage house back at White Acre, and for her herbarium, too. It was like a holiday for her, the week her shipment arrived; she spent days in nostalgic absorption, unpacking it all. She had missed every item and volume of it. She was blushingly amused to discover, buried in the bottoms of the trunks of books, all her old prurient reading material. She decided to keep the lot of it—though she was sure to keep it well hidden. For one thing, she did not know how to dispose of such scandalous texts respectably. For another thing, these books still had the power to stir her. Even at her advanced age, a stubborn tug of brazen desire lingered within her body, and still demanded her attention on certain nights, when, under the coverlet, she would revisit her familiar old quim, remembering once more the

taste of Tomorrow Morning, the smell of Ambrose, the urgency of life's most stubborn and unrelenting urges. She did not even attempt to fight these urges anymore; by now, it was evident they were a part of her.

Alma earned a respectable salary—her first—at the Hortus, and she shared an assistant and a clerk with the director of mycology and the overseer of ferns (all of whom became dear friends—the first scientific friends she'd ever had). In due course, she made a reputation for herself not only as a brilliant taxonomist but also as a good cousin. It pleased and surprised Alma not a little that she adapted so comfortably to the bustle and tumult of family life, given that she'd always lived such a solitary existence. She delighted in the clever repartee of Dees's children and grandchildren at the dinner table, and took pride in their many achievements and talents. She was honored when the girls would come to her for advice or consolation about their thrilling or terrible romantic disturbances. She saw bits of Retta in their moments of excitement; bits of Prudence in their moments of reserve; bits of herself in their moments of doubt.

Over time, Alma came to be regarded by all the van Devenders as a considerable asset both to the Hortus and to the family—which two entities were utterly indistinguishable, in any case. Alma's uncle gave over to her a small, shady corner of the palm house, and invited her to make a permanent display called the Cave of Mosses. This was both a tricky and a satisfying assignment. Mosses do not like to grow where they are not born, and Alma had difficulty orchestrating the necessary and precise conditions (the correct humidity, the right combination of light and shade, the proper stones, gravel, and logs as substrates) to encourage the moss colonies to flourish in these artificial surroundings. She successfully executed this feat, though, and soon the cave thrived with moss specimens from all over the world. It would be a lifelong project to maintain the exhibit, which required continuous misting (achieved with the help of steam-powered engines), needed to be cooled by insulated walls, and could never be exposed to direct sunlight. Aggressive and fast-growing mosses had to be kept in check, so that rarer, more diminutive species could advance. Alma had read of Japanese monks who maintained their moss gardens by weeding with tiny forceps, and she took up this practice, as well. She could be seen every morning in the Cave of Mosses, removing one tiny invasive strand at a time, by the light of a miner's lantern, using the tips of her fine steel tweezers. She wanted it perfect. She wanted it to glitter like emerald fire—just as that extraordinary moss cave had glittered for her and Tomorrow Morning, years before, in Tahiti.

The Cave of Mosses became a popular exhibit at the Hortus, but only for a certain type of person: the type who longed for cool darkness, for silence, for reverie. (The type of person, in other words, who had little interest in showy blossoms, mammoth lily pads, or crowds of loud families.) Alma enjoyed perching in a corner of the cave and observing these sorts of people enter the world she had made. She saw them caress the pelts of moss, and watched their faces relax, their posture loosen. She felt an affinity with them—the quiet ones.

During those years, Alma also spent a considerable amount of time working over her theory of competitive alteration. Uncle Dees had been urging her to publish the paper since he'd read it upon her arrival in 1854, but Alma had resisted then, and she continued to resist. Moreover, she refused to allow him to discuss her theory with anyone else. Her reluctance brought nothing but frustration to her good uncle, who believed Alma's theory both important and very probably correct. He accused her of being overly timid, of holding back. Specifically, he accused her of fearing religious condemnation, should she make public her notions of continuous creation and species transmutation.

"You simply do not have the courage to be a God-killer," said this good Dutch Protestant, who had attended church quite devoutly every Sabbath of his life. "Come now, Alma—what are you afraid of? Show a little of your father's audacity, child! Go forth and be a terror in the world! Wake up the whole barking dog-kennel of controversy, if you must. The Hortus will protect you! We could publish it ourselves! We even could publish it under my name, if you dread censure."

But Alma was hesitating not from fear of the church, but from a deep conviction that her theory was not quite yet scientifically incontrovertible. A small hole existed in her logic, she felt sure, and she could not deduce how to close it. Alma was a perfectionist and more than a little bit of a pedant, and she certainly was not going to be caught publishing a theory with a hole in it, even a small hole. She was not afraid of offending religion, as she frequently told her uncle; she was afraid of offending something far more sacred to her: *reason*.

For here was the hole in Alma's theory: she could not, for the life of her, understand the evolutionary advantages of altruism and self-sacrifice. If the natural world was indeed the sphere of amoral and constant struggle for survival that it appeared to be, and if outcompeting one's rivals was the key to dominance, adaptation, and endurance—then what was one supposed to make, for instance, of someone like her sister Prudence?

Whenever Alma mentioned her sister's name, with respect to her theory of competitive alteration, her uncle groaned. "Not again!" he would say, pulling at his beard. "No one has heard of Prudence, Alma! No one cares!"

But Alma cared, and the "Prudence Problem," as she came to call it, troubled her mind considerably, for it threatened to undo her entire theory. It especially troubled her because it was all so personal. Alma had been the intended beneficiary, after all, of an act of great generosity and self-sacrifice on Prudence's part almost forty years earlier, and she had never forgotten it. Prudence had silently given up her one true love—with the hope that George Hawkes would marry Alma instead, and that *Alma would benefit from that marriage*. The fact that Prudence's act of sacrifice had been utterly futile did not in any way diminish its sincerity.

Why would a person do such a thing?

Alma could answer that question from a moral standpoint (*Because Prudence is kind and selfless*), but she could not answer it from a biological one (*Why do kindness and selflessness exist?*). Alma entirely understood why her uncle tore at his beard whenever she mentioned the name Prudence. She recognized that—in the vast scope of human and natural history—this tragic triangle between Prudence, George, and herself was so tiny and so insignificant that it was almost farcical to raise the subject at all (and within a scientific discussion, no less). But still—the question would not go away.

Why would a person do such a thing?

Every time Alma thought about Prudence, she was forced to ask herself this question again, and then watch helplessly as her theory of competitive alteration fell apart before her eyes. For Prudence Whittaker Dixon, after all, was scarcely a unique example. Why did *anyone* ever act beyond the scope of base self-interest? Alma could make a fairly persuasive argument as to why mothers, for instance, made sacrifices on behalf of their children (because it was advantageous to continue the family line), but she could not explain why a soldier would run straight into a line of bayonets to protect an injured comrade. How did that action bolster or benefit the brave soldier or his family? It simply did not: through self-sacrifice, the now-dead soldier had negated not only his own future, but the continuation of his bloodline, as well.

Nor could Alma explain why a starving prisoner would give food to a cellmate.

Nor could she explain why a lady would leap into a canal to save another woman's baby, only to drown in the process—which tragic event had just occurred, not long ago, right down the street from the Hortus.

Alma did not know whether, if so confronted, she herself would ever behave in such a noble manner, but others inarguably did so—and fairly routinely, all things considered. Alma had no doubt in her mind that her sister and the Reverend Welles (as another example of extraordinary goodness) would unhesitatingly deny themselves food that another might live, and would just as unhesitatingly risk injury or death to save a stranger's baby, or even a stranger's house cat.

Furthermore, there was nothing analogous to such extreme examples of human self-sacrifice in the rest of the natural world—not so far as she could see. Yes, within a hive of bees, or a pack of wolves, or a flock of birds, or even a colony of mosses, individuals sometimes died for the greater good of the group. But one never saw a wolf saving the life of a bee. One never saw an individual strand of moss choose to die, by giving over its precious water supply to an ant, out of simple beneficence!

These were the sorts of arguments that exasperated her uncle, as Alma and Dees sat up together late into the night, year after year, debating the question. Now it was the early spring of 1858, and they were debating it still.

"Don't be such a tiresome sophist!" Dees said. "Publish the paper as it is."

"I cannot help but be, Uncle," Alma replied, smiling. "Remember—I have my mother's mind."

"You tax my patience, niece," he said. "Publish the paper, let the world debate the subject, and let us rest from this wearisome, long-nosed fault-finding."

But she would not be swayed. "If I can see this hole in my argument, Uncle, then others will surely see it, and my work will not be taken seriously. If the theory of competitive alteration is indeed correct, then it needs to be correct for the entirety of the natural world—humanity included."

"Make an exception for humans," her uncle suggested with a shrug. "Aristotle did."

"I am not talking about the Great Chain of Being, Uncle. I'm not interested in ethical or philosophical arguments; I'm interested in a universal biological theory. The laws of nature cannot admit exceptions, or they cannot stand as laws. Prudence is not exempt from gravity; therefore, she cannot be exempt from the theory of competitive alteration, if that theory is, in fact, true. If she *is* exempt from it, on the other hand, then the theory cannot be true."

"Gravity?" He rolled his eyes. "My goodness, child, listen to you. You wish to be Newton now!"

"I wish to be correct," Alma corrected.

In her lighter moments, Alma found the Prudence Problem almost comical. During the entirety of their youth Prudence had been a problem to Alma, and now—even as Alma had learned to love, appreciate, and respect her sister enormously—Prudence was a problem *still*.

"Sometimes I feel that I would like never to hear the name Prudence spoken in this household again," Uncle Dees said. "I've had it up and down with Prudence."

"Then explain her to me," Alma insisted. "Why does she adopt the orphans of Negro slaves? Why does she give her every last penny to the poor? How does this advantage her? How does this advantage her own offspring? Explain it to me!"

"It advantages her, Alma, because she is a Christian martyr, and she relishes a bit of crucifixion from time to time. I know the type, my dear. There are people, as you surely must realize by now, who take every bit as much pleasure in ministration and self-sacrifice as others do in pillage and murder. Such tiresome exemplars are rare, but they decidedly exist."

"But there we touch upon the heart of our problem again!" Alma retorted. "If my theory is correct, such people should not exist at all. Remember, Uncle, my thesis is not called 'A Theory of the Pleasures of Self-Sacrifice.'"

"Publish it, Alma," he said wearily. "It is a fine piece of thinking, all in one piece. Publish it as it is, and let the world argue this point."

"I cannot publish it," she insisted, "until the point is *inarguable*."

Thus the conversation rotated and circled and ended as always, stuck in the same frustrating corner. Uncle Dees looked down at Roger the dog, curled up in his lap, and said, "You would rescue me if I were drowning in a canal, wouldn't you, my friend?"

Roger thumped his interesting version of a tail in reply.

Alma had to admit: Roger likely *would* rescue Uncle Dees if he were drowning in a canal, or trapped in a fire, or starving in a prison, or pinned beneath a collapsed building—and Dees would certainly do the same for him. The love between Uncle Dees and Roger was every bit as enduring as it had been immediate. They were never to be seen apart, man and dog, not since the moment of their introduction. Very quickly after their arrival in Amsterdam four years earlier, Roger had given Alma to understand that he was no longer her dog—that, in fact, he had never been her dog, nor had he ever been Ambrose's dog, but that he had been Dees's dog all along, by force of pure and plain destiny. The fact that Roger was born in distant Tahiti, whereas Dees van Devender resided in Holland, had been the result, Roger appeared to believe, of an unfortunate clerical error, now thankfully rectified.

As for Alma's role in Roger's life, she had merely been a courier, responsible for transporting the anxious little orange fellow halfway around the world, in order to unite dog and man in the eternal and devoted love that was their rightful due.

Eternal and devoted love.

Why?

Roger was another one Alma couldn't figure out.

Roger and Prudence, both.

The summer of 1858 arrived, and with it a sudden season of death. The sorrows began on the last day of June, when Alma received a letter from her sister, delivering an awful compendium of sad news.

"I have three deaths to report," Prudence warned in the first line. "Perhaps, sister, you had best sit down before you read on."

Alma did not sit down. She stood in the doorway of the van Devender residence on Plantage Parklaan, reading this lamentable communication from distant Philadelphia, while her hands shook in distress.

Firstly, Prudence reported, Hanneke de Groot was dead at the age of eighty-seven. The old housekeeper had passed in her rooms in the basement of White Acre, safe behind the bars of her private vault. She appeared to have died in her sleep, and without suffering.

"We cannot conceive of how we shall carry on here without her," Prudence wrote. "I need not remind you of her goodness and value. She was as a mother to me, as I know she was to you."

But scarcely had Hanneke's body been discovered, Prudence wrote on, than a boy arrived at White Acre with a message from George Hawkes that Retta—"transformed these many years by madness, beyond all recognition"—had expired in her room at the Griffon Asylum for the Insane.

Prudence wrote, "It is challenging to know what one should regret more arduously: Retta's death, or the sad circumstances of her life. I strive to remember the Retta of long ago, so gay and carefree. Scarcely can I see her in my imagination as that girl, before her mind became so dreadfully clouded . . . for that was so long ago, as I have said, when we were all so young."

Then came the most shocking news. Not two days after Retta's death, Prudence reported, George Hawkes himself had died. He had just come from Griffon's, straight from making arrangements for his wife's funeral, and had collapsed on the street in front of his printing shop. He was sixty-seven years old.

"I apologize that it has taken me more than a week to write you this unhappy missive," Prudence concluded, "but my mind is beset by so many thoughts and distresses that it has been difficult for me to proceed. It staggers one's mind. We are all grievously shocked here. Perhaps I have delayed so long in writing this letter because I could not help but think: Every day that I do not tell my poor sister this news, she does not have to bear it. I search my heart for a peppercorn's worth of comfort to offer you, but find it difficult to come by. I scarcely can find comfort for myself. May the Lord receive and preserve them all. I am at a loss for what else to say, please forgive me. The school continues well. The students thrive. Mr. Dixon and the children send their abiding affection—most sincerely, Prudence."

Now Alma did sit, and she put down the letter beside her.

Hanneke, Retta, and George—all gone, in one sweep of the hand.

"Poor Prudence," Alma murmured aloud.

Poor Prudence, indeed, to have lost George Hawkes forever. Of course, Prudence had lost George long ago, but now she had lost him again, and this time forever. Prudence had never stopped loving George, nor he her—or so Hanneke had told Alma. But George had followed poor Retta to her grave, bound forever to the destiny of the tragic little wife he had never loved. All the possibilities of their youth, Alma thought, all run to waste. For the first time, she considered how similarly her fate and her sister's had unfolded—both of them doomed to love men they could not possess, and both of them resolved to carry on bravely despite it. One did the best one could, of course, and there was dignity to be found in stoicism, but truly there were times when the sadness of this world was scarcely to be endured, and the violence of love, Alma thought, was sometimes the most pitiless violence of all.

Her first instinct was to return home with all haste. But White Acre was no longer her home, and even to imagine walking into the old mansion without seeing Hanneke de Groot's face made Alma feel sick and lost. Instead, she went to her office and wrote a letter in reply, searching her own heart for peppercorns of comfort, and finding them scarce. Uncharacteristically, she turned to the Bible, to Psalms. She wrote to her sister, "The Lord is near unto them who are of a broken heart." She spent the entire day behind her closed door, bent quietly in half by grief. She did not burden her uncle with any of this sad news. He had been so pleased to know that his beloved nursemaid Hanneke de Groot still lived; she could not bear to inform him of this death, or the others. She did not wish to lay any trouble upon his good and cheerful spirit.

Only a fortnight later, she would be glad of this decision, when her uncle Dees contracted a fever, took to his bed, and died within the space of a day. It was one of those periodic fevers that swept through Amsterdam in summertime, when the canals grew stale and fetid. One morning, Dees and Alma and Roger shared breakfast together, and by the next breakfast Dees was gone. He was seventy-six. Alma was so ruptured by this loss—on the heels of the others—that she barely knew how to contain herself. She found herself pacing her rooms in the night, pressing one hand against her chest, for fear her ribs would cleave open and her heart would fall to the ground. Alma felt that she had known her uncle for such a short while—not nearly long enough! Why was there never enough time? One day he had been there, and then, the next, called away. All of them had been called away.

Half of Amsterdam, it seemed, gathered for the funeral of Dr. Dees van Devender. His four sons and two eldest grandsons carried the casket from the house on Plantage Parklaan to the church around the corner. A bundle of daughters-in-law and grandchildren clutched each other and wept; they pulled Alma into their midst, and she drew comfort from this press of family. Dees had been much adored. All were bereft. What's more, the family pastor revealed that Dr. van Devender had been a quiet paragon of charitable works for all his life; there were many in this crowd of mourners whose lives he had aided or even saved over the years.

The irony of this revelation—in light of Alma and Dees's interminable midnight debates—made Alma want to cry and laugh at the same time. His lifetime of anonymous generosity certainly placed him high on Maimonides's ladder, she thought, but he might have mentioned it to me at some point! How could he have sat there, year after year, dismissing the scientific relevance of altruism, while at the same time secretly dedicating himself to it quite tirelessly? It made Alma marvel at him. It made her miss him. It made her want to question him and tease him—but he was gone.

After the funeral, Dees's eldest son, Elbert, who would now be taking over directorship of the Hortus, had the good grace to approach Alma and pledge to her that her place, both within the family and at the Hortus, was absolutely assured.

"You need never worry for the future," he said. "We all wish for you to stay."

"Thank you, Elbert," she managed to say, and the two cousins embraced.

"It comforts me to know that you loved him, as did we all," Elbert said.

But no one had loved Dees more than Roger the dog. From the first moment of Dees's illness, the little orange mutt had refused to move from his master's bed; he would not leave after the corpse had been removed, either. He planted himself in the cold sheets and would not budge. He refused to take food—not even the *wentelteefjes* Alma had prepared for him herself, and which she had tearfully tried to feed him by hand. He turned his head to the wall and closed his eyes. She touched his head, spoke to him in Tahitian, and reminded him of his noble lineage, but he did not respond in the least. Within a matter of days, Roger was gone, too.

Were it not for the black cloud of death that swept across Alma's landscape in that summer of 1858, she almost certainly would have heard about the proceedings of the Linnean Society of London on July 1 of that year. She generally made a point of reading notes from all the more important scientific gatherings across Europe and America. But her mind was—forgivably— much distracted that summer. Journals piled on her desk unread, as she grieved. Looking after her Cave of Mosses absorbed whatever scant energy she could muster. Much else went unattended.

And thus she'd missed it.

In fact, she would hear nothing of it until one morning in late December of the following year, when she opened her copy of The *Times* and read a review of a new book, by Mr. Charles Darwin, entitled *On the Origin of Species by Means of Natural Selection, or the Preservation of Favoured Races in the Struggle for Life.*

Chapter Thirty

Of course Alma knew of Charles Darwin; everyone did. In 1839, he'd published a quite popular travel book about his journey to the Galápagos Islands. The book—a charming account—had made him rather famous at the time. Darwin had a light hand on the page, and he'd managed to convey his delight with the natural world in a comfortable and friendly tone that had welcomed readers of all backgrounds. Alma remembered admiring that talent of Darwin's, for she herself could never come close to writing such entertaining, democratic prose.

Reflecting back on it now, what Alma remembered most clearly from *The Voyage of the Beagle* was a description of penguins swimming at night through phosphorescent waters, leaving, Darwin wrote, a "fiery wake" in the darkness. *A fiery wake!* Alma had appreciated that description, and it had stayed with her these last twenty years. She'd even recalled the phrase during her voyage to Tahiti, that marvelous night on the *Elliot*, when she had witnessed such phosphorescence herself. But she did not remember much else about the book, and Darwin had not distinguished himself to any extraordinary extent since. He had retired from travel to a life of more scholarly pursuits—some fine and careful work on barnacles, if Alma recalled correctly. She had certainly never considered him the major naturalist of his generation.

But now, upon reading the review of this new and startling book, Alma discovered that Charles Darwin—that soft-spoken barnacle aficionado, that gentle penguin lover—had been hiding his cards. As it turned out, he had something quite momentous to offer the world.

Alma put down the newspaper and rested her head in her hands.

A fiery wake, indeed.

It took her nearly a week to get a copy of the actual book from England, and Alma waded through those days as though in a trance. She felt she would not be able to produce an adequate reaction to this turn of events until she could read—word for word—what Darwin himself had to say, rather than what was already being said about him.

On January 5—her sixtieth birthday—the book arrived. Alma retired to her office with enough food and drink to sustain her for as long as necessary, and locked herself inside. Then she opened *On the Origin of Species* to the first page, began to read Darwin's lovely prose, and from there fell downward into a deep cavern that resounded from every side with her own ideas.

He had not stolen her theory, needless to say. Not for a moment did that absurd thought even cross her mind—for Charles Darwin had never heard of Alma Whittaker, nor should he have. But like two explorers seeking the same treasure trove from two different directions, she and Darwin had both stumbled on the identical chest of riches. What she had deduced from mosses, he had deduced from finches. What she had observed in the boulder fields of White Acre, he'd seen repeated in the Galápagos Archipelago. Her boulder field was naught but an archipelago itself, writ in miniature. An island is an island, after all—whether it is three feet or three miles across—and all the most dramatic events in the natural world occur on the wild, competitive, tiny battlefields of islands.

It was a beautiful book. She wavered, as she read it, between heartbreak and vindication, between regret and admiration.

Darwin wrote, "More individuals are born than can possibly survive. A grain in the balance will determine which individual shall live and which shall die."

He wrote, "In short, we see beautiful adaptations everywhere, in every part of the organic world."

She felt an upswell of complicated emotion so overwhelming, so dense, that she thought she might faint. It hit her like a blast from a furnace: she had been correct.

She had been correct!

Thoughts of Uncle Dees swarmed her mind, even as she continued reading. Her thoughts of him were constant and contradictory: If only he had lived to see this! Thank God he had not lived to see this! How simultaneously proud and angry he would have been! She would never have heard the end of it: "See, I *told* you to publish!" Yet he would have celebrated this great, endorsing confirmation of his niece's work, as well. She did not know how to digest this circumstance without him. She longed for him terribly. She would have gladly suffered his scolding for some of his comfort. Inevitably, too, she wished her father had lived to see this. She wished her mother had lived to see this. Ambrose, too. She wished she had published it herself. She did not know what to think.

Why had she not published?

The question stung her—yet as she read Darwin's masterpiece (and it was, quite obviously, a masterpiece) she knew that this theory belonged to him, and that it needed to belong to him. Even if she'd said it first, she could never have said it better. It was even possible that nobody would have listened to her had she published this theory—not because she was a woman or because she was obscure (although these factors would not have helped), but merely because she would not have known how to persuade the world as eloquently as Darwin. Her science was perfect, but her writing was not. Alma's thesis was forty pages long, and *On the Origin of Species* was more than five hundred, but she knew without question that Darwin's was by far the more readable work. Darwin's book was artful. It was intimate. It was playful. It read like a novel.

He called his theory "natural selection." It was a brilliantly concise term, simpler and better than Alma's bulkier "theory of competitive alteration." As he patiently built his case for natural selection, Darwin was never strident or defensive. He gave the impression of being the reader's kindly neighbor. He wrote of the same dark and violent world that Alma perceived—a world of endless killing and dying—but his language contained not a trace of violence. Alma would never have dared to write with such a gentle hand; she would not have known how. Her prose was a hammer; Darwin's was a psalm. He came bearing not a sword but a candle. Everywhere in his pages, moreover, he suggested a spirit of divinity—without ever evoking the Creator! He summoned a sense of miracle through rhapsodies on the power of time itself. He wrote, "What an infinite number of generations, which the mind cannot grasp, must have succeeded each other in the long roll of years!" He marveled at all the "beautiful ramifications" of change. He offered up the lovely observation that the wonders of adaptation made every creature on the planet—even the humblest beetle—seem precious, astonishing, and "ennobled."

He asked, "What limit can be put to this power?"

He wrote, "We behold the face of nature, bright with gladness . . ."

He concluded, "There is grandeur in this view of life."

She finished the book and allowed herself to weep.

There was nothing else she could do, in the face of an achievement so splendid and so devastating, but weep.

Everyone read *On the Origin of Species* in 1860, and everyone argued about it, but nobody read it more carefully than Alma Whittaker. She kept her mouth closed during all the drawing room debates on natural selection—even when her own Dutch family took up the subject—but she followed every word. She attended every lecture on the topic and read every review, every attack, every critique. What's more, she revisited the book repeatedly, in a spirit as probing as it was admiring. She was a scientist, and she wanted to put Darwin's theory under a microscope. She wanted to test her theory against his.

Of course, her paramount question was how Darwin had managed to solve the Prudence Problem.

The answer quickly emerged: he hadn't.

Darwin had not solved it because—quite cannily—he avoided the subject of human beings altogether in his book. *On the Origin of Species* was about nature, but it was not overtly about Man. Darwin had played his hand carefully in this regard. He wrote about the evolution of finches, of pigeons, of Italian greyhounds, of racehorses, and of barnacles—but never did he mention human beings. He wrote, "The vigorous, the healthy and the happy survive and multiply," but never did he add, "We, too, are part of this system." Scientific-minded readers would arrive at that conclusion for themselves—and Darwin well knew it. Religious-minded readers would arrive at that conclusion, too, and find it an infuriating sacrilege—but Darwin *had not actually said it*. Thus, he had protected himself. He could sit in his quiet country house in Kent, innocent in the face of public outrage: *What harm can exist in a simple discussion of finches and barnacles?*

As far as Alma was concerned, this strategy constituted Darwin's single greatest stroke of brilliance: he had not taken up the *entire* question. Perhaps he would take it up later, but he had not done so now, not here, in his careful, initial discourse on evolution. This realization dazzled Alma, and she nearly slapped her own forehead in dumbfounded marvel; it never would have occurred to her that a good scientist need not tackle the *entire* question right away—on any topic whatsoever! In essence, Darwin had done what Uncle Dees had tried for years to persuade Alma to do: he had published a beautiful theory of evolution, but only within the realms of botany and zoology, thereby leaving the humans to debate their own origins.

She longed to speak to Darwin. She wished she could dash across the Channel to England, take a train down to Kent, knock on Darwin's door, and ask him, "How do you explain my sister Prudence, and the notion of self-sacrifice, in the context of the overwhelming evidence for constant biological struggle?" But everyone wanted to talk to Darwin these days, and Alma did not possess the necessary sort of influence to arrange a meeting with the most sought-after scientist of the age.

As time went on, she gleaned a clearer sense of this Charles Darwin, and it became evident that the gentleman was not a debater. He probably would not have welcomed the chance to argue with this obscure American bryologist, anyway. He probably would have smiled at her kindly and said, "But what do *you* think, madam?" before shutting the door.

Indeed, while the entire educated world strove to make up its mind about Darwin, the man himself stayed amazingly quiet. When Charles Hodge, at the theological seminary in Princeton, accused Darwin of atheism, Darwin did not defend himself. When Lord Kelvin refused to embrace the theory (which Alma thought unfortunate, as Kelvin's would have been such a credible endorsement), Darwin did not protest. He also did not engage his supporters. When George Searle—a prominent Catholic astronomer—wrote that the theory of natural selection seemed to him quite logical, and posed no threat to the Catholic Church, Darwin did not respond. When the Anglican parson and novelist Charles Kingsley announced that he, too, felt comfortable with a God who "created primal forms capable of self-development," Darwin spoke not a word in agreement. When the theologian Henry Drummond tried to work up a biblical defense of evolution, Darwin avoided the discussion entirely.

Alma watched as liberal-thinking ministers took refuge in metaphor (claiming that the seven days of creation, as mentioned in the Bible, were in actuality seven *geological epochs*), while conservative paleontologists such as Louis Agassiz went red-eyed with anger, accusing Darwin and his supporters of vile apostasy. Others fought Darwin's battles for him—the mighty Thomas Huxley in England; the eloquent Asa Gray in America. But Darwin himself kept a gentlemanly English distance from the entire debate.

Alma, on the other hand, took every attack on natural selection personally, just as she felt secretly buoyed by every endorsement—for it was not merely *Darwin's* idea that was being scrutinized; it was *hers*. She thought at times that she was becoming more distressed and excited by this debate than was Darwin himself (another reason, perhaps, that he made a better ambassador for the theory than she ever could have). But she also felt frustrated by Darwin's reserve. Sometimes she wanted to shake him and make him fight. In his position, she would have come out swinging like Henry Whittaker. She would have had her nose bloodied in the process, to be sure, but she would have bloodied some noses along the way, too. She would have fought to her stumps to defend their theory (she could not help but think of it as "their" theory) . . . if she had published the theory at all, that is. Which, of course, she had not done. So she had no prerogative to fight. Therefore, she said nothing.

It was all most vexing, most engrossing, most confusing.

What's more—Alma could not help but notice—nobody had yet solved the Prudence Problem to her satisfaction.

As far as she could see, there was still a hole in the theory.

It was still incomplete.

But soon enough, Alma grew distracted, then increasingly captivated, by something else.

Dimly and incrementally, as the entire Darwin debate raged on, she became cognizant of another figure concealed along its shadowy margins. In the same way that Alma—when she was young—would sometimes catch a glimpse of something moving on the periphery of her microscope slide and struggle to focus on it (suspecting, before she knew what it was, that it might be important), now, too, she could see something strange and perhaps significant hovering in the corner. Something was out of place. Something existed in the story of Charles Darwin and natural selection that should not exist. She twiddled the knobs and raised the levers and aimed her complete attention upon the mystery—and that is how she learned of a man named Alfred Russel Wallace.

Alma first saw Wallace's name when, out of curiosity, she went back to explore the first official mention of natural selection—which had been on July 1, 1858, at a meeting of the Linnaean Society in London. Alma had missed the notes of that meeting's proceedings when they'd originally been published, owing to her period of mourning, but now she went back and studied the record quite carefully. Immediately, she noticed something peculiar: another essay had been presented that day, just after the introduction of Darwin's thesis. That other essay was titled "On the Tendency of Varieties to Depart Indefinitely from the Original Type," and it had been written by one A. R. Wallace.

Alma tracked down the essay and read it. It said exactly the same thing Darwin had said, in his theory of natural selection. In fact, it said exactly the same thing Alma had said, in her theory of competitive alteration. Mr. Wallace argued that life was a constant struggle for existence: that there were not enough resources for all; that population was controlled by predators, illness, and food scarcity; and that the weakest would always die first. Wallace's essay went on to say that any variation in a species that affected the outcome of survival might eventually change that species forever. He said that the most successful variations would proliferate, while the least successful would be rendered extinct. This was how species arose, transmuted, thrived, and vanished.

The essay was short, simple, and—to Alma's mind—extremely familiar. *Who was this person?*

Alma had never before heard of him. This was unlikely in and of itself, for she made an effort to be aware of everyone in the scientific world. She wrote letters to a few colleagues in England, asking, "Who is Alfred Russel

Wallace? What are people saying about him? What happened in London in July 1858?"

The stories she learned intrigued her only more. She discovered that Wallace had been born in Monmouthshire, near Wales, to middle-class parents who later fell on hard times; and that he was more or less self-educated, a surveyor by trade. As an adventurous young man, he had shipped off to various jungles over the years, and became a tireless collector of insect and bird specimens. In 1853, Wallace had published a book entitled *Palm Trees of the Amazon and their Uses*, which Alma had missed entirely, as she'd been traveling between Tahiti and Holland at the time. Since 1854, he had been in the Malay Archipelago, studying tree frogs and the like.

There, in the distant forests of the Celebes, Wallace had contracted malarial fever and had nearly died. In the depths of his fever, focused upon death, he'd had a flash of inspiration: a theory of evolution, based on the struggle for existence. In a mere few hours he'd written down his theory. He then mailed his hastily penned thesis all the way from the Celebes to England, to a gentleman named Charles Darwin, whom he'd met on one occasion, and whom he much admired. Wallace, quite deferentially, asked Mr. Darwin if this theory of evolution might perhaps have any value. It was an innocent question: Wallace had no way of knowing that Darwin himself had been toiling on this exact idea since approximately 1840. In fact, Darwin had already written nearly two thousand pages of what would become *On the Origin of Species*, but had shown his work to no one except his dear friend Joseph Hooker, of the Royal Botanic Gardens at Kew. Hooker had for years been encouraging Darwin to publish, but Darwin—in a decision that Alma could well appreciate—had held back, from lack of confidence or certainty.

Now, in one of the great coincidences in scientific history, it appeared that Darwin's beautiful and original idea—which he had been privately cultivating for almost two decades—had just been expressed, almost word for word, by a nearly unknown, thirty-five-year-old, malaria-suffering, self-taught naturalist on the other side of the planet.

Alma's sources in London reported that Darwin had felt compelled by Wallace's letter to announce his theory of natural selection, afraid that he would lose ownership of the entire notion if Wallace were to publish first.

Quite ironically, Alma thought, it appeared Darwin feared being *outcompeted* over the idea of competition! Out of gentlemanly courtesy, Darwin had decided that Wallace's letter should be presented at the Linnaean Society on July 1, 1858—right alongside his own research on natural selection—while at the same time putting forth evidence that the hypothesis had belonged to him first. The publication of his *Origin of Species* had swiftly followed, less than a year and a half later. That rush to publish now suggested to Alma that Darwin had panicked—as well he should have! Wallace was closing in! As do many animals and plants under threat of annihilation, Charles Darwin had been forced to move, forced to take action—forced to adapt. Alma remembered what she herself had written in her own version of the theory: "The greater the crisis, it seems, the swifter the evolution."

Reviewing this extraordinary story, there was no question in Alma's mind: natural selection had been Darwin's idea first. But it had not been Darwin's idea *uniquely*. There was Alma, yes, but there had been somebody else, too. Alma was beyond amazed to learn of this. It seemed an utter intellectual impossibility. But it also brought her strange comfort, to know that Alfred Russel Wallace existed. She drew warmth from the knowledge that she was not alone in this. She had a peer. They were Whittaker and Wallace: comrades in obscurity—although Wallace, of course, had no idea that they were comrades in obscurity, because she was even *that much more obscure than he*. But Alma knew it. She felt him out there—her strange, miraculous younger brother of the mind. If she had been more religious, she might have thanked God for Alfred Russel Wallace, for it was that small sense of kinship that helped her move gracefully and safely—without debilitating resentment, despair, or shame—through all the clamoring commotion surrounding Mr. Charles Darwin and his colossal, transfiguring, world-changing theory.

Darwin would belong to history, yes, but Alma had Wallace.

And that, at least for now, was comfort enough.

The 1860s passed. Holland was quiet, while the United States was riven by an unthinkable war. Scientific discourse carried less weight for Alma during those terrible years, with the news from home of endless, appalling slaughter. Prudence lost her eldest son, an officer, at Antietam. Two of her young grandsons died of camp diseases before even seeing a battlefield. All her life, Prudence had fought to end slavery, and now it was ended, but three of her own had been lost in the fight. "I rejoice and then I grieve," she wrote Alma. "After that, I grieve some more." Again, Alma wondered if she should return home—and even offered to—but her sister encouraged her to remain in Holland. "Our nation is too tragic at the moment for visitors," Prudence reported. "Stay where the world is quieter, and bless that quietness."

Somehow, Prudence kept her school open through the entire war. She not only endured, she took on yet more children during the conflict. The war ended. The president was assassinated. The union held. The transcontinental railroad was completed. Alma thought perhaps that was what would keep the United States sewn together now—the rough, steel stitches of the mighty railroad. These days America seemed, from Alma's safe distance, to be a place of uncontrollable, ferocious growth. She was happy not to be there. America was a lifetime ago; she did not think she would recognize the place anymore, nor would it recognize her. She liked her life as a Dutchwoman, as a scholar, as a van Devender. She read every scientific journal, and published in many of them. She had lively discussions with her colleagues, over coffee and pastry. Every summer, the Hortus granted her a month's leave to go gathering mosses across the Continent. She came to know the Alps quite well, and came to love them, as she tramped across their majesty with her cane and her collecting kit. She came to know the fern-damp woods of Germany, too.

She had grown into a most contented old lady.

The 1870s arrived. In peaceful Amsterdam, Alma entered the eighth decade of her life, but remained committed to her work. She found it difficult to hike anymore, but she tended to her Cave of Mosses, and gave occasional lectures at the Hortus on the subject of bryology. Her eyes began to fail, and she worried that she would no longer be able to identify mosses. In anticipation of this sad inevitability, she practiced working with her mosses in the dark, to learn to identify them by touch. She became quite adept at it. (She did not need to *see* mosses forever, but she would always want to *know* them.) Fortunately, she had excellent help with her work now. Her favorite young cousin, Margaret—fondly nicknamed Mimi—revealed an innate fascination with mosses, and soon became Alma's protégée. When the girl finished her studies, she came to work with Alma at the Hortus; with Mimi's assistance, Alma was able to complete her comprehensive, two-volume *The Mosses of Northern Europe*, which was well received. The volumes were prettily illustrated, though the artist was no Ambrose Pike.

But nobody was Ambrose Pike. Nobody ever would be.

Alma watched as Charles Darwin became ever more the great man of science. She did not begrudge his success; he deserved the praise, and carried himself with dignity. He kept at his work on evolution, which she was pleased to see, with his typical blend of excellence and discretion. In 1871, he published the exhaustive *The Descent of Man*—in which he finally applied his principles of natural selection to humans. He was wise to have waited this long, Alma thought. By this point, the book's final determination (*Yes, we are apes*) was almost a foregone conclusion. In the dozen years since *Origin* had first appeared, the world had been anticipating and debating "The Monkey Question." Sides had been drawn, papers had been written, and endless rebuttals and arguments had been brought forth. It was almost as though Darwin had waited for the world to adapt to the unsettling notion that God might not have created mankind from dust, before delivering his calm, well-ordered, carefully argued verdict on the matter. Alma, once more, read the book as closely as anyone, and much admired it.

Still, though, she did not see a solution to the Prudence Problem.

She never told anyone about her own evolutionary theory—and about her own small, tenuous connection to Darwin. She still was far more interested in her shadow brother, Alfred Russel Wallace. She had watched his career carefully over the years too, taking vicarious pride in his successes, and feeling distress at his failures. At first, it had seemed that Wallace would be forever Darwin's footnote—or even footman, insomuch as he spent a good part of the 1860s writing papers defending natural selection, and, by extension, Darwin. But then Wallace took an odd turn. In the middle of that decade, he discovered spiritualism, hypnotism, and mesmerism, and began exploring what more respectable people called "the occult." Alma could nearly hear Charles Darwin groaning at this development from across the Channel—for the two men's names were forever to be linked, and Wallace had taken off on a very disreputable and unscientific flight of fancy indeed. The fact that Wallace attended séances and palm readings, and swore that he had spoken to the dead, was perhaps pardonable, but the fact that he published papers with such titles as "The Scientific Aspect of the Supernatural" was not.

But Alma could not help but love Wallace all the more for his unorthodox beliefs, and for his passionate, fearless arguments. Her own life was becoming ever more sedate and circumscribed, but she took such pleasure from watching Wallace—the wild, unbridled thinker—cause academic mayhem in so many directions at once. He had none of Darwin's aristocratic propriety; he spilled over with inspirations and distractions and half-baked notions. Nor did he ever stay on a single idea for long, flitting instead from whim to whim.

In his most transcendent fascinations, Wallace inevitably reminded Alma of Ambrose, and this made her fonder of him than ever. Like Ambrose, Wallace was a dreamer. He came down strongly on the side of miracles. He argued that nothing was more important than the investigation of that which appeared to defy the rules of nature, for who were we to claim that we understood the rules of nature? Everything was a miracle until we solved it. Wallace wrote that the first man who ever saw a flying fish probably thought he was witnessing a miracle—and the first man who ever *described* a flying fish was doubtless called a liar. Alma loved him for such playful, stubborn arguments. He would have done well at the White Acre dinner table, she often thought.

Wallace did not completely neglect his more legitimate scientific explorations, however. In 1876, he published his own masterpiece: *The Geographical Distribution of Animals*, which was instantly celebrated as the most definitive text on zoogeography yet produced. It was a stunning book. Alma's young cousin Mimi read most of it to her, for Alma's sight had grown quite dim by now. Alma enjoyed Wallace's ideas so much that during certain passages of the book, she sometimes even cheered aloud.

Mimi would look up from her reading and say, "You do quite enjoy this Alfred Russel Wallace, don't you, Auntie?"

"He is a prince of science!" Alma smiled.

Wallace soon undermined his own rescued reputation, however, with an increased involvement in radical politics—fighting vociferously for land reform, for women's suffrage, for the rights of the poor and the dispossessed. He simply could not stay above the fray. Friends and admirers in high places tried to secure him stable positions at good institutions, but Wallace had become known as such an extremist that few would risk hiring him. Alma worried about his finances. She sensed he was not wise with his money. In every way, Wallace simply refused to play the part of the good

English gentleman—probably because he was not, in fact, a good English gentleman, but rather a working-class firebrand who never thought before he spoke, and never paused before he published. His passions made for a certain amount of chaos, and controversy stuck to him like a burr, but Alma did not want him ever to back down. She liked to see him needling the world.

"You tell them, my boy," Alma would murmur, whenever she heard of his latest scandal. "You tell them!"

Darwin never publicly spoke an ill word about Wallace, nor Wallace about Darwin, but Alma always wondered what the two men—so brilliant, and yet so opposite in disposition and style—truly thought of each other. Her question was answered in April of 1882, when Charles Darwin died and Alfred Russel Wallace, per Darwin's written instructions, served as a pall-bearer at the great man's funeral.

They loved each other, she realized. They loved each other, because they knew each other.

With that thought, Alma felt deeply lonely, for the first time in dozens of years.

Darwin's death alarmed Alma, who was now eighty-two years old, and increasingly frail. He had been only seventy-three! She had never expected to outlive him. The sense of alarm stayed with her for months after Darwin passed away. It was as though a piece of her own history had died with him, and nobody would ever know it. Not that anyone had known it before, of course, but a link was undoubtedly lost—a link that meant a great deal to her. Soon Alma herself would die, and then there would be only one link left—young Wallace, who was then nearing sixty, and maybe not so young anymore, after all. If things went on as they always had, she would die never having known Wallace, just as she had never known Darwin. It felt unbearably sad to her, quite suddenly, that this might come to pass. She could not allow it to happen.

Alma pondered this. She pondered it for several months. Finally, she took action. She asked Mimi to write a nice letter, on Hortus stationery, asking Alfred Russel Wallace to please accept an invitation to speak on the subject of natural selection at the Hortus Botanicus in Amsterdam, in the spring of 1883. A honorarium of nine hundred pounds sterling was promised for the gentleman's time and trouble, and all travel expenses, naturally, would be covered by the Hortus. Mimi balked at the fee—this was several years' wages, for some people!—but Alma calmly replied, "I will be paying for everything myself, and what's more, Mr. Wallace needs the money."

The letter went on to inform Mr. Wallace that he was more than welcome to stay at the van Devenders' comfortable family residence, which was conveniently situated just outside the gardens, in the prettiest neighborhood of Amsterdam. There would be plenty of young botanists about the place who would be happy to show the famous biologist all the delights of the Hortus, and the city beyond. It would be an honor for the gardens to host such a distinguished guest. Alma signed the letter, "Very sincerely yours, Miss Alma Whittaker—Curator of Mosses."

A reply came swiftly, from Wallace's wife, Annie (whose father, Alma had been thrilled to learn, was the great William Mitten, a pharmaceutical chemist and first-rate bryologist). Mrs. Wallace wrote that her husband would be delighted to come to Amsterdam. He would arrive on the nineteenth of March, 1883, and would stay a fortnight. The Wallaces were most grateful for the invitation, and praised the honorarium as very generous, indeed. The offer, the letter hinted, had arrived at just the right time—as had the money.

Chapter Thirty-one

Ｈe was so tall!

Alma had not expected this. Alfred Russel Wallace was as tall and lanky as Ambrose had been. He was not far from the age Ambrose would have been, either, if Ambrose had survived—sixty years old, and in fine health, if a bit stooped. (This was a man who had plainly spent too many years bent over microscopes, peering at specimens.) He was gray-haired, with a heavy beard, and Alma had to resist the urge to reach up and touch his face with her fingertips. She could not see well anymore, and she wanted to know his features better. But that would have been rude and shocking, so she restrained herself. All the same, as soon as she met him, she felt she was welcoming her oldest friend in the world.

At the beginning of his visit, though, there was such a bustle of activity that Alma was a bit lost in the crowd. She was a large woman, true, but she was old, and old women do tend to get pushed aside at big gatherings—even when they have footed the bill for that gathering. There were many who wanted to meet the great evolutionary biologist, and Alma's young cousins, all enthusiastic young students of science themselves, took much of his attention, crowding him like hopeful beaux and belles. Wallace was so polite, so friendly—especially with the younger set. He permitted them to boast of their own projects, and to seek his advice. Naturally, they wished to parade him about Amsterdam, too, and thus several days were occupied with silly tourism and civic pride.

Then there was his speech in the Palm House, and the ponderous questions afterward from scholars, journalists, and dignitaries, followed by the requisite long, dull dinner in formal dress. Wallace spoke well, both at his lecture and at the dinner. He managed to avoid controversy, answering all the tedious and uninformed questions about natural selection with thorough patience. His wife must have coached him to be on his best behavior, Alma thought. *Good girl, Annie.*

Alma waited. She was not one who was afraid to wait.

In time, the novelty surrounding Wallace's visit died down, and the clamoring crowds thinned. The young moved on to other excitements, and Alma was able to sit next to her guest for a few breakfasts in a row. She knew him better than anyone, of course, and she knew that he didn't want to talk about natural selection forever. She engaged him instead on subjects that she knew were dear to his heart—butterfly mimicry, beetle variations, mind-reading, vegetarianism, the evils of inherited wealth, his plan to abolish the stock exchange, his plan for the end of all war, his defense of Indian and Irish self-governance, his suggestion that British authorities beg the world's forgiveness for the cruelties of their empire, his desire to build a four-hundred-foot-diameter scale model of the earth that people could circle in a giant balloon for educational purposes . . . that sort of thing.

In other words, he relaxed with Alma, and she with him. He was a delightful conversationalist when fully unfettered, as she had always imagined he would be—willing to converse on any number of wide-ranging subjects and passions. She had not enjoyed herself this much in years. Because he was so kind and engaging, he inquired about her life, as well, and did not merely speak of himself. Thus Alma found herself telling Wallace about her childhood at White Acre, about collecting botanical specimens as a five-year-old on a silk-draped pony, about her eccentric parents and their challenging dinner-table conversation, about her father's stories of mermaids and Captain Cook, about the extraordinary library at the estate, about her almost comically outdated classical education, about her years of study in the moss beds of Philadelphia, about her sister the brave-hearted abolitionist, and about her adventures in Tahiti. Incredibly—though she had not spoken to anyone of Ambrose in decades—she even told him about her remarkable husband, who had painted orchids more beautifully than any man who ever lived, and who had died in the South Seas.

"What a life you have lived!" Wallace said.

Alma had to look away when he said this. He was the first person who had ever said so. She felt overcome by shyness, and also by the urge, once more, to put her hands on his face and feel his features—just as she felt moss these days, memorizing with her fingers what she could no longer adore with her eyes.

She had not planned when to tell him, or what to tell him, exactly. She had not even planned that she *would* tell him. In the last few days of his visit, she came to think that she would probably not tell him at all. Honestly, she felt it was enough merely to have met this man, and to have closed the gap that had divided them all these years.

But then, on his final afternoon in Amsterdam, Wallace asked if Alma would personally show him the Cave of Mosses, and so she took him there. He was patient about walking across the gardens at her achingly slow pace.

"I apologize that I am so pokey," Alma said. "My father used to call me a dromedary, but these days I grow weary after ten steps."

"Then we shall rest every ten steps," he said, and took her by the arm to help guide her along.

It was a Thursday afternoon, and drizzling, so the Hortus was mostly deserted. Alma and Wallace had the Cave of Mosses to themselves. She took him from boulder to boulder, showing him the mosses of all the continents and explaining how she had woven them all together in this one place. He marveled at it—as would anyone who loved the world.

"My father-in-law would be fascinated to see this," he said.

"I know," said Alma. "I've always wished to bring Mr. Mitten here. Perhaps someday he will visit."

"As for me," he said, sitting on the bench in the middle of the exhibit, "I think I would come here every day, if I could."

"I do come every day," said Alma, joining him on the bench. "Often on my knees, and with tweezers in hand."

"What a legacy you have created," he said.

"That is kind praise, Mr. Wallace, from one who has created quite a legacy himself."

"Ah," he said, and brushed away the compliment.

They sat in pleasant silence for a while. Alma thought of the first time she was alone with Tomorrow Morning in Tahiti. She thought of how she had said to him, "You and I are—I believe—more closely affixed to each other's destinies than one might think." She longed to say the same thing now to Alfred Russel Wallace, but she was not certain if it would be correct to do so. She would not want him to think that she was boasting about her own theory of evolution. Or—worse—that she was lying. Or—worst of all—that she was laying challenge to his legacy, or to Darwin's. It was probably best to say nothing.

But then he spoke. He said, "Miss Whittaker, I must tell you that I have thoroughly enjoyed these last few days with you."

"Thank you," she said. "And I have enjoyed you. More than you can know."

"You are so generous, to have listened to my ideas about anything and everything," he said. "Not many are like you. I have found in life that when I speak of biology, they compare me to Newton. But when I speak of the spirit world, they call me a weak-minded, babyish idiot."

"Do not listen to them," Alma said, and patted his hand protectively. "I have never liked it when they insult you."

He was quiet for a while, and then: "May I ask you something, Miss Whittaker?"

She nodded.

"May I ask how it is that you know so much about me? I do not wish you to think I am offended—on the contrary, I am flattered—but I simply cannot make sense of it. Your field is bryology, you see, and mine is not. Nor are you a spiritualist or a mesmerist. Yet you have such familiarity with all my writing across every possible field, and you also know my critics. You even know who my wife's father is. Why could that be? I cannot put it together . . ."

He trailed off, fearing, it appeared, that he had been impolite. She did not wish him to think that he'd been rude to an elderly woman. She did not wish him to think, either, that she was some unhinged old bat with an unseemly fixation. That being the case, what else could she do?

She told him everything.

When she was finished speaking at last, he was silent for a long while, and then asked, "Do you still have the paper?"

"Certainly," she said.

"May I read it?" he asked.

Slowly, without further conversation, they walked through the back gate of the Hortus, to Alma's office. She unlocked the door, breathing heavily from the stairs, and invited Mr. Wallace to make himself comfortable at her desk. From under the divan in the corner, she retrieved a small, dusty, leather valise—as worn as though it had circled the world several times, which, indeed, it had—and opened it. Inside was but a single item: a forty-page document, handwritten, and gently swaddled in flannel, like an infant.

Alma carried it over to Wallace, then settled herself comfortably on the divan while he read it. It took him a while. She must have dozed—as she did so often these days, and at the strangest moments—for she was startled awake by his voice sometime later.

"When did you say that you wrote this, Miss Whittaker?" he asked.

She rubbed her eyes. "The date is on the back," she said. "I added things to it later, ideas and such, and those addenda are filed away in this office somewhere. But that which you hold in your hands is the original, which I wrote in 1854."

He considered this.

"So Darwin was still the first," he said at last.

"Oh yes, absolutely," said Alma. "Mr. Darwin was the first by far, and the most thorough. There has never been any question about that. Please understand, Mr. Wallace, I do not pretend to have a claim . . ."

"But you arrived at this idea before me," Wallace said. "Darwin beat us both, to be certain, but you arrived at the idea four years before me."

"Well . . ." Alma hesitated. "That is certainly not what I wish to say."

"But Miss Whittaker," he said, and his voice grew bright with excitement and comprehension. "This means there were three of us!"

For a moment, Alma could not breathe.

In an instant, she was transported back to White Acre, to a fine autumn day in 1819—the day she and Prudence first met Retta Snow. They were all so young, and the sky was blue, and love had not yet grievously injured any of them. Retta had said, looking up at Alma with her shiny, living eyes, "So now there are three of us! What luck!"

What was the song that Retta had invented for them?

We are fiddle, fork, and spoon,
We are dancing with the moon,
If you'd like to steal a kiss from us,
You'd better steal one soon!

When Alma did not respond right away, Wallace came over and sat beside her.

"Miss Whittaker," he said, in a quieter voice. "Do you understand? There were three of us."

"Yes, Mr. Wallace. It appears that there were."

"This is a most extraordinary simultaneity."

"I've always thought so," she said.

He stared at the wall for a while, silent for another long spell.

At last he asked, "Who else knows about this? Who can vouch for you?"

"Only my uncle Dees."

"And where is your uncle Dees?"

"Dead, you know," said Alma, and she could not help but laugh. This was how Dees would have wanted her to say it. Oh, how she missed that stout old Dutchman. Oh, how he would have loved this moment.

"But why did you never publish?" Wallace asked.

"Because it was not good enough."

"Nonsense! It's all here. The entire theory is all here. It's certainly more developed than the absurd, feverish letter I wrote to Darwin in 'fifty-eight. We should publish it now."

"No," Alma said. "There is no need to publish it. Truly, I do not have a need of that. It is enough, what you just have said—that there were three of us. That is enough for me. You have made an old woman happy."

"But we *could* publish," he pushed on. "I could present it for you . . ."

She put her hand on his. "No," she said, firmly. "I ask you to trust me. It is not necessary."

They sat in stillness for a while.

"May I at minimum ask why you felt it was not worth publishing in 1854?" Wallace said, breaking the silence.

"I did not publish because I believed there was something missing from the theory. And I will tell you, Mr. Wallace—I *still* believe there is something missing from the theory."

"Which is what, exactly?"

"A convincing evolutionary explanation for human altruism and self-sacrifice," she said.

She wondered if she would have to elaborate. She did not know if she had the energy to dive fully into the giant question again—to tell him all about Prudence and the orphans, and the women who pulled babies from canals, and the men who rushed into fires to rescue strangers, and the starving prisoners who shared their last bites of food with other starving prisoners, and the missionaries who forgave the fornicators, and the nurses who cared for the insane, and the people who loved dogs that no one else could love, and all the rest of it beyond.

But there was no need to get into particulars. He understood immediately.

"I've had the same questions, myself, you know," he said.

"I know that you have," she said. "I've always wondered—did Darwin have such questions?"

"Yes," Wallace said. Then he paused, reconsidering. "Though I never knew exactly what Darwin concluded on the matter, to be honest. He was so careful, you know, never to make proclamations about anything until he was absolutely certain. Unlike me."

"Unlike you," Alma agreed. "But not unlike me."

"No, not unlike you."

"Were you fond of Mr. Darwin?" Alma asked. "I've always wondered that."

"Oh, yes," said Wallace easily. "Quite. He was the best of men. I think he was the greatest man of our time, or, indeed, of most times. To whom can we compare him? There was Aristotle. There was Copernicus. There was Galileo. There was Newton. And there was Darwin."

"So you never resented him?" Alma asked.

"Heavens no, Miss Whittaker. In science, all merit should be imputed to the first discoverer, and thus the theory of natural selection was always meant to be his. What's more, he alone had the grandeur for it. I believe he was our generation's Virgil, taking us on a tour through heaven, hell, and purgatory. He was our divine guide."

"I've always thought so, too."

"I tell you, Miss Whittaker, I am not at all distressed to learn that you beat me to the theory of natural selection, but I would have been terribly cast down to have learned that you had beat Darwin. I so admire him, you know. I would like to see him keep his throne."

"His throne is in no danger from me, young man," said Alma mildly. "No need for alarm."

Wallace laughed. "I quite enjoy it, Miss Whittaker, that you call me a young man. For a fellow in his seventh decade, that is quite a compliment."

"From a lady in her ninth decade, sir, it is simply the truth."

He did indeed seem young to her. It was interesting—the best parts of her life, she felt, had always been spent in the company of old men. There were all those stimulating meals of her childhood, sitting at the table with the endless parade of brilliant aged minds. There were the years at White Acre with her father, discussing botany and trade late into the night. There was her time in Tahiti with the good and decent Reverend Francis Welles. There were the four happy years here in Amsterdam with Uncle Dees before his death. But now she herself was old, and there were no more old men! Now, here she sat with a stooped graybeard—a mere child of sixty—and she was the ancient tortoise in the room.

"Do you know what I believe, Miss Whittaker? Regarding your question on the origins of human compassion and self-sacrifice? I believe that evolution explains *nearly* everything about us, and I certainly believe that it explains absolutely everything about the rest of the natural world. But I do not believe that evolution alone can account for our unique human consciousness. There is no evolutionary need, you see, for us to have such acute sensitivities of intellect and emotion. There is no practical need for the minds that we have. We don't need a mind that can play chess, Miss Whittaker. We don't need a mind that can invent religions or argue over our origins. We don't need a mind that causes us to weep at the opera. We don't need opera, for that matter—nor science, nor art. We don't need ethics, morality, dignity, or sacrifice. We don't need affection or love—certainly not to the degree that we feel it. If anything, our sensibilities can be a liability, for they can cause us to suffer distress. So I do not believe that the process of natural selection gave us these minds—even though I do believe that it did give us these bodies, and most of our abilities. Do you know why I think we have these extraordinary minds?"

"I do know, Mr. Wallace," Alma said quietly. "I've read a good deal of your work, recall."

"I will tell you why we have these extraordinary minds and souls, Miss Whittaker," he continued, as though he had not heard her. "We have them because there is a supreme intelligence in the universe, which wishes for communion with us. This supreme intelligence longs to be known. It calls out to us. It draws us close to its mystery, and it grants us these remarkable minds, in order that we try to reach for it. It wants us to find it. It wants union with us, more than anything."

"I know that is what you think," said Alma, patting his hand again, "and I believe it is quite an inventive notion, Mr. Wallace."

"Do you think I'm correct?"

"I couldn't say," said Alma, "but it is a beautiful theory. It comes as close to answering my question as anything ever has. Yet still you are answering a mystery with another mystery, and I cannot say if I would call that science—though I might call it poetry. Unfortunately, like your friend Mr. Darwin, I still seek the firmer answers of empirical science. It is my nature, I'm afraid. But Mr. Lyell would have agreed with you. He argued that nothing short of a divine being could have created a human mind. My husband would have loved your idea. Ambrose believed in such things. He longed for that union you mention, with the supreme intelligence. He died searching for that union."

They were quiet again.

After a while, Alma smiled. "I've always wondered what Mr. Darwin thought of that idea of yours—about our minds being excluded from the laws of evolution, and about a supreme intelligence guiding the universe."

Wallace smiled, too. "He did not approve."

"I should think not!"

"Oh, he did not like it at all, Miss Whittaker. He was appalled whenever I brought it up. He could not believe—after all our battles together—that I was bringing God back into the conversation!'"

"And what would you say?"

"I tried to explain to him that I had never mentioned the word *God*. He was the one who used the word. The only thing I'd said was that a supreme intelligence exists in the universe, and that it longs for union with us. I believe in the world of spirits, Miss Whittaker, but I would never bring the word *God* into a scientific discussion. After all, I am a strict atheist."

"Of course you are, my dear," she said, patting his hand again. She was so enjoying patting his hand. She was enjoying every moment of this.

"You think me naive," Wallace said.

"I think you marvelous," Alma corrected. "I think you are the most marvelous person I have ever met, who is still alive. You make me feel glad that I am still here, to meet somebody like you."

"Well, you are not alone in this world, Miss Whittaker, even if you have outlived everyone. I believe that we are surrounded by a host of unseen friends and loved ones, now passed away, who exert an influence upon our lives, and who never abandon us."

"That's a lovely notion," said Alma, and she patted his hand once more.

"Have you ever been to a séance, Miss Whittaker? I could take you to one. You could speak to your husband, across the divide."

Alma thought over the offer. She remembered the night in the binding closet with Ambrose, when they had spoken to each other through the palms of their hands: her one experience with the mystical and the ineffable. She still didn't know what that had been, really. She still wasn't entirely certain she hadn't imagined it all, in a fit of love and desire. Alternatively, she sometimes wondered if Ambrose truly had been a magical being—perhaps some evolutionary mutation in his own right, simply born under the wrong circumstances, or at the wrong moment in history. Perhaps there would never be another one like him. Perhaps he had been a failed experiment himself.

Whatever he had been, though, it had not ended well.

"I must say, Mr. Wallace," she replied, "you are most kind to invite me to a séance, but I think I shall not do that. I have had a small bit of experience with silent communication, and I know that just because people can *hear* each other across the divide does not mean they can necessarily *understand* each other."

He laughed. "Well, if you should ever change your mind, please do send word."

"You may be sure I shall. But it is far more likely, Mr. Wallace, that you will be sending word to *me*, after I am dead, during one of your spiritualist meetings! You should not have to wait long for such a chance, for soon I will be gone."

"You will never be gone. The spirit merely lives inside the body, Miss Whittaker. Death only separates that duality."

"Thank you, Mr. Wallace. You say the kindest things. But you needn't comfort me. I am too old to fear the great changes of life."

"Do you know, Miss Whittaker—here I am, expounding upon all my theories, but I have not paused to ask you, a wise woman, what you believe."

"What I believe is not, perhaps, as exciting as what you believe."

"Nonetheless, I would like to hear it."

Alma sighed. This was quite a question. What *did* she believe?

"I believe that we are all transient," she began. She thought for a while and added, "I believe that we are half-blind and full of errors. I believe that we understand very little, and what we do understand is mostly wrong. I believe that life cannot be survived—*that* is evident!—but if one is lucky, life can be endured for quite a long while. If one is both lucky and stubborn, life can sometimes even be enjoyed."

"Do you believe in an afterworld?" Wallace asked.

She patted his hand once again. "Oh, Mr. Wallace, I do so try not to say things that make people feel upset."

He laughed again. "I am not as delicate as you may think, Miss Whittaker. You may tell me what you believe."

"Well, if you must know, I believe that most people are quite fragile. I believe that it must have been a dreadful blow to man's opinion of himself when Galileo announced that we do not reside at the center of the universe— just as it was a blow to the world when Darwin announced that we were not specially crafted by God in one miraculous moment. I believe these things are difficult for most people to hear. I believe it makes people feel insignificant. Saying that, I do wonder, Mr. Wallace, if your longing for the spirit world and an afterworld is not just a symptom of a continued human quest to feel . . . significant? Forgive me, I do not mean to insult you. The man whom I dearly loved had this same need as you, this same quest—to commune with some mysterious divinity, to transcend his body and this world, and to remain significant in a better realm. I found him to be a lonely person, Mr. Wallace. Beautiful, but lonely. I do not know if you are lonely, but it makes me wonder."

He did not answer that.

After a moment, he merely asked, "And don't you have that need, Miss Whittaker? To feel significant?"

"I will tell you something, Mr. Wallace. I think I have been the most fortunate woman who ever lived. My heart has been broken, certainly, and most of my wishes did not come true. I have disappointed myself in my own behavior, and others have disappointed me. I have outlived nearly everyone

I ever loved. Remaining alive to me in this world is but one sister, whom I have not seen for more than thirty years—and with whom I was not intimate, for most of my life. I have not had an illustrious career. I had one original idea in my life—and it happened to be an important idea, one that might have given me a chance to be known—but I hesitated to put it forth, and thus I missed my opportunity. I have no husband. I have no heirs. I once had a fortune, but I gave it away. My eyes are deserting me, and my lungs and legs give me much trouble. I do not think I will live to see another spring. I will die across the ocean from where I was born, and I will be buried here, far away from my parents and my sister. Surely you are asking yourself by now—why does this miserably unlucky woman call herself fortunate?"

He said nothing. He was too kind to reply to such a question.

"Do not worry, Mr. Wallace. I am not being facetious with you. I do truly believe I am fortunate. I am fortunate because I have been able to spend my life in study of the world. As such, I have never felt insignificant. This life is a mystery, yes, and it is often a trial, but if one can find some facts within it, one should always do so—for knowledge is the most precious of all commodities."

When he still did not reply, Alma went on:

"You see, I have never felt the need to invent a world beyond this world, for this world has always seemed large and beautiful enough for me. I have wondered why it is not large and beautiful enough for others—why they must dream up new and marvelous spheres, or long to live elsewhere, beyond this dominion . . . but that is not my business. We are all different, I suppose. All I ever wanted was to know *this* world. I can say now, as I reach my end, that I know quite a bit more of it than I knew when I arrived. Moreover, my little bit of knowledge has been added to all the other accumulated knowledge of history—added to the great library, as it were. That is no small feat, sir. Anyone who can say such a thing has lived a fortunate life."

Now it was he who patted her hand.

"Very well put, Miss Whittaker," he said.

"Indeed, Mr. Wallace," she said.

After this, it seemed their conversation was over. They were both pensive and tired. Alma returned her manuscript to Ambrose's valise, slid the case under the divan, and locked her office door. She would never again show it *497* to anyone else. Wallace helped her down the stairs. Outside it was dark and foggy. They walked slowly together back to the van Devender residence, two doors down. She let him in, and they stood in the hallway and said their good-nights. Wallace would be leaving the next morning, and they would not see each other again after that.

"I am so very glad you came," she told him.

"I am so very glad you summoned me," he said.

She reached up and touched his face. He allowed her. She explored his warm features. He had a kind face—she could feel that he did.

After that, he went upstairs to his room, but Alma waited in the hallway. She did not wish to go to sleep. When she heard his door close, she took up her cane and shawl again and returned outside. It was dark, but that did not matter to Alma anymore; she could scarcely even see in the daylight, and she knew her surroundings so well by feel. She found the back gate to the Hortus—the private gate that the van Devenders had used for three centuries now—and she let herself in to the gardens.

Her intention had been to return to the Cave of Mosses and contemplate matters for a while, but she soon grew short of breath, so she rested a spell, leaning against the nearest tree. My goodness, but she was old! How quickly it had happened! She was thankful for the tree beside her. She was thankful for the gardens, in their dark beauty. She was thankful for a quiet spot in which to rest. She remembered what poor little mad Retta Snow used to say: "Thank heavens we have an earth, or where would we sit?" Alma was feeling a bit dizzy. What a night this had been!

There were three of us, he had said.

Indeed, there had been three of them, and now there were only two. Soon, there would be only one. Then Wallace, too, would be gone. But for now, at least, he was aware of her. She was *known*. Alma pressed her face against the tree, and marveled at it all—at the speed of things, at the amazing confluences.

A person cannot marvel in dumbstruck amazement forever, though, and after a while Alma found herself wondering what tree this was, exactly. She was familiar with every tree in the Hortus, but she had lost track of where she was standing, and so she did not remember. It smelled familiar. She stroked its bark, and then she knew—of course, it was the shellbark hickory, the only one of its kind in all of Amsterdam. Juglandaceae. The walnut family. This particular specimen had come from America well over one hundred years earlier, probably from western Pennsylvania. Difficult to transplant, because of its long taproot. Must have come as a tiny sapling. A bottomland grower, it was. Fond of loam and silt; friend to quail and fox; resistant to ice; susceptible to rot. It was old. She was old.

Lines of evidence were converging upon Alma—lines from every direction—driving her toward her final, formidable conclusion: soon, exceedingly soon, her time would come. She knew this to be true. Maybe not tonight, but some night soon. She was not afraid of death, in theory. If anything, she had nothing but respect and reverence for the Genius of Death, who had shaped this world more than any other force. That said, she did not wish to die quite this moment. She still wanted to see what would happen next, as much as ever. The thing was to resist submersion for as long as possible.

She clutched the great tree as if it were a horse. She pressed her cheek against its silent, living flank.

She said, "You and I are very far from home, aren't we?"

In the dark gardens, in the middle of the quiet city night, the tree did not reply.

But it did hold her up just a little while longer.

ACKNOWLEDGMENTS

For their assistance and inspiration, the author wishes to thank: the Royal Botanic Gardens, Kew; the New York Botanical Garden; the Hortus Botanicus Amsterdam; Bartram's Garden; the Woodlands; Liberty Hall Museum; and Esalen; also Margaret Cordi, Anne Connell, Shea Hembrey, Rayya Elias, Mary Bly, Linda Shankara Barrera, Tony Freund, Barbara Paca, Joel Fry, Marie Long, Stephen Sinon, Mia D'Avanza, Courtney Allen, Adam Skolnick, Celeste Brash, Roy Withers, Linda Tumarae, Cree LeFavour, Jonny Miles, Ernie Sesskin, Brian Foster, Sheryl Moller, Deborah Luepnitz, Ann Patchett, Eileen Marolla, Karen Lessig, Michael and Sandra Flood, Tom and Deann Higgins, Jeannette Tynan, Jim Novak, Jim and Dave Cahill, Bill Burdin, Ernie Marshall, Sarah Chalfant, Charles Buchan, Paul Slovak, Lindsay Prevette, Miriam Feuerle, Alexandra Pringle, Katie Bond, Terry and Deborah Olson, Catherine Gilbert Murdock, John and Carole Gilbert, José Nunes, the late Stanley Gilbert, and the late Sheldon Potter. Special recognition is due to Dr. Robin Wall-Kimmerer (the original gatherer of mosses) and, indeed, to all women of science throughout history.

> Rest assured, dear friend, that many noteworthy and great sciences and arts have been discovered through the understanding and subtlety of women, both in cognitive speculation, demonstrated in writing, and in the arts, manifested in manual works of labor. I will give you plenty of examples.
>
> Christine de Pizan,
> *The Book of the City of Ladies*
> 1405